THE
GUINEVERE'S TALE

TRILOGY

FULL SERIES

NICOLE EVELINA

Lawson Gartner Publishing
PO Box 2021
Maryland Heights MO, 63043
www.lawsongartnerpublishing.com

Printed in the United States of America
First Printing 2018

ISBN
978-0-9967632-8-8 (print)
978-0-9967632-9-5 (e-book)

Library of Congress Control Number: 2018954315
Editor: Cassie Cox, Joy Editing
Cover Design: Jenny Quinlan, Historical Editorial
Layout: Qamber Designs and Media

Publisher's Cataloging-In-Publication Data

Names: Evelina, Nicole.
Title: The Guinevere's tale trilogy / by Nicole Evelina.
Description: Maryland Heights, MO : Lawson Gartner Publishing, [2018]
Identifiers: ISBN 9780996763288 (print) | ISBN 9780996763295 (ebook)
Subjects: LCSH: Guenevere, Queen (Legendary character)—Fiction. |
        Great Britain—History—To 1066—Fiction. | Queens—Great Britain—
        Fiction. | Lancelot (Legendary character)—Fiction. | Man-women
        relationships— Great Britain—Fiction. | LCGFT: Arthurian romances. |
        Historical fiction. | Fantasy fiction.
Classification: LCC PS3605.V424 G95 2018 (print) | LCC PS3605.V424 (ebook) |
        DDC 813/.6—dc23

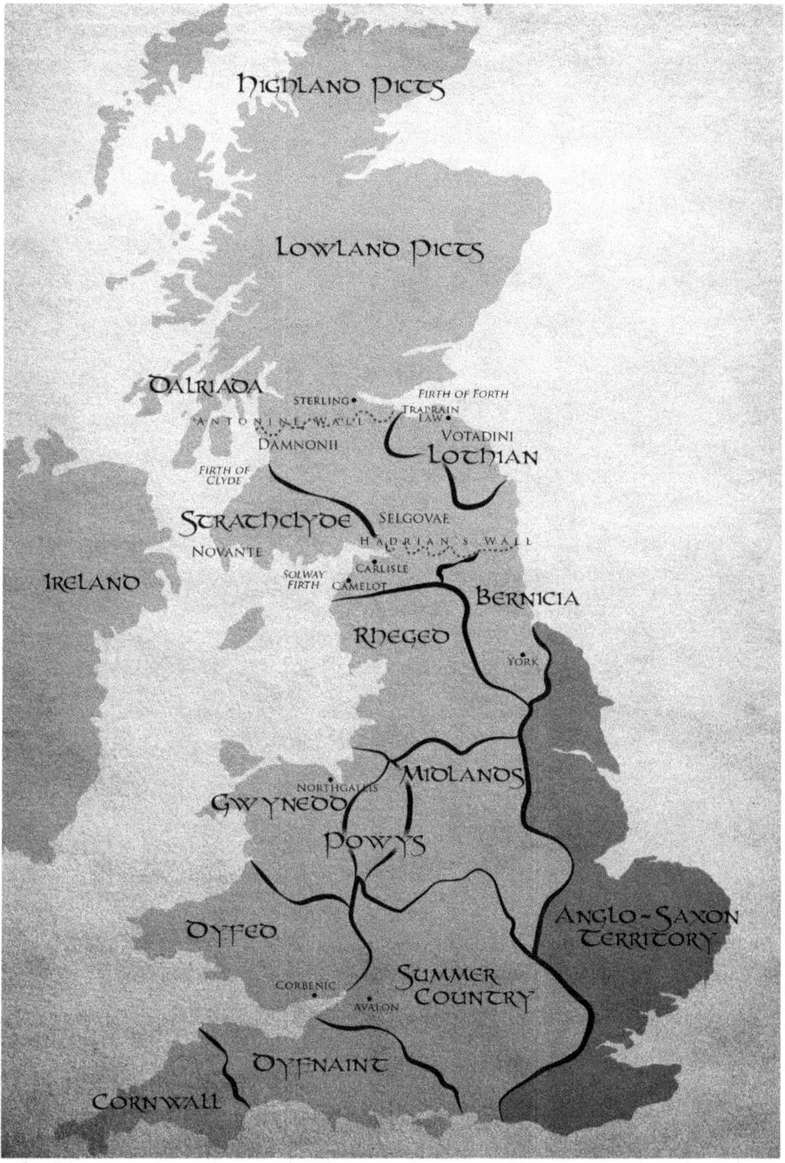

HIGHLAND PICTS
LOWLAND PICTS
DALRIADA
STERLING
FIRTH OF FORTH
ANTONINE WALL
TRAPRAIN LAW
VOTADINI
DAMNONII
LOTHIAN
FIRTH OF CLYDE
STRATHCLYDE
SELGOVAE
HADRIAN'S WALL
NOVANTE
IRELAND
SOLWAY FIRTH
CARLISLE
CAMELOT
BERNICIA
RHEGED
YORK
MIDLANDS
NORTHGALIS
GWYNEDD
POWYS
ANGLO~SAXON TERRITORY
DYFED
CORBENIC
SUMMER COUNTRY
AVALON
DYFNAINT
CORNWALL

DAUGHTER OF DESTINY

BOOK ONE OF GUINEVERE'S TALE

I am Guinevere.

I was once a queen, a lover, a wife, a mother, a priestess, and a friend. But all those roles are lost to me now; to history, I am simply a seductress, a misbegotten woman set astray by the evils of lust.

This is the image painted of me by subsequent generations, a story retold thousands of times. Yet, not one of those stories is correct. They were not there; they did not see through my eyes or feel my pain. My laughter was lost to them in the pages of history.

I made the mistake of allowing the bards to write my song. Events become muddled as ink touches paper, and truth becomes malleable as wax under a flame. Good men are relegated to the pages of inequity, without even an honest epitaph to mark their graves.

Arthur and I were human, no more, no less, though people choose to see it differently. We loved, we argued, we struggled, all in the name of a dream, a dream never to be fulfilled. Camelot is what fed the fires that stirred us to do as we did. History calls it sin, but we simply called it life.

The complexity of living has a way of shielding one's eyes from the implications of one's role. That is left for others to flesh out, and they so often manipulate it to suit their own needs. To those god-awful religious, I have become a whore; Arthur the victim of a fallen Eve; Morgan, a satanic faerie sent to lead us all astray. To the royalty, we have become symbols of the dreams they failed to create and Arthur is the hero of a nation, whereas to me, he was simply a man. To the poor, we are but a legend, never flesh and blood, a haunting story to be retold in times of tribulation, if only to inspire the will to survive.

We were so much more than mute skeletons doomed to an eternity in dust and confusion. We were people with a desire for life, a life of peace that would be our downfall. Why no one can look back through the years and recognize the human frailty beneath our actions, I will never understand. Some say grace formed my path; others call it a curse. Whatever it was, I deserve to be able to bear witness before being condemned by men who never saw my face.

It ends now. I will take back my voice and speak the truth of what happened. So shall the lies be revealed and Camelot's former glory restored. Grieve with me, grieve for me, but do not believe the lies which time would sell. All I ask is that mankind listen to my words, and then judge me on their merit.

PART ONE

Isle of Glass

Chapter One

Spring 491

One more step, and there would be no turning back.

I glanced hesitantly at Viviane, who waited in the belly of a small boat at the edge of the gray-green lake. A slight breeze lifted her long, dark brown hair around her face to frame the crescent mark of a priestess tattooed on her brow. She stood patiently, one pale hand on the scrolling prow of the boat, which curved like a swan sleeping with its beak nestled under its wing. The vessel seemed to disappear in her wake, the other end obscured by a dense fog that rolled and curled in a sinuous dance that made it impossible to see what lay beyond. The air was thick with the heavy, choking fumes of the tar that turned the boat black, protecting it from the waters that lapped incessantly at its base and sides.

I looked down at my reflection; the gentle current pulled at the image of a girl hovering between youth and womanhood, fists balled nervously into the fabric of a green dress, wisps of black hair escaping from a long, tight braid flung over her left shoulder. She looked back at me with uncertain eyes, not emerald as they should be, but nearly black in the odd half-light where the spring sunshine gave way to the dower mists.

Who are you? she seemed to ask.

I wasn't sure how to answer.

If I stepped aboard, I was no longer Guinevere, daughter of King Leodgrance of Gwynedd, but Guinevere, acolyte of the Goddess. The boat would take me to Avalon, away from the only life I had ever known and into a place of great mystery. I remembered my nursemaid, voice full of awe and reverence, describing Avalon as an earthly paradise—a holy place of temperate breezes and unending sunshine, where disease was unknown and crops needed no tending to produce a bountiful harvest each year without fail. Some of our servants even believed the hillsides teamed with faeries, dragons, elves, and all manner of mythical creatures that only came to ordinary mortals in their dreams.

Now I had to make a choice. Did I wish to go this place and learn to control the visions haunting my waking hours, or return to the familiar security of my home at Northgallis, despite the constant threat of Irish raids?

As if in answer, my sight clouded over against my will and a devastated seaport village arose before me, an unfamiliar place. My inner vision did not see the attack, but the aftermath lay before me as though I were there—the burned-out hulls of overturned ships, bodies being carted to the countryside by black-robed mourners for burial, crumbling houses laying bare the broken lives within.

I clenched my eyes closed, but the images remained, and they would come again, as they had so many times before. There would be no respite anytime soon if I didn't go with Viviane and learn from the priestesses on the isle how to control this ability, this gift—as my mother called it—that I regarded as more of a curse.

Taking a deep breath, my decision made, I willed myself to lift my right foot, clad in a thick leather boot against the last of winter's chill, from the sand and place it in the boat. I took Viviane's cool, reassuring hand and let her help me aboard. She untied the mooring from a dock shrouded in fog and sank a thin pole into the invisible water. The boat glided smoothly across the lake, which scarcely seemed disturbed by its passage. As we moved, the world around us became even more engulfed in mist, until the shore was swallowed up and we floated in a land of milky vapor.

My stomach tightened. Had I made the right choice? What was I getting myself into? I was only eleven years old, not yet mature enough to foresee how such a decision might affect my future life and still enough of a child to already miss my family terribly. I fidgeted with my tunic as worry swam through my mind. What if the priestesses did not like me, or worse, what if the darker rumors were true?

I bit my thumbnail apprehensively as I thought about what I had heard—the priestesses were keepers of powerful magic that could influence the weather, bring forth life from the barren, or curse the wretched with unspeakable suffering, according to their will. Most common folk considered the priestesses harmless, but a vocal minority cowered in fear, regarding them as dark seekers of unnatural forces who, according to a few accounts, chose to roam the countryside in animal form, transforming back into humans only to cause mischief. What if they were right? What would these women do to me? I shivered at my own horrible imaginings of bloody sacrifice and evil magic.

No, I would not choose to indulge in such dark tales. Viviane had been nothing but kind to me, so I was determined to believe the same of the rest of Avalon's inhabitants. I'd made my choice; now I had to see it through.

Straining to see beyond the mists, I tried to perceive the path Viviane followed with ease, navigating through the maze of sandbars and other perils as only a trained priestess could. Nature had provided a perfect ward against those who would do harm to the inhabitants of the isle. Like the tides that responded to the urgings of the moon, every morning, the mists rolled out across the lake, cutting off access to the uninitiated; each evening, they contracted around the Tor, the tallest, most sacred hill on the island, providing a thick blanket of protection to those who slumbered in the darkness below.

Eventually, the boat stilled and Viviane lifted the pole into the boat, a trail of water dribbling after it. She gave a sharp whistle, which was answered a short distance in front of us. I nearly toppled over as the boat was heaved forward by unseen hands.

⚬⚬⚬

Once ashore, the veil of mist thinned and I caught my first glimpse of Avalon. The land dipped lower as my eye moved inward from the lake. The shoreline gave way to damp marshes, slim clusters of reeds, and wetland grasses in which stately silver herons and colorful kingfishers played and hunted for fish, heedless of the activity around them.

Mountains and low hills veiled in shadow appeared brown, purple, and gray on the far horizon, acting as a screen separating Avalon from the outside world, while directly in front of me, the sun shone brightly on a cluster of buildings, giving their white-gray stone a radiant appearance. Beyond them, the sun warmed colorful gardens and vast green orchards that in a few months would be heavy with fragrant fruit. Farther to the east, a soft, cool breeze stirred tall golden grasses in the open plains, and shadows played hide-and-seek with the sun on the outskirts of tall forests of oak, ash, elm, and other sacred trees.

To my right, the sacred Tor loomed above the flat land, its

humped shadow reflected in the still waters of the inland lake encircling its base. A spiral path wound around the hill, and nine pairs of evenly spaced pillars marked stations along the way. As my eyes traced the pathway upward, I was surprised to find the summit was ringed with standing stones, the two taller portal stones capped by a horizontal slab, much like the Druid's circle several days ride to the east.

I was immediately caught up in the buzz of activity generated by the throng of brightly clad women preparing for some great event. A few younger women dressed in robes of forest green helped secure the boat, while young and old alike scurried up and down the stairs of a tall, stately columned building, and others carried supplies to the long, flat houses that lay adjacent. I marveled at their organization. In the flurry of activity, none seemed to lose sense of her purpose. Even my father's army could not boast that.

Viviane followed the line of my eyes and smiled, her blue eyes twinkling. "These are your sisters now, Guinevere. They will be your only friends and family for many years. You will be introduced to them later. Come."

She took my hand and showed me into one of the flat houses near the gardens. I met a short dark-haired girl, who I guessed to be one or two years older than me.

"Mona, this is Guinevere, our newest candidate. Guinevere, Mona will help you become acquainted with the isle," Viviane said by way of introduction.

Mona gave me a welcoming smile as Viviane departed. Then, with a fluid gesture, she ushered me inside to a small bedroom where I washed the dust from my hair, feet, and skin and changed into a pure white gown, just like the one Mona wore.

Snatching up my discarded traveling clothes and a ball of soap from the bedside table, Mona strode across the terrace overlooking the lake. She was halfway down a gently sloping hill before she paused then turned, a small frown creasing the otherwise smooth skin between her eyes.

"This way," she said, beckoning before she wound her way through a series of herb, vegetable, and flower gardens. She walked along the edge of an apple orchard to a clear, softly flowing stream.

I remembered hearing that waters such as those were rumored to heal every illness and even grant eternal youth. I glanced about in awe. Were the stories true?

Mona handed me my tunic, which I held dumbly. I watched as my tan cloak turned the color of freshly tilled earth as she submerged it in the water. She wrung it out, laid it flat against the surface of a large, smooth stone, and began running the fragrant lavender soap over the material, working it into the fibers with her fingertips.

I was utterly transfixed. At home, we had servants and slaves who took our soiled linens and then returned them to us clean. I had never thought to question how it happened.

Mona looked up at me with eyes as dark as her hair, the ghost of a smile playing at her lips as if she could read my thoughts. "Go on," she said encouragingly, gesturing toward the tunic I still held balled between my hands. "You will have to learn to clean your own clothes. You will have only three tunics, two for daily use and one for rituals, so take good care of them. You will need to learn to mend them too, but that is a lesson for another day."

My heart twisted at the thought of having to do menial labor, and the better part of me wanted to refuse. I opened my mouth in protest, but Mona's gaze silenced me. I knelt down beside her and plunged my tunic into the stream. I gasped, not expecting the water to be icy cold. Mimicking what Mona had done, I lifted my dress out of the water and twisted the sodden lump of material between my reddened fingers, nearly drenching myself in the process.

Mona grabbed my hands and pulled my arms out straight. "Hold it out, away from you," she instructed, "unless you want to take a bath at the same time." She giggled, not unkindly, at my ineptitude.

I spread out my dripping tunic on Mona's chosen rock and began to soap it. She looked at my hands with curiosity, no doubt wondering why they resembled the rough, callused hands of a warrior in training instead of the smooth, silky skin of most noblewomen. I could sense the unspoken question she was too polite to ask.

"My mother," I began, throat constricting with emotion as I pictured her face, "has been training me to wield a sword since I was old enough to feed myself. She is a Votadini from the lands far to the north. It is a tradition of her homeland that all the women of the tribe be trained to fight alongside their men in battle."

"Are you good at it? The fighting?" Mona's interest came through as pure excitement.

I dipped the frothy material back into the water, fighting the current and the leaden heaviness of the cloth as I tried to rinse it clean.

"I thought I was," I said quietly, disappointment slowly creeping into my voice as I spoke, "but I could not even defend myself when we were attacked. I nearly lost my life, but my mother saved me."

Mercifully, Mona asked no more questions. I told myself it was all in the past now. No acts of violence were allowed on the isle, so I would have to let go of my training and the horrors of the day it failed me, just as I would have to relinquish my noble rank.

By the time we completed our task, it was late afternoon. Instead of taking me back to the house where I had changed clothes earlier, Mona guided me through the maze of trees to a long, single-story building of white-gray stone, one of the ones that seemed to glimmer from the shore.

"This is the House of Nine," she explained on tiptoe as she draped my wet garments over a sturdy branch of white-barked birch about half a foot above her head. "If the Lady deems you a worthy student, you will live here with me and seven other girls. We are all about the same age." She glanced over her shoulder. "That is Grainne peeking out from the doorway."

The golden-haired girl shrank back momentarily at the sound of her name, seemingly embarrassed at being caught spying on us, but then she came bounding toward us like an excited puppy. Trailing hesitantly in her shadow was a small brunette girl who exuded peace and calm in equal amount to Grainne's energy.

"You must be Guinevere," Grainne said by way of greeting. But before I had time to reply, she asked, "So is it true you were kidnapped by Irish raiders?"

"You told me they were landless tribal outlaws." The smaller, dark-haired girl scowled at Mona before introducing herself as Rowena.

"Then you must have misheard me," Grainne shot back. "I said no such thing."

For a moment I couldn't respond, shocked they had been gossiping about me before I even arrived.

"In the House of Nine, there are no secrets," Mona whispered in my ear. "We know every scrap of one another's business."

Grainne and Rowena looked at me expectantly, clearly waiting for my answer.

"Well, I yes," I began. "I was attacked—"

The tinkling of a soft bell cut me off. Viviane appeared in the doorway and bid us to follow her.

"Where are we going?" I asked, unsure of what activity might begin when the sun was fast sinking below the horizon.

"To meet the Lady of the Lake," Viviane answered.

Viviane escorted us into a massive temple-like building that lay open to the lake and world of mists beyond, and she led us up a set of steep stairs. How silent the structure seemed to be, although the air around us vibrated with a low hum. After passing through a small foyer, we entered a large square room with ceilings as high as the tips of ancient oaks. As my eyes adjusted to the light, I began to make out figures in the room behind us. At first they appeared as phantoms without faces, but after a moment, we were surrounded in a semi-circle by a crowd of women dressed in brightly colored gowns of forest green, pearl white, and the same ocean blue Viviane wore. She led me to stand in front of a throne-like chair at the far end of the room.

The wall behind the chair was lined with pots of sweet-smelling incense, its lazy haze blending with the orange flames from rows of candles that glowed like the midday sun. From the ceiling hung brass containers of fire, probably fed by small charcoal bricks. Craning my neck, I peered between the curious women to my right, just catching a glimpse of flower petals floating on the surfaces of bowls of water surrounded by scores of seashells on a small table. In the opposite window, the one facing east, bronze wind chimes adorned with feathers hung limply from their strings, silent due to the lack of a breeze. Glancing over my shoulder, I was startled to see the Tor framed perfectly in the doorway behind us. All of the elements—earth, air, water, and fire—were represented here, all in perfect balance.

As the moments trudged slowly by, I grew increasingly uncomfortable. Everyone seemed to be staring at me as if I came from another world. A few whispered to each other, no doubt talking about me. I began to nervously twirl a strand of my hair in order to combat the sickening fear welling up inside me.

"Guinevere, stop that." Viviane swatted at the fingers knotted in my hair. "It does not befit a student of Avalon to fidget like a child," she said, her voice sharper than I'd ever heard it.

I dropped my hand to my side. Just then, a small wooden side door creaked open, and I jumped in fear. The murmuring ceased as every woman in the room snapped to attention at once.

An aged, stately woman emerged from the dark interior room and took her place on the throne. Her hair was a rich auburn streaked with heavy bands of gray, her face lined and furrowed from many years of living, but her eyes were bright and perceptive, like a hawk's. She wore a blue gown similar to Viviane's but decorated with intricate spiraling patterns. A single glittering crystal bobbed from a silver chain around her neck, and a thin silver circlet rested on her head, just above the mark that signaled her rank as High Priestess—the three visible phases of the moon drawn in blue ink. Her crown mirrored the mark so that the waxing and waning moons peeked out from her hair on either side of an opaline full moon.

As I watched, awestruck, every woman in the circle around us, including Viviane, dropped to one knee in unison and touched the thumb of her right hand to her forehead, lips, and heart—the same gesture my mother had made to Viviane when she arrived at Northgallis. As one, they whispered, "May the Goddess grant me wisdom, may the God govern my speech, and may my heart be filled with their love."

I looked around nervously, unsure if I should do the same, and fumbled a slight curtsy instead.

"Her name is Argante, but always address her as Lady," Viviane whispered.

The old woman smiled slightly at my attempted reverence but then just as quickly resumed her serious disposition. "Viviane, for what reason have you gathered us here?" Her voice was stern and authoritative.

Viviane stepped forward and nudged me toward the Lady. "Sisters, I have brought with me a new candidate to be counted among our number." She placed a hand on my shoulder, turning to address the woman on the throne. "Most blessed Lady of the Lake, this is Guinevere of Northgallis, who wishes to be named a servant of the Goddess."

Viviane had warned me on the journey here that in Avalon, when speaking in general, all the goddesses of our people were collectively referred to as the Goddess, and likewise, all the gods as the God. Avalon welcomed people of many tribes and traditions, each with their preferred deity names and mythologies. This way, they avoided confusion and arguments over exactly which deity was being referenced or whose gods were better. Here, all were equal and, except on feast days sacred to a specific deity, all were worshiped according to individual preference. Personally, I favored the horse goddess Rhiannon, worshiped in my homeland, and the sun god Lugh, patron of my mother's Votadini tribe.

Argante's eyes met mine with an all-knowing gaze that pierced my soul and laid the entire contents of my being out on the floor for her examination. As her eyes searched mine, I trembled and said a private prayer to my gods, terrified she would find in me some imperfection, some reason to send me back to my father in shame. Argante reached forward, placed a hand on my brow, and my eyes involuntarily snapped shut. Moments passed in silent darkness, and then wood creaked as she sat back in her chair. When I opened my eyes, she appeared pensive.

The women in the assembled crowd shifted their weight restlessly, and tears began to prick at the back of my eyes. I feared this lengthy pause was a sign of disapproval; surely if I was pleasing to her, the Lady would have made it clear without delay. I searched the air between us for Viviane's hand, and she gave mine a gentle squeeze before leaving me once again on my own.

"This child is pure of heart," the Lady said at long last, her voice far-off and intense, as if it was not she who spoke, but someone greater through the medium of her voice. "Her innocence and faith please me greatly. I see in her no duplicity or capacity for betrayal, only a strong desire to love and serve. In her blood the sight runs strong, and she will be for Avalon a great asset." She paused, and a slight frown played on her lips. "However, she will not ascend to greatness on this isle. Another crown sits on her brow, one that will secure the safety and prosperity of many, but at a great cost, both to herself and to those she holds dear."

A whisper of concern ran through the circle as I knitted my brows together, trying to puzzle out the meaning of her words.

"But that is the future and its lines are not writ in stone, only hinted at by an uncertain sight interpreted by the human heart." Argante looked at me lovingly now, seeming much more human, her voice softer. "Do not fear what is to come but embrace it, following the Goddess's voice—which you shall not fail to hear in your heart—and trusting she will lead you on the right path. Guinevere, you have been chosen by she who created life itself and now you must prove your devotion by stating your intent. Why have you come to the isle of Avalon?"

I shifted my gaze to the floor in embarrassment, unsure how to reply.

"Answer from your heart," Viviane whispered.

I raised my eyes to meet the Lady's. "To serve the Goddess, who has protected me since before my first breath." My voice issued forth strong and clear, as if propelled by a will other than my own. "My mother promised me to this isle in thanksgiving for our safe deliverance from her difficult labor. Now I fulfill the vow she made eleven years ago."

In truth, this was my fate, but I purposefully neglected to mention my visions in such a public arena. Argante likely knew about them already, and I feared the judgment of the others.

Argante nodded in understanding. "Honorable as that is, it does not compel you to stay. Do you come here free of coercion and choose to remain here of your own will?"

"I do."

"Look around. The women gathered here are your sisters. Do you promise to treat them as such, harming none and living in love and trust so strong that you give freely of yourself when needed and accept their aid when offered to you? Will you treat each woman as you would treat the Goddess, your own mother, or yourself?"

I looked out over the sea of strange faces. "I will."

Argante caught my gaze and held it, impressing on me the seriousness of what she was about to say. "Know that the vows you now take are not binding and you may be released from them at any time, should you so desire. They are, nevertheless, a promise, and you will be held to them by value of your word, as it is your source of honor."

Uncomfortable, I wanted to look away but could not break her gaze.

"Do you vow to serve the Goddess and God with all of your mind, heart, and soul and preserve your maidenhead until such time as you take your final vows or part ways with our community?"

I swallowed, sensing the sacrifice required in assenting to these terms. "I do."

Argante smiled at me with all the warmth of a doting grandmother and leaned forward to kiss me on the forehead. "Welcome to the sisterhood, Guinevere."

CHAPTER TWO

Summer—Winter 491

Life in Avalon—a life equal to, rather than above, everyone else—was more difficult than I expected. I cried myself to sleep for a month.

No amount of protesting, tears, or will power could change the orders dispensed daily by the Lady's authority. Argante had no time for temper tantrums and flatly ignored them. Complaints only ended in a sentence of silence for the remainder of the day, and if I refused to obey a command, I found myself without supper or barred from the evening's ceremony, a great humiliation in this sacred place.

When my attention wasn't fully focused on the task at hand—such as when I was helping to clean our communal living quarters or learning to cook a palatable meal—I found myself longing for home. As my parents' only surviving child, I had rarely been away from them, following in their footsteps to learn how to rule the kingdom I would one day inherit.

But now I faced years without their love and attention, and I missed everything. Sparring with my mother and male cousins had been replaced with chasing the other girls across the hillsides and racing to climb trees. Quiet evenings learning new embroidery patterns by the firelight with my lady's maid were replaced by solemn rituals I barely understood. I even missed sitting with my parents at council meetings, where the western lords would lament High King Uther's inattention to their kingdoms now that he was focused on the invading Saxons. Those practical lessons in politics and governance now gave way to endless language and writing classes, which were followed by studies of the lore of the gods and practice of how to worship them on each of the eight great festivals.

Every morning began with sunrise salutations on the holy Tor. Then while the other girls scampered off, laughing and joking, to their lessons in familial groups, I followed Viviane to her quarters for private study. It was unusual for a first-year student to learn control of the sight—that usually came after a series of tests designed to assess our mental preparedness—but given my situation, Viviane thought it best for me to begin with that skill.

"You will not be able to give your other studies full attention if your mind is clouded with visions," Viviane explained on our first day.

That had been several weeks ago. Now I was used to the pattern of each lesson, although that didn't stop my hands from shaking as I washed my face and hands in the cool, clear water collected from the white spring. Sitting with my legs crossed beneath me, I closed my eyes and took a series of deep breaths, focusing my attention on my heartbeat.

I dreaded these meetings. My fear was in part because I knew they were separating me from the friendships I was trying so hard to forge. Even though they never showed it, I heard the other girls' spiteful whispering that I was getting preferential treatment. But even more, I feared the painful memories and horrifying images that each session unearthed. Even when the visions were unrelated to me personally, the experience left me feeling raw and ragged.

"Tell me when you feel the sight coming on," Viviane directed, her voice gentle and musical like the tinkling of bells.

She had already taught me the signs preceding each vision—the disorienting feeling like I was floating above my body and the now-familiar tingling in the center of my forehead, the very spot all priestesses were marked upon their consecration.

"Now," I exclaimed, the area between my brows prickling.

She settled to the floor behind me, her voice almost directly in my right ear. "This time, instead of replacing what you see with a pleasant memory, as we have done before, will the image to go away, simply because you desire it to."

At first, I thought I was succeeding because I couldn't see anything. But before I could draw my next breath, I was reliving the day my mother and I were attacked in the woods near Northgallis, the moment that had led me here. My mother's scream rang in my ears as they descended on us, a pack of foreigners with strange markings on their left forearms. I tried to defend myself, but there was an arm around my throat, crushing my windpipe. I was dragged from my saddle onto another horse by one of the men. My arms were wrenched behind me, leaving me defenseless. Even now, the stench of his skin filled my nostrils.

"I can't. It isn't working," I cried to Viviane, only half aware what I was seeing was not real. My panic rose with the pace of my breath.

Viviane placed a hand on each of my shoulders. "Yes, you can. Imagine the scene collapsing in on itself like folded cloth. When that is done, frame what remains in an open doorway. Shut the door tight. You can even lock it, if you like."

I concentrated on the vision as it played out before me, my mother and captor battling with me trapped between them, their blades clashing dangerously close to my nose. Slowly and with much effort, I covered the scene in reams of gray wool, first over my stunned captor, his face eternally contorted by the last thing his eyes saw—my mother's sword buried in his stomach. I folded that in over the memory of my wounded mother, blood streaming from gashes in her arm and side. One more fold to make that image disappear, and I slammed shut the door of my mind. Now there was nothing but the chirping of the birds outside Viviane's walls.

I opened my eyes in relief, still panting from the effort.

Viviane's pale eyes searched my face. "It is over. It may take some time and you may have to repeat the exercise, but eventually you should be free. As long as you keep that door closed in your mind, the vision should not trouble you again." She put an arm around me.

I reached behind me to complete the embrace.

"In a few years, I will teach you how to open your mind without letting that memory back in, so have no fear. For now, it is probably best to shut off the channels of the sight until you can control them."

Laughter echoed outside as the women moved from one task to another, interrupting our private moment. Viviane poked her head out the door and waved to Mona.

Turning to me, she said, "You have missed your Ogham lesson for today, but I have no doubt you will catch up. Off with you." She shooed me out the door.

I followed Mona to Argante's hut where we would learn from her great wisdom.

⁂

My days began to pass quickly. Spring gave way to summer's heat, and we spent nearly every pleasant day outdoors, getting to know every inch of the island and learning to feel the subtle shifts in energy as the seasons progressed in their endless cycle. Romping through the forest and over the hillsides, we were taught to identify every herb and flower that took root in the land and how to use it in healing.

Today, however, we stood in a large rectangular garden spread out behind Avalon's main cluster of buildings. Tiny blooms of chamomile magnified the sun while tall reeds of dill nodded their hairy stalks and seeded starbursts over thick carpets of fragrant thyme and marjoram. In the far shadows of the wall, foxglove bells stood sentinel over purple-winged wolfsbane, perky clumps of larkspur, seductive nightshade, and other herbs not meant for untrained hands. Those were the herbs of the Goddess, which, like her power, could bring life or death, depending on the intent and skill of the one using them.

While every one of the herbs cultivated here could be found growing wild across the isle, this garden kept the most commonly used ones near to hand, in case of emergency. It also served as a teaching ground for new students.

On the opposite end of the garden, a tall, thin girl with bright red hair and skin like fresh cream was pointing at herbs as Viviane named them off, a test we each took to determine who could advance to more complex lessons and who still needed more study.

I toyed with the finger-like fronds of a fern whose name would forever be etched in my memory. It was the only one I had misidentified. Unfortunately, had the situation been real, my mistake would have killed the recipient. Viviane was displeased, to say the least, and there was no question she would tell Argante. I was desperate to win their approval, so this setback troubled me deeply.

I eyed the girl engrossed in the test, who was now squatting over a spray of tiny pink flowers at Viviane's feet. "I wager she is right on each," I muttered to the girls waiting impatiently with me. "She always is."

Rowena snorted. "Herbs come as easy to Morgan as does breathing."

"But she's part fey, so she has an advantage," Grainne chimed in.

I narrowed my eyes at the bright-eyed girl with wavy, golden tresses. "You don't really believe that rot, do you?" Although I thought I detected a slight lilt in Morgan's voice when she spoke, I didn't think for a moment she was part of an ancient, mystical race from across the sea in Ireland. I had been living with Morgan for months now, during which time she had proven herself very much mortal, although she would be loathe to admit it, content as she was with her reputation for Otherworldly perfection.

"Oh yes." Grainne scooted closer to me, leaning in as though confiding a great secret, and the other girls inclined their heads to listen. "One of the old priestesses told me Morgan has lived here most of her life, but no one can remember her coming here. There was no boat ride through the mists for her; she just appeared." She made a popping sound with her lips.

I looked back at Morgan, noting with a pang of jealousy the blossoming approval on Viviane's face as they moved from plant to plant. She was outshining me again.

Everyone seemed to have their own theory about Morgan's origins. Other whispers named her the lone survivor a slaughtered tribe, or worse yet, a changeling or the abandoned offspring of some unholy union. But more than likely, the tongues which told such tales were simply jealous of Morgan's intelligence and aptitude in the magical arts, if not of her great beauty. I assumed she had been promised to Avalon much like myself, or taken out of kindness from the arms of a mother who could not care for her.

"No, I think she is very much human." I turned back to Grainne. "I just wish she were more forthcoming. I never know what she is thinking, and that unnerves me."

Grainne smirked as a placid, lightly accented voice floated over my shoulder. "I think it is unkind to speak of others outside their presence."

I whirled around. Morgan had materialized silently behind me, her slate blue eyes flashing. Maybe Grainne was right about her otherworldly bloodlines.

An amused smile played on Morgan's lips. "Viviane told me to tell you we all passed the test."

The others whooped and hooted with joy.

"There is only room for one favorite among us," Morgan quietly added to me. "That title is mine, and I intend to keep it. You'll have to try much harder if you wish to best me."

⟡

As summer wore on, Morgan's declaration of dominance ate at me. I was used to getting my way unchallenged, and to make matters worse, I was also used to being the best and brightest of the cohort my mother instructed back home. So I was ill-equipped to endure my rival's constant assertion of superiority.

At first, I took the passive route, hoping she would be satisfied, forget me, and move on to hating someone else. I let her think she was superior even when I knew my skill to be greater and frequently resorted to false flattery, but Morgan saw through me every time. To truly win her over, I would have to openly admit my inferiority before the rest of the House of Nine, bowing and scraping like a slave before her master. That was the one thing I would not do, and she knew it.

So our competition slowly became a battle of wills. We found tiny ways to trip one another up or gain advantage—petty things like toppled ink pots, missing vials of herbs, and well-timed pinches that forced one another to break the solemnity of ritual—childish pranks we thought went unnoticed by anyone else. That is, until one day in early winter when Argante asked us to remain with her after our lesson ended.

We were learning the basic tenants of law, which at our early level consisted of memorizing categories of possible dispute—property, contracts, and crimes—along with their corresponding value or punishment. After eight months of study, we could easily recite the equivalent value of a cumal of rich farmland versus one of poor, rocky soil, or how to determine the honor price owed to a father for a bride. While not as exciting as divination or as entertaining as learning epic bardic poetry, it was equally important. Someday, as priestesses, we might be called upon by kings or lords to settle matters of law they did not want or were unqualified to decide themselves.

Argante had just returned from such a journey, where she'd adjudicated several cases for the new lord of the Summer Country, a young tribal prince named Malegant who, according to rumor, had managed to overthrow his own mother, as well as kill or subdue nearly a dozen siblings who contested his right to the throne. The resulting kingdom was a blend of three previous tribal holdings, and peace was tenuous at best. He'd had the foresight to call on Argante for aid, and she had been using some of the examples from his court to instruct us.

"I have called you apart from the others because I have a special case to present to you, one I would normally pose only to advanced students. I believe because of your superior skills and wit, you will rise to the challenge. Imagine yourselves the judges of this scenario. A man takes a second wife—"

"Does that happen anymore?" I asked, not realizing I had voiced my thought aloud, until Argante pinned me with an outraged expression that answered louder than her voice ever could have. I'd better not interrupt her again.

"A man takes a second wife," she repeated. "His first wife is displeased and kills her. Is she to be held guilty or not?"

This situation was a matter of tradition, one told in bardic lore from ages long past, before the coming of the Romans, so we were familiar with the idea, even though our studies had not yet reached that level of complexity.

"Does he have sons? When did the murder take place?" Morgan asked.

"Ah, now you are getting to the heart of the matter." Argante gestured with her index finger as she spoke. "He had no sons, and the murder took place two days after his second wedding."

Morgan wrinkled her brow. "Then no, she is guilty of no crime and no punishment should be given. If the second wife dies within the first three nights of marriage, then the primary wife is held blameless, regardless of her actions."

"The primary wife would have to pay a fine to the victim's kin, whether or not she was within her rights," I corrected Morgan.

Argante turned to me. "And if the second wife's family seeks vengeance?"

"If the family takes revenge, they do so at their own peril, unless they hire outlaws to do their bidding," I answered.

"And why is that permitted?" Argante asked Morgan.

"Because outlaws are not held to the same code as those with tribal ties. The only way to impose the law on a band of outlaws is to hire your own, and even then, they may turn on you."

"Exactly." Argante nodded and clapped her hands together, pleased. "Now what if the husband kills the first wife out of anger for her act? How is he to be punished? Is he put to the sword, or does he pay a heavy fine and enter slavery for a number of years? Or is there another alternative?"

Morgan and I looked at one another, puzzled. That was well beyond our ken. I decided to keep silent.

Morgan attempted to form an answer but never made it beyond

stuttering, "I-I-he..."

Argante fixed us in her solemn gaze. "I did not expect you to know the answer. You see, ladies, you have just proven you are equals both in knowledge and ignorance. Stop trying to best one another, and concentrate on your studies. You only hurt yourselves by directing your attention elsewhere. Now go join your sisters."

Morgan was silent as we made our way out the door, but then we moved out of earshot of our teacher.

"We are *not* finished," she sneered.

⁂

Hours later, in the deep stillness of night, I woke with a startled gasp, one hand pressed protectively over my racing heart, the other clamped in a fist at my side, still holding my one piece of home—a small wooden dog that had been my going-away present.

Sometimes the door of my mind would not stay shut. Most of the time it was locked to even gales, but in my weaker moments, just the slightest whisper of a memory was enough to release the lock and let the sight slip in like a winter draft.

Fighting to see through the cobwebs left behind by my nightmare, I sat up and gazed around at the other girls sleeping soundly all around me. Rowena was facing me in the next bed, a slight smile upon her lips, one arm tucked beneath her head, the other thrown carelessly above it. At least I had not woken them in my fright.

I lay back down, focusing on my breathing as the snow swirled outside the window facing the Tor, blanketing the isle in a glimmering cape of white. Slowly, I went through the steps of shutting my mind to the sight, trying to forget the terror that came with it.

That was one of the strange things about visions that came unbidden. Even after the images faded, the emotions they conjured remained. Tonight it was the bittersweet dregs of the Holy Grail, with its sanguine promise of peace offset by the rumbling threat of destruction. This was a dream that had haunted me for as long as I could remember. I suspected it was my confession of this dream, more than my recurring visions or my mother's vow, which had prompted Viviane to bring me here. The Grail was one of Avalon's clandestine treasures, and anyone who knew of it belonged here, safe behind the mists.

I shivered and drew the blanket closer around me. In the months that had passed since I came to Avalon, my visions had dwindled in number and more time elapsed between them, but they did not cease as Viviane had hoped. Argante told me they probably never would but echoed Viviane's promise that with training, I could control them. However, she warned that I would never be totally in control. Weakness, she said, was the strongest trigger, even for a woman of many years like herself. Each one of us, just by being alive, was subject to its many whims. Even with all the training Avalon could provide, illness, fatigue, or even strong emotions such as love or fear could render us powerless to the sight.

I bit my lower lip, trying to decide what had prompted this dream. I was healthy and my initial fear of life on the isle had faded, so that left one possible trigger—some strong emotion. Even without much thought, I knew what it was. Hatred. It burned in my belly even as I turned the previous day's events over in my mind. Morgan's refusal to let go of her quest for dominance over me, even after Argante's strict admonition, set me on edge. I was done fighting, but Morgan never would be, at least not until she saw me trod down once and for all.

Suddenly, a sound as soft as the tease of a feather captured my attention. I lifted my head slightly off the pillow. It came again, more distinct this time, a small cry almost like the mewing of a kitten. I lifted myself onto my forearm and scanned the beds. One was empty. Wrapping the heavy fur blanket around me, I followed the sound, my bare feet swishing softly on the cold floor.

I could just make out a small figure hunched on the thick white rug in front of the fire. As I drew nearer, I recognized Mona's silhouette.

I crossed my ankles and sank down silently beside her, wrapping my arm and half of the blanket around her. She nestled into my embrace like a baby bird beneath its mother's wing. Neither of us spoke, for we both knew the source of her grief. Whether by design or malevolent coincidence, Mona had been named after a holy island off the coast of my father's kingdom of Gwynedd, which had been home to the Druids before its inhabitants were slaughtered by a power-crazed Roman governor, an event she frequently relived in her dreams.

When I first joined the House of Nine, I thought her a banshee, but by now, I was so used to her screams in the night that I usually turned over and went back to sleep whenever she woke me. But something was different tonight. Maybe it was because of my own nightmare, but I wanted to keep watch with her, to hold her until her tears ceased and she finally succumbed to sleep.

After a long silence, Mona spoke, hiccupping through her tears. "I asked Argante today why I am cursed."

"What? Why?"

"By the nightmares, I mean. She told me the sight works differently in every person. Some can see the future, while others are given the gift of seeing distant things as they occur or, in my case, long after."

"But I still do not understand. It seems pointless to repeat the same events over and over again, even if only in our minds." I stroked her hair, gazing off into the distance as I thought of my own visions and felt anew the frustration of reliving tragic events and portents without any understanding of why.

"That is exactly what I thought, so I asked her what value there is in seeing the past. She did not really answer me but went into one of her lectures."

"What did she say?"

Mona shifted around so she was facing me. Distracted by her story, she had finally stopped crying. She adopted a dignified pose and mimicked Argante's regal voice, quoting her while being careful not to wake the others. "'How can we ever plan a better future if we do not learn from our past? If you burned your hand but did not remember the pain, how would you know not to touch the flame again? It is the same in battle or politics. If no one remembers the successes and failures, then our lives are but one pointless circle with no hope that future generations will advance. Knowing someone's past gives special insight into their motivations, which is much like being inside their minds. Do not discount the gift you have been given. If you develop it properly, it is a blessing that could prove very useful.'"

We were both silent for a moment.

"How very"—I searched for the right word—"cryptic. Do you feel any better?"

She shook her head. "Not really, but at least I know Argante sees potential in me, in my condition. What is that?" She pointed at the object clutched in my left hand.

I opened my palm, having completely forgotten I was holding anything. In it lay the small wooden carving of a dog. Peredur, the young son of my lady's maid, had given it to me as a farewell present on my last day in Northgallis. It had been a gift from his own father to help him conquer his fear of the dark. My palm was still etched with its imprint, made as I was clutching it in my sleep.

"This"—I gave Mona a squeeze—"is a magic wolfhound. He protects you from all your fears. I have been sleeping with it to combat my homesickness, but maybe you should keep him for a while."

Mona took the toy from my hand and examined it in the firelight. "I think he is one of Ellen's own," she said with awe, referring to the goddess of all journeys, even in the land of dreams.

"He doesn't appear much of a protector," interjected a bored voice from the dark depths of the room.

We both turned. Morgan stood in the shadows, her blanket trailing after her like a cape.

"Considering you are both awake, I would say he is not doing his job," she said, sitting down on Mona's other side.

"And what is your excuse?" I countered, annoyed at her interruption of a private moment.

Morgan narrowed her sleep-ringed eyes at me. "Who could sleep with the two of you chattering away like squirrels?"

"Have you been listening long?" Mona asked, a mixture of embarrassment and distrust in her voice.

"Long enough. I-I came over to ask you a favor." Morgan inclined her head to Mona and pursed her lips, as though unsure if she should go on in my presence.

"You could simply ask, if you want privacy," I pointed out to Morgan. I rose, leaving my blanket with Mona. I would take the one from her bed. "Good night, Mona. I hope you feel better."

She waved the wooden dog at me. "Of course I do."

I padded back to bed, slowing my pace just enough to catch a hint of Morgan's request.

"I heard what Argante told you. Will you try to see my past? It would mean very much to me to know where I come from."

Mona's voice lost its edge and once again radiated her natural warmth. "I don't think it works that way, but I will try."

I pulled Mona's blanket around me as I padded back to my bed, pondering this turn of events. So the rumors were true. Perfect little Morgan had a weakness after all—she was an orphan, at least as far as she knew. That meant she had no kin, no tribe to return to, no life save that which she had built on this isle. She was utterly beholden to the whims of Avalon. No wonder she was so anxious to secure her place as favorite daughter.

Well, she would have to fight me for it. I knew it was wrong, but I couldn't help but smile inwardly at the possibilities and plot ways to use my newfound knowledge to my advantage.

Chapter Three

Autumn—Winter 493

Two years came and went in the ceaseless rhythm of sacred festivals and lunar cycles. In the House of Nine, change began to unleash its unsettling force as bodies began to blossom. The Goddess saw fit to give Morgan ample curves, while I had little more than budding breasts and barely perceptible hips beneath my gown. But my moon time came first, and with that sacred milestone, I was finally able to trade my white robes for the forest green of a second-degree initiate.

Were I still at home with my mother, a different kind of ceremony would have marked my entrance into womanhood, one which had been passed down from mother to daughter for countless generations among the Votadini. I imagined my mother at her mortar and pestle, crushing leaves of woad, adding them to a tiny steaming cauldron of water, copper, and other substances which she would not divulge until I had a daughter of my own to mark, then carefully straining the liquid to produce a dark blue ink. I imagined myself lying facedown in her chamber at the new moon as a cluster of thin, sharp bones like teeth slowly pricked the symbol of our tribe, a horse whose body formed an endless knot, into the flesh of my left shoulder blade. She would lovingly bandage the tender flesh and embrace me, now officially a woman of our tribe, though I lived far from our ancestral home.

But those were the memories of a person I had chosen not to become. My life was here, in Avalon, among the ranks of the acolytes struggling to understand our new roles in ritual and study. We were learned, but not yet masters, and stood as assistants to those who trod the path of the Goddess before us. Gone were the carefree days of childhood; we now had to adjust to the growing demands of adulthood and increasingly complex temporal and spiritual studies.

A sharp autumn breeze shook the tips of the fiery oaks and

rustled our gowns. We were supposed to be concentrating on the circular boards in front of us, carefully set with gleaming crystals in a purposeful formation, but my mind kept drifting to my friends back in Northgallis. We were all nearing marriageable age now, and they would be preparing to leave their childhood homes for the beds of powerful men they barely knew. At one time, I would have envied them, but now I was grateful to be here, learning about one of Avalon's most sacred forms of divination.

As Argante had explained it, Holy Stones originated with the Druids who had ruled our tribes long before the Roman eagle made her nest on our shores. Comprised of two sets of twenty-one stones aligned in a triangle formation facing off across an empty field, it was primarily used to predict the outcome of battle and advise clan leaders of strategy. Stones with different properties were used to represent troops—footmen, archers, or cavalry—protecting the two most important pieces: the king and the queen. The battle or situation in question was simulated using these stones, performed over and over as the seer received strategic advice from the gods. Once the best strategy with the most positive outcome was determined, the Druid would advise his or her leader.

Although capturing the king was the point of the exercise and the only way victory could be claimed, the queen—a red stone symbolizing the Goddess, lifeblood, and the power behind the throne—was the most important piece. Known by names such as the Sovereignty Stone or Lady Fortuna, the queen was the only piece that could move anywhere on the playing field. The queen also had the ability to sacrifice herself to save the king or "heal" captured troops and return them to the board, but no more than three times in any game. The only piece that could actively capture a queen was the opposing queen.

Outside of Avalon and the Druids' isle, Holy Stones was primarily a game of strategy for the wealthy and well-educated, and few knew its true power or purpose. Some of my earliest memories were of playing this game with my father. He often played it as a way to clear his mind when he needed to think. The tenderness and patience with which he'd taught his "little warrior" how to protect the queen on an oak board with polished gemstones was as clear to me now as when it happened.

Today, however, it was more than a game. We were learning how to use this seemingly secular cover to reach out to the world beyond the lake and its marshes to gather information useful in advising those in power. We had each been given a different situation and were now asked to play it out and relay what strategy would most benefit our ruler.

I was paired with Morgan. She sat across a long wooden table on which rested five sets of boards. In our scenario, High King Uther faced a challenger to his supremacy—one of his own lords from the Midlands who had recently allied with the Saxons.

Morgan and I faced off just as they would have but played out our moves and counterattacks with stones instead of lives. We had taken about an equal number of each other's troops, and I was waiting for her to make her next move. To my right, Grainne and Mona were moving their pieces at astonishing speed—forward, back, off the board, and on again as each of their queens asserted her healing power—eyes unseeing, concentrating on the visions that directed their every move.

"Are you going to make a decision before the sun goes down?" I asked Morgan.

"Be quiet and let me concentrate. I can't help divination doesn't come as easily to me as it does to you," she sneered, fingers vacillating between two groups of stones.

I was about to retort that the sight often passed from mother to daughter—an admittedly cheap dig at her unidentified maternity—when Argante drifted in our direction, checking on each pair's progress.

"Remember, ladies, true power, true skill is not about doing one better than one's sister. All things thrive in balance, and for that to be maintained, each must focus on what she is best at and on her own destiny, not that of her sister."

She was speaking to the whole group, but her chiding glance was clearly meant for me.

Argante noticed Morgan's hesitation and paused behind her, placing a gnarled hand on top of the one Morgan held in mid-air. "Stop for a moment, Morgan. Do not try, just be. What you see before you is not a wooden plate and scattered stones, but two armies on the field of battle. You are the war goddess Morrigan, directing battle through the eyes of her ravens perched in the treetops and awaiting the final outcome. You know the strong and the weak. You call some to glory and others to death. Breathe deep, and tell me what you see."

Morgan's eyes became distant, but I did not need to hear her words to know what images flashed before her, for I saw them too. On both sides, the soldiers were badly wounded and tiring fast. Blood streamed from gaping holes in chests and abdomens or congealed into dark patches around slashes to faces and limbs. Some collapsed from their injuries while others fought on without an eye, an ear, and even a hand. Beneath the soldiers' feet, the ground was thick with bodies.

I suddenly understood this was the turning point. The next few decisions would determine the outcome, whether the troops returned victorious to their wives, died in battle, or ended their days as slaves to foreign masters.

Morgan's hand shot out, and she advanced an archer, putting him in firing range of my foot soldiers but also leaving him unprotected.

It was a decoy. The move was meant to draw my attention to the obvious kill and away from her increasingly vulnerable king. If I wanted a prolonged siege, I could have stayed back, picking her men off one by one, but I saw an opening. Her right flank was weak, and I surged forward, ignoring her archer. In this state of heightened awareness, I knew it was better to sacrifice a few troops to protect the many.

The unexpected onslaught threw Morgan, who struggled to keep pace. She eventually faltered, leaving me free to replace her queen with mine and, in the next move, capture her king.

We both sat back, breathing heavily. The visions had cleared, but my head buzzed with the exertion. Around us, the afternoon was advancing, the declining sun making the crystals scattered about our boards gleam merrily in the last gasp of day.

"Very good," Argante lauded us. "You have both done well. Remember, when we practice this way, one of you must always lose. But when you use this method of divination in real situations, be sure to control your sight so that you may see both your best advantage and your enemy's every weakness. It is the only way to assure victory for your side."

Morgan threw her an acerbic glare, clearly displeased about losing, but fortunately for her, Argante had already turned her back.

"Guinevere, I would like to speak with you in private." She guided me to the shade of a nearby oak, leaving Morgan to sulk at the table. "I did not make this known, but each of the scenarios I set before you was a real battle, one I could use to measure your skills because I know the tactics that were used, as well as the outcome."

Argante leaned heavily on her cane. "The battle you and Morgan just completed was the one exception. We received word last night that King Uther was contemplating just such a move against an insurgent and wished to see the possible outcomes before advising him. So we set our two strongest seers in opposition—you and Morgan—and you have given us the key to the battle. Because of the number of casualties you anticipate, I will warn him to avoid any confrontation whatsoever. If he is foolish enough to defy my advice, at least I can tell him how to come out alive. Congratulations, Guinevere. You have just saved the life of your king and many of his men." She patted my shoulder and hobbled back to the table, leaving me to contemplate her words in stunned silence.

☙ ❧

Morgan towered head and shoulders over me now, having shot up like a weed over the last lunar year, and she took no small pleasure in being able to literally look down on me. Mona too had grown, though she was still considerably smaller than Morgan, while it appeared I was destined to mirror my mother in petite stature. Even Grainne, so child-like in appearance, was slightly taller than me. Though I felt like a dwarf compared to them, I was glad to share the Neophyte Hall with those women. The rest of our sisters from the House of Nine had already left us, bound for marriage or ministry in the outside world, a world I scarcely remembered though I had called it home less than three years before.

A year and a day—that was all that remained before our period of study ended. After that, the Goddess could summon us at any time to the mysterious ceremony that preceded our final vows. We all intended to remain on the isle and serve the Lady here, but that was not entirely in our control. If our families wished to have us back, they could call for us, or if Argante became aware of a need for our skills, we could be sent anywhere in all of Britain. As an uncertain future loomed before us, we made the most of our time together, taunting and teasing, fighting and laughing as though we were related by flesh and blood.

Late one winter morning, Argante was summoned to High King

Uther's court in Carlisle by a rare personal invitation. Although she rejoiced at the king's choice to consult the keepers of ancient wisdom in such turbulent times, the chill weather had taken a toll on her health, so she appointed Viviane as emissary in her stead. Late season snows still clogged the passes and trails of the Mendips, which led north out of Avalon, so Viviane sent word that it would be several weeks before she could safely undertake the journey.

To fill the time between, Argante commissioned a tapestry for the king in praise of his wise decision to include Avalon in his circle of closest councilors. The motif chosen was representative of the mysteries of Avalon, the very same mysteries Uther himself had sworn to uphold many years before when he took the Druidic oath upon his initiation into their mysteries. In this way, the tapestry would be not only a gift; it would also serve as a reminder of the old ways in a court increasingly populated by unsympathetic Christian priests.

It could have been woven on one of Avalon's many looms, but Argante insisted the tapestry be hand-stitched in ancient decorative tradition. She decided such a task would be perfect for the neophytes, and so Grainne and Mona were given the assignment of preparing and weaving the base fabric, while the elaborate embroidery would fall into the more dexterous hands of Morgan and myself. We worked for what felt like months, and as winter warmed into early spring, our labor was nearly complete.

The evening before Viviane was to leave for the northern country, only two blocks of sewing remained. The pattern was rapidly taking shape, my tired hands sewing what remained of the Goddess's gown. Next to me, a stool sat empty but for multicolored threads brushing the floor as Morgan had left them hanging the night before. Only one of the God's feet and the grass on which he stood remained to be sewn; an hour or two more of stitching, and her wearisome job would be done.

But Morgan was nowhere to be found. She had disappeared not long after breakfast and never showed up to complete her task. Where could she be? Not for the first time, I found myself resenting her ability to do as she pleased with little or no consequence.

I will likely be the only one to note her absence as long as she comes to the evening's ritual on time. One thing is for certain, I will not do her portion of the work for her. Let her feel Argante's wrath for once. It would only be fair.

The sun was just beginning to slip below the horizon when I buried the final knot in my section. Breathing a sigh of relief, I snipped off the excess thread and sat back, admiring the results of our work. Finally, it was all done, except for Morgan's block. I stretched my aching arms, pinched out the candle flame, and made my way toward the door, intent on resting before the twilight ritual.

I didn't even make it out the door before Morgan came rushing up the stairs, face white, hair flapping wildly behind her.

"Morgan, kind of you to make an appearance. Do you not think you are taking quite a risk? Many threads demand attention, but little time remains."

She threw a biting look in my direction in response to my mocking. "If you must know, *Guinevere*"—she said my name like it was bitter to her tongue—"I came to fetch your help."

I feigned surprise. "*You* are asking *me* for help?" I started toward the door. "You made your bed, Morgan; now you must sleep in it. I will not aid you one stitch."

Morgan's hand clamped around my arm, forcing me to face her. "No, you silly cow, I do not need your help with the sewing. Ailis has found her way up a tree near the lake and cannot get down again."

How did Viviane's young daughter manage to climb up a tree? There was little time for speculation. Viviane would have all our hides if her only child were to suffer any misfortune.

"Where is Viviane? Does she know?"

"I don't know. I came here because you were closer—"

I didn't wait around to let her finish her excuse. My feet carried me swiftly across the plains of waving grass to the shore of the inland lake. I scanned the trees lining the water's edge. Sure enough, there was the sobbing lass, a tiny version of her mother save for her auburn hair, clinging to a tree branch that stretched its fingers out over the lake.

Morgan had been right to summon help. Ailis had not yet learned to swim, so if she fell, she would drown. And from the vise-like grip she had on the bobbing branch, I guessed she did not have the dexterity or courage to back down the tree either.

"Ailis! Ailis, stay where you are. I will come and get you."

The girl did not respond, only continued to wail.

Without a second thought, I scampered toward her, plowing through the foliage that separated us. The base of the tree was surrounded by clumps of tall plants with spiked stems and tooth-like leaves, whose berry-like purple and green flowers appeared harmless from a distance. Only now that I was standing in them, arms and legs prickling like I was being attacked by bees, did I recognize the plants for what they were—stinging nettle. No doubt I would pay for my good deed later with an itchy rash.

Grumbling to myself that I should have known better—it *was* one of the plants we'd had to identify in our first herbalism test—I climbed up the tree, using the outcropping branches to support my ascent. I inched forward, wincing as the skin pricked by the nettles was irritated by the tree bark, until I had the wailing child in my arms and we were once again safely on the ground.

Even before I set Ailis down, the tiny poisonous teeth hooked into her dress told me she had been playing in the nettles long before I arrived. Not wanting to expose anyone else to the irritating plant, I bathed Ailis in the lake, hoping the water would lessen the severity of her outbreak. As her tears slowly subsided, she began to tell me about the colorful songbird that had caught her attention, inspiring her to scale the tree to have a closer look. Once she was dry, I returned her to Viviane's care, but only after making her promise never to do such a thing again.

The sky was almost completely dark by the time I neared my quarters, so I would not have enough time to change my clothes before the ritual began. As I passed the weaving room, I heard Argante speaking with Morgan and peeked my head in to see her reaction to my earlier work.

At first, I could not understand the distress and concern etched in Argante's face. But then I looked down and saw its source. All of my long hours of stitching had been ripped out of the hanging as if I had never completed them, and the lower left corner—Morgan's block—was burned, pieces of blackened thread and crumpled cloth the only testaments to the tragedy. Nearby, a soot-stained taper lay in a pool of wax, as if someone had franticly flung it away from the tapestry.

"What happened here?" I asked incredulously, crossing in front of Morgan to finger the thread that made up all my missing stitches.

"Your irresponsibility caused this girl's work to be ruined," Argante growled coldly. "That is what happened here."

"What?" My astonishment echoed off the stone pillars and

silent loom.

"When I came in, some of the ribbons were hanging down from your block, dancing precariously close to the candle flame," Morgan explained, picking up a charred thread as evidence. "I tried to intervene, but a gust of wind tipped the flame, igniting the cloth. All I could do was put it out." Her wide blue eyes were filled with innocent astonishment.

My blood boiled. How dare she blame this on me! Did Argante really believe that story? Surely she could see through Morgan's lies.

Struggling to contain my rage, I faced Argante. "But that is not . . . I am certain I extinguished the flame—" I began, unable to collect my thoughts.

"No, I will hear no excuses from you, Guinevere," Argante cut me off. "Look at you, scraped and covered in dirt. If you had been here doing what you were supposed to be instead of cavorting through the hills, none of this would have happened."

I listened to her berate me in utter shock. So that was how it happened. Morgan needed a way to blame her absence on someone else, and the child's peril proved a convenient means. She might even have encouraged Ailis to climb that tree. Now she was turning her thoughtlessness on me. I had to make Argante understand.

"Lady, please listen to me. I did no such thing. Morgan—"

Argante turned on me with steely eyes. "I said no more!" She clasped her hands and surveyed the burned material. "The damage is unfortunate, but it is repairable. As you know, Viviane leaves at first light for her meeting with the king, so all the work must be completed by then. Guinevere, you will stay here and mend what your carelessness has ruined, as well as complete your allotted portion of the embroidery. Morgan will assist me in tonight's ritual in your place. In addition, to ensure you learn to take your responsibilities seriously, you will scrub the sanctuary stairs in the morning."

I opened my mouth to protest once again, but Argante ignored me and walked away, as did Morgan, but only after casting a wicked grin in my direction.

So that was it. I had no choice but to endure Morgan's punishment while she plied everyone else with lies. *Damn her!* I raged inwardly while I completed the tedious work. The moon rose and set, the stars shone brightly and paled into dawn, and all the while, my heavy eyes squinted at endless rows of stitching until at long last, the final thread was knotted and hidden away.

Argante woke me with a gentle pat just after sunrise. I had no memory of falling asleep, but she said I had done so a few hours earlier. She inspected my work, nodding approvingly as she ran her fingers across the needlework.

"Your stitching is well done," she commented, inspecting a complex pattern.

I began to pack away the spools of thread. Slowly, I became aware of Argante's silent gaze and looked up.

"Where did you get those?" She gestured to the trail of red, inflamed blisters that wound their way up my arm.

Involuntarily, my face flushed. "Yesterday, after I finished my sewing, Morgan came rushing in, telling me Ailis was trapped in a tree and in need of my rescue. I rushed to help her without paying heed to the plants at its base. It is—"

"I know what it is," Argante said, clearly irritated. "Most of Ailis's body is covered in blisters. At least now we know where she was exposed to the plant." The old woman sighed. "Now if you will excuse me, I need to speak with Morgan." She stopped in the doorway and turned. "Mona has gathered all you will need to tend to the stairs. In the meantime, make a poultice of sorrel and mud to apply to your rash. It will help relieve the itching."

⚬⊙⧉⊙⚬

When I arrived, bathed and medicated, to complete the last part of my unjust sentence, I was surprised to see Morgan leaning against one of the pillars at the top of the stairs, her expression as sullen as the gray, frostbitten morning.

"Morgan? What are you doing here?"

She shot me an icy look. "Always so innocent, aren't you?" She pointed toward the pail and bristle-brush sitting at her feet. "I, too, am to play scouring maid today. And I suppose I have you to thank for that. Am I right?"

I raised an eyebrow at her and dipped my brush into the bucket. "If anyone is to blame, it is you. Why did you burn the material, Morgan?"

She turned away, toying with her own brush. "I have no idea what you are talking about."

"Yes, you do. Why did you do it?"

She ignored my question and raised her voice in a mocking, sing-song tone. "High and mighty Guinevere, daughter of the great King Leodgrance. Are you afraid the hem of your gown may be dirtied by a little hard work? Nothing less than perfection for you, oh pristine one."

Her sarcasm stung. I flung the brush back down into the bucket, sloshing soapy bubbles at my feet. "Do you really think me that much a fool? Have you learned nothing about me in the last three years? I have no fear of hard work—no one here does, or she would not survive." As I advanced on Morgan, my mind briefly flashed back to my first washing lesson with Mona. "But unlike you, I would never betray my sister just to make myself look better in Argante's eyes."

A wicked smirk spread across Morgan's face. "Is that so?" she asked doubtfully. "We shall see. But bear this in mind, *my lady*. Not everyone has had your privileged life. Some of us must do what we can to survive."

"Survival at the cost of others is cruel," I retorted. "Although I suppose I should expect that from you by now. Perhaps it isn't your fault, since you had no parents to teach you respect."

Morgan turned on me with the venom of a viper. "I had twenty priestesses as my mother and the Archdruid as my father. Avalon is *my* home. Not that my upbringing is any concern of yours. As for what I may or may not have done, someone had to put you in your place. I cannot help it if you finally saw your inferiority to me and cannot live with the consequences."

With that she turned and began scrubbing in the opposite direction, the conversation closed.

As the silence became a wall between us, I could only wonder what her next move would be and how I would suffer for it. I had, after all, exposed her greatest vulnerability. If I knew one thing about Morgan, it was that she would not let such a deep insult go unpunished.

Chapter Four

Spring 495

In early spring, when I was barely fifteen, during the impossibly cold nights on which the ewes gave birth, they came for me— nine priestesses of the isle. I needn't be told what was about to happen; I had waited four long years for this night.

As I followed behind the solemn procession to the top of the Tor, I tried to recall the tales told of the initiation of a priestess. No one who had successfully passed the tests had ever spoken of them, for they were sworn never to reveal the secrets to the uninitiated. Still, rumors followed every initiation ceremony, and before the crescent was set onto the new priestess's brow, tales of horror and adventure floated through the House of Nine, leaving the young ones petrified yet excited at the prospect of one day bravely facing the unknown challenges.

As we passed through the entrance to the circle of stones, the other priestesses emerged from the shadows into the flickering torchlight to surround us. I knelt before Argante, who seemed this night to be more goddess than woman.

"Guinevere of Northgallis, you came to these shores a child seeking to become a servant of the ancient ones. Now, as a woman, is that still your wish?"

"It is."

"Know then that the gods require great sacrifice of those sworn to them. Before you may give your life to the Goddess and the God, you must prove yourself worthy of such an honor."

She stepped aside, revealing the altar stone, which was laden with symbols of earth, air, water, and fire. I knew then that, like the Druids, I would be tested by each of the elements.

"A priestess must be able to feel and manipulate the energies around her. Draw from the clouds rain which will soak the land with healing waters," Argante commanded.

The clear night sky stretched out beyond the Tor, stars winking defiance from the heavens. To an outsider, it would seem preposterous to try to make a cloudless sky rain, but I had enough training to know nothing was impossible.

I took a deep breath, willing the roots of my being downward, and closed my eyes, drawing the power of the Tor deep into myself until the very heartbeat of the earth was within my veins. I raised my arms, and the naked branches around us shivered. Concentrating on the void before me, I turned nine times sunwise, faster and faster, willing the energy up through my feet and out of my hands. The wind increased with each turn, so that by the time I opened my eyes, the stars were obscured by thick clouds. I brought down my hands with force, and raindrops followed. In the distance, a crack of lightning was answered by the peal of thunder.

Argante nodded. With an outward sweep of her arms, she commanded the rain to cease, though the clouds remained. She led me back over to the altar stone where a brazier burned brightly in the center.

"With power comes great responsibility. I ask you now to demonstrate your trust in the gods you serve by reaching into this fire and withdrawing a coal without fear."

I swallowed hard. We trained for many hours to be able to accomplish this task, one which signified our ability to let go of ourselves and place the needs of others before our natural inclinations. My hand shook as I reached toward the fire, but I willed myself not to feel the burning heat. *Fire is only a spark fed by air. I am much more—a being of spirit above all.* The heat grew more intense as I reached toward the coals, coloring my skin a deep scarlet. But instead of burning me, it traveled around my hand with comforting warmth, as if I was wearing a thick, protective glove. With a final prayer, I grasped the coal, which weighed heavy in my hand but bore no more heat than a sun-drenched rock. With a sigh of relief, I presented it to Argante, unharmed, and set it down on the altar stone.

Argante's face remained impassive. "Your success is a sign of great fidelity, and I am pleased. As one final scrutiny, I bid you prepare the sacred brew from the fruits of the earth that will draw down the Goddess into this mortal frame, that you may swear your vows directly to her."

Facing north, I looked down at the altar stone, on which one of the priestesses had strewn a variety of herbs. I knew some of them were not part of the sacred drink meant to induce a trance, so my ability to complete this task successfully was crucial.

My mind flickered back to the garden and my first test of herbal knowledge, where I had made a fatal mistake. What if I did something wrong and accidentally poisoned the Lady of the Lake? Would they slaughter me right here, using my blood to atone, or merely banish me from the isle to live my life in shame?

I cast aside the herbs I knew to be a trick and set to work grinding the others, separating valuable buds from deadly leaves. Water from the white spring bubbled in a small cup placed over the brazier. I added the herbs and a heady, sweet scent emerged, a clear sign I had done well.

Viviane strained the liquid and gave it to Argante. She drank, swayed a little while speaking the words of invocation, and then seemed to shrink and disappear into the force that inhabited her body.

I blinked. Her hair had transformed from gray into a lustrous auburn, and her skin was now smooth and unlined. On each side of her stood a ghost-like white horse as insubstantial as smoke, snorting puffs of fog from their nostrils and pawing at the ground, forming tiny clouds beneath their hooves. This was the goddess Rhiannon, protector of my tribe and line.

Holding their reins in one hand, she reached out to me with the other. "I am the Great Mother, she who is at once Maiden, Mother, and Crone, mistress of the silver moon, she of a thousand names, who holds the powers of life and death at her command. Guinevere of Northgallis, do you truly wish to serve me?" The voice that issued from her lips was young, strong, and confident, not the raspy growl that had instructed me all these years. There was no doubt this was no longer the Lady of the Lake, but one far more powerful and ancient.

"I do."

"With full understanding that the vows you are about to make are irrevocable and will forever bind you to my service, even beyond this lifetime, pledge now your life to me."

I knelt, and the words cascaded from my lips without hesitation. "I swear to always obey the Goddess and her consort and to uphold the mysteries of Avalon with all of my being, even laying down my life for them if it is so required. I promise to perform all of my actions with love and trust in the Goddess's guidance, as I am now her earthly representative. Above all, I pledge to love and serve the Goddess and God even through my dying breath and to respect all forms of worship that give them honor."

The goddess stepped forward and placed a kiss on my brow, on my lips, and on my heart. Rhiannon raised my chin to face her, placing her hands on top of my head. "Receive now the blessings of the Great Mother and arise a priestess of Avalon."

When I looked up again, a young man stood in her place. His hair was radiant like the midsummer sun, eyes as blue as the sea. In his left hand he held a spear, and on his right forearm rested a shield. I knew him immediately to be Lugh, the sun god of my mother's people.

"You have pledged yourself to my service, daughter, and for that I commend you. Though I cannot promise you a life of joy, I can promise you one of merit. Seek my wisdom, and you shall not fail. Be blessed, child of the Votadini, and be clothed a priestess of Avalon."

He bent down and placed his lips upon my forehead. Heat like the kiss of the sun shot through my being, and I closed my eyes to shield them from the radiant light. What seemed like an instant later, I opened them to find the sky already brightening to soft orange and pink through breaks in the clouds.

The god and goddess were gone, but I was far from alone. Surrounding me were a circle of priestesses. As the sun began to color the eastern horizon in a pale glow, my forehead, lips, and heart were anointed with rose oil, and with great ceremony, the blue robes of priestesshood were wrapped around my shoulders.

The women laid me face up on the altar stone. I welcomed its cold, solid surety after the ethereal nature of my tests and vows. Argante was still under the influence of the sacred drink, so Viviane bent over me, chanting softly in an ancient language as she set about marking my brow with the crescent tattoo. Our mark was the waxing crescent moon, a sign of ever-increasing power and growth, but as I struggled to remain motionless under the biting tips that created the shape, I wondered if that was simply wishful thinking.

I shivered with sudden cold that had nothing to do with the icy stone. Viviane sighed and put a firm hand on me, bidding me be still, but I barely noticed. I was remembering Argante's prophecy on the day of my admittance.

"Another crown sits on her brow, one that will secure the safety and prosperity of many, but at a great cost, both to herself and to those she holds dear."

Deep down, I knew this moment set in motion forces that would validate her words. What I could not foresee, even with the aid of the sight, was how.

Chapter Five

The new moon following my consecration brought with it a flurry of activity to Avalon's shores. Late one night, the Druid astronomers noted something strange in the sky—a comet, unlike any seen in a generation, soared above a triune of sacred stars. The comet was bright and its tail slender and long, causing it to take on the appearance of a firedrake. It was said that the same sign appeared in the heavens when Britain was in peril before the reign of Uther Pendragon. Because of its prophetic timing, the comet had been known as the Kingmaker.

The reappearance of this celestial sign was taken very seriously, and all unnecessary activity was suspended. The Druids invaded our shores from their own sacred land in an unprecedented journey that made the elders talk of the great wonder that was sure to follow.

For the next two moons, days were spent in Avalon's great library, consulting star charts or speaking with the elders, researching the Kingmaker's last appearance. Our nights were a tireless pursuit of the great star. It had not reappeared since the night following its first sighting, but we all knew it would come again. So that no skill would go untapped, Argante and Merlin, the Archdruid, decreed that Druids and priestesses should work in groups or pairs to pool their knowledge to uncover its meaning. When night fell—except on the full and new moons, when each sex kept to its own mysterious ceremony—young and old alike would fan out in groups to designated sites across the isle where the lines of energy intersected and, with weary eyes, perform their craft.

And so it was on a mid-spring night not long after the equinox. The air was unseasonably warm, the land hushed in drowsy slumber. Creatures of the night sang their soothing lullaby. All across the hillside, small fires twinkled, marking the spots where priests and priestesses tried to divine the will of the gods.

My companion lay on the tall grass a few feet away from me, head resting on his intertwined fingers, dark eyes cast heavenward, while I sat next to the sacred spring, leaning heavily upon a large boulder on its bank.

I studied him with keen interest. Aggrivane was seventeen, the second son of the great King Lot who ruled the wild kingdom of Lothian far to the north in my mother's homeland. That much Argante had told me before she sent us off into the woods. Over the past several months, I had learned much more about this tall, handsome man. Aggrivane spoke of his dreams of becoming a warrior, dreams that would have to wait to be fulfilled, out of obedience to his father. King Lot insisted he learn the path of peace before espousing a life of violence.

"He told me it would be to my benefit to calm my willful and stormy nature," Aggrivane had explained with a smirk.

I'd seen him for the first time on the day of the Druids arrival. Our paths crossed as he labored to unload one of their boats, and he regarded me warmly with chestnut eyes fringed with thick lashes, the corner of his lips turned up in a self-conscious half-smile.

Just as they were now.

Oh no, he knows I was staring at him. I turned away, and my cheeks flushed with embarrassment. I had believed him to be asleep. Hastily, I forced my attention back to the pool and stared into its depths as if the waters could wash away my humiliation.

Amused, Aggrivane sat up, brushing back his wavy, dark brown hair. "Enjoying the view?" he asked, eyes crinkling with mirth in the way I found so attractive.

He was only teasing me, but I could not bring myself to answer. Words died soundlessly in my throat, and I did my best to shield myself from his penetrating gaze by letting my hair fall as a screen between us. I had no experience with men, so I did not know how to conduct myself in this unfamiliar situation.

"Guinevere, look at me." He seemed remorseful, even slightly hurt I had not taken his joke as intended. "Merlin and Argante sent us here to work together—not to hide from one another. Please, let us make peace." He reached out a hand toward me.

"I am sorry," I stammered, my voice barely a whisper. "It is just... we so rarely receive men on these shores. . ."

Aggrivane nodded but said nothing, his look turning pensive.

I feared I had offended him in some way. But before I could give voice to my fears, he came over to sit by my side. His rich, dark eyes searched my face.

"You are a newly consecrated priestess, are you not?" His finger grazed the blue crescent on my brow, only recently healed. His touch was like fire that left a tingling trail in its wake. "Is it true that the comet first appeared on the night you took your vows?"

My eyes widened and I nodded slowly. Few people knew of that. "It is," I replied, more warily than I would have liked. "But I did not see it."

"Of course not." He studied my face with a concentration he usually reserved for the stars.

The intensity of his gaze was making me uncomfortable. Warmth spread from my face to my breasts and was slowly creeping down my torso.

"Perhaps then"—his voice was soft and sweet as nectar—"the firedrake heralds some greatness for you."

A trill of nervous laughter escaped my lips. "I fear you regard me too highly."

"Perhaps," he mused. "Or perhaps not." He smiled sweetly at the thought. He returned his attention to the stars and moments passed in silence before he spoke again. "How long have you been on this isle, Guinevere?"

"I was brought here just after my eleventh birthday, about four years ago."

"How did you come to this vocation?"

"My mother promised me to the Goddess at birth. I was brought here when I started showing signs of the sight." Without realizing what I was doing, I moved closer to him and began to slowly trace the image of a serpentine dragon that wound its way up his dominant arm—the sign of his clan. "What about you? You said it was your father's wish that you study with the Druids. Do you regret it?"

His eyes followed my hand as he began to gently caress it with his own. Then he let out a slow, deep breath. "No, I do not. My father is a wise man. The path of peace is the best training a warrior can have because it teaches you love and the value of life. Because of what I have learned, I will never kill for sport or pleasure, only out of duty to my king or in self-defense. There would be much less bloodshed if all soldiers were trained to follow the holy path."

The hypnotizing motion of his fingertips stopped.

"And you, my little priestess." He clasped my hand. "Have you any regrets?"

Images of an alternate life—the one I would have led had I stayed with my family—raced through my mind. I saw myself with my childhood friends at play in Northgallis or studying under the watchful gaze of a tutor.

I shook my head. "My life here has taught me to have faith in that which I cannot see"—I found myself leaning into him as I spoke—"in what can only be felt."

We fell silent, lost in the energy that pulsed in the scant space between us. I tried to convince myself that it was the power of the intersecting ley lines, but to no avail. This energy, this blinding, throbbing force drew me toward Aggrivane; in my innocence, I did not understand it, but I was powerless to resist it.

Overhead, a shooting star illuminated the velvet sky. Startled, we both looked up.

Aggrivane's face lit up with a different kind of fire. "It is the first herald," he exclaimed. "Three shooting stars in the vicinity of the triune precede the comet's appearance." Then his face clouded over with disappointment. "Now is the time for us to work our magic if we are to gain access to the answers we seek."

Absorbed in what had passed between us, I had almost forgotten the reason for our nocturnal vigil. Hastily, I slipped out of his arms and over to the edge of the spring, where I peered purposefully into its depths.

The waters shone inky blue and green in the dim light of midnight. In the soft light of the slender moon, I caught a glimpse of the smooth stones lining the bottom. I inhaled deeply, determined to free my mind to the will of the Goddess. A soft breeze caressed my cheek, and I breathed in the heavy perfume of honeysuckle from a hedge somewhere nearby. Slowly, my consciousness sank into the murky depths of the nothingness that separated our world from the celestial plane. Deeper and deeper down I forced my mind, but I still saw nothing but darkness.

Frustrated, I looked up in time to see the second herald paint the sky the color of dawn with its shimmering streak of light. Aggrivane was performing complex mental calculations known only to the Druids, eyes on the sky, darting to and fro in rapt concentration.

I closed my eyes and breathed deeply. I projected my senses outward until the vibration of the Tor behind me pulsed in my veins. I willed myself free of my body and allowed my soul to sink into the void between worlds—into the silent depths of eternity that existed before the Goddess gave birth to the world. Again, I reached the point where visions should start to form, but they did not. I could not seem to pierce the veil.

I cursed under my breath.

Without taking his eyes from the sky, Aggrivane reached out to me. "What is it? What do you see?" he asked, standing to get a better view of the sky.

"Nothing," I replied, defeated.

"Why don't you try one more time?" he encouraged. Without waiting for my answer, he knelt down on the grass behind me, placing his arms around my waist, hands on top of my own.

"But what about the stars?"

He gave a small laugh. "I can see them in the reflection of the water. Have no fear." He pulled me to him and murmured into my hair. "Remember the power that was given to you when you were made a priestess."

His voice was soothing, and I slowly melted into a trance. I relaxed against him and breathed in his scent, the smell of oak and apple wood. Soon my heart beat the same slow, two-note rhythm drumming in his chest.

His fingers intertwined with mine. "You know the power of the Goddess. Invoke her into you and let yourself be free."

The surface of the water rippled with his breath and my vision turned inward; I no longer had need of any sense save that of touch. Everywhere Aggrivane's body met mine, we seemed to be as one, exchanging energy as if there were no bounds between us—no space, no clothing, not even skin. His lips grazed my neck, the stubble around his mouth tickling my skin invitingly, and suddenly the veil that separated me from the spirit world was lifted.

"The third herald," Aggrivane said softly.

His voice reached me as if from a great distance. While the star lit the sky, in the depths of the water danced a vision older than the standing stones. Fires blazed in low pits on the hillside. A man more animal than human stood on the edge of the forest, naked but for the antlered crown on his brow and the blood painted on his flesh.

Above him on a hill stood a woman, also nude, her billowing hair radiant as the sun, her bare breasts mirrors of the full moon that shone in the sky above her.

The woman came to him and bade him to drink from a golden cup, after which she did the same and led him to a secluded grove. There she opened herself to him, and he poured out his seed in the fertile plain of her body.

"The old ways must be kept. Remember the old ways," a chorus of voices chanted in my mind.

I came back to myself suddenly, panting as if I had run the length of the isle, my body held upright only by Aggrivane's arms, strong as the trunks of a pair of ancient oaks. Saying nothing, I spun around and kissed him full on the mouth. He seemed surprised but willing. Too soon, light like the midsummer sun pierced the darkness behind my closed eyes. Squinting, I opened one eye and pulled away.

"The firedrake!"

We both stared in awe at the wonder before us. The firedrake was many times larger than the heralds that preceded it, and even the moon seemed dim in comparison. Its long tail stretched across the sky, led by a fiery head that resembled a snarling dragon. It streaked through the night, accompanied by a shriek that could have raised the ancients from their resting places. Then, just as quickly, it was gone.

◦◦◦

Merlin gathered everyone together the next morning following sunrise salutations. He sat on the top of the sanctuary stairs, holding court with Argante and Viviane. The other Druids and priestesses gathered around on the steps below. Their voices blended into a low buzz as they speculated on the meaning of the firedrake and the mysterious visions and other phenomenon reported following the comet's appearance last night.

I watched Merlin, in awe of his power of attraction, a gift that flowed as easy as breath. He was a lodestone, able to draw anyone to him when he wished, but equally capable of keeping them away when he willed it. This gift, or illusion, as some called it, never failed to both thrill and unsettle me when he was near.

As Merlin held council with the isle's eldest and most powerful, he appeared perfectly comfortable in his role as the youngest Archdruid in living memory, directing and counseling with the wisdom of a man who had seen six decades, rather than only three. Though he bore great responsibility, his face remained unlined, pale as fresh milk, intense, with knowing eyes the color of the lake. Some said his bright copper hair, which in many ways reminded me of Morgan's, marked his bloodline as descended from the earliest races of our land, those who were part fae and bore greater resemblance to gods than men. Maybe that was where his commanding presence came from. He certainly could inspire fear and awe in equal measure, depending on his mood.

Tearing my gaze away from Merlin, I chanced a glance at Aggrivane, who stood next to me. I was doing my best to hide my nervousness and pretend nothing had changed between us, but we both knew it had. I was finding it difficult to meet his eyes without immediately flushing, but every so often he would catch my gaze and hold it with a smile that made my heart melt. Hesitantly, he brushed my fingertips with his and I nearly gasped at the spark that ran up my arm. Looking up at him with a timid smile, I entwined my fingers with his and bit my lip, bashfully turning my attention back to the activity at the top of the stairs.

Merlin's long red hair shone in the early morning light as he leaned in toward Viviane, the two whispering in an intimate manner. We all knew Merlin fairly well because he visited the isle several times a year to conduct business with Argante. But it was not just her he came to see; he seemed to have a special affection for Viviane, and the two were never far from one another's side when he was here. It was never spoken of, but I strongly suspected Ailis—the girl I rescued from the tree two years earlier—was his daughter and Viviane his wife, though I doubted a legal contract was what bound them to one another.

Regardless of the truth, Merlin never singled out Ailis; he treated her with the same fatherly respect and affection he bestowed on each one of us. No matter how brief his visit, Merlin never failed to inquire about us, as concerned for the welfare of Avalon's priestesses and neophytes as he was for the Druids in his own care. Witty and eloquent, he often regaled us with mythical or historical tales or fanciful riddles, and sometimes even taught us a little of the Druid's lore. As I grew into womanhood, I came to treasure his visits and appreciate the confidence he showed in me, for I viewed him much like a second father and wished never to disappoint him.

Merlin stood, his bright eyes sweeping the crowd as he prepared to speak. "Druids of Britain, priestesses of the Goddess, I bid you good day. And an especially good day it is, for we have the privilege of carrying out Divine orders, beginning this very morn."

All around me, heads turned as neighbor whispered to neighbor, questioning or positing a personal theory on what Merlin's words meant.

"As you have no doubt heard, and perhaps embellished in the retelling"—he chuckled—"many signs and wonders were given to us last night as the firedrake made what I believe to be its final appearance. Alone, your experiences may seem odd and perplexing, but that is because they are but fragments of a greater whole. Taken together, the Lady and I believe they reveal the will of the God and Goddess.

"This we know: from this generation shall arise a great king and so a great sign, the firedrake, has been given to herald his ascent to power. As in days of old, the Goddess wishes this man to be hallowed in both the heavens and on earth, in a ceremony that can only take place on this holy isle between one of her priestesses and the man she deems worthy. This being so, on Beltane we will enact the most holy of rituals ever to be performed—the Sacred Marriage. By coming together in the life-generating, creative act and emulating the love of the God and Goddess, this pair shall assure the great king is wedded to the land—man to woman—priest to priestess—Otherworld to Earth—and the blessing of the Goddess shall be bestowed on him and on our land.

"We know, too, that the Goddess wishes the treasures of Avalon no longer lie hidden in the mists but be returned to the outside world, beginning with the sacred sword. The king will be vested with this symbol of power by the Lady herself when he comes forth to be hallowed."

And so it was to be. The Druids departed our shores for their home within hours, charged with the task of finding this great king before the festival. The priestess who would embody the Goddess would be chosen from our own number in a few short weeks.

I smiled inwardly as I looked around our sleeping chambers that night before retiring. From the expression on many faces, it was clear mine was not the only heart the Druids had taken with them.

CHAPTER SIX

Summer 495

On Beltane morning, all the daughters of Avalon—young and old—shivered in the chill air as night slowly gave way to dawn. As we traversed the tender grass carpeting the plains between the confluence of the white and red springs, our feet were washed in fresh dew, a silent absolution from the earth herself.

We reached the summit of the Tor in silence and joined hands, feeling the subtle shift of energy as light broke over the horizon. This was a sacred day, one of the most holy of all holidays celebrated by our people. Today was the beginning of summer, the day honoring the union of the Goddess and God and the fertility of all the land.

On Beltane night, every woman was said to be the Goddess incarnate and every man the God. Their sexual union reflected that of the two aspects of Deity, and any child born of such a union was considered blessed by the gods. However, in rare years when the Sacred Marriage was performed, those terms increased ninefold for the couple who invoked the God and Goddess into their bodies in ritual, as well as for their offspring. Today one of us would be chosen, set apart by the Lady to act in her service.

Mona's clear voice broke the silence in a high, worshipful note as she saluted the rising sun in song, speaking the language of our ancestors. We responded reverently and fell to our knees in unison. Mirroring the actions of the others, I ran my palms across the grass and placed them on my face.

"Through the tears of the earth, may the Goddess grant me health and long youth," I quietly prayed, echoing the words whispered by each priestess as she washed.

I glanced over in time to catch Morgan shrinking away as Grainne swiped at her hair, trying to get it wet or dirty—I wasn't sure. I couldn't help but smile. We were all vowed priestesses now, but in many ways we were still children, still prone to the same mischief as the day we came to the isle.

Rising, I turned to face the circle of standing stones that surrounded us, towering twice my height in some places. Somewhere down below, deep in the forest, Aggrivane and the other Druids hunted. I had heard the low blast of their horn as we gathered at the springs. They had their own sacred rites, their own duties particular to this day and to the ceremony that would be enacted tonight. Under the shelter of the oaks, ash, and elm, they fought to determine who would be the Sacred King.

When I closed my eyes and listened, I thought I could hear them chanting and the occasional cry of one being tested. I tried to center myself and send forth my mind to see their progress, but my efforts were interrupted as Viviane and Argante made their way to the center of the circle.

Argante opened her arms wide and addressed us in a tone of authority. "The Druids have chosen the men from whom will be selected the Sacred King according to the ancient tests. So too have we chosen the one who shall take up the mantle of the Goddess and perform the role of the Virgin Queen." She inclined her head to the copper-haired priestess next to me. "Morgan, the responsibility has fallen to you. Though this is a great honor, it comes at a heavy price. Do you agree to sacrifice your maidenhead in service to the Great Mother and to do so with utmost humility?"

Morgan nodded silently, barely able to contain her excitement.

"So be it then. Come with me." Argante gestured for Morgan to follow her out of the circle. "I will prepare you for the ritual."

Morgan began to follow but then stopped. Slowly, she turned toward me, a triumphant smirk on her face. "Look who is the victor now," she whispered in my ear. "Lineage or no, it seems I have won our little competition after all. While I am taking part in the most sacred of our rituals with the God himself, you will have to be content whoring away your virginity with a common man." She shrugged. "But perhaps that is how it should be. The Goddess never errs, you know."

This, then, was her ultimate revenge—taking the top honor, one that would not be bestowed again, at least not to our generation. I wanted to kill her in that moment, to wrap my hands around her neck or strangle her with the braided rope of her own hair. But Grainne, sensing my tension, held my arms as Morgan gave me one last gloating sneer and swaggered away down the hillside.

I forced my mind back to the present and made myself breathe deeply. "Sweet Mother, give me strength," I muttered, trying to calm the poisonous brew of hatred and jealousy boiling in my belly.

As I fought for control, the first ray of sunlight peaked over the crest of Pen Hill. It shone directly on the altar stone only twice a year—today, the festival of life, and on Samhain, the day of death. Viviane had placed a polished crystal at an angle on the stone and it captured the light, serving as a natural lens to ignite the tinder beneath. From this tiny fire, she lit a series of small white tapers, which were presented to each of the remaining virgins.

As I held mine, I suddenly realized what was to come tonight— the full significance of the candle. It was permission to take a lover, to engage fully in the festival. This flame, lit not by human hands but by the sun, the symbol of the God, was the flame of passion which drew him to the Goddess. Its heat seemed to travel from my finger-tips, up my arm, and through my veins, warming my blood. I felt my cheeks flush and my breasts tingle. An unfamiliar stirring below my belly told me I was ready to experience the full extent of the mystery this night would bring.

⌘

As we traipsed through the forest, we sang ancient festival songs and others made up on the spot, gathering wands and flowers, weaving them into garlands and wreaths, bedecking one another and any sacred tree, stream, or well we could find. Some of the Druids had begun drinking already, so to them, everything was sacred and deserving of a floral crown.

"They say the Sacred King is quite a strapping man," Mona said above the boisterous laughter. "Good thing I wasn't chosen for his queen or he'd have crushed my delicate frame." She swept a hand down the length of her slender body to emphasize her point.

"You'll have no such problem from Connor," teased one of the Druids, poking a smaller man in the ribs. "Wiry as a stork, he is."

Connor grabbed the teasing Druid around the neck playfully and pretended to bash in his head.

"Guinevere, did you hear Aggrivane took second?" Grainne yelled over her shoulder to me, never loosening her grip on the man at her side.

"He did?" That meant Aggrivane was the Sacred King's champion, and thus allowed to choose his mate from among the virgin priestesses. It was not as holy an office as the Sacred King, but an honor nonetheless. Suddenly, I was afraid. What if he wanted someone else? Worse yet—what if I, in my innocence, was a disappointment to him? All of my earlier confidence drained away, and I began to wonder if attending the ritual was such a good idea.

"Where is he anyway?" asked a man whose name I did not know. "It is unlike any son of Lothian to miss a celebration."

We continued on, the boys harassing the girls like children and making jokes that on any other day would have been considered lewd. From time to time, a couple lingered behind to steal a few kisses or inspect a grove or meadow and claim it as their own for later in the night.

We were nearing the apple orchards when we crossed paths with another group, Aggrivane among them. He smiled when he saw me and motioned me off the path into a small stand of trees. I followed in breathless anticipation, palms sweaty, heart thumping.

When we were alone, he drew me toward him. I ran my fingers through the thick mass of dark curls at the base of his neck and smiled, breathing in his scent. It took me a moment to notice there was something in his right hand. A golden arrow with a crystal tip shimmered as the wind waved the branches overhead. It was his prize as second.

"I have made my choice," he whispered into my hair, kissing the top of my head.

"And I, mine." I melted into his arms, reveling in a state of pure bliss.

⁎⁎⁎

An hour later, the sun was high overhead. The wind had stilled, holding its breath in imitation of the crowd.

At the center of the clearing, the two opponents stood, facing one another on the axis of a great circle drawn in the dirt. On one side stood the morning's victor, a large man who had been transformed into the Oak King, naked save for a loincloth the color of tree bark and the oak leaves twined in his yellow hair. Tiny painted vines and leaves wound their way around his sinuous flesh, tracing the contours of toned muscle in his arms, legs, and torso. His face had been painted green, so his identity was unknown to all but a select few.

Across from him, sweating in fur as white as snow, was the Holly King, a crown of prickly green leaves and bright red berries upon his brow. Merlin, being the last man to hold the office of Sacred King, fulfilled this role. Just as each year light conquered darkness, so too would this newcomer have to defeat him in order to claim the favor of the Goddess and restore the balance of power in the heavens and on the earth.

As I stood at the edge of the circle, Aggrivane's arms protectively encircling me, I caught a whiff of roasting flesh from the stag sacrificed by the Druids, our food at the feast that would follow. I shivered, suddenly aware of the pungent reminder that although this battle was mock, it served a great significance in the cycle of life and death.

Argante stood in the circle between the two men, cloaked in silver from head to toe, the goddess of the stars who directed the wheel of time and decreed all things. She attentively watched the midday sky, waiting for the precise moment between day and night when all things hung in perfect balance.

Looking at her now, I could see no trace of the illness that had kept her confined to her hut the last several weeks. Worried that the ritual might further damage Argante's health, Viviane had asked to take her place, but Argante insisted on fulfilling the role that was her due as Lady of the Lake.

Soundlessly, she gave the signal and glided out of the circle. The two men began to shift, testing one another as in a real duel. As prescribed by the ancient ritual, each man was armed only with a staff made of the wood whose spirit he embodied. Neither was allowed to cross his half of the circle, for it represented the light and dark halves of the year, which twice annually stood in equilibrium but never overlapped.

The combatants poked at one another with their staffs until they reached the center of the circle. Then their branches crossed, crackling and popping as each tried to overtake the other. The sound brought back memories of a forgotten life—a time in my youth when the young boys and I would practice fencing with blunted wooden swords under my mother's direction.

They danced along the center line, bobbing and weaving to avoid each other's swings, while trying to find the weakness in the other, the opportunity to overpower. It did not take long for the stalwart Oak King to topple the lithe Holly King, though Merlin was a much better fighter than I had anticipated. He had a speed and skill belied by his size. Still, that was not of much consequence when he lay supine on the ground, the Oak King's foot resting lightly on his throat.

"The Holly King has died! The Oak King is reborn! The light ascends once again!"

The cry echoed through the isle as the victor helped Merlin to his feet. The time for ritual drama was at an end; the time for celebration had begun.

☙ ⬥ ❧

In the valley at the foot of the Tor, hundreds of bonfires lit up the night, surrounded by circles of merry priestesses in pale blue ritual robes, Druids in white and royal blue, and nobles loyal to the ancient ways spanning every color in between. Fire was everywhere. It lit up the night and ignited the spirits of the revelers. A handful of men and women made their way through the crowd, twirling staffs with blazing tips, while some brave souls were rolling fire wheels down the hillside into the lake.

Everywhere drums echoed the heartbeat of the earth, whipping us into an ecstasy of wild abandon. Laughter and lively conversation mingled with smoke and the intoxicating scent of ritual herbs, a potion of joy carried on the warm night breeze. A makeshift musical troupe of harpists, pipers, drummers, and singers gathered to play traditional songs of the twelve ancient tribes. Some of the more intoxicated revelers were singing along, while the more sober conversed, told off-color stories, or continued the luck-bestowing tradition of jumping over the smoldering embers from the fire that had cooked the ritual meal.

In the center of the valley was the largest fire, built of the nine sacred woods. Around it, the Archdruid, the Lady of the Lake, Viviane, Morgan, and the Sacred King sat, breaking their ritual fast on the flesh of the fallen stag. The shadows in which he sat made it difficult for me to see the Sacred King clearly, but I could tell that he was now dressed in animal pelts and his face was painted with sacred markings.

While I was watching them, grateful to have claimed Aggrivane as my own but still a tiny bit jealous of Morgan, the drummers shifted to a lively tune. Aggrivane tossed off his cloak and grabbed my hand, easily whisking me to my feet. I laughed and stumbled as he pulled me toward the center of the festivities and we joined a train of dancers whirling between the bonfires. I lifted my skirts in my right hand and struggled to hold on to his with my left as we spun between the bonfires in a dizzying dance of freedom. Faces swirled past—Mona, Grainne, Rowena, Druids I had come to recognize but whose names I did not know—each one seemed more joyous than the last. Finally, the song came to an end, and Aggrivane scooped me up, breathless, in his arms.

"Look." He pointed at the main fire. "The Sacred Marriage is about to begin."

The drums ended on a sharp beat, and silence settled over the valley. The high note of a bell rang out, and the Virgin Queen was led forward by the Lady of the Lake. I would not have guessed it to be Morgan had I not already known. Her face was hidden from view by a gauzy white veil, but her hair flowed softly over her shoulders, blazing brighter than the bonfires, and upon her head rested a crown of spring flowers. A flowing white skirt concealed her thighs from view, but her breasts remained bare, revealing that each of her nipples and her navel had been adorned with paint in the shape of a small blue spiral. After a few instructive words from Argante, she stood barefoot before her consort.

She bestowed her blessing upon the Sacred King, anointing him with the blood of the stag and investing him with the sacred sword of Avalon, the first of the treasures to be returned to the outside world, according to the Goddess's decree. He, in turn, gave her the lingering kiss of knowing, which signaled the start of the most sacred part of the evening.

The couple was blocked from my sight as Merlin and Argante stood in front of them, conducting the rest of the ritual in secret. I could only guess that what was taking place was a magnified version of the ritual the spectators were about to perform in pairs. After the sacred couple was led off to the area reserved for their union, other pairs followed suit, fanning off to secluded groves, caves, and other private areas across the island.

Aggrivane led me by the hand down through the orchard along a winding path, his boots making soft indentations in the dirt in front of me. The apple blossoms breathed their perfume into the air as we passed. My heartbeat quickened with each step.

"Where are we going?" I asked.

Aggrivane chuckled but did not reply.

He led me to a small copse of dense oak trees. Their base formed a nearly perfect circle, roots intertwining deep in the ground beneath. A carpet of soft moss blanketed the base, nurtured by the shade of the branches above. Moonlight filtered down through the leaves, throwing glittering shadows before us.

The grove would have been breathtaking alone, but it had been decorated for the feast. Strings of white hawthorn blossoms hung from the lowest branches overhead, and a rainbow of wildflower petals were strewn among the moss and ferns, making the grove appear much like a faerie queen's bridal bower.

"I found this place not long after we arrived to await the fire-drake," Aggrivane explained. "It has been my own personal paradise. I had no way of knowing if you would say yes, but I wanted to make it special, just in case." He scratched the back of his neck nervously as he spoke.

"It is beautiful." I could say no more, emotion choking my voice. That he would do something so thoughtful reassured me that whatever passed between us tonight would be something much greater than lust incited by the festival.

Aggrivane cocked his head to the side as the tempo of the far-off drums shifted. They were softer now, but somehow more insistent. He removed his cloak and laid it on the ground before pulling me to him and cupping my cheek in his hand. I was suddenly paralyzed with nerves, but as I gazed in to his eyes, I knew I was safe.

The thrum of ritual became like a dance as we moved ever closer, drawn in by the steady musical pounding and the pulsing of blood in our veins. His fingertips sent shivers up my spine as he ran them up the length of my body, from hips to shoulders, bringing the fabric of my dress along with them. I reached out a shaking hand to untie his belt and remove his clothing, aided by his more knowledgeable hands.

For a moment, we simply stood, marveling at the sight of one another. Then Aggrivane took a small step toward me, closing the gap between us. Gently, he brushed his lips against my skin in the sacred triune kiss, lightly touching the crescent on my brow, pausing to taste my lips, and trailing down to my heart.

I ran my fingers through his hair, every nerve begging him to remain there, to do what he willed. But mindful of my sovereignty, he looked up, wide eyes seeking permission to continue. I smiled softly and nodded, sending a private prayer to the Goddess to guide me as I trod unknown paths.

His lips closed on my breast, and I arched my back in unexpected pleasure, grateful for the circle of his arms around my hips to keep me upright. As if sensing my thoughts, Aggrivane slowly eased me to the ground, where his cloak waited to enfold me.

He eased himself down on top of me, slowly tracing his way down my body with a litany of kisses and delicate caresses, each one increasing my longing. As the heat of his skin seeped into mine, I lost all sense of space and time, until the boundaries between us melted away.

A quick stab of pain followed as the veil within me was rent and we became one with the heavens and the earth. He was the velvet black of midnight enfolding and embracing me. I was the silver moon that called the tides of our joining and lit up his darkness. Together, we feverishly fought against the coming dawn, only too aware it would tear us apart forever.

ஒஒ ஓஓ

Far too soon, the pale light of morning began to erase the night. We clung to each other, shivering, unwilling to do what must be done. The ecstasy of the festival had long since faded, and with it, the surety of divine expansiveness. I keenly felt the insignificance of my humanity, how small and helpless I was in the face of the cruel fate that befell all couples of the festival fires.

In the distance, the low moan of the Druids' horn broke the silence.

"They are calling me," Aggrivane whispered, lips grazing my cheek.

"Calling us to part." I said what he did not. Then I kissed him slowly, imparting my unspoken emotions in that single act.

The horn sounded a second time, and Aggrivane reluctantly pulled away.

"Do you see that?" He pointed toward the eastern sky, where a single star still glowed with the fierce brilliance of midnight. "That's the morning star, named by the Greeks for the goddess of love. When you see it, think of me and I will think of you."

"No." I shook my head, wondering how many other lovers were now making that same pledge. "That star is the herald of the dawn that now takes you from me. I don't wish to relive this pain, nor should you. I will think of you on the rising of its counterpart, the one that signals the coming darkness, for it was under that starry veil our love was conceived and consummated."

He held my hands between his and kissed them. "My love, most of the year they are one and the same star. Just as we cannot think of one another without remembering our parting, neither can they be separated. But as you will it, so shall it be. I will think of you when the stars emerge from their daylight retreat."

With one last kiss, he was gone and I was alone in my despair, certain this moment was the worst I would ever experience.

CHAPTER SEVEN

One full moon cycle later, I watched the light slowly drain from the sky as I traversed the seven rings of the Tor with the other women of Avalon. I clung to Aggrivane's parting words as though they would bring him back to me. I was supposed to be thinking of the ritual, but instead I sought out the night star, as I would every night until the end of time.

"Airanrhod, Branwen, Brigid, Rhiannon, Cerridwen, Great Mother," the priestesses uttered in rhythmic unison. The chant echoed off the terraced side of the Tor as we wound our way in and out of its turns, slowly ascending.

"Hear us," responded the acolytes.

The wood chips lining the path crackled underfoot as we passed. We moved like the tide, first closer and then farther away from our destination, which was the summit of the Tor, the center of the labyrinth. Unlike a maze, it had no dead ends or trickery—only a beginning and an end. The complex journey of ascent that began our ritual was meant to free our minds of all care and focus our spirits. When we descended at the close, it would slowly release us from our spiritual state and bring us back to the world.

I pushed all thoughts of Aggrivane from my mind and concentrated on my breathing. Regardless of my mood or mindset when I entered the gate, I always found peace along the way. This walking meditation had been one of the few ways I had found solace during my early days in Avalon. To this day, I marveled at how symbolic the pattern was. As in life, the farther I seemed from the goal, the closer I was, and when I thought it lie just around the next bend, I was at the opposite point.

"Airanrhod, Branwen, Brigid, Rhiannon, Cerridwen, Great Mother," we called.

"Hear us," the younger ones replied.

"Airanrhod, Branwen, Brigid, Rhiannon, Cerridwen, Great Mother."

"Hear us."

I gradually fell under the spell of the chant and lost the ability to distinguish my own voice from the rest. Around me, the rosemary, lavender, and night-blooming flowers that clung precariously to the side of the Tor's rings exhaled their fragrance, coaxed by a gentle nudge from the hem of our gowns. Above, the rotund Honey Moon ruled the clear night sky, sparkling stars surrounding it like dutiful courtiers.

I was so absorbed in the procession that I scarcely noticed when we reached the top.

Across the circle, Morgan's copper hair reflected the silver moonlight with an odd luminosity. By now it was clear she was not with child as was hoped. Still, Argante said the Sacred Marriage was not a failure; she insisted the Goddess had a greater purpose in mind.

Four of the women raised their arms to honor the elements, then Viviane recited the sacred prayer to the Goddess of the moon. As her last words died out, the wind stirred, fanning the flames of the ritual fire toward the heavens. Argante gave the signal. It was time for the invocation.

Viviane stepped forward and assumed the position at the center of the circle normally occupied by Argante. This was the first time in anyone's memory that Argante had not acted as the mouthpiece of the Goddess. It was not a good a sign. Argante's lingering illness— the one that had taken hold before Beltane—had progressed to the point that she had been carried up the Tor on a litter. She was far too weak to withstand such powerful forces, so Viviane performed the ritual in her stead.

Viviane faced the moon. Morgan and I moved to flank each of her sides, serving as attendants to her every need. Viviane raised her arms, closed her eyes, and the air around her grew perfectly still, as if time had stopped. An ancient chant passed her lips in a language of time immemorial, and her head tilted back as her body received the spirit of the Goddess. Morgan and I braced both of her shoulders, but Viviane shrugged away our hands, indicating she needed no assistance. Slowly, she opened her eyes and turned, regarding each priestess with distant eyes.

"Great Mother, may your wisdom forever guide us." Argante

leaned heavily on her cane as she posed the first of the ritual questions to the Goddess. "What say you of this land?"

"The red dragon is poised to return to the realm of spirit, but another shall succeed him. The hallowed one has received the blessing of the land, and so shall it prosper under his guidance. Although malevolent forces threaten from without, the bear shall be victorious and all shall bow at the sound of his name." The voice that issued from Viviane's mouth was not her own, but one like liquid silver.

Argante seemed unfazed by the strange reply. "Thank you, Mother." She continued on in the traditional way. "May your goodness be forever praised. What say you of this sacred place?"

"Soon the final passage shall be crossed by one of great power, allowing the lily to emerge from shadow and bloom in the light. An unlikely rose is transplanted to this isle and blossoms in its rich soil. But beware the rose and handle her carefully, for her thorns threaten to pierce the bud of the lily, thus causing the whole garden to die."

A murmur rippled around the circle, but Argante paid no heed.

"We thank you for your wisdom. May your protection be forever on us. What say you of these, your servants?"

"These here gathered serve me well, and I am pleased. But the day will come when sister shall oppose sister, both in this sacred place and without. Loyalties will be tested and betrayed, so heed my warning. That which is birthed in jealousy shall not give life but infect all who draw near. Therefore, act with love and not out of spite. Only then shall you escape the fate the stars foretell."

Silence followed. Around the circle, my confusion was mirrored in all but a few faces. Argante, however, seemed to have comprehended the Goddess's enigmatic words fully, for she leaned against her cane, nodding as if in agreement with what she heard, eyes shining with newly formed tears. Morgan too appeared to have gleaned some knowledge from the prophecy, for she once again bore that sly, cat-like expression that made me suspect she knew more than she let on.

We bid the Goddess farewell and Morgan led Viviane aside to recover from the strain. I was called forward to gaze in the well of seeing. Every month, a different priestess took her turn scrying in a cauldron filled with water from the confluence of the sacred springs. Sometimes her visions elaborated on the prophecy given by the Goddess. Other times they yielded a message that pertained to one or more of the priestesses present, while sometimes nothing was seen at all.

I stood over the cauldron, gazing at my own reflection and breathing deeply, trying to calm myself enough to open my perception. As I leaned forward and exhaled, my breath ruffled the surface of the water, shattering the mirror image before me. A mass of colors swirled in the water, and I sent my consciousness downward through them, into the depths of the dark. I breathed out once again and my hair fell forward, separating the watery oracle from the rest of the world around me. Slowly, my spirit rose up and escaped my body. Smoke-like tendrils of gray mist began to dance on the surface of the water. Then the visions came.

At first, all I could see were shapes, but then I became aware of enough details to know what I was seeing. It was Northgallis. I recognized my father's sign—an eagle with a thistle blossom clutched in its talons—flying high above the watch towers. The sight of the familiar walls made my heart soar, but that joy was short-lived. My father came into view first, unkempt and unshaven, tears etching canyons in his cheeks. On his shuffling heels followed a tall blond man whose ritual robes marked him a Christian priest. My lady's maid, Octavia, trailed behind, scarcely able to stand, so great was her grief.

Bringing up the rear was an honor guard transporting a bier. The body was shrouded and covered in a black cloth, but I recognized the symbol embroidered on it immediately. It was a knot work horse, the symbol of my mother's clan. Beside the bier, a young man carried a small box draped in matching cloth but bearing my father's standard. It was a baby's coffin; this woman had died in childbirth. Somewhere in the recesses of my heart, I knew who she was, but my mind could not bear to admit it.

The vision splintered to pieces as stabbing shards of light filled my eyes. From somewhere far away, a banshee's high-pitched wail shattered the night. It was only moments later, as my hand struck the cauldron and sent it tumbling to the ground, that I realized I had been the one screaming.

My knees could no longer support me, and my mind threatened to collapse as well. I sank to the ground, heedless of the steaming waters that soaked my skirts. A merciless claw squeezed my heart so hard I thought I would die. I struggled to breathe but could not take in air. Cold, stiff fingers like those of the Death Mother herself pawed at my arms, trying to help me to my feet.

"Guinevere, what is it? What have you seen?" The voices echoed from a great distance.

I swallowed, fighting back the blackness that threatened to engulf me. "My mother—she is dead."

PART TWO

World Beyond the Mist

After seventeen miserable days tracing old Roman roads north from Avalon with Morgan and a handful of guards, this was not the homecoming I had envisioned. I expected to be greeted warmly at the gates by my family and long-estranged friends, but there was nary a soul present to welcome us home, not even a wandering dog.

Our guards shouted out our arrival. A moment later, the entry doors opened and we were ushered quickly inside the gates with only the merest of polite greetings, as if those inside feared to speak with us. While the others hurried quickly indoors, I lingered in the doorway, drawing comfort from the feeling of protection the thick walls of the fortress gave me.

"My Lady, do come inside."

My thoughts were interrupted by the nasal Midland accent of a blond serving girl who had mysteriously appeared by my side. She tugged on my arm with outrageous familiarity not befitting a woman of her rank. I thought to chastise her for it, but she quickly whisked me away before I could speak.

The fire popped and crackled in the hearth as we stood in the foyer, anxiously awaiting some acknowledgement of our presence. Morgan and I avoided eye contact, still refusing to speak to one another, clinging to the grudge that had begun to fester on Beltane and had only grown worse with time. I still harbored a pit of jealousy over her selection as the Virgin Queen. She had grown secretive and developed a bitter edge in the aftermath of the ritual—I guessed because she had not fulfilled her duty by conceiving a child—using her long-practiced hatred of me as an outlet, never letting me forget she had been chosen and I swept aside. We were only together now because she was ordered to accompany me. I could not wait to bid her farewell.

Time passed slowly, and I began to wonder if my father was

even in residence at the moment; perhaps that was why we were so coldly welcomed. Finally, the maid reappeared in the doorway and announced the master of the house was otherwise engaged, but we were all to bathe and rest; my father would entertain our company at dinner.

It was strange that my father would not come to welcome me himself, but it had been many years since I was a resident of this house. Schedules and decorum could change in far less time.

Though I needed no assistance finding my way up to my old chamber, the maid insisted on accompanying me. I planned to return to Avalon after our mourning period, but Argante had insisted I bring a small bag with me. Without thinking, I began to unpack what remained of my life on the isle: a few sundry mementos and the two blue robes I was given to wear when performing my duties as a priestess at births, funerals, and other sacred events.

"Please, my Lady, allow me."

The squeaky, small voice of the maid pulled me out of my memories. For a moment I simply looked back at her, uncomprehending. Then I realized I had grown so accustomed to doing things for myself in Avalon, I forgot the same actions were unthinkable in this world.

Unsure of how to comport myself, I busied myself by admiring the tapestry hanging on the wall above my bed. The hanging depicted a beautiful young maiden befriending a unicorn as a host of faeries and other nature spirits looked on. It was a scene from one of my favorite childhood stories—a tale my mother recounted on many dark winter nights in front of the fire. She and I had just begun constructing the tapestry shortly before the Irish raid and the whirlwind that whisked me away to Avalon. It pleased me to see she had completed it in my absence. I could only wonder if each stitch gave her comfort in knowing she had set her daughter on the path the Goddess intended, or if each dip of the needle pricked at her heart, tormenting her conscience over sending her young daughter so far away.

Alas I would never know; she was not here to ask.

I wiped a tear from my cheek and, without a word to the maid, fled from the room on silent feet, seeking sanctuary, somewhere familiar to get my bearings. Rushes, stone, and dirt passed as a blur beneath my toes, and when I next raised my head, I found myself in the armory.

It was strangely quiet, so I knew I was alone. But if I stopped and listened, I could hear the soldiers practicing not far away.

Their grunts and clamor carried on the wind. For a moment, I even fooled myself into believing my mother's authoritative voice commanded and corrected them, but when I really attuned my ears, I found that Rhys, captain of my father's guard, had taken her place as drill master.

Little had changed in this land of iron, bronze, and leather. Gear for each man was still neatly stacked on shelves against one wall, ready at all times for battle, while scores of javelins, swords, daggers, polished bronze-and-wooden shields, and other weaponry lined the racks. I inhaled, savoring the unique bouquet only the close quarters of an armory could produce—the heavy scent of tanned hides, stale sweat, the sharp tang of polish, and just a little wood smoke from the temporarily silent forge. Strange as it may have seemed, this was the scent of home.

Of course my feet would lead me here; it had been my favorite place as a child. Before I was old enough to walk, my mother carried me as she inspected the equipment. I was fascinated by the glimmer of sunlight on the metal objects that surrounded me, entranced as though in a crystal cave. Later, once I could feed myself, she gave me a tiny blunted dagger, which eventually gave way to a wooden sword when my lessons began. Then finally, only two years before I went to Avalon, she bestowed on me my first real sword, a miniature version of her own. I could still picture the intricately crafted pommel and feel the twists of braided metal in my clenched fist.

I sought out my sword now, as eager for its reassuring touch as a babe for her favorite blanket. In the far corner, the tall chest containing my father's arms and armor stood slightly ajar. But its twin, which had held my mother's fighting paraphernalia, had been removed, as had the small trunk that housed my sword and child-hood armor. Dismayed, I picked through my father's things, hoping he had decided to store it all in one case, but I found only his belongings.

Glancing wildly about me, I began searching for the treasure I could not believe was gone. But then I caught my reflection in one of the polished brass shields that hung on the wall and froze. I was not alone after all. Standing behind me to my left was a dark-haired woman. For a moment I thought it the shade of my mother, but when the figure advanced on me, it proved to be very human.

Turning slowly, I tried to ignore the cold sweat blanketing the back of my neck at being caught where I ought not be.

"Octavia!" I exclaimed in a sigh of relief. My lady's maid would give me up to no harm. I ran to her side and enveloped her in my arms, suddenly feeling so weak and weary that I had to draw my strength from her.

"Blessed child, you have returned to us." Octavia smiled at me warmly, though her face still betrayed the sorrow in her heart. "Come, let us go outside. This is no place for a reunion."

She led me into the sunlit courtyard, and we stood watching the warriors spar while she insisted on hearing every last detail of my time in Avalon. While I was happy to oblige her with tale after tale, somewhere in the back of my mind I knew we were both simply delaying an inevitable conversation. Finally, in a moment of silence, I could take no more.

"Oh, Octavia," I cried, a surge of hot tears racing down my face. "I wish Mother were here so she could know all that has happened to me." I clung to the older woman's shoulders, surprised at the force of my own emotion. Burying my face in her long black ringlets, I choked on my tears.

"I know. So do I." She placed her hands on my shoulders and tipped up my face to meet her eyes. "But one thing is for certain, she hears you now, and she is very proud of you."

"Do you think so?"

"I know so." She kissed me on the forehead.

I smiled weakly. "Octavia." I licked my suddenly dry lips. "I have to know. The baby—was it my brother or my sister?"

"It was a boy." She hesitated a moment. "That is why your father was so upset. It was the heir to the kingdom he had been praying for. Now it will likely pass to your cousin Bran."

I thought I was the heir to his kingdom. I frowned. I would bring this up with my father when I next saw him.

Octavia saw my puzzled expression and attempted to explain. "Your father has placed a greater emphasis on his Roman heritage, of late. Despite all of the pregnancies your mother lost and babes who died young, your father had always hoped for a son to pass his kingdom on to, so that it would not fall into another lord's—your future husband's—hands upon his death."

I started to protest.

Octavia waved away my rebuttal. "I know your mother intended you to inherit, but Northgallis is a long way from the traditions she endorsed, so your father had a valid concern. Then with the death of the boy child and of your mother, all of his dreams fell apart. You were so far away. He felt he had nothing."

"Nothing?" Anger flared within me, heating my cheeks and quickly drying my tears to an invisible crust. "Is that what I am? Is that why my mother's arms are gone, so that not a memory of her remains? And what of my sword? Have I no say in the placement of my own possessions?"

Octavia clasped my hands in hers and regarded me gravely. "Your mother's sword is buried with her, as is her right of honor. As for yours. . ." She hesitated. "Your father melted it down. He wishes no more training of the kind for you."

I gaped and attempted to interrupt, but Octavia held up a hand to silence me.

"Guinevere, your father is not the same man you left here all those years ago. He has changed so much. Many things, many traditions died with your mother. You must realize that. Take what I have told you into consideration when you see your father, and do not be too hard on him. Have pity on him instead."

The weight of her words lay on my shoulders like chain mail. I could not respond. I had hoped to return to a place of warmth and love, but instead found myself in a house full of perplexing strangers.

Could four years really change so much?

◦◦

Late that night, when the candles burned low and all the servants had gone to bed, I padded barefoot along the corridors, searching for my father. He had not shown up to dinner, so Octavia, Morgan, and I ate our meal in awkward silence amid the gaping stares of a handful of servants I did not know. They were obviously curious about me, and more so about Morgan—especially given the tension that sparked the air between us—but fortunately knew their place well enough not to ask questions.

Later, as I lay my head on the pillow, willing the racing questions in my mind to cease, I finally accepted sleep would not come until I saw my father again. He was not in his room and his attendant was fast asleep, so I set out to find him, stealing through halls that seemed much smaller than my childhood memories would have me believe.

The kitchen was abandoned, as was the great hall, so I began to trace the corridors, peeking into unlocked storage areas and long-abandoned living quarters. With every beat of my heart, my conviction grew. I had to see my father, to know that he still cared for me, despite his recent change in attitude. He was my last living link to my mother, and I his. As the thought skittered across my mind, I began to wonder if that was why he had yet to greet me; maybe I reminded him too much of her.

I slowed as I neared a room near the end of the hall on the uppermost floor. The soft flicker of candlelight spilled out through a door slightly ajar. It took me a moment to orient myself and then my heart stopped as I realized where I was. This was my mother's chamber.

I leaned against the wall and closed my eyes, steeling myself with a few deep breaths. Splinters pricked my fingertips as I clawed at the wall and squeezed my eyes tight, fighting back memories of all the times I played in my mother's wardrobe or sat on her footstool while she braided or brushed my hair. She had nursed me in that room through many ailments, insisting I would rest easier sleeping in her bed, with her warmth to soothe me. A shiver shimmied down my spine. She died in that bed. It was only natural my father would be there.

I pressed my lips together and tiptoed over to the door. I could barely make out my father's silhouette in the pale light of the single candle burning on the windowsill like a beacon, silently calling my mother's soul back to the place she so loved. I took another deep breath. I had thought myself prepared to face my father and all our missing years, but I was not ready to face my mother's ghost as well.

I took a tentative step into the room, knowing my father would soon be able to see me out of the corner of his eye. "Father," I called softly as I approached, not wanting him to mistake me for a specter.

He lifted his head and looked at me, at first unseeing as though I had roused him from a waking dream. Then slowly, comprehension dawned and he smiled, brushing away the tears staining his cheeks. "Guinevere," he breathed. "Daughter, my heart warms to see you."

I raced over to him and hugged him tightly, alarmed to feel fragile bone rather than the hard muscle of the warrior king I remembered. After a moment, he released me, holding me at arm's length and squinting to consider me in the dim light.

"You are not a little child anymore." He sighed.

I reached for a blanket draped over the edge of the bed and wrapped it around my shoulders. "That is true, but even grown women have need of their fathers," I said, climbing up into his lap just like I did as a little girl.

He wrapped his arms around me, as if he feared I would disappear like the smoke rising from the candle wick. I closed my eyes and laid my head on the crook of his neck. His hair, now turning gray, still smelled of the same imported citrus oil that punctuated my youngest memories.

"You look just like her, you know," he said in a small, soft voice. He paused thoughtfully before adding, "I miss her."

"So do I," I answered, tears streaming freely now.

In the silence, I could almost forget the years that had passed, that I was now fifteen and we were grieving the death of someone so dear. I could almost make myself believe I was still the little girl who had climbed into his arms after a terrible nightmare. And in some ways, I was, for this was the worst nightmare either of us could imagine.

"Please don't leave me," my father whispered in an unfamiliar tone of grief. He had always been so confident, so strong, but now he was broken, pleading. "Don't go back to Avalon. I. . . I need you here."

I pursed my lips, realizing he was right. Unfamiliar as it first seemed, this was my home. "I will stay. You will need someone to keep the servants in line."

He laughed, the first joyful sound I had heard since coming home.

◈◈◈

The following morning, I discovered Morgan had an ulterior motive for making the long journey to Northgallis. Not only was she seeing me safely returned to my family's care in Viviane's stead, but she was also under the Lady's orders to accompany another of our household to her new life in Avalon. Octavia's youngest, Nimue, a small plump girl who had inherited her mother's thick mass of dark hair and her father's haunting green eyes, was expressly requested to return to Avalon as its newest acolyte.

As Octavia and I watched them depart, memories of how quickly I bonded with Viviane came rushing back. If Nimue adored

Morgan and clung to her as a mother figure like I had to Viviane, Nimue had little chance of emerging from her period of study with her innocent soul intact. Poor girl. I prayed for her sake she would take to some of the more kind-hearted priestesses like Grainne or Rowena instead. But I dared not voice this to Octavia. She was fretting enough for both of us.

"Nimue is too young. I should not have let them take her yet," Octavia berated herself as she led me down a path over a gently sloping hill to the grove where my mother was buried. "A few more years and she would have been the same age as you were. She would have been old enough, prepared enough to survive this. First I sent Peredur off to be fostered. Now Nimue is gone too. Although I fear I had little choice. Not only did the Lady of the Lake request her presence, I could not very well let her grow up here. Your father would have sent her to a convent before the spring anyway."

I stopped cold at her statement. "What did you say?"

She turned around at the sound of my voice, her pained expression making it obvious she knew she had transgressed. "Guinevere, I have told you your father is a changed man. It is time you knew the full extent."

She led me into the grove of yew trees and sat me down on the soft grass before venturing into further explanation. "Your mother meant so much to Leodgrance that her death nearly drove him insane. For days he would neither eat nor sleep, only sit in her room and weep, uttering only a single word—why?—when visitors came to tend to him. For three days, he refused to allow her to be buried, insisting that she was not really dead. Then the fourth morning, he unexpectedly joined us at the breakfast table and announced she should be buried according to the rites and customs of her people. And so, she was laid to rest here."

Octavia pointed toward the western end of the grove, where a large stone tablet protruded from the bare earth, which was stained red by ochre, a smattering of white quartz stones scattered at its base. The stones and pigment were talismans of the dead to my mother's people, meant to ease the soul's journey to the spirit world.

Slowly, painfully, fearfully, I made my way over to the burial site. Although my mother's burial was performed according to her native traditions, the tombstone that marked her grave was set up by my father in the traditional Roman fashion of his ancestors. It bore the carved image of a slender, long-haired warrior woman in native dress, surrounded by thistles, her eyes cast to the heavens. I ran my hand over the rough surface of the stone, tracing the grooves as if doing so could bring her back again. Beneath the image was an inscription, which began—as all other Roman memorials did—with the words "*Dis Manibus,*" addressing the gods of the shades. It continued, "*Corinna of the Votadini, wife of the king of Gwynedd, daughter of King Cunedda.*" The memorial ended with the traditional Roman attribution naming the deceased's patron. "*Her husband Leodgrance set this up in her memory.*"

I could no longer deny it. My mother really was dead. It was written in stone in front of me for the entire kingdom to see. The world around me faded in a blur of tears, and I dissolved in grief. Eventually Octavia's arm encircled me, her warmth breathing life back into my frigid bones. I looked up, my eyes now parched from so much crying, never more grateful for this woman who, although officially a servant in my father's employ, was also at once my confidant and dearest friend, more like family than many of my blood relations.

Octavia turned toward the fortress, shielding her eyes from the amber rays of the setting sun. "We must return home soon, Guinevere, but I have not yet finished what I wanted to say. I brought you here not only because you needed to come, but so you might better understand your father. You can see in this stone the love he possessed for your mother. After her burial, he was lost like a sailor without a star to guide him. He returned to his habit of sitting in her chamber. He spoke often of the dream that had prompted him to let her body go, though he would reveal its details to no one. We all knew he was still holding on to Corinna in spirit and feared what damage this would do to him. As he would speak to no one else, and your party from Avalon had not yet departed the isle, the local Christian priest was sent for in the hope that perhaps Leodgrance would speak to him."

I bristled at the word *Christian.* I felt no enmity toward them as a group. In fact, they shared the Tor with us, also considering it sacred but for very different reasons. They believed Joseph of Arimathea, a follower of Jesus, settled there after Jesus's crucifixion and brought with him magical relics of their savior. Today, they lived in crude huts of woven branches on the edges of the marsh, just beyond where the mists gave way to the outside world. But I had heard enough tales to know that not all Christians lived such humble, holy lives. Many considered the religion of Avalon in direct opposition to Christianity and, like the Romans before them, sought to destroy it. That fear was what made the hairs on my neck and arms stand at attention every time I heard the word.

Octavia noticed my reaction and patted my hand. "We did what we thought was best." She sighed. "As it turned out, our good intentions only made things worse. The young priest, Father Marius, who came to our door did get your father to return somewhat to normal, but he also convinced him that his dream was a sign your father should give up the religion of his ancestors and embrace this new god, this Christ. Your father was so taken with this priest and his promises of an eternal life that he willingly agreed, intent on dragging the rest of us along with him."

She pulled me to my feet, continuing her story as we ambled back to the hall, where we would soon be expected for the evening meal. "Of course, I would not go along with this outrageous notion, and I told him so. He was not pleased and threatened not only my position in his house but the future of my child as well, decreeing she would be reared in a Christian convent as soon as arrangements could be made. It was then I determined that my little rose would be transplanted to Avalon when you returned. Anything would be better for her than being raised in this household, such as it is now."

Octavia's words tore at my heart as surely as if she had stabbed me. Not only had I lost my mother, but my father, despite his love for me, had become a stranger as well, and I now faced a life in a home that did not recognize the religion I was vowed to serve. As we returned through the yawning castle gates, for the first time, I feared my future life at Northgallis.

Chapter Nine

Autumn 495

Every evening, my father, Octavia, and I ate dinner at dusk in the great hall, quietly discussing our day and any news that filtered in from the village or countryside. After the trenchers were cleared, we passed the hours of early evening by sewing, writing letters, playing games, or telling stories—catching up on the lost years I was away in Avalon. I treaded carefully, still unsure of my position in this new world, but all went well. It was a quiet life, but one doing much good to heal our wounded hearts.

However, this mid-autumn evening was anything but routine; for the first time since my mother's death, we were having guests at dinner.

The household was abuzz with activity, preparing for the arrival of Lord Evrain, ruler of the kingdom of Powys, which bordered my father's lands. Though Evrain possessed only moderate power in the overall hierarchy of the country, maintaining a pleasant relationship with him was of utmost importance because of the location of his lands. Should he ever turn against my father, the proximity of his kingdom would give any enemy perfect staging grounds for an invasion of our less-fortified eastern border. This being so, I was admonished to be on my best behavior.

Even though Lord Evrain was considerably late in arriving, I was still rushing to tuck my hair beneath the cream-colored veil my father had insisted I wear low over my forehead. Apparently the visiting lord was a very religious Christian, so the sight of my sacred crescent would not make for a very good first impression. I was dismayed by having to conceal something I had worked so hard to attain and was so proud of; in my mind, the mark was a part of me, but I had no choice.

Voices carried in from the courtyard below, muffled greetings of peace. Evrain and his men were finally here.

"Guinevere, make haste!" Octavia hissed.

I turned to face her, and she scowled, pulling at the veil until it brushed my eyebrows.

"Be certain you do not let it slip," she warned. "Your father is in a foul temper as it is."

Octavia escorted me firmly by the arm as we descended the staircase into the great hall, falling into her proper place behind me only when we came within sight of Lord Evrain and his small cluster of attendants. I took a deep breath and wiped my clammy, trembling hands on the sides of my gown. Having been away in Avalon for so long, I had forgotten the rules of courtly life. *Dear Goddess, please let me make my father proud.*

I stepped forward out of the shadows, careful to stay a distance behind my father. Once the men had been formally introduced to one another, my father gracefully slid his arm behind me and gently nudged me forward.

"Lord Evrain, this is my only child, the Lady Guinevere."

I curtsied low before the silver-haired man, not daring to meet his eyes.

"Indeed, she is a beauty," he said to my father as he reached to take my hand and assist me to rise. "Lady Guinevere, I am most honored to meet you."

He had addressed me, so now I could raise my eyes. "In truth, sir, the honor is mine."

Lord Evrain released my hand and gestured to the young man on his right. "Allow me to present to you my son Fergus. He is my youngest and the only of my sons yet to take a wife."

Evrain glanced purposefully at my father as his son stiffly stepped forward. He was thin and tall, his arms and legs far more than his still-growing body could manage.

He is barely more than a boy.

Fergus roughly clasped my hand in his puppy-like paw. "I am grateful to be a guest in your home," he croaked in the uneven voice of one not still a boy but not yet a man. He shot an uncertain look at his father, who nodded in encouragement. Fergus swallowed before continuing. "And I feel most privileged to present this token to you," he stammered, fumbling to untie a pouch from his belt. "It pales in comparison to your beauty."

Out of the corner of my eye, I saw Fergus's father smile delightedly.

Oh no. This is more than a gift. Evrain is trying to make a match.

I fought to hide my fear and disgust behind a smile of surprise as Fergus removed a delicate golden chain from a small velvet bag. I tried to catch Octavia's eye but found my father's warning stare instead. I quickly returned my gaze to the man-boy in front of me. As he struggled to fasten the golden rope around my wrist with his bulky fingers, the rubies suspended from the chain caught the torchlight, reflecting dully on the ashen surface of his face.

When the bracelet hung securely from my wrist, I clasped Fergus's hands in mine, as was expected of me. "My Lord, I am most flattered." My smile tightened to cover my true emotions as I looked into his lifeless, nervous eyes. "Your gift is truly a treasure, one that I will cherish for years to come. I only hope I will be judged as valuable to you as the gift you have given me."

Lord Evrain clapped his hands together, pleased by the exchange. "Hurrah! Now that the introductions are done, shall we sup?" He took my father by the arm and started toward the long table in the center of the room.

From somewhere behind Evrain's rust-colored cape, a man cleared his throat. Lord Evrain turned. His annoyed scowl was artfully replaced with an apologetic smile as he gestured toward a young man previously hidden in the throng of attendants.

"It appears I have forgotten someone after all," Evrain said.

The man glided forward when he was introduced, but I did not need to hear his name to know who he was. Before me stood Aggrivane of Lothian, my lover from the Beltane fires. When his dark eyes met mine, they registered the briefest moment of shock, which faded into joyful recognition coupled with a slight upturn of his lips before he could discipline his features and pretend to be introduced as a stranger.

Evrain seemed a bit embarrassed by his guest, explaining away Aggrivane's presence as an act of charity to a fellow king. "He is the son of an inconsequential barbarian who wears a crown only by right of inheritance. He is a guest in my court, studying how to govern. Pay him no mind; he is here to learn, not to socialize." Evrain turned to me and added, "Until he wins or inherits land, he is more a servant than a noble. He is certainly not fit to be in the company of such a gracious lady."

Was I supposed to take that as a compliment? It seemed more of a veiled warning.

⁕ ⁕ ⁕

By the time the main course was served, I was beginning to wonder if it was possible to die of boredom. My father and Lord Evrain disagreed over everything and especially seemed to enjoy arguing over the most trivial matters. I tried to force myself to pay attention to their discussion, but I kept finding every excuse possible to steal a glance in Aggrivane's direction. Judging from the way he tightened his jaw and kept his body angled away from me, he was doing everything he could to pretend to be uninterested in me, but every so often his resolve weakened and he fleetingly returned my gaze.

Perhaps it was our time apart or pure imagination on my part, but Aggrivane seemed to have grown more handsome since the last time I saw him. Everything about him made my body twinge: the way the light reflected off his glossy hair, the gleam in his dark eyes, the way his whole face lit up when he laughed. Nothing would have pleased me more than to spend the entire evening admiring him and indulging in secret memories of our night together. But I was brought back quickly to the present by a sharp pinch on my thigh. I scowled at Octavia, my lust-addled mind not yet comprehending the reason for her action.

"Guinevere," she hissed quietly, amid the din of servants changing courses and the clattering of dishes. "You'd best get control of yourself, or your father will have your hide."

"But, Octavia, he is—"

"I remember his name from your stories. I know full well who he is. But Lord Evrain does not, and it is in your best interest to keep it that way. Aggrivane is to be of no consequence to you. Do you understand?"

I nodded dumbly.

Instead of enjoying a reunion with the man I loved, I had been sentenced to the company of Lord Evrain's socially inept son. I had been attempting all night to engage the boy in some type of conversation, but he seemed just as afraid of me as he was of his father. Every time I asked him a question, he gave me the simplest possible answer and then returned to staring at his plate or at the floor. "The weather is quite fine, yes" or "I do agree that the meat is cooked perfectly." I could get no opinion or interest out of him whatsoever.

Desperate for some relief from the tedium, I tried one last topic.

"How do you find living with your new guest? Do you dislike Lord Aggrivane as much as your father?"

Fergus's eyes widened, and he put down his knife. "Oh no, I like him very much. He is so kind to me."

Thrilled I had finally found a subject that interested him, I was eager to keep him talking. "How so?"

"He is the only one willing to listen to me, to teach me what he knows. I hope to be as smart and skilled as he one day. He is the best storyteller. You should hear him recite the great triads. His words are magic."

As Fergus prattled on about Aggrivane, I couldn't help but let my gaze wander in his direction. I was rewarded by a jab in the ribs from my serving maid that brought my attention back to our enamored guest, but only temporarily. I had a feeling by the end of the night, my entire side would be black and blue from Octavia's admonitions.

⁕⁂⁕

Throughout the insufferably lengthy meal, the two lords talked mostly of things long past or those that I cared not for, but late in the evening, the subject changed to politics and I began to take notice of the conversation.

"The villagers are bursting with gossip about Uther's successor," my father noted, cutting another slice of meat as he spoke. "They say he is little more than a boy. What do you know of him, Lord Evrain? Can he be trusted to lead the country?"

Curious now, I looked up from my plate, intent on stealing yet another fleeting glance at Aggrivane. Instead of meeting his twinkling gaze, my eyes were drawn to Lord Evrain, who, now deep in his drink, was gesturing wildly as if to match his booming tone.

"So you have heard of our young king-to-be, have you? He is quite a lad," Evrain bragged as if speaking about his own son. "He is Lord Ector's son, or was," he corrected himself.

"What do you mean?" my father questioned with a wrinkle in his brow. "Has something happened to Ector?"

"Bless him, no. Oh, it is quite a tale. How is it that you have not heard? Does news not travel past the Cambrian Mountains? Surely you must know."

If the twitch of muscle in his jaw was any indication, my father was beginning to get annoyed with his drunken guest. "I assure you, my lord, we do not. Would you be so kind as to recall the events to us?"

Evrain beamed. That was just the invitation he had been waiting for.

"Father," Fergus interrupted as all eyes turned to him, shocked at the intrusion from the quiet boy. "Should not Aggrivane tell the tale? He *is* as a bard under your command." Fergus flushed visibly, squirming under his father's blazing stare. To me, he added in an aside, "He tells it so magnificently."

"Be quiet, boy," Evrain roared, gesturing violently toward his son and sloshing wine onto the table in the process.

My father grimaced. "Perhaps your son has a good idea. We have heard little from your guest this evening. It would be refreshing to hear him speak."

Evrain's eyes bulged with disbelief and anger. "He is not here to speak or to entertain. He is here to observe and to serve. I will hear of no such thing." Evrain set his jaw resolutely, as if to say there would be no budging him from that position.

Before I could cast a sidelong glance her way, Octavia had already risen and taken hold of a pitcher of wine. She sauntered over to Evrain's side and bent down to his level.

"My good lord, surely you will allow the boy to tell one simple tale." She batted her eyes flirtatiously as the liquid flowed into his cup. "What harm can it do? If he is truly as in need of learning as you say, his speech can only magnify the splendor of your own. Besides"— she bent lower, giving everyone at the table an unobstructed view of her cleavage—"it will give you a chance to relax. All this discussion of politics must have made you weary." She ran her free hand across his shoulders, rubbing them gently.

Evrain was clearly entranced by Octavia's charms, openly ogling her. He patted her hand but then quickly recovered himself. "I do not normally take advice from servants." He gave her a scathing, yet passionate look. "But perhaps you are right. Go ahead, Aggrivane. Tell us all of the boy who would be king." He turned to face Aggrivane, regarding him coldly, letting him know he already expected him to fail. "It is, in a way, your story to tell, after all."

For a moment, Evrain's words perplexed me. But then I remembered something Aggrivane had told me during one of our nights together in Avalon. His father was Uther's chosen successor. If Uther had changed his mind at the last moment, Aggrivane would be telling the tale of his own family's undoing—how he went from being third in line to the throne of the high king to having his name struck from the possible line of succession. Of course, Evrain would use this opportunity to humiliate him. It took all of my willpower not to shoot Evrain a disgusted look.

Unfazed, Aggrivane sat up straight in his seat and cleared his throat, his eyes passing briefly over me, just long enough to let me to know he hadn't forgotten me. "The account you are about to hear comes straight from a knight who guarded King Uther and fought alongside our new king," he said, by way of preface.

Then he cocked his head slightly, as though he was listening to music only he could hear—a gesture not uncommon among bards settling into their roles—and began to weave his tale.

"It was nearing sunset in a valley near the fort of Tremontum in the wild lands of the country to the north." Aggrivane inclined his head toward me ever so slightly in acknowledgement of my lineage. "The sky was ablaze in all the colors of the dying day. The reds and oranges of evening were at war with the blue and pale yellow of day. Down on the ground, however, things were not so lively. The battle between Uther's troops and the merciless Saxons was at an impasse; both sides had retreated to camp, and it looked as if they would have to call a halt for the night and risk the possibility of defending against a sneak attack under the cover of darkness.

"The men were tired, and many were wounded. Morale was flagging under the strain of many days of fighting. Alarm spread quickly through the ranks as Uther threw down his sword in a fit of rage and retired to his tent. Most other nights he stood vigil with Merlin and his advisors, planning the next day's battle by the light of the moon. But not this night.

"The moon rose and traveled through the heavens, spreading her pale light across the camps of invader and native alike. Still there was no word from the king, no nightly orders of who was to watch and who was to sleep. The men began to grumble.

"About midnight, Merlin joined Uther in his tent. He found the king reclining on his mat, his face ashen and covered in sweat.

"'My King, what ails you? How may I be of service?' Merlin bowed low in genuine concern for his ruler and friend.

"Uther smiled slightly, the gesture barely masking his grimace of pain. 'Lord of Light, Walker between the Worlds, that is what they call you, do they not? Then indeed, you already know I am not long for this world. I suspect the spirits have told you.' He grimaced as another wave of pain racked his body and his breathing grew labored.

"'Indeed, they have.' Sorrow weighed down Merlin's voice.

"'Then we haven't much time. There is something you have long known, a secret buried deep within our hearts that must now be revealed to the one who will inherit my crown. Merlin, call my son to me and bid him bring me my sword.'

"Merlin assented with a low bow. 'As you wish, sire.'

"The night watchmen stirred as Merlin strode out of the tent and inquired of the captain the whereabouts of one of the young soldiers. He was directed to a tent on the outskirts of the encampment where the women who followed the battle slept.

"Arthur begrudgingly untangled himself from his bedmate's embrace and was directed by Merlin to a pile of boulders in a grassy patch near the king's tent. 'Your king has damaged his sword,' he said, pointing at the blade wedged between two rocks. 'He desires it returned to him, and I was told you have the strength to remove it.'

"Puzzled, Arthur regarded Merlin as one who had lost his senses and grabbed hold of the hilt. A shower of amber sparks lit up the night as the broken blade scraped against the stone. Arthur displayed the useless weapon to Merlin without a word and followed him into the king's tent.

"By this time, the whole camp had grown tense, the warriors sensing something amiss in the balmy west wind, as if it had been sent from beyond the seventh wave. Some whispered that the west wind was an omen of death, while others listened, watched, and waited for some sign from the Saxons or from their absent king.

"As Merlin and Arthur ducked below the door flap of the tent, Uther's impending death was apparent. Though the wind whistled roughly through the trees outside, the air inside had grown still. Uther's breathing was coming in shallow gasps, his face holding a mere shadow of the great power it once possessed.

"Shocked and distressed at his king's condition, Arthur knelt before him, presenting the sword. 'I have brought your sword, my lord. Tell me, what is your will of me?'

"The dying king smiled. 'It is your sword now, my son.' His eyes closed and he grasped his chest, fighting through another wave of pain. 'Take it and defend our land against those who would hold us captive, for my power is now yours.'

"Arthur knelt speechless before Uther, searching his face for meaning he could not comprehend. Finally, he turned to Merlin for explanation.

"'Uther is your father, Arthur. Soon, you will be high king.'

"Uther reached out to his son. 'I beg you bear me no ill will for concealing this from you. You'—he fought for breath—'have always had my love, and your protection was my greatest concern.'

"The king looked up suddenly, regarding them with unseeing eyes. 'My ancestors call me home, my son. I bid you farewell. May the gods be with you, and may you only die in battle.'

"One final spasm shook his body, and Uther breathed his last.

"Merlin bowed his head. 'The high king is dead,' he declared to the guards within the tent. He removed the ring of office from Uther's hand and placed it on Arthur's finger. 'And the new king is born. Hail, High King Arthur!' he cried.

"The cry was taken up by the men in the tent and echoed by those outside. Confusion reigned as word spread from one end of the camp to another. But soon the ravens began to crow, and the commotion was drowned out by shouts of the night watchmen. The Saxons were marching toward camp."

Aggrivane leaned forward and his voice grew more intense. "I tell you, it was as if the Saxons had planned the whole sequence of events themselves. Right at the moment of transition, the moment of greatest weakness, our men were being attacked. Arthur seemed unaware of this coincidence; he was strangely focused, having shaken off his shock and clothed himself in the mantle of power. Once the men were hastily armed and battle formations in place, he called them all unto him, scanning the assembled warriors with eyes of bluest fire.

"'A few hours ago, I was one of you, and now I find myself called to lead you. I do not yet ask for your loyalty, but I do ask for your trust. Allow me to lead you in this battle to secure our country's future, and then you may evaluate my worthiness to be your king. One thing I beg of you—do not allow your grief, anger, or personal grievances to cloud your minds. Think only of turning this horde of murderers away from our shores. You have all sworn an oath of allegiance to Uther. Consider victory in this battle to be his final command.' Arthur raised his father's damaged sword high over his head and, with the other arm, brandished his own. 'To arms, men of

Britain! To arms!'

"Arthur's men were ready for the onslaught when the Saxons rained down upon them. Having lost the element of surprise, the Saxons were weakened, though they fought hard. Many brave men lost their lives, following Uther as his honor guard into Otherworld. But many others won great honor. As dawn brightened the sky on the first day of Arthur's reign, the Saxons were defeated, hundreds killed in all. The royal army—and the nation—were left to grieve for their fallen warriors and their dead king and to come to terms with the sudden rise of another. So began the rule of the great King Arthur."

The grand hall was silent but for the crackling of the fire in the hearth. I could not move, could not tear my eyes away from Aggrivane. Though I did not look at them, the utter stillness around me indicated everyone was as spellbound as I, living the events brought to life through Aggrivane's words.

My father was the first to stir. "Good sir, that was a fine tale. I beg you tell me where you learned such skill."

Evrain moved to interject, and Aggrivane took note.

"Truly, my lord, it is of no consequence." He dropped his gaze to the floor. "Nor am I."

Evrain seemed pleased by the show of humility, but I was not. I could not believe that Aggrivane would so willingly deny his talent and the years of Druidic training that had brought him this far. I was about to voice this thought when I caught Aggrivane's eye. He was silently begging me to keep quiet.

I slumped back in my seat as the talk returned once again to our new king.

"Now that we have heard the fantasy, what do you think to be our king's chances, eh?" Evrain asked, draining yet another cup.

"He will have a tough road ahead of him," my father said gravely. "Who upholds his sovereignty?"

"I have heard that allegiance has been sworn by Cador of Cornwall, the king of the north country, and Pellinor of Dyfed. I know he aims to gain your loyalty as well, my lord. But not all are so quick to cower before the mighty Arthur." Evrain pounded the table with his fist. "King Lot has declared war upon the whelp. He had been appointed Uther's successor long ago and rightly feels cheated of his office. He was the only lord present the night of Uther's passing who refused to kneel and swear fealty to Arthur."

Aggrivane shifted uncomfortably in his seat at the mention of his father's disloyalty. He glanced out the window and then his stool scraped loudly as he rose suddenly from his seat. "Forgive me, my lords, but the candles burn low. I must see to the horses."

Evrain motioned toward the door dismissively. "Yes, yes, be off to your duties." The tone in Evrain's voice made it clear that he was glad to finally be rid of his guest.

"We bid you good eve," my father said, rising.

"Thank you, my lords." He bowed to both kings and threw me a fleeting glance filled with longing before departing.

CHAPTER TEN

ours, minutes, days—I could not tell how much time passed before I was finally able to beg permission to retire for the night. A long argument about Arthur's right to the throne had followed Aggrivane's departure, and then I was subjected to the torment of a dance with the gangly Fergus. The full moon was already high in the night sky when I bid our company good night.

I turned to Lord Evrain and his son and curtsied to them. "Good sirs, I am honored to have had the privilege of your company this eve. I wish you pleasant dreams."

Evrain took my hand. "After a night such as this, how can they be anything but pleasant?" he asked with a not-so-charming implication.

"My lord, you flatter me," I whispered modestly before bidding Fergus good night.

The lanky boy kissed my hand and pawed at the bracelet with its drops of fire dangling from my wrist. "If I had known the beauty of your eyes, I would have made these emeralds," he said with an uncomfortable grimace that betrayed the lack of confidence behind his words.

I smiled, greatly amused. "Fergus, did your father tell you to say that?"

He merely blushed wordlessly and bobbed his head in a gesture of farewell.

⁂

The drunken laughter of my father and Lord Evrain wafted out from the great hall as I slipped silently across the courtyard to the stables. I pulled my heavy cloak closer around me to stave off the cold night air, praying the tower guards would take no notice of my fleeting presence, or if they did, that they would mistake my simple garb for that of a serving girl.

My breath was coming in short, impatient puffs by the time the low, long building came into view. The sweet odor of hay mixed with the tang of the horses greeted me as I pulled open the heavy door. A faint glow illuminated one of the far stalls. My heart raced. He had waited for me.

"I was wondering when—if—you would arrive," Aggrivane said, looking up from the shining chestnut stallion whose coat he was gently brushing.

The lantern light caught the expressive gleam in his eye, and I sighed aloud, rushing toward him, eager to enfold myself in his arms. He quickly dropped the curry comb he was holding, and within moments, his lips met mine.

Pulling away, I cupped his cheeks in my hands and looked deep into his eyes. "I feared I would never see you again." Tears welled in my eyes, bringing all emotions to the surface.

"I would wait an eternity for you," he whispered softly. He pulled me slowly down to a pile of fresh hay heaped in one corner of the stable. "It is not exactly the lush grasses of Avalon." A crooked smile played across his lips, and the memory of our night together was reflected in his eyes.

I smiled in return. "My love, it will do, I assure you."

I buried my head in his chest, taking comfort in his heartbeat. For just this one moment, I longed to be back in Avalon again, to be free.

I turned my face up to him. "Why do you stay with Lord Evrain when he treats you so? Why do you not go back to your father?"

Aggrivane frowned. "I am a nobleman's son. That means I must learn to be both a warrior and a leader from a lord other than my father. My father sees alliance with Lord Evrain as crucial to future peace within our lands. Do not underestimate him; Lord Evrain is more cunning and powerful than many give him credit for. In order to prevent a feud between our two houses, I was sent to live with his family and learn from him."

I shivered in the cold. "But what can you learn from a boor such as him? Lord Evrain is evil and cruel!"

Aggrivane smirked as he pulled me nearer, leaning in so that his lips brushed my ear as he spoke in the slightest whisper. "Lord Evrain is a bitter, self-important man. He dreams of ruling the whole of this land but knows he lacks the power to do so. That is why he vehemently opposes Arthur, who is living out the dream he has secretly harbored for so long. In order to make up for his own weaknesses, Evrain uses what power he has to manipulate the other lords around him. Why else do you think he paid your father a visit? He knows that his own sons will not make strong enough rulers to continue what he has started. But if Fergus marries you and Evrain can control your father, he has indirect control of the whole of Gwynedd."

I stared at him incredulously. "Is it true?"

He nodded.

"But why does Lord Evrain hate you so?"

Aggrivane shrugged and ran his fingers through my hair, sending chills down my spine. "My mother is Arthur's sister. That makes me royalty of higher station than Evrain can ever dream. Therefore, he uses his place as my temporary superior to try to make me subservient to him. He has never allowed me to forget that I am the second of five brothers and likely will not inherit but will have to earn my lands and title." The devilish smile returned to his face. "Besides, I daresay he fancies you not so much for his son but for himself."

I swatted his chest playfully. "Do not say such things, good sir, for my innocent ears will not abide them!"

He nipped one of my earlobes. "Innocent, eh? I do not recall them being so innocent when last we parted. Perhaps I should see what can be done to refresh your memory."

All thought of the cold night air and the meeting taking place in the castle vanished as I melted into his arms, allowing their strength to refuel all that I had lost over the previous months. His kisses were like enchanted nectar; the more I tasted, the greater my desire. One of his hands caressed my breast through the fabric of my gown, while the other searched hungrily beneath the folds of my skirt.

Over the months we spent studying the stars in Avalon, I came to know every inch of Aggrivane's body by sunlight and starlight. Now, in the near darkness, I found that I could trace each scar that raised his skin and took comfort in the familiar contours of his body. His kisses grew more intense and I happily yielded my body to him, safe and content in his arms.

When the moments of pleasure had passed, we drowsed in each other's arms, dreaming of a life together as a faraway nightingale sang his nocturnal hymn.

"Why do you not ask my father for my hand?" I asked Aggrivane. "You are a lord in your own right, not a slave like Evrain would have you believe. My father would be happy to rid his house of me, I assure you."

He laughed. "I doubt that to be true." He fell into silent contemplation. "I could not ask your father in front of Lord Evrain. That would break the pact he made with my father, and Evrain would declare a war of honor upon us."

I sat up on my arms and gazed at him hopefully, my mind racing. "Perhaps you could find some reason to stay behind when Lord Evrain leaves. He would be happy to unload you into the care of my father. We both know that."

All that remained was the unanswered question—why? Why would my father allow Aggrivane to stay? I listened to the chirping of the crickets and the soft snuffling of the horses, praying for an answer. Somewhere in the distance, the low murmur of voices signaled the changing of the guard and, suddenly, I knew.

I grabbed Aggrivane by the shoulders, and the words tumbled out in a rush of excitement. "Rhys is the best swordsman in Northgallis. My father has forbidden me to practice the arts of battle, so I know Rhys would have room for an additional student. You could study with him for a few months in exchange for teaching my cousin Bran some of the knowledge you gained on the Druids' isle. Besides, Bran would love to have someone near his age to spar with."

Aggrivane regarded me warily. "But would your father allow my teaching? He seems set against all you learned in Avalon. Plus, I hear tell of a priest that trails at your father's heels. He is not likely to accept another of the old faith into your household."

I waved a hand dismissively. "Then do not teach him the secrets of the isle, but entrust to him the knowledge of language, reading, and the written word. Every lord should have such training, but with the constant threat from the Irish, there has been little opportunity to school Bran in such things. As for Marius, I have yet to meet this deity made flesh, but no man has ever held sway over my father, least of all a priest."

Aggrivane kissed my lips softly. "You are not going to stop until I agree to present this proposal to your father, are you?"

I grinned and shook my head.

"Well then, it is settled. Upon the dawn, I will ask for a private audience with your father and tell all to him."

I kissed him hard on the mouth. "Let us then thank the Goddess for our good fortune." I pulled him down to the soft straw and closed my eyes, reveling in the joy that this man would soon be my husband.

৽৹৹৹

"I assure you, my lord, no finer animal ever walked the earth."

Aggrivane and I froze, clasped together in fear. Had we slept? Somehow we had missed the lords' approach and were likely to be discovered. Evrain's drunken slur was unmistakable. The voices were quickly drawing near the stables.

Aggrivane's eyes had grown large, and I could tell by the tilt of his head that he was listening to sounds my untrained ears could not hear.

I slipped on my dress, looking around wildly like a trapped animal, but there was no way to escape. There was nowhere to hide, and the men were nearly at the only door.

"What do we do?" I hissed at Aggrivane, trembling in fear.

Aggrivane hastily pulled on his tunic. "Hide your face with your hair and bury your head in my chest. I will speak to them, and if the gods are with us, we will escape unharmed."

He kissed the top of my head one last time before the door swung open and Lord Evrain burst in, incoherently bragging about his horse, followed by the confident stride of my father and a lighter, shuffling footstep that I could only assume belonged to Fergus.

"Pure Eastern blood, I tell you. Sired by a Pegasus and stolen from a Saracen warrior. He was shipped here by the tradesmen in my employ. Many a lord has offered a handsome sum for his offspring, but I—"

Evrain had obviously seen us. I could imagine the look on my father's face.

"Well, what have we here?" Evrain bellowed.

I clung ever tighter to Aggrivane and willed myself to be completely still and silent.

"It appears our young ward has found himself a willing serving maid."

I felt Evrain step closer and said a silent prayer of thanks that Octavia had thought to outfit me in one of her old dresses to fool the guards in case I was seen coming here.

Evrain fingered my hair, and I could not suppress a cringe as I turned my face farther away from him.

From his tone, Evrain sounded to be appraising my worth. "Dark hair, strong body. Is she related to that Roman woman who served us at dinner?" He chuckled salaciously to himself. "If she is, then you have found yourself one fine wench, lad."

Aggrivane dropped his gaze to the floor. "Truly, I do not know, sir. We have barely spoken."

Evrain howled with laughter and gave Aggrivane a hearty slap on the back. "That's the way, my boy. The less they say, the better they are. Isn't that right, Leodgrance?"

My father cleared his throat and mumbled a polite agreement.

"My lord," Aggrivane addressed my father, "forgive this woman for not bowing to you as you deserve. She is embarrassed and fears punishment." He positioned himself between the lords and me.

"Indeed, I see no need for retribution. It is late, and we should all to bed," my father responded.

Something in his tone told me that my father knew that the woman trembling behind the curtain of black hair was no serving maid. I breathed a sigh of relief as I heard them turn toward the door. Just then, I felt something crawling up my arm, its many legs tickling my skin. Without thinking, I shook off the spider and the sleeve of my gown fell back around my elbow.

"Wait!" Evrain roared. "What is this?" Evrain stalked toward us and jerked my wrist, wrenching me away from Aggrivane's protection.

He held up my arm, and Fergus's bracelet bled ruby teardrops in the lantern light.

Damn! How could I have forgotten to remove that vile trinket?

"My lord," Evrain called, "it appears your maid is not only a strumpet, but a thief as well."

He pulled me roughly toward him. His breath stank of drink and decay as he leered at me through the raven strands that separated us. "Now, let us see what kind of creature you have trapped, Lord Aggrivane."

He yanked back my hair as if he meant to pull it out by the roots. I summoned all my courage and raised my face to him. His eyes bulged as he beheld the mark of priestesshood on my brow, and recognition spread across his face.

⚜

"Is this how you raised your daughter to behave, my Lord Leodgrance?" Evrain spewed rage like a boiling kettle. "I knew when you married that northern savage she would be no example to your children, and then God cursed you with a daughter as your only living child."

It was nearly dawn. Evrain had been raving for what felt like hours, pacing the length of the audience chamber under the watchful gaze of Father Marius, my father's newfound savior. Aggrivane stood at a distance, his stoic silence masking the pain and fear buried deep within his troubled eyes.

"My poor son lies in his chamber, distraught by her betrayal." Evrain pointed an accusatory finger toward me.

More likely you locked him there.

"And she has disgraced me, a guest invited on your honor. My lord, she is blight on your entire house. She must be punished."

"She is also my daughter," my father said angrily.

Evrain knew he had overstepped his bounds. "I beg your pardon, my lord." He paused, steepled hands pressed to his lips in thought. "But the fact remains that these two were caught in an immoral embrace." He regarded Aggrivane coldly. "My son was openly courting your daughter. By the agreement I struck with the Lord of Lothian, this boy had no right to take what belonged to my son."

Aggrivane surged angrily toward the throne. "Guinevere belongs to no one, especially not your son." He faced Lord Evrain squarely with more fierceness than I had ever seen. "And especially not to you. If she belongs to anyone, it is me, the man to whom she swore her intention to marry and to whom she freely, willingly gave her heart."

"And her body," Evrain added with a leering snarl. "Lord Aggrivane, you have broken the agreement I made with your father, and so you will leave my house in disgrace and return to him. I will ensure your father pays dearly for your insolence." The promise of retribution lit his eyes with manic intensity. He turned toward my father. "I demand punishment of his paramour. Without it, there can be no peace between our lands."

I looked with suspicion upon the man who threatened my future. Aggrivane was right; there was more to his plan than healing a breach of honor. Evrain was fishing for something.

The morning cock crowed as my father sat staring into the distance, considering his options. Father Marius too seemed to be weighing the alternatives, his milky blue eyes hardening in meditative concentration.

"There is one solution that I believe will be pleasing to all parties," my father stated.

I jumped at the sudden breech of silence. My father motioned me forward to stand before him like a prisoner receiving her sentence.

"Lord Pellinor of Dyfed has extended an offer to allow you to live with his family. I was not going to ask you to leave so soon, but your behavior has left me no choice. Perhaps under their guidance you will learn how to behave like a lady—a *Christian* lady."

My heart was pounding, blood rushing in my ears. I could no longer contain the fury that was building inside me. "Have I no say in my own fate? When did Northgallis become a kingdom of tyranny?" I directed his attention to the sacred mark upon my brow. "I made my choice long ago, Father. I have chosen to live my life with Aggrivane, following the ways of our ancestors—of my mother's people—the way of Avalon, free from the oppression of Rome." I locked my arm possessively around Aggrivane's.

My father's face darkened with rage. "Child, I am your father, forget not that! My father was a Roman, and by virtue of that lineage, I am free to invoke Roman law, under which you are my property to do with as I please! I could have you killed or sold into slavery or prostitution if I so chose, without even the slightest question or repercussion falling on me."

He rose from his chair and bent down so he stood face to face with me, gripping my shoulders. Terrible strain marred his bloodshot eyes. "Be thankful I think so highly of you, Guinevere. All I have chosen is for you to live in the house of a kind nobleman who will see that you are well treated and well prepared for your future role as wife. Is that so much to ask, daughter?"

I should have remained silent, but the willfulness I inherited from my mother would not let me. "And who here would enforce that Roman law you threaten me with, Father? Rome hasn't given us a thought in over half a century. From whom do you draw your authority?"

That was the wrong thing to say.

"It was Rome who gave Britain an understanding of herself as a nation rather than a land of scattered tribes." My father was in his full battle fury now. "It was from Rome that Britain learned to combine her scattered forces effectively. It was by her lesson that our clans learned to live under single rule. Without Rome, our high king could not now be contemplating his united kingdom. The past glories of imperial ties spark within our family blood. You are no one to criticize Rome!"

I broke away from his grasp before he could strike me, retreating to face him from the far corner. "You never treated me like a Roman daughter when I was growing up. If you had, I could accept this now. You always gave me the freedom and respect that first drew you to my mother and her people. But now that she is dead, all that must end."

My father looked as if I had just broken his heart. He opened his mouth to speak, but no words followed.

"Leodgrance, do not forget that your wife died possessed by the devil," Father Marius said softly. He had been waiting for this very opportunity. In a flash of scarlet robes, he stood between us, bidding me be silent with wave of his hand.

"Liar!" I lunged toward him, intent on scratching out his eyeballs, but Aggrivane restrained me in a firm grip.

"Foolish child, I speak the truth." Father Marius spat his words at me with none of the compassion with which he claimed to mark his faith. "All women scream in childbirth in reparation for the sins of the flesh, but Corinna's extreme suffering could only have come from the devil, sent to punish her for giving her daughter over to the pagans instead of to the Church."

I struggled against Aggrivane's grasp, but he held me fast.

"Do not make things worse for yourself, love," he whispered.

Marius was clearly enjoying himself. "Why else would the child inside her have died? The devil runs wild in this savage country, causing old women to claim to see visions of the future and men to be morally repugnant." He cast an accusatory eye to Aggrivane before returning his attention to my father. "Why, this new king of ours is nothing more than the devil's own puppet—advised as he is by the high priest of heathens. No, Leodgrance, there was no hope for your wife. When she gave her daughter to the evil isle, she gave up her very soul. The only thing that could have saved her would have been a life of penance and austerity in the cloister. Even then she may have suffered in the afterlife."

He turned his bitter eyes toward me but refused to look into my face. "Your child here is already following the same path, wanton as she has proven herself to be. Do you wish her to suffer the same fate?"

My father suddenly looked old and weary. He sighed, the sound of a defeated man. "No, I do not." He sank back into his chair. Summoning his strength, he issued the final verdict. "Guinevere, you will live with Lord Pellinor's household until such time as a husband is chosen for you. Lord Evrain, I beg your forgiveness for any affront caused by the events of this night." He pounded his fist on the arm of his throne, sending a heavy blast echoing off the walls. "This is my will, and as I have proclaimed, so it shall be."

Father Marius regarded me with an icy stare. "I will pray that your party makes it to Dyfed before the first snowfall," he said, but there was no sincerity behind his words.

Chapter Eleven

I hardly noticed the journey south.

I had lost everything I had ever loved: my family in Avalon, my mother, my lover, and now my father. Even Octavia was forbidden to accompany me. Once again, I was alone, facing the prospect of another new home; it seemed like each time I traveled somewhere new, my heart became heavier, weighed down by another form of pain.

Life had just begun to feel normal again. The homesickness I had felt for Avalon had begun to fade; the shock and blinding grief that gripped my soul at my mother's death had begun to loosen just enough to let me breathe again; even my father had shown a flicker of his old genial nature—and then all the wounds were slashed open in a single instant.

My horse trod the miles without prodding or direction, as if he was as resigned to his fate as I was mine. The countryside passed without my knowledge. All I could see in my mind's eye was Aggrivane. The memory of him was the one thing that enabled me to draw breath—the light of his smile, the softening of his eyes each time they found mine, the warmth of his breath.

When Aggrivane and I parted in Avalon, I'd accepted it was unlikely we would ever see one another again. Of course I missed him, thought of him, dreamed of him, but that was all it was; it seemed more fantasy than reality. But when I saw him standing in the entryway of Northgallis, an unexpected beacon in my dark world, he had been real, as was our love—overwhelmingly, tantalizingly, achingly real. As our bodies came together, so did our hearts, our souls, permanently intertwined among our limbs like mistletoe in the boughs of an oak. When he whispered that he would marry me, my world was complete once again.

No matter what my father or that horrid priest said, he would always be mine. I couldn't let him go, but I couldn't be with him either, and it was tearing me apart.

The fissure in my heart seemed to expand every time I thought of him returning to Lothian. Surely his father would be merciful, would he not? Lot was widely known as a man of great integrity and strength of will. Aggrivane spoke highly of his father and it was clear that they loved one another, so he would understand; he had to. Perhaps Lot would even see the injustice that was done to us and send his men to rescue me from my prison. Then we could be together forever, just as we had intended.

Even now I could feel Aggrivane's hand in mine as we wound our ways to unknown fates. I knew with absolute certainty that as my body drew ever closer to Dyfed, a small shard of my soul journeyed northeast to Lothian with him.

◈◈◈

I could barely breathe as I waited outside the large oak doors of the great hall. Corbenic was a large holding, much more imposing than my own home, and standing here surrounded by guards did nothing to make me feel welcome. Inside, Lord Pellinor and Lady Lyonesse were holding court. With a murmur of voices, they attended to the room full of courtiers, common folk, and emissaries, each with their own agenda or case to plead.

The men around me shifted anxiously and stomachs rumbled audibly as the minutes ticked by. My feet were beginning to get stiff and sore when a servant emerged from the suddenly silent room to beckon us in. When I stepped through the doorway, I was greeted by a press of people on either side, strange faces peering at me with open curiosity or obvious distain. I began to sweat under the weight of their judgment, and I tried to ignore the feeling I was being paraded in front of the entire court like a criminal.

Pellinor's tall, thin frame came into view first. He was standing in front of his throne with a warm smile on his face. A few new wrinkles creased his face and less of his close-cropped black hair was visible along his forehead, but otherwise he appeared much the same as when I had seen him last, two summers before I went to Avalon.

"Guinevere, welcome." He came forward when we reached the dais and embraced me warmly. "I am so happy your father accepted my invitation. It has been far too long since we have had the pleasure of your company." He regarded me with sincere appreciation, the way I had expected my own father to receive me.

Ignoring the gaping crowd, he continued in his familial tone. "My, you have grown. You are not the only one who has come of age in the passing years." He put out his arm, and a beautiful girl about my age with long strawberry-blond hair trotted to his side. "You remember Elaine. The last time the two of you were together, you were covered in mud, do you remember?" He laughed lightly.

Elaine grinned at me, and although my body was visibly shaking, I couldn't help but be warmed by her presence. I remembered quite clearly. It was Elaine who had led us into the bog, chasing after one of her many fantasies. Time had dulled the particulars, but I remembered enough.

My heart was beginning to warm and the slightest hint of a smile tugged at my lips when I caught the eye of the woman perched in the throne next to Pellinor. She had draped herself in such a way as to appear larger, more imposing than I knew her to be. With a sudden chill, I understood it was she who was holding court and that she was simply indulging her husband's kindness. Her eyes were fixed on my forehead, and her jaw was taut. It was clear she had not been forewarned about my religious views and was not pleased.

Having held my gaze long enough to make her authority clear, Lyonesse rose and embraced me stiffly. "Welcome, Guinevere." Her words were kind, but her greeting held no warmth.

Lyonesse had never been overly affectionate, but her actions were much more formal than I recalled from my last visit. Her brief embrace threw me off balance, and I stumbled as she released me and we both returned to our places.

Pellinor too took his seat beneath a large painting in which a woman lovingly gazed on her child while the father watched serenely but protectively from behind them. In the background, an older man and woman raised their eyes skyward in silent prayer of thanksgiving. I would have thought it a portrait of Pellinor's family, if the child had not been a boy.

"Gentlemen," Pellinor said to the assembled guards, "I release you from your service. You may tell Lord Leodgrance that his daughter is safely in my care. My men will show you to the barracks, where you may dine and rest before beginning your journey back to Northgallis in the morning."

As the clamor of armor and footsteps receded, I was pleased to note the crowd had grown considerably smaller. Besides Pellinor's family, there now remained only a few people I did not recognize, among them a strikingly beautiful woman with porcelain skin and a wild curly mane of hair that was more orange than red, brighter even than Morgan's in the sunlight. She observed me with a strange mixture of emotions, as if she knew enough to pity me yet was dying to learn more. Her nearly concealed smile told me that she was amused by my situation.

I stood silently, still trembling before Pellinor and Lyonesse, unsure how to proceed. If I should speak, I could not; my throat was dry and my tongue seemed glued to my palate.

Lyonesse gazed down at me, her sapphire eyes hard and disapproving, still boring into my forehead as though she could remove the crescent by force of will. It was then that I realized she made me more uncomfortable than Argante had on my first day in Avalon. That thought sent a shiver down my spine, while beads of cold sweat made an appearance on my forehead and on the back of my neck. I looked to Pellinor and Elaine for reassurance, but Lyonesse quickly drew my attention back to her, exactly where she wanted it.

"I must admit I had serious reservations about allowing you to live here—and I still do—but my husband promises me you will behave with the utmost decorum and mind your place. Is that correct?" Her voice was grim, as though she held little hope regarding my ability to comply.

I nodded mutely.

She seemed the tiniest bit assuaged and relaxed slightly in her chair. "I know the story of how you came to be here, the real reason why our invitation was accepted." She eyed her husband accusingly.

Pellinor was nonplussed, but I had a feeling it was all an act.

"With the addition of you to the household, we now have three mouths to feed and three husbands to find." She gestured to her daughter, who immediately blushed scarlet. "Elaine, of course, will be no problem, but I question the influence you and the other one may have on her, especially together." She threw the curly-haired woman a look of repugnance.

Why does she not call the girl by name? That simple act of disrespect rankled me.

"I do not want our home to become a house of ill repute. Given your history"—it was clear that she was speaking now both to me and the curious girl in the corner—"that could be a very difficult assumption to avoid."

"Be reasonable," Pellinor interjected. "Isolde and Guinevere have done nothing to earn your ire. Past offenses are nothing to us now. What good is it for Guinevere to have come here if she is not given a chance to begin anew? Even our Lord and Savior did not turn away the Magdalene from his companions, and he often dined with prostitutes and tax collectors. We owe Guinevere the same compassion and forgiveness."

Inwardly, I took offense at Pellinor's scriptural reference, but he meant well, so I ignored him.

"But those people were repentant of their sins, husband," Lyonesse retorted, her voice becoming higher and harsher with each word. "Guinevere has done nothing to indicate she regrets what she has done or to show firm purpose of amendment. Therefore, we must be on our guard." Her attention was back on me now. "You will be the model of righteousness while you live within our walls, do you understand? If I hear even the faintest whisper that you have done or even thought of anything that may be morally questionable, I will turn you out without a second thought." Her eyes blazed fire. "I advise you to have as little interaction with Elaine as possible until you have proven yourself to be true to the path of virtue—"

"Lyonesse, you cannot forbid two friends from being together," Pellinor interrupted, exasperated. "It is against nature, and it is not compassionate. Think how you would feel if someone did the same to you. Guinevere and Elaine are practically kin; you cannot rend the garment of family without displeasing God."

For a moment Lyonesse was speechless, thrown by Pellinor's accusation of un-Christian behavior, but she recovered and quickly changed the subject. "So be it. But your visits must be supervised."

She stood, descended two of the three steps that separated us and stood glowering down at me. Silently, she scrutinized my face, my dress, and, I suspected, my body beneath. She took a deep breath and let it out with an exaggerated sigh.

"You seem to be in good health, and you are comely enough. It *will* be a challenge finding a good Christian man willing to marry you since you are a branded woman." She started to touch the mark on my forehead with trembling fingers, but then pulled away, as if she feared being burned. "But I have faced bigger challenges in my time, and I am determined not to fail.

"The mark may mean little if we can show that you have changed and embraced the true faith," she said, more to herself than anyone else. "But the bigger problem lies in your virtue, or lack thereof." She smirked. "Normally I would call the healer and have her publicly certify your virginity, but since we all know that would be a fruitless gesture, we will have to improve your spiritual virtue instead. It will be cold comfort when a man realizes he has been bound to a used woman, but it is the best we can do under the circumstances."

Pellinor started to object once again.

Lyonesse silenced him with a wave of her hand and went on. "We attend Holy Mass at dawn every morning. I expect you to accompany us and show the proper respect. Perhaps you will even learn the meaning of true faith."

I desperately wanted to remark that my chances were better of learning it from a sermon than from her actions, but I bit my tongue.

"It is late and you must be tired from your journey," Lyonesse said, showing compassion for the first time. "You." She snapped her fingers at Isolde. "Show her to her chambers."

Isolde threw Lyonesse a look of clear distain as she emerged from the shadows near the wall and took my arm, leading me up the stairs like a lamb to slaughter.

❧ဎ❧ဎ❧

I closed the door behind me and leaned against it, trying to comprehend what had just occurred.

"Is that their idea of a welcome?" I was trying to reconcile the warm memories of my youth with the odd greeting I had just received.

Isolde shrugged. "It's normal, if that is what you are asking. Pellinor is a just man ruling with patience and compassion, while Lyonesse is ever lording her self-importance over everyone around her. They *are* rather judgmental of those who do not conform to their standards, though." Isolde opened one of my trunks and fished around in the contents. "I dare say that an Avalonian priestess is nearly as bad as Irish royalty in their minds. But I would think you would have anticipated as much."

I shrugged. "No, I did not. I—I cannot remember them acting

like this when my family came to visit." A stab of pain hit my heart at the word "family," and my brow furrowed involuntarily. "Maybe I was just too young to notice, but I think they have changed."

Isolde turned from the bed to face me. "That was nothing. When I first arrived, Lyonesse would have had me shackled and handed over like a prisoner." A sly smile spread across her face. "But she had to receive me like a second daughter, with all the pageantry and circumstance accorded to my rank, and it nearly killed her." She was grinning.

Curious now, I raised my head to meet her green eyes. "How *did* the heir to the Irish throne come to live in the kingdom of Dyfed?"

Isolde stopped unfolding my garments and looked off into space, cocking her head to one side and pursing her lips. "Actually, that is one thing we have in common. It was your father's idea."

My confusion must have been plain to read because she smiled.

"Do you not remember? You were there when my fate was sealed, or so they tell me. All of nine years old, you were sitting at your mother's knee when the council of western lords met with my mother's ambassador and agreed to trade my freedom for a promise of peace between Ireland, Gwynedd, Dyfed, and Cornwall. My presence here, and the promise of a strong marriage to some unnamed British noble, is all that stops my people from devouring this coast. Your father offered me up then to protect his seaports from plunder just as he offered you up to placate that Powys pig, Evrain."

I looked down at the floor, seeking the shadow of my feet in the firelight. "So we mean nothing to them, any of them?" I asked in barely a whisper.

Isolde snorted and I started. "Oh, we mean plenty to them. We are the most valuable currency there is to Christian men." She thought for a moment. "Well, we'd be more valuable as virgins, but you understand my point."

I met her gaze. "So you're not. . ."

"No."

"But what about Lyonesse's test?"

Isolde laughed, a hearty, throaty sound of genuine joy. "You believed that nonsense? Guinevere, did all those years on that isle rot your brain? Lyonesse is all talk, a liar determined to sell her shell of Christian perfection to everyone, including herself. But Pellinor is her biggest mark. Sometimes I think she fears he would send her away at the slightest hint of imperfection. So she overcompensates. There is no healer, no test. And even if there was, such things are easy enough to fake," she said with a dismissive wave of her hand.

I eyed her suspiciously, wondering how she came to such knowledge.

Isolde put aside the item she had picked up and looked at me purposefully. "Life in this house is one extravagant game. You will learn to play it, and I will teach you how." She wiggled her eyebrows. "It's actually kind of fun."

She sat down on the bed, motioning for me to join her. "But to win the game, you must first understand the other players." She looked impish. "You were probably too young the last time you were here to understand the details. Let's start with Pellinor. He claims to be a descendant of Joseph of Arimathea, the man in whose tomb their Christ was buried. According to legend, he was a tin trader, and after the death of Jesus, he escaped along the trade routes to Britain, where he hoped Roman law wouldn't be able to find him."

Isolde grew serious, her eyes distant as she recalled the tale she had no doubt heard countless times. "As Pellinor tells it, the prophecy of the Grail was spoken by the apostle John after Christ was laid to rest. In appreciation for Joseph's generosity, the seventh child of the seventh generation after his would bear a man of unparalleled purity, second only to Christ himself, and that man would bring the world the gift of the chalice of Christ. Some say that the one who bears it will never die, while others claim it will bestow everlasting peace on the land in which it is held."

"But that is ridiculous," I said. "It is no relic of their god but one of the treasures of Avalon. It is highly symbolic in our faith, but it has no magical properties, at least not that anyone in Avalon speaks of."

Isolde glared at me warningly. "Do not let those words, or any like them, escape your lips in this house. If you do, Pellinor will send you back to your father before you have had the chance to blink." She gripped my shoulders, looking me square in the eye. "You must understand that this prophecy is all that Pellinor has. His sons have disappointed him, so he has no hope for a stronger kingdom until Elaine marries, and given his high standards for her, that is unlikely to be any time soon."

My eyebrows knitted together in frustration. I was about to ask her to clarify when she interrupted with a question.

"Did you see the painting behind Pellinor's throne?"

"Yes, I assumed it was of his family—ancestors perhaps."

She nodded. "You are correct, in a fashion. You see, that is a painting of what the Christians call 'the holy family.' The man is Joseph, foster father of Jesus the Christ; the woman is Mary, his mother; and the child is Jesus. But what makes this painting unique is that it also contains two others: Joachim and Anne, the parents of Mary."

I stared at her, thoroughly confused, despite my basic knowledge of Christianity. I failed to see what that had to do with Pellinor.

Isolde sighed, seeing I was not making the connection. "To Pellinor, this painting represents his past, present, and future. He believes he is related to a man who performed a great service for this savior-child. He is the sixth generation since that fateful event. Elaine is the seventh child of the seventh generation, if you count all of Pellinor's children, living and dead. Therefore in Pellinor's mind, his progeny—Elaine—is fated to bear the man who will discover the Grail. That makes poor Elaine sacrosanct, for she will bear the most perfect man to live since Christ. In a way, she is to Pellinor a reflection of the Virgin Mary, which makes him and Lyonesse like Joachim and Anne."

I nodded. Somehow this was beginning to make sense. "But who then will be Joseph? You cannot mean to say that Pellinor believes Elaine will conceive miraculously? I do not think that their god would allow a wonder of that magnitude twice—if he even did once."

Isolde laughed. "No. Pellinor's mind is still partly anchored in reality. He knows she must have a husband for the child of prophecy to be born. That is why he has already begun compiling a list of possible suitors. Lyonesse says they will be brought to Dyfed to interview for her hand as soon as Elaine's monthly courses begin."

"And Elaine? What does she think about all of this prophecy? That must be a mighty weight to bear."

Isolde shrugged. "It is hard to say, really. Pellinor keeps her locked away in her room most of the time. I keep her company when I can, but that is only when Lyonesse is out. She wouldn't want her daughter associating with one such as me. Honestly, I think Elaine is a little . . . well, eccentric. If you had that pair as parents, you would be as well. All of that time alone has made her prone to mistake her imaginings for real events—although that could partly be my fault too." She smiled sheepishly, and her cheeks reddened.

"What?" I stammered, taken aback. "What do you mean?"

She ducked her head and stood, pacing to avoid my gaze. "As a good Christian lady, Elaine is not allowed any books other than those the tutor supplies her and the lives of the saints the nuns let her borrow—all rare and valuable resources that must be returned in a timely manner. I noticed when the bards come to entertain, she is enraptured by their tales of romance and adventure, so I started sharing with her the legends of my homeland, the very same stories of tragic love and magical creatures I was told as a child. The difference is that as I grew, I learned what was real and what was not. I don't think Elaine has the same ability." She paused, facing me now. Her brow was creased with concern. "I think she believes some of the stories are true. Maybe she has convinced herself she is one or more of the characters, I don't know. Not long ago, she told me she had seen a vision of her future husband in her mirror."

I cocked an eyebrow. "But doesn't that run contrary to her faith, seeing such things?"

Isolde shook her head. "Elaine is well-versed in the extraordinary abilities attributed to some holy men and women. She believes her god has blessed her with a special gift. I believe she needs companionship. It is good you are here. She is not a danger to anyone, but the more you can draw her out of her fantasy world and into her real life, the better off everyone will be."

"If Lyonesse lets me," I corrected her, grimacing at this new responsibility.

"Oh, she will; just give her time to warm up to you. All you have to do is be good for a while." She winked.

"Does no one else notice her behavior? Certainly Lyonesse must be aware."

"Elaine is adept at keeping to herself anything that might upset her parents," Isolde explained. "She knows what best suits her strategically. Her parents love her in a way I will never understand, and she returns that love by being to them exactly what they want—the model of virtue. But every so often, her carefully crafted mask slips, mostly in private. Beware of her jealousy and remember you are dealing with a mind more fragile than most," she warned darkly. "But she has been well lately, so hopefully she will not cause us any grief."

Isolde grew silent, no doubt ruminating on the slim likelihood of a peaceful winter with us all cooped up under one roof. I seized the opportunity to change the subject.

"Why do you let Lyonesse treat you like a slave?" I asked bluntly, surprised at how easily I spoke my mind around this girl.

"It is her way of teaching me humility," she answered with a deep sigh, showing no sign of offense. "I've grown used to it. I matured faster than Elaine and Lyonesse began to see me as a threat—or rather, as competition for her daughter," she corrected herself. "That was when she began insisting I walk behind her family and ordering me about." She exhaled loudly through her nose. "I'm surprised she still lets me dine at table with them. I go along with whatever she wishes—attending Mass every morning, doing tasks she finds distasteful during the day, and praying on my knees every evening with the rest of the family." She pointed a slender, pale finger at me. "You'd do well to take a lesson from me in that. The same will be expected of you. You may be a future queen, just like me, but in this house, you are little more than a servant."

I stood, crossing to stand in front of her, enraged by the future her words painted. "*I* am no servant. *You* may have accepted your fate, Isolde, but I will do no such thing! I am a priestess of Avalon, and I will *not* pretend to worship their god. I will demand the respect I deserve as an equal to their daughter in all things." My face was hot, blood boiling. "I may not have come here under my own volition, but that does not mean I will relinquish control of my life."

To my great annoyance, Isolde smirked. "To whom will you protest? Your father? He sent you here, believing it best for you. To Avalon? They have no say in matters of family. Your life is not being threatened. You are not being harmed." She shook her head, exasperated. "You are missing my point. You do not fight them—that is what they want. Rail against them in your mind all you like, but do not show it; they sense rebellion like a falcon knows his prey. If you want to live in peace, you will keep your thoughts to yourself and go along with them until such time as someone asks to be betrothed to you."

The mention of an engagement sent another stab of pain through my heart and my eyes welled with tears, deflating my self-righteous anger. I had been engaged only a few days ago. When I looked up into Isolde's eyes, a connection formed between us, two prisoners bonded by a common fate.

"And you," I asked quietly. "When will Pellinor find you a mate?"

Her eyes grew soft, watery. I had hit a nerve. "Who knows? Elaine is his top priority and now with you here. . ." Her voice trailed off and she began to pace again, a thoughtful silence spreading out between us. "If they do not match me soon, my family will be angry."

She was so quiet I had to strain to hear, and I wondered if she was merely thinking aloud, talking to herself, but she paid me no heed.

"If I were at home, my mother would have me engaged by now," she continued in the same low tone. "That was the whole point of the peace treaty, to unite Britain and Ireland through marriage. But I have resources. My people have watchmen stationed throughout the city." She ran the knuckles of her right hand along her mouth, thinking. "Should too much time pass, any one of them could whisk me away under cover of darkness and the treaty would be void because Pellinor failed to uphold his end of the bargain and obtain for me a husband. Then I would be free to marry whomever I choose." She stopped at the window, looking out over the sea toward Ireland. Her eyes were glittering now, a plan forming in her mind. "My mother would not deny me love. Then someday, when I am Queen of Ireland, I will be able to repay what Lyonesse and Pellinor have given me. They will regret treating me so."

Suddenly, she seemed once again aware of my presence. Her attention focused on me, and she let her hand fall to her side. "I suppose we all live in a fantasy world from time to time," she said apologetically, her lips twisting into a half smile, half frown.

Gracefully, she descended into the window seat and I joined her, suddenly weary.

"We are going to cause quite a stir in their pious little world, I can feel it." There was conspiracy in her voice. "Now, if it won't cause you too much pain, I'd love to hear about the man who was worth risking your inheritance for."

While the cold, soaking rains wrenched the last of the leaves from the trees, Isolde and I spent time getting to know one another. When I asked about her life before she came to Corbenic, she was evasive, but I learned she had a mother she practically worshiped, a younger sister she adored, and a younger brother she loathed. She, in turn, was very interested in my childhood, asking about every detail. As a result, I found myself forgetting she was Irish—and therefore, my enemy—and telling her things I would otherwise keep to myself.

"The thing I miss the most is being able to hold a sword," I told her one quiet afternoon. "I cannot find the words to explain it, but when I do, nothing else matters. The weapon and I dance, and the rest of the world falls away." I remembered my last lesson with my mother and cousin Bran, only days before the attack that shook my life to the core. Although Bran was taller than me by an arm's span and twice as strong, I had disarmed him in only three moves. "My mother would be highly displeased if she could see how my skills have deteriorated, thanks to Avalon's policy of nonviolence and my father's prohibition."

"Maybe she can." Isolde's eyes were glimmering when she looked up at me. "And I may have a solution for you." She wiggled her eyebrows at me.

Mine arched in response. "Isolde—" I said her name slowly, as though approaching an unfamiliar animal. "I don't know what you are thinking, but I know I do not like it."

She slid off her seat, graceful as a cat, wagging her index finger at me as she approached. "Don't be so quick to judge. It so happens that the son of Pellinor's weapon's master owes me a favor. I may be able to talk the master into training you. If"—she touched me lightly on the nose—"you promise to keep it a secret."

I was at a loss for words. Isolde had a solution for everything. "Of course," I croaked, eventually. "How soon do you think you can arrange it?"

Her grin signaled she was already up to no good. "I will talk with him tomorrow. My guess is you'll be sparring again before the week is out."

I still do not know what words Isolde used to charm Guildford, the weapon's master, but she was true to her word. He agreed to give me covert lessons if I agreed to teach his son to read. He didn't know what terms were specified in his own contract with Pellinor and did not want his son to suffer the same fate. He had dreams for Liam to become a warrior and win his own land one day. If he could read, his lot in life would be all the stronger.

The next evening, Isolde and I met the well-muscled swordsman and his boyishly handsome son in the barn of a farmhouse just outside the castle gates. It was close enough for us to sneak there unnoticed—it seemed Isolde knew a myriad of ways in and out of the castle—yet far enough from the prying eyes of court to evade suspicion. After all, who would question the ringing of blades on the weapon's master's property? Passersby would rightly assume someone was getting in some extra practice. What they would never guess was who.

We would occasionally vary our location so as not to arouse suspicion—one day the lower paddock, the next a clearing in the woods—but as the days went by, the barn proved to be the place with the least interruption or cause for prying eyes.

Nearly a month into my training, on a cold, clear morning, we reached the safety of the barn just as the sun broke over the horizon. I usually sparred with Liam while Guildford instructed, so I was surprised to see Guildford suited in leather armor, warming up with basic footwork and a few practice swings.

"Blessings of the day to you, ladies," he greeted us in a warm baritone.

"And to you as well," Isolde answered, sneaking a quick peck on Guildford's cheek before he could protest.

I smiled, still shy in the presence of so great a man. Guildford's name was known along the western coast of Britain from Cornwall to Rheged because he had trained most of the men who successfully fought off the Irish for the last twenty years. The irony of Isolde being my means to him now did not escape my notice.

Though his shoulder-length hair was streaked with gray and his face deeply lined, he had the agility and strength of a man half his age, and the prospect of facing off with him made my stomach clench.

Guildford must have read my expression. "Come on now, lass. We have only until the church bells toll. Get ye ready."

I threw Isolde a questioning look as I shed my cloak, tucked the hem of my tunic into my belt, and donned my own protective leather breastplate.

She read my meaning and casually asked what I had been too intimidated to ask. "I thought Liam was challenging Guinevere today?"

"Liam needs time to study what Guinevere taught him when last we met. He's been needed to help secure the last of the harvest and mind the slaughter. Isn't that right, son?"

Liam looked up from the board on which he was slowly tracing letters with a crude stylus. His cheeks and throat reddened at the attention. "Yes, Father. More hands keep the beast of winter at bay, or so Mother says."

Isolde sauntered behind him, trailing her finger across his shoulders as she passed. She bent low over his left shoulder and surveyed his work. "He's doing well. Guinevere will have him reading and writing in no time." Her breath ruffled the hair at his ear.

Liam's blush deepened.

Isolde sat down on the bale of hay next to him, guiding his hand when he struggled.

As I went through my own brief warm-up, I wondered at the nature of the favor Liam owed her. He wasn't yet old enough to join Pellinor's army and I hadn't seen him about the castle, so how had they met? It really could have been anywhere, given that Isolde had lived here for so many years, and by her own admission, Lyonesse's guard was not always as close as it was now. But since he was obviously attracted to her, I could only assume she had used that to her advantage.

Guildford skimmed the tip of my sword with his own, a subtle bid for my attention. As we did with each new technique, he took me through the whole sequence once, explaining both offense and defense as we flowed through the movements.

I began with my shield outstretched, sword drawn high as I readied to strike. I brought down my sword, aiming for Guildford's head, but he stepped forward, blocking me with his shield, and putting me on the defensive. He held my sword fast, pushing against it with his shield so that I could not release it to strike again. Quickly, he raised his own blade, thrusting at my face, and I instinctively raised my shield arm to deflect. The jolt shot down my arm and into my teeth as the sword glanced off. Guildford took advantage of my momentary shock to change tack, using the motion of my defense to propel his sword toward my thigh, while also swatting aside my sword with his shield.

"That is only half the sequence, but I want you to learn both sides of it now. Once you've practiced, we'll put it together with the pattern I showed you at our last instruction and see if you can disarm me."

Leaving me to practice as both fighters in this duel, Guildford sat on a barrel, halfway between Isolde and me, so he could correct my technique as I practiced.

"Do you really mean what you said last week?" Without preamble, he resumed the conversation they let fall last time we scurried back to the castle. "How could it possibly be done?"

"Of course." She waved a hand airily as if swatting away a fly. "I would not offer if I was not intending to keep my word. When I return home, at least one of you will come with me. I will send for the others as I can."

I wanted to stop and consider the implications of what Isolde was saying, but to do so was a potentially dangerous distraction. I tried to focus on my training as their conversation whirled around me like so many dragonflies.

"But how will you do it while keeping Lyonesse in the dark? You know if she found out, she would lash out in ways you cannot even imagine."

Isolde shook her head. "She need not know. I have connections in the kitchens, the stables, even in her own bedchamber. The family will not discover my plan until it is too late to stop it."

Liam paused in his studies. "You will break Pellinor's heart, you do realize that."

I stopped then, sword mid-swing, and turned to the boy, surprised at his astute interjection. He was gazing at her with a strange combination of infatuation and concern for his father's master.

Isolde, for her part, appeared shaken, a tiny line of worry marring the space between her eyes. She bit her lower lip as if the thought hadn't crossed her mind. "I know," she finally responded in a small voice. She swallowed hard. "It pains me to betray him so, but I cannot let years of injustice go unpunished." She looked up at Liam, eyes seeking his approval—or maybe it was his forgiveness she wanted. "I put no one in danger by what I am planning to do. I could easily wage war, but instead I chose a more subtle form of revenge."

Guildford made a sarcastic sound. "Yes, how noble of you. You merely rob their household of the best servants and craftsmen, weaken them from within."

I went back to dueling with my shadow then, uncertain whether Guildford meant his words in jest.

"Do you wish me to send for you or no?" Isolde's tone was haughty. She clearly thought him serious and was hurt by the thought.

"I do, I do." Guildford sighed. "I simply wish I did not have to betray my master in the process."

He must have stood silently, for in the next moment, I heard the crunch of his boots as he came toward me.

"Ready?" He picked up his sword, assuming a standard opening stance.

I nodded, mirroring him.

We went through the sequence again, in the same roles. When we reached his jab for my thigh, I blocked it and brought up my sword, forcing him back. I swung horizontally around my right side, and Guildford lifted his sword and shield in response, using both to absorb the brunt of the blow. Stepping to my left, I repeated the strike on the other side, harder, forcing his defenses upward, exposing his now vulnerable groin area. I touched the tip of my blade to the area just below his armor to signal where my thrust would have landed.

Guildford clapped his hands together. "That was well done indeed."

Isolde put an arm around me as I bent to examine Liam's writing, my chest still heaving from the exertion of the fight. My eyes had made it only halfway down the page before a bell tolled in the distance, signaling the beginning of the morning prayer that preceded Mass.

"We must be off. There is little time to change before we meet Lyonesse and Elaine for daily devotions," I said. No matter how many times we did this, I would never lose the fear of being caught, the sheer panic at the thought of Lyonesse's reaction to my forbidden activity.

But Isolde was as calm as ever. While I stripped off my armor and did my best to straighten my wrinkled dress, she tousled Liam's hair and pecked him on the cheek. "Be a good boy and practice your letters—for me."

Liam smiled self-consciously. "Anything for you."

I embraced Guildford. "Tomorrow, then?"

He nodded. "Indeed."

"Remember, I keep my promises," Isolde called over her shoulder.

That's what I'm afraid of. I began my morning prayers then and there, begging the gods as I ran toward the castle that whether Isolde left for Ireland as a new bride or struck out on her own as she had threatened to do, it would not bring calamity on Pellinor's house. For I was part of that house now, and as much as I was growing to love her, I did not want to see her thirst for vengeance bring pain to those who held my future in their hands.

Chapter Twelve

Winter 496

Snow was gently falling from the pre-dawn sky, covering man and beast alike in a thin film of white powder. We were gathered in the courtyard outside Pellinor's castle in the early morning darkness, along with the rest of the village, to celebrate Candlemas, the first day of spring, though it came in what felt like the depths of winter. In my religion, it was a day dedicated to the goddess Brigid, who was the patroness of women's mysteries, especially childbirth, as well as fire and all forms of poetry and inspiration. In the Christian world of Corbenic, however, the feast commemorated the day the Virgin Mary, obedient to the laws of her own religion, went to the temple to undergo ritual purification after giving birth and present her son to God and the temple elders.

"Why, oh why, must this tradition be conducted outdoors?" I muttered to myself through chattering teeth. I stomped my frozen feet on the equally frozen ground and noted a little less feeling in them. I had been cold all morning, for we woke to find all of the fires in the house extinguished. As was custom, they would not be lit again until after Mass.

"Mortification, is that what they call this?" I asked Isolde, who was nearest to me in the long line of white-cloaked, half-frozen women.

She smiled. "Appropriate, is it not? We are liable to catch our death out here."

I knew she was only commiserating with me; Isolde did not even seem to feel the cold, so great was her excitement. She hadn't slept more than an hour last night; this was her favorite feast—mainly because it was the only one performed nearly the same as it was in her homeland. It was the one time of year she could erase the miles separating her from her family.

"Wait until you see it, Guinevere; it is truly beautiful. The ritual may be Christian, but the actions and the words are practically the same. Only at home, we don't carry a statue of stone. We fashion a likeness of Brigid out of straw and carry her in a litter made of rushes."

Isolde was practically bouncing in place as she spoke, her eyes wild with passion and memory as she watched the cluster of people at the front of the line struggling to lift a heavy stone statue. Lyonesse, for her part, tried to squelch Isolde's enthusiasm and make her display the proper demeanor. But Isolde didn't even hear her. To her, reverence and happiness were one and the same; her joy was her prayer.

Among the small crowd were Pellinor and Elaine, who was dressed in white like the rest of us, but her head was veiled in lace and crowned with rushes.

Isolde looked at Elaine with a mixture of envy and sadness, an expression I recognized from my Beltane competition with Morgan.

"I always wanted to be that girl," she said wistfully.

Her words surprised me. "Did you not take her role in your homeland? You are the eldest royal daughter, so I thought that would be your right."

A small, bitter laugh escaped her blue lips. "It would have been had I stayed. My mother insisted the representative of the goddess be at least twelve years old so she would be mature enough to understand the ritual and treat the office with respect. I would have been the most devoted Bride anyone had ever seen." Her eyes searched the western horizon. Did she see the castle walls or the mountains or the icy ocean in between? No, she was searching for home.

Isolde sighed and she was present once again. "Of course, here, Lyonesse would sooner accept the Goddess before she would let me lead the procession." She paused, looking impish. "Although I hear she came from a pagan family, so there may yet be hope!"

"So if even *you* have a chance, does that mean it is not always a member of Pellinor's family who is chosen?" I could practically see my words formed by my icy breath in front of me.

Isolde's eyes widened and her face shaped into the expression I had come to associate with frustration when she had to explain something to me that she took for granted. "Oh, no. This is Elaine's year because she is fourteen, marrying age." She sniffed, a haughty sound that I couldn't be sure was caused by the cold. "Sadly, rather than treat this holy day as a source of devotion, Pellinor and his princes use it as an excuse to parade their eligible daughters through the streets." She rolled her eyes.

A slight pain tugged at my heart for Elaine as I watched her take her place in line, reverently balancing the cross and the candle with which she had been entrusted. The poor girl thought she had been chosen for her virtue, when really it was her body on display, not her soul.

The bells tolled, announcing the dawn of the day. The line lurched forward, led by Elaine. Following close behind were Pellinor and three of his lords, each holding one corner of a heavy stone statue depicting the Virgin Mary seated with her divine child in her lap.

The snow crunched softly beneath our feet as we walked in silence, each bearing a candle lit by the priest. We wound our way out of the castle gates, through the village, and into the countryside beyond. People lined the streets, waving rushes, peculiar equal-armed crosses, and dolls made of straw. As the procession passed, many fell to their knees, crying out "thrice be blessed, noble lady!" or asking for the blessing of the goddess Brigid or the Virgin Mary.

By the time we arrived at the church, my hair was wet with matted snow and I scarcely felt the floor beneath me. The litter on which the statue rested was covered in evergreen boughs, seeds, and bowls of milk, offerings of the devotees.

As the church doors swung open to admit us, the small cluster of monks began chanting in Latin.

Pellinor and his companions placed the statue and its offerings on a special altar near the front of the little church. After giving the cross to the priest, Elaine deposited her candle directly in front of the statue, and each of us followed suit, forming a circle around the tall center candle. When Isolde stepped forward to make her offering, her face was glowing with reverent love. I did not miss the slight inclination of her head or the soft bow she made before the statue, and neither did Lyonesse. The latter nodded approvingly, not comprehending the true source of Isolde's devotion.

The priest swung a censor around all sides of the statue, filling the room with a sweet, pungent odor that seemed out of place in the bitter cold. Elaine came forward and stood next to the statue, her face now completely obscured by her veil. She held the bowl of cold, clear water the priest had just blessed and sprinkled each member of the assembled crowd as they came forward to pay their respects.

Slaves, servants, and poor workers laid their tools at the feet of the Virgin, along with the seeds they would begin planting once the earth thawed. Finally, one member of each household—a female servant, slave, or the eldest daughter—came forward and lit a candle from the one Elaine had held, carrying with it the Virgin's blessing. From this one light, each hearth fire and lamp in Pellinor's kingdom would be lit; the light had come once again to the earth to melt its frozen soil.

As Mass began, I wished it could also thaw my frozen feet.

⌘

The great hall was warm, the air thick with smoke and the scent of mingled food, wine, and ale, and buzzing with the sound of merry chatter and the tinkling of dishes. Each year, on the evening of Candlemas, Lord Pellinor held a great feast for his subjects. It was another of his rituals of penance. To atone for the sins his wealth brought upon him and to imitate as closely as possible the generous heart of Christ, on this night, he feasted the poorest of his people. Farmers, tradesmen, orphans, homeless, thieves, and prostitutes, all were welcome with open arms. Each was given a sumptuous meal, and if they lived far away or had no homes to return to, he paid the nightly fee at a nearby inn so they could slumber free of worry or fear.

Although this was not an entirely new idea—many lords held similar celebrations on Christmas or Easter—I had to admire Pellinor for doing it, and not just out of obligation; he seemed to truly enjoy himself. He went around to each table, speaking freely with every guest, asking about their wants or needs. A scribe followed quietly behind, noting what was said so it could be acted upon at daybreak. Many times I saw him discreetly press a fistful of coins into a needy hand, to be met with stunned silence, a whispered blessing, or tearful gratitude.

This is the definition of Christian love and mercy, not the doctrine of fear and guilt Father Marius proclaims in my father's house.

I had been thinking of them both a great deal lately, and as I wrestled the meat from a chicken bone, I wondered at my father's welfare. There had been no news, which was not surprising, given the bitter winter weather, but still I worried for him, alone in Northgallis with only his memories and that wretched priest to keep him company.

Elaine too looked preoccupied. She stared at her plate, mindlessly pushing at her food with her knife rather than eating it. She looked tired and very apprehensive. Perhaps Isolde had told her of her father's intentions of showing her off, or maybe she had figured it out. One thing was certain—something weighed heavy on her mind.

Isolde appeared to be enjoying herself, chatting merrily with one of the household servants. She was only a few seats down from where I sat, so I could hear snippets of their conversation. Earlier she had explained to the baker's black-haired daughter that this was the only day of the year she felt at ease; despite the title she held in her native land, it was the only time she'd felt equal to everyone else in the room. Now, a few cups into the evening, they were apparently discussing lovers past and presently desired, and were in the midst of a lengthy discussion about the physical merits of the blacksmith's son.

I turned away, embarrassed to overhear some of their more unguarded comments. I said a quiet prayer of thanks that Lyonesse was seated at the opposite end of the long wooden bench, where Isolde's drunken discourse could not reach her ears.

My eyes followed my thoughts, involuntarily seeking out Lyonesse's face. There was no head table tonight, no dais, as all were to be equal at this feast, so Lyonesse had nowhere to which she could escape. She looked absolutely miserable, sitting rigidly amidst the wives of the innkeeper, the blacksmith, and some of the soldiers, all of whom were raucously celebrating. Her pale hair was piled high and tight on her head, making her look harsh, an effect only magnified by her scowl.

I bet she would crawl through her own skin if it meant she could escape the gaggle of joyful women around her. She caught my eye, and I braced myself for the dart sure to be thrown my way, but to my surprise, rather than glare, Lyonesse smiled. It was just a twitch of her lips, but it was the first positive gesture she'd shown me since I arrived.

Pleased and shocked, I grabbed the nearest serving girl and instructed her to keep watch over Lyonesse's cup. Perhaps the atmosphere was finally rubbing off on her. Or maybe it was the wine. Whatever the solution, I wanted to keep her happy for as long as possible.

After the dishes were cleared, the court minstrels struck up a lively tune, giving everyone the chance to dance for a bit before the evening drew to a close. The baker's daughter had found a dance partner and so had Isolde—the blacksmith's son, judging by her earlier description. She whooped audibly as he spun her past my table. I couldn't help but smile. Even Elaine had timidly accepted the hand of a young soldier. I had seen him earlier today during the procession. Tall, strong, and dark-skinned, he was the son of one Pellinor's underlords, one of the many who had turned out to see Elaine on display. Now, as she hesitantly held his hand and let him lead her through the steps, she looked to Lyonesse for approval. The latter nodded encouragingly.

I had no desire to dance, and fortunately, no one seemed to notice me. As the night went on and the candles burned low, my thoughts turned to Aggrivane, as they so often did when my mind was not otherwise occupied. He would have loved an evening such as this, where one was free to be at ease, where customs and rules did not apply. He might even have taken the idea as a model back to his father in Lothian. We certainly would have done the same in our kingdom, had we married.

My brooding was interrupted by the sight of Pellinor approaching Lyonesse and softly taking her hand. She blushed at whatever he said and rose from her chair, smiling. They too began to dance, whispering in one another's ears whenever the steps brought them close. I had to look away; the intimacy of their exchange made me feel as though I was intruding on a private moment.

I rested my head on my arm to avoid seeing any of the dancers. Instead, I focused on the music and indulged my thoughts of Aggrivane. How I would have loved to have joined in the dancing were he my partner. I imagined him guiding me assuredly across the dance floor, pulling me close and then spinning me around until I dizzily fell into his waiting arms.

The Goddess brought us together twice. I had to trust she would do so again. It was the only thing keeping me from losing my mind in this strange house of piety and politics, where I was forced into a mold that I did not fit because it could never contain my soul.

But the Goddess also took him from you twice, answered a dark voice somewhere in the recesses of my mind.

But I am her priestess and must adhere to her will, no matter how loathsome it may be, I reminded myself.

Then you must realize you may never see him again, it answered, sending an icy fissure through my heart.

CHAPTER THIRTEEN

I didn't know when I fell asleep, but the next thing I knew, the hall was quiet, nearly empty. It must have been well after midnight.

I rubbed my aching head—perhaps I had one glass too many—stretched, yawned, and looked around. Elaine and Isolde were having an animated conversation in the corner. From their wide grins and excited eyes, I guessed they were discussing their respective dance partners. Lyonesse was flitting about, loudly directing the servants who had stayed behind to clean up, her good mood having faded along with the effects of the wine. In another corner, Pellinor was gently removing the last of the loitering guests, a particularly troublesome man who it appeared would need more than persuasive words to convince him to leave.

"My good sir, the night draws late and snow falls deep. Will you not please accept an escort back to your home from one of my men? If you have no lodging, I will provide one night's rest for you in town," Pellinor was saying, his voice tender with compassion.

"A generous offer, my lord," the hooded man replied, looking up for the first time. "But would Christ turn his own kin out into the cold?"

As the man removed his hood, Pellinor turned a sickly shade of gray, and I gasped, recognizing Merlin at once.

"Come now, brother," he continued. "Has it been so long that you have forgotten me?"

Pellinor struggled to regain his ability to speak. "Taliesin—Merlin," he corrected himself from Merlin's given name to the Archdruid's official title with much effort. He gulped and staggered backward onto a bench. "You come only when there is news." He looked worried, aging well beyond his years in only a few moments. "What news?"

Lyonesse, Elaine, Isolde, and I rushed to Pellinor's side, blinking dumbly at one another, unsure of what to do.

Merlin held Pellinor's gaze, obviously enjoying his discomfort. "Greetings of peace to you as well." He almost laughed, extending out a strong hand to Pellinor. "Please, you must introduce me to your extended family. Your company has grown since last we met."

Once the introductions were made, Pellinor dismissed the servants and we all took seats, eager to find out the cause of Merlin's unexpected visit. Lyonesse was on my left, Isolde on my right, and Merlin took the seat directly across from me. His bronze hair gleamed in the low light of the fire that cast shadows over the planes of his face and accentuated his high cheek bones and smooth, unwrinkled skin.

While the men exchanged pleasantries, I leaned over to Lyonesse, who finally had managed to close her mouth and was now clenching her jaw as if foresworn never to open it again.

"Why does Merlin call him brother?" I asked.

"They are kin—cousins, I think, related through the maternal line. They have spoken to each other as brothers as long as I have known them," she whispered in disgust.

I smiled to myself. So the saintly Pellinor was related by blood to the Archdruid of Britain. I could not have asked for a more interesting turn of events. I wondered how Pellinor kept this family secret quiet and what advantage the silence brought to Merlin.

"You asked if I bring news," Merlin was saying. "Indeed, I bring great news. I have come to tell you of the coronation of your high king." More quietly he added to me, "And I have a message for you."

Isolde and Elaine sat up straighter and regarded me with wonder. Lyonesse leaned forward on the table, giving me a look that could only be described as lethal. If I valued my life, it said, the message better not bring any scandal upon her house—and she silently demanded to know what it was.

Pellinor, who had missed the aside, sat back, glowering. "That was two months ago, Tali—Merlin. Why do you bring this news to us now?"

"Why were you not present to witness it yourself?" Merlin countered, his hands steepled in front of him, elbows resting lightly on the table.

"Yes, Father, why did we not attend?" Elaine asked, her face aglow with curiosity.

It was the first time I'd ever heard her speak out of turn.

"Glynis, Lord Lansdowne's daughter, said it was the grandest spectacle in three generations," she added a bit peevishly.

Lyonesse's expression had cooled from murderous to livid. "Yes, husband, tell me why I was the only tribal queen who did not witness her high king's installation."

Leave it to Lyonesse to make this about herself.

Pellinor shifted in his seat, clearly uncomfortable. "I thought it best to send a representative in my stead. The weather was beginning to turn poor," he explained feebly, "and Strathclyde is such a long journey—"

Lyonesse cut him off, fuming. "You made the journey many times when Uther had need of you. What made this time any different?"

Pellinor stood, enraged by the accusation in her voice. He brought his palm flat down upon the table. The smack reverberated around the deserted hall. "How would it look for a Christian king to attend the coronation of a man who is at best unknown and at worst a heathen bastard?" His voice was somewhere between a growl and a roar.

Merlin regarded him calmly, untroubled by Pellinor's outburst. "It would look like you were in unity with your high king, and that was all anyone was asking. Arthur does not demand that his subjects agree with all that he does or believes. He simply asks for your trust and your loyalty."

As he realized Merlin was right, Pellinor sank back into his seat. The fire in him had gone out.

"So what happened? What did we miss?" Elaine asked eagerly as though the previous exchange had not taken place.

Merlin chuckled at her enthusiasm as he reached behind his back to remove his harp from beneath his cloak. "I will tell you everything that took place, down to the last detail, but it is better if I do so with this." He ran his fingers lovingly along the bow in the wood. "The ancients say that one note of a song is twenty times more powerful than a single word, and that only in song can truth be clearly perceived, for though words can harbor lies, music cannot abide them."

He strummed an opening note.

"Wait." Elaine put out a delicate hand to stop him. "Please. Before you begin, will you kindly tell us of our high king's appearance? No one here has ever seen him, and it would help us visualize your tale." Elaine's eyes were wide, her cheeks flushed. She was sitting so far forward on the bench I feared she would fall off. She looked happier than I'd seen her during my whole visit.

Merlin grinned, obviously amused by Elaine's interest in the subject. "Actually"—he turned to me—"Guinevere has seen him, though I doubt she remembers it."

Elaine shot me a look of pure envy.

"When did I see him, my lord?" I regretted my regression to Avalonian formality as soon as the words escaped my lips. The others did not appear to notice. They were too eager to hear the answer to the question.

"He came to the Beltane fires. Think, Guinevere, and you will remember." Merlin squinted at me as though willing my mind to give up the memory.

I slowly shook my head. When I thought of that night, all I could see were Aggrivane's loving eyes.

"No matter, you will meet him soon enough." He turned back to the others. "Your king is a man of great strength, large in build and tall. He stands a full head higher than I and is twice as strong. I have no doubt he could wrestle a pack of wolves to the ground if it came to that."

Elaine gasped and Isolde giggled, grasping my wrists with clammy palms as she listened.

Merlin's smile widened, and he held Elaine's gaze, nearly hypnotizing her. "Indeed, lass, you do well to be awed. Your king's nickname is 'the bear,' due to his great size and strength, but do not be fooled—he is not a brutish man. He is known for his grace and agility, and he is an accomplished swordsman."

His gaze shifted respectfully over Lyonesse to Isolde. "But I doubt those are the details *you* are after." His eyes lingered on her as he spoke.

Her cheeks flared in response.

"His features are fine-chiseled and strong, for he is Roman on his father's side. His mother, Iggraine, can count the generations of her people in this land back to the Belgae, who called his land home for thousands of years. He received from her a kindness of heart not commonly encountered. He is not yet seventeen years old." He'd lowered his voice just slightly and regarded the three of us. "Nearly the same age as all of you, and has yet to take a wife." He looked at each of us meaningfully.

Elaine looked like she would faint.

"Enough. We have indulged your dramatics," Pellinor groused. "Get on with your tale, for the hour grows late." He faked a yawn. Elaine threw her father a nasty look. Had either he or Lyonesse seen it, she wouldn't have been able to sit down for a week.

"Perhaps I have been a little too loquacious," Merlin apologized. He picked at the strings of the harp again and a soft melody slowly took shape. "Lords from every kingdom descended upon Arthur's ancestral home, the seat of his father, Uther Pendragon. Add to them villagers and country folk from three kingdoms in every direction, and you will begin to understand the size of the crowd. Shoulder into back, elbow to elbow, they stood crammed along passageways, craning their necks to see the king in the dim light of rows of torches as he approached the inauguration stone. The stone, larger than three men's heads, even when weathered by the ages, stood atop the same hill on which it had been deposited by the gods before time began. Some say it has been in Arthur's mother's family since before the Romans came."

His story now established, Merlin began to tap out an accompanying beat with his boot on the flagstones underfoot. "At exactly the stroke of midnight, they raised him up, the Lady of the Lake supporting one elbow, the bishop the other, and his mother behind him representing his ancestors."

I imagined Viviane – who became Lady of the Lake after Argante's passing not long after I left Avalon – in her formal robes of office, silver crown and milk-white moonstone glittering in the firelight. I knew not who the bishop was, but I surmised he was a better man than Father Marius if the king trusted him enough to request his assistance.

"The crowd went silent, eagerly anticipating the response of the gods. Some say the stone cried out, proclaiming him the true high king of Britain, while others say he glowed with the light of the gods. Some even say Uther himself appeared and gave his son his blessing."

Across the table, Pellinor rolled his eyes.

"Whatever the truth, the moment had come. The contract between Arthur and the land had been established. I stood, and in a loud voice proclaimed his right to the throne. 'Arthur, son of Uther Pendragon, who was brother to Aurelius Ambrosuis, both of whom were sons of Imperator Constantine, you stand before us seeking to be wed to the land and henceforth hold it in your care. Is that so?'

"Arthur nodded solemnly.

"'Then I ask the goddess of sovereignty if she accepts this man as her mate.'

"The Lady of the Lake approached the stone, her gait smooth and sure, her back straight, head held high. She had called upon the Goddess, and now her face was not her own. She was youthful and carefree, the light of the stars in her eyes. She stood before him, taking his hands like a lover.

"'Man of clay and bone, you are but dust in my eyes. I am the spirit of the land you seek to rule. What is it that you offer me in exchange for my approval?'

"Arthur knelt before her, looking up into her infinite eyes, and proclaimed his vow to all. 'I pledge to you and to all my people my undying loyalty, from this moment to my very last breath. I swear to uphold the laws of this country and protect its land and its people, even with my own life. I promise to reign with justice and mercy, treating all with equanimity, and to defend this land from all who would seek to do it harm.'

"The Lady faced the assembly, her eyes closed, perfectly still. The crowd held its breath in anticipation."

I realized in that moment that I was doing the same.

"She opened her eyes and proclaimed her judgment for all to hear. 'I accept your vows, Arthur, son of Uther. You have my blessing. In exchange for your loyalty, I place upon you one geis, on pain of honor, which you may never break. You must always uphold my ways while remaining respectful of other's beliefs, for all are my children and though they may tread different paths, all return to me in the end.'

"'This do I swear,' Arthur replied.

"'Arise then, High King of Britain, and be armed for battle, for as even the most placid sea is subject to storm, your reign will not be without struggle.'

"The Lady then gave him the royal regalia, a white wand made from a sacred branch from Avalon and the sword of sovereignty—called Caliburn—its intertwined snakes a symbol of the light and dark aspects of power. From her hands he took the red cup of lordship and drank from it, his eyes watering and lips puckering, for its contents were both bitter and sweet, for so too is power. He returned to the stone, placing one foot upon it, the other firmly planted on the earth. The crown of Britain was taken up both by myself and the priest. Each whispering a blessing—his in Latin, mine in the tongue of our ancestors—we placed the diadem upon his brow.

"'Dux Britanniarum!' some in the crowd proclaimed, while others bestowed upon Arthur the ancient title of 'Arddurex' before we even had the chance to declare him high king.

"One by one, the kings in attendance came forth to pledge their service—Mark of Cornwall, Gerent of Dyfnaint, Malegant of the Summer Country, Cadwalla of the Midlands, Uriens of Rheged, Evrain of Powys, Cador of Bernicia, Guinevere's father, and Pellinor's representative. Even the lands of Gore, Dalriada, Brittany, the four northern tribes, and your mother"—he smiled at Isolde—"sent emissaries to bring the new High King greetings of peace."

Merlin stopped strumming, and with the music went all of the life in the room. His face darkened. "Noticeably absent was Lot of Lothian, who believes, as husband to Arthur's sister Ana, he is the true heir to the throne. I would advise you to have no dealings with him. He can be of a dark temper and no doubt will attempt rebellion."

Pellinor yawned—genuinely this time. "Have no fear, brother. I have no esteem for that man or his progeny."

I chose to ignore his barb against Aggrivane, still trying to pry the memory of having seen Arthur in Avalon from the recesses of my mind. Lyonesse was drowsing, chin resting on her chest. Elaine, lulled to sleep by Merlin's song, sat with her head upon her mother's shoulder, a slight smile upon her lips. I guessed she was dreaming of Arthur.

Pellinor, however, seemed in no mood to sleep. In truth, he looked like he was aching for an argument. I sat up in my chair and stretched, willing myself to stay awake despite the gnawing headache I longed to stifle with sleep.

"Merlin, you say our king was crowned by both you and a Christian priest. That is quite a break from tradition—and I must admit, more than a little confusing. To which faith is he sworn?"

Merlin regarded Pellinor carefully, fully aware the man was angling for something. "Our king," he said with great emphasis, "is Druid-trained, taught by my own hand. His foster father, Lord Ector, sent him to study with us on the sacred isle a few years ago.

He was never meant to take our vows, only to learn from our wisdom. Like his father, he serves the lord of light—the one whom some call Mithras, Apollo, or Lugh. However, he refuses to disparage the Christian religion because he can see in it the same marks of his own faith, but also because his mother took the habit of a Christian nun after Uther's death. To insult Christianity would be to insult her. Therefore, he upholds both his native religion and that of his mother." Merlin sat back in his chair, clearly satisfied with his answer.

Pellinor made a pensive grunting sound. "A very well-rehearsed account, but I have my doubts. The boy seems too good to be true." He muttered his next statement, but it sounded like something about no man being able to serve two masters. "Honestly, brother," Pellinor continued his complaints a little louder now, "if he lacks the sense to embrace the one true faith, how can we be sure he has sense enough to be our king?"

Merlin sighed, looking weary of this circuitous argument. "Pellinor, we all know your views, and it is obvious that nothing I can say will appease you."

Pellinor looked hurt.

"All I can do is tell you the truth. I cannot force you to believe it. While Ector always maintained he had no knowledge of Arthur's paternity, he made certain that Arthur received an education fit for an heir apparent. In addition to his Druidic training, Arthur learned the dialects of all the native tribes, is fluent in Latin and Greek, and has even taken it upon himself to learn the language of the Saxons. He is trained in arms and military strategy and can recite the names and titles of all the ranking men of the eleven tribes, should he one day need them as allies. Does that satisfy you?"

Pellinor frowned. He obviously was not expecting the king to be so well-qualified, or at least, Merlin to have such a thorough answer. "I suppose it will do."

Elaine and Lyonesse had awoken.

"Father," Elaine jumped in, seeing a lull in the conversation. "May we go to bed now?"

Her voice was so like a little child, I had to stifle a giggle.

Pellinor seemed only then to realize the rest of us were in the room. "Why yes, of course."

As we all made our way to our chambers, Elaine's preoccupation returned. I touched her shoulder and she stopped, turning to face me. Her forehead was wrinkled with worry and her eyes were heavy, morose.

"What is wrong, dear heart? Are you tired?" Truth be told, I was feeling a little unsteady myself.

She nodded. "Of course. Are you not?" She hesitated, unsure whether to elaborate. "It is only that all of this revelry and hearing about our new king has made me sad."

"Sad?" I was shocked at her response; it was the opposite of what I expected. "Why is that?"

"It made me realize how lonely I am."

With no more explanation, she turned away and ascended the stairs, leaving me gaping behind her.

༄༺ ༻༄

As I continued toward my own room, Merlin stopped me.

"Is there somewhere we may speak in private?" he asked.

I led him back into the now-empty hall, which seemed abnormally large in the silence following the feast. I wearily sank onto an abandoned bench and motioned for him to do the same.

"Guinevere, there is something you need to know," he began.

I probed his face, searching desperately for the meaning my heart sought. "Yes? Is it about Aggrivane?" The words tumbled out, buoyed by hope.

"No." He seemed torn between regret and amusement at my optimism. "It is about Morgan."

My heart sank into my feet. Why would he go through all of this to talk to me about the one person I never wanted to think about again?

"I know she is not your favorite person, but you need to know this. She has been banished from Avalon."

"What?" I nearly fell off my seat. "Why? What happened?"

"It is complicated." He took a deep breath and began to explain. "There was a competition among the priestesses to determine who would be Viviane's second, now that she has assumed the office of Lady of the Lake. It is a long tradition in Avalon. I wish you could have taken part. You would have done well. During the three days of the full moon before the equinox, the priestesses displayed their skill at all of the ancient arts—divination, control of the elements, spell casting, mastery of the sight, and ritual. I served as judge, so

Viviane could not be accused of partiality. The final test was healing. Morgan had done the best, and everyone expected her to easily win this event as well."

I involuntarily flinched, recalling her skill in that area, and the old jealousy reasserted itself. My stomach roiled, and I tasted bile.

"But when it came time for the judging, something unexpected happened. As was custom, each priestess had to drink from the cup prepared by her partner as a sign of trust. When Rowena drank from Morgan's cup, she immediately fell to the floor in a fit."

I gasped and covered my mouth with my hand. "Is she. . . did she. . . is she well?" My eyes filled with tears at the thought of my dear friend meeting such a horrible end.

"Yes, she eventually recovered. Viviane was able to give her an antidote, but we don't know what the effects will be. No one knows if it was an accident or if Morgan did it on purpose. She seemed as shocked as everyone else and has always maintained her innocence. But she was immediately suspected of poisoning Rowena because she was the closest competition. You of all people should know how Morgan treats people whom she perceives as a threat."

My mind drifted back to the day I rescued Ailis from the tree above the lake. I could still smell the burned tapestry thread and feel the puffy red blisters. Without realizing what I was doing, I scratched at the phantom sores on my arm that had long ago healed.

"But surely you do not believe she poisoned Rowena, do you? She lived with us in the House of Nine. She was our sister. Even Morgan would not—"

"When we analyzed the contents of Morgan's brew, there was an obvious error in ingredients, two herbs that should never be mixed together. You know how talented she is. It was a mistake she would not have made."

"But even she can err." To my own amazement, I found myself defending my old rival. "Perhaps she was fatigued or distracted or maybe someone wanted it to look like—"

"What is done is done," Merlin interrupted. "It was the judgment of the council—myself, Viviane, and the elder priestesses— that regardless of her intent, Morgan broke the vows she made at her consecration. By using the arts for harm, she failed to uphold the sisterhood and therefore had to pay the price. Viviane banished her from Avalon for a year and a day. After that time, she may return, if she wishes. But they had an intense row before she left, and with Morgan's pride, I doubt she will acquiesce to return."

I could scarcely believe my ears. Merlin was so calm, he could have been telling me about the weather. I could not comprehend his attitude. "So that is it then?" The frustration I was trying to suppress burst out in a fit of rage. "You sent her off the isle with nowhere to go? She has no family to return to, no friends. Avalon was her home!" I was shaking, a cold sweat blanketing the back of my neck and shoulders.

Merlin jumped to his feet, tipping his bench backward. He towered over me with such ferocity that I shrank back, heart pounding. For the first time since he arrived, I felt like I was in the presence of the Archdruid.

"Do you really think us that unkind or uncaring? After so many years with us, do you really believe us capable of turning her out on her own? We contacted several houses—prominent families, mind you—who were willing to take her in. They expected her, but she never inquired at a single one. We sent her with a guard intended to see her safely from house to house until she found employment, but she dismissed them—or rather, escaped them."

"So where is she then?"

Merlin hung his head, an uncharacteristically humble gesture. "We do not know. We have searched everywhere we are welcome, and she is not to be found. She has simply vanished."

"Much like the fey they say she came from," I whispered to myself.

"Viviane was just trying to teach her a lesson—instill some humility." Merlin continued as if he did not hear. He was thinking aloud. "No one expected her to react so rashly."

Had they not been paying attention her whole life? Morgan had always been unpredictable. What did they expect?

Merlin righted his bench and sat back down. "Guinevere, I want to share something with you, a theory I have told no one except for Viviane. Do you swear you will not repeat it?"

My breath caught. "Of course." I willed myself to be calm. I was suddenly very hot, though whether with the intimacy of Merlin's request or my nagging need for sleep, I could not tell.

"Do you remember the strange prophecy Viviane spoke during your last full moon in Avalon?"

My brow furrowed as I tried to recall the words, but all that rose to my muddled mind was something about animals and flowers.

Seeing my difficulty, Merlin recited the three verses from memory.

"*'The red dragon is poised to return to the realm of spirit, but another shall succeed him. The hallowed one has received the blessing of the land, and so shall it prosper under his guidance. Although malevolent forces threaten from without, the bear shall be victorious and all shall bow at the sound of his name.*

"*Soon the final passage shall be crossed by one of great power, allowing the lily to emerge from shadow and bloom in the light. An unlikely rose is transplanted to this isle and blossoms in its rich soil. But beware the rose and handle her carefully, for her thorns threaten to pierce the bud of the lily, thus causing the whole garden to die.*

"*These here gathered serve me well, and I am pleased. But the day will come when sister shall oppose sister, both in this sacred place and without. Loyalties will be tested and betrayed, so heed my warning. That which is birthed in jealousy shall not give life but infect all who draw near. Therefore, act with love and not out of spite. Only then shall you escape the fate the stars foretell.'*"

He continued breathlessly. "I believe I know to whom it was referring. We now know the red dragon was Uther and the Goddess foretold his passing and the rise of Arthur as king. I told you many people call him 'the bear' because of his size, and that is how he is identified in the prophecy. We also know that the final passage was Argante's death. That leads me to believe that Viviane is the lily, who has how taken her place of power as Lady of the Lake."

I nodded, amazed at how much sense that made, like pieces of a child's puzzle fitting into place. "But who is the rose? The terrible threat to Viviane?"

"We don't yet know. Only time will reveal her. But one thing we do know is the Goddess warned of enmity between priestesses. That is why I'm sharing this with you. I want you to be on your guard with Morgan. I believe you will see her again, and you should be prepared for when you do. By knowing what has happened to her, I hope you will feel a little more compassion toward her. I would hate for your jealousy to bring the prophecy to pass."

Looking into his eyes, which were now to me a scrying pool, I saw the future he feared. Morgan was standing with her arm draped protectively around a young boy, about ten years old. She sneered as though she could see me, and then the scene changed. A hooded woman delicately unlaced the praying fingers of a priest and placed a vial in his palm. He held it up to the light, and its contents glinted with malevolence. He nodded, and she turned to leave, a single stand of fiery hair betraying her identity. Morgan again. Then there was nothing but thick, choking smoke.

Merlin was still talking when I came back to myself, but I could not hear him over the shrill ringing in my ears. I grabbed the bench to steady myself as a wave of dizziness overcame me. The room swayed, and darkness beckoned. The last thing I heard was Merlin's startled cry as I collapsed at his feet.

Chapter Fourteen

The images floated in and out of my view, sharper than dreams, but they were no longer of Morgan. They were of war. Men on horseback, hundreds of them, swords glittering in the fading evening light, horses braying and whinnying as the men chased something—or someone—I could not see. Before I could blink, the whole scene melted as my vision blurred.

Shapes and colors were all I could make out now. It was as if someone had draped a gauzy veil in front of my eyes. Light and darkness alternated as I struggled to get my bearings.

"She is beginning to awaken." An echoing voice spoke from somewhere across a great void.

I tried to tell the voice to leave me alone, but my mouth wouldn't work. This was all so strange. Why wouldn't my lips move? Where was the rest of my body? All I could feel was an odd tingling engulfing my other senses and the sensation that my head was on fire.

"Guinevere, love, I'm here." The voice spoke again, washing over me in waves. "You are ill, but I will take care of you, I promise."

My eyes slowly began to focus. I could now make out the form of a girl about my own age sitting next to me. Her hair looked like my head felt. I knew this girl. Who was she? I searched around in my addled mind, sifting through names that refused to attach themselves to the faces that stared back at me.

Isolde? Was that it? I must have said it out loud.

"Yes, and Elaine and Merlin are here as well. We were very worried about you."

Her smile was warm, concerned. As she spoke, something cold and comforting skimmed over the fire in my head, momentarily causing it to sputter. In that moment of relief, my mind was clear. I remembered my conversation with Merlin about Morgan and my disconcerting visions.

I looked around, seeking Merlin. He was at the foot of the bed, watching me closely.

"Guinevere," he said softly, "you fainted. I brought you to your room. It appears you are quite ill. Your illness has weakened your resistance to the sight. You've been mumbling about your visions for some time now." He rounded the bed so he stood over me and bent down close. "It is best not to fight it. Your body needs rest, and if you resist, all you will do is weaken yourself more. Just give in and let the Goddess show you what she wills."

His last words echoed in my head, pounding to the same rhythm as the pulse of my blood as I struggled to remain conscious. I was losing, and I knew it. I was being sucked into an eddy, helpless to fight the swirling disorientation that had captured my senses.

From somewhere in the back of my mind, a loose strand of memory floated free, Argante's ominous warning from the day I was called before her to demonstrate mastery of the sight.

"For the remainder of your life, the sight will come to you of its own bidding when one to whom your soul is bonded is in peril."

I fought my leaden eyelids, wanting to ask Merlin if Argante was right. I was beginning to think so. First, the vision of my mother's death. Now the nonsense about Morgan. But was the sisterhood bond enough to count? I shivered despite, or perhaps because of, my fever. The sight beckoned. What was to come?

As if she could hear my thoughts, Isolde squeezed my hand. "I will not leave you," she pledged.

It was last thing I heard before darkness dragged its cape over my eyes and the visions began again.

ﻌﺨﺨﻌﺨ

I could hear his thoughts, this man whose dark complexion marked him as a descendant of Britain's ancient tribes. I knew him at once. The resemblance was too certain for him to be other than Lot, King of Lothian, father of my estranged lover. And he was plotting rebellion—treason.

It had been far too easy to get to this point, simpler than anyone could have ever imagined. Clandestine meetings with others of like mind, whispered words of treachery concealed in darkness; alliances formed as gold flowed from one hand to another.

His claim to the throne was legitimate, if one followed the

ancient laws of the land, which passed title and power through the matriarchal line. Because Uther had no living sisters, his wife's daughter, Ana—Lot's wife—was next in line, even though she wasn't related to the high king by blood. Through her, Lot and his sons had as much claim to the throne as Arthur, perhaps more. This, coupled with the widely known understanding between Uther and Lot that upon Uther's death, Lot would assume the throne until his eldest son came of age, was why Lot refused to swear loyalty to Arthur.

The problem was that everyone believed Merlin's account of Uther's deathbed scruples—which Lot doubted ever took place, though no one could deny Arthur's skill in guiding the bereft army to victory. On top of that, no one knew what rule Arthur followed. Being half Roman and half Belgae, he seemed to follow whatever tradition suited him best at the moment.

These young upstarts have no sense of loyalty. Lot glowered.

Lot's supporters were smart enough to stay silent, at least in public. Some had even taken oaths of loyalty to Arthur. But those taciturn allies were growing in number daily, thanks to the network of spies and mercenaries Lot had employed to sow the seed of doubt in the minds of the most powerful men from one end of the island to the other.

Those who did not join his cause willingly were subjected to harsher measures. When loyalty couldn't be bought, it was coerced. Many of the tribes' most powerful men and women had been lax in obeying their own laws. Lot smiled as he thought of the power contained in the slightest bit of shameful information. A few illegitimate children, a throng of indiscreet lovers, a couple of misplaced alliances, and a handful of murders had given him support from within almost all of the key kingdoms.

However, the most drastic measures had been reserved for Arthur's staunchest supporters. They began disappearing three days ago, taken from their own homes by brute force. The price of ransom spread across the land like wildfire: the lords would only be returned upon Lot's coronation, after they had publically declared an oath of allegiance to him.

I could see them now—Lot's soldiers. Banging on doors in the middle of the night or disrupting households at the break of dawn, dragging out by force the lords and clan chiefs who resisted Lot's cause. The soldiers were under strict orders to harm no one during their raids. Lot insisted this be a bloodless revolution. He couldn't risk the people regarding him as a tyrant. No, he would not be branded another Vortigern; he would be their savior.

The element of surprise gave Lot's men leverage, but every so often, someone would resist, and one key player had escaped. That was why they were here, hidden amidst the foliage of the forest southwest of Lothian, lying in wait for the king.

A young boy approached them from behind. Without turning to look at him, Lot grabbed the boy by the throat of his tunic, his eyes trained steadily on the road.

"What news?" he rumbled.

The boy was taken off guard by Lot's swift action and the tightness of his grip. "The king. . ."—he struggled to breathe—"approaches from the south. He—"

Lot relaxed his knuckles.

The boy sucked in air. "He will cross us as his party emerges from Eildon Pass."

Lot nodded, still fixated on the narrow path that wound its way out from between mountains. "Does he suspect?"

The boy shook his head, although he knew Lot was not watching. "No, my lord."

"And the second unit?"

"In place, sire. As soon as the king's party halts, they will surround them, cutting off any chance of escape."

"Good." Lot released his hold.

The boy quickly scampered away, deep into the trees.

A few moments later, the steady clomp of hooves and the clattering of disturbed stones broke the silence of the forest. A small posse of men had made it through the pass and spilled out into the clearing. Before I could even search their faces, Lot's men sprang out, weapons drawn like a band of robbers.

Curses and oaths filled the air as the men reeled from the surprise and took a defensive stance, their own weapons at the ready.

Fearless, Lot approached the group, his black eyes singling out the largest warrior. Thanks to Lot's ruminations, I knew without looking who this man was, but I still gasped in disbelief at the sight of him.

King Arthur looked just as Merlin had described him, but his armor and traveling cloak made him look even more imposing. His tanned face and clothes were stained with grit from the road, and the aggravated expression on his face made me fear for Lot; Arthur was not a man I would want to cross.

"Arthur, so good of you to join us," Lot purred, as if he were greeting guests at a feast.

Arthur raised a hand, and his guards relaxed their stance but left their weapons trained on the opposing party. "I remind you, Lord of Lothian, I am your king, and you would be wise to address me as such." His voice was surprisingly deep and gravelly through his tightly clenched jaw.

Lot made a show of looking around. "King, you say? I see no king here but myself."

"Then your eyes deceive you," Arthur rebutted, "for I stand right in front of you."

Lot pretended to refocus his eyes. "No. All I see is a man who stole the mantle of power from his own kin by contrived tales and trickery. This man is no king. I am the true heir to the crown of this country, and I am here to claim what is mine." Lot drew his sword and pointed it straight at Arthur.

At the same instant, Arthur mirrored the motion.

Lot's men edged in closer, itching for the battle to begin.

Arthur again signaled his men to stand down, many of whom were shuffling their feet and trembling with the effort to keep from rushing their king's aggressor.

"Lot, I do not wish to kill your men. Shedding their blood would only needlessly create widows and orphans." His rich indigo eyes scanned the opposing force, halting abruptly. "Uriens, will you too betray me?" he asked a gray-haired combatant with the intensity of a far younger man. "My brother-in-law has always opposed me, but you swore an oath to me."

"I am supporting the true claimant to the throne," Uriens stated confidently.

"Then I regret I must oppose you as well, friend." Arthur sounded truly pained. He turned his attention back to Lot. "I have heard of your plans—and of your claims. If it is a war you want, you have picked the perfect way to start one, but I doubt that is your intent." He studied Lot, appraising his opponent's every reaction. "No, you are a man of peace; despite your recent actions, you will not be satisfied if this road runs red today. It is I you desire, and so you shall have your chance. I accept your challenge of combat."

Lot snarled. This was not a turn he had been expecting. He was an excellent fighter, but to cross swords with Arthur was a dangerous proposition. He had been counting on someone else to do that part of the work. Now Arthur gave him no choice. It was either fight or lose face in front of his troops.

"Move away, men," he ordered.

Both sides fell back to give the combatants room. Arthur waited patiently, reflecting Lot's every move to give him little advantage. Lot swung first, his sword easily glancing off Arthur's shield. Arthur responded, and the dance went on. Finally, Arthur landed a blow to Lot's shielding arm, causing him to drop his defense.

The tide was turning rapidly against Lot, and he knew it. He made a pretense at following strategy, but soon struck out in desperation, slashing at any area of Arthur's exposed skin. It was the wrong move; Arthur nimbly avoided him and quickly had Lot on the ground, sword to his throat.

Lot's men shifted their weight nervously, unsure if they should rescue their fallen leader.

Arthur's back was toward them, but he understood their quandary. "If none of you make an aggressive move, you will be allowed to return to your homes in peace and without charge. Any other action will be considered treason."

Lot's men sheathed their weapons.

Arthur heaved Lot upright so that he was kneeling, facing Arthur's men. "The law states that I should take your life," he said plainly. "But I am hesitant to rush to judgment."

Lot's eyes bulged; he was incredulous that he had not already been slain.

Arthur began to pace in a circle around Lot, the point of his sword never losing contact with Lot's flesh. "You see, I am intrigued by your mind. It took an astonishing grasp of strategy to plan and execute so brilliant a coup. It seems such a waste to kill you."

Silence reigned for a long moment.

"But then again, I would be a fool to let you go outright, so I am asking myself, what is of the most value to you?" He mused aloud as he paced, clearly enjoying the tension his delay in action created. "You no longer have any money or power—I have seen to that."

"What?" Lot choked, unable to keep the requisite silence. He immediately shrank back, anticipating Arthur's violent rebuke.

But Arthur merely stopped and looked Lot square in the eye. "You did not know?" A wide grin spread across his face. "You mean to tell me that with your contingent of spies and informants, no one told you my reason for traveling north?" He gave a dubious laugh and then his face turned to granite. "I was coming to your kingdom to personally deliver your formal censure. Your treasury has been turned over to the crown for proper dispensation in light of your own misuse."

Lot's face was ashen, his mouth open wide like a drawbridge.

"Yes, I was a step ahead of you. Even if this unfortunate situation had not occurred, I was taking steps to cripple your power." Arthur looked up, like a thought suddenly occurred to him. "That reminds me, I also have in my possession a decree stripping you of all your authority and awarding it to your wife. She will rule in your place."

Lot was processing the information as fast as he could. Ana? But she was Arthur's sister—she would never betray him. The realization hit him like a bolt of lightning. That was the point. Arthur had severed the artery that fed Lot's influence; he would never again be able to plot an insurgence without someone knowing. A string of curses and foul words flowed through his mind.

"But all of this was going to happen anyway," Arthur continued. "I am back to asking myself, what is the most fitting punishment for your crimes?" He said it almost as if he were expecting Lot to answer. Then his face lit up with inspiration. "If I do not take your life, perhaps this will illuminate for you where your loyalty should lie."

At the slight incline of his head, one of Arthur's men came forward, grazing his own blade against Lot's neck. Arthur rushed into the throng of men, disappearing from view. When he emerged, he dragged forward two men with tattooed right arms. He shoved them to the ground at Lot's knees. Two other men with identical markings were treated the same by one of Arthur's guards. The hands of all four were bound, and each now had daggers to their throats.

Had I voice in this realm between worlds, I would have screamed. One of them was Aggrivane.

"Your sons came to warn me of your treachery and voice their opposition. They accompanied me on this journey to witness your censure. Now I find they may be more useful than I expected. Perhaps the sons should indeed pay for the sins of their father."

Arthur turned his back to Lot, and one of the guards applied pressure to his blade, drawing a thin trickle of blood from Lot's eldest son, who flinched but remained silent.

"It is your choice, Lot. Your life or theirs. And by the way, I know where my sister and your youngest are staying at the moment. Tintagel, isn't it? It would be a shame if your boy had an accident."

The threat behind Arthur's words was so real I could almost see it come to life: a young boy, an untried horse, a mountainside trail, and bloodied rocks below.

Lot wrestled with himself internally, fighting two opposing instincts. His sense of self-preservation urged him to sacrifice his sons, but his impulse as a parent was to save his progeny. Compromise. There had to be a compromise.

"Is there no other way—no middle ground?" he finally said, and as he did so, his demeanor cracked.

Arthur only watched impassively as tears seeped from his prisoner's eyes. Behind him, Lot's sons bowed their heads, sharing in their father's anguish.

"So be it then." The words were the last breath escaping from a dying man. "Take me," Lot answered. "I have sealed my own fate."

Arthur approached, and as he drew his sword, Lot lowered his head. He waited, resigned, but the death blow never came. He opened his eyes and slowly looked up. Arthur stood before him, naked sword at his waist, tip to the earth.

"Lot of Lothian, I will take your life but not your mortality. Swear to me now an oath of loyalty, and you shall live."

Lot pledged his fealty, kneeling at Arthur's feet and kissing his hand. He acknowledged Arthur as the one and only high king of Britain, swore to uphold and defend him, and to remain true to him to his dying day. His words were repeated by all of the men who joined him in revolt. They had seen to what lengths their king was willing to go to preserve his title and were not willing to stand in opposition of him.

"All of my former conditions regarding your treasury and your right to rule remain in place," Arthur said. "And I will release your sons on one condition—"

"But they have done nothing wrong," Lot protested, back to his belligerent self now that the danger had passed.

Arthur silenced him with a single glance and continued as if uninterrupted. "They will take up permanent residence at my court. I know they will appreciate the opportunity, and should you ever decide to rebel again, they are easily within my reach."

Arthur's threat—or was it a promise?—weighed heavily on my mind until I finally slipped into complete unconsciousness.

Chapter Fifteen

Spring 496

I remained in an unresponsive state for the better part of a week, alternately restless in my dreams—as Lyonesse chose to call them—or sleeping so still and silently that several times they thought me dead from fever. They had even called in Father Joseph to give me the final blessing.

"That's when the real fun began." Isolde smiled slyly at the memory as she sat at my bedside one cold, sunny morning. "Father Joseph examined you and declared you very much alive, though gravely ill. That was when I gave you the diluted drop of wolfsbane." Her tone held the slightest hint of remorse. "I know it was dangerous, but you were already more among the dead than the living . . ."

I gently placed my hand on top of hers. "Isolde, you did very well. It was probably that tiny drop that brought me out of my illness. Viviane used to tell us that wolfsbane was one of the few herbs that could draw a soul back through the veil and release it from the grip of death." As if on cue, a rumbling cough welled up in my chest, leaving me breathless.

Isolde looked away, embarrassed, and continued with her story. "Anyway, Lyonesse had received word that morning that what you were seeing about Lot and the high king really was true. The letter even confirmed Arthur's bitterness at Uriens' betrayal—"

A shock raced through me. My eyes widened. "What did you say?"

Isolde cocked her head to the side and scrunched up her forehead in confusion. "That Arthur is upset Uriens sided with Lot." She continued without letting me respond. "The letter also said that when it was over, Arthur took away Uriens' right to rule the town of Carlisle. They say it will be Arthur's new capital."

I wasn't listening. As she prattled on about Arthur using the town to keep a close watch on the aged ruler of Rheged, I went through our earlier conversation in my head. I had told her about Lot's revolt and the anguish I'd felt at seeing the king threaten Aggrivane's life, but as for Uriens' involvement . . . I was still trying to figure out why he was there.

"I never told you that," I interrupted Isolde mid-sentence.

"What?"

"When I recounted my visions to you, I never told you Uriens was there." An accusatory edge crept into my voice unbidden.

Confusion clouded her face, but then just as quickly cleared into another sunny smile. "No, silly, not then. You told me that while the sight was upon you. You practically narrated everything you were seeing."

I was stunned silent. I saw the visions as clear as day, but as though I was out of my body. I had no connection to it, no way to make it work, which was why I could not scream.

I shook my head. "That is not possible. I tried several times to speak before I knew what was happening. I tried to call out to Arthur, to Aggrivane, to react to what I saw."

Isolde's eyes were bright with wonder as she tried to reconcile what she had experienced with what I was telling her. "But you did, Guinevere. You screamed like you were being murdered. That must have been when you saw Aggrivane," she whispered, almost to herself.

"But how could I have been telling you what I saw?"

"You answered every question I asked you, responded to my voice . . . did you not hear me?"

"You were questioning me? I heard nothing but the sound of my visions. I would have remembered your voice. I am sure it would have brought me back to you." As soon as I spoke, I heard the affection in my own voice. I was truly growing to love Isolde.

She caught the inflection and blushed in response. "It was the same with Islene," she said quietly.

"Who?"

She looked uncomfortable now. "Islene, my sister. She has the sight. Growing up, I used to coach her through each one of her visions, asking her what she saw, drawing more description out of her. It became so ingrained in me that when I realized you were not merely dreaming like Lyonesse thought, I automatically began asking you questions. And you responded just like Islene used to." Her words rushed out, pensive and hushed as they always were when she was thinking aloud, a frequent habit. "But your gift is different than hers. Islene can see the future. You seem to be able to see things that are happening in the moment, but far away. It's almost like you can be in two places at once." Her voice wavered with emotion.

I leaned forward hoping she would go on.

"Islene told my mother not to send me here, not to sign the treaty. But no one listened to her—no one ever did." Her eyes brimmed with tears.

I patted her shoulder gently, intending to comfort her, but she winced, distracting me from my intended question about Islene's visions. "What is wrong?"

She wiped her eyes with her hand and looked down. "Nothing. I have gotten away from my point. We were talking about Lyonesse and Father Joseph."

Isolde was forcing herself to be cheery, that much was clear, but her grimace hadn't escaped my notice. I yanked back the neck of her gown, ignoring her feeble attempt to pull away. A pattern of swollen, red flesh crisscrossed down her back.

She batted my hand away, as angry now as the patchwork of scars that marred her flesh. "It is no struggle to guess at whose hand I received these. I caught her at an inopportune moment, and she called me a witch for trying to heal you. That is all you need know." Her eyes flashed a warning that made it clear I was not to ask any more.

I opened my mouth to respond.

"Father Joseph gave you a general blessing," she said, cutting me off as she turned back to the original point of our conversation. "He was nearly out the door when Lyonesse stopped him. Since it seemed you were going to live, at least for a little while, she told him about your strange dreams and said she thought you were possessed by a demon. She demanded that he perform an exorcism on you. Naturally, Father Joseph refused. He emphatically stated that your body was ill, not your spirit, and what you needed was healing and love, not fear and paranoia. He told her she would have to find another priest if she wanted that ritual performed. This, of course, infuriated Lyonesse. She commanded him to baptize you instead." Isolde leaned toward me, her previous irritation forgotten.

I could tell she was enjoying spinning this yarn. She had a gift of being able to recount things in a way that made me feel that rather than being an unconscious presence in the room, I had actually wit-nessed them. I could understand why Elaine was so enraptured by her.

"I have never seen a Christian priest come so close to assaulting a woman before. In a split second, Father Joseph went from a patient servant of God to an impassioned defender of the faith."

She deepened her voice in imitation of the normally mild-man-nered priest. "'My lady, I care not what title you claim upon this earth; no one can command another who has reached adulthood to be baptized. That most holy of sacraments must be conferred by free will and a genuine desire to embrace our faith.'

"He gritted his teeth and laid into Lyonesse like no one had ever dared, advancing on her without fear. 'This woman has obviously made her choice.' He gestured to the mark of priestesshood on your sweaty brow. 'Our Lord is much more gracious and understanding than you could ever comprehend. She will be saved by her own faith, should He call her home, so you need have no concern for her soul. I advise you to pay as much attention to the state of your own spirit and leave hers to her conscience. I bid you good day!' And with that he strode out of the room."

Another coughing fit shook my body, but after a few minutes, I managed to clear my lungs enough to speak. "I am sorry I missed that."

Isolde picked up a small vial from a nearby table and shifted her weight so she was sitting fully on the bed now, facing me. She uncorked the bottle and began rubbing the pungent oil on my chest. The woody, heavy scent threatened to overwhelm me, but I immedi-ately felt a little relief. Pine oil. Whoever taught her the healing arts had trained her well.

"Oh, but it gets better. Lyonesse tried to baptize you herself after that."

"She did?" My mouth dropped open, eyebrows knit in disbelief.

She laughed. "Yes. And you screamed at the exact moment she tried to bless you with the holy water." She was laughing so hard now she was almost in tears. "Guinevere, you could not have planned it better. You scared the wits out of her. She has not been back to visit you since."

CHAPTER SIXTEEN

Spring/Summer 496

Once it was clear I would live, life at Corbenic returned to normal, or at least what passed for normal in Pellinor's household. He went back to interviewing, berating, and sometimes forcibly removing Elaine's endless suitors one by one.

But for once, the house was quiet. In a small antechamber, Pellinor was penning a letter to my father. Lyonesse was studying her prayer book, and Elaine was humming quietly to herself as she stitched. I was toying with my own needle but not really accomplishing anything. I was wishing I could find a way to sneak out and track down Guildford for another lesson. Liam had learned to write the alphabet and spell a few simple words, and I was anxious to resume his lessons after the break caused by my illness. I also was eager to begin rebuilding the muscles that had atrophied from my time in bed.

I tried to catch Isolde's attention—the artful Irish princess always was helpful in providing an excuse or distraction when one was needed—but she was too involved in a whispered conversation with two of the lady's maids to pay me any heed.

I stood, stretching my stiff limbs, and drifted over to the window, intent on searching the grounds for any sign of Guildford's whereabouts. I hadn't taken three steps when the chamber door flew open, followed by a flushed servant who almost toppled into Pellinor in his haste.

"My lord, I told him the family was not to be disturbed. I told him to wait, but I could not stop—"

Before the puffing boy could finish speaking, a stately man appeared behind him. The visitor ambled in casually, as if he had been invited and was expected.

The intake of breath from every woman in the room was audible as we surveyed our handsome guest. Even from a distance, I could tell he was taller than Pellinor. He had dark hair and pale eyes that glinted merrily, as though they found pleasure in each and every object they took in. His complexion was clear and soft and he was finely dressed, from his polished boots to the colorful, embroidered cloak secured over his left shoulder. The circular brooch that pinned it in place was a familiar symbol to me—a stylized horse whose limbs became part of an eternal knot. It was the same symbol my mother had borne on her left shoulder blade—the one by rights I should bear—the symbol of the Votadini bloodline.

"My lord Pellinor." The elegant foreigner turned to Pellinor, who had leapt to his feet, hand on his sword, at the intrusion, and addressed him with the greatest politeness. "I am Galen of the Votadini tribe, eldest son of Chief Donel the Bold. I apologize for arriving unannounced, but I was told a messenger would precede me and be sure all the proper arrangements were in place. But obviously that has not occurred." An edge of irritation crept into his voice but was as quickly covered by cautious formality tinged with warmth. "Nevertheless, I come to your home seeking the hand of your daughter." He swept into a low bow before Pellinor.

Pellinor, clearly shocked, made a slight movement as if to speak, but before he could do so, Galen turned from him and approached Isolde. I cringed, stealing a glance at the equally transfixed Lyonesse, expecting him to make the grievous blunder of mistaking Isolde for Elaine.

Galen smiled at Isolde, taking her hand in his. At his touch, Isolde's breathing hitched, bosom fluttering as she struggled to maintain her composure. She beamed back at him, effervescent eyes and alluring smile brighter than a thousand suns.

"A wild Irish rose," he declared, clearly appreciating her beauty.

Isolde blushed violently in response and dipped her head in acknowledgement of his assessment.

Galen reached back as if to stroke her wild hair but instead produced a perfect white rose in full bloom.

Isolde gasped and took the bud tenderly, gazing, speechless, back and forth from the flower to its benefactor.

"A reminder of your homeland." Galen held her gaze.

She seemed most content to revel in it.

I rolled my eyes. *More likely pilfered from someone's garden on your way in.* As attractive as the man was, I couldn't help but wonder on how many other women he had used that trick. How long had he been watching us to know where she was from? Or had he sent a spy to gather information? I looked again at Lyonesse, but she seemed just as taken as everyone else, her left hand resting lightly over her mouth, frozen by the wonder of Galen's gift.

He approached me next, eyes glinting much like a cat playing with its prey. His smile was sly, as though he knew I suspected him. He took his time studying my face, memorizing my features. Despite the protests of my mind, I felt my body growing hot under his gaze.

"If I am not mistaken, you are descended from the same race as I," he stated seriously, followed by a chuckle at the astonishment that must have registered on my face.

It took me a moment to find my voice. "Yes, my mother was from the north, from the Votadini tribe."

"We of the untamed, ancient land always recognize our own." He winked at me and produced from beneath his cloak a flawless lowland thistle.

My jaw dropped. How had he procured this? Even making the best time, he would have had to have picked this days, if not weeks ago. Yet the flower showed not the slightest blemish or sign of wear. Its bud was strong and green, the lavender spikes within firm and straight. I was beginning to wonder if he was some sort of magus or even one of the fey.

Still chortling, he turned from me to Elaine, who was now visibly trembling. He stopped in front of her and clapped his hands together silently, bringing them up to his lips in thought.

"Dear lady, you are more beautiful than anything in nature, so I can offer you no tangible token of my admiration."

Elaine seemed not to know how to take his words, her visage wavering between joy at his compliment and disappointment that she was the only one not to receive a gift.

"However," Galen continued, "I can offer you something far more dear—my life and my heart—or if you will not accept those, accept at least my humble prayers, for I will pray for your soul until the day I die." He knelt at her feet and took her hand, kissing it gently.

Part of me knew I should be revolted by the obvious display of calculated charm and overwrought spectacle, but I could not. Galen had captured my heart despite my better instincts, and it was obvious the rest of the family felt the same.

Galen completed his circuit around the room and was now speaking quietly with Pellinor and Lyonesse, the latter of whom clutched a small wooden cross to her breast, no doubt procured from the same mysterious purse as all the rest. Pellinor had been appraising Galen's livery as he beguiled each of us and was now inspecting the papers he presented. After a few moments of consultation with his wife, Pellinor called the forgotten servant over to him.

"Erwyn, please show Lord Galen to the guest quarters in the gentlemen's wing."

The servant indicated Galen should follow him, and the maids skittered out the room behind them, no doubt off to spread the word to the rest of the castle and half of the surrounding countryside.

Elaine, Isolde, and I met each other's gaze, thrilled that the unexpected suitor had been invited to stay. While we all knew he was there to court Elaine, the tension that fizzed between us in that moment meant only one thing—the women of Caer Corbenic were at war.

Although men often were considered the chief strategists and architects of war, they had nothing on the cunning of a determined woman when her heart was on the line. It didn't take long for us to figure out that although Galen was there for Elaine, Isolde and I also had a chance. Despite his protestations of love, we all knew Galen simply was looking for a well-bred wife. I was the same rank as Elaine, and perhaps more attractive due to our shared Votadini heritage and the dowry of Votadini lands near Stirling I had inherited upon my mother's death, not to mention the numerous gold mines that dotted my father's kingdom. Isolde, on the other hand, was heir to the throne of Ireland, making her the highest-ranking of all of us, and therefore, also the most dangerous.

Unfortunately, Lyonesse and Pellinor were perceptive of this as well. They did all they could to keep Elaine and Galen together and away from their less desirable wards. He accompanied the family to Mass—which Isolde and I were oddly no longer required to attend—and at other times indulged him with all manner of sport and entertainment.

The positive outcome was Corbenic was a livelier place than I had ever seen it. However, Isolde and I could do little but watch from the shadows. With the little freedom we had, the two of us angled to spend time with our charming guest. During his first months at Corbenic, I was able to grab a few disparate moments once in a while, but had little luck otherwise. Isolde fared even worse during daylight hours, being fully treated as a servant now, her time taken up with an endless list of chores. To her credit, she fulfilled them with little complaint, but the fury grew behind her eyes. Because she was absent from her bed most nights, I could only speculate that she chose to trade sleep for Galen's empty hours and perhaps fill his bed in the process.

One morning I awoke to find the castle strangely silent. Guessing the family had gone to Mass, I dressed and ventured down to the kitchen to break my fast with whatever scraps I could find. Lyonesse never allowed her family to eat until after receiving the sacrament, and by the time they returned, she likely would have some diversion for me that would not indulge my aching belly.

I had just emerged from the pantry, arms full of slightly stale bread, hardened cheese, fruit, and a half-empty flagon of wine, when a shadow fell across my path. I recognized its owner just in time to stifle my scream and save my breakfast from being ruined among the greasy rushes.

"Galen!" I gasped. "You startled me. What are you doing here? I thought you would be out with the others."

He courteously relieved me of my burden, moving it to a low table and keeping one apple for himself, tossing it in the air, a glint in his eyes, only to catch it a moment later. "Pellinor was going to take me hunting—he wanted to show off Lyonesse's new pair of hounds—but he left in haste to resolve some sort of dispute among two of the northern chieftains. The messenger who summoned him said it was likely to turn deadly soon."

I sat in silence across the table from him, eating my breakfast, still slightly unnerved at being so unexpectedly alone with him.

The quiet was broken with a crunch as he bit into the apple. "In case you were wondering, Lyonesse and Elaine are in town. They went to meet with the sisters to help with some service to the poor. I offered to join them, but Lyonesse said that the sisters would object to the presence of a man within their walls, so I was not permitted to come. She sent Isolde off to market with a list so long, two servants had to accompany her to bring it all back. I doubt they will return for several hours."

So we truly were alone then? Well, except for the kitchen maid tending the fire, who seemed greatly amused by the situation, though she pretended not to listen. I knew her well enough to know she could be trusted.

And why would she need be? It was not as though something inappropriate was going on; we were just talking. And eating. Eating was safe, right? So why were my cheeks reddening more each second?

I chanced a glance at Galen. His eyes were sparkling. He smiled when he caught me looking at him. I dropped my gaze, embarrassed. I wished I had left my hair down so that it could hide me from him, like I used to do with Aggrivane.

I cleared my throat nervously. "So how were you planning to spend your day, then?"

"Well, actually, I had hoped to go riding."

I nodded, stood, and began clearing the table.

Galen grabbed my arm, and I whirled instinctively to confront him, surprised. He glanced over his shoulder to make sure the maid wasn't listening.

"I was hoping you would join me. My horse is already saddled for the hunt."

My heart leapt into my throat, missing several beats. My mind was suddenly numb. "I—I, cannot," I stammered. "Lyonesse dislikes me enough already. If it were known I went out alone with you—"

"We needn't be alone," he answered smoothly, his hand still on my arm. "Bring your lady's maid."

"I haven't one," was all I could manage to reply. My mind was beginning to scatter at his nearness. He had a fresh, wild scent like lowland heather.

He flashed a captivating grin at the kitchen maid. "I see here with us a lady who also is a maid. Will she not for a few short hours substitute as a witness that we engaged in no impropriety?" He turned to the maid. "Do you ride?"

"Yes, sire," she responded, trying to hide her joy at this exciting turn of events.

My stomach lurched. The maid was Isolde's friend, so I knew she would find out about everything that happened—as would half the household—but Lyonesse trusted her, so she was an asset in that respect. I was taking a risk, but I did not have the strength to turn him down.

"So be it," I acquiesced.

⋅◦҉◦⋅

The early morning sun caressed my skin as we set out. Galen led us east toward the Forrest of Dean and away from town, lest we be spotted by prying eyes. The maid followed discreetly behind us, clearly enjoying a rare day out of doors. All around us life was bursting forth, from the budding trees and blooming flowers to the myriad of woodland creatures who sang in the trees overhead or, frightened by thundering hooves, cleared the path before us.

We slowed to a canter as the path grew narrower, and Galen allowed my horse to fall into step with his. I could not find the courage to look over at him, but I knew he was watching me.

Self-consciously, I tucked a loose strand of hair behind my ear. The tension that held fast between us was not the sensual pressure that boiled between lovers, but also not the awkwardness common among strangers; whatever it was, it was driving me mad. Galen, however, appeared at ease. Like Isolde, he always seemed to be playing with his environment, squeezing the most out of every situation—always in control.

The breeze rustled the tender leaves, and the jays called from the treetops. Finally, I could stand the silence between us no longer.

"How did you hear Pellinor was looking for a husband for Elaine?" I blurted out the least dangerous of the questions demanding resolution in my mind.

Galen smiled playfully. "You wound me, my lady. I hoped you would ask about me."

I glared at him. "Well, I am, in a roundabout way."

He chuckled. "You would be surprised how fast word of a young virgin bride spreads across this land, especially when she is the daughter of a lord such as Pellinor." He leaned in closely, as if confiding a secret, lips nearly grazing my ear. "We men have a spy network that runs from one tip of the island to the other, and we can track the scent of an eligible woman like a fox."

I turned to look at him, to judge his sincerity, and found his face only inches from mine. Though his tone was serious, his eyes told he was teasing. I could not help but smile, although I pulled away a bit, guiding my horse just slightly to the right.

"Forget I asked then."

"No, seriously, we do," he insisted. "I was traveling in the south of Rheged, just about to cross into Powys, when I heard about Elaine."

My skin rose to goose pimples. Something about his story did not seem right. "That would have been, what, just after Candlemas? Is that not fairly early in the season to be so far from home? Were you not worried about late season snows?"

"No. It was a warm winter in that area, and the threat of dangerous weather had long since passed." His answer was as airy as if I had asked about the trees. "And in case this was going to be your next question, I was in Rheged on an official visit for my father. He has trade relations with many of the officials in that area. They provide coal, and sometimes salt, and we give them wool from our sheep. It is much higher quality than anything than could be sheared from those sorry beasts they raise." His expression dared me to ask any more questions.

His answers, while precise, seemed a little too rehearsed.

"But if you were so far away, how did you know so much about the three of us when you first arrived? And where did you get those gifts?"

Galen stopped his horse across the track in front of me, forcing me to a halt. "My lady inquisitor has an impressive list of questions," he observed, his jaw taut with irritation. "I will answer, but you must do the same for me first. I'll bet my life you pressed that thistle with a cold iron and have it stashed somewhere safe. Am I right?"

I glowered at him.

He gave me a sardonic look, taking my silence for agreement. "As for those gifts, a man's courtship methods are his own business, and you will get no more from me on the subject. But I will tell you this. It was not difficult to learn all I needed to know about the lot of you. The closer I drew to town, the more I heard. Have you ever slept in the common room of an inn?"

He let a few heartbeats pass, and when I didn't respond, he grinned at me. "I doubt you have. Well, cheap liquor loosens lips, especially in close quarters. Many rejected suitors stayed the night in town before returning to their homes. At first, they were reluctant to speak of their embarrassing experiences at court, but I made sure the ale flowed without interruption, and as the night wore on, they began to reveal details that eventually painted a very interesting picture. Few had actually seen Elaine, but she was rumored to be beautiful. They all agreed her father was a force to be reckoned with and her family was very religious. Then I began hearing comparisons between the chaste daughter and the amorous Irish houseguest and of their mysterious friend from Gwynedd. It was not difficult for me to determine who was who when I presented myself to Pellinor. You actually aided me by all being in the room at once—removed the guesswork." He winked.

"And what did you hear about me?" I was terrified of the answer, but vanity compelled me to ask.

He shrugged and pulled his horse around, continuing forward. "Not much really. Only that you had joined the household a few months before at your father's bidding. Rest assured that many men consider you lovely, but you need not fear for your virtue, not with the Irish one around. Of course, I knew you to be a child of the north as soon as I saw you. No one else on the whole of the island is as fair of skin as we"—he scrutinized me closely—"although you have a deeper complexion than I would have imagined."

"My father is Roman," I answered.

"I won't hold that against him."

Even the maid laughed. Her giggling filled the air a few paces behind us.

I was interested now. "I wonder if you knew my mother. She was only thirteen when she came to Gwynedd, but her family still lives near the Firth of Forth, not far from Stirling."

"Ah, so you *are* a true lowlander, then. My clan is farther west, near Loch Lomond, but still within the jurisdiction of Stirling." Galen pulled up his sleeve and extended his right arm, revealing his clan tattoo. A falcon in flight, beak open in a silent hunter's cry, deadly talons at the ready, encircled his arm, just as the dragon marked Aggrivane's family. "Who ruled your mother's clan?"

I had to think hard. It had been years since my mother and I had spoken about her family, and my time in Avalon had dulled a lot of memories. "I'm unsure of who holds power now, but when I was young, my mother spoke of a king named Culhwch. He was her half-brother."

"Culhwch?" Galen was thunderstruck. "That means your mother must have been the woman called Corinna."

I was not certain if that was a question or a statement. "Yes. Did you know her?" Then another thought sent ice down my spine. "Are we kin?"

His eyes were distant; he was lost in thought but answered anyway. "No. At least, it is not likely. But my mother lived at court in Stirling and spoke often of your mother."

He stopped both of our horses by putting out his hand. His eyes scrunched up curiously. "Do you know the story of your family?"

I was confused. "I know that my mother married my father as

part of a peace treaty." The similarity to Isolde's situation suddenly struck me. "I know they loved one another very much, but that is all."

"Oh, Guinevere, there is so much more. Your parents are spoken about in lore throughout the four lowland tribes."

My mouth went immediately dry, and my stomach twisted warily. The only way so many diverse people across such a wide area could know the same tale was if the bards sang it, and the bards bestowed only two kinds of fame—heroism and infamy. The only way I was going to know which dogged my lineage was to hear their story for myself.

"Tell me."

alen insisted we stop and give our mounts rest and water before continuing the story. I had the sense this was simply a ploy to keep me interested, now that he had me on the hook. The maid took charge of the horses, while we walked along the marshy shore of a small river, being certain to stay within her range of sight. Playing the perfect gentleman, Galen had even asked her to point out the farthest thing she could see so that we knew when to turn around.

I knew enough not to trust him, but that amount of precaution was insulting. It was clear no matter how much he flirted, Galen had no intentions of impropriety with me, or at least none he wanted known. I couldn't help but glower inwardly that Elaine was good enough for his heart and Isolde his bed, but all I warranted was a supervised jaunt to the river and back.

He took no notice of my foul temper as we walked among the tender shoots that would grow with summer heat into reeds and grasses, mud squishing under our boots.

"Your family is quite remarkable. I am surprised you know so little," he said.

I did not answer. So many lost years, time stolen from us by Avalon and my mother's early death. *How much more would my mother have told me, how much more would I have learned if things had been different? Or would she have said anything at all?* At the moment, all I could feel was stinging betrayal that all the tribes of the north knew my family better than I. I took a deep breath and signaled with a slight incline of my head for him to begin.

"Even before the betrayal of the Saxons, old king Vortigern was paranoid and feared any ruler who might entertain the idea of challenging him. So he ordered the men of the northern tribes to come within the boundaries of his kingdom and, hence, within his control.

Vortigern used the excuse that he needed their strength and skill to defend against the Irish, which was at least partly true.

"As the story is told, your grandfather, King Cunedda, believed that complying with Vortigern's wishes would prevent Votadini bloodshed. So he made the agonizing decision to leave his wife and her newborn child—your mother—to settle in northern Gwynedd. He intended to send for them as soon as he was established in his new home. But your grandmother knew what dangers lay ahead for her husband, so she did not expect to be quickly summoned. She contented herself with remaining in her homeland, rearing her child according to the traditions of our tribe. They say she was a fierce war-rior—your mother."

I smiled at the memory. "Yes, she was. It was she who taught me the arts."

"Did she now?" Galen seized my hand, turning it palm up, examining the calluses. "Ah, yes, you have the hands of a fighter." He traced lightly over each of the darkened patches of skin worn tough by repeated grasping of the sword pommel.

"Lyonesse thinks they are from the work she sometimes makes me do," I said, feeling the nervous need to explain even though he hadn't asked.

"She is fond of treating her guests as servants," he mumbled to himself.

I winced, his words confirming intimacy with Isolde, at least in conversation; they were clearly confidants.

He was still intent upon my hand. "We shall have to have a spar to see if our people are correct that women make equal partners on the battlefield as in the bedroom."

I froze. "Please, no. It is forbidden. If Pellinor or Lyonesse knew I wielded a weapon within their walls, they would turn me out."

Galen must have seen the fear in my eyes because he relented. "Your secret is safe with me." The words were murmured softly in my ear as his arms closed around me for a brief moment, and he lifted me effortlessly over a fallen tree trunk.

It was then that I caught the veiled intention behind his quip. I lost my mind at the touch of his body. It had been so long since I had felt the heat of another that I almost collapsed in his arms.

Whether he failed to notice or was concerned about the maid watching, I knew not, but he righted me very professionally, keeping a light hand on the small of my back as we continued to pace the riverbank.

"To return to my story—or rather yours." He winked. "Once your grandfather was in Gwynedd, he realized Vortigern's deal was somewhat of a trick. No land or authority automatically came with this compliance, and what was worse, his title meant nothing in this new country. He could have returned to his family, but Cunedda was still convinced they were safer if he stayed where Vortigern wished and carried out his commands. In a show of sincerity, he went to Vortigern's court to ask some assistance in setting up a new life. While Vortigern was pleased Cunedda had acquiesced to his demands, he was not one to dole out charity and so sent Cunedda away empty-handed.

"However, several prominent lords had heard him plead his case and took pity on him as a just man. One of them was your father's father, a man of Roman stock named Lucian. Lucian wished to give Cunedda a title and some holdings in his own territory of Gwynedd, but Cunedda feared this would only anger Vortigern and bring his wrath needlessly upon Lucian's house. Instead, Cunedda asked not to be treated as Lucian's equal, though he was, but as any other unlanded soldier seeking his kindness. Lucian admired your grandfather's honesty and humility, so he took him in and gave him shelter and employment fighting against the Irish invaders.

"Years passed in this arrangement, and Lucian took your grandfather ever deeper into his confidence. He confessed to Cunedda that, unlike Vortigern, he despised the bloodshed caused by the constant fighting among the tribes of the north and the Romans with his own people. One day he came to Cunedda with a proposal. Lucian's son, Leodgrance—your father—would marry a Votadini of royal lineage, preferably one of Cunedda's relatives. Both tribes would agree to live in peace, and Lucian would ensure Gwynedd was a place the Votadini could dwell safely under Vortigern's rule. Seeing the wisdom of this plan, Cunedda offered his only daughter, Corinna, to Leodgrance as act of gratitude for Lucian's years of protection and kindness.

"When it was announced Leodgrance and Corinna were to be married, there was much rejoicing among the tribes at the peace that would follow. However, Lucian's overlord, a powerful man named Julian who exercised control over much of the western coast, did not approve of the plan. Julian despised the thought of tainting pure Roman blood with that of our kind, so he ordered Lucian to kill Cunedda, the bride, and her immediate family when they arrived for the wedding, thus eliminating the royal Votadini line and demonstrating power over their tribe. Although Lucian loved Cunedda like his own kin, he was very much afraid of Julian and reluctantly agreed to do as he was commanded.

"But Lady Fortuna was with your family, for Leodgrance found out about the plot. Like his father, he was a man of peace, but he would do what he must to save Corinna and her family. He may not have set eyes on his bride yet, but he was beginning to love her just by her actions. She was risking much to marry him—bravely leaving her home, her title, her people, all to unite with him in a treaty that was ideal in theory but would be difficult to maintain. He couldn't let her die, especially not as an innocent victim of someone else's machinations.

"On the night before the wedding, when all of the men were gathered together in celebration, Leodgrance made certain that Lucian and Julian received poisoned cups. They died, but no one ever suspected your father. He and your mother were married, and well, I think you know the rest of the story." He fell silent, leaving me to absorb the epic that had resulted in my birth.

I halted, suddenly seeing my father in a whole new light. For the first time, I was touched with pity for him. I had always known of his affection for my mother, but I never suspected how deeply his love ran or that he was capable of murdering his own father to save her. Suddenly the broken man, half crazed with grief, I left at Northgallis made much more sense. I still could not fathom what he saw in Father Marius, but at least now I understood the reason for his desperate search for comfort and redemption. He had done unspeakable things to save my mother, and she had been taken from him as violently and as suddenly as if Julian's plan had been fulfilled so many years before.

Heartache filled me at the thought of what my return so soon after my mother's death must have done to him. There I was, a younger version of the woman he just lost; I probably appeared to him much like my mother did when she came to Gwynedd to marry him. With a shock, I realized that his coldness had not been meant for me, but as a defense against the pain caused by having to face the ghost of his dead love in my eyes.

Unable to speak, I stared at Galen like a simpleton.

"Have I said something wrong?" His features were etched with genuine worry.

"No, I am fine," I croaked, trying to recover my voice. "Your story made many things about my family very clear to me, things I never expected and could not possibly explain." I took a step forward. "Please let us speak of other things. Tell me how you like Elaine. I hardly ever get to see her anymore."

"Oh, Elaine is a wonderful girl," Galen said as we resumed our walk, the forced emotion in his voice making me wonder how he really felt about her. "She is very beautiful. I've never seen hair quite like hers before—golden, yet woven with strands of red, like silk stitched with gold thread. And her eyes are so pure, so innocent." His voice softened as he searched for an apt metaphor. "In so many ways, she is like a young doe. Her eyes hold such wonder about the world, about me, about everything. Unlike most people, she sees the good, or at least the potential for good, in everyone. I am so afraid of letting her down."

His confession caught me off guard. Did Galen really have feelings for Elaine?

"Why would you let her down?"

"I am not who she thinks I am, Guinevere."

I hadn't expected him to admit this so candidly. "What?"

The tenderness in Galen's smile was almost heartbreaking. "No one is. She sees everyone as she thinks they should be. She has in her mind this false image of me—the embodiment of her fantasies of a man who is pure, who will be her savior and her one true love. I am human. I have made mistakes—grave ones—and I will continue to do so. It is in my nature to be a bit of a knave, not a saint. I cannot possibly live up to her expectations of me."

He really did love her—that much was clear. But I doubted he loved her with the fire of a paramour or the romance of a fated soul. Galen's love for Elaine was that of a protector; he abhorred the idea of shattering her innocence, but knew, just in the course of living, that he would have to. Still, she could do worse than being paired with a man who held her in such high esteem. She need never fear abuse or cruelty by his hand or any other he could control.

"So you intend to marry her then?"

His brow creased, and he regarded me quizzically. "Of course. Why else would I be here?"

I wanted to ask him when, if he loved Elaine so much, he planned to evict Isolde from his bed—although I still had no proof of that—and stop dallying with me in the forest.

I took a deep breath. "Galen, I do not understand you. Why come all this way to court Elaine when there are plenty of noble women in your own country or in other kingdoms? Yes, Dyfed is a rich land, but it will offer you little but trouble, by way of the Irish, especially when Isolde becomes queen. Why risk that fate? You have admitted you cannot possibly be the spotless knight Pellinor expects to wed his daughter. What is in it for you? What are you really after?"

His eyes flashed with anger, and he turned on me. "Why do you suspect me at every turn? You barely know me, yet you accuse me of dishonesty. From whence does this mistrust spring? I have done nothing to wrong you, nothing to offend you, yet you insist on treating me like a criminal." He snapped his fingers. "Ah, I know what it is. You are jealous. A man who is not paying attention to you is much like a toy you want but cannot have. Do you honestly believe that simply because you are daughter of the king of Gwynedd, all men will fall at your feet? You have too much virtue to be taken as a whore, but little better probability of being chosen as a wife. Your attitude will be your downfall; no man wants a haughty, distrusting wife, no matter how beautiful."

His words stung me into silence. *Perhaps my inquires had gone a little too far.*

But Galen was so engrossed in his own anger he barely registered my lack of rebuttal.

"Did it ever once occur to you that your questioning may offend me?" he demanded. "What exactly were *your* intentions when you agreed to come riding with me today? Am I to cast aside your friend and choose you instead? If you were trying to entice me or hoping I would seduce you, you not only lack understanding of what is attractive to men, but sound judgment as well. You lost any chance at winning my heart the moment you berated me with your questions. You are worse than a fishwife!"

We had reached the horses now and the maid was watching us with open curiosity, but I cared not who heard us. I felt bound to defend myself.

"I accept no blame for you being threatened by an intelligent woman. You should be used to my kind by now—no doubt you were reared by one. I was raised according to the traditions of your homeland, which bid me speak when I suspect a liar. You may be able to charm and dazzle everyone else in this household, but you have not fooled me. I may not know exactly what you are playing at, but I know you to be untrue. Good thing you will find no resistance from Elaine, as she was raised to be the docile woman you seem to so desire. I wish you both well, but I pray we never cross paths again."

Before he could recover from my rebuttal, I grabbed the reins of my horse and mounted. The startled maid quickly followed suit. I knew those roads well but gambled that, as a foreigner, he did not. He would be dependent on me to find his way back to the castle.

"Use your charm to get you home—see how far that gets you," I called over my shoulder as we galloped off. "I have no need of you, but I doubt you can say the same."

Chapter Nineteen

Summer 496

Someone had been caught, but I was not sure who.

When I retired the following night, Lyonesse locked Isolde and me into our room, promising to liberate us after they returned from Mass at dawn. For a few moments after the bolt slipped into place, we stared at each other in silent shock. I had thought we were in the clear; Lyonesse seemed pleased that Galen and I refused to exchange more words than politeness required, and he gave no indication that our tryst had ever taken place. Had the maid spilled our secret? Worse yet, had Galen told them everything? After I pushed him so far, he would have little to lose, especially if he implicated both Isolde and me while remaining an innocent victim in their eyes, a deception I had no doubt he could accomplish. Horrible as that seemed, it would explain Lyonesse's desire to keep us both under lock and key.

"What does she know?" I asked quietly.

Isolde shook her head slowly, contemplating the options. "I'm not sure."

I sank down on the bed. "We could be ruined."

"We?" Isolde scoffed. "What have you to account for? Lust within your heart is not a punishable offense, and it most certainly will not get you turned out into the street."

Isolde was rarely cross with me; her jab at my lack of success with Galen was a clear sign of how worried she really was. I turned down the bedclothes and slipped beneath them.

"And you? What have you to fear?" I asked.

Isolde blew out the candle on the bedside table. "Guinevere, you are a perceptive woman. I believe you can guess without my telling you."

"So that *is* where you were each night." I stared up at the shadows on the ceiling, my stomach twisting as my suspicions were confirmed. "But you have not left our room in nearly a month."

"He has rejected me." Her voice was small, frail.

I had been watching the life drain out of Isolde for some time now. Here in the darkness, it seemed as though she had given up completely. Sick with guilt, I wondered how much of her present pain was due to my allegations. Surely Galen had told her what had happened, what I had said. If I saw through him, it would stand to reason he would fear others would soon come to the same conclusion. Better to leave her now than be caught in a sin he could not deny.

"Isolde, I am so sorry."

"You did nothing. I knew what I was getting into when I warmed his bed. A lovers' tryst is built to destroy itself; they all end in time." She was trying to remain strong, but her voice was wavering.

"Did you love him?"

She shifted in the darkness. She was on her side, facing me, silent tears caught by the pale moonlight. "I could never fall in love. My heart is not here; it is at home with the radiant roses and emerald hills. It is chasing the deer and embracing the sweet smell of the meadows. My life here is not my own, but I take happiness where and from whom I can get it. Will you condemn me for that?"

I had no answer for her. I had done enough damage already; I was the reason she lay here in pain, imprisoned in what should have been her home. I could only assure her of my love and hold her as she cried herself to sleep.

⁂

Our confinement lasted only a few more weeks, during which time Isolde displayed a surprising skill at being able to pick locks and move about the castle unseen so that we could continue our scheduled meetings with Guildford and Liam.

"This is not the first time they have kept me under guard. You learn what you must to survive," Isolde explained while deftly jiggling the back side of the lock on our bedroom door, which could be opened from both sides if one knew how. "This one is at least a challenge; I had a duplicate key to my former room." Her impish smile was back.

Once the danger of Beltane had passed—a night full of grief at lost love for the both of us—Isolde seemed to rally, showing incredible resilience and strength. At the same time, Pellinor began "forgetting" to lock us in until it became clear he would not do so again if we would pretend nothing had changed.

One morning, Isolde and I were playing a game of Holy Stones with a set she had brought from her homeland when Lyonesse and Elaine entered the castle below after Mass. I could not tell what she was saying, but Lyonesse was angry, honking at Elaine like a goose.

As Lyonesse chased Elaine up the stairs, their voices became clearer. Apparently Elaine's crime was to return Galen's gaze during Mass when he smiled at her.

Lyonesse was still hitting Elaine with her veil when they barreled into the room.

"How dare you, you little strumpet! During holy Mass, your eyes should only be on one of two men: the priest or God. And as I do not think you can see God—you can't, can you?" Lyonesse's tone was tinged with curiosity and hope.

Elaine shook her head, incredulous at the question.

"Blessed be God for those whose daughters can," she muttered, casting a holy glance skyward before continuing exactly where she left off. "Your actions are sure to cause scandal among the whole village."

Isolde rolled her eyes and stifled a snicker, but not in time.

"You dare mock me, you ungrateful little wretch?" Lyonesse wheeled on her, unleashing the remainder of her fury. "'Tis no wonder Elaine is showing signs of immodesty with you around. I will be dead and buried before we find a Briton willing to marry one as ill-mannered and unrepentant as you."

In the time I had been here, I had seen Isolde undeservedly bear the brunt of Lyonesse's anger many times. But she had been laying into Isolde as often as she could lately, no doubt out of frustration that she had yet to see Elaine married.

I could stand it no longer. I rose to my feet, advancing on Lyonesse in defense of my friend. "Have you no comprehension of the law? Who she marries matters not. Isolde will be Queen of Ireland one day, and that means she could destroy your whole kingdom and everyone in it." I gestured to Elaine without breaking my hold on Lyonesse's eyes. "If she put her mind to it."

"Guinevere, please. I do not need you to defend me." Isolde raised her palm in a gesture of peace and turned her attention to Lyonesse. "Lyonesse, I apologize for my lack of respect. But what Guinevere says is quite true." She held Lyonesse's gaze, daring her to continue.

At that moment, Galen and Pellinor joined us, completely

unaware of what had transpired. They appeared to have been arguing as well, and their whispered disagreement continued after they settled into seats near the window. My back was toward them, but I could hear them well enough.

"It has been four months," Pellinor insisted. "You are content to eat my food and sleep under my roof, yet you make no promise to my daughter. What more time could you need to know that we are true? Surely Elaine has proven her virtue to you by now."

"That is not the issue and you know it," Galen answered. "If you will not agree to allow my tribe safe haven in Dyfed, then I will not wed your daughter."

"But you have no need of my kingdom." Pellinor was fighting to keep his voice down. "Leodgrance already assures safety in Gwynedd for all Votadini who desire it."

So that was Galen's excuse for not yet signing the marriage contract—the only step that remained before he and Elaine would be formally wed.

"Not anymore," Galen said with more than a touch of bitterness.

I considered the implications of that. If my father decided to no longer honor his agreement with the Votadini—yet another tradition that had died along with my mother—he could be courting war. It all depended on how much importance it held for the current Votadini chief and how loudly his people clamored for it.

Isolde snapped her fingers in front of my face and called my name twice to summon my attention back to her.

"Sorry," I muttered. I moved one of my archers in position to take one of Isolde's foot soldiers. "What are they squabbling about over there?" I craned my neck to see around Isolde. Lyonesse and Elaine continued to pick at one another as they both pretended to be saying their after-Mass prayers. I smiled at the irony of the situation.

Isolde's hand hovered over her king. "Lyonesse says she had a revelation while at prayer during Mass. She is worried that Galen is not the man spoken of in the prophecy because he is a foreigner. According to her, the prophecy makes no mention of the man being from another land." She advanced her king on a group of my knights, proudly defending her mother's marble queen, her most prized possession.

I gave up on her foot soldier and moved my troops in position to defend against the advancing king. "What did Elaine say to that?"

Isolde laughed. "She calmly replied that nowhere in the prophecy does it state that he must be a Briton, either."

"Good for her! I bet Lyonesse had no reply."

"No." Isolde maneuvered her queen out from among her ranks and into conquering position of my queen. "But Lyonesse has started in on any little fault she can think of. It is like listening to two little girls quarrel."

I was fairly certain there was little I could do to defend my queen. I went to move a knight in between her piece and mine but rubbed my forehead instead. I was so used to using this game as a method of divination that the sight wanted to come to me now. It was taking all the strength I had to resist it; after what I had seen while I was ill, the last thing I wanted was more visions.

When I looked up again, Isolde was watching Galen. "I think you may be right, Guinevere."

"About what?"

"About Galen. I wonder if he can be trusted."

"Isolde, you are still upset because he left you."

"No," she insisted. "He told me what you asked him, and I think you are on to something. Why *is* he here if not to marry Elaine?" Isolde reached for my queen.

I began to relay what I had overheard moments before but was cut off by a bang when the door burst open, startling everyone.

A messenger entered and strode over to Pellinor, handing him two letters. "Urgent messages for you, my lord."

Pellinor looked down at the rolls of parchment and then up at me. "Guinevere, this one is for you."

My heart leapt. This had to be the news I was longing for. It was Aggrivane—I knew it. The other would be from his father or my father, telling them I could return home because Aggrivane wanted to marry me.

I tore at the wax seal without really looking at it. As I read, my heart sank. The letter was from my father.

> "My beautiful daughter, I miss you so very much. I was wrong
> to send you away in such haste. Please forgive me."

I wondered what had prompted his change of heart, especially given Galen's revelation that Gwynedd was no longer a safe haven for the Votadini.

"You should know that I fought with our king against the Saxons near the town of York. I am happy to report that we were victorious and are now constructing earthen dams to keep the filthy mongrels at bay.

But that is not why I send this message to you. During the battle, I was grievously wounded."

My eyes misted over, and I had to remind myself that if he had written this letter, he was not dead. I scanned the page faster.

"I would have certainly died, were it not for the heroic actions of our king. He saved my life, and I owe him a great debt."

I did not get to finish reading the last paragraph because Pellinor had finished his letter and jumped to his feet.

"The king, he is coming here," he stuttered. "He wishes to hold a tournament."

"Why? When?" Lyonesse seemed as frantic as Pellinor looked.

"He did not give reasons. He is already in Gwynedd. He will arrive just before Lughnasa."

Lyonesse clapped a hand to her mouth. "But that is in less than a month!" she exclaimed, and then began muttering to herself. "I wonder why he chose not to stay in Gwynedd. Oh, Northgallis is much too small. Thank goodness, we have much more room for accommodations. A royal visit! I must tell my sister; she will be so envious!"

Pellinor was already scribbling out a reply.

"Ladies, come, we must prepare," Lyonesse commanded.

Isolde made her winning move and grabbed my queen before leaving the room. "Don't worry. You'll have plenty of time to win this back," she teased, unfazed by the turn of events.

I looked down at the last paragraph of my letter.

"You will be seeing me soon, as King Arthur wishes to hold a tournament in Dyfed and I will accompany his party. He has already written to Lord Pellinor advising him of the situation. I hope to bring you good news when I arrive."

Good news? Perhaps all had been forgiven and my hopes were not in vain. All I could do now was wait.

Chapter Twenty

Autumn 496

Chaos ruled Corbenic. With less than a month to prepare for the royal visit, plus all of the guests it would entail, every person was busy, all hands valuable. Elaine and Galen's courtship was temporarily overshadowed as their attention was diverted to the tasks at hand. Lyonesse used Elaine as her right hand in overseeing preparations and training the additional servants that would be needed, while Galen assisted Pellinor in managing the lodging and security logistics that came with a royal visit. I had become a servant like Isolde, cleaning long-neglected guest rooms, scrubbing linens, baking countless loaves of bread, and doing whatever was asked of me.

The king, his lords, and other visiting nobles began arriving during the week prior to the tournament, sometimes one household at a time, other times in caravans of two and three families who had traveled the long distance together for safety. The work only increased with their arrival, as there were more mouths to feed, more people to get in the way, and children and dogs underfoot.

Time slipped away rapidly, and before any of us could catch our breath, Lughnasa dawned bright and clear. It was a beautiful morning, but the sunshine brought with it the promise of oppressive heat.

My feet and arms ached from long trips to and from the market, laden down with bushels of supplies, and my hands were red and chafed from the lye used in the laundry. The last thing I wanted to do today was stand out in the sun and watch a bunch of men attempt to kill each other; I wanted to sleep. As I dragged myself out of bed, I had to remind myself that today I would meet the king, a rare honor, one for which I should be grateful.

Isolde seemed no better off than me. Deep circles rimmed her eyes, though she had not strayed from her bed at night in months. She seemed to sleep well, yet rest had little impact on the weariness that showed in her face.

We dressed for the tournament quietly, trying to balance our display of finery with material that would not suffocate us in the stifling heat.

Isolde was ready much too quickly, full of what I assumed was nervous energy. As she waited on me, she regarded herself in polished shield that was our mirror, brushing a hand over lackluster skin, frowning at her reflection.

I caught her eye in the silver disk. "Are you unwell?"

"I am fine, merely tired," she answered with an uneven voice. "Have *you* found it easy to sleep with those men carousing all night?" When she turned to face me, her smile was forced.

"If it matters, I do not believe you," I responded to her first statement, ignoring her attempt at diversion.

"It matters." She gave me a peck on the cheek. "But you are still wrong."

Before I could answer her, she was out the door, and I was forced to follow, still fastening my belt as I ran.

⁘

A meadow to the east of the castle had been cleared for the tournament. Grass stripped away, the horses pawed at the dirt, sending puffs of dust into the thick air. Clumps of early spectators milled about, angling to establish their claim on areas with the best view. We were directed to a raised dais, where we would sit with the king in a place of honor, as part of the host family.

In the oval competition ring, men of all ages practiced their skills with a variety of weapons. Each was hoping to win the favor of the king and to be invited to fight with him against the enemies of the crown, which grew more numerous with each passing day. They would be given rank today, a segregation that would determine who would be accepted into the king's inner circle of compatriots and friends, and who would be forced to curry favor from without. Those yet untested would show their skills to the king, and if they met his approval, would be invited to pledge their loyalty and be trained as knights. The younger boys, whose families wished them to be trained under Arthur's tutelage, would fight in a cordoned area with wooden swords and blunted spears.

I eyed Pellinor as he watched his own warriors sparring on the borders of the ring. Although it was an honor, this royal visit came at great cost to him. The expense to replace the candles, torches, and rushes, and build up the stocks of food, wine, ale, hay, and other items for the guests and their horses must equal, if not exceed, his yearly household expenses, yet he did not seem troubled. Though Lyonesse had nearly lost her voice by shouting orders at everyone, including him, Pellinor had never seemed more serene. I suspected that he expected something from the king in return for his generosity—and I had a feeling it somehow involved Elaine.

While Lyonesse fretted over the cost of the visit and what such a high capacity of guests would do to her home, the surrounding town was thriving under the increase in revenue. Only the highest lords and their families were invited to stay at Corbenic; the others were taken in by lesser nobles from the surrounding countryside or lodged in one of the town's many inns. This meant much needed income not only for the honest innkeepers and merchants, but for the thieves, beggars, and prostitutes of Dyfed as well. Pellinor's security battalion was doing their best to keep order in the town, but even now, purses no doubt were being picked and unsavory propositions made.

I spotted Guildford among the growing crowd of warriors. He was giving last-minute pointers to Liam, who caught my gaze and waved. I returned the gesture. I was surprised to see with him my cousin Bran, now a grown man I barely recognized, and a few of the boys with whom I had sparred as a child under my mother's tutelage. With a smile, I wondered what the king would think if I stepped out into the ring and took up my own sword. The thought of Lyonesse's horrified face made me laugh out loud.

"What are you giggling at?" Isolde wanted to know.

"Nothing." I was struggling to catch my breath. "Only an amusing thought."

"And you are not going to share?" She stuck out her lower lip in an adorable pout.

From far below, a voice carried on the wind.

"Lothian, do not think victory will be yours this day. I shall not fall to your sword a second time." The speaker was a tall, dark-haired man with tan skin and imposing features.

"Who is he?" I asked Isolde.

"Accolon, son of Uriens of Rheged. He is cousin to Lothian

royalty. He is very handsome."

Rather than scrutinizing Accolon, my eyes eagerly sought out the object of his taunt, desperate to know to which of the brothers it had been addressed. Another tall, dark-haired man gave Accolon a rude gesture in response. It was not Aggrivane.

"Oh heavens," Lyonesse groaned. "Must those Lothian men be so coarse? Savage barbarians." She turned to the ladies seated around her. "I wonder why Accolon is fighting for his father instead of Owain. After all, Owain is the elder son. It is his duty."

The ladies tittered in agreement. Lyonesse's lips curled up in a slow smile as she began gently flapping a small hand fan of swan feathers, not so much to cool herself as to show off her latest purchase and the wealth it implied.

Isolde rolled her eyes and whispered an answer to me. "Owain is the strategist in the family; Accolon prevails with the steel." She explained this as plainly as if she was a member of their household.

"Isolde, how do you know all of this?"

She cast a sidelong glance at me. "I have my ways."

"You have your spies, you mean."

"Call it what you will," she said airily.

The sun was nearly overhead now; the competition was soon to begin. I swept the ring one final time, looking for Aggrivane. I finally spotted him with his father and brothers. Aggrivane's back was toward me, but I breathed a sigh of relief knowing he was there, hale and whole despite whatever may have passed since we parted. I wanted to run down to him and wish him luck, but I knew better than to make such a foolish mistake.

Seeing Aggrivane reminded me there was one other person I had not spotted in the crowd. "Elaine, where is Galen? He is supposed to compete, is he not?"

Elaine looked startled that I had spoken to her.

"I am certain he is here somewhere," Lyonesse cut in. Her tone was cold and carried a warning that I should not pursue the subject further. She craned her neck to see over the massing crowd. "I cannot even find some of our own men in this throng."

Elaine looked worried. Actually, she looked like she was going to cry, and I instantly regretted my foolish question. Maybe Galen was right. Perhaps I did assume too much.

My thoughts were interrupted as the low vibration from a trio of bronze horns announced the king's arrival. Their commanding baritone rumbled in my ribcage as I turned with the rest of the crowd toward the entrance of the ring. One row at a time, we genuflected in unison as the king and his court appeared.

I sucked in air and audibly gasped when I saw him. Even from a distance, Arthur was much more striking in person than in my visions. Towering over everyone in his party, he exuded an air of power and confidence that could not be mistaken. I fell into a deep curtsey but could not lower my eyes from his face. His high cheekbones, broad nose, and chiseled jaw were softened by kind, intelligent blue eyes framed by gently sloping golden eyebrows only slightly darker than his long, straight blond hair.

"Remind me to thank the Goddess for creating him," Isolde whispered breathlessly.

I swatted her playfully as we all rose. Arthur was handsome, I would give her that, but in a carnal way that was at odds with my personal taste. I far preferred Aggrivane's poetic soul.

Arthur stood before his place, only a few removed from my own, and gestured for everyone to be seated.

"I wish to thank every one of you for attending these games today," he began, his deep voice strong, clear, and calm. "As you know, I called this tournament to invite the best of my subjects to prove their mettle and show their desire to serve with me in defending our isle. We have enemies on many fronts, and even within our land." His eyes rested briefly on Lot. "But today we are all friends.

"The tournament will proceed as follows. To separate the wheat from the chaff, we will begin with a general melee involving all adult competitors. No blood is to be spilt; if you are hit, you are to fall to your knees, raise your hands, and yield. My men"—Arthur raised his hand, and several men on the field, each wearing a bright yellow sash, did the same—"will be assisting in judging. Anyone who violates the rules will be disqualified.

"After that round of fighting, the names of the remaining warriors will be taken down, and each will fight in single combat until only two remain. In this round, you may draw blood, but you must stop before delivering what would be the fatal blow. The final ten warriors will be awarded prizes, and the winner will have the honor of assuming the role of my second."

A murmur echoed through the crowd, and Arthur paused to let

them quiet.

"On this, the feast of Lugh, the warrior god and Sun King, I wish you all blessings and the best of luck." His full lips raised into a slight smile. "For my sake, try not to kill each other."

The crowd laughed, and Lyonesse grimaced, no doubt more at the pagan reference than at the inevitable bloodshed.

Isolde and I eyed each other joyfully. This was going to be fun.

∘꩜ ꩜∘

The general melee was over surprisingly fast. When the horn sounded, men came at one another in a dizzying kaleidoscope that changed faster than I could follow. Oaths flew through the air, along with spears and javelins, as one after another, warriors sank to their knees and then trudged, disappointed, off the battlefield.

I was saddened to see Liam among them. He had been trapped into defending himself against two much older men, a situation even his skill could not have prevented; only experience would have saved him. When he reached the sidelines, Guildford clapped a hand on his shoulder, obviously proud despite the defeat, and led him away.

There was a lull as the remaining men lined up, the scribes recorded their names, and they drew lots to determine the order of combat. Once they were sorted, the men returned to a holding area beneath our stand to rest and tend any minor injuries. This gave us a clear view of each man, and Isolde and I amused ourselves by critiquing them.

Galen appeared, and Elaine breathed a sigh of relief.

Eventually, Aggrivane led his brothers into the pen. I wanted with all of my heart to cry out to him, but I did not dare due to the close supervision I was under. Lyonesse had stiffened, well aware of who was a mere stone's throw away. All I could do was stare at Aggrivane and pray he noticed.

He must have felt me watching him because he looked up, pausing in disbelief. Once he was sure I was who he thought, he inclined his head slightly in greeting and smiled the crooked grin that had illuminated my dreams for the last year.

Our joy was short-lived, however, as the horn sounded once again and the men lined up for one-on-one combat. The first to spar were two of Lot's sons, Gawain and Gaheris, paired by chance. Gawain was the victor.

A litany of nobles followed, most of whom I did not know. Gawain and Accolon held a lengthy duel, at the end of which Accolon was forced to concede defeat; a lanky blond from Cornwall named Tristan battled Galen and emerged the victor, much to our family's disappointment; and a brawl ensued when an unruly Parisi nearly decapitated one of Pellinor's men. Both were disqualified, the Parisi for this disruptive action, and the Dyfed warrior for his extensive, bloody injury.

Although Arthur cheered with great joy and conviction at each round, eyes bright with mounting excitement, I could not match his enthusiasm. My concentration was beginning to wane when one of the men in the next pair was called by a name I hadn't heard in years—Peredur of Gwynedd, Octavia's son.

That couldn't possibly be correct, could it?

I strained to see the features of the muscular man with curly blond hair. If I looked at him just right and peeled away the years in my mind, before me stood the young boy I had bid farewell so many years ago.

I calculated in my head. Peredur was seven when I left him and his mother behind for the isle. I was in Avalon roughly four years, and it had been almost a year since I arrived in Dyfed. That meant Peredur couldn't be more than twelve or thirteen years old, at least a year younger than the minimum age to compete as an adult. *He must possess incredible talent to be allowed an exception to the rule. Either that or whomever he fights for is very powerful.*

Peredur wielded his sword with a skill and grace well beyond his years. The crowd stilled to silence as he danced across the dirt, blade held horizontal in his gloved hand as he defended against the long reach of his opponent's spear. He barely seemed to be making an effort, while his dumbfounded opponent fought with all his energy, trying to keep Peredur at bay and land a blow. In the end, Peredur defeated him with expert precision, using an attack that began by advancing on his opponent in a series of quick, short steps, and then deflecting his spear off to the left in an arc, which opened him up for the final blow. Peredur's blade sliced a long line through his opponent's armor and into his ribs. The warrior dropped his weapon, and Peredur held him captive. The tournament advanced to the semifinal round, crowd roaring its approval as the fighters changed places.

Isolde poked me in the ribs and inclined her head toward Arthur, whose gaze was fixed in our direction.

"That is the third time he has looked this way. Who do you think has captured his attention?" she asked, hope obvious in her voice.

I almost laughed when I imagined what we must look like to him—Elaine, Isolde, and I—all sitting here in a row, prize geese for the picking. We could not be more different in appearance—Isolde, tall with flaming curls, bursting with lust for life; Elaine, the petite, blue-eyed, blond definition of demure; and me, a short, raven-haired jumble of Roman and Votadini. Whatever his taste, odds were one of us would be to his liking. Even though I probably should have felt honored by that, I could not help but feel a little like a whore on display in a brothel.

I met his eyes only briefly, but long enough to see him smile just slightly. I returned his gesture with a slight inclination of my head and a soft upturn of my lips, a pleasant expression I hoped would convey kindness and respect, before turning back to Isolde.

"I think he is watching all of us," I whispered, not wanting her to know Arthur's attention was on me. I chanced another glance at him.

His eyes had shifted to Elaine.

"Actually, he seems to be concentrating on Elaine."

"Not if I can help it," Isolde muttered under her breath and sent him a smoldering look. "Will you look at those muscles? I bet he would be fun to take to bed." Her fantasies played out in her expression.

"Behave yourself," I admonished in jest, stealing one last look at Arthur. *She is right. He is a handsome man.*

Just then, Aggrivane's name was announced, and I whipped around. He stepped into the ring to face an unfamiliar opponent. The man, a foreigner from Brittany called Lancelot, was dark-haired like Aggrivane, but his eyes were a captivating shade of blue that reminded me of the wildflowers that dotted the hillsides in this part of the country.

Isolde grabbed my clammy hand and held it so tightly I thought she was going to break it. She was bouncing nervously beside me, an action that was not helping my anxiety any.

As the men circled each other, I took a deep breath and did not let it out. Not only was my love part of this duel, it would determine which one of the two men would go on to compete to be Arthur's second. Every sinew in my body was singing Aggrivane's name, willing him to victory.

They rounded each other for a while, posturing and testing like feral dogs. Finally, Aggrivane's sword lashed out like a snake. But Lancelot blocked him and parried with a technique I had never seen, a nimble flick of the arm he must have learned in Brittany. From that moment, Aggrivane was on the defensive, never able to regain the upper hand.

Lancelot fought with a grace I did not know possible; it was as though his sword were merely an extension of his arm. He followed Aggrivane's every move, hawk-like, calculating his next several moves in response. Whenever Aggrivane changed tack, Lancelot had a response that kept him off balance.

Lancelot eventually forced Aggrivane up against the hay bales forming the perimeter of the pitch. As they fought nose-to-nose, Aggrivane abandoned his sword for a long dagger hanging at his belt.

"Brilliant!" I whispered, quietly congratulating him on his ingenuity. There was no rule against multiple weapons, though few had brought more than one into the pitch. But before I could get too excited, Lancelot had wrenched it from Aggrivane's grasp and had his sword at Aggrivane's throat.

The breath whooshed out of me as I exhaled in disappointment. I felt terribly for Aggrivane and wished I could comfort him, resenting more than ever the shackles of propriety that bound me to my seat. Isolde rubbed the small of my back comfortingly, and I placed my head on her shoulder, ready to be done with the tournament.

The final two combatants, Lancelot and Kay, Arthur's foster brother, paced at the edge of the ring, waiting for the king to give the word.

I lifted my head from Isolde's shoulder. Beside us, Elaine was wringing her hands, a habit she had when she was trying to make a decision. She called her maid over to her, removed one of the flowers from the garland in her hair, and handed it to the woman. Elaine spoke a few words to her before the maid departed, but I could not hear them.

The maid fought her way down to the edge of the ring and attracted Lancelot's attention. She said something to him, pointed toward us, and handed him the flower. He raised his hand in our direction and smiled. Though the gift had come from Elaine, I could have sworn he was looking directly at me.

"What was that?" Isolde asked warily.

"I'm not sure, but it worries me." It was very uncharacteristic of Elaine to make any bold moves, especially in so public a venue. "Did Lyonesse or Pellinor see?"

Isolde looked over my shoulder. "No, they are deep in conversation with your father."

"Oh." I didn't know whether to be relieved that they had not witnessed the strange turn of events or worried that they were speaking with my father. The last conversation they had had brought me here, so I was fairly certain I did not want to know where this one would lead.

Chapter Twenty-One

everal hours later, I opened the door to my chamber, expecting to find Isolde there. Before the investing ceremony, during which Lancelot turned down the position at court he had rightly won, Isolde had said she was going to try to get an audience with the king and insinuated I should use the time to find Aggrivane. She disappeared into the crowd, and no one had seen her since.

The room was empty. My heart fell, and I worried over her whereabouts as I stepped out of my sticky dress, washed, and put on a fresh garment. I was just reaching for my comb when I saw it—a small pouch lying on my pillow.

I picked it up cautiously, curiously, mind racing with who could have left it and what it could possibly contain. I slid apart the drawstrings and turned the bag upside down. Two round red stones and a small roll of parchment fell into my palm. I turned the stones over in my hand. Two queens. I knew without touching the paper who the message was from.

I sank down on the bed, tears already welling in my eyes. Reluctantly, I opened the tiny scroll and steeled myself to read its contents. It was Isolde's handwriting, as flowing as her enthusiasm but cramped on the small page.

> *Guinevere,*
> *I am fine, and you will be too. Breathe. I know you do not*
> *understand now why I have gone, but you will.*

I smiled. It was like she was standing right next to me. The tears began to fall of their own accord.

> *I have returned home, to a place where I am loved and*
> *where my future is assured. Galen is with me, but it is not what*
> *you think. It is not what they will accuse me of. Please know*

that I am doing this for a very good reason, and I will explain as soon as I am able.

As you can see, I have returned your queen—you won it back today by your strength. Please accept mine as a gift. I no longer have need of it, but I pray you will find in it—and in the memory of me—the ability to endure your circumstances. You may return it to me when we next meet. I am certain we will.

Please take care of Elaine. She needs a companion, Guinevere, especially now that I have stolen away her love. I do not wish to break her innocent heart, but believe me when I say I had no choice. She will hate me bitterly for what I have done, but I tell you truly that by hurting her now, I have saved her from a much deeper pain.

I may not possess the sight, but I know you are destined for greatness. It was not by accident that I chose my gift to you. Whatever the days ahead may hold, remember that you create your own happiness; do whatever it takes to make life worth living.

Thank you for your kindness and friendship. Your presence has made the last year the brightest of my life. I love you as if you were my sister. You are in my heart always.

Isolde

For a long time after I finished reading, I could not move. I could not see or think. My mind kept recalling Isolde's smiling face and replaying the events of the day. I had been by her side nearly all day. How could this have happened? How could she have just disappeared? It would take a long time for me to truly understand she was gone.

It was my duty to inform the others, so I returned the two stones to their pouch and secured it to the belt at my waist. That way Isolde always would be with me. I hurried down the stairs to the hall, where the family had agreed to gather.

Pellinor's agitated voice reached me before I entered the room. "In truth, I know not where Galen is."

I barged into the room, letter in hand. "I know where he is."

Silence greeted my confident declaration, and I looked up, noticing with a start that the family was not alone. Four burly, dark-haired men with full beards were standing in a line before Pellinor.

Their colorful, richly embroidered cloaks proclaimed them from the tribes of the north—those between Hadrian and Antonine Walls—like Galen. Each wore a brooch representing one of the four tribes.

"She is one of them; maybe she can tell us if what they say is true." Lyonesse scoffed at me with unusual distain.

I had no idea what was going on or what Lyonesse meant. I was one of whom? I scanned each face in the room, searching for answers. Elaine looked pale, Pellinor was growing redder by the minute, and Lyonesse wrinkled her nose at her guests as though they emitted a foul stench.

One of the men handed me an official-looking document.

As soon as my eyes fell upon it, I understood part of the confusion. It was written in their native language, which was more a series of glyphs than letters, so no one else in the room was able to read it. It had been many years since I had studied my mother's native tongue, but I understood enough to decipher its meaning.

"It is a ban of marriage," I stated, still uncertain what this meant.

"Yes," one of the strangers replied. "You will see that the bride is Fia, daughter of Brennen of the Selgovae."

I nodded, seeing her name.

"And please tell us who is listed as the husband."

My eyes dropped to next line, and I gasped. "Galen, son of Donel the Bold, of the Votadini."

I looked up at Elaine in astonishment. For a moment, she mirrored my shock. Then she began to cry.

"He is married?" I could scarcely force the words past my lips.

"Yes, lady," the tallest of the men addressed me. "And he is a wanted man. Not only did he abandon his wife, he has impregnated and deserted at least two other women in the lands between his home and here. We have come to take him to face his punishment."

"But we do not know where he is," Pellinor interjected, his face ashen now.

"I do." I held up the letter. "He has fled to Ireland."

Elaine began to sob.

"With Isolde," I added. I couldn't bear to meet Elaine's gaze.

Elaine let out a cry so guttural and heart-wrenching, I thought she was going to collapse on the spot. I expected Lyonesse to comfort her, but instead she curled her fingers around the arms of her chair, digging her fingertips into the wood in anger, knuckles turning white. It was Elaine's maid who took the poor girl into her arms, pulling her off to the corner of the room.

"Gentlemen," Pellinor's voice was sober as he passed Isolde's note to the foreigners, "as you can see, I have no power where he has gone. I assure you that he was these many months engaged to marry my daughter, and I had no hand in aiding his escape. I suggest you take your grievances to the Queen of Ireland."

The Votadini regarded one another, jaws clenched in frustration. One of them nodded, and they all bowed to Pellinor in unison. Their leader thanked Pellinor for his time, and without another word, they departed.

The tension in the room eased, but only minutely. Elaine's sobs punctuated the silence at intervals. I quickly stashed away the note before it could be taken from me.

Lyonesse crossed the room to where Elaine stood, supported by her maid, the woman's arms the only thing keeping her upright. Lyonesse reached out to Elaine and I thought she would embrace her grieving daughter, but was startled when her hand came down full force across Elaine's cheek. The crack echoed in the silence that followed.

Lyonesse circled her daughter like a wolf. "I put my faith in you, in your virtue, and you bring me a philanderer for a son?" she thundered.

Elaine stared at her mother with red-rimmed, bewildered eyes. Her tears were silent now.

"Will you now have me believe that you still possess any shred of virtue? That you could possibly still be pure?"

Elaine raised her arms against any further physical assault from her mother and answered with a quavering, pleading voice. "I assure you I am. He did me no harm at all. I am as pure as the day you birthed me!"

"A day I will forever regret if your words are lies," Lyonesse spat.

"Stop it!" Pellinor roared. "We have a bigger problem than the question of our daughter's virtue."

Every head in the room turned from Elaine to her father.

"Isolde's departure violates the treaty. We are no longer safe from the Irish. As soon as she reaches their shores, we become vulnerable. I must speak to the king."

❧❧❧

The possibility of trouble with the Irish compelled Arthur to remain at Corbenic and, with him, a council of his most trusted nobles.

Elaine spoke to no one for days, a ghost amid the feasting and festivities that accompanied the king's extended visit. When her presence wasn't required, she remained closeted in her chambers, weeping out her pain and frustration.

Even when she began to come around, Elaine spoke only when she was addressed and kept to herself as much as possible. Judging by her past behavior, this should only be a transitory phase, yet I was concerned. A light had gone out from behind Elaine's eyes, and I was afraid it signaled some permanent destructive change in her.

One evening when we were alone—Pellinor off in council with Arthur and his men, Lyonesse entertaining the ladies—I convinced Elaine to go for a walk with me. As we wound through the village streets in the cool night air, I tried to get Elaine to talk to me.

"I have nothing to say to you," she said coldly as we passed an inn where the revelers were spilling out into the street. "Were it not for you, I would be married now."

I could hardly believe my ears. "How could this situation possibly be my fault?" Isolde's? Yes. Galen's? Certainly. But me? She was mad.

"You were the one who read the document, Guinevere. Why did you not lie and tell my father those men were imposters or that the document said something else? Anything else! I loved him!" She was in a rage again, spewing vitriol as easily as she had shed tears.

"What would you have me do, Elaine? Let this scoundrel take you as his concubine?" I raised my voice in response to hers until we were both yelling. People passing us in the lane were beginning to stare, but I did not care about creating a spectacle. "Where would that leave you three moons from now when he had taken your money and your lands and left you alone and pregnant?"

She turned on me, incensed. "He would do no such thing!"

"Elaine, you heard the men. He has done it two times before, not counting his wife. What makes you any different?"

She had no reply and so lashed out like a child. "You just don't want me to be happy! You cannot find love, so no one else will either. *That* is your plan."

I halted and stared after her, shocked. "How can a heart of so few years be so dark?"

Elaine whirled and took three steps toward me so that her face was only inches from mine, her eyes dark and menacing. "Do you not understand that lack of love can blacken a heart just as quickly as loss of it?"

Her face was strained, pulled tight by the pain in her heart. "I am never allowed to love, never free—a bird trapped in a cage. I would be happier if Father gave me to the cloister. At least then Christ could be my spouse." She grabbed my forearms with surprising force, fingers digging into my flesh as she spoke, eyes straining to shed tears her body was too weary to produce. "My heart yearns for the love my mind knows exists. Everyone but me is allowed happiness. Isolde was sent here to marry. Even you, who were exiled because of love— you know the joy of its fulfillment. I have nothing."

My heart was breaking for the poor, innocent girl before me. I pulled her out of the street and into an alleyway to give us some privacy.

"You have your God," I said, thinking that reminder would bring her comfort.

"What little good He does me," she muttered.

The bitterness in her voice took me aback.

"I have faith, yes—that His will is truly what is best—but it is cold comfort when all speak of me dying barren and alone. You have no idea of my life, Guinevere." She spat my name with such hatred, she briefly reminded me of Morgan.

"Who says such things, Elaine? I have heard nothing of the sort."

She released my arms violently, flinging them away from her. "Of course not. You live in your own little world, you and Isolde, off having your fun while I am trapped in a life not of my own making."

She turned away, her back toward me as she watched the setting sun.

"Do you really think we would have chosen the lives we live?" I asked her. "I was exiled here, torn away from the only people I ever loved. I have no one here, Elaine. What kind of life is that? Isolde had no say in her placement in your house and, from what I can tell, was never welcome. Your mother treated her as a slave, and she endured it until she was forced to flee."

Elaine turned back to me, eyes flashing dangerously. "She *chose* to leave with *my* intended. Tell me, were they having an affair the entire time, or did the whore have a last-minute flash of inspiration?

I cannot make myself feel sorry for her, and I never will. She deserves everything that is coming to her, and so do you."

So much for making peace with her; it seemed I had gained another enemy.

After my confrontation with Elaine, I was restless, not yet ready to return to that empty room that may as well have been a prison cell. I needed to breathe in the night air, to feel free for however many minutes I could snatch from time's grasp.

I headed deeper into the village, seeking the open fields beyond the castle walls. I knew not where I was going, but it mattered little. Had my father not been nearby in counsel with the king, I would have run away tonight, to some distant town, back to Avalon, or maybe even boarded a ship to Ireland. Until now, I had not realized how much I missed Isolde, how much I had depended on her joy, her playful outlook on life to give me hope. The last few weeks, trapped with Elaine's anger and depression, had been horrible. I could almost feel her sadness leaching into my bones, threatening to burn away my soul and turn me into a bitter shell.

As I neared the turrets of the outer wall, I began to consider asking my father to take me back home. It would mean capitulating to Father Marius and admitting guilt I did not feel, but it was an opportunity I would not see again. Once my father returned to Northgallis, I would be stuck here indefinitely. I still had the option of running later if he sentenced me to more time in Pellinor's house. As I walked, I made my mind up to speak with him in the morning.

As I rounded the corner and turned onto the main road that led away from Corbenic, I froze. Someone was coming toward me. Someone I recognized as if from a long-forgotten dream. As the figure grew nearer, my heart picked up speed. I knew that gait, the sound of those footsteps. It was difficult to make out his features in the shadow of the tower, but I didn't need eyes to know who approached.

Aggrivane. I did not know if I thought his name or whispered it aloud, but he stopped. He seemed to be regarding me with the same disbelieving awe that emanated from every pore of my skin.

Hesitantly, we each took a step forward. That was enough for a patch of light from the dying sun to fall upon us and confirm the hopes we dared not speak. We rushed into each other's arms like the reunited lovers of a fairytale.

Arms, hair, lips, clothing all entangled like seaweed at the ocean's edge. The heat from our breath won out over the cool breeze that swirled around us as we kissed, bodies crushed together, eager hands confirming this was more than a fanciful dream.

Finally, our lips parted.

"I thought you returned to Carlisle with your brothers," I breathed, staring into the chestnut eyes I thought I would never see again, scarcely able to believe he was here, in my arms.

"I did," he answered, "but my father called me back a few days ago. I did not know if you were still here—or if you would be able to see me."

"I am here. And I will not leave your side." I kissed him gently on the cheek. "But we should take care not to be caught—again. Lyonesse is worse than Evrain could ever dream of being."

Still locked in each other's arms, we looked around for some means of escape, a shelter in which we could hide, if only for a few stolen moments. "I know a place. Follow me." Inspiration had struck when I asked myself what Isolde would have done. The question was not *what would she have done*, but rather, *what did she do?*

I took him by the hand and led him through a winding series of side roads to a small building huddled in the shadow of the great main keep. The front door would be securely locked, but with the right encouragement, the side door should give way.

It opened just as I expected, and we slipped inside. In the dim light, I could make out just enough of the floor to get us where we needed to be.

"You brought me to an apothecary?" Aggrivane asked as we passed rows of hanging dried herbs and racks of vials containing multi-hued liquids that glinted with sinister intent in the slats of pale light that slipped through the boards in the shutters.

I laughed. "No, silly. Thanks to Pellinor's paranoia, nearly everything in the castle is connected. The cellar of this building leads up into the main structure."

"I call that sound strategic planning, not paranoia."

In the dark, I doubted he could see the sardonic look I cast in his direction, but I did it anyway. "You don't know Pellinor."

I led Aggrivane by the arm down through a series of winding tunnels beneath the walls of the castle. We had to navigate by touch as neither of us possessed any source of light. It had been much easier the first time I made this journey; Isolde had brought with her a torch when we were forced to sneak out to meet Guildford and Liam. I could still hear her matter-of-fact answer when I asked how she knew such a place existed.

"I had a lot of free time during my first few years here. They did not know enough yet not to trust me." Her clever smile illuminated my mind's eye. "They kept Elaine so closely guarded that she was only rarely a playmate to me, so I went exploring. I found more than a dozen passages on my own. The existence of this one, however, was revealed to me by one of the guards—he is dead now—but I will be forever grateful to him. It has saved my hide many times."

"Does anyone else know this is here?" Aggrivane asked as though reading my mind, his inquiry tinged with apprehension.

I shrugged. "I suppose some of the guards know. Isolde said that Elaine knew about a few of the passages but always was too scared to go into them."

I wondered from whence Elaine's fear emanated—the dark, unfamiliar terrain or imaginings of her mother's reaction if she were caught. Probably a combination of the two.

I was so deep in thought I nearly missed the subtle change in the ground beneath our feet that signaled we were approaching the other end of the tunnel.

"Wait," I said.

We both stopped walking. I ran my hand along the wall, feeling the cold foundation of the castle. My hand hit upon a wooden support beam. "This is it." I led Aggrivane a few steps west, fingertips on the low ceiling above us. "Do you feel it?"

"I do," he whispered as his fingers trailed over the hinges on the door overhead. "Where does it lead?"

"A tiny library tucked away in the southwest corner of the ground floor. Most of the books were smuggled out of Rome generations ago or given to Pellinor as gifts from the more literate parts of the empire. Almost no one uses it anymore, but Lyonesse likes the statement of wealth the collection affords. Although with all the people here, it would not surprise me if someone sneaked away for some peace and quiet. Be careful—the door is covered by a rug, so we will have to push it clear."

Aggrivane chuckled as we heaved upward on the door. "I think we will be safe. Most of the lords cannot read or write. You and I are fortunate to be Druid-trained, remember? Other than our fathers and the king, I cannot think of another literate man on the council."

I wanted to remind him that Pellinor's family was taught by the Christian priests, but I thought better of it as both the door and its covering gave way.

"We are right below a table, so watch your head," I warned him as quietly as possible.

Once we were on our feet, I brushed a few bits of spider web out of his wavy brown locks. I let him take the lead, as he recognized where we were as soon as we peeked out into the deserted hallway. I held my breath, and within minutes, we had made it to the threshold of the old servants' quarters in which he was staying.

I let out a sigh as I stepped inside, willing my pounding heart to calm. We were safe.

Aggrivane followed close behind. He swung the door closed, but it was forcefully stopped by someone's hand before it shut.

Aggrivane motioned for me to retreat farther into the cramped room.

I looked around, searching for some means of concealment or escape. A small table with a basin and water jug stood to my left, a large storage chest just opposite, and the tiny raised bed directly in front of me, one side against the wall. There was nowhere for me to go, not even a closet. Seeing no other alternative, I wedged myself between the bed and the floor, scooting as close to the outer wall as possible.

"Retiring so early, Lothian?" It was Uriens' son, Accolon. I recognized his voice from the tournament. "I thought you may fancy a late-night gamble." He shook something that rattled like it contained tiny bones or pebbles of some sort.

"No, thank you, cousin. Another time, perhaps," Aggrivane responded politely.

"Shame. I was rather hoping to avenge my loss to your house at the tournament."

I imagined Aggrivane rolling his eyes.

"You do realize that had I won," Accolon rambled on, clearly pleased with the sound of his own voice, which was dripping bravado, "I would have challenged the king in defense of my father—fought the duel Arthur denied him during Lot's revolt."

Aggrivane's reply was muted from my hiding place, but I was grateful Accolon seemed oblivious to my presence. The hinges on the door squeaked as Aggrivane opened it to let his cousin pass through.

"In quite a hurry to be a-bed tonight, are you not?" Accolon teased. "Do you perhaps have someone waiting for you?"

A footstep too heavy to be Aggrivane's crossed the threshold in my direction. Though I was facing the wall, Accolon's presence filled the room now, the pungent oils he used to keep his black hair from hanging in his face strong. His feet shuffled as he turned around, looking for where Aggrivane's mystery woman could be hiding.

I held my breath, realizing too late that I had inhaled a lung full of dust. It tickled my throat as I fought to stay silent.

I stiffened as a draft of air passed over me. Accolon must have knelt down to get a better look. I closed my eyes, praying that my black hair and brown dress would blend into the shadows.

The moments ticked by in silence. My lungs began to burn as the dust scratched at my throat, nose, and mouth, daring me to cough and divulge my location.

Finally, Accolon's footsteps retreated and the door clicked shut.

I waited a few moments, and once Aggrivane had barred the door with the storage chest, I slowly began to scoot my way out from under the bed, careful not to hit my head amid hacking coughs.

"Did he see me?" I asked when my coughing fit had ended and I was upright once again.

Aggrivane burst out laughing and brushed a hand across the top of my head, sending a shower of dust flitting to the floor.

"At least I know what you will look like when you are old and gray." He handed me a small mirror about the size of a brick. "No, I do not think he saw you. I could barely spot you, and I knew you were there."

I held up the disc of burnished metal in front of me. My hair was indeed gray, and the left side of my face looked like I had been sweeping the chimney. I looked down. The entire front of my dress was covered in dust. I tried to wipe it off, but that only made matters worse.

"Now, this will not do." Aggrivane clucked his tongue disap-provingly, shaking his head. "I will not have a woman who frequents the dustbin in my bed." He was trying to repress a smile as he saun-tered to the table and poured water into the basin.

I reached for the cloth, but he grasped my hand instead.

"Let me."

Aggrivane dipped the cloth in the water and slowly drew it across my hair, his eyes never leaving mine as he worked. The musi-cal tinkle of water droplets told me when he submerged it and wrung it out, but I never broke his gaze to look.

Even more gently, he slid the soft, moist surface down my face and neck, smooth like a caress. Each pass was followed by a kiss, and sometimes the warm trail of his tongue, until the cloth was forgotten and we were lost in each other's arms.

After a few moments, he stopped me by placing a finger on my lips. A single word passed through his. "Tunic."

I quickly unfastened my copper belt, pulled the dirty fabric up over my head, and let it fall to the floor. I stepped toward him to remove his clothes, but he again placed a fingertip on my lips.

His hand went back into the water. I shivered as he stroked my breasts with the cloth. The water was cool, yet somehow invigorat-ing, and I arched my back in pleasure.

Aggrivane's lips met mine as he continued to bathe my naked body. His beard burned where it grazed my skin, igniting my senses. I dug my fingers into his skin, trying to make us permanently insepa-rable. He responded with crushing kisses, and I was vaguely aware of a sense of weightlessness as he carried me across the room. Before I knew it, I was intertwined with him on the bed, his tunic and breeches long since abandoned on the floor next to my dress.

✦✧✦

Hours later, we lay drowsing in the small bed. He was softly stroking my forehead. I felt so safe in his arms, like the past year had been nothing more than a horrible nightmare from which I had finally been awakened.

"I almost died without you," I whispered.

"I felt the same way."

We spent a long while gazing into each other's eyes. I was not even aware that I was tracing the outlines of the dragon embedded in his right arm with my fingertips until I encountered a smooth, raised line above his elbow. How many other scars had he gained while we were apart?

I propped my head up on my left arm. "What happened after my father separated us?" *How did you get this?* was what I really wanted to ask.

He made a sarcastic sound. "Which part of the story do you want? It is more complicated than a bard's tale."

"Start with yours. Where did you go?"

"Lord Evrain's men escorted me home. My father was furious, although I daresay it was more aimed at Evrain's manipulation than at me. To placate Evrain, my father sent me to the Saxon front. I cannot begin to tell you how difficult that was—facing my first real battles against so savage an enemy." His eyes took on a strange hue at the memory, a mixture of pain and suppressed fear. "I nearly lost my life a thousand times, but there was always someone there to heal me, to take away the pain until I was strong enough to fight again."

I dropped my eyes to the homespun sheets. "Camp women."

"Yes," he answered, lifting my chin with his index finger so that I had to look at him. "But not in the way you think. The women who follow the army are more than the prostitutes common gossip would have you believe. Without them, many good men would have died, myself included. There were even a few I recognized from the sacred isle, branded as they were with the mark of the Goddess."

My eyes grew wide.

"They provide our meals, clean our clothes, tend our injuries," Aggrivane hastened to explain. "How else do you think a busy camp runs? We do not have time to mend our gear, learn strategy, and tend to our basic needs all at once. They have nowhere else to go, and we gladly pay them for their services."

He laughed at the look I gave him, only then realizing the irony of his words.

"Not those services. There were many who offered such pleasures, but I partook of none." He kissed me on the forehead. "My heart and my body belong to you and no other."

I smiled up at him. "I believe you."

The corners of his mouth turned upward briefly, but then his face hardened as the memory returned. "I tell you truly, I learned more in those months than I would have in years under Evrain's tutelage. As we fought our way southeast, it was the memory of you that kept me going. Every step, every breath that I took brought me closer to the moment when I would see you again.

"We were not far from the ancient Brigante capital when Gaheris, my younger brother, caught up to our regiment and told me of our father's traitorous plan. We knew from past experience how dangerous he could be when his mind was set on something, so we went to warn the king. Arthur was grateful for our loyalty and brought us along to Lothian to witness the sanctions he would place upon our father. But Father was waiting for us. We were ambushed just beyond Eildon Pass."

"I know. I saw it," I interrupted.

He sat up. "What?"

My cheeks flushed as I understood his confusion. "I was deathly ill at the time, and the sight took over. I saw Lot's insurrection as though I was there with you."

He gave me an incredulous look. "You did?"

I nodded and relayed to him all I had seen, while he sat motionless, unable to comprehend what I was telling him, details I had no other way of knowing.

"I was scared to death when Arthur dragged you and your brothers out of the crowd. I really thought he would kill you," I said, concluding my tale.

Aggrivane had regained some of his composure. "So did I. When he took us, Arthur whispered to each of us not to fear, said that our lives were in no danger. But when Gawain began to bleed, I questioned both his sincerity and his sanity."

I smirked. "Arthur does drive a hard bargain."

"Indeed. But it worked. I have never seen a man so loyal as my father since that day. He even fought alongside the king and your father at York."

"I heard rumors of that, but was never able to confirm your fate." I placed a hand on his temple. "I feared you died."

Aggrivane mirrored my gesture. "I am safe, love. As you can see, we were victorious, though at a high cost. Were it not for Arthur, your father would have perished at the hands of the Saxons. He owes Arthur his life."

"He mentioned that in his letter, but I have not had much chance to speak with him about it."

"I would not bring it up." Aggrivane's voice grew serious. "Your father is a proud man who does not like to be reminded of his weaknesses, much less that he is in debt to another. I have no doubt he will find a suitable way of repaying our king for his kindness."

"I suppose," I said, unable to suppress a yawn. I pulled Aggrivane back down to the covers, suddenly weary of talking. "Let us sleep now, my love. We can speak of this more upon the morrow." I gave him a long, lingering kiss. "Hold me in your arms tonight and let us dream of future happiness."

As the castle fell silent around us and dreamers took to their beds, I allowed myself to hope this time would be different. Our next sighting of the morning star would mark the beginning of our lives together, just as it had once heralded our separation. Only this time there were no Druids, no priests, to keep us apart. All we had to do was make sure we were not caught. But the more I thought about that, the more difficult it seemed, especially in a house that bred spies like lice. We would have to be very careful.

CHAPTER TWENTY-THREE

The next several weeks passed in a blur of alternating pleasure and fear, one emotion when I was with Aggrivane and
the other anytime anyone else was near us. I was so frightened someone would discover our affair and tear us apart again,
something my long-neglected heart, only recently stitched up by
Aggrivane's love, would not abide.

Some nights I carried a change of dress with me as I prowled the
halls, praying to make it safely from one bedroom to the other. On
others, when Aggrivane had an early morning call to duty, I dared
ferry only myself across the border between the ladies' and gentlemen's chambers. I felt like a thief in my own home, stealing minutes,
hours of happiness from a family that seemed adverse to its very
nature. No matter how many times I sneaked back to my room, I
would never lose the fear of being met by a guard before I could get
inside, or worse yet, finding Lyonesse waiting for me when I thought
I had made it safely.

Each night as I sank down into the bedcovers, I resolved to apologize to Isolde the next time I saw her. During my weeks of intrigue,
I developed an appreciation for what she went through each time
she sought joy in this house, and slowly began to realize what a hypo-
crite I had been. I had condemned Isolde for exactly the same behavior with Galen that I now so willingly embraced with Aggrivane.

❧❧

We lay together in the cramped bed, gazing at the flames dancing in
the fireplace, casting flickering shadows on all four walls of the small
room.

"I am sorry I cannot offer you better accommodations," Aggrivane
said. "This is certainly no Beltane bower."

I smiled at his concern. "But it is not the stables, either."

I felt his laughter before I heard it.

"I forgot that Lyonesse is well aware of who you are," I admitted. "I should be grateful she lets you lodge here at all. There is little love for your family under this roof."

Aggrivane turned his head so he could see me. "Ah, but the king favors me, so she must, as well. But I am surprised you can get away from your chambers. I figured they would have barred the door."

I giggled. "They did that for a while when Isolde was here. But she found a way out. I would have too. Nothing can keep me from you." I kissed his nose. "Though I don't think he knew for sure we escaped, Pellinor made Lyonesse swear she would never do such a thing again. That is probably why it has not happened." I reconsidered for a moment. "That, and I doubt they think I would be so bold with my father under the same roof."

Aggrivane shook his head. "A year's time and they do not know you at all, do they?"

"My true nature has never mattered much to them. They simply cast me in whatever light suits them best at the time. Now that I am out from under Isolde's corrupting influence, they choose to imagine me more like their sainted daughter. But what they do not know is that Isolde taught me many of her tricks. After all, she *is* the reason I am here with you."

Aggrivane's eyes held a kind of wonder. "You speak of Isolde often. She must have meant a great deal to you. I wish I could have met her."

I smiled at the memory of my friend. "She seems to think we will meet again, so maybe you will still have the opportunity."

We both fell silent for a while, lost in our own thoughts. Outside, the watchman announced the midnight hour.

"You said there were many sides to the story of what happened after we parted. I know what happened to you. Now what about Evrain?"

Aggrivane sat up and stretched. "He is one man I wish I could send to the Saxons. He would not last a minute, and that would be fine by me."

I had never heard his voice so bitter.

He lay down on his back, hands supporting his head. "While I was off trying not to get myself killed, my brothers, Gawain and Gaheris, were attempting to negotiate peace with Evrain. Of course, he wanted none of it, refusing all efforts on the grounds that neither of my brothers were landed lords and therefore were beneath his dignity. Arrogant cur. One of these days I will repay his many affronts to my family. Anyway, he refused to speak with anyone other than my father, who, as you know, was busy at the time, plotting to take over the throne. As Gawain tells it, one night Father had an epiphany and stormed out of the castle well after dark, intent on visiting Evrain. The result is that Evrain is now related to the king, or so he thinks."

I turned over to face him. "Say that again?"

He grinned. "You heard me. In exchange for his loyalty and forgiveness of my offense, Father offered Evrain—a widower at the time—the hand of his daughter, Amelie."

I was confused. "His daughter? Is she not also your sister?"

"No, not fully. She is a bastard some six years younger than me and was reared by her mother in another city. Up until the tournament, I had never even met her. But Evrain does not know that. He thinks she is my mother's child and, hence, niece of the king. You see, my father figured out Evrain's weakness—his ambition. He saw that Evrain was trying to use the tension between him and Arthur as an excuse to make his own bid for power. So my father offered him something more valuable than he ever could have imagined— the chance to be related to the king. He knew that Evrain would think that having Arthur's niece in his family could be a suitable device to manipulate the king. He was right. Evrain happily joined my father's cause, all past grievances forgotten."

I was awestruck. "Does your father's ambition ever end?"

Aggrivane smiled but said nothing.

"What is it? What is on your mind?"

He turned to face me. "I spoke to my father today."

I sat up, pulling him with me, our hands clasped tightly. "And what did he say?"

Aggrivane composed his features, looking more serious than I had ever seen.

My stomach knotted.

"He is not certain of your fidelity to me."

My heart leapt into my throat. I started to defend myself.

"He wants to know," Aggrivane continued, his face like stone, "if you were the one who sent the flower to the Breton bastard who defeated me at the tournament."

Slowly, I realized he was joking. Relief rushed out of me in a spray of saliva as I exhaled.

"Sorry." I dried his cheeks with my thumbs then affected my most proper voice. "You may tell your father that it was not I who behaved so rashly, but my dear friend Elaine."

Aggrivane caught me up in his arms and showered my face with kisses. "He is very amenable to our engagement and gives his blessing. He likes you, Guinevere—"

I stopped him mid-sentence, kissing him with more force than even I anticipated.

Aggrivane submitted happily and then finished his sentence as he pulled me into his lap. "Although I think he likes your dowry more."

"The lands south of Stirling? Let him have them if it means we can be together."

"Do not speak so lightly of them just because you have never seen them," Aggrivane chided. "Those lands make you a very valuable wife because they mean you have influence over the Votadini, and through them, the whole area. You—"

I stopped his thought with a kiss whose meaning could not be misinterpreted. I wanted nothing of politics at that moment, only to be lost in him.

I lost track of time in the aching passion that followed, but soon he was holding me again, both of us breathless.

"So is it true? Are we really to be wed?" I asked.

"Yes, it is, if you will have me."

"Of course I will."

"My father promised to speak to Leodgrance and obtain his permission as soon as possible, but it may take some time. As you know, this must be approached with utmost delicacy, given the household we are in and what is known of our past transgressions. But he swore to me he will not fail, and I have complete faith in him," he said, confidence in his voice.

I smiled and reached up to stroke the thin line of hair that ran along his jaw, nuzzling my cheek into his chest. I wanted nothing more than to remember this moment forever.

Chapter Twenty-Four

The autumnal equinox came and went without a single word from the Irish. The council formulated a plan that would go into effect if any hostility was detected, so Arthur decided it was time to return to his own lands. Pellinor, ever the gracious host, insisted on organizing one final celebration to honor the king before he left.

As the first light of dawn colored the horizon, I joined some of the servants in the kitchen to gather supplies for the hunting party. I found them speaking animatedly in hushed tones. From what I could gather, one of them had received word from Isolde, who had arrived home safely some weeks before.

"She is keeping her promise," someone said.

That was all I was to know. All conversation ceased when I entered the room, a spy in the enemy camp.

But the absence of the kitchen maid who had accompanied Galen and me on our ride did not escape my notice, nor did Liam's sudden departure, allegedly to work in another household. Isolde's conversation with Guildford during my fighting lessons so long ago drifted through my mind, and suddenly it all made sense. Isolde had begun her revenge by slowly poaching Lyonesse's servants. But how far would she go? I pushed the troubling thought from my mind and busied myself seeing to the provisions for the hunt.

By mid-morning, the sun shone brightly in the clear sky overhead and we reached the summit of the hill from which we would watch the action. The maids unpacked our wares, and Elaine and I spread a cloth over the dying grass, still damp with dew.

"You were saying your husband takes full responsibility for the breach of peace?" inquired one of the ladies, whom I thought to be the wife of Arthur's foster brother, Kay.

"Yes," Lyonesse said as she arranged herself on the blanket. "He sees now that it was through his fault that the misguided girl left. He really was hard on her—treating her like a servant simply because she was foreign, with no regard to her nobility whatsoever. It is a shame really; she could have prospered under a more charitable hand. I cannot tell you how many times over the years I said to him, 'My lord, do you not think we should accept her as a daughter and treat her with the respect accorded to her station?' But he nearly took my head off at the very suggestion."

The ladies who had gathered around Lyonesse tittered disapprovingly. I busied myself with unpacking the supplies so that my tongue would not be tempted to set her straight. As usual, she was projecting her own harsh actions onto her innocent husband.

"I tried my best to instruct her." The drama built in Lyonesse's voice as she continued. "I think she was coming along until that Pictish brute darkened our door. Oh, how he had us all fooled—a demon wrapped in the guise of an angel! I told Pellinor that had he not placed all of his attention on Elaine and Galen during that time, the girl would not have acted so rashly, but he refuses to see it."

Of course, Lyonesse refused to call Isolde by her name, and I bristled in response. She continued to disrespect her even now.

Lyonesse sighed sorrowfully. "All the poor girl ever wanted was a father, and not finding one within our walls, she took flight with the devil. I doubt God will have much mercy on her soul in her homeland, filled as it is with the stench of pagan lies."

"All you can do is pray for her soul," one of the women replied earnestly.

At that I nearly lost my composure and dropped the basket I was carrying. Lyonesse turned and regarded me coldly, but only Elaine was able to see my face. I had thought her still cross with me, especially on this subject, but to my surprise, she smiled in empathy.

"And then there is the matter of the treaty," Lyonesse continued. "I doubt her people will see it as we do. It was not a sign of antagonism on our part. We had nothing to do with the actions of a disturbed child. We have sent word to them that we still desire peace, but I dread to think what such a breach of charity will do to this house."

Yes, Lyonesse, make the entire situation about yourself. You always do.

Disgusted with the turn of events, I sneaked into the woods. I could listen no more to the lies that Lyonesse crafted as naturally as breathing. The sad thing was that over the past year, I had come to learn she truly believed what she said; no amount of testimony to the contrary would convince her that reality was different from what she had fixed in her mind. Therefore, she was an angel of mercy, her husband an unrepentant sinner, her daughter an innocent victim, and I of no consequence.

I followed the sound of the hunt north, the rumble of the horses and the baying of the hounds not far below. Now and again, I would catch sight of one of the men, a muted blue or burgundy cloak standing out against the dull bark of a dying tree or a patch of tangled bracken. Through the last of the season's leaves, I could see my father's hair, still bright despite a generous dusting of gray, standing out from the others. He was laughing and talking with Lot. My stomach fluttered in anticipation of what they could possibly be discussing.

With a whoop and a sudden thunder of hooves, Arthur, Aggrivane, Gawain, Kay, and Pellinor took off ahead of the others, following the trail of Kay's falcon, who was dutifully stalking their prey from the sky. As I ran to keep up with them on a parallel path, I kicked at what I thought to be a stone in the grass, only to feel a squish and a slight wetness at my toe as my boot made contact with a half-rotted apple. Cursing, I dragged my foot along the grass to clean my shoe and noticed more fruit lying on the ground. Looking up, I discovered I had stumbled upon a small copse of apple trees.

Below, the quintet of hunters slowed. I wasn't sure if they were just listening or had lost the trail. I swung myself up into one of the trees to watch them, a habit my body happily remembered from Avalon. Smiling, I recalled many afternoons spent among the branches of kin to these fragrant trees with my sisters, all of us young girls with heads full of faerie tales and dreams.

When Aggrivane removed the bow from his shoulder, I realized my dreams were coming true. If our parents were discussing what I suspected, tonight we would be able to announce our intentions publicly.

A snap reverberated through the trees, and the king's horse shifted nervously. Arthur calmed the beast and cocked his head to one side, signaling to the others to remain silent. The snap came again, followed by several smaller cracks; each seemed to be closer than the last. I listened intently, holding my breath along with the hunters.

"Guinevere! There you are."

I started and clung to the branch overhead to keep from falling. I looked down. Elaine stood at the base of the tree.

"Elaine! You startled me." My heart was pounding.

"Sorry. I saw you leave the camp and was wondering where you went. May I join you?"

"Certainly." I warily extended a hand and helped pull up her small frame onto the branch opposite me. What were her motives? As far as I knew, she was still mad at me, in spite of her earlier smile.

She rummaged in her pouch. "I almost forgot. This is for you." She handed me a small roll of vellum. "I thought you may want it, and I surely have no need of it."

I unrolled the paper slowly, uncertain what it might contain. Staring back at me was a startlingly life-like charcoal drawing of Isolde. Elaine's talent was rare for one of our people, who preferred spiraling, abstract images with no clear beginning or ending. But Elaine favored her Roman tutors in this regard, drawing in a classical style that, should her parents ever see evidence of it, would surely see her punished for putting undue emphasis on human images. By offering one of her drawings to me, Elaine was giving me the power to betray her, should I choose.

I looked up at her, speechless. I had seen drawings like this before, lining the walls of her bedroom—which no one but Isolde and I ever entered, and even then in defiance of Pellinor's orders. Most of those were images from her imagination, scenes from the epic poems of the bards. I had no idea she had been drawing us.

I suppose this means she's forgiven me for whatever role she thinks I played in Galen's escape.

Elaine was never one to offer an overt apology when she realized she'd done wrong. She preferred some small gesture of amity. I recalled a time when, as young girls, we quarreled over which of us had more royal blood and she had called my mother a series of dishonorable names she could have only learned from her mother's lips, insulting me by association. She hadn't apologized then either, just showed up the next morning with a fistful of daisies, which she thrust at me, all enmity forgotten.

"Thank you," I finally croaked, still shocked at her peace offering.

Elaine giggled and settled herself against the hollow of the branches as if nothing had ever transpired between us. "This reminds me of when we were little."

Elaine's cheerful disposition today was one in a series of fluctuating moods she had displayed in the past few months. They ranged from the bitter rage and pain she had displayed when yelling at me to such joyful optimism that I began to wonder if she had taken to drinking. No one could predict her humor; it changed with the wind, often oscillating severely in the course of a single day. She had always been a moody child, given to fits of temper, but never in such extreme.

"Do you remember the time we followed those two merchants out of town?" she asked, swinging her legs merrily.

I laughed, seeing clearly in my mind's eye younger versions of ourselves stowed away on the back of a cart. One of the merchants had a son whom we both fancied. Our plan had been to ride along unnoticed until the merchants stopped at an inn for the night. What we were going to do then, I could not recall. I doubt we had thought things through that far.

"We made it nearly to the next town before we were discovered. We are just lucky the merchants were friends with your father—who knows what could have happened to us." I shivered at the thought. "I thought your father was going to kill us when we turned up back at Corbenic at twilight."

"I think my rump is still sore!" Elaine exclaimed, rubbing her backside at the memory.

"It is not half of what we deserved."

In the valley below, the rest of the hunters caught up with Arthur's party. They seemed to be discussing what to do next.

"Guinevere, can I tell you something?"

"You can tell me anything. You know that," I said absently, plucking an apple off the branch next to my head.

When Elaine did not speak, I looked up. She was wringing her hands again. I raised my eyebrows, willing her to speak whatever was vexing her.

"I—I am not sure where to begin, how to say—" she stammered.

I bit into the apple. "Just say it, Elaine."

"I think I have met my husband."

Her words tumbled over each other so fast I had to take a moment to decipher what she said. I stopped chewing. "Tell me more."

Elaine's face was as scarlet as her dress. "Please do not think me mad, but last autumn, I was in my room praying and I happened to glance over at my mirror. The light from one of the candles caught the edge of the metal, and there was this bright spark. Then it seemed to me that a face was staring back at me." She stared off in the distance, her face placid with the memory. "I could not see him clearly, but his face shone like the sun, his eyes the color of the sea. At first, I thought it was an angel, but then I was given to understand that this man was real and that he was coming for me. Guinevere, he is the man of the prophecy."

She turned to me, her eyes lit up like a child seeing a beloved relative return safely from war.

So Isolde was serious about that. I had to respond carefully. One wrong word and she might crack, spiraling into tumult as easily as she now shone. I made sure my voice was measured and even.

"Dear heart, are you sure you were not imagining things? Or mistook your own reflection? Perhaps you fell asleep and were dreaming."

"I wondered that too. But then Galen appeared. For a long time I thought he was the one. I kept trying to reconcile his face with the image in my mind, but something did not fit right. Then when he disappeared, I knew my instincts had been right. He was not the one. But then I saw him again—the man from my vision—at the tournament."

Oh no, I think I know where this is leading. The flower. That's why she gave him the flower. I swallowed my mouth full of fruit and lowered my head, looking up at her. "And who was that?" I asked, knowing full well the answer she would give.

"Lancelot, the man who won the tournament." She looked sheepish now, much younger than her years. "On impulse, I sent one of my maids to him with a blossom from my coronet. I know it was not much, but I wanted him to have a reason to remember me."

I nodded, pretending to understand, wondering what the best approach was to take with her. "No wonder you were so upset when he refused the position in Arthur's house. Have you any idea where he went after that?"

She shook her head slowly. She was gazing off over the treetops again. "He probably took to the road again. He said he likes being a nomad warrior, remember? But he will come for me. Someday he will proudly take my hand, and my heart."

There was a sudden commotion from the hunting party below, and we both jumped. The dogs were baying again, chasing an animal up the hill not far ahead of where we sat. The men abandoned their horses, scrambling after the dogs on foot up the rocky terrain.

Elaine and I looked at each other. If we started running now, we would cross their path in little time. We leaped down from the tree and took off in the direction of the hunt. Excitement escaped from my heart as a whoop of joy as we ran.

Soon the shouts of men were nearby and we slowed to a walk, not wanting to disrupt the hunt or spook the animal.

I was still trying to understand all that Elaine had said. "So if you know this man—Lancelot—will return, why do you sound so worried? What is there to fear?"

"The problem is that my maid overheard Arthur and my father discussing a dowry last night." She grabbed onto my arm, forcing me to halt. "Guinevere, I think the king is going to ask me to marry him!"

I considered that. Arthur had been paying a lot of attention to Elaine, and Pellinor had looked very pleased with himself lately. If the king was planning to leave soon, it would only stand to reason he would take his future wife home with him. It also would explain the hunt and tonight's feast.

I blinked, unable to resist the grin the thought brought with it. "Elaine, I think you are right. Forget about the shadows of the past and things that have yet to be. Do you understand what this means? You are going to be queen!"

"Do you really think so?" Her expression flickered from uncertain to one of serious consideration. "Queen." She repeated the word like it was foreign on her tongue. "It is certainly a higher rank than I ever imagined." Then she laughed. "Perhaps I was wrong. Maybe *this* is my fate. My mother is going to be so proud!"

⁕

We met up with the hunting party before they crossed the ford. Pellinor and Arthur were walking at the head, chortling at some joke we had missed. Elaine curtsied to both.

"Come, daughter, walk with us," Pellinor invited, wrapping an arm around her.

I gave her an encouraging smile.

Lot and my father followed, once again in deep conversation. To my delight, my father paused to embrace me before continuing on. I considered that a very good sign.

As I passed on down the line, I met Kay and Gawain, who were carrying the deer, which was tied to a log by its front and back legs. A line of knights followed, merrily singing a common drinking song. No one noticed that Aggrivane and I lagged at the rear, quietly holding hands behind our backs.

"Have you spoken with your father?" I asked, keeping my voice as low as possible.

"I have." Aggrivane grinned, tilting his head in so our foreheads touched. "He reiterated his support and said he would confirm this with your father."

"Did he?" I bit my lower lip in anticipation of his answer.

"He said an announcement would be made at the celebration tonight."

I stifled a squeal by stealing a quick kiss and then made sure the proper distance was between us in case anyone thought to glance back. It took every bit of control I could muster to keep from skipping back to the castle.

⋅⊗⋅⊗⋅

Corbenic had never seen such a feast.

As we dressed for the evening, Elaine ran in and out of the room, peeking down over the balcony every few minutes and keeping me up-to-date with constant status reports.

"Oh, Guinevere, you should see the flowers! I've never seen so many blooms in one place before. They are practically raining from the ceiling," she said breathlessly, as her maid caught her by the arm, forcing her to stand still.

"She will soon enough if you stay in one place long enough for me to dress you," her maid said sharply.

When we finally arrived in the hall, I gasped. Elaine had been right. While we were away, the servants had done a spectacular job decorating the hall for the farewell celebration for the king. Brightly colored autumn leaves, gourds, berries, and flowers of every shade lined every available surface and candles glittered merrily in between.

Lyonesse sat at the high table, looking out across the hall filled with revelers. She was practically purring with delight. Her daughter had been given a place of honor next to Arthur and was now engaging him in what appeared to be delightful conversation. Her husband sat on Elaine's other side and Lyonesse next to him. She looked every inch the queen tonight.

As a ward of Pellinor's household, I had the fortune of being seated only two places to the left of Arthur. My father sat between us, Kay and Arthur's other companions following on down the line.

Kay had just begun to recite an amusing poem one of the court bards had created about one of their less graceful courtiers when my father gently touched my elbow. He nodded toward Arthur, who stood, goblet in hand.

The room fell silent by degrees as people took note of their king.

"I would like to thank Lord Pellinor for his gracious hospitality over the last several moons. I and my court placed an unexpected burden on him by coming here and then staying longer than expected, so this feast is more than I could ever have asked from anyone. You have been a most cordial host, and your generosity will long be remembered." He raised his cup to Pellinor. "Long life and many blessings to you, friend."

I repeated the toast with the rest of the assembly and drained my glass.

Arthur smiled and gazed out over the crowd. "As many of you know, there is a tradition among the people of this land that when the king partakes in a hunt, the head of the stag is awarded to the fairest lady. In this court, I find many worthy candidates, but my decision is clear."

A trio of servants wheeled out the stag's head, dressed as a trophy and adorned with chrysanthemums and garlands of rosebuds. A golden chain was wound between its horns, and from it dangled a sparkling emerald the size of a man's eye.

"Elaine of Corbenic, please do me the honor of accepting this token of your king's appreciation. Your kindness has touched my heart. I swear you will never be forgotten."

Arthur took Elaine's hand and raised her to her feet. He removed the jewel from its perch and secured it around her neck.

The crowd erupted in applause, and Elaine blushed in response.

Arthur kissed the top of her hand gently before helping her back to her seat.

As the servants began to serve the main course, I caught Aggrivane's eye. He was sitting at a lower table with his father and brothers. He smiled and winked at me, and butterflies took flight in my stomach. Tonight would be something grand.

We ate heartily, the fallen deer providing some of the best meat I had ever tasted, succulent and tender, perfectly paired with sweet squash, savory salads, and other late-autumn delights.

Throughout the meal, Elaine, more jovial and outgoing than I had ever seen her, held Arthur's attention. Her sapphire eyes, accentuated by the color of her gown, sparkled invitingly, and I was not surprised that Arthur could not tear himself away.

Only once did he look in my direction, a stolen glance that first was directed at my father, then lingered on me. I was transfixed. The power and grace that emanated from the king was palpable. I could do little but stare and drop my gaze shyly to the table when he finally looked away.

By the time the plates were cleared, my face was flushed with joy, and I was feeling the effects of the wine. For once, I partook with abandon, letting it carry away my cares on a current of heady optimism. Kay kept me in stitches throughout the meal with an endless stream of humorous remarks about everyone and everything and showed little signs of stopping. He had even managed to procure my permission for a dance later in the evening.

Amid the buzz of conversation, Arthur stood again. Someone rapped on the underside of the table, and silence fell over the hall.

"I promise, this is the last time tonight you will have to listen to me speak," Arthur said.

A smattering of laughter followed.

"Many of you have made it quite clear you feel it is time for me to take a wife. I tell you tonight that I have decided to take your advice."

Another murmur rippled through the crowd as everyone looked around, wondering who the lucky woman could be. Many eyes were fixed on Elaine, who looked like she would faint. Next to her, Lyonesse was practically bursting with anticipation.

"The woman I have chosen is not someone many of you know well, as she has modestly kept to herself these many years. But in exchange for a service I would freely render to any of my subjects, her father has offered me the most valuable of gifts, his only unmarried daughter. I believe she is well prepared to lead our land in these uncertain times and can influence those I cannot. I will admit that until recently, I was unaware such a creature of beauty and learning existed in our midst, but from the moment I saw her at the tournament, I knew I wanted her to be my queen."

My father squeezed my hand, and I looked at him, confused. Out of the corner of my eye, I saw Lot lean in toward Aggrivane and whisper something in his ear. Aggrivane's face went white and he started to rise, but Lot held him fast.

I was still watching them when Arthur's words reached my ears.

"Guinevere of Northgallis, will you do me the honor of becoming my wife?"

The world slowed. I could hardly believe what I had heard. *Me? Didn't he mean to ask Elaine? There must be some mistake.*

Frantic, I looked to my father for reassurance. He grasped both of my hands and was grinning broadly.

No, there must be an explanation. Service? What service? Oh no. No. No. No. Arthur was not referring to the counsel he gave Pellinor, but to saving my father's life. I am repayment of his debt. No, this cannot be happening.

My eyes darted to Elaine, who sat frozen in shock, a single tear dripping down her cheek. Lyonesse stared at me, murderous hatred naked in her expression.

In that instant, I could almost hear the response that was expected—nay, required—repeated in the thoughts of the hundreds of onlookers.

I scanned the room for Aggrivane, to plead with him to do something to make this madness stop, but he was already gone. All I could see were the expectant expressions of my father and Arthur. I was alone in this trap, and there was but one way out. My response was not a choice but rather the submission of one already condemned.

My lips said yes, and cheers erupted all around.

I beamed back at my betrothed, but inside my heart was screaming, *I am so sorry, Aggrivane.*

As the commotion continued, I prayed my false expression would hold and not betray the anguish in my heart. All of my hopes and dreams had fled with Aggrivane, along with my freedom. Though others saw me as a fortunate woman, I felt like little more than a prisoner, transferred from one dungeon to another. I knew almost nothing of this man who was to be my husband, and yet I was supposed to happily accept him. My heart rebelled in painful spasms. To marry without love was to embrace the cold emptiness of the tomb, only without the sweet release of death.

I looked around the room with trepidation, suddenly realizing my assent to be Arthur's wife meant more than the loss of my maidenhood. If Arthur willed it, I would become high queen, and these people, my subjects. With a jolt of alarm, I realized Argante had predicted this very moment when I stood before her as a mere girl hoping for acceptance to Avalon.

Another crown sits on her brow, she had said, or rather the Goddess through her.

Part of me wanted to collapse in the rushes, to beat my fists on the floor like a petulant child and wail at the injustice done to me. But I had made a vow when I became a priestess that I would follow the Lady's will, no matter where it led. If she wished me to be with this man, then I had even less choice than I had imagined.

I squared my shoulders and took a deep breath before gliding to Arthur's side, arranging my expression into one of pleasant shock. I felt nothing but distain for him—and for my father—for treating me like a brood mare, but I could not let that show. There would be plenty of time for confrontation later, in private. Now, I had to play the part of the future queen.

Tentatively, I took Arthur's hand, and he stepped back, presenting me to the assembly. Avoiding the malevolent glares of Lyonesse and Elaine, I lifted my head high and willed the power of priestesshood to emanate from me. This might not have been my choice, but it was my destiny, and I was going to face it on my own terms.

CAMELOT'S QUEEN

BOOK TWO OF GUINEVERE'S TALE

PART ONE

Fledgeling

Chapter One

Winter 497

The sigh of a reed pen across parchment, one jagged line of ink. That was all it took to betray my king and myself.

My signature, made with trembling hands, may have made me Arthur Pendragon's wife, but it couldn't change my heart. He'd asked for my assent to this marriage, and I gave it, but it was a lie.

Marrying him was my duty. That much I had resigned myself to in the two months since Arthur proposed, shattering my dreams of a life with Aggrivane of Lothian.

I watched with hollow detachment from my place next to Arthur as our marriage contract was sealed in the snowy courtyard of the old Roman fort of Carlisle, the stronghold of Arthur's father, the previous high king, Uther.

Arthur stood facing my father, back to the gate of the castle. His breaths were small puffs of white in the frosty air. "King Leodgrance of Gwynedd, by the signing of this contract, I bind myself to you and your kin through the hand of your daughter, Guinevere. As proof of my fidelity, I bestow upon you the price of her honor." Arthur extended a wooden box of coins, ornately wrought gold brooches, and jewels—my bride-price, the money that assured Arthur's sincere backing of our union but which would become mine should we ever part ways.

"I thank you, Your Majesty," my father said with a humble bow. "You are now my son as well. My gift to you is a symbol of my tribe, the people who are your most loyal servants."

My father held out his hand, and a servant placed the reins of a bridle into them. He passed them to Arthur. At the other end was a coal-black steed, a reminder of the days when brides were sold for cattle or land rather than gold. The stallion was muscular and strong but calm, indicating he was well trained and would be a valuable addition to Arthur's growing cavalry.

Arthur handed the reins to one of his attendants and clapped my father on the shoulder. "All of Britain is indebted to you for the most precious gift of your daughter, who, in a moment, will become our queen. I thank you for giving her into my care."

My eyes welled with stinging tears. To anyone in the assembled crowd, I likely appeared overwhelmed now that the deed was done, but my heart burned with a mix of emotions. Some small part of me knew this was the same transaction that would have taken place had I married Aggrivane as I'd intended, but my heart said this was all wrong. I should have been standing next to a man I loved, one with whom I couldn't wait to share my life, not the stranger who had stolen my dreams.

But those were the ruminations of a lovesick, petulant girl, not a level-headed ruler. As Merlin approached me with a pot of fragrant rose oil in one hand, the crown of Britain in the other, I forced myself to think like the high queen I was about to become. I was married to the High King of Britain, a position most women would kill for, and I'd had to do nothing to obtain it thanks to my father's willingness to use me as payment of his life-debt to the king.

I glanced at Arthur. His kind gaze held not a hint of temper or malice; he would not abuse me. Plus, he was allowing me to be crowned queen instead of simply naming me his royal wife, which meant we would rule as equals. Those facts had to be enough to trump whatever hurt and pain I still felt. Besides, though I would never openly admit it, part of me wanted to be high queen. I had been raised to rule and govern, and now I had a chance beyond my wildest imaginings.

I fell to one knee before Merlin, touching my right thumb to my forehead, lips, and heart—the sign of Avalon—in acknowledgement of his office as Archdruid.

Merlin's smile reflected our long friendship, forged from my years in Avalon under the tutelage of the Lady of the Lake. He leaned in close, his voice soft in my ear as he said, "No one is more deserving of this role than you. But take care your heart does not lead you astray."

I pulled back, regarding Merlin quizzically. I had no idea what he meant. For a moment, his eyes held the glassy, faraway look of prophecy, then he blinked, and it was gone. Before I could be sure

I had really seen it, Merlin turned away as though nothing had ever passed between us.

To the waiting crowd, he proclaimed, "Guinevere of Northgallis, priestess of Avalon, and now wife to High King Arthur Pendragon in accordance with his will, this day I anoint you High Queen of Britain."

Bowing, I willed myself not to shake, though my legs felt as if they would give way beneath me.

"May you be blessed with purity of mind and judgment by the Maiden"—he anointed my hair—"with love of your people from the Mother"—he drew small, sticky shapes on my cheeks—"and with the wisdom of the Crone"—he covered my hands in the warm oil—"and may she of a thousand names bless you and keep you always."

He placed the glittering circlet upon my head, secured a heavy braided metal torque around my neck, and knelt. "May I be the first to pledge my loyalty to you, High Queen Guinevere."

The crowd genuflected as one with a soft rustling of furs and other fine materials.

Arthur came and stood by my side, taking my gloved hand. Loudly enough to be heard by all, he said, "These are your people, my lady. From this day forth, they are in your care. You are my equal in war as in peace. Will you fight by my side to defend their honor with your person and your very life?"

The full weight of responsibility was a stone in my stomach as I looked over the bowed heads of Britain's nobility—the kings and queens of our thirteen kingdoms and countless tribes—along with Arthur's most trusted warriors and advisors. A flurry of movement caught my eye, and I glanced over just in time to catch my father yanking Father Marius, his confessor and advisor, to his knees. The pious troll had never borne me any affection. In fact, he had tried to ruin my life a few years earlier, so seeing him forced to prostrate himself before me gave me no small pleasure.

I turned my gaze back to Arthur. "I will. From this moment on, I honor and care for them as I would my own children, for they are children of the gods. I am privileged to lead them."

A cheer went up, growing louder as the group rose to their feet. In a moment, they would come forth one by one to pledge their allegiance to me, but there was one thing left for me to do—our union must be sealed with a kiss.

I turned to Arthur. My stomach clenched as I looked into his deep blue eyes. I saw naught of malice, only affection and hope—hope for the future of Britain, for us. As our lips met for the first time, I told myself the past was done. What mattered now was our future and the future of our kingdom.

⁕

As the sun set on the old Roman fort, nobility from across the country and emissaries from all of the surrounding lands toasted our health and welfare. Arthur and I were seated above the rest, on a dais at the center of a long table. Our families trailed off like ribbons on either side.

The hours sped by in a haze of ale, music, laughter, and good cheer. Dish after dish of delicacies were placed before us and removed, finely dressed pheasant giving way to fish in pungent sauces, roasted boar with herbs followed by sweetmeats, candied nuts, and baked apples. All the while, wine and ale flowed freely—so freely some even said the fountain in the courtyard dedicated to the god of victory spurted wine in our honor.

Amid the clatter of plates as courses changed, Isolde, heir to the throne of Ireland and my dearest friend, came to my side and embraced me tightly.

"See, I told you my queen would bring you good fortune," she teased, referring to her piece from the game of Holy Stones we'd played on and off for over a year.

I reached into the pouch beneath my gown and retrieved the gleaming red orb. "Is this occasion enough to return it to you, or do you wish to win it back?" I held it out to her on my open palm.

She considered for a moment, green eyes dancing with mirth. "I believe you have better things to do tonight." As though the implication in her voice were not enough, she threw a longing look at Arthur. "It is my turn to be jealous, I suppose."

My elbow caught her ribs just as she snatched up the stone. "Speaking of jealousy, how is Galen?" Galen was the one-time betrothed of our friend Elaine whose heart Isolde had broken when she ran away to Ireland with him.

She rolled her eyes and sighed. "It is far too long a story to relate tonight, but I will tell you this—I knew what I was doing when I agreed to let him come with me. He has proven to be valuable leverage for my family."

Slightly fearful of her thirst for justice, I wondered what fate she planned for him.

She read my expression and continued, "I have plans that will benefit both his country and mine."

I shook my head, in awe of her determination and strategy. "You are a formidable ruler already, and the crown has not even passed to you yet."

She flashed her impish smile. "I learned young it is never too early to read your allies and enemies and uncover what each one most needs. If you can provide it or deny it, you hold the power." Her gaze flickered across the room to the lanky, fair-haired warrior called Tristan. I remembered him from the tournament as part of the house of Cornwall. "Speaking of which, I have allies to make."

I wasn't sure if she meant politically or personally. Knowing Isolde, it was probably both. We gazed at each other for a long moment, knowing we likely wouldn't see one another again before she returned home.

"I will write as often as possible. You will make a great queen." She squeezed my hand and glanced at Arthur. "Do yourself a favor. Forget about what is past and enjoy the role fate has given you." She arched an eyebrow. "I certainly would."

Her laugher trailed behind her, and I couldn't help but echo it.

Arthur turned toward me. "This is the happiest I have seen you since the night we were betrothed," he said, sounding slightly astounded.

I dropped my gaze to my lap, embarrassed. "Isolde brings out the best in me."

Arthur raised my chin softly with his finger. "If the roles were different and I could have her at court, I would command it in a heartbeat, if only to see more of your beautiful smile."

I blushed, uncertain what to say. Since our betrothal, we had been under the same roof less than two weeks, so the awkward tension of strangers had yet to melt into familiarity.

I fidgeted with the torque encircling my neck. Made of intricately twisted strands of gold, silver, and copper, it was the symbol that proclaimed me queen to all who held to our people's beliefs; the crown I wore was mere pageantry. Tipped on one end with a highly polished black lodestone and on the other with an opaque orb of moonstone, it was a constant reminder of the light and dark responsibilities of queenship while also acting as a conduit to the wisdom of the gods.

I lifted one of the finials from the skin I was convinced it was bruising. "Please tell me we don't have to wear these every day."

His gaze followed my hand, and he smiled. "Only on formal occasions." He adjusted the weight for me.

We were so intent on each other neither of us noticed a visitor had approached until she spoke. "Patience, brother. You'll have time enough later for undressing your new bride."

We both looked up, startled, into the placid eyes of Ana of Lothian, Arthur's older sister. Her expression was playful.

"I swore my loyalty to Guinevere earlier, and now I would like to offer you both my love." She fixed her gaze on me. "And my apologies. I am truly sorry for the circumstances surrounding your engagement. If I had known your intentions—"

Arthur's brow wrinkled. "Ana, what are you apologizing for?"

My eyes snapped to him, and I searched his face for some hint of malevolence or deception, some indication this was a cruel joke. But all I found was genuine confusion.

"You didn't know." The words were a gasp, hardly above a whisper as they escaped my lips. I'd assumed he was aware of the circumstances but had simply done as he pleased. This turn of events shook my perception of him, prodding my reluctant heart toward compassion.

Ana covered her mouth with her hand. "I thought—I thought for sure you knew, that Leodgrance told you and you overruled him." She looked at the floor, unable to face either of us. "Guinevere and my son Aggrivane pledged their troth shortly before you asked for her hand. My husband was supposed to secure her father's consent, but you succeeded first."

Arthur looked between Ana and me, surely searching for something in my eyes to confirm or refute her words. Then his gaze became distant, as though he was envisioning his own stolen future.

A moment later, he gave me a sorrowful look. "I did not know. I am sorry. I do not ask your forgiveness, for an offense of such a nature will take a long time to heal, but I beg you to try not to hold this misunderstanding against me."

I looked at Ana, pleading with her to give me a sign or tell me what to say, but her gaze was still on floor, her cheeks flushed with embarrassment. So this was to be my first test. How would I respond to an impossible request without anyone to guide me?

I cleared my throat before placing my hand on Arthur's and giving him a soft smile, just as a queen should. "Of course I forgive you, husband. It was a tragic misunderstanding but one that brought us to this night. Let us dwell not on it but enjoy our feast."

Those pretty words were required of me. In my heart, shock, confusion, and misery warred. I had no idea which one would win out.

⚬⚭ ⚭⚬

The long meal finished, our guests reveled in earnest. Musicians filled the hall with lively song while jugglers, bards, and entertainers of every ilk roamed among the guests, delighting and mystifying them with colorful tricks and witty verse. The tables were pushed against the walls to create an ample dance floor, which quickly filled with tipsy couples.

Arthur led me into a lively round where we stayed side by side for most of the dance. Something had been bothering me since our conversation with Ana, and I took advantage of the situation to unburden myself.

"Arthur, if you intended to ask me to be your wife, why did you award the stag's head to Elaine?"

His expression showed he thought the answer was obvious. "Pellinor was my host; I could not insult him. Besides, he is a valuable subject."

"I thought you were going to ask her to marry you."

He laughed. "So did almost everyone else. Perhaps I was a little too charming, but she is a sweet girl and thrived on my attention. What was I supposed to do, warn her ahead of time?"

I narrowed my eyes at him. "A hint would have been polite. The poor girl was crushed." Arthur grunted, and I glanced around his shoulder at Pellinor, who certainly didn't appear upset that his daughter had been passed over. "Her father looks to be quite recovered from the disappointment."

Arthur winked at me. "Gold cures most ills, trust me."

The song ended, and we milled among the crowd, accepting even more well-wishes. Within a few minutes, I felt as if the false smile I had maintained all day would stiffen and set, as permanent as the crescent mark of Avalon on my brow.

A young couple approached us, and my stomach twisted. He was Lord Malegant of the Summer Country. I had learned his identity when he pledged his fealty to me during my coronation. Then I had been dazzled by his handsomeness, but all night something had needled at me, a tiny voice insisting I had seen him before.

Malegant was tall and muscular, wavy dark blond hair tied at the base of his neck with a royal blue cord identical to his cloak. His skin was ruddy with drink. He led a small woman by the arm—a child really, perhaps all of fourteen—and gracefully maneuvered her in front of him as they reached us. She dipped into a low curtsey, and he bowed.

"Well met, Lord Malegant." Arthur clapped him on the shoulder.

"My king, allow me to introduce my wife, Fiona."

Fiona raised her head, revealing amazingly large hazel eyes. "I am honored to be in your presence, my lord." She smiled shyly at me and added, "Yours as well, my lady."

Malegant took my hand and kissed it, his slight beard gazing my skin. "Your Majesty." His eyes glinted with a look that was truly magnetic.

With a sharp intake of breath, I realized I knew that look, and the memory came flooding back.

It was during my third year in Avalon, before I had attained priestesshood. Normally I wouldn't have been allowed on the other side of the mists, but one of the marsh women had gone into early labor and I was asked to accompany one of the priestesses as her assistant midwife.

I had been standing on the shore of the lake, waiting for my companion to finish her business inside, when he emerged from one of the little huts at the base of the Tor. I'd expected to see one of the wild hermits who were part of the community of Joseph of Arimathea, but instead this well-groomed noble fixed his irresistible eyes upon me. I remembered thinking I would melt and be swept away by the waters of the lake.

When I described him to my priestess companion, she knew immediately who he was and warned me in a motherly tone to stay far away from him. He was known to cause trouble for women, especially those vowed to the isle, she said. But I never understood why because she refused to say more.

But before I could speak, Malegant led the doe-eyed girl away, his hand clasped just a little too tightly around her arm. Caught up in my own thoughts, I had missed the whole conversation plus any opportunity to find out more about the Lord of the Summer Country. Uriens called Arthur's name, and my husband excused himself.

I was heading back to my chair, still wrapped up in half-remembered rumors about Malegant's questionable reputation, when a voice stopped me in my tracks.

"Well, well," it said.

I could almost see the catlike smile in the lilting voice. It was a sound straight out of my nightmares. I knew the speaker even before I turned. "Hello, Morgan," I said as cheerily as I could manage.

We regarded one another coldly, each taking the other's measure. She was little changed, the candlelight making her skin glow and highlighting the crescent mark of a priestess on her forehead. Wherever she had fled couldn't have given her too hard a life.

She settled into a mock curtsy. "Your Majesty." She nearly choked on the words.

I gave her a triumphant smile. "Last I heard, you slipped Avalon's guard and went missing. What ill star directs you to darken this happy occasion?"

Morgan shook her head and clicked her tongue disapprovingly. "Still bitter about being second best, I see."

"You know my role, yet you dare call me second best?"

She was nonplussed by my outrage, which only irritated me more. "I've always been better at understanding the will of the Goddess than you."

I sucked in air to reply, but then I noticed how her hand hovered protectively over her abdomen, which, now that I looked closely, was swollen. She was pregnant.

I tried to cover my astonishment. "And whom did the Goddess direct you to marry? Or do you just rut like a sow and see who the child most resembles?"

Morgan's smile was indulgent, as if she was dealing with an especially simple child, but her tone was frosty, biting. "My husband is Uriens of Rheged, brother-in-law to the king. Welcome to the family, Guinevere."

⁕

I plopped down in my chair with a huff, mind still reeling from Morgan's revelation. An orphan who did not know her lineage had managed to infiltrate the highest levels of Briton nobility—and now she was my sister by marriage. That meant I would be spending much more time in her presence, no doubt the subject of her constant conniving. I'd thought I left that behind when we parted ways in Avalon, but the Goddess had willed us together again whether I liked it or no.

Sensing my displeasure, my life-long attendant, Octavia, flitted to my side and replaced my cup with a fresh one. I smiled, grateful for her constant concern and friendship. I brought the cup to my lips, intending to drain it in one gulp, but the sharp smell stopped me. It was unlike any wine or ale I had ever encountered, nor was it cloying like mead. I sniffed it warily, its bitter bouquet stinging my nose.

Octavia saw my confusion. "It is a drink from your mother's native land. Some of the Votadini ambassadors brought it to toast your queenship. You *are* one of them after all. Your father and some of the knights are partaking of it liberally in the adjoining room—and enjoying themselves immensely, I might add."

I raised an eyebrow at her and took a slip. It was bitter but slid smoothly down my throat, its peppery tail burning like a comet. I shuddered, intending to push the cup away. But the warmth that followed made me reconsider. This strange drink heated me from the inside out, making me feel comfortable for the first time all day, as though I was wrapped in my mother's old blanket. A few more sips and I barely remembered talking to Morgan or any of the pain of the last few months.

Lost in this tingling fog, I scarcely noticed when the crowd began to thin. Eventually Arthur returned to my side, a little worse for the wear. He was laughing and smelled of the same strange brew. I wondered when they had pulled him into the other room.

The tone of the music changed, becoming slow and sensual, and with it, the entire tenor of the room shifted. Now it felt more like a Beltane ritual than a wedding feast. Arthur's closest friends and many of his knights were teasing us, telling lewd jokes with base gestures that openly indicated what was to come. Soon the entire room descended into debauchery.

Kay was more than happy to fulfill his duty as Arthur's first man. When the appointed hour came, Kay wriggled his eyebrows at me, picked me up, and threw me over his shoulder, symbolically kidnapping me. He carried me into the bridal chamber as I flailed and screamed with laughter for him to put me down. His bravado faded, however, as soon as he set me on my feet. He took his leave with a stiff bow, but not before swatting me on the backside. I thought I heard him stifle a drunken giggle as he passed over the threshold.

Turning into the room, I froze. The bed, with its double-layer feather mattress, was finer than anything I had ever seen. The expensive sheets were strewn with rose petals and fertility herbs, and a bough of mistletoe hung over the pillows, prepared to receive the newlywed lovers.

Octavia slipped in to prepare me. She lovingly removed my clothes and bathed me in perfumed water, whispering advice and a few pointers I was embarrassed she knew. She clothed me in a simple white shift and quietly ducked out of the room, leaving me alone to wait for my husband.

I heard the horde of men even before the door opened to a chorus of whoops and whistles, and Arthur stumbled in, having been shoved by his enthusiastic friends.

"No listening in the hall," he called after them as the door closed and the lock clicked. He regarded me uncertainly, the firelight glinting off his freshly oiled chest.

Nervous laughter escaped my lips. "You look ready for a wrestling match."

Arthur lifted an eyebrow. "If that is how you would like it." He stepped closer and removed the chaplet of flowers from my hair. "And you are fit for a ritual, not a wedding bed."

"Is it not every man's dream to lie with the Goddess?" I teased, the drink making my tongue bold.

His face darkened, and he looked away, mumbling, "I prefer my partners mortal."

Silence stretched on for a few moments as we each tried to decide how to proceed. I finally decided to be honest with him, to tell him all the things building in my heart since the fateful night he had proposed. If the truth wasn't spoken now, it might not ever be.

"You really didn't know?" I asked, barely above a whisper.

"About Aggrivane?"

Arthur shook his head, watching me carefully. "If you had it to do over again, would you choose me?"

How could he even ask me such a question? He was the king. What was I going to say—no? "Would I have a choice?"

Arthur stepped toward me, hand outstretched. "Of course. You've always had a choice."

I stepped away from him. "Have I? You asked for my hand in front of the entire court of Dyfed, already having secured my father's agreement."

Arthur dropped his hand, balling it into a fist at his side. "Guinevere, I understand your pain. You are not the only one who has lost something. I had a completely different life before I became king—plans, dreams which will never be fulfilled. This is a duty I never asked for."

"Neither did I."

"But you're here now." His smile was tender.

Before I could respond, he leaned in and kissed me gently. Then he pulled back and searched my eyes as if looking for permission to continue.

My tension eased, shoulders sagging as I realized he was right. I was here now, with my husband. No matter what had come before, I'd made my promise to him. I had a duty now, to him and to my people. In answer to his questioning eyes, I kissed him back, with equal tenderness and no small amount of awkwardness.

He ran his hands over my hair, down my neck and shoulders, to my waist as our lips danced, gradually learning one another's pace and preferences. When his hands reached my hips, he removed my shift and lifted me effortlessly. We made love with the uncertainty of strangers, the act slowly forming a bond between us even as we struggled to find pleasure in our forced coupling.

When it was over, Arthur lay his head on my chest and his breathing slowed to the even pace of a dreamer. I kissed the top of his head.

"I suppose being married to you will not be so bad," I whispered before closing my eyes.

CHAPTER TWO

A week later, we set off for Camelot, Arthur's permanent home some miles west of Carlisle. We took the two-day journey at a leisurely pace but rose early on the third morning at Arthur's insistence. We arrived just as the eastern clouds were slowly breaking, the first light of dawn glowing rose and gold in their underbelly.

Arthur lowered my hood and kissed the top of my head, whispering into my hair, "Behold your kingdom, my queen."

My breath caught in my throat as we rounded a bend and the land ahead came into view. High above, on a lofty hill, a massive fortress made of gray stone held court. Its elegant square turrets reached like arms into the sky while graceful arches stretched across courtyards like limber sinews and glazed windows winked in the morning light.

This was nothing like the fortress I had called home as a child or even Pellinor's vast estate. Out of necessity, we had fortified our wooden palisades with stone, but it was not meant to enhance the appearance of our homes. This castle, on the other hand, with its ethereal beauty, looked as though it had grown right from the mountainside at the command of some otherworldly force. Some might say it looked like an imagining out of a bard's tale or an enchanted palace built by the fey, but to me, it was the star castle of the goddess Arianrhod, who rules the heavens.

My eyes followed the zigzagging line of ramparts separating the living quarters from the town, the town from the market, and the market from the military defenses. A burgeoning community spilled out from the castle's inmost walls in a patchwork of thatched and timber roofs. Along the sides of the road and in the main courtyard outside the castle gates, merchants stacked the last of the orchards' apples in precarious piles, butchers hung the remnants of their slaughtered charges in attractive displays while others arranged bas-kets, bread, and other wares in rows of stalls.

As trades were made, wagons rumbled through the outer gates and down to the docks on the edge of a large harbor. There, trade ships prepared to cross the waters to do business with the Caledonii, who lived on the distant northern shore. Miles away, the bay gave way to the Firth of Clyde, and the Firth melted into the sea.

The woodland through which we had passed embraced the entire area, stretching all the way from the shore to the farthest reaches behind the castle. As I took in the dense stands of wooly fir, emerald pine, and the shivering branches of oak and elm, I could scarcely believe this breathtaking place was real. Dizzily, I clung to Arthur, searching his face for some sign I was dreaming.

He merely smiled softly. "Welcome to Camelot, Guinevere."

⁂

We followed a hidden path to the castle and entered through a pri-vate side gate so as not to attract the attention of the townsfolk. There would be time to meet them later.

I couldn't help but crane my neck in awe, taking in the vaulted ceilings, towering columns, and Roman arches that defied nature as they held up massive stone blocks heavy enough to crush a man should they fall. Arthur led me through the maze of corridors into the heart of the castle.

"My father had long dreamed of a fortress to rival even the great-est built by Rome," Arthur explained, "one none of our enemies would dare attack."

I heard his voice but couldn't tear my eyes away to look at him. He didn't appear to mind, guiding me as patiently and gently as one leading the blind.

"He spent most of his life studying Roman and Greek architec-ture and even the engineering of the strange lands far to the east of Rome. This place was his life's work, but even had he lived one hun-dred years, he could not have completed this alone."

"He had Merlin's help," I said softly, as sure of that as I was of my own name.

I had seen Merlin's powers of persuasion firsthand. The Arch-druid had a way of convincing people to do his bidding, yet he left them with the certainty that it was their idea, that they had volunteered for whatever backbreaking task he had in mind.

"How many years did it take to build?" I looked at Arthur for the first time.

"Several decades from what Merlin has said. I was living with Lord Ector, so I know little of what occurred in the royal family before my father's death."

We stopped in a circular portico that stretched out beyond the main walls of the castle. Watching over it at even intervals were four giant statues, each several times larger than any mortal man.

"Your tribal gods?" I asked, thinking this room was a sort of shrine.

Arthur shook his head. "My family." He pulled a large golden ring from the smallest finger of his left hand and held it out for me to see. "This ring tells their story."

The band was thin, capped by a square with rounded corners. The square was divided into twelve triangles filled with smoky quartz. A large round sapphire dominated the center, braced at four corners by smaller blue stones. Encircling the whole was a wreath of ornately wrought gold resembling eight crescents of lace. At the center of each, capping the spokes of the triangles, was a large gold orb.

"It's beautiful," I exclaimed, holding the ring up and turning it this way and that in the sunlight.

Arthur nodded. "Indeed. It was hard won over many generations."

He took my hand and approached the first statue, a stoic man with sharp features and a hawklike stare. He wore a Roman toga, its dark gray marble nearly purple in the shadows, and a wreath of laurel was chiseled around his head.

"This is the Emperor Constantine the Third, my grandfather, the last Roman ruler of this isle. He was proclaimed emperor by the Britons, but he had quite a bit of trouble with your mother's people, I'm told," he said.

My mother had come from the Votadini, one of the four tribes who lived just north of Hadrian's Wall. "We don't enjoy being told what to do," I said matter-of-factly.

Arthur grinned. "So I've noticed." He pointed at the center stone in the ring. "This sapphire was part of the booty Constantine collected upon conquering the city of Arles, which was part of Gaul, southwest of Brittany. But at that point, it was only a stone."

"How did it come to be like this?" I asked, touching the ring and letting my hand rest on his.

"Ah, to answer that, I must introduce you to my uncle."

Passing a wide window that reached from floor to ceiling, we came to the next statue, a man with slightly gentler features and a pleasant expression. He held a book and a map.

"This is Aurelius Ambrosius, second eldest son of Constantine. Aurelius was considered a great diplomat, and he was the first to try to unite the ancient tribes. To a certain extent, he succeeded. Were it not for him, my father would not have been able to claim the title of high king."

"But Vortigern held the throne between Constantine and Aurelius, did he not?" I asked, turning from the statue to my husband.

Arthur was pleased. "They taught you well in Avalon." Then his face clouded, and he clenched his jaw, making a muscle jump. His eyes hardened, turning as cold as the marble statues. "The tyrant Vortigern..." Arthur exhaled. "He usurped the throne in the chaos surrounding Constantine's death. You see, Constantine's sons were too young to rule, so they fled to Brittany to seek safe haven, and Vortigern swooped in to fill the void. He was king of Powys at the time. Idiocy must run in the blood, for from what you tell me of your encounters with him, Vortigern's current progeny, Evrain, is no wiser than his great-grandfather. All Vortigern got in return was a knife in the gut, betrayed by the Saxons at his own peace council. Some say he died—"

"Others say he sleeps still under the mountains of Snowdonia," I whispered. In my mind's eye, the icy peaks rose to the north of my childhood home, and I recalled the fanciful tale that said Vortigern's breath melted the snows in spring each year. I also remembered it was he who had convinced my maternal grandfather to settle in Gwynedd, an act that eventually led to my mother marrying my father. Because of that, I was in some small measure happy Vortigern had had his moment of triumph.

Arthur interrupted my reverie by continuing his tale. "Vortigern's son, Vortimer, reigned for a few months before being poisoned, but I can promise you my family had no hand in that. We simply took back the title that was rightfully ours. Aurelius had the sapphire set in a brooch. The story goes that the triangles represent the ancient tribes, those who held the most power during Aurelius's time."

Arthur led me onward around the room. Another window, a twin of the first, separated Ambrosius from his brother. I looked up into features that bore a distinct resemblance to my husband's. I knew before Arthur even spoke that this was Uther Pendragon.

Arthur put an arm around me and gently urged me forward. "Father, may I present to you my wife, Guinevere of Northgallis."

Smiling with a mixture of embarrassment and admiration for my husband, I curtsied before the mute figure. "My lord, I only wish I could have met you in this world."

As I raised my head, I took in the image next to Uther, the only woman in the group. I recognized her immediately for I had met her only a short time before. This was Queen Iggraine. In her full regal regalia, strong and confident, she stood in stark contrast to the docile nun who had witnessed my marriage and coronation while shrouded in heavy black robes.

Arthur seemed to understand my musings. "My mother was a mighty queen, or so they tell me. She ruled her family's ancestral kingdom of Dyfnaint with her first husband, Goloris, for several years. When my sister was about seven or eight—I can't remember now—Uther visited Tintagel. As Ana tells it, Uther was smitten with my mother when he first laid eyes on her. I'm not sure how Ana could have known that at such a young age, but to this day she maintains her certainty.

"Uther called on Goloris and his men to help defend against the Saxons as they were pushing west from the old Regni lands and soon would threaten Dyfnaint. Uther's army was victorious, but Goloris perished. My mother eventually wed Uther, becoming high queen. This ring was his gift to her, forged from the brooch, as a wedding present." Arthur took the ring and slipped it onto the largest finger of my right hand. "And now I wish you to have it. You are part of this family and part of its story now." He kissed both of my hands. Arthur's gaze turned from me to the image of his mother. "I hadn't intended to tell you my whole family history today, but there you have it. I hope to come to know yours sometime."

"You will," I assured him. My attention was drawn to an empty niche beyond another pair of windows. "What is this for then?"

Arthur looked into the shadows of the alcove. "That place is reserved for my own statue." He turned to me. "And I hope yours as well."

My cheeks flushed as I embraced him. "I would be honored."

"Come." He tugged on my arm. "I want to show you why I did not bring you here for the wedding."

We traversed yet more hallways leading deep into the center of the castle. Arthur paused before opening a single door. As we stepped into an enclosed courtyard, a rush of cold air raised my skirts, bringing goose pimples to my legs.

I gasped. Before me was a perfect replica of the labyrinth that coiled around the Tor in Avalon. Borders of stone and bush formed the boundaries of the gravel pathway, which wound inward rather than up as the one on the Tor did. Outside the circle was a carpet of grass bordered on three sides by the castle. A high wall guarded the fourth side, affording complete privacy.

"The garden was just completed. I was waiting for word before bringing you here. I have no doubt it will be prettier during the growing season," Arthur said by way of excuse for the plants that had long since turned inward to become reedy skeletons during the cold months.

"I think it is wonderful," I gushed as I pulled him along the path behind me.

"Viviane told me how much walking the labyrinth in Avalon helped you think. I fear that as queen there will be much on your mind, so the least I could do was provide you with a place of sanctuary."

I stopped, turned, and kissed him.

After some time, he pulled away, grinning, and urged me onward. When we reached the center, I clapped a hand over my mouth. A lone apple tree shivered in the breeze, waving a few stubborn pieces of withered fruit at us in greeting.

"From Avalon's own orchards," Arthur proclaimed proudly. He drew up close behind me so I felt his warm breath on my ear.

"Viviane?" I asked.

"And Merlin," he added.

"Of course."

Arthur bent forward and embraced me tightly. "I hope you will feel welcome here, Guinevere."

"I already do."

⁂

Once the Yule celebrations were over and I had met the entire court, as well as half the populous—or so it felt—Arthur and I retreated into the warmth of his study. The small room was located above his bedroom and accessible only by a hidden staircase that led from one room to the other. Here we would not be disturbed.

As the snow fell deep and ice coated the land below, I set about learning all I could about the vast island for which I now had responsibility. On the table, Arthur had spread out a large map depicting each of the kingdoms, their intersections with ancient tribal boundaries, and areas of possible conflict. I traced the carefully drawn lines with my fingertips—green land, blue water, red battle lines—remembering the large tapestry map that hung in my father's council chamber. The borders had changed little since then, and unfortunately, neither had the conflicts.

"The Saxons have all but given up fighting for the winter," Arthur explained, "but we do have a small contingent holding out near Badbury Hill. Our men are well supplied at the fort there, so I believe they will make it through the winter with few casualties. But I can't say the same for the Saxons. They know if they cripple us there, they will have a clear path into the Summer Country and Salisbury Plain. That's why they are willing to starve. And starve they will." He growled the last sentence like an irritated bear.

He stabbed a finger at one of the many forts lining Hadrian's Wall to the northeast of us. "The tribes between the walls appear to be our next concern. My men at Corastopitum report increased activity in the area and believe Chief Caw of the Damnonii is planning something." He sank back in his chair. "As for our western foes, the Irish are quiet for now, and if King Mark follows my advice, they are likely to remain placated."

I raised an eyebrow at him. "What advice?"

Arthur's smile was full of mischief. "I told him it would be wise for him to make alliances—of the marital variety."

I considered the possibilities. I knew of several unmarried noblewomen Mark could choose from, including the docile Elaine, whose neighboring kingdom of Dyfed could possibly present a united front with Cornwall against the Irish. But even that didn't suggest a strong enough alliance to keep them at bay. Surely Arthur couldn't mean Isolde, could he? Mark was handsome, but she would never suffer his arrogance. I imagined the arguments that would surely arise from that union and smiled.

I was still giggling as I readied the board of Holy Stones, a divination tool of the Druids that most people considered merely a game. As I set the two clusters of twenty-one stones in their places, I said a quick prayer of gratitude I had been taught how to use the sight to draw deeper meaning from the game. Even if I didn't know the politics of the realm as well as Arthur yet, at least I could prove my worth this way.

I arranged the stones to mirror a battle with the Damnonii. The four tribes that made up the area between the Hadrian and Antonine Walls were normally peaceful, allied with us even though they weren't subject to Arthur. But like anywhere else, it only took one poor decision to plunge them into war. If Arthur thought they were a threat, they likely were.

I stared at the stones, letting the sight take over. Flashes came to me as I moved the pieces, which represented different groups of warriors, trying over and over to find the point of greatest advantage for our troops. Our men were more formally trained than the Damnonii, but the northerners were quick and fiercely determined. They knew if they could get our men off their horses, they evened the fight. Plus, they had been raised on the land, felt it their souls, and could use every hiding place and ambush point to their favor.

"I've been thinking," Arthur said some time later, jolting me out of my trance.

I blinked, forcing my mind back to him. "About what?"

"We are fools if we don't learn from our predecessors," he said, flicking away the latest missive from one of his advisors.

"I agree. But to what end? What are you proposing?"

He rose and came to stand beside me, studying the board. "Claudius just completed his survey of the old Roman forts. He sent a report by messenger. It made me think we are lacking something in our defenses." His hand hovered over the defending army, and he moved a company of spearmen.

I swatted his hand and moved the pebble back; my plan would be completely derailed if I lost that group of men. "My visions are showing the same." I gestured to the board. "I'll show you."

Arthur leaned forward on his arms, and the table groaned.

"Our horsemen should be our strongest asset." I indicated a group of blue stones currently clustered around the queen. "They are powerful, fast, and difficult to defend against, so why do we lose so many? From what I can see, they have two main limitations—they are easily unseated and those who are not are often grievously wounded.

If we could give them a more secure base from which to fight and strengthen their armor, they could truly be a force to be feared."

Arthur sat next to me, studying the stones. "I see your point. The Breton boy who won the tournament—what was his name?"

"Lancelot."

"Yes. Lancelot had some interesting thoughts on modifying saddles that I am curious to test. He pointed out that some of the strongest armies in the world employ a foothold on either side to keep their men from slipping from their steeds. It's in part how the Scythians and Sarmatians earned their fearsome reputation."

I shivered at the mental image of the wild horsemen who had many times terrorized Rome and most of the continent, leaving a bloody trail in their wake. If we could learn from them, we stood a better chance of keeping our attackers at bay, perhaps even defeating them for good.

My thoughts turned to Lancelot and how he had shocked everyone at the tournament by turning down the honor of being named Arthur's second. Arthur had politely accepted his refusal, but it was an embarrassment, so I'd expected Arthur to treat it as an insult. But here he was waxing poetic about Lancelot's wisdom. I shook my head. I still had a lot to learn about my husband.

Beside me, Arthur rambled on, oblivious to my musings. "Claudius also reports there may be some advantage to returning to the old tribal armor. Have you ever seen it?"

I nodded, remembering the weight of the thick layer of interlocking metal rings on my chest and shoulders as I learned weaponry from my mother. A few tribes still used it, but in general, it had been abandoned because of the expense and time it took to produce.

"We could never afford to outfit every man with it," Arthur said, "but I think it may be worth trying on our most elite forces even though they will need a little time and training with it. I am certain we still have some metalsmiths left who know the craft."

I looked at the pieces on the board, seeing men in their place. "Arthur, I think you are on the right track. Look."

I shuffled pieces across the board, engineering an escape to open land for the mounted army. They fanned out, keeping the queen safe behind their impenetrable line. They swallowed up the contingents of footmen, easily deflecting blows from spears and other missiles, cutting down whole ranks in mere moments. A few perished, but only a few turns later, they had captured the king and were in striking distance of the opposing queen. It was only a matter of time before she was taken.

I looked up at Arthur, proud to have finally found the path to victory. "If this army had the improvements you suggest, they would easily overpower their opponents."

"And with your strategy, they would be certain to win." His eyes were alight with hope and satisfaction.

Slowly, I realized he was proud of me, his battle queen and partner, his wife. I had gained some measure of respect, passed a test neither of us had known was looming.

I pushed myself up, standing just enough so I could kiss him gently, tacitly, as I measured his interest. His kisses were warm, but the nails he ran down my arms suggested he was in the mood for something more sporting than our usual soft lovemaking. I nipped his lower lip in answer and moved my hips against his.

Groping blindly behind me, Arthur shoved the contents of the tabletop to the floor, letters falling like autumn leaves in my peripheral vision. He bent me backward until I was half standing and half lying on the table. Before he could even grab my dress, I went for his trousers, peeling them off to expose his swollen manhood. Starting at his knee, I ran my tongue up his inner thigh and took him into my mouth. Arthur grunted his pleasure.

When he could take no more, he stopped me, leaned me back again, and entered me with such force I cried out. My body, more than wakened by the act I'd just performed, accepted him willingly. It wasn't long before we were both panting and spent, lying in each other's arms on the floor.

But that didn't last long. As soon as he recovered, Arthur kissed each of my breasts and rose to his feet, fastening his trousers.

"Where are you going?" I called as he bounded down the stairs to his bedroom.

"To find the Breton boy. We have to get the men and horses trained before anyone else attacks."

I flopped back down, using my arms as a pillow. So this was the life of a queen, abandoned by my husband for his men and horses. Yet I smiled. I was happy after all.

Chapter Three

Spring 497

By the time the first blossoms appeared on the trees, I was pregnant. I was wary of telling Arthur for I had already lost one child over the winter. I went little more than a month without bleeding then had a harder time of it when it did come. But there were signs any priestess would recognize, and I knew.

I had been using certain herbs to encourage conception, the antithesis of those I had used to prevent it when I was with Aggrivane. It appeared they were working, but I was still frightened this one would not last, so I kept my happy little secret and spent time every night praying to Brigid, the divine midwife and healer, that the child within me would grow strong and live to open his or her eyes to the world.

Finally, I could wait no longer. My breasts had swollen, along with my belly, and it looked as though the child was destined to live. One clear evening near Beltane, Arthur and I stood on one of Camelot's many terraces, watching the sun settle to its rest in the bosom of the mountains. As I watched him contemplating the peaceful land below, my mind ran through a million ways to tell him, hundreds of phrases, but none of them conveyed the growing sense of hope within me.

I took his hand, and he looked at me, immediately noticing the preoccupation in my eyes. Before he could ask, I put a finger to his lips.

"My love, I am with child," I said quietly.

A flicker of confusion then the dawn of clarity came into his eyes. A wide smile lit up his face. "Truly?"

I nodded, my eyes filling with tears. "By the end of the year, you will have an heir."

He picked me up with a whoop of joy and spun me around then set me gently on my feet. He embraced me with a tenderness I would not have expected from a man of his tall, broad stature.

I stood with my head resting on his chest, listening to his heartbeat. This was supposed to be a moment of great joy and anticipation, but I already felt panic dulling the happiness. It coiled around my heart and slithered down my spine, leaving an icy trail in its wake. I grabbed Arthur's hands and squeezed them.

"I have never been so scared," I admitted in a small voice.

Arthur leaned back and tipped my face up toward his. "Why?"

I pulled away from him and paced, willing my heart to slow though it seemed determined to beat faster with every step. "My mother bore thirteen children—did I ever tell you that? I was the only one to live more than a few years. Most died shortly after birth and some well before. And my mother"—my voice cracked—"she died in childbirth. They tell me she screamed for days before my father finally had the child cut from her body in the hope of saving him, but it was too late. What if the same fate befalls me? The goddess of fertility is not kind to the women in my family, Arthur."

To his credit, Arthur listened to my rambling patiently and didn't try to stop me.

My eyes fixated on a puffy pink cloud as the ghost of a memory danced in the back of my mind. "I remember having a brother. I wasn't much older than he when he succumbed to some sort of illness. The saddest thing is that one day he was prattling at my feet, and the next he was dead. All that life, all of his potential, gone in the blink of an eye."

Arthur wrapped his arms around me from behind and rested his chin on the top of my head. "The same misfortune will not befall you. It is terrible your parents suffered so, but your life is your own. You are young and strong and nothing bad will happen to you. I will not let it. I promise."

I tipped my head back to look at him. He was beaming with pride. I forced myself to smile, letting the panic ebb away under his touch. "So who do we tell first? Your family or mine?"

He grinned. "We tell the world."

⚜

As the weather warmed and buds began to dot the trees, I set out to get to know my people. I longed to visit the innkeepers, midwives, blacksmiths, carpenters, bakers, tanners, and families of all trades. Just as Pellinor had on Candlemas, I wished to introduce myself personally and hear about their daily needs not important enough to lay before the court in formal petition.

Just before I left the fortress for the town, Arthur broke away from a conversation with Kay, Bedivere, and Malegant to catch my arm.

"Since you have not yet named your champion and have no one to guard you, you should take one of my men with you," he said.

"Why? I can defend myself if need be."

Arthur looked down, scratching the base of his neck. "Oh, I am well aware. But it's not just you I am concerned with." He placed a hand on my belly. "We have enemies all around, my love. I would feel better knowing you had someone watching over you. Plus, you could devote more of your attention to listening to the people if you didn't need to constantly be on your guard."

"He makes a valid point," Kay put in.

"I volunteer to accompany you, my queen," Malegant interjected with a slight bow and a gracious smile.

"Do you now? And why should I choose you over the other men here?"

"Because I speak three languages and am knowledgeable in trade from the diversity of my own kingdom. Think of me more as an advisor."

"One with a very sharp sword." Arthur snickered.

"Indeed. Plus, it will give us the chance to get to know one another better. After all, I too am one of your loyal subjects." Malegant's eyes sparkled with mirth.

I laughed despite myself. "That is what I asked for, is it not? Very well." I eyed Malegant with mock suspicion. "But do not get in my way," I teased.

⚬⚭ ⚭⚬

It didn't take Malegant long to prove his worth. By noon, he had already physically turned away one man whom he'd deemed a threat to my safety, discussed the competitive price of shellfish up and down the coast with a fishmonger, and by nightfall had taught a young apprentice how to load amphore without spilling the contents.

"How does the Lord of the Summer Country know such things?" I asked the next day as we wandered through the town again.

Malegant raised a tawny eyebrow at me. "Do you think I've spent my years only yelling commands and counting my wealth? I have had many adventures, lived many lives." He took my forearm and guided me through a particularly crowded lane. "You see, my family has a bit of a turbulent past. When my father was killed, I was forced to flee my tribe and seek fosterage elsewhere. When I came of age, I had the skill but not the power to defeat those who sought my blood. So I worked where I could, learning and gaining respect as I went. Now I know a little about a great many things."

With his vast knowledge, Malegant became an advisor to the people in addition to my personal guard. We spent many mornings together, seeking to learn the ways of those who lived in the shadow of Camelot.

Once the rains ended and seeds were sown, the market returned, and I spent most of my spare time among the milling crowds, visiting vendors from the surrounding countryside. I quickly learned it was they, not the townspeople, who were the most reliable source of information. Free of Camelot's walls, they came bearing news from three kingdoms in every direction.

Those glorious, sun-dappled spring mornings, when the harbor breeze carried the scent of lilacs and salt and the world felt full of possibilities, were also perfect for loosening lips as everyone wanted to bask in the sunshine and spread the latest gossip. In one morning, I learned from a woman selling freshly picked greens that Morgan had given birth to a son, a tanner told me of rumors that a new Christian missionary was due in town, and a hunter setting up shop to peddle his pelts relayed that the Saxons were recruiting any mercenaries and outlaws they could find. That was chilling confirmation of what Arthur's spies had long suspected. Arthur's attempts at diplomacy had failed; soon there would again be war.

But that was not the only disturbance pricking at my mind. Malegant's behavior was beginning to concern me. When he'd first taken to defending me from those who would clamor for a piece of their queen––those who rushed at me or if a crowd pressed in too close––I attributed his zeal to overprotection. But as the weeks passed, I noted he was enjoying his role of enforcer a little too much, sometimes shoving and tossing men aside when a polite word would have done.

When I spoke to him of it, he promised to reign in his temper, but I wondered if he could hold to it, especially after the heated argument he had instigated that very morning with another nobleman who offered to take his place at my side.

The memory was still fresh in my mind when a group of young

men, chieftains' sons judging by their finery, called to Malegant to join them in the alehouse.

Malegant waved them off. "I'm afraid that must wait for another time. For today I am the queen's protector."

All eyes turned to me. It didn't take long for one of the boys to kneel, his friends following suit. The first looked familiar, tall and lanky with big brown eyes that made him appear younger than he likely was. Something in his awkward gestures tugged at my memory. Perhaps we had met before.

"Please, my lords, rise. I do not require such gestures every time someone lays eyes on me."

They stood, and the tallest ambled over to Malegant. "How does Pudicitia Fur become the queen's guardian?" He elbowed Malegant. "Who did you have to bribe to get that position?"

I turned to Malegant, who had gone rigid, his nostrils flaring. "These are your friends, yet they call you 'the virtue thief'? Pray tell me how you came by that name."

"He is known for taking what he wants," one of the men answered for Malegant, either not catching or ignoring the joke in my voice.

"That's an understatement," snorted another. "Liked Fiona so much he stole her right out from under her father's nose."

The familiar man tensed. "You speak of my sister. Show some respect," he said through gritted teeth.

"I could say the same to you," Malegant stated. "Show your betters their due, Fergus."

Fergus. It all clicked into place. The familiar man before me was the grown-up version of the Powys boy to whom Lord Evrain had tried to match me nearly two years earlier. Being the youngest son, he was of lower rank than Malegant, who ruled his own kingdom, thus Fergus was expected to demonstrate deference.

"You are no better than I and certainly not worthy of Fiona," Fergus growled.

"Hey, little pup, don't get your hackles up over me," Malegant taunted.

"Gentlemen, that is enough," I warned them.

Fergus paid me no heed, advancing on Malegant. "And why not? You kidnapped my sister, forced her to marry you, and now you ensure her allegiance through fear. I've seen her bruises. I know what you do to her. What you've done to them all."

I didn't like the way this was going. Soon they would come to blows. I should have just left them to it for it was no business of mine what they did, but Fergus's words stirred something in the back of my mind. What was it the priestess had said when I first sighted Malegant outside of Avalon all those years ago—that he had sullied more than one priestess and was not to be trusted?

Malegant leaned toward Fergus, so close his breath stirred Fergus's beard. "Be careful what you say, boy, or I shall be forced to put you in your place."

"And where is that? At the bottom of a bog with your last wife?"

Malegant's face turned scarlet. Before I could step between them, he was grappling with Fergus like a wrestler. His friends were no help; rather than helping me break up the fight, they cheered Malegant and Fergus on.

A crowd gathered around us, yelling and placing bets, as I looked for an opening to put an end to this childish behavior. Malegant knocked Fergus to the ground and landed a blow to his gut. Fergus kicked back, and I was able to wedge myself between them, shoving hard at the shoulders of both men.

"That is enough, both of you. You are lords in your own right, not children." I shouted Fergus and his friends away. "Go on about your business. If you don't, I will have you imprisoned for endangering my welfare."

The three of them scampered into the crowd.

I turned to Malegant. "I shall require a new protector, one who can hold his temper. Rest assured Arthur will hear of this. You have proven yourself an embarrassment to the crown."

Malegant opened his mouth, presumably to defend himself, but I didn't let him.

"Move," I commanded the onlookers, who dutifully parted to let me through.

As I stormed back to the castle, I was certain of two things: Arthur would not deal kindly with Malegant's transgression and Malegant's anger toward me would take a long time to flare out. He was a proud man, and I had just publicly shamed him. Were I any other woman, I might have feared his wrath, but my position protected me from any revenge he might seek. Or so I chose to believe.

Chapter Four

Summer 497

Combrogi—that's what he called them. It was an ancient word meaning "fellow countrymen," but to Arthur, it meant much more. Those men were his most trusted advisors, his brothers. They were also the strongest warriors in the land. Led by twelve prime members, each represented his own tribe and took Arthur's decrees back to their lords. It was a relationship based in mutual trust. He hid nothing from them and listened to their thoughts, in return expecting them to respect his decisions and be open with their opinions. If that bond were broken, so too would be the tenuous peace that united us as one land.

They were more than a war council and something other than a team of advisors. Together the decisions the Combrogi made had to take into account the temperament of their lords, the needs of the peasants, threats from within and outside our borders, and still reconcile conflicts between generals in such a way they would supply Arthur's needs for men, horses, and supplies.

As queen, I was now one of them, attending my first of their quarterly meetings held on each of the solar festivals. The Combrogi gathered in Arthur's circular meeting hall, the area I had mistaken for a shrine on my first day at Camelot. Arthur and I sat in thrones raised slightly above the other seats. All others were equal in their places. A few chairs stood empty, waiting for the return of men who were out on assignments for the king.

Today my father occupied one of the open spaces. He was not technically a member of the Combrogi, but since he was visiting, he had insisted on sitting in. Arthur wasn't pleased by this, but because Northgallis's support would be crucial in the upcoming war, he'd acquiesced. He had, however, drawn the line at allowing Father Marius to accompany my father. Arthur had explained that not even Merlin attended these meetings and if Leodgrance felt the need for spiritual direction, he could obtain it in private, just as Arthur did.

As Gawain began his report on how the adoption of the stirrups and chainmail was progressing, I caught sight of a shadow drifting from left to right, right to left beneath the chamber doors. If I listened closely, I could hear the almost imperceptible sweep of fabric across the stones followed at even intervals by the whisper of Latin.

Marius. I smiled. It must have been killing him to wait outside, two armed guards barring his entrance. At least this was the last time he'd darken our doors for a while. He was leaving for Rome in the morning, called there by the leader of his religion to report on the spread of Christianity in our fair isle. With any luck, they would keep him there.

"The men are adapting to the new armor much better than the horses are to the new saddle and stirrup, my lord," Gawain was saying when my attention returned to the room. "We are having some difficultly training them to it."

"Perhaps if you didn't beat them into submission, they would respect you rather than fear you," I answered, temper rising quickly.

Horses were sacred to my family as a symbol of the Goddess. Call her Epona, Rhiannon, or any other name, horses were her animals, and I could not bear to see them harmed. I had never seen them mistreated until I came here. In Gwynedd, we loved our horses, letting them warm to us, and earned their trust over time. What resulted was a lifelong bond that was broken only by death. During one of the Irish attacks, I had even seen a horse turn on an enemy soldier when his rider was threatened.

In contrast, these northern men knew no way to get an animal to do their bidding other than to break its spirit. Horses, oxen, dogs—it didn't matter; they wanted to dominate them all with whips and brands. I suspected they used the same tactics on their women.

I had hoped my position would help end their barbaric practices, but I could do little to make Arthur see reason. I had even demonstrated to the Combrogi how I'd learned to train my own horse and showed them how he could be taught to tolerate the modified saddle. But my advice had fallen on deaf ears, and the reason was always the same—"It takes too much time. Time we do not have."

Arthur shot me a reproachful look. "Guinevere, we have discussed this. If anyone can show me an effective way to tame the stallions that does not take months of work, I will gladly employ his methods, but until then, we must continue with what we know. It is imperative that both horse and rider learn to accommodate our new offenses as quickly as possible."

Gawain wisely moved on to another subject before I could respond. But he wasn't talking for long before the chamber doors burst open and my heart stopped. Sweeping through the door with great agitation was my former fiancé, followed by a man whose angelic gaze took my breath away.

Aggrivane bowed before Arthur, ignoring me completely. "Your Majesty, my lords, I apologize for the interruption. But word reached me you were looking for this man." He jerked his thumb over his shoulder at Lancelot. "I have found him, and I now happily deliver him to you."

Something in Aggrivane's voice told me he was still smarting from Lancelot's victory at the tournament in Dyfed two summers before. The pair had obviously not bonded on their journey here.

Lancelot bowed, first to me then to Arthur. "I am pleased to be of service to you, High King. Please tell me how I may help." His accent made every word sound as though it tumbled on a light breeze.

Arthur gestured for the two men to sit. The only empty chairs left were on either side of Tristan, directly opposite me, so I had no choice but to look at the two of them. Lancelot smiled warmly at me, but Aggrivane still refused to acknowledge my presence.

Arthur addressed Aggrivane. "I thank you for doing what no other of my subjects seem capable of—" He nodded at Lancelot. "Harnessing the wind. As a gesture of my thanks, Aggrivane, you may take a place among my Combrogi, if you wish."

I stopped breathing. *No, no, no, no, no. This isn't happening. This can't be happening.* Arthur knew our history. He couldn't be so thick as to name Aggrivane one of his most trusted men, could he?

But then I remembered Arthur's deal with Lot, who had led an unsuccessful rebellion shortly after Arthur came to power. As punishment, Lot's sons were forever under Arthur's control, and Arthur preferred to keep them as close as possible. I let out a silent sigh, sagging in my chair. It looked as though I would have to get used to having my former lover around, something I was not comfortable with. As much as I had learned to be happy with Arthur, part of my heart still belonged to Aggrivane.

Aggrivane looked at Arthur with great surprise. Apparently he hadn't expected so kind a reception either. "My Lord, I am honored to accept."

Arthur narrowed his eyes to steely darts directed at Aggrivane. "My offer is, of course, based on the provision that you have kept your word to me."

I looked from the man I'd thought would be my husband to the one who was. As far as I knew, they hadn't seen one another since the night Arthur proposed to me and sent my life crashing down around me. I had no idea what promise Arthur could have extracted from Aggrivane.

Arthur's features relaxed as Aggrivane nodded slowly. "Good. I look forward to seeing proof of your fidelity." He turned his attention to Lancelot. "I assume my lord Lothian has told you I have taken your advice on how to improve our forces? You are well-known for your skill with horses, are you not?"

"Oui," Lancelot answered, somewhat perplexed.

"Then you will join us in the stable yard at noon. We are all eager to see what you can do." Arthur banged his fist on the table three times, and the meeting was adjourned.

◦ೊ಄ ಄ೊ◦

"What did he mean, 'proof of your fidelity?'" I demanded as the door boomed shut behind me.

Aggrivane didn't look up from where he sat, drinking deeply from a cup of what smelled like strong red wine. The shutters were shut, blocking out the daylight, so the only illumination came from the fire pit. But in that subtle glow, I saw him wince.

"Why do you not ask him yourself? He is your husband." The words were forced through gritted teeth.

"Aggrivane, do not do this. Do not behave like this," I begged.

"How am I behaving? Like a jilted lover? No, I have no right to that title."

His sarcasm stung. I crossed my arms defensively, as if to ward off his anger.

"Tell me, how long after I left that night did it take you to fall into his arms? Or his bed?"

I ignored his question. "Need I remind you that you left me? You left me to face my unwanted fate all alone. The least you could have done was stand by my side and fight for me."

He wrenched the cork from a bottle and poured himself another glass of wine without looking up. "What good would that have done? He is High King. I am nothing in comparison. From what I hear, your fate was sealed long before that night. You were never intended to be with me."

"Arthur was not aware of our relationship. Did you know that?"

Aggrivane met my gaze then, apparently speechless.

"If you had stayed, if we had faced him together, none of this would have happened. We might be together now."

Aggrivane swallowed hard, the shadow of what could have been darkening his eyes. "Might is the operative word. He could just as easily have dismissed me and taken you to wife anyway. He bears no love for my family, remember? Even now he uses my father's attempted rebellion to hold me to foolish promises."

I bent in front of him to grasp the arms of his chair. "Exactly what proof does he expect to see?"

"You do not want me to answer that, my queen." His face was only inches from mine, but he kept his eyes trained on the crimson bottom of his cup.

"Aggrivane, please stop with the formality. It is only the two of us here. Remember us?" My mind flashed back to the night we were reunited at Corbenic and our frantic lovemaking. My cheeks flushed, but I doubted he saw it. "Answer the question."

"Fine." He let the silence stretch out before meeting my gaze with cold, emotionless eyes. "Arthur wishes to meet my wife."

I recoiled as though he had punched me in the gut. "You are married?"

The words hung in the air like a bird gliding on the wind.

Then he shot them down with the only arrow that would find the mark. "And you are pregnant."

My hands automatically went to my belly. It wasn't yet obvious through my clothing, so someone must have told him. "Yes, I am."

I moved away and opened the shutters.

He squinted at me through the bright light. "Well, we make quite the pair, do we not? Both married to people we do not love and you with a child on the way."

"I never said I do not love Arthur," I said automatically, then the full meaning of his words hit me and my stomach clenched. "Wait—you are not in love with your wife?" I sat across from him, unconsciously leaning toward him.

"Do you really think I could fall in love with someone in such a short time?" He sounded hurt. "I do love Camille but not the way I loved you."

I cringed. Camille? What sort of name was that? It sounded fitting for a cat or maybe a prize dairy cow.

"When my father sent me away, it was back to the Saxon border where he knew my mind would be preoccupied with other things, like staying alive. Sometime later, I heard of your wedding. That was a grim time for me, and I will not insult your intelligence by saying I spent that night alone. It was easy to find comfort in the arms of a stranger."

Hurt bubbled up inside me. Telling me he had been with a whore or his wife was a whore, whichever the case may be, was not helping.

"A short time later, a messenger from the king arrived, instructing me not to return to court for at least six months, and even then I could not return without a wife." He cocked his head at me. "It seems your husband wanted to neutralize any threat I may be to his new marriage."

I glowered at him, silently willing him to get to the point.

"Once the snows cleared, I'd had enough of battle and decided to visit the court of my uncle Uriens. Aunt Morgan says hello, by the way." He raised his glass to me mockingly.

I gave him a derisive smile. He was clearly enjoying himself.

"I walked into a hornet's nest there, but it all turned out well." He swung his feet up onto a footstool, set his glass down, and laced his hands together on his abdomen, waiting.

He clearly wanted me to ask him to continue, but I wouldn't give him the satisfaction. Moments passed as we stared at one another, neither willing to budge. I considered the appropriateness of labeling anywhere Morgan was a hornet's nest. She would have been their queen bee.

Finally, I gave in with a heavy sigh. "And what was so interesting in Rheged?"

For the first time since he'd arrived, Aggrivane smiled. "My wife."

I thought I was going to vomit, and it had nothing to do with my pregnancy.

"I will wager you did not know Uriens had a daughter, did you? Well, she is adopted. Her parents died in a fire when she was a child.

She still has scars on her hands. She spent some time in a convent, but with no family to provide for her expenses, they could not let her stay. So Uriens took her in. It is a shame the nuns could not keep her; she would have made a great nun, wanted nothing more in the world.

"Anyway, she was caretaker to Accolon's sons and Morgan's new baby when I arrived. She was content too, but Uriens insisted she marry. He said without a husband, she was a drain on the family's resources."

"So she married you," I concluded, happy to have his drawn-out tale finished.

Aggrivane wagged a finger at me. "Eventually yes, but not yet. Let me finish the story."

"I wish you would."

"You see, Camille is a Christian." He waited for me to blanch, but I carefully kept my face neutral. "She believed she belonged to Christ just as much as if she had taken vows in the convent. She refused to marry and, in an act of rebellion, cut off all her hair."

My mouth dropped open. "But the only women who wear their hair shorn are slaves. It is sign of bondage."

"Yes, it is. For Camille, it was a sign of bondage to Christ. She was his slave, so she made certain no man would want to marry her."

"But you did."

Aggrivane dropped his eyes to his cup again. "When I arrived, Uriens was threatening to sell her into a brothel or let her starve on the streets. I couldn't let that happen."

Don't act as if this was all charity on your part. I almost said it, but something in his expression stopped me.

"But you also saw a solution to Arthur's provision," I reminded him.

"Yes, it worked out well for us both."

My browed furrowed. "How did you convince someone so bonded to Christ to give up her virginity to you? That is still a condition of marriage in her faith, isn't it?"

A small rumble echoed in Aggrivane's throat. "Religion be damned. The marriage was not consummated, so it is not valid in that way, but it is still legally binding. However, if you tell anyone what I have shared with you, Camille and I are ruined."

I briefly considered shouting it from the rooftops. Slowly, I understood that his risky admission was Aggrivane's way of apologizing. If I wanted to ruin him and have him removed from court—and Arthur's good graces—I could. He'd willingly given me the key.

Aggrivane rose and slowly advanced on me. "I allow Camille to live as a spouse of Christ, and she enables me to be here. Once Arthur has met her, she will return to Rheged and help raise Uriens' children and grandchildren. Do you understand? We live a lie because it suits us. She is there, and I am here. I am here because I—"

He was interrupted by a light rapping on the door.

"Enter," I said, thinking it was one of the guards calling me to the stables.

The door swung open, and a young woman with dark hair and eyes entered. Her face lit up at the sight of Aggrivane, but she immediately dropped into a curtsy when she noticed me. Her short, uneven hair prevented her veil from lying flat on her head, and she wore thin gloves. This was obviously Camille.

"Your Grace, they told me I might find my husband here. I am—"

Her voice was as placid as her eyes, but in spite of Aggrivane's confession, I couldn't stop jealousy from surging through me. I cut her off. "I know who you are. Your husband was just telling me all about you."

The threat was meant for Aggrivane, but Camille's frightened expression said she'd perceived its meaning as well.

They both bowed as I swept from the room.

⁊⊙ ⊙⁊

The sun was shining merrily, birds were chirping, and people were joyfully calling to one another as they readied for the midsummer festivities beginning at sundown. After my encounter with Aggrivane, I was in a foul temper, and the last thing I wanted to do was stand around with the Combrogi and watch some boy charm horses, no matter how attractive he was.

As Arthur approached the stables with Lancelot, his arm slung around the Breton in friendship and their heads close together in conference, I reconsidered my assumptions. Maybe it wasn't fair to call Lancelot a boy. He had to be near my age, perhaps a few years younger, but he had a face so open, an expression so innocent, I doubted even the most evil spirit would dare assault his virtue. Not that I was under any illusion he was as unsullied as he appeared; enough wandering warriors has passed through Northgallis and Corbenic for me to know better. In his years on the road, chances were good Lancelot had warmed the fur-lined beds of queens and lain down in flea-ridden brothels—and chances were equally good he was at home in either place.

The Combrogi, a few of their wives, and a smattering of servants, stable hands, grooms, blacksmiths, and the like were gathered round as Kay led one of the more troublesome young horses out into the courtyard beyond the stalls.

"Ho there, handsome. Let us see you work your magic," a woman called to Lancelot from deep within the crowd.

Lancelot did not respond, only smiled self-consciously.

Arthur bid him to begin. "Her name is Danu," Arthur told him of the horse.

Lancelot stood still for a long moment, watching the animal, noting her every move from the flick of her ears and the twitch of her tail to the way she pawed the ground and how her muscles rippled as she took in his scent. It reminded me of the way he had sized up his opponents in the tournament.

Slowly, Lancelot raised one arm, holding his hand out to the horse as though asking her to dance. The filly snorted and pawed the dirt again, but Lancelot moved forward, never taking his eyes from the animal's. He approached at an angle so as not to frighten the beast, pausing if the horse backed away, and when he was nearly in front of her, Lancelot crooned to the animal in his native tongue.

"Aw, isn't that sweet? He's whispering sweet nothings in her ear." Malegant laughed derisively while someone else made kissing noises.

Arthur shushed Malegant and his friends with a warning glare, but Lancelot didn't notice. He was stroking the mane and muzzle of the filly. Several men muttered amongst themselves in disbelief at how quickly the two were taking to each other.

"The only misunderstanding that ever comes between horse and rider is born from spoken language," Lancelot spoke to us. "Believe me, they understand your intention, know your every move before you do. Nothing is lost on them, but we fail to have a way to clearly communicate our desire through words.

"Your king tells me many of you resort to violence to make your wishes known." He shook his head reprovingly. "How many of you would beat your wives if they did not understand you?"

A ripple passed through the crowd.

"Ah, perhaps that is the wrong question to ask here. Let me put it to you another way. How many of you would harm a child who was only learning to speak?"

The crowd was silent. Lancelot had their attention now.

"Horses are much like children," he explained, not bothering to look at us as he stroked the horse. "Though I have known several who surpass men in their intellectual capacity"—he glanced at the pair who had made fun of him and fixed them with an unfriendly stare—"we must approach them as we would a child. Because as with our young, we cannot simply tell horses what we wish them to do. We must show them, earn their trust, and they will learn from us."

Lancelot motioned for Kay to hand him the saddle. Lancelot opened his palm to the horse, who greedily snuffled something out of it, and I swore she looked at Lancelot with appreciation. "You are all experienced riders. Certainly you know a treat will put your horse at ease just as a sweet pacifies an ill-tempered child."

Lancelot held up the saddle in front of the horse, showing it to her and motioning his intention to heave the burden onto her back. The horse snorted and her nostrils flared, but she only stamped in place. Lancelot whispered to her again, and the animal steadied. Slowly, with all the care of a mother dressing her child, Lancelot secured the saddle on the filly's back, giving her another handful of oats to reward her good behavior.

Lancelot stepped back. "It is not the stirrup they fear but you. A saddle is a saddle, but because of the way you introduced it, they associate it—and you—with pain and humiliation. I tell you this— if you continue in this way, your horses will rebel and you will lose your cavalry completely."

"Arrogant arse. Thinks we do not know our own horses," Malegant muttered.

"I think he makes some good points," Gawain replied.

I rolled my eyes. I had told them the exact same things only weeks before. But would they listen to a mere woman? No. But a foreigner whom they barely know? Of course. He had proved himself worthy of attention by besting them all at the tournament. Plus, it was clear he had Arthur's backing, something I could not manage.

After another few words of encouragement, Lancelot slipped his boot into the stirrup, mounted the horse, and led her in a tight circle.

"Bollocks!" Malegant cried, still firmly on the side of flogging.

Lancelot raised an eyebrow at him. "Indeed? You have not seen enough? Would you like to try, or shall I show you again?"

Malegant only crossed his arms and grimaced.

The horse shied and bucked slightly when Lancelot urged her forward, and Lancelot was smart enough to know when it was time to give the animal a break.

"I will see to her myself," he said to the grooms. "Continuing the flattery into routine grooming is very important. It lets her know you are there for her in all things, both unusual and mundane." He smiled. "Somewhat like a romance."

Several of the women giggled, and a blush warmed my own face. Try as I may to dismiss his charms, I was smitten. Lancelot began to lead the horse inside, ignoring the tittering onlookers.

Arthur called after him. "Lancelot, wait. A moment of your time, please."

"Wait for me inside," Lancelot instructed the grooms who led the horse away.

Arthur clapped Lancelot on the shoulder. "What you have done here today is nothing short of miraculous. You have accomplished more in mere moments than we have in months, all with no harm to anyone. Will you do me the great service of staying on at Camelot as my master of the horse? My men will learn much from you."

Behind Arthur, I made a face. If he had listened to me, we'd have had no need for this new prodigy and would be well on our way to having the horses trained by now.

"Ah, oui," Lancelot answered with a humble smile. "Yes, gladly."

"Excellent. Tonight at the festival, you will swear allegiance to me and my queen and take your place as a member of the Combrogi."

Malegant scowled. He had been jockeying for that position since Arthur was crowned. He huffed away through the crowd, a bitter grudge taking shape with each step. Lancelot was proving quicker to make enemies than friends.

Lancelot stared after him. "Perhaps we did not get off to the best start," he said as I neared.

I watched Malegant's receding figure stalk back toward the castle.

"I think not." I placed a reassuring hand on Lancelot's arm and took a deep breath, trying to decide the most delicate way of saying what was on my mind. "Malegant is a proud man. He does not take kindly to correction, so you will need to be diplomatic in your dealings with him. You should be gentle in your interactions with all of the Combrogi. Brothers in arms though they may be, they eye one another suspiciously even on the best of days, so think how much less trust they have for a foreigner, especially one who begins by telling them they are wrong."

"She is right, you know," Arthur put in.

Lancelot nodded, apparently seeing my line of reasoning. "I fear I have painted myself a fool."

We advanced slowly toward the great stables so Lancelot could finish his work.

"I would not say that, but it would be wise for you to try a different tack, something less chastising and more encouraging," Arthur said.

"As you noted, they are experienced soldiers and horsemen, not green squires who do not know their way around a saddle," I said. "In your new role, they will be forced to look up to you, like it or not, so it is important you give them a reason to respect you." I glanced at Arthur. "We will do everything we can to help persuade them toward you."

It hadn't rained in weeks. Not a single drop had fallen since after midsummer, and soon Lughnasa would be upon us. In the withering fields and cramped stables, cattle and horses swatted at biting flies, and dogs lolled in alleyways or nipped at one another in the streets, irritated to restlessness by the oppressive heat.

Indoors, the Combrogi were little better. Malegant picked yet another fight with Lancelot, who was being vigorously defended by Garheis, Aggrivane's youngest brother and Lancelot's strongest devotee. At least Tristan wasn't there to stir the pot. King Mark's decision to call him back to Cornwall was fortuitous. Tristan disliked Malegant but regarded Lancelot even less kindly, so he would have done all he could to egg them both on.

Today was pleading day, the one day of the month when anyone—slave, servant, freeman, or noble—could lay their suit before us in open court. Because of Arthur's continued time in council with them, the majority of the Combrogi also were present, ready to accept any complaint of behalf of their lords. Most months saw an onslaught of petitioners who waited hours to stand before the throne, but on this day, few arrived to make their cases. The nobles most likely didn't wish to sully their trousers with sweat by leaving their dwellings while the poor were in the dehydrated fields, scratching in vain at the unyielding ground for some source of water to quench the thirst we all felt.

I had tried several times to call down a shower from the clouds to no avail. Some part of me knew it would take more than my power alone to break the stranglehold of this heat, but I had to try. I had summoned rain when I became a priestess and a hundred times before, but it seemed the baby was diverting my energy. The most I could muster was a few wispy clouds that dissipated as quickly as they gathered. So I was awaiting word from Avalon, where I had sent Viviane an urgent request for a rain ritual on our behalf. I didn't know how the rest of the country was faring, but if Camelot's condition was any indication, we were all well on our way to ruin. I prayed that was not the case.

From my seat on the dais, I watched Gawain charming, or rather harassing, one of the courtiers on the far side of the room. At first she seemed taken in by his smile and whatever seductive words he spoke softly into her golden hair, but when his hands roamed a little too freely, she turned and smacked him hard across the cheek.

Peredur burst out laughing, applauding her courage, and Arthur snarled for all of them to settle down. Sometimes I felt as if I was living in a castle full of overgrown children. Finally Arthur kicked them all out, saying he and I would wait out the last of the pleading hours alone.

Lancelot and Malegant slunk out down opposite hallways as soon as Arthur's tirade ended. Peredur and Gawain were making plans to meet in the tiltyard when we heard the alarmed voices of the guards outside.

"Messengers for the king," one cried while the rest was garbled by chaos we could not see.

We all jumped to our feet and advanced toward the door, but it opened with a thud before any of us could reach it. A body slumped into the room, another slightly less injured man following and hovering over the prone figure before us. Arthur swore, and I recognized the distinctive uniform worn by the soldiers from the milecastles, small forts along Hadrian's Wall. Arthur circled the bleeding husk of a man, and I knelt to examine his wounds.

"It's a miracle he survived the journey, but I fear he will not live to tell his tale," I said, shaking my head sadly as the soldier's life drained out at my feet.

"He doesn't need to," Arthur said grimly, pointing the toe of his boot at the man's uniform, which was more toga than tunic. "Nor was he meant to. This was the message we were meant to receive. He is Tremonium's general, so if he is here, chances are good there is no one left to save at the fort." He rounded on the mute second man, clearly the horseman who had carried the general to us. "How did you escape with your life?"

The man looked at Arthur with a mixture of horror and shock etched into his ashen features. He was shaking and could only stare.

I fetched him some wine, and he drank what he could with unsteady hands. The rest spilled onto the floor where it became indistinguishable from the general's blood.

"Chief Caw," he sputtered, unable to say more.

Even behind the emotion, the horseman's voice had a familiar inflection it took me a moment to place. He was Votadini. Why would the Damnonii chieftain send a Votadini man as a courier from a fort mostly populated by Strathclyde Britons? The hair on the backs of my arms raised. It made no sense yet could not be without meaning.

The solider had found his voice again but only just. "Dead, every one—men, women, horses too."

Arthur growled and struck a vase with his fist, sending it shattering to the ground. He ignored the shards grinding into the stone beneath his boots as he paced. "He would have known that fort was more than a garrison. It was a shelter for lowland villagers in times of distress. If there had been any whiff of trouble—and I promise you he gave them one—they would have headed for the safety of its walls like sheep. Heartless bastard."

The servants around us stood like statues, shocked by Arthur's outburst.

Recovering myself, I gestured to the women nearest to me. "Ladies, please take our wounded messenger to the infirmary and see he be tended to."

As for the general, there was nothing anyone could do.

"We ride to Tremonium then," Kay resolved, already heading toward the stables.

Arthur put out a hand to stop him. "No. Not now. That is exactly what Caw expects us to do. He's counting on us to swoop in on a rescue mission. It would make us easy targets, well-contained for his hordes. No, I will play this out in my own time." He continued to pace. "Now we wait. Let them grow restless, unsure. Let them wonder. Did the general die on the road to Camelot? Did Caw's dramatic message fail to make it to the king? Was the king unmoved? Better yet, does the king now lie in wait for him? I want all of these questions, all of these fears, to be chasing their tails around his mind before we move to retaliate."

When he finally halted at the base of the dais, I expected to see the familiar gleam of triumph in his eyes, but instead he turned a look of great distress upon me.

"He's heading to Lothian," Arthur said. "Why else send a Votadini with the general? They share tribal bounds with Lot and are his strongest allies. This was no random act of terror but a show of power to indicate what is to come. He's plotting to overthrow the kingdom and seize power for himself."

I was struck dumb by Arthur's words. If that was true, then Chief Caw had gone mad. The Votadini and the people of Lothian wanted nothing of war. I highly doubted this move had Damnonii backing either. The peace they had built was far too precious for any of them to risk.

Bedivere must have been thinking along a similar track. "Arthur, do you see what he is doing? If Lothian falls and the Votadini cower, nothing is stopping him from marching south to sack York, which is already weakened thanks to repeated Saxon attacks. From there he would have free rein into Brigante territory and would have amassed a force great enough to bring down even Camelot. It's not an original plan, another fool tried it about three hundred years ago, but it is a formidable one."

Arthur moved into action. "Then we have little time. Gawain, Aggrivane, send our fastest messengers on the most direct route to your mother and make her aware of the situation. Caw has a few days on us, and I do not want Ana taken by surprise. Follow the messengers with our strongest forces and meet us at Traprain Law, but do not take the main roads. I don't want to risk the Damnonii anticipating our movements. And summon Tristan from Cornwall. Tell him to ride night and day. We will need his skills."

He turned to Kay and Bedivere. "Since the two of you know the area the best, I am sending you as scouts up to Tremonium. Look around and see if you can gauge what we are in for, where the threat is greatest. I'm not sure if they will have moved on to Lothian yet, and if so, with what percentage of their forces. Even if they have split, if we can take down part of their army, we will be stronger for it."

"Best not appear as soldiers though," I warned. "Disguise yourselves as farmers or shepherds. Pretend to be picking around the ruins for scraps of stone or whatever else you can find to enlarge your pens. If the Damnonii insurgents even suspect who you are, their archers will pierce you through before you can draw breath."

For the first time since the general's arrival, Arthur relaxed a little as he recognized the advantage of having a battle-trained wife to relieve some of his burden. "A very wise bit of advice you'd do well to heed. I would like to see you both returned to my presence alive."

The two men regarded each other with familiar humor, and Bedivere looked down at the stump of his deformed left arm. "I guess this means I am your servant again. Just once I would like to be the master but have yet to find anyone who believes me a proper threat."

"Until they have your javelin sticking in their gorge, that is," Kay added with a hearty laugh. He was clearly looking forward to the adventure.

"The rest of you," Arthur addressed the remaining crowd, "brief your men, make your preparations, and say your farewells. We ride with the morning star."

⁂

It took me all night to convince Arthur to let me come with him to Traprain Law. He sought to exclude me only out of love and concern, but it rankled me nonetheless. These were my mother's people, and her influence had made me loathe to be kept out of any situation in which my skills could be of use. Even more, I had to admit I feared being left home alone, useless like a dairy maid, while Arthur and everyone I cared about risked their lives. I was a battle queen, and I was going to act like one, pregnant or no.

"You are in no condition to make such a long journey. We will be riding fast and hard, and I will not risk the life of our heir to appease your self-worth," he said, seeing my intentions for what they were.

I should have been more concerned about the fate of my baby, but I believed that as long as I stayed out of the thick of battle and atop my horse, we would both be fine. And like it or not, Arthur needed me there as strategic collaborator.

"I am not yet so heavy with child that I cannot sit upon a horse. Even Octavia will attest to that," I retorted.

Arthur's look warned me he was growing tired of our argument. "Would you have me trundle across the country in a chariot with you? Or perhaps you would prefer a cart? I will not slow us down or place you in any danger, Guinevere." His voice was laced with the guilt he would feel should any misfortune befall us.

But in the end, he succumbed, and I took my place next to him at the head of the line. Following my warning to Kay and Bedivere, Arthur split up our forces into reasonably sized groups and had us all outfitted to appear as bands of pilgrims on holiday to the holy springs and lakes that dotted the northern lands. He kept us off the old Roman roads and led us down a series of ancient byways and trails, navigating based on the expertise of a Combrogi named Bors who had spent his life in the area.

After an exhausting three-day journey, we rested at Traprain Law, a little more certain of our safety with our two armies combined. But now there was the question of how to proceed. We had anticipated a quick confrontation with a definite outcome, but that did not appear to be the way things were working out.

Kay and Bedivere returned from Tremonium the same day. They found the fort exactly as we had feared—torched to the ground with no survivors and very few clues left to tell what, or who, had brought down the once-mighty citadel. Although they had spotted a few lightly armed warriors patrolling the area, Kay and Bedivere were left in peace and did not think they were followed.

So it appeared Caw's war band had moved on, but Ana had not had any overture from him that indicated he was near. Much like with the undying heat, we were at an impasse, unsure of how to force the arm of change and even less certain how to ensure it came down in our favor.

Arthur grew more and more frustrated with each passing day. I wondered if part of Caw's plan was to drive Arthur to rash behavior, but I didn't dare voice it. Penned inside the fortress walls, Arthur behaved very much like the bear for which he was named, and I had no desire to feel his wrath.

As soon as Tristan arrived, he ordered the Cornish knight to accompany the scouts on a tracking mission. They returned with news that Caw and his men were holed up somewhere within the outskirts of the Caledon forest.

The seam of the wood was just visible from the guard towers on the northeast side of the castle. Arthur, Kay, Bedivere, Lot, Ana, Tristan, and I met in one of the larger square rooms while the rest of the household slept, trying desperately to think of some solution to the quagmire.

"They won't attack the castle," Tristan declared. "I didn't see any evidence of siege weapons or any indication they were building any, so I doubt they have the manpower."

Lot shook his head. "So why come all this way, exert all this effort, if they're unwilling to do the one thing necessary to overthrow us?"

"You forget," Arthur said, "that they need not destroy the town to claim victory. In fact, it is to their advantage to keep it as intact as possible for their own use. All they need is one of our heads."

Lot snorted. "So what are you suggesting, that we walk out there and let them take their pick? Or should I dispatch you right now and save them the trouble? Perhaps if I presented your corpse to them politely, they would show me mercy."

Ana's face reddened in a rare display of anger. Lot's swagger made it easy to forget that she was still in charge, as Arthur had long ago decreed. "Enough, both of you. This is not a boyhood brawl we are facing. It is the future of our kingdoms. The way I see it, if you do not think they will attack, we have three options." She ticked them off on her fingers. "One, we could try to wait them out, which does not seem wise considering the drought has already undermined our resources and they have the water of the swamps and bogs at their disposal, disgusting as they are. Two, we could do as our frustration bids us and charge in blindly, but that gives Caw the advantage of not only seeing us coming but being able to savor the chaos in which we die. Or. . . we can find a way to flush them out."

"I still favor standing at the edge of the wood and shouting, 'Here I am. Come and get me,'" Lot whispered to me, and I had to suppress my laughter.

Though amused by her husband, I was proud of Ana for her level-headedness and ability to see clearly through the emotionally charged situation. But then again, she was the daughter of Queen Iggraine and the famous warrior Goloris.

I turned her words over and over in my head. "Flush them out," she had said. But how? I tried to think of every angle, to see the impending clash from their point of view and determine what would drive me out were the roles reversed, but my mind moved in the same maddening circles. Arthur, Lot, and Kay's ideas grew more and more fanciful as the night wore on. I closed my eyes and tried to block out their voices, to summon the sight or call upon the Goddess, but it seemed that avenue of inspiration was as closed to me as my ability to draw down rain.

I opened my eyes with a sigh just in time to see a sheet of heat lightning illuminate the eastern horizon, revealing the contours of tall puffy clouds that looked like ship's sails. Suddenly a thought shifted in my brain, a single grain of sand set free to tip the whole balance. The sky flashed violet once again, and I knew Ana was right. We could force them out. And the earth was telling us how.

"What would happen if that lightning were not contained within the clouds, if it were set free?"

For a long moment, no one responded to my peculiar question. Six pairs of eyes blinked at me blankly.

"It would strike something," Ana answered warily.

"And say it struck a tree. It would catch fire, right?"

"I presume so, yes."

I turned away from the window, a plan rapidly forming in my head. "So why can we not be the fire? Burn them out. I have seen it used on small game in the hunt, so why not extend the metaphor and make it a little bigger?" I rushed over to Arthur, eager to make him to share in my excitement. "Think about it. They are shielded from our sight and our weapons by walls of trees—dry, brittle wood, thanks to this merciless summer. What difference is there from the fort they just destroyed? What would you do if they were hidden within a wooden castle?"

"Burn it down," he said, slowly beginning to understand.

"But there is a serious flaw in your plan," Lot protested. "Caledon Wood is not a defined structure. You cannot simply set it ablaze and let it burn. You would destroy the countryside for miles with absolutely no control over where it burns. You would be risking the lives and livelihoods of my people."

From his solitary perch on the northern windowsill, Tristan watched me carefully, green eyes narrowed in concentration. "Not necessarily. Ana, you said there are bogs and swamps hidden within the trees, right? Has anyone ever mapped them? Do we know where they lead?"

"To the river and then to the sea," Lot said. "A series of canals more or less connects the heart of the wood to the water. My family has been ruling this land for countless generations. There is not much about it we do not know. Yes, the marsh would divert the fire and perhaps control its spread, but it also would provide Caw with a safe place for shelter and a possible method of retreat."

"Not if we block it off." Tristan was on his feet now, bent over the table, fingers rapidly sketching out a drawing of the areas he and his team had surveyed. Lot supplemented what he could recall of the locations of the marshlands. Tristan stabbed a finger at one edge of the map. "If we wait for a night with a southern wind and focus on this area, it will carry the flames exactly where we want them to be, forcing Caw to retreat into this clearing just beyond the periphery of the woodland. If we can get our troops in place before we start the blaze, we will have the best chance of ambush as they flee from the flames."

◦◦ ◦◦

We moved contingents out of the fortress over the next three nights, when the moon hid her face and the land was shrouded in darkness. Placed at key points around the wood, each was a self-contained unit of fighters comprised of cavalry and infantry, equally capable of success as a cohesive entity or as highly skilled individuals. The weakness of our army was the strong individual pride that ran in veins more used to clan allegiance and self-reliance than the precise formations demanded by Roman strategy. We had to be certain that even if the unit broke, the men would survive to defeat their attackers.

I agreed to remain behind with Ana and her family, far from danger, while Arthur, Lot, and their forces plunged in headlong. Occasionally an eagle-eyed Damnonii would spot our army's movements and leave camp to investigate, but not one of them returned. I had to wonder what Caw made of his slowly dwindling numbers or if he even noticed.

As the feast of Lughnasa passed, still without a single rain shower, a strange pressure built in the land as if the earth itself would soon begin to boil. If we were restless within the relative safety of Traprain Law, I had to wonder how the foot soldiers in the field, exposed to the elements and all their heat-induced hallucinations, were faring.

Then one evening, in the dead of night, the winds shifted, their southern heat unmistakable. Huddled in the highest level of the hill fort, Ana and I watched as Caledon Wood went up in flames. The trees themselves seemed to combust, some as though set off by the very dirt in which they grew as torches were flung into their roots, others with hair on fire from flaming missiles. I said a silent prayer for forgiveness to the spirits of the trees that were now sacrificing their lives for our cause.

Smoke rose rapidly, obscuring any view of the pandemonium we might have glimpsed. For once I was thankful for the loss of sight, both physical and mystical, for I had no desire to know the suffering that must have been taking place below. All I could do was pray that Arthur and our men were safe and that our destruction of this magnificent wood would not be in vain.

The people housed within Traprain Law had been instructed to stay within the well-guarded walls of the castle, but they quickly clogged the ramparts, climbing on anything they could find to get a better view of the spectacle. Their shouts and exclamations only added to the madness.

Confusion reigned until the air cooled as dawn approached. I watched the eastern sky for some sign of light and soon realized that though the night was done, no brightness was forthcoming. It was as though the ash had choked out the sun. Then the first cool drops stung my skin, rapidly increasing until they created tiny rivulets in the ashy grime that coated me from head to toe. The sun was not gone, merely masked by clouds. At long last, it was raining.

Ana and I hugged as the drops became a downpour. The Goddess, and perhaps the priestesses in Avalon, had heard our prayers and deigned to help us dampen the fire. As the clouds continued to pour forth their libation, we all waited to learn the final outcome of the battle—anxiously at first, then with increasing dread as time dragged by. I clung to the damp window, praying with all my heart I would not return to Camelot a widow or spend my remaining days grieving for the Combrogi, certain in the knowledge I had orchestrated their deaths.

By the time the smoke cleared and sky lightened, most of the fire had been dowsed. The remaining trees, bereft of their leaves, stood in somber silence like tombstones, marking the loss of life for both their kind and ours. The quiet stretched on, interrupted at odd moments by a crack as a charred branch gave way and tumbled to the blackened brush below, a sharp cry as a crow spotted carrion or a confused songbird sought an incinerated nest.

Slowly the wood stirred as men emerged, some seemingly unharmed, others limping, blackened with soot or stained by dark splotches of blood. They appeared one at time or in pairs, but occasionally a group would stumble into the clearing, carrying a fallen brother or dragging an inert prisoner. At first they were all strangers to me, probably Lot's men, but then came faces and bodies I recognized. I was somewhat shocked and slightly mortified by the gratitude I felt that I didn't personally know any of the dead.

One by one, the Combrogi returned, shaken but relatively unscathed. Peredur was limping, Malegant and Gawain were clutching bleeding wounds, and Tristan held a broken arm, but none appeared to be in danger of death. The worst of the fighting had to be over because more and more men followed, their spirits buoyed by the sight of safety and shelter. They called out to loved ones on the ramparts and swooped them up in joyous embraces at the gates. A few held aloft the remains of their enemies, cursing and taunting the spirits of the dead.

The knot in my stomach tightened as I scanned the outline of the once-great forest for any sign of Arthur. Every few moments, my gaze swept the mounting crowd below, hoping I had missed him. Where is he? Has he been injured? Or even. . . I couldn't dare think the word.

My heart sank as I watched Kay and Bedivere guide an injured Lot through the gates. I rushed down to meet them, Ana close at my heels. She was making an odd choking sound by the time we reached them.

Lot held up a hand to calm her. "It is all right. I will be fine. It is only a broken leg."

"Had a tussle with one of the bogs," Kay explained in my ear, "fell right in."

So much for knowing everything about them. "And Arthur? Where is he?" I couldn't keep the edge of hysteria out of my voice.

Kay and Bedivere exchanged a glance I couldn't read.

"He'll be along," Kay said.

Ana left me so she could attend Lot, and the two soldiers headed for the barracks for some much-needed rest. I found myself standing alone in the midst of the crowd, uncertain what to do or even what to think. I hugged myself protectively and watched, unseeing, as the jubilant armies of Camelot and Lothian rejoiced at the Damnonii defeat. As more time passed, I fought the urge to sink to my knees in the mud and give in to the terror that threatened to engulf me.

"The living grieve only for the dead, and I do not think many tears will be shed for him."

My head snapped up when I heard the familiar gravelly voice

that held just a hint of irony. Astonished, I peered into Arthur's twinkling eyes, dumbly processing in some part of my mind that he was here, safe and alive. As this awareness dawned, I realized that Caw's severed head was dangling from Arthur's raised hand, twisting to and fro like a child's toy.

Shoving away Arthur's burned knuckles and, with them, his trophy, I pulled him to me, caressing his sodden, blistered skin. As the reality of Arthur's safety and our victory dawned, I felt another very intimate shock. I gasped as the babe in my womb moved, landing a sharp kick beneath my ribs followed quickly by a second further down in my abdomen.

Arthur bent over me in alarm. "What is it? Are you unwell?"

In his expression, I read the manifestation of all the anxiety he had put aside to allow me to accompany him here.

I shook my head, laughing. "Hardly." I placed his broad palm along the curve of my belly and waited. It wasn't long before he flinched in surprise as the child moved again, a second flutter following shortly after. "Arthur, I believe we have sired warrior children."

"Children?"

"Yes, I feel two distinct presences. I believe I am carrying twins."

Chapter Six

Autumn 497

A fiery shower of reddish-orange leaves fluttered from the oak trees surrounding us as I looked out over the assembled men, many of them my friends, all of them my sworn subjects. From their number I had finally chosen my champion, and they were here, in a sacred grove protected by the Druids, to hear his name declared in one of our few rituals that mingled the secular with the sacred.

It had been my right, or more accurately, my responsibility, to choose a champion from the moment I was crowned queen. Arthur could not serve as both king and champion because doing so would have divided his loyalties between his wife and his realm, so I needed to choose a protector. But a champion was more than a bodyguard; he was in essence an extension of my will, vowed to follow me in all things. I had to trust him with my very life for he was sworn to protect me above all else, even the king. Together with Kay, Arthur's champion, this man would protect my children as they were fruits of my body. I could have chosen randomly from the strangers I'd met at my coronation, as some queens had done before me, like a child drawing lots for a game. But I didn't want to make such an important decision before I'd had the chance to get to know the temperaments and proclivities of those from whom I chose.

Some of them had openly courted me for the position, which had the opposite of the intended effect. I could not entrust my life to a man who desired the position for its status; I had to trust him implicitly, which I could not do with knowledge of his ulterior motives. Even those who'd employed more subtle tactics—I firmly believed that was the reason behind Malegant's early efforts to accompany me in public—had hurt their chances. With each meeting of the Combrogi, and even some chance personal encounters, the pool of possible contenders had dwindled.

I'd made my decision that summer. I couldn't say that a single event had cemented my choice, nor could I tell exactly when it had been made, but one day I looked at him and I knew. Perhaps it was the sum of a string of small moments, a kind word here, a gesture there, but as I thought back over our time together, the answer was clear. He was a dangerous choice, and one that likely would prove unpopular, but my mind was made up.

One thing still haunted me as I began to chant, letting go of myself and calling the Goddess into me—Merlin's reaction when I had disclosed my choice the day before. He had turned his sapphire gaze on me, and I suddenly felt chilled. His pupils contracted as his gaze retreated inward, and a brief shadow clouded his face. It was a look I knew well—it signaled a flash of the sight.

Merlin's eyes had focused on me as he came back to himself, but they lost none of their iciness. "Tell me, how can you be sure you've made the right decision?"

"Are you saying it is not?" I countered with equal steeliness. As much as I cared for and respected him, I could not abide his meddling in my personal affairs. It was my right to choose whom I willed. He was Arthur's advisor, not mine, and I preferred him to stay out of my business.

He stood directly in front of me, towering over me. "I am saying all actions have consequences, and I have seen the result of the one you are contemplating. You tread a slippery hillside, Guinevere. If you do not guard yourself well, you may go tumbling down and drag us all into the mire with you."

I pulled myself to my feet, no easy task with my protruding belly, and faced him down. Most people wouldn't have dared challenge the Archdruid, but sometime in the last year, I'd lost the awe that had held me in fear of him. Maybe it was the familiarity of spending so much time with him or the fact that I now held a position of power as well, but I no longer felt compelled to cower in his presence.

I stepped toward him, forcing him to retreat slightly. "If you have seen something of such great import, *Archdruid*"—I laced his title with as much contempt as I dared—"tell it to me in plain terms; do not hide behind the vaguery of visions and prophecy."

Merlin shook his head. "Alas, I cannot. You know as well as I that the future is fluid, ever changing as the sea. If I name what I have seen, I risk impugning innocent men *and women*"—his tone made sure I knew he was referring to me—"for trespasses they may never commit. I can only warn you that this reaches well beyond who carries a sword in your name."

That was his last word on the subject. Now, with my eyes closed, I could feel him to my left, but I no longer sensed any hostility. He was doing his job as Archdruid, submitting to the will of the gods and no doubt praying they would change mine.

I made myself forget the past and focus on the present. This was as close as I would ever get to experiencing the power of the Lady of the Lake. Today, I was the Goddess in her role of Sovereignty, she who grants and removes temporal power. I was to invoke her just as fully as during any Avalonian ceremony but without the aid of the sacred drink for I still needed my human faculties. I was to be at once goddess and queen, the supreme symbol of womanhood, both mortal and divine.

I said a silent prayer for guidance and let my consciousness slip downward in the quiet. At first, nothing happened, then a silver glow, like liquid moonlight, filled me with warmth. I felt her within me, a quiet, gentle, reassuring presence.

I opened my eyes, and the awe on the assembled faces made me realize I must appear to them every bit the Goddess incarnate. Merlin had dressed me in the pure white gown of the Maiden, which was cinched by a thick black cloth belt, symbolizing the wisdom of the Crone, and covered in the rich crimson cloak of the Mother. That I was nearing the end of my pregnancy only added to the effect.

I opened my arms wide and addressed them. As I spoke, I wasn't sure if it was in my own name or that of the Goddess or both. I had the strange sensation of remembering the ritual, rather than reciting it, as though it were as familiar to me as breathing. "I have called you here today for one purpose—the arming of a champion. This role is second only in sacredness to that of kingship. As such, it is a privilege only I can grant, and once sanctified, none may contest.

"Many of you are worthy, but only one can hold the office. I have searched my own heart and endeavored to know yours. Know the one whom I have chosen is not peerless, nor should he seek to place himself above the rest. I choose him because he is, to me, best suited for the role. It is an honor, yes, but the man who takes on this mantle also shoulders a great burden, so do not be envious of his station."

In unison, the assembled men knelt. I regarded each man with new perceptiveness, seeing them with the vision of the Goddess. My eyes passed over Kay and Bedivere, whom I could never choose because they were Arthur's men through and through and their loyalty would always be to him; to Bors, Malegant, Accolon, and a few others I liked but mistrusted for reasons I could not name; past Aggrivane, with whom my tangled past would forever be a stumbling block; and finally to Owain, Tristan, and many others I knew had greater loyalties to their lords than to me.

Finally I found the face I sought. "Lancelot du Lac, arise and stand before me."

Merlin closed his eyes and bowed his head in disappointment and submission. I gestured Lancelot forward, and the men murmured to one another uneasily. Hesitantly, and slightly self-consciously, Lancelot did as he was bidden.

"I have chosen you for my champion. Do you accept this office?"

He smiled and dipped his head humbly. "I do."

Before I even had the chance to ask, Aggrivane was on his feet, shouting, "I invoke the right of challenge."

His words were greeted by an audible gasp from the crowd, followed by cheers of support. Lancelot hadn't made many friends since his arrival. Many of the men would have been happy to see him publicly defeated.

When I'd made up my mind, I foresaw this might happen, but challenge was Aggrivane's right. At the time of first investiture, any man might challenge the chosen one and the two had to do battle. The winner would be the queen's champion, but the loser was allowed to renew his petition each year on Lughnasa for seven years. If the challenger was ever successful, the title would pass to him. If not, the title would remain for life with the original winner. I could only hope Aggrivane wouldn't hold a grudge for long.

The human part of me was mortified and afraid that Arthur would take Aggrivane's outburst as a sign of lingering affection for me, but the Goddess within saw the justice. I had no choice but to let them proceed.

I nodded, speaking the words of the Goddess. "Men have long fought for love of me. Lay on, but draw no blood within this sacred circle."

Weapons were not allowed within the sacred grove, so they would have to fight hand-to-hand, a skill I knew Aggrivane possessed.

I was unsure of Lancelot as I had only seen him do battle with a sword. Amid cheers from their supporters, they both removed their shirts and shoes and rolled up their trouser legs. The crowd quieted and formed two camps, leaving the combatants in full view of where I stood.

As they circled each other like wolves, Lancelot taunted Aggrivane. "I have already bested you in front of the king and court once. Do you really wish to have me humiliate you in front of the Combrogi and the Goddess as well?"

Aggrivane's answering grin was thick with malevolence. "It will be all the more sweet to avenge that affront before such an audience."

Then he lunged at Lancelot and grasped him around the shoulders, seeking to throw him off balance. Their brawl reminded me of two spiders fighting, an indistinguishable tangle of limbs. They struggled not only against one another but against nature herself, unable to find true purchase on the wet, leaf-strewn ground. One moment one seemed to have the upper hand, then fickle Fortuna would smile upon the other and he would rally, flipping his opponent and pinning him but never for long.

Their grunts and groans were nearly drowned out by the cheering Combrogi, who had forgotten they were still at a ritual rather than a game of sport. Most supported the son of Lothian, but a few were on Lancelot's side. For my part, I held my breath and tried to abandon my will to the Goddess who floated unperturbed inside me.

Finally, Lancelot wrestled Aggrivane to the forest floor and held him down. Merlin begrudgingly declared him the victor. Aggrivane snatched up his shirt and returned to his place, growling. I thought it cruel that he now had to watch as another man yet again took his place by my side, but I was powerless to change tradition.

Brushing leaves, dirt, and acorn shards from his hair and pants, Lancelot dressed and once again took his place in front of me.

"Lancelot du Lac, so named as the son of the Lady of the Lake in the forest Broceliande, you have declared your willingness to serve as my champion; now swear your allegiance to me."

Lancelot knelt and touched his thumb to his forehead, lips, and heart in recognition that his vows were to both queen and Goddess. "My lady and my queen, I thank you for selecting me as your champion and defender. Though I know I am not worthy, I humbly accept this honor and pledge myself to you. I vow to use all that I am, all that I know, and all that I may acquire in your service. Anything you ask of me, I will do. If you are in peril, I will rescue you; if you are reviled, I will defend you; if you are threatened, I will fight for you, even unto death. My life is now forfeit; do with me as you will."

Arthur stepped forward and drew his sword, the legendary Caliburn, one of the treasures of Avalon given to him by the Lady of the Lake when he became king. He held it flat, shining blade resting against on his open palm, hilt of intertwined golden dragons in the other. He held it out to Lancelot, saying, "Know that you defend my queen in my name and with my power. Anyone who opposes you opposes me."

Lancelot bent his head to receive Arthur's blessing. As Arthur sheathed his sword, I handed another to Lancelot. It was a specially forged replica of Caliburn, the only difference being that the jewels in the dragons' eyes were a bright emerald rather than ruby. The similarity was meant to remind Lancelot, and anyone unfortunate enough to face his might, that he fought in defense of the house of Pendragon. As Lancelot accepted the weapon, the sun bounced off the blade, illuminating its inscription: "In Her names and by Her power, I defend this land." A reminder of these very vows.

As Merlin blessed Lancelot and consecrated his sword, the Goddess departed from me, her purpose fulfilled. The tranquility and peace left me in a rush like an exhalation, and just as quickly, my usual worries flooded back in. I looked over the Combrogi, wondering how they were reacting to the news that Lancelot was now not only master of the horse but my champion as well. Part of me wished I could hear their thoughts, but I knew it was best I could not. They were no doubt filled with resentment. Every one of them hoped to be elevated to a higher position in Arthur's court, and as far as they were concerned, its two highest honors had been given to an unworthy outsider. I hoped they would come to understand in time.

I couldn't help but watch Aggrivane. Even as Merlin said the closing words, Aggrivane shifted from foot to foot, understandably uncomfortable. After Merlin's final blessing, Aggrivane shot through the trees and out of sight just as he had the night he lost me to Arthur.

Merlin shooed everyone out of the grove so he could purify the site for its next use by the Druids. The men dispersed, some talking excitedly in groups, others striding off to the horses, anxious to begin the long ride back to Camelot. But Lancelot lingered at my side.

"Thank you for this honor, my lady. It is truly unexpected, and I will be forever grateful," he said as we followed others to the horses.

I kicked up leaves like a child as I walked. "You are best suited to defend me in all things, and I trust you implicitly."

As we passed Merlin, I expected him to ignore me, but to my surprise, he put out a hand to bar my path. He glanced up at Lancelot and then back to me.

"What is done is done," he said without preamble. "I suggest you find Aggrivane and try to make him see reason. He stormed off in that direction." He pointed east. "You are the only person he will listen to right now, and we cannot afford to make an enemy of him."

Without another word, he entered the circle and began paying homage to each of the oak trees as though I did not exist.

I gave Lancelot an apologetic look. "He's right. I should go and find him. Please wait for me here. I will not be long."

◦ৎ№ ৯ை◦

Aggrivane had made no effort to cover his tracks. Following his footprints, deep and unmistakably stamped with rage into the muddy depths of the forest, I picked through clumps of mutilated leaves and swept past decapitated branches, the innocent victims of his anger, until I came to a small clearing at the edge of a stream.

His back was toward me as he faced the water. "You should not have come."

"But you knew I would." I couldn't see his face, but I imagined how he would close his eyes and smile ruefully by way of answer. He was determined to ignore me, so I crossed the clearing in a few purposeful strides then tugged on his shoulder in a vain attempt to force him to face me. "What would you have me do, Aggrivane? Choose my former lover as my champion? How would that look to Arthur? To the court?" I was almost yelling, my voice raw.

He had to see reason. He had to know I'd had no other choice. Because I hadn't, had I? I wrapped my arms protectively around myself. Suddenly I wasn't so sure.

For a long while, Aggrivane said nothing, and sounds of the forest returned as the birds decided my outburst was not aimed at them. Then slowly he turned, his face a stony mask, but I saw pain reflected in his eyes.

"Yes," he whispered. "That is exactly what you should have done—selected the one you wish to have always by your side, not a substitute to distract you from your true feelings."

The candor of his words struck me to the core as surely as if he had buried an arrow deep inside my heart. Tears dampened my cheeks before I could find my voice, and I turned away. My mind was working feverishly to deny the truth of his words.

"I am no longer the girl you met in Avalon. My actions. . ." I took a deep breath. "Are watched by everyone." I winced inwardly as I realized how close I had come to repeating Merlin's words about my actions having consequences. "To have named you my champion would only have given my detractors something to use against me."

"Did Lyonesse teach you that, how to make excuses for any subject?" Aggrivane spat, referring to the malicious woman I had lived with during the latter part of our courtship.

I whirled around, ready to retort, but he stopped me by holding up his hand.

"Everything you have said to me since I returned has been one gigantic justification." His eyes narrowed, inspecting my face. Then he firmly gripped my shoulders, forcing me to look directly into his eyes. "Why do you refuse to acknowledge that you are still in love with me even to yourself?" His eyes searched mine so thoroughly I felt naked before him. "Do you know what I was about to say to you the day Camille interrupted us?"

I was about to reply, but he rushed on. "I was about to tell you that I was still in love with you. Married or no, neither of us can deny what flickers deep within no matter how hard we try to hide it or snuff it out."

Aggrivane cradled my cheeks, and my heart cracked all over again, just as it had when my father separated us, just as it had when I futilely searched for his face in the moments after Arthur proposed. I closed my eyes, trying to deny what my heart so readily understood. My head spun with a million thoughts, the loudest being a voice shouting, *No, this cannot be happening. He did not just say those words.*

You are dreaming; this is not real, I kept repeating, but I knew it wasn't true. I tried to force the feelings down, and I let out a strangled gasp as they nearly choked me. I did still love him, but to admit it, to say it out loud, would have been treason. And once I gave voice to those feelings, there would be no going back—no controlling the torrent that came with them.

The words were hanging on my tongue, each beat of my heart bringing them closer to my lips. I pulled away, head bowed and eyes on the grass slowly dying beneath my soles. I knew what I had to do, what had to be said, but every fiber of my being railed against it. I swallowed hard and forced myself to speak, my voice sounding foreign to my ears. "This has to end, Aggrivane. We can't continue to live like this. I do not want to lose you, but there can be no illusions about what is or ever will be between us."

Aggrivane cleared his throat and shuffled his feet. I didn't dare look up. I knew by his silence that his expression would rend me beyond repair.

"If that is what you wish," he said, clearly struggling to keep his voice steady. "But promise me one thing."

I answered without hesitation, "Anything."

I suddenly remembered how he had looked the night we first kissed, the way the wind rippled his black locks into shining waves and how his dark eyes twinkled like the stars in the midnight sky. I would have given anything to be able to go back to that moment, to start things over and live the life destiny had stolen from our grasp.

"Promise me no matter how much you love your husband or esteem your champion, no matter how many others you burn with passion for, you will reserve a small place in your heart only for us. It can be in the darkest depths of your soul, but I need to know there is some part of you no one else can touch, a place that is purely mine."

I stared at him, wishing I could tell him such a place already existed, sealed from all others by wounds that would never fully heal, scars that marked me as his as clearly as if he had carved his name into my heart. But all I could do was nod and wipe away the tears as they fell. "I promise."

His smile was as tender as his touch as he ran his fingertips down my cheek from my temple to jaw. "So do I."

As he embraced me one last time and kissed my forehead, I knew my love for him would haunt me forever.

Chapter Seven

Winter 498

With one sharp stab, my entire world changed.

We were in the middle of a cordial dinner with Cador, lord of the western kingdom of Bernicia, when I felt the first sign of distress. At first I thought I'd just eaten too much venison or the leek soup had disagreed with me, so I continued my conversation with Cador's wife, laughing heartily at her impression of an impudent servant.

But then a second twinge bit at my ballooning belly. I sucked in air and dropped my knife, hands instinctively fluttering to the sore spot in my side. I looked at Arthur in alarm, and he slowly ceased chewing as understanding dawned across his features. A moment later, I felt a soft trickle of warmth ooze down my thigh.

I grabbed Octavia's arm as she leaned over my shoulder to refill my goblet and whispered in her ear, "I think my time has come."

Ignoring the sudden silence and alarmed expressions of Cador and his wife, I allowed Octavia help me to my feet and usher me toward the door. I prayed my womb would hold the remainder of its waters until we were out of their presence.

"Lord Cador, it appears you and your wife may have the honor of being present at the birth of my first children . . ." Arthur's voice held a mixture of astonishment and pride.

Halfway down the hall, I had to grip the wall near a window as another spasm caught me off guard, and the seal of my womb broke in a watery rush. I had just enough time to notice the large flakes of snow falling in the deepening shadows before another of my maids came running to support my other arm. She and Octavia helped me shuffle the rest of the way to the room prepared for the royal birth.

Chaos broke out all around as soon as I was safely ensconced in childbed. Octavia called for the servants and sent one to fetch Grainne, who, on Arthur's orders, had been staying at Camelot for the last month so she could assist when my labor pains began. He had originally insisted that Viviane act as midwife, but she'd successfully argued that the High Priestess of Avalon could not be withheld from her duties to wait on the whim of unborn children, no matter how royal. Arthur's expression of consternation that someone would dare disobey his orders had been so outrageous it made me smile even to remember it.

But my joy was short-lived. I grimaced and took a deep breath as another cramp began, though I willed myself through it. I had been present at enough births to know this was just the beginning. But I could already feel tiny fissures of fear breaching the calm I endeavored to maintain.

The pain rose and abated as the evening progressed. Servants flitted about me, preparing reams of cloth, heating water, and fussing over details real and imagined. Outside, the snow mirrored their frenzy, coating treetops and turrets in a thick white blanket as the sky hardened from lead to pitch. All the while, Octavia sat by my side, holding my hand and cooing encouragement as the pain rose along with my screams and my determination diminished.

As the birthing process took hold, everything became hazy, disjointed like when I'd had the fever in Pellinor's house, except this time, instead of being numb, I was acutely aware of every nerve in my body. My throat was raw from screaming, my legs cramped from holding the muscles taut, and I could scarcely take a breath between the spasms in my womb.

I wasn't sure when I began calling for my mother—it must have been sometime between when a servant told Octavia a crowd of townspeople had gathered to hold vigil in the courtyard and when Grainne said it was nearly time to push. Even though I cried out for her, the thought of my mother did little to calm me because with it came the memory of her many trials in childbed. I tried not to give in to the terror that threatened to consume me, but pain had weakened my resolve. Soon I lost all grip on reality.

I was oblivious to the world around me, lost in a thrumming buzz that was everywhere and nowhere all at once. Eventually Octavia's voice cut through the din, commanding me with every ounce of her Roman authority to push. I took a deep breath, gritted my teeth, and bore down hard.

"The baby's head is nearly out. Push again, my love," Grainne encouraged.

I grunted and pushed harder, again and again, until an odd sense of relief and release washed over me, and the child slipped out from between my thighs.

"You have a son," Grainne shouted jubilantly.

But just as quickly, her face fell. Instead of a lusty cry, there was silence. No one spoke as I searched each face, each one more concerned than the last. I knew something was terribly wrong.

"What is it? What is wrong with my baby?" I croaked.

Grainne only shook her head and handed the child to the young priestess acting as her assistant. She clutched my son, patting his back and holding him as near to the fire as she dared. It was then I noticed there was no rise and fall in his chest. My baby was not breathing.

Before I had a chance to protest, to beg my child to draw breath, a new wave of pain rocked my weakened frame, and I cried out.

"Guinevere, you have another baby who seeks the light of life. You must find the strength to push again."

My mind was in tatters, hardly able to comprehend what she was saying, torn between my silent son and his sibling waiting to be born. I gave a mighty heave that felt as though it broke me entirely.

"Very good, Guinevere," Octavia coached. "I know you are tired, but this little one cannot be born without your help. Try just one more time."

I tried to focus on what she was saying, but my mind kept wandering to the hearth, trying to understand what was happening to my son. Somewhere in the lucid recesses of my mind, I recognized what the young priestess was doing. My child had been born dead, and she was cleaning him, swaddling him not for his first hours of life but for the grave.

I hardly noticed as another convulsion shook my deflating belly. All around me, Octavia, Grainne, and the other women urged me on. I pushed one final time. Then there was nothing left to give.

Grainne was cursing at me in several languages as she struggled to pull my second child free. I shook my head weakly, tangled black locks whipping the sides of my face, and sank into the sweat-soaked sheets, utterly defeated.

I was numb, and my spirit was slowly detaching from my body. Soon I swam in a sea of darkness as soft as gosling down. Higher and higher I flew until nothing remained of my former life.

The last sound I heard was the fragile, mewling cry of my daughter.

࿐ ❧ ❦ ࿐

Where I was was utterly silent, calm and peaceful like the quiet of a soft winter snowfall when the whole world is at rest. But I was not in the world; that much I knew. I was somewhere in-between and outside, not unlike the ethereal borderland of mists shrouding Avalon. But I was not there either. This place had none of the humming vibration that was felt rather than heard as the boat slipped through the mists. No, this place was somewhere else entirely.

I was moving forward yet standing still at the same time. I had no sensation of walking or even thinking that I wanted to move, yet there was motion all around me. I tried to close my eyes and reopen them to balance myself and refocus, but it made no difference. I looked down to find I had no arms to guide me, no legs supporting me.

I had the vague sense I had been somewhere similar to this before, perhaps in one of my many meditative journeys as part of my training in Avalon. Slowly, like a babe opening its eyes for the first time, I realized this was the land of the spirit, where no corporeal body could follow. If I'd still had lungs to fill with air, I would have sighed in relief. Never before had I realized what a burden it was to carry around a body or retain a lifetime of thoughts and memories. Gone were the worries and anxieties of life, the expectations, misplaced priorities, anger, and grudges. All that was left was the true essence of myself.

I had always expected to come face-to-face with the dark aspect of the Goddess when my soul departed this life, to have a terrible moment of reckoning before meeting the mighty Ceridwen and her cauldron of death and rebirth where I would either be granted access to the eternal joy of the Otherworld with my ancestors or plunged into the depths of her cauldron to be reborn again.

When I heard my name called, it was as though the sound came from both outside myself and within my mind at once. Still following my human instincts, I turned, expecting to behold the Goddess. But there was no one there.

Like a dreamer gradually waking from slumber, I began to sense dull colors and formless shapes, though I could make no sense of them. It was as though my inner eyes were adjusting after the transition from the physical world. Slowly, the world formed around me, or rather, revealed itself to me one sparkling grain of light at a time.

As the jumble of hues and wild figures coalesced, I found myself in a grassy sunlit meadow dappled with bashful violets, stately poppies, and clusters of tiny golden wildflowers. Their colors were so much more intense than anything I had seen on earth, their scent more heavily perfumed.

And suddenly I was no longer alone. The presence I had sensed from the first moment of darkness but had not dared to name took form before me. A woman with glistening raven hair, slightly lined pale skin, and gentle green eyes that were straight out of my memories stood before me. After all of my tears and pleading, she had come at last—too late to save my body but perfectly timed to soothe my bewildered soul.

"Mother," I breathed, instinctively rushing toward her, wanting to embrace her.

"My sweet daughter," she crooned just as she had when I was babe. I was certain she would have embraced me if it was within her power in this incorporeal state.

"Mother, I missed you so much. Where am I? Is this the Otherworld? Where is the Goddess?" The words tumbled out in a rush.

My mother smiled, a lovely, luminous gesture that filled my whole being with the sunshine of loving acceptance. "She is here. She is everywhere." She regarded me with appraising eyes. "But you are asking the wrong questions. It matters not whether your heart still beats. What you should be asking is do you wish it to? Are you ready to leave your life behind and stay with me?"

I began to shake. My mind whirled through everything I had lost in the last few years—her, Aggrivane, and for all practical purposes, my father. I could abandon it all because there was nothing left for me in the world. But then I thought of Arthur, and for a brief moment, I could see him, collapsed by my bedside next to the pale, fragile body I barely recognized as my own. His head was bent as if in prayer, his hands clasped so tightly over the motionless bones of my arm that his knuckles were white. Long strands of hair, flecked gold at odd intervals in the somber candlelight, curtained his face from sight, but I could tell from the quaking of his large frame that he was sobbing, grieving for the wife he thought was dead.

Perhaps I was. I looked back at my mother in confusion, more uncertain than ever what was happening.

"Can you leave him?" she asked as two children appeared next to her.

One was a confident, proud young boy, perhaps two years old, the other an angelic girl of the same age. Both had identical bright green eyes and long tawny locks.

"Your children are safe and happy here. I will take care of them just as I did you."

A bittersweet blend of joy and sadness washed over me. So they had both died. I was certain I would have been crying if I'd had tears to shed in this world between worlds.

"May I see them?" I asked tremulously, almost afraid of the answer.

My mother nodded, and they scampered to me, so calm and comfortable I was certain they knew I was their mother. I sank down so my eyes were level with theirs, and to my great astonishment, I felt two small, sticky hands around each of my arms, and I was able to hold them against my heart, which I now felt beating faintly.

Somewhere in the back of my mind, I knew what was happening. Without realizing it, I had made my decision as soon as I had witnessed Arthur's pain, and I was slowly returning to life. It also meant I was slowly losing my children all over again.

I looked into their eyes, determined they would know just how much I loved them. Somehow being able to hold them and gaze into their eyes was all the communication I needed. The spirit spoke without words.

After a long while, the boy squeezed me tight, and the girl placed a dainty kiss on my cheek. Then a host of other children appeared— the brothers and sisters I had never known. Some had the stormy gray-blue eyes and defined chin of my father, while in the faces of others, I saw my mother or even my paternal grandmother looking back at me. With a final look at me, my twins darted off to the edges of the meadow to play, shrieking the earsplitting yelps of joy only children can produce, tumbling over one another but never getting hurt.

My mother took a few steps forward and encircled me in her arms, warmth radiating through all my limbs. "You must return now. But know I love you for all time. I promise to watch over you and welcome you to the Otherworld when your time comes. Have faith and trust in the God and Goddess to whom you have pledged your life."

I nodded, tears scalding my cheeks. "I will. I love you."

A dull humming noise, like the crescendo of a wordless chant, rose in my ears, and the edges of my vision blurred. I turned, facing a portal of shimmering golden light. All I had to do was step through, and I would be back in my body.

I glanced over my shoulder in time to catch one final glimpse of her, now holding my children like an image of the Mother Goddess.

"Good-bye, Mother." The words I had been deprived the chance to say in life echoed behind me as I fell through golden rain into the darkness of unconsciousness.

ↄ℮ ℮ↄ

They told me Arthur kept vigil at my bedside from the moment Octavia's call of distress had brought him to the birth that had gone badly. As the servants replaced the bloody bed linens, he lifted my lifeless body, begging me in strained whispers not to abandon him. Long after the servants had slipped back to their quarters, eyes red-rimmed and shoulders sagging with fear, grief, and guilt, long after Grainne had prepared my babes for their burial and placed a soft hand on Arthur's shoulder, telling him my spirit was all but gone, Arthur remained. Stubborn as the bear for which he was named, he refused to accept my death.

When I surfaced from the black depths separating the worlds, eyelids fluttering in the golden light of a new day, Arthur stirred, disbelieving. He lifted his head from where it rested on my belly and stared at my face, rubbing his eyes like one convinced he dreamed still. I smiled weakly, raising the first three fingers on my right hand in an attempt to reach him.

"Guinevere," he breathed, tears sliding down his cheeks. "The gods be praised. My prayers do not go unheeded."

He embraced me as gently as he dared and called for Grainne, who appeared prepared to conduct a funeral, if her somber expression and lowered eyes were any indication. She nearly dropped her candle at the sight of me sitting up and blinking, weakened but very much in the realm of mortals.

Once she had given me a thorough examination and declared I would live, her attention returned to the most dreaded of all priestess' duties—a child's funeral. I had been unconscious a full two days, but they had delayed the royal burial out of concern I would need to be interred with my children.

They were to have their funerary rites at sunset as was custom. Arthur had decreed his children should be entombed with his father in a nearly inaccessible valley at the base of the highest of the Western Fells. It was an ideal royal resting place for few would be brave enough to venture in and do the graves harm, and it was fast becoming Camelot's royal cemetery.

I wasn't well enough to travel to the funeral, and truth be told, I didn't want to. I had said good-bye to my children in the Otherworld. But that wasn't enough to keep the sight at bay. Weakened by grief and my childbed travails, I was defenseless against it. Against my will, it transported me to that final, terrible ritual as clearly as though I were at Arthur's side.

Most of the city, as well as nobles from three neighboring kingdoms, turned out to bid farewell to the future of the realm, the prince and princess they'd never know. From Camelot's gates to the entrance to the valley, noble and peasant stood shoulder to shoulder. In more populated areas, people lined the streets so thickly the Combrogi had to ride ahead of the bier, cutting a path for the wagon to pass, and guards lined every side, doing their best to keep villagers from touching the caskets, which the peasants believed held some magical power.

Still, by the time its wheels stilled in the muddy, snow-dappled basin, the funerary cart was laden with gifts from the people: sprays of late season flowers, berries, and leaves; evergreen boughs symbolizing life after death; and bracelets and trinkets of gold, bronze, and silver. They were offerings made on the children's behalf, which Arthur dropped into the sacred stream that sliced through the valley.

When the time came, Merlin led the prayers over the bodies with Grainne acting as his assistant. With gentle, trembling hands, Arthur placed our babies in their graves, arranging their bodies in the traditional posture—pointing north on their left side, knees curled up and arms crossed over their chests in an attitude of sleep, heads facing east to look toward the promise of rebirth. He folded the funeral shrouds over them but could do no more. Sinking to his knees, he wept so hard his entire body shook. It was left to Kay and Bedivere, his trusted companions, to place our funerary gifts at their sides and fill in the graves.

Arthur kept watch with our son and daughter as day faded into night.

Finally, when the moon had risen and the frigid air made icicles in Arthur's beard, Merlin put an arm around him. "It is time to depart, old friend. Let them rest in peace. You kingdom awaits your return."

Throughout the long visions, my eyes were dry. My heart clenched in agony, but silent sobs were the only outward sign of my grief. As I lay curled in bed, seeking to hide from the visions and the pain, my body betrayed me, breasts leaking milk for mouths that would never taste it. I felt the emptiness of loss with every movement, keenly aware that those who had so recently inhabited my body now rested in the womb of the earth.

PART TWO

Hunted

Chapter Eight

Summer 500

I didn't need to hear the words to know what everyone was saying. I sensed it in their pitying glances, saw it cloaked in the eyes of courtiers, scented it on the wind that carried the servants' secrets beyond the alleyways, and in my darkest moments, I even tasted it on my husband's tongue. In the alehouses and barracks, ripening fields and desolate moors, they all whispered the same refrain—"the queen is barren."

Two years had passed since my children were born dead, and still my womb refused to allow life to take root. Grainne had assured me from the moment I regained consciousness that there was no reason I could not have many more children, but even then I had been suspicious. As a midwife, I had on occasion lied to a grieving mother, especially when I sensed that telling her the truth would mean taking away all she had to live for.

If that was the case for Grainne, I would not hold it against her. It was my highest duty to produce an heir. If she saw some merit in giving me false hope, then I would credit the cloud of deception in her gray-blue eyes to my own untamed imagination.

For a while, I was able to convince myself she was right, especially when, a few months after I had recovered, my moon time came and went without a drop of blood for three straight months. In that small bloom of anticipation, my world was right once again. But hope was drowned in a rush of crimson that returned with every new moon to remind me of my failure to my husband and my country.

"Arthur, we must decide what to do if this continues. We cannot leave the country without an heir," I told him late one night as we lay in bed.

He grunted his agreement. "I have thought upon that much since our children died. We could pick up the plan my father abandoned and name one of Lot's sons to the throne. Gawain would make an excellent king."

"But what of those who believe the throne should pass through my line? My nearest relative is my cousin Bran."

"Does he wish to take the throne?"

I thought hard. As a member of the Combrogi and ruler of Gwynned, Bran was known well to both of us. Though he was a capable fighter, he had not the stomach to take on a larger kingdom, much less the entire country. "No, I do not believe so."

"Then we must approach the house of Lothian and, failing that, pick another of the Combrogi. I would like to watch Mark's nephew Constantine. Like Tristan, he is a strong strategist and a capable fighter. After Gawain, he may be our wisest choice. Let us allow time to reveal the answer."

As we grappled with the real possibly of a childless future, life at Camelot continued. This month we held pleading day outside in the courtyard rather than in the Great Hall to capture the blessed relief of occasional breezes tossed up from the harbor. However, the winds could scarcely reach us, blocked as they were by the sour bodies gathered around us. The crowd was attracted by the oaths and screeching of our last case, a loud quarrel between two lordlings who came to blows before Arthur and I could render judgment.

Before we could call forth the next petitioner, a man emerged from the crowd, the ragged, coarse material of his tunic dragging behind him. Sobbing, he fell to his knees at our feet, mumbling something that sounded like "forgive me" over and over. He clutched and clawed at our legs as though we could save him from whatever plagued his mind.

I clambered back in my chair, seeking to move out of his reach. I sent Kay and Lancelot a warning glare, ready to call them into service to remove the intruder.

He was trembling, eyes rolling about uncontrollably as he begged, "Mercy, my lord, have mercy."

Arthur leaned toward him, placing a hand on his bony shoulder. "What crime have you committed? How may I show you mercy?"

The man looked up, and his eyes cleared for one awful moment, holding in their depths the chilling resolve only madness could create. "Murder."

Kay and Lancelot inched closer, but Arthur paid them no heed. His deranged subject held all of his attention. "Whom have you killed? Why come before me?"

The man shook his head as if loathe to confess the nature of his crime. He stared at us for a long moment. Then slowly he pointed at Arthur, speaking so softly we had to lean forward to hear him whisper, "You have the eyes of the dead."

My skin prickled, and I caught the flash of steel, but before I could react, a dark-haired woman leapt out of the throng and tackled our claimant, sending him sprawling with a cry of pain. The crowd let out a collective gasp and backed quickly away. Arthur and I were on our feet, weapons drawn, while half the Combrogi surrounded our attackers.

"What is the meaning of this?" Arthur roared.

"I have just saved your life," the woman announced.

We stepped cautiously toward where she lay, still holding our claimant. She lifted his left arm, which dangled uselessly in her grip, and revealed a thin blade pressed against his palm and wrist, concealed beneath a tattered sleeve. It was the same hand he had held out to Arthur.

"This was inches from your throats, and neither of you saw it." She looked at us, accusation plain in her stunning black eyes.

For a moment, neither of us moved. Then involuntarily, my hand went to my throat.

"How do we know you are not involved, merely part of the trick?" I asked.

"Because if I were," she said with a look of disdain, "you would be dead by now."

Arthur recovered himself, expression blossoming as though he had just been made party to the plot of some elaborate joke. "Indeed, Sobian can be lethal when she puts her mind to it."

I stared at him, openmouthed. "You know this woman?"

Arthur laughed, a hearty sound that began in his chest and escaped as a joyous rumble. He extended a hand to the woman and helped her to her feet. "Kay, take this man away." He kicked the madman with the toe of his boot.

"Gladly." Kay pulled our would-be killer roughly to his feet. "I have additional business with you." His voice held the promise of dreaded things to come.

I was still speechless, trying to comprehend what had just taken place. This woman had come out of nowhere to save us from a madman bent on killing us both but whom neither of us, trained in the arts of war, had suspected. Now it appeared Arthur knew her.

I took Arthur's hand, suddenly unsteady. "What is going on? Who is this woman?"

Arthur's smile brightened. "Guinevere, meet Sobian, Scourge of Sidhe."

Sobian brushed off her deep golden cloak and sank into a curtsey. "I am honored to be of service, my queen."

I took in the stunned crowd standing around us, as unsure of how to react as I was. "I—how do you know one another?"

Arthur's gaze followed mine. "That is a story best told in private."

Bedivere and Lancelot set about dispersing the crowd while Arthur invited Sobian inside. He sent servants ahead with orders for strong ale and water so Sobian could wash. I followed on their heels, still confused and feeling suddenly displaced by our guest.

Arthur and I sat in a small meeting room just off the main hall, waiting as Sobian cleaned the dirt from her clothes and skin. Octavia brought in the ale then hovered protectively at my side, just like the second mother I'd always felt her to be. I put a hand reassuringly on the one she laid on my shoulder.

"I am fine," I told her between long draughts of ale. "Really."

Her eyes narrowed. "Keep telling yourself that and eventually you may believe it, but I don't. I can feel you trembling."

Was I? I stilled myself for a moment. Wild energy still coursed through my veins from the attack, but beneath that, yes, I was shaking. And why should I not be? Some lunatic had just tried to kill us both, and I never saw it coming. I took a deep breath and tried to arrange my thoughts. Best start with the most pressing issue. "Arthur, who *is* this woman? Why do you trust her so?"

Arthur smiled, his face taking on a dreamy air as though he recalled a cherished memory. "Let's just say that during my time in Uther's army, I grappled with her on more than one occasion. Sobian is, to this day, one of the most fearsome creatures I have ever encountered."

"More fearsome than I?" I quirked an eyebrow at him, daring him to give the wrong answer.

His smile widened, and he leaned forward to kiss me. "Of course not."

I gestured for him to continue. "Get back to your story. I want to know who this woman is before she returns."

"This woman, as you call her, has always gone by the name Sobian, though I've never believed her to be Irish. She used to be a river pirate. I first encountered her when I was stationed at Caerleon near the Bristol Channel. Uther sent a contingent of men because she was causing a lot of trouble on the Sabrina. If you were foolish enough to fall for her charms, you'd lose your purse faster than your pants." Arthur chuckled. "They called her the Scourge of the Sidhe because she had the ability to slip on and off of ships with her crew as stealthily as the fey and the charm to convince the captain he'd given her his goods of his own free will."

"It's hard to believe one woman could possess such charm," I said dryly.

"Oh, I assure you, she does. Wait a bit. I'm sure she'll turn it on you. Women certainly aren't immune."

"Immune to what?" Sobian entered the room as Octavia quietly slipped out.

"I was just telling my wife about your reputation."

She gave me a dazzling smile. "I knew I was not ever far from your mind, my king." She curtseyed to Arthur, lowering her long lashes at same time as her bosom.

I did my best to hide the glower her shameless flirting brought to my face before she looked up.

"Please sit with us and have a drink. It is the least we can do for you." He held out a cup to her, and she obliged his request. Arthur leaned toward her across the table. "How did you know what that man was going to do? Do you think him genuinely mad?"

Sobian's reaction was guarded as she watched me over the rim of her cup. "Let's just say I had been tracking him for some time and knew better than to believe what I saw."

Her vague answer did nothing to improve my opinion of her. "How exactly does a river pirate know how to spot an assassin?"

"I left that profession many years ago. Now I earn my keep in many ways."

Arthur arched an eyebrow. "So you are an honest woman now?"

Her amusement came out as a trilling laugh. "I would not say that, but I am no longer a criminal if that is what you mean."

"What *do* you do?" I asked.

"I have been a warrior, a spy, and even an outlaw for a time."

"And an assassin," I added.

Sobian's eyes grew wide, and she made to protest.

I held up a hand to silence her denial. "Don't bother. I was trained by one of the best warriors on this isle and know you have to be aware of what to look for in order to spot someone as convincing as our criminal."

Sobian was dumbstruck. She turned to Arthur. "I would never—"

"I know. Please forgive my wife's rudeness." He shot me a scathing look. "She does not know you as do I. In fact, I was thinking that we can use a woman of your skills."

It was my turn to be incredulous. I set down my cup with more force than I intended. "We can?"

"Yes." His tone brooked no argument. "Today has shown us our security is weak, and I cannot have that. Sobian, you have seen the law from both sides. You know its holes. I believe you can help me improve my ability to protect myself, my wife, and my people."

Sobian took a long drink. "What exactly are you asking of me?"

"I would like you to lead my cadre of spies. You will learn everything you can of our friends and enemies."

I cringed at the thought of having this woman around regularly. "Kay already acts as your second, and I have Lancelot as my champion. What more protection do we need?"

Arthur's exasperation came out in a flare of temper. "Guinevere, you have a strategic mind. If you let go of your petty fear that I will give you up for Sobian—which will not happen, I assure you—you will be able to see the wisdom in my choice. Kay and Lancelot protect us daily, but someone needs to be in command. Until now, I have filled that role, but it is becoming clear I cannot handle that duty in addition to governing my country. Sobian has already proven her loyalty to us. Who better to employ?"

My cheeks reddened. I could not believe he would call me jealous in front of her, no matter what their history. "First of all, *husband*, I have no fear of this woman. If need be, I will prove that to you in the sparring ring. Second, will it not appear strange that a woman is suddenly in charge of our guard? I do not think your men will take kindly to taking orders from her."

Arthur regarded me calmly, a challenge in his eyes. "Nor do I. That is why her true role will only be known to us and our champions. Sobian, you are well versed in subterfuge. Do you believe you could pretend to hold another role while acting in this one?"

Sobian looked back and forth between us, chewing the nail of her littlest finger as she weighed her options. "Of course."

Arthur stood, motioning for us to do the same. He placed my hand in Sobian's. "Meet your new lady's maid."

I coughed, choking on the ale I was swallowing. "Arthur, you must be joking."

"Not at all. It is the perfect disguise. She will have every right to be near us."

"I already have Octavia. What do you suggest I do, turn her out? And what will people say when Sobian is seen meeting with you in private?"

"Octavia will continue to fulfill the same duties she always has. She will simply appear to have more help." He cast a flirtatious look in Sobian's direction. "As for what people will say, kings have had dalliances with maids since time began. The more they believe that, the less likely they are to suspect the truth."

I shoved Arthur with both hands, knowing the act wouldn't budge him, but it made me feel better. "I am simply supposed to go along with this, is that right?"

Arthur said nothing.

I looked from one to the other, knowing I was trapped. Arthur's plan was sound, but I did not like the idea of living in close company with a woman Arthur had obviously befriended in the past any more than I liked knowing people would think he was disloyal to me. Arguing with him would do no good. Perhaps I could tolerate the situation until I found a reason to have Sobian removed. "If you two will excuse me, I would like to lie down."

I was halfway out of the room before Sobian came trailing after me. "Let me assist you, my lady," she offered, amusement clear in her voice.

"I do not require your services," I spat over my shoulder.

◦◦◦

I made it to my room and slammed the door. Alone at last, I leaned against the door, struggling to catch my breath. Tears spilled over as the enormity of the day finally sank in. I slid down to the floor and ran my hands through my hair. How could my life have changed so much in only a few hours? I thought Arthur had grown to love me, but he had just accepted a former lover back into his confidence after only having been reunited with her for a few hours. What did that mean for my marriage?

I didn't know how long I spent contemplating my situation, but just as quickly as the tears had come, I started laughing. I was being ridiculous. Arthur had had to learn to live with Aggrivane at court long ago. Granted he'd sent my former betrothed on missions away from Camelot as often as possible, but he had still learned how to cope with his presence. I was behaving like a child. Galen had been right the day we argued in the forest so many years before. I really was as bad as a fisherman's wife. And worse, I had changed little with the passage of time. I stood, straightening my dress and mentally preparing myself to apologize to them both.

After a few deep breaths, I went back down to the meeting room, expecting to find Arthur and Sobian discussing the finer points of her new role. But to my surprise, the room was empty. Octavia came in, holding a tray to collect the ale pitcher and our used glasses.

"Do you know where Arthur went?"

She eyed me carefully. "He is in his room. Alone." She emphasized the word, knowing I would wonder. "They told me about her new role. Are you in agreement that it is wise?"

"I will be," I reassured her.

Octavia made a noise indicating she wasn't so certain then busied herself cleaning up the table. That was when I saw the lone sheet of paper. Thinking it to be notes from Arthur and Sobian's discussion, I bent over the table to get a better look.

My blood turned to ice. The letters were formed of patterns made by varying lengths of horizontal, vertical, and diagonal lines. It was written in Ogham, the ancient language of the Druids, so it could not have come from Arthur. He hadn't studied with them long enough to have learned it. Plus, its message was not one a husband leaves his wife.

I ran to Arthur's room, rubbing my hand over the goose-pimpled flesh of my arm. "You may wish to rethink your decision," I said as I entered.

He looked up. "Why is that?"

I held the paper out to him. "This was left in the meeting room." I shivered again.

He plucked the paper out of my hand and turned it in several directions, trying to figure out how to read it. "Ogham. That's unusual. What does it say?"

I grabbed it back, irritated beyond decorum. After what had happened with the madman and Sobian, I didn't think I could take much more.

"That's the problem. I think it's a threat. *'My queen, you may close your eyes to the one you scorned, but that will not keep me away. I will breathe your last breath so that you will live on forever in me.'*"

Arthur's face darkened. "Only one man could claim such a thing."

I looked at him quizzically, brow furrowing. "How do you know Sobian isn't party to this? It appeared right after she did in the very room she last occupied."

Arthur sighed, clearly frustrated that I didn't trust Sobian implicitly as he did. "Because this isn't her way. As she said, if she wished you dead, you would be. She has no need for idle threats."

"Who then?"

"Think about the message." His tone took on a condescending air I did not care for. "Someone you once rejected? Who did you give up to marry me? You may not want to see it, but the answer is right in front of you."

He didn't have to say the name. Suddenly I knew exactly who he blamed. His menacing gaze was fixed on my former lover.

Guilty or not, Aggrivane was in serious trouble.

⁖⁙⁖

Within the week, Aggrivane was given a special assignment as an envoy in Brittany, and Camille chose to go with him. In many ways, it was easier for me not having him around, not being reminded of what would never be, especially with Camille's recent pregnancy. That had been a surprise given Aggrivane's insistence on their love being chaste. Plus, while I'd never suspected Aggrivane, I breathed a little easier knowing he was out of easy reach of Arthur's wrath.

But despite this move, the notes continued appearing as summer progressed, which meant Aggrivane couldn't have sent them. They came at odd intervals, frequently enough that the sender had to be nearby—messages didn't travel that quickly from Brittany— but inconsistently enough that I could never anticipate them. Or rather, I was *always* anticipating them, always on edge, as I was sure my hunter intended. Each one was more threatening and found in a more intimate location than the last. The fear they provoked built along with summer's heat. These were no mere mind games; whoever was doing this had a point to prove—he or she had, or could gain, personal access to me. It had to be someone in our inner circle, but I had no idea who it could be or why this was happening.

Then on the night of the full moon, after Grainne and I completed our ritual, I found a tattered page tied to the apple tree in the center of the labyrinth at the very heart of Camelot. Without reading its sinister message, I crumpled it with a snarl and marched straight to Arthur's quarters.

"I cannot take any more of this. I am the queen. I will not have one of my subjects threatening me. If you will not act to find out who is doing this, I will."

Arthur stood. "What will you do?" he asked with a mocking chuckle. "Interrogate each man of the realm until one finally confesses? I'm already doing everything that can be done, wife. Sobian is investigating. Give her time." He marched over to me, towering above me. "And if you ever speak to me like that again. . ."

I looked up at him, steel in my eyes. "You'll what? Divorce me? Hit me? In the former, you cannot, and in the latter, you forget I can and will take you on any day."

"Is that so?" He picked me up and carried me to his bed. "Let us see how well you fare."

◦◦◦

It was Sobian's idea to gather the kings of the tribes, their lordlings, and the Combrogi at Arthur's southern power base, a scarred hill fort called Cadbury. Officially, we were together to celebrate Samhain—the night the old year gave way to the new—but what only those closest to the crown knew was that Sobian had reason to believe this area was linked to the source of the chilling notes.

"When I was a pirate, I amassed a vast collection of valuable paperwork along with the other booty," she explained. "Naturally, I kept any correspondence written by those in power in case it would ever prove useful leverage. In time, I noticed these pages had common characteristics, such as the way the vellum was prepared or even the color of the ink, little signatures that betrayed a common maker. By matching those with the name of sender, I could usually narrow down the location of origin." She tapped one of the threatening notes against her hand. "I believe this came from somewhere in the south-central part of the Summer Country."

We couldn't accuse anyone based on that idea, but it was a place to start. Sobian suggested we gather everyone in the area and observe them in the abandon of the feast when they would be most at ease.

Situated atop a towering hill overlooking the Somerset Levels, Cadbury had one of the most impressive views I'd ever seen. From its walls, farmland, bogs, and untamed wilderness stretched to the horizon in every direction. Anyone foolish enough to attack this fort would be seen long before they glimpsed the castle and its four terraced earthen banks and ditches surrounded by thick stands of trees. Even if they did manage to overcome those obstacles, the castle itself was ringed by a wooden palisade with several gatehouses full of archers and armed troops. Arthur had chosen his location well.

Cadbury was even more impressive from the inside. The great hall, a massive structure separate from the fortress's other buildings, was larger than any I'd ever seen, even Camelot. Above me, its support timbers stretched like ancient oaks into darkness even hundreds of candles could not penetrate. Based on the number of bodies milling about, I was fairly confident it could hold nearly a thousand people without strain.

At a signal from Arthur, Kay rapped on the underside of the table, indicating to the crowd they should quiet down—and for a moment, I was back in Corbenic the night Arthur had proposed and turned my life upside down. I shook my head to clear it and pushed my goblet out of arm's reach. Whatever Arthur had them serving was too strong for me to consume without measure. I needed my wits about me if I was to observe whatever actions Arthur suspected would be brought out as our guests drank themselves into unsuspecting candor.

Arthur stood, watching imperiously as his guests settled and turned their faces to him. "I promise you will not have to listen to me overmuch this night—"

"Aye, we all know how you love making speeches," Bedivere interrupted from his table below the dais, brotherly grin bright enough to light the night.

Arthur acknowledged him with an expression colored by a mix of amusement and annoyance before turning back to the assembly. "It is by no coincidence I picked this night to bring you together. It is the new year, and as the wheel of time turns once more, it is a time for celebrating, a time for new beginnings and unity. In that same spirit of brotherhood, I wish to introduce all of you tonight to our newest member. As many of you know, Mark of Cornwall has ruled the kingdom of Dyfneint in addition to his own land since his brother's passing into the Otherworld. This night, he wishes to formally pass control of Dyfneint to his nephew, Constantine." Arthur raised his hand, indicating the two men should rise.

Mark looked around at the assembled lords. "I could have passed the crown to my nephew in private, but I wanted all of you to know he takes this throne with my blessing." He stepped forward and kissed his nephew, removing a golden torque from around his neck and placing it around Constantine's throat. He turned back to the crowd. "My fellow lords, regardless of your quarrels with me, if you recognize my nephew as the rightful ruler of Dyfneint, please stand that I may see you."

Arthur remained standing, and I joined him, offering Mark a compassionate smile. One by one, each of the lords, including Ana, silently rose.

Mark nodded his thanks. "In that knowledge, I bid you all peace." He and his nephew took their seats.

Before Arthur could speak again, Malegant stood. "My king, if we are using this feast as a public stage for private matters, I wish to speak."

Beside me, Arthur stiffened. He still hadn't forgiven Malegant for his embarrassing tussle in the market all those years before, for which Malegant had been banished from court for three months. "Lord Malegant, I remind you this is not pleading day. If you have a case to lay before the court, I suggest you come to Camelot on the next full moon with everyone else."

"But this isn't just any case. And I too wish the full witness of the court to its outcome."

Arthur pursed his lips behind folded hands. "I have a feeling if I forbid you to speak you will do so anyway, and I have no desire to eject you from my court *again*. You may proceed, but be brief." He sat down hard on the bench, hunched shoulders and taut muscles clearly displaying his displeasure.

Malegant bowed with dramatic flourish. "Thank you, my king."

Arthur made an impatient gesture, commanding him to get to the point.

"Quite simply, I am here to lodge a formal complaint that Lord Uriens still holds approximately one hundred of my men captive in his lands. I have petitioned this court multiple times against him, and still they languish rather than being reunited with their families."

Before Arthur could issue a rebuttal, Uriens was on his feet, rushing toward Malegant with the virility of a man half his years. "You attacked me, remember? Do you truly expect no punishment for your breach of peace? Did it ever occur to you that our king has taken no action because he feels me justified in my acts?"

Malegant shot Arthur a disdainful look. "If that is so, then he is not only cowardly but a disgrace to his role."

The collective intake of breath in the room was audible. Many of the men in the crowd stood, loyalty and instinct bidding them to protect their king.

Before I could blink, Uriens had his eating dagger drawn, blade at Malegant's throat from behind. "I could split you open from ear to ear here and now, and no one would lift a finger to stop me, you traitorous bastard!"

Weapons were not allowed at the quarterly meetings, but still Combrogi rushed forward to do what they could to prevent any further violence.

Malegant grinned evilly. "Go ahead, old man."

Uriens flicked his wrist and blood ran from Malegant's throat, but the younger man spun away before the blade could do any serious damage. Malegant picked up his own utensil and caught Uriens in the side. Blood blossomed in a crimson stain on Uriens's tunic.

Malegant laughed, a cruel sound of dark glee. He wielded his dagger at the others. "Who else wishes to oppose me?" He turned his manic eyes on Arthur. "Do you dare challenge me, king?"

"Surrender or I will kill you myself," Arthur yelled.

Malegant made a show of thinking. "I rather like my odds."

He turned and melted into the now turbulent crowd, most of whom were trying to stop him. He dodged bodies and gloved fists as though he had trained for this very moment, shoving some men aside, tripping and punching others until he was free.

Arthur motioned to Kay, Lancelot, and Sobian. "Take your troops and be sure he leaves this city in worse shape than he entered it. And if he happens to stop breathing in the process, bring me his head on a pole."

୭୬୧ ୨୧୧

I sat dumbfounded in the chaos that followed, unable to do more than watch as Morgan tended to her injured husband and groups mobilized to ensure Malegant was apprehended.

Arthur sat equally silent, a vein in his neck pulsing rapidly.

"Owain and Accolon will kill him for that," I finally said.

Arthur grunted, a masculine sound I had grown to associate with disapproval. "If they can find him. That slippery bastard has more holdings in this part of the country than there are chambers in a beehive."

"Do we still hold the feast, or would it be better to postpone?" I asked.

"No, we will proceed. Sobian still wants to see how everyone acts when deep in their cups. Now I must be her eyes." Arthur motioned Bors over. "Tell the servants to bring out dinner. That should tempt everyone back to order." He winked at me. "If I know one thing, it's that rumbling stomachs sooner obey the call of food than ears listen to any order. Uther's army taught me that."

Arthur was right. At the first whiff of food, the remaining lords who had chosen not to chase after Malegant turned their attention from their plans and arguments to peer over one another's shoulders, hoping to catch a glimpse of what delicacies were being laid on the table. Soon, all were seated, their earlier proclamations quieted to a hushed buzz of conversation.

I had just taken my first bite of roasted meat when a serving maid approached us from behind.

The girl bowed her head. "Forgive me, my king, but I am sent to find the queen."

"I am here. What need have you?"

The girl kept her eyes on the ground. "My lord Aggrivane has need of your skills for his wife and child lie ill in the next building."

I wondered why I had not seen them among the crowd. As much as I disliked Camille, I wouldn't have wished her ill health. I looked at Arthur, trying to gauge his reaction.

He nodded. "Go, but take Gareth with you. I will not have you alone with so many revelers and madmen about."

I touched his hand in thanks. "If Morgan returns, send her as well. We may have need of her. . . specialized skill." I choked out the compliment. "I will meet you back here when I am finished."

The girl and I found Gareth then fled into the cool night, a fine spray of mist falling from the moonless sky. I shielded my eyes from the unexpected brightness of dozens of leaping bonfires. As my eyes adjusted, the courtyard came alive with dancers, hundreds of people packed into the confines of the thick castle walls.

"Forgive me, my lady," the maid said demurely then grabbed my wrist before leading me into the fray, Gareth following close behind.

I quickly understood why she had risked touching me. If she had not, I would have quickly lost her in the shifting throng. Everywhere I looked was a whirl of light, color, and sound. The flash of a blue cloak gave way to the giddy laughter of a group of young girls enjoying their first festival and the cry of a vendor hawking skewers of meat. Faces whirled past, some painted into masks, others unrecognizable under hoods, everyone's eyes gleaming wildly. We veered to the left, and a cup of some rank drink was thrust into my hand, but before I could see who had given it, they were swallowed up in the press of people. We wove right, dodging a knot of rowdy men, and I yelled my apologies as I stepped on someone's foot. I turned back just in time to narrowly miss colliding with a brazier.

I was panting by the time we reached the doors of the next building, a long, low structure like the ones in which we lived in Avalon. Gareth took up his post outside. Without pausing, the maid—whose name I still did not know—opened the door and led me to the chamber where Camille and her young son were staying. His cries were audible before the door more than cracked open.

The poor thing must be miserable.

Camille was visible as soon as I entered the room. She leaned against the windowsill, clad only in her shift despite the cool dampness of the breeze. It clung to her, fixed in place by sweat. She held her screaming son on her right hip, propping herself up with the other. The strain in her features said she was using all her energy to stand upright.

Camille looked up, her face pale and drawn, hair plastered to her forehead and neck. "I can't get him to stop crying." Her voice was thin and weak.

"Here"—I reached out to take him—"let me try."

Her hands barely brushed mine, but it was enough to confirm she was burning with fever. Her son's forehead was equally hot, his tiny, clenched palms clammy as he beat against my shoulder.

"Shhh. . . all will be well, little one," I cooed, stroking his hair, careful not to bounce him and upset what likely was a delicate tummy. "Camille, please lie down." I pulled the sheets back from the bed. I turned to the maid. "Has she anything else to wear?"

The maid removed another thin tunic from a chest and helped Camille into the dry clothing.

Camille lay back. "I wonder why you bother when I will just sweat through it too." She spoke through cracked lips that looked painful even from a distance.

I turned to the maid. "Water some wine and bring it back here for her. Then go to the kitchen and bring back some yarrow and feverfew, honey, a flagon of wine, a small cooking pot, a mortar and pestle, and as much willow bark as you can find."

The maid curtsied and scampered off without a word.

I smiled at Camille. "I will make a tea that will hopefully help both of you sleep and bring the fever down. How long have you been ill?"

Camille's eyes fluttered closed as she lost her battle to keep them open. "I felt strangely upon rising this morning and grew weaker throughout the day. Llew became restless only a few hours ago. He is why I did not attend the feast."

I looked at Llew, who had finally stopped screaming and trying to beat me into making him feel better. He was worn into submission, a cranky mew the only indication he was still fighting whatever illness held him in its grip.

The maid returned with the wine and some of the supplies. She helped Camille drink while I struggled to grind the herbs with one hand and keep Llew secure in my other arm. Once the maid was gone again to fetch the rest, I looked at Camille, who had sunk into sleep, her breathing shallow but even.

"Your mother needs her rest, little Llew. And so do you. Sleep now." I abandoned the mortar and rubbed the top of his head, willing his tiny eyelids to grow heavy. "The Goddess guard you as you slumber." I kissed his tiny limp hand as he finally drifted off.

I didn't know how long I sat there holding him before a voice cold as ice woke me from my reverie.

"Does it pain you to know he could have been yours?"

I looked up to see Morgan draped in the doorway, arms crossed defensively.

She was right. He could have been my son had Aggrivane and I married. I shifted Llew's weight in my arms. Now that she mentioned it, it did hurt, but I wouldn't let her know.

"Does it pain you to be such a shrew?" I snapped back.

Morgan pushed off the doorframe and moved back to let the maid through. "Suit yourself. I don't have to help you."

I would have let her go if Camille hadn't woken right then, mumbling incoherently. I handed Llew to Morgan and rushed to her side, cupping her forehead. "Her fever is worsening."

Morgan laid Llew next to Camille in the bed. Without a word, she stripped off her cloak, rolled up the sleeves of her tunic, and rattled off yet another list of supplies for the poor maid to fetch. Then she hung the pot over the fire and poured in the honey, which caught the light and reflected it onto her face, making her glow like some Otherworldly being.

Like the fey they say she hails from. That rumor had been around before I set foot on Avalon's shores and had dogged her ever since. Sometimes I wondered if it was true.

I picked up the mortar and pestle and continued grinding. "How is your husband?"

She threw me a look that clearly questioned my motives for asking. "He is resting nearby. The wound is serious, but there is nothing else I can do for now." She stirred the honey before setting the spoon down with a bang.

Llew woke, whimpered, and I scooped him up.

Morgan turned on me, scooping the herbs out of the mortar and flinging them into the pot without so much as glancing down. "Why did Arthur let him go? If my husband had done that to"—she struggled to say Malegant's name but could not—"anyone, he would have been arrested on the spot. Why not the same punishment for *him?*"

"We tried, Morgan. You were there. He escaped."

Morgan gave me a chiding sidelong glance. "Is that really the best you can do? Do you think me so dim-witted that that explanation will suffice? I'll go after him myself if I have to." She began pouring the amber liquid into two cups.

"No, don't. He's dangerous."

She snorted. "You think I don't know that? I've dealt with him before. I know how changeable his alliances are. He's in league with whoever benefits him."

"Much like you." The words slipped out before I realized I was even thinking them.

Her eyes widened, and she stopped pouring. "Is that what you think of me?"

"Does it really surprise you? You've always lived for yourself—you have said as much."

"Believe what you will." She paused as if thinking, then her mouth curved into a vindictive sneer. "You'd better enjoy holding that little boy because he's the last child who will ever fill your arms. Your bloodline dies with you. But mark my words—one day my child will be greater than even you. You may think I am concerned only with my own well-being, but you know nothing. Absolutely nothing."

I tipped one of the cups into Llew's tiny mouth, too stunned to respond. He gurgled and attempted to spit out the contents, but I wouldn't let him. When he finally swallowed, I put him back into bed with Camille, who woke only long enough to drink her own dose.

"I will stay with them," Morgan said. "Go back to your husband. I should be here, close to mine." I took a few steps toward the door before Morgan called after me. "Be on your guard. Evil spirits roam this night."

I rolled my eyes. Of course they did. It was the feast of the dead, the night when the veil between the worlds was the thinnest. But I was a trained priestess with one of Aggrivane's younger brothers as a guard. I had nothing to fear.

◦◦◦

By the time Gareth and I emerged into the courtyard, the evening's drizzle had intensified to a light shower, but it wasn't stopping the revelers. The music had grown primal, fed by the deep vibrations of horns and punctuated by the rhythmic booms of drums. Around the central bonfire, a group of men and women chanted in a language ancient and dark. Although I did not understand the words, it felt somehow appropriate to invoke the ghosts of Samhain.

Even more people packed the courtyard now, so I no longer bothered to ask pardon for barging through groups or stepping on toes. Nor did they seem to care. Caught up in the ecstasy of the night, they only had eyes for one another and the spirits only they could see.

Past the painted woman decorating drunken couples with spirals and swirls, through the knots of undulating couples around the bonfires, and beyond the brawny twins hawking ale, I scurried, head bent to shield me from the rain. Then a hand shot out from a tangle of dancers, and I was caught up as they swirled through the crowd. Forced to keep up or be trampled, I was passed from one partner to another. The black eyes gazing back at me were eerily similar from one to the next.

When they finally let me go, the door to the great hall was in sight, but Gareth was not. I craned my neck, peering through the swirling mass of people to catch sight of his dark curls. Once I thought I saw him, but it turned out to be only the tanner. I was still looking for Gareth when I heard my name, spoken by a voice I recognized but could not immediately place. For a moment, I thought Gareth had caught up to me.

I turned instinctively and found myself looking up at a hooded man. When he angled his head to meet my gaze, the firelight flickered on his face, which was painted from temple to temple in red spirals. The effect was shocking, making him appear more demon than man, and obscured his identity as much as the Sacred King's had been at my first ceremony.

He leaned down so he was closer to my level. "Do you not recognize me?" He clucked his tongue disapprovingly.

I backed up, seeking escape, uncomfortable from his nearness and familiarity. Only a handful of people would have dared speak to me in such an informal way, but his build and voice did not match any of them.

"Do I know you?" I finally asked, frantically searching for the door that had been nearly within reach before he distracted me but now had vanished into thin air.

He chuckled. "Maybe this will jog your memory—'*As the dreamer dreams of solace, so I dream of you. Come with me now into the city made from earth and ashes, from which there is no escape.*'"

For a moment, I couldn't place his words. But then, with an icy chill, I realized he was quoting one of the notes, one of the ones no one else knew about.

"How? Why?" I stumbled back, unable to comprehend being face to face with the man who had stalked me for months. I edged back again but was met with cold, wet stone at my lower back. One glance down told me I had backed into the well. I struggled to keep my balance as he leaned into me.

"I told you I could get to you anytime, anywhere. And here we are." He cocked his head to the side. "Do you still not recognize me?"

He pulled back his hood, giving me a clear view of his decorated face. It took me a moment to see through the maze of markings, but when I did, a scream rose up in my throat. It was seized by panic, and I was able only to squeak out his name.

"Malegant."

He grinned mirthlessly. "That's right. And now you're coming with me."

He grabbed my wrists, preventing me from fighting back. I tried to kick my way free, but he avoided my blows just as he had avoided those in the hall. His other hand, clad in a glove, clamped over my mouth. Instinctively, I gasped, inhaling an astringent odor foreign to the leather that made me want to gag. But instead of letting me go, he pulled me close, spreading his fingers so they covered my nose as well.

My head tipped forward as I gasped for air, suddenly light-headed. The world spun around me as I fell, helpless, into his arms.

"That's it, my queen, just give in," he purred into my ear as he pulled me along.

To anyone with the presence of mind to pay us heed, we probably looked like every other drunken couple, one supporting the other as we danced ourselves into oblivion. I tried to speak, to cry out, to wrench my arms away, but I could not move. I was completely under his control. And I was slipping away, giving in despite my best efforts to fight whatever foul concoction was tempting my body to sleep.

My eyes began to close. The last thing I saw was him yanking off the glove and tossing it into the bonfire, where it was consumed by the flames.

Then there was nothing but darkness.

⁘⁙⁘

Waking was much slower than falling into the void. I was aware first of a rocking sensation and an occasional bump. Mind still addled, I mistook the rhythm for a cart or even a boat, but then I breathed in sour horse sweat. With a jolt, the events of the night came back to me. I struggled to open my eyes, heart pounding, breath heaving with the knowledge I was under Malegant's control.

My vision was hazy, marred by whatever drug Malegant had used on me and made worse by the steady rain. As we continued slowly, a blurred kaleidoscope of brown, green, and black marched with us. I tried to reach up and wipe away the rain clinging to my eyelashes, to clear my sight, but I found my hands were bound together and tied to the horse's saddle.

Then I felt it. Another heartbeat behind my own. The warmth of human contact. The familiar scent of wood smoke from the bonfires and just a slight remnant of the acerbic potion that beckoned me back to darkness even now. I fought back a wave of nausea as the realization of who was holding me upright dawned on me. Slowly, I raised my head, unable to make myself turn to look him in the face.

A low chuckle deep within his chest, a sound I felt rather than heard, was the only verbal acknowledgement he gave to my being awake, though his grip on me tightened.

There was almost no sound as we picked our way slowly down the slick, muddy track. We were still descending the steep path from the castle to the road below, so I couldn't have been unconscious long. We weren't so far away from the castle I couldn't escape. I just had to figure out how.

I breathed deeply, willing my mind to clear and fighting back a rising tide of panic. Being bound and still sluggish, escaping would not be easy, but I vowed he would not take me beyond Arthur's reach. I took stock of my situation. It was raining, so the road was wet. If our horse faltered, I would topple along with him and only gain Malegant's wrath for my efforts. He knew I was awake, so I had no element of surprise either. Nor did I have a weapon with which to wound. There was at least one horse ahead of us and one behind judging from the muddy squash made with every step of the animals' hooves. I had no way of knowing how many men were making the journey on foot. Malegant was too smart to leave me loosely guarded. He had seen me fight and knew my capabilities.

As I tried to think, the rain increased, sending streams of green paint into my eyes. So that was how he had slipped me past the tower guards. I was just a woman in a painted mask, a passed out reveler like so many others.

Inwardly, I cursed. How was this possible? Arthur had his best men, including an assassin, on Malegant's tracks, yet he'd walked out the main gate with me unconscious in his arms. It was a testament to the power of distraction. Chances were good no one was expecting him to hide in plain sight. What were the chances they were following us now?

I twisted around, straining to look past Malegant's broad shoulders for any sign we were being followed.

"No one is there. We're all alone, you and I, and my men will be of no aid to you," Malegant purred into my hair, his lips brushing my temple as he pulled me even tighter against him. I wriggled and turned my face away, trying to avoid his advances. His grip on my shoulders increased, fingertips digging bruises deep into my tense muscles. "Fighting only makes me want you more."

As if to prove his point, Malegant reined his horse to a stop and dropped the reins. His left arm slid to my waist, and he tipped me backward, pinning my arms between his body and mine as he leaned over me. I sucked in air and tried to squirm away, but he held me fast.

His lips came down on mine with surprising force, his voracious hunger forcing my lips apart until I gagged on his tongue. Summoning all my strength, I pitched forward against the solid wall of his chest and bit down hard on his tongue. He cried out and recoiled but not before I tore at his lower lip, drawing more blood.

He dragged the side of his hand across his gushing lip, yelling a string of epithets that would have made even Arthur blush. Before I could blink, the back of his hand hit me squarely in the jaw, sending me reeling, vision suddenly alight with stars and lightning. I was falling, the muddy ground quickly approaching my head, when his fingers wrapped around my calf, stopping my descent. Stinging pain spread across my scalp as he wrenched me back onto the horse by my hair. One of the gold combs that had held it in an intricate twist was lost in the mire. The strand of hair it had been responsible for fell over my face, sticking fast in the blood streaming from my nose and mouth.

His men had surrounded us, frantic to ensure I didn't escape. Their torchlight illuminated Malegant's face and his swollen lower lip. I saw myself reflected in his eyes—bloodied but far from broken.

Over his shoulder, the Tor was visible through a clearing. Its bonfires winking through the mists were an odd reminder of the feast we were supposed to be celebrating. But it also reminded me of the one weapon I possessed, one I doubted he would ever suspect.

Malegant yanked the black strands from my face, scrutinizing my eyes. He wanted me to cower and collapse, that much was clear. But he was dealing with a woman used to physical pain, trained to endure it. I would never give him the satisfaction of knowing how badly he had hurt me.

Instead, I laughed, a primal sound that stunned us both. Maybe it was the aftereffect of whatever floral essences he had used to render me unconscious or a side effect of his blow, but it was genuine. I had an idea of how I could escape.

"Bloody woman is crazy," one of Malegant's men said.

Malegant said nothing, just signaled for us to continue. His arms around me—certainly not weak before—became strong as two iron chains. There was no way I'd be able to budge until he wanted me to. But I didn't need to.

I waited until we had gone some distance and were out on the open road leading away from Cadbury before I relaxed against him. Let him think the fight had gone out of me or, better yet, that I had passed out from my wounds. I closed my eyes and breathed deeply, shutting out all sound, all sense of what was going on around me. I was aware of the energy of the night, of the feast, but as I searched deeper, I felt the familiar pulse of the Tor deep within the earth below us. I concentrated on matching my heartbeat to it, becoming one with it. As I inhaled, I drew it in, allowing the energy to pool in my fingers. Then I began to move them, slowly, subtly, drawing the mists toward me.

Once I was certain I had control, I opened my eyes. A short time later, we entered the forest. It had stopped raining but only recently. On either side, trees hugged the road so closely their dripping leaves still sent rills of freezing water down my back and between my breasts.

When we were sufficiently deep within their gnarled embrace, I let the force flow from my fingers. At first, only a ribbon of mist was visible here and there among the trees, not an unusual sight so near to dawn. But as we advanced, speeding toward our unknown destination, the fog grew subtly denser, obscuring the trees then crawling and whirling over the road like a sinister snake. It slithered upward, reaching from root to treetop until we could no longer see the coming dawn. Finally Malegant and his men slowed their horses, proceeding as though they feared the spirits hidden within the mists would accost them at any moment.

All the while, I worked the ropes binding my hands, ignoring the burn as they bit into my flesh. I nearly had enough slack when one of Malegant's men spoke up.

"My lord, there is evil magic here. Should we continue or take another route?"

Malegant tensed behind me. He stopped his horse, and the others followed suit. With one last burst of will, I brought the mists in so they surrounded us in a wall of white on all sides. I was just about to jump when Malegant seized my shoulder, forcing me to twist to face him.

He growled, low and menacing like a dog taunted past endurance. "What was your plan, priestess? To baffle us? Make us lose our way? Or did you simply hope we would turn tail and run in fright?" He clenched my fists, squeezing my fingers until I cried out. "You forget, woman, that I was married to two priestesses. I know all of your tricks. And I also know what you require to perform them."

Malegant's smile was cruel. He nodded to the guard nearest us. "Break her fingers—each one of them."

⋅֍֎⋅

Pain shot through my hands as though shards of glass were flowing in my veins. I wanted to scream, but my sore, swollen jaw would not let me speak, much less cry out. Waves of nausea ebbed and flowed, but I sensed we weren't moving anymore. That must have meant I was wherever Malegant had intended to take me.

When I opened my eyes, I expected to be chained in a dark, dank cellar. But I was lying in a soft bed in a square room with a high timbered ceiling that met at a point in the center. Above me, candles flickered in a round iron chandelier. Slowly, mindful not to exacerbate the throbbing in my temples, I turned my head. A tall wooden chest swam into view, followed by a table and chair on one side of the bed and a small fireplace on the other. A breeze swayed the shutters on either side of the small window, carrying in the earthy, cave-like scent of moist rock and flowing water.

I tried to sit up, forgetting my injuries, and yelped as I unwisely pressed my weight onto my hands. I collapsed back onto the sheets, panting, blanketed in cold sweat, and fighting my rebelling stomach. My head began to ring.

"Now, that was not wise." Malegant clucked his tongue chidingly.

I jumped, unaware I wasn't alone. He must have been sitting somewhere outside my view.

He came toward me, his eyes reproachful. "Imogen worked so hard to set and bandage your fingers, and here you go trying to undo all her efforts."

Imogen? I recalled a flash of graying auburn hair and kind brown eyes amid the darkness. Perhaps I did have some memory of her.

Malegant grasped my upper arms and helped me to a sitting position, seating himself on the bed so his hip touched my leg. As I had on the horse, I tried to scrabble away, but every movement brought increased pain that threatened to hurl me back into the void of unconsciousness.

Once the dizziness passed, I looked at my hands. No wonder they felt five times their normal size. They were bound in reams of thick, strong cloth so bulky they resembled the heavy protective gloves worn by blacksmiths and bakers. Fascinated, I held up one hand and tried to move my fingers. The effort sent a jolt of pain through my hand, but my fingers remained immobile.

"Harming you was never in my plans; you made me do this when you tried to escape." Malegant carefully guided my hand back down to the bed. "Do not try to use them. Imogen is here to help you as you heal." He leaned toward me, weight forcing me onto my back once again. "Besides"—a spark of lust lit his eyes—"this way you can't fight back."

In a flash, he was kissing me just as hungrily as before. With a sickening chill, I knew what he intended to do. My lips went dry, my limbs began to shake, and my stomach, already unsteady, audibly voiced its willingness to void itself in any way it could. As he worked his belt loose, I tensed my muscles and prepared to fend him off, suddenly wishing I had paid more attention to my mother's lessons on hand-to-hand combat.

I forced my face to the side. "Please, no," I mumbled through my swollen jaw.

He pinioned my chin between his thumb and fingers, forcing my face back to his. He continued kissing me, smothering my breath with his lips. I knew better than to bite him again, even if my jaw would have let me, so I twisted my hips, hoping to gain some leverage to push him back. Wrenching an arm free, I aimed an elbow at the base of his neck and tried to bring my knee up between his legs while he was distracted.

But he was too strong, too quick. He caught my elbow and pinned both forearms behind my head, the weight of his body holding me down. I writhed beneath him, still seeking escape, but when his naked flesh touched mine, I quickly learned all I was doing was arousing him more.

I screamed silently as he thrust into me. Tears sprang from my eyes as he ripped me apart from the inside. I clenched my eyes shut as if that act alone could make him stop. I found myself fading away, no longer able to feel the pain or hear Malegant's grunts of pleasure. It was strangely like manipulating the elements, falling into the void between worlds. Only this time, instead of gaining power, it was being taken from me.

Something inside my mind shattered. The physical violation was one level of horror, but the truth of what he was doing did not lie solely in the act. He had taken my sovereignty, the right of every woman, every priestess—and especially the queen—to choose her lovers as she willed. Had he killed Arthur, taken my crown, and left me for dead, he couldn't have rendered me any more powerless. It was that thought, so much more damaging than my physical exhaustion, that made me stop struggling and simply endure what was being done.

Eventually I felt the sweet relief of his weight releasing me as he rolled off to one side.

Still panting, he kissed my cheek softly. "Thank you, wife. Let us see how quickly you can bear me a son."

I froze. *Wife.* I suddenly remembered the story of Malegant taking Fiona from her homestead to make her his wife. *He seeks to invoke ancient laws by which I am now his legal spouse.* But what about Fiona? Was he going to take two wives? And did he not know I was barren? Perhaps he didn't believe it. I closed my eyes and swallowed hard. *This was nothing like the attack I suffered as a child. Then I was a valuable commodity to be traded and bargained. Now I am owned. I am his property to do with as he pleases regardless of my will or commitment to the man who is his king.*

That was when I knew this nightmare was far from over.

Chapter Nine

Winter 501

As the days passed and Malegant's abuse continued, I began to dread the dark because I knew he would come.

It wasn't uncommon for him to be out of his mind with drink, which only served to hamper his performance and prolong my torment. Sometimes when he couldn't satisfy himself sexually, he would beat me until my eyes were bloody and my body shredded by his fingernails and teeth.

Imogen helped me visit the latrine and conduct my business—a humbling experience to be unable to perform such basics without aid—then lifted me back into bed, stroking my hair and holding me as I sobbed and shook. She never spoke, only communicated with her eyes and a few simple gestures. I assumed she had been born mute, but I did not have the heart to ask, nor did I know how she would explain. Somehow, her silence comforted me.

Each morning, Imogen would help me wash, brush my hair, and feed me spoonfuls of pottage as though I were a child. We spent the interminably long days in each other's company, she knitting or spinning, me sleeping or staring out the window at the lake far below or the mountains towering above.

Each night, Imogen would again help with my ablutions and see me settled into bed before retiring to her own mat. Only when Malegant came, which he inevitably did, did she leave the room.

In time, as my wounds began to heal and I regained my strength, I grew restless and paced the length of the chamber, for there was little I could do without the use of my hands. One morning, Imogen surprised me by removing the bandages from my hands.

"What are you doing?" I asked, only to feel foolish because she could not reply.

Imogen fixed me with a determined stare. *It is time,* her eyes seemed to say. *Trust me.* Slowly, carefully, she moved the smallest finger of my right hand.

I sucked in air in anticipation of the pain, but it did not come. Only when she applied a slight pressure to my knuckle to make my finger bend did I want to scream. Still holding my gaze, she repeated her tortuous routine on each of my fingers. By the time we were finished, my brow was slick with sweat, and I was lightheaded.

Imogen patted my thigh, as if to tell me I had done well.

Every day for a week, we repeated this exercise once at dawn and once at dusk. After a few days, the pain was tolerable, though I didn't yet dare try to move my fingers on my own.

One week after starting to exercise my fingers, she gestured for me to try. Hesitantly, like a child attempting her first steps, I bent my right index finger. When it didn't hurt, I nearly whooped with joy. I tried my other fingers. They all worked. I couldn't help but laugh. Soon I was wiggling my fingers in front of me, a child discovering her hands once again.

The following day, Imogen produced a collection of small objects from a pouch at her waist: a small wooden block, a stylus, a rock, and a ball of yarn. She indicated each in turn, grasping it in her hand then handing it to me. After a few minutes, I understood. She wished me to get used to holding objects of various sizes and weights again.

Everything went smoothly until I tried to shift the rock from my right hand to my left. It hit the floor with a thud, a chip skittering across the wooden planks and under the bed.

Embarrassed, I bent to pick it up.

So did Imogen.

We knocked heads as we straightened.

I laughed, rubbing my forehead. She made a gargling sound that I could only assume was laughter and massaged her brow.

It was then I saw it, light as a shadow, delicate as a whisper. In the center of her forehead was the ghost of a waxing crescent moon, long ago faded into nothingness.

Tenderly, I traced its shape, a soft smile forming on my lips. "You are a priestess," I said softly. "Just like me."

In response, Imogen touched her thumb to my forehead, lips, and heart.

I embraced her, feeling at once the bond of sisterhood that joined all priestesses of Avalon. My mind raced. No wonder she had taken such good care of me. Her expertise was the only reason I was slowly regaining use of my hands.

"Thank you." It was not the first time I had spoken my gratitude since waking in this accursed place, but I felt it stronger now than ever before. "How—" I wasn't even sure what I wanted to ask. "How did you come to be here?"

A moment after the words escaped my lips, we heard approaching footsteps.

Imogen placed a finger to her lips as if to say, *Keep this between us. We will discuss it later.*

I shivered, knowing what would be expected of me. Malegant had his own ideas of how I should practice using my hands.

⁘

The weather grew colder as each day passed until one melted into another like the ceaseless snow that covered the fortress with a thick white veil. One morning, when the snow was falling gently, I gathered up my courage and stuck my head out of the window. Looking up, I was pelted with thousands of icy feathers, but I saw enough to know we were on the uppermost floor of a castle made from a single wooden tower. In some ways, it resembled a granary more than a fortress. I twisted back around and braved a look down. Far below, the lake was churning with icy waves.

In the distance, I could just make out the edge of a thin bridge connecting the tower to some anchor on the far shore. The snow and ice made its rope railing look more like a giant cobweb. A fierce gust of wind rocked the castle, and I pulled my head in a little. The bridge was swaying. I couldn't help but imagine that anyone caught on it would feel much like an insect in a spider's snare.

Shivering, I climbed down off the ledge and tacked the fur lining tightly over the window. I sat in front of the fire and combed my hair with my fingers, relishing the heat. I had been here—I counted the full moons—three months, and this was the first time I'd dared think of escape. Why hadn't it occurred to me sooner? *You were in no condition,* my mind answered. *Only now are you strong enough.* Yes. I was finally strong enough to fight back. But how? There had to be a way out beyond the locked door. If Imogen could come and go, so could I.

I was still contemplating the possibilities when Imogen entered with our midday meal: freshly baked bread and bowls of hardy, dark stew. I ate my portion hungrily, especially grateful for the heat that made its way leisurely down my throat and into my stomach. My tongue tingled with hints of sage, rosemary, and wild onions mixed with the sweetness of parsnips, turnips, and something gamey—not venison, something wilder. "Imogen, this is wonderful. Did you cook it yourself?"

She nodded proudly.

After we had eaten our fill, she signaled it was time to begin my therapy for the day. We had progressed beyond holding simple objects to performing complex patterns. She showed me a set of movements, first placing the fingers of her left hand horizontally across her shinbone then touching certain points on the fingers of her right hand.

I copied her, pleased at both my dexterity and ability to recall the pattern she presented. After suffering so many blows at Malegant's hand, I had feared I would have lasting damage to my mind, but as each day passed, the likelihood of my fear coming true lessened.

Imogen clapped excitedly then touched the pads of two finger-tips to the side of her nose, repeating the pattern she'd performed on her leg.

As I mimicked her movements, something tugged at the back of my mind. This exercise was familiar somehow, though its meaning was lost in the fog of my memory. Was it a game my mother had played with me? Or some kind of code Elaine and I had invented on one of our childhood adventures? No, it was neither of those. As we repeated the pattern over and over, the fog slowly lifted. Avalon. That was where I knew these movements from. She was a priestess, and so was I.

I repeated the pattern once more, very slowly, realization beginning to dawn. I could translate the gestures into words.

I can speak to you, but Malegant must not know.

Imogen was speaking to me through cossogam, sronogam, and basogam—the three types of signing Ogham. They were named for the body parts used to speak: the leg, nose, and palm. Written Ogham was taught early in our training, but only the priestesses who remained for advanced studies learned manual Ogham in preparation for the silence and isolation of the final days before consecration.

"How, how—" Now that we could communicate, I suddenly found myself speechless.

My son does not know I remember Ogham. He never pursued advanced studies, so he cannot sign, though he can write it.

I held up a hand to stop her frantic signing. "Wait. I must have misunderstood you. Did you say 'son'?"

She nodded. *Your captor is my son. For that I am deeply ashamed. Please forgive me.*

My legs turned to jelly, and I sank to the floor, unable to process what I had just learned. Not only could Imogen speak to me in her own way, but she was Malegant's mother. "But you helped me. . ."

Imogen sat in front of me, using nose Ogham so I would be sure to see her. *I wish you no harm. I myself am a prisoner here. If I could help you escape, I would. I do not condone the things my son does.*

"I need time to think about this."

I understand, she signed. *Just remember that in front of him, I am mute. If he finds out the truth, he will kill us both.*

"Or at least cut off our hands," I said, half in dark jest.

We were silent for a long while. I stared into the fire, trying to rearrange what I now knew of my world—the nature of the land where I was being held, Imogen's relationship with Malegant, and my ability to talk to her—with what little information I had gleaned during the months I was bedridden. Putting it all together was like trying to solve a riddle without all the clues. I needed to know more.

I turned to Imogen. "Where is Fiona? Why have I not seen her?"

She shook her head, eyes brimming with tears. *She is dead.*

I gasped. My eyes pricked. "Was it. . .was it. . .?" I could not bring myself to ask if my captor was to blame.

Imogen nodded.

Fiona had been such a sweet, innocent girl. She was so docile, there was no way she could have provoked him into deadly rage as I easily could. "What happened?

Imogen hesitated. *She knew too many of his secrets, as did I. He killed her and cut out my tongue.*

I clasped my hands over my mouth, horrified. "But you are his mother!"

She gestured for me to keep my voice down. *And he is a demon.*

⚬⊛⊛⚬

Not long after my fingers healed, Malegant insisted I begin living with him on the main floor. "After all, you are not my prisoner. You are my wife."

And so my life developed into a new routine, one of serving, kneeling, and obeying Malegant's every whim. That very morning, I took on the duties of both wife and slave, although considering Malegant had made me his wife by kidnapping, I was willing to bet the two were one and the same in his mind. There were few others in the castle, so I assisted Imogen in preparing each meal. The thought crossed my mind that a quick end could be made to all of this with a simple "slip" of the wrong combination of herbs, but Imogen warned me against it.

I have thought of that as well, but so has he, she signed while carefully slicing carrots for the stew. *He will make you eat your portion first. Only once he sees you suffer no ill effects will he deign to eat.*

I shivered. So this man who held me captive was not only cruel and mad, he was clever, which made escaping his grasp that much more difficult. Maybe that was why Fiona had submitted. But I could not. I would not. The blood of queens sang in my veins. I could not let them down.

About two weeks later, in a lull between snowstorms, our little hideaway received its first visitors. From my vantage point in the kitchens, I could just make out two men, burly and wooly as bears, speaking with Malegant. Their unkempt appearance and guttural tongue were all I needed to place them as Picts. What they were doing so far south, however, was a mystery.

"My wife is very hospitable," he said. But then he caught sight of me, excused himself, and stalked in my direction. Without losing eye contact, he grabbed me by the throat, his fingers digging into my airway. "If you so much as make eye contact with my guests"—his breath was hot in my ear—"I will make certain you cannot walk, much less use those beautiful hands of yours. Do you understand me?"

I tried to speak, but all that came out was a strangled gurgle. I settled for nodding, but all that did was make the pain in my throat worse and rob me of what little breath I had left.

"When you serve us tonight, you will cover your face and answer to the name Fiona. While we eat, you will kneel in the corner until we have need of you."

Stars were beginning to dance before my eyes. I nodded again. Finally he let me go, and I bent over, coughing and my eyes streaming. When I looked up, he was gone.

Beneath the gauzy black veil, my face was covered in sweat. Every step I took was measured, every movement carefully carried out. I willed myself not to trip, my hands not to shake, as I placed the platter of lamb on the table and returned with a bowl of sauce.

Around the long table, Malegant and his guests paid me as little mind as they would a specter. All, that is, except for a woman I had not seen earlier. Her flaxen hair was loose, flowing down to her trim waist. She was dressed as though for battle, a long, menacing sword hanging at her side. Something was familiar about her, but I could not place what it was.

One of the men held up his cup, and I hurried to refill it.

"Why does your wife not show us her pretty face?" one of the men asked. "I do so enjoy a beautiful woman." He punctuated his statement with a sharp pinch to my backside.

I had to fight my instinct to smash the pitcher of ale over his head.

"Maybe she's not as pretty as he says," the woman scoffed. "Some men have to settle for less than the best."

Malegant pointed at her with a bone. "Like your husband?"

The men chuckled, and her cheeks reddened with rage.

"Watch your tongue, Lord Malegant." She toyed with her dagger under the guise of slicing a chunk off the shank before her. "Or you shall lose it."

Malegant sat back in his chair, a smug smile playing at his lips. "Aine, I'd love to see you try. Or do you not recall the outcome of our last tussle? I remember you pleading with me to spare your bloody carcass."

Aine was distracted from their exchange as I took away her used trencher and replaced it with a fresh one. She grabbed my wrist and removed the sapphire ring Arthur had given me from my finger. "Pretty bauble," she sang, looking right into my veiled eyes. "I think I'll keep it." She shoved me away.

"You never answered my question, my lord," insisted the man who had assaulted my backside.

"Her brother recently passed through the veil, and she doesn't wish others to witness her mourning," Malegant said dismissively. "But you did not come here to discuss our woes."

I retreated to the corner, adopting the submissive pose Imogen taught me—kneeling back on my heels, palms on the floor, head bent low to the ground. I wasn't sure how I was supposed to know when they needed me to serve, but if this was what Malegant wanted, I would do it.

As the night went on and the visitors fell under the spell of Malegant's thick, strong ale, they switched from the common tongue to the visitors' native language. I was fairly certain Malegant was aware I would be able to understand some of what was said, their tongue being not so different from my mother's native language, but he did not so much as cast a glance in my direction. While I couldn't understand every word, I understood enough to follow the conversation.

"He's left Camelot in the hands of his second and has declared Cadbury his capital until such time as she returns," one of the Picts said.

Arthur. They were talking about Arthur. He was still looking for me.

"But surely he can't have many men left," Malegant protested. "How many of them would last for extended periods outdoors in the deep of winter?" There was irritation in his voice and perhaps the slightest hint of fear.

"Many of the knights have returned to Camelot, Cadbury, or been wounded," one of the Picts conceded. "But there are a few who continue to search."

"Let them come," Malegant said with sudden vigor.

"What makes you think they will come after you?" Aine asked.

"Arthur hates me already. I did kill one of his lords, a member of the Combrogi. I would think I was first on his list of suspects." Malegant sounded almost proud of his state of disgrace.

My stomach tightened. I had not known Uriens had died from his injuries. Tears welled in the backs of my eyes, and for once, I was grateful for the veil so no one would see me weep—ironically the very reason Malegant had given for its use.

The woman said something I did not understand. Everyone laughed.

The Picts pulled wineskins from their belts and passed them around. Everyone poured some of the cloudy brown liquid into their cups, and they toasted, but again I couldn't understand what they were cheering about. Slugging down the drink, Aine sauntered around the table to Malegant. Her eyes glowed with a lustful fire.

"Dear sister, do not be so bold in front of our guests," Malegant chided, this time in our native tongue, but his heart clearly wasn't in the rebuke.

"I am no sister of yours. Your mother always underestimated her control over her husbands' cocks." She traced a finger down his chest then began painting Malegant's face with the remnants of the jelly still on his plate from the final course. He pushed her away playfully. "Oh, but you are, sweet sister." He took her finger in his mouth and sucked off the jelly.

That was when I placed her. The woman sitting on Malegant's lap was the girl who had been painting the reveler's faces and bodies on Samhain. I froze, wondering if she knew full well who was sitting in the shadows beneath the veil. It couldn't be a coincidence that she had been there when I was taken and was also here now.

The Picts grinned. "You aren't the only ones who should have some fun tonight. What about them?" One indicated Imogen and me with a jerk of his thumb. "Are they for sale?" Malegant looked us over as if assessing our value. "The one in the veil is my wife, so no, she is not for the taking. But this one"—he indicated Aine—"would likely take you both, or you can share her with the other woman, if you like."

They studied Imogen carefully then each chose a companion. After one more slug of liquor, they each dragged a woman off toward the sleeping chambers.

Malegant was no less gentle with me. He tugged me to my feet and flung me over his shoulder. "Be grateful I think so kindly of you, wife, and know I will treat you far better than my guests. They have. . ." He paused in the middle of the hall, searching for the right word. "More brutal tastes."

⋘ ❦ ⋙

A fortnight passed, each day a forgery of the last. Imogen came stumbling into the bedroom, bruised and bloody, the morning our guests were due to depart.

She signed frantically. *I have been through a lot in my life, but I cannot take being used as a whore any longer. Last night, those dogs abandoned Aine and both came at me at once.*

It was my turn to tend her injuries. I swabbed her bleeding thighs and gave her herbs against pain and disease.

"What was the shape of the tattoo on their right arms?" I asked, hoping to ferret out which of the tribes raised such brutes.

Tattoo? she asked, apparently dazed from pain. *Which one? They are so covered with them it would take close and careful study to tell one from another.*

So they were Highlanders then. That was even worse than I'd suspected. Malegant had kept me away from the majority of their discussions, but I'd gleaned enough to know they were negotiating some sort of bargain.

Imogen looked at me. *It is time. We must get out.*

"But how?"

She grasped my hand and smiled. *We will figure it out. Together.*

⚬⚬⚬

The next night, Malegant fell into bed next to me, deeper in his cups than I had ever seen him. He stank of that strange Pictish brew. They must have left the remainder of it with Malegant's sister. Whatever they had been bargaining for, her return had been payment.

"You must be happy to have your sister back," I said, trying to be pleasant when all I wanted was for him to pass out.

"My sister," he mumbled into the feather pillow, "is worthless. All of them are. First Leigh fails to kill Arthur, and now Aine can't even secure a simple exchange of lands. At least she was good for delivering the notes."

I sat up. That was a revelation. At least now I knew how he—or rather she—got in and out of Camelot to deliver me notes without being seen. I wanted so badly to ask him who Leigh was, but I was more afraid of sparking his temper by revealing too much interest in his motives.

Malegant turned his face toward me, head still glued to the pillow. "Aine claims I don't trust you and I never will. I should prove her wrong by explaining myself to you, not that I owe you even a drop of information." He narrowed his eyes at me. "But you have a strategic mind, so perhaps you will appreciate the brilliance of my plan. After all, it won't be long before the whole of Britain marvels at its intricacy, bowing before the brilliance of its new king."

I closed my eyes. So he *was* planning to overthrow Arthur. I'd suspected as much, but to have such a plan confirmed was another matter. But he had done more than prove me right; he given me another key to how his mind worked, another possible way too thwart him. His pride, which he so highly valued, could be turned against him.

"I would be honored to be the first to know." I swallowed hard, willing myself to say words I knew would please him. "As your wife, it is my right, is it not?"

He propped himself on one elbow and regarded me closely. "You are finally coming to understand. Good. Yes, it is time you know all."

"Who is Leigh?" I asked, bringing him back to his previous line of thought.

"One of my many half brothers. I used him to try to have Arthur killed, but then your spy or maid or whatever she really is interfered, so I had to change tack. Luckily, I have no shortage of half siblings who owe me their lives and therefore must do my bidding. I told you long ago how I was fostered for my own protection. When I returned, my mother had taken power, and I found I had a brood of younger brothers and sisters sired by the chieftains of the other six ancient tribes. But she was law-bound to none of them, so each made his own claim against me."

"What did you do?" I asked with mock concern, stroking his hair.

He shrugged. "What any man would do given the situation. If I was to take my rightful place as head of my tribe, I would have to kill each one of them. The eldest I killed with my bare hands, the entire village cheering us on. By the end of the year, my arms were bloody up to the elbows, my skin furrowed with scars. I was so crazed with blood and revenge I threatened even the babes. I remember pressing a dagger to the chest of a screaming toddler, threatening to cut out his heart. I think I would have done it too, had they not relented. In the end, the families I did not overthrow with steel paid me their loyalty in exchange for the lives of their youngest. Aine and Leigh were among them."

I lay in stunned silence, sifting through what he had just revealed. No wonder this man was so brutal—he'd always had to be. For him, brutality was a way, *the* way, to stay alive.

Malegant kissed my stomach, dragging his lower lip up to the cleft between my breasts. I thought he was going to begin his nightly work on me, but he laid his head on my breast instead.

"You and I have quite a history, you know," he drawled, tracing a finger over the muscles in my abdomen. "I was your mother's pupil.

You were too young to remember, only able to wobble on fat baby legs. I remember three of your brothers and a sister. She was a lot like you, you know—same piercing green eyes and haughty attitude. She was already promised to another, but I vowed to myself that when you came of age, you would be mine."

I tried not to recoil from the thought of this man desiring me from childhood. There were taboos against such a thing for a reason. "Is that why you tried to have Arthur killed? Because he wed me and you did not?"

Malegant laughed. "It is so much more complex than that, but yes. You see, the man in whose house you lived, Lord Pellinor, sought to control all of the Summer Country. As I had no interest in his simpering daughter, I convinced him that if he arranged your marriage to me, I would cede some of my power. He was a useful tool, the old, pious fool. And your father wasn't much more formidable. All I had to do was remind him of my training with your mother, and he practically welcomed me like a son. Everything was arranged. I had already paid your right of purchase and price of virginity—what a farce that was."

His voice trailed off as his lips met mine, tenderly for once, and he began to move against me slowly, as though stoking his own pleasure.

"Your father owes me, Guinevere." He planted a line of kisses from one end of my collarbone to the other. "Were it not for that damned honor debt, you would have been my wife of the highest degree years ago. But then that fool Uriens told Arthur about you, and he swooped in and stole you from my grasp. But now the old man is dead. So"—he leered at me—"how do you think I should best extract payment from your father, from Arthur?" His hand closed around my throat.

"I can give you all the money owed you and then some, you know that." My voice shook, though I tried to temper it.

"But that's not really the issue, is it? No, your father did more than cheat me out of money. He cheated me out of my rightful wife. Then the king not only did the same—he sullied my name as well. This is revenge on many levels, Guinevere, a substantial righting of wrongs." He forced me onto my stomach, grabbed me roughly by the hair at the nape of my neck, and entered me with his usual force.

I cried out in pain. He twisted one hand in my hair and continued to pull, his other hand digging sharply into my right buttock. If only I could have associated pain and pleasure the way he did, I would have been in ecstasy.

"A son," he panted. "That will be the ultimate recompense. Then I will be the one with a legitimate heir." He bit my earlobe. "Arthur is a dead man, and I will get what is owed to me."

⚬⚬⚬

bering his diatribe from the night before. The impending snowstorm that had driven away the Picts arrived, so we spent the day in close quarters, holed up against the cold and wind. I was on edge all day, waiting for Malegant to make some comment or show some sign of regretting what he'd said, but he treated me as though nothing had happened. The only difference was that he took Aine to bed that night.

I tried hard not to think about that. I still didn't know for sure that Aine was related to Malegant by blood, only that he thought she was and she vehemently denied it. Maybe she was right. But then again, this man broke every prohibition in our culture without a second thought. It made my skin scrawl to think he believed her to be his sister and yet saw nothing wrong with their relationship or, worse, carried on anyway. But I couldn't bring myself to ask Imogen the truth— I really didn't want to know.

Imogen interrupted my thoughts with a swift tap on my wrist.

Guinevere, I am afraid if we do not do something soon, he will tire of you. My son is like a cat with his prey. He toys with it until he grows bored. Then he goes in for the kill. I can already see the joy fading from his eyes.

"Then what do we do? We have to escape."

For a while, we were both silent, caught up in our thoughts. I twisted what I had learned around in my mind, trying to find some weakness, some chink in the armor of Malegant's plan we could use to our advantage. We were in a tower on an island surrounded by deadly cold water in a valley between mountains. The fortress was nearly impenetrable.

There was no way the two stout Picts would have crossed that string of a bridge that swayed in the wind outside the window, and neither could we. It was far too icy to try. There had to be another way in. And if there was, there was another way out.

"How did the Picts get into the castle?" I asked.

By boat, she signed after setting a mug of tea in front of me. *But it is heavily guarded.*

I brought the mug to my lips and breathed in the steam. It was earthy, heavy with the loam of the forest and berries forbidden to mortal lips. I breathed in again, trying to identify the scent. The distinctive smell of burning dried leaves—sage—was the first to assault my senses. Woody rosemary, marjoram, and thyme followed, chased by the sweeter aromas of mint and imported hyssop.

Imogen smiled. *I learned this blend from Argante when she was a young priestess. It opens the centers of the sight and will give us knowledge we seek. Let us drink in honor of our gods.* She held up her mug.

I let the warm liquid flow past my lips. On the whole, it had a pleasant taste, reminiscent of a salad of early spring greens, but once swallowed, it bit back with sharp spiciness that made me want to gag.

I closed my eyes and breathed deeply, allowing the liquid to flow through my veins. As it took effect, I relaxed for the first time in months. A second mouthful brought with it the sight—a vision of the tower burning while we rowed away to the safety of the far shore.

I opened my eyes.

What do the gods say?

"We set the tower on fire and escape in the boat. But how can that be? You said it was heavily guarded."

It is, but not at night. We don't have enough guards to keep watch at all hours.

I swallowed the dregs of my tea, tossing around the basic elements of our plan—fire, the boat. What else? How did it turn into action?

Fire, travel by water. . . I found myself invoking the goddesses associated with our quest—Ellen, the guardian of the ways; Nehalenni, patroness of travelers; and Brigid, the goddess of fire and forge.

That was when it hit me. Brigid. She was the key.

I grabbed Imogen's arm. "The feast of Brigid nears. On that night, the moon is full and will be eclipsed by the sun. That will afford us both distraction, as all cower inside against evil omens, and protection in the darkness. Once we have cleared the lake, we can invoke Brigid and burn this place to the ground."

She smiled. *Then we must make ready.*

Chapter Ten

Over the next several weeks, we took measures to be certain we would be prepared for our journey. Imogen sewed small pouches of herbs in our skirts so that we would not be without aid if one of us became sick or injured. On washing day, we smuggled warm cloaks and a change of clothes out of the castle with the soiled linens, using a hollow tree stump at the edge of the lake as a hiding place for our supplies. It was my job to see that a certain amount of food was set aside, along with a few wineskins. Finally, Imogen procured two small daggers—purloined from the Picts, she said—as a means of protection and for use in hunting.

When all was in place, we waited for the appointed hour. Like everyone Druid-trained, Malegant would be using the feast coupled with the eclipse, the time of greatest power, to perform acts of divination. According to Imogen, his men—in whom he had instilled sufficient misinformation—would be cowering in terror and begging the gods to bring back the moon. That meant we only had to evade Aine to be clear to escape.

We made certain the day went like any other—serving at meals, sewing, and minding chores—while Malegant and his men sparred and negotiated matters of politics. Once night fell, we ate a quiet dinner, but I didn't fail to notice Malegant glancing expectantly out the window every few minutes, anticipating moonrise.

When he finally stood, I made to follow him to bed, but he held me at arm's length. "You are a priestess. You of all people should know I will sleep alone tonight, with only the bones for my company."

I lowered my eyes. "As you wish."

Imogen and I retired to the room we shared, and the tower went eerily silent. For a long time, all we could hear was the pop of the logs in the fire and the creak of the walls as they resisted the wind. We had just gathered our things and donned our cloaks when an eerie keening broke the silence. The hairs on the back of my neck stood on end. Beside me, Imogen stiffened.

We slowly inched along the darkened corridor toward the sound.

"That is old magic," I whispered. "Dark magic."

I felt it coiling around me, drawing me in like a rope. It was so seductive, so alive. It was the same power I'd tasted on the rare occasions I cursed our enemies, and part of me longed for more. When we reached Aine's door, the keening reached a feverish pitch. Without thinking, I put my hand on the door to peer inside.

Imogen pulled me back.

I could not see her signing in the dark, but somehow I knew she was telling me to resist the temptation to watch. She shoved me past the door toward the staircase leading down to the dock.

Away from danger now, we lit a small oil lamp. Imogen was frantically weaving her fingers, a message that came in fits and starts, as though her hands could not keep up with her mind.

She was calling the Callieach. You had to step away, else she enter you by mistake. The Dark One is not particular about her vessel. That is magic no one in this land has practiced for centuries. She must have learned it in the Highlands.

"Is Aine truly yours?" I asked as we neared the door barred tight against intruders.

Imogen nodded. *Her father was my link to Icini gold. Though she never admits it. She believes herself a child of Eire.* She shrugged as if to say there was nothing she could do about it.

We struggled to lift the heavy beam from its catch. Above us, Aine's keening continued, though it was slowly morphing into a guttural chant. For a moment, I could not move. All I could do was listen, mesmerized by the sound of something my blood remembered though my mind knew it not.

I started from my trance as Imogen freed the beam with a thud that reverberated throughout the house. We both froze, hearts pounding. Aside from Aine's uninterrupted chanting, there was not a single sound.

We opened the door to a cold, clear night. Far above, in the black veil of night, the moon was turning a sickly shade of rose as the sun's shadow slid slowly across its surface. The wind buffeting the castle tore at our cloaks with icy fingers, as though determined to stop us from reaching the dock.

Somewhere, an animal's desperate screech punctuated the silence, the cry of a soul that knows it's about to reach its end. It could have been deep in the woods across the water, but I had a sinking feeling it came from Aine's room as part of whatever arcane ritual she was performing.

We plucked our bundles from the tree stump and headed for the water. But when we drew near, it was clear the boat was not where we'd expected it. Where there should have been depth and shadow, we saw only a reflection of the waning light of the eclipse.

Imogen stamped her foot and cursed with her fingers.

"I don't understand. You said it was always moored here at night."

It is. She looked around. *He must have locked it up against the wind.* Her eyes grew wide. *Or he knows.*

We returned our packs to the stump in case we weren't successful in finding the boat, and I followed her back into the tower. There was only one place large enough to house a vessel.

Off to one side was a storage room used to house the provisions delivered monthly by a local fisherman whom Malegant paid handsomely for his discretion. Bags of grain sat next to sacks of sprouting onions and nuts, half eaten by the mice, while piles of firewood made an impassable fortress to the far end of the room. Above us hung rows of cheeses and bouquets of herbs. Barrels of salt fish and ale lined the opposite wall. But no boat.

Imogen stood with her hands on her hips, turning in circles as though the boat was there and had simply been rendered invisible.

"It's not here. Let's go. We can try again another night," I hissed. I had the increasingly terrible feeling we had been set up.

We could try the bridge, Imogen signed.

In my mind's eye, I recalled the thread of rope and wood being tossed about in the wind. No, we should not dare try to cross it this night. Even if I could have used my powers to calm the wind, in her altered state, Aine was likely to sense the magic and raise the alarm. Silently, I shook my head and edged back into the main room without waiting for Imogen.

Aine's chanting had slowed into what could probably have been best described as crooning. She sounded as if she was singing a lullaby. Distracted by the sound, I didn't see Malegant until I ran into him, forehead knocking painfully into his chest.

"My love, why are you wearing your heavy cloak in the house?" he asked, fingering a fold of the material.

I was sweating, highly aware I had been caught. I shivered in fear. "I was cold. I—I can't get warm."

Malegant turned my face toward him with a finger at my chin. He scrutinized my face. "Your face *is* clammy, and you are deathly pale."

"What are you doing down here?" I asked.

"Aine called me. I might ask the same of you."

Aine's crooning drew my attention again, so it took me a moment to register his words.

"I—I don't know," I said, pretending to be dazed with fever.

He grasped my hands, and my shaking increased.

"Your hands are freezing. Let's get you into bed." He put an arm around me and guided me up the stairs to our room, calling for Imogen as we walked.

I would never know how she reached the room before us, but when he opened the door, there she was, as placid as though he had merely interrupted her knitting.

"I believe Guinevere is ill. Stay with her, will you?"

Heaviness filled my head as though I really were ill. Imogen helped me into bed, and I lay there, watching the candles blaze and illuminate Malegant's attempts to see the future in the patterns formed by sun-bleached bones of birds, oxen, and other animals I couldn't identify.

Aine soon stopped crooning, and I fell into an exhausted sleep, relieved neither she nor her brother appeared to suspect anything.

◈ ◈

That night, I dreamed of strange things. In my dreams, Aine was still chanting, though I could not see her. Her voice was all around me, coming from everywhere and nowhere. I was flying high above the tower and its island, then past the mountains and trees, then over open countryside. As I passed by, cairns burst open, the dead rising in their shrouds, some still carrying the weapons and finery with which they had been buried. They followed me to the sea, where I landed on a rocky beach. From the water came a cloud of ashes that slowly formed into a procession of souls.

"Find her!" they commanded. "Find her before *She* does."

Then the dream shifted. Merlin sat up in his bed, drenched in sweat. It was early morning. Without bothering to dress in more than a simple tunic, he ran, barefoot, to find Arthur. My husband was still in bed, and he looked up in alarm at Merlin's intrusion.

"Great magic, the like of which I've never seen, has woken our ancestors. They come with a grave warning." To my utter shock, Merlin went on to relay the exact contents of the earlier part of my dream.

"Who should we find, and who should we fear?" Arthur asked, confused.

Merlin leveled him with an impenetrable gaze. "I am not certain, but I think they are telling us to find Guinevere. And in answer to your other question—pray my suspicions are wrong."

My perspective shifted again, and I was in the throne room. Merlin was describing something to Arthur, Sobian, Lancelot, and Gawain.

"The auguries confirm it. This is the location of the magic I felt. It was ancient and dark, enough to drive the ancestors from their resting places with a warning. Whatever its source, it must be stopped. I beg you brave men, and woman, to join with me in finding this castle in the glass."

As they armed themselves to depart, I saw their destination. It was the very fortress in which I now slumbered.

Chapter Eleven

Spring 501

A few weeks later, as spring was beginning to paint the forest with its first blush of green, Malegant came to our morning meal dressed in his riding boots and traveling cloak.

"I am going out to begin collecting taxes in the nearby villages," he announced.

Imogen threw me a hopeful look behind his back.

"I am going with you," Aine pronounced.

"No, you are not. Someone needs to stay here to guard her." He gestured to me with his tankard of ale.

"But I'm bored."

"What do I care?" he asked around a mouthful of bread. "Besides, the fisherman should be here tomorrow with the next moon's supplies. Someone has to pay him."

Aine sat in a huff, her arms crossed like a petulant child's. "Isn't that the duty of your wife?" Suddenly she looked up. "You still don't trust her." It was a statement, not a question. "And you probably never will," she added more quietly.

After the dishes were cleared, Malegant led me upstairs to the room in which he'd first held me prisoner. "Please forgive me for this, but I can't have you getting any ideas about running away while I am gone."

He produced a length of thick chain with twin shackles affixed to one end. The other end was bolted tightly to the wall. He seized my hands and bound them in the iron manacles.

Immediately, fear formed a leaden lump in my stomach. My hands shook beneath his grasp, but I couldn't stop them. "What is the meaning of this? In the six moons I have been here, you never once chained me up. Have I done something to affront you?"

His face hardened. Before I could blink, he struck me full force across the cheek with the back of his hand. I stumbled back, knocking my head against the wall.

"You heard what I said. It was either this or break your hands again. Which would you prefer? Or maybe your feet too this time?" His voice was cruel as he raised an eyebrow and patted me twice on the cheek. "I didn't think so." He kissed me roughly and backed away. "Imogen will be instructed to treat you as before. She will bring your meals three times a day. There is a bit of sewing and a book for you to pass the time. The chain is long enough for you to reach the bed and the necessity pot but not to leave the room. I will return in a few days."

When he was nearly through the door, he turned. "Who knows, we may find another use for those chains when I return."

I glared at him, but he was already gone. I slid down the wall and sat on the floor, listening as he unmoored the boat and departed with the splashing of oars. No doubt he had a horse waiting on the other side of the lake to take him wherever he wished to go.

It was odd, but now that I was shackled with little freedom of movement, I finally felt like a prisoner. Maybe it was because I was free from the constant threat of beatings and rape, free from my fear of him. I hadn't realized it, but it was that fear, my fight for survival, that was keeping me sane. Before I realized what was happening, I began to sob, hysterical spasms over which I had no control. Curled up in a ball on the floor, I buried my head in my knees, clenched my fists in my hair, and wept.

For the first time, I realized the gravity of my situation. I was Malegant's prisoner, his "wife" of the lowest degree according to ancient tribal law. I had been violated and subjugated in the most horrible ways possible, robbed of all the dignity due to me as a queen and a priestess.

And what of rescue? Arthur surely would have sent all of the forces at his command to rescue me six months ago. They would have combed the forests and glens, rivers and mountain passes, for me. Six times the moon had waxed and waned, yet no one had found me. He'd probably even issued a reward so the people would be motivated to look or turn over any evidence they had. Briefly, I wondered how many false claims he fielded each pleading day, how many dark-haired daughters were passed off as imitations of the queen in the hopes of monetary gain. At the thought and the image in my mind's eye of Arthur's annoyance, I laughed as uncontrollably as I had cried.

The laughter buoyed my spirits a bit. I chewed on a morsel of a thought. If Arthur truly had issued a reward, I could use that to my advantage—if only I could get access to other people. Imogen had as little hope of escape as I, and Aine—well, I had the feeling she would rather see me dead than returned to Arthur, no matter the sum.

That left who? The guards? I hadn't had many interactions with them, but they were no ordinary mercenaries—of that much I was certain. It took a certain loyalty or compulsion to remain in an assignment as remote and joyless as this. So either they believed in Malegant so strongly they were willing to kill for him or he had some kind of leverage that made them obey his every whim. There might be an opening there, but it would take time and much effort, not to mention careful avoidance of their master, to feel them all out.

Exhausted, I eventually drifted off to sleep. When I woke, stiff and sore from my awkward position, the first thing I saw was that dinner had been set on a tray within arm's reach. Imogen must have had to return to the kitchens to prepare Aine's meal.

I stood and stretched, thanking the gods that at least Malegant had shown me the kindness of being able to move around. Munching on a leg of whatever poor bird adorned my plate, I went over to the window and looked out. The sun was sinking fast, turning the lake to a pool of blood, but the sound of the water lapping the shore was at least relaxing. I looked down. The dock was empty. We were all trapped here until Malegant returned.

I was about to give up hope and climb into bed when a new thought crossed my mind. Malegant had mentioned the fisherman was supposed to deliver supplies in the coming days. Perhaps if I could get free, he would recognize me or I could convince him I was being held under duress.

It was a weak plan, but it was more than I'd had a few hours before.

I fought against the shackles for a few moments, trying to slip my hands from their unyielding grasp. Somewhere deep in my mind, I knew this would do no good, but still I strained to make my hands narrow until my skin was raw and my wrists threatened to dislocate.

I decided to change tack. Holding my wrists up to the light, I inspected the locks on my manacles. They were the simplest type of barrel lock—not surprising since Malegant didn't know about the skill I had obtained from Isolde. Had Malegant been wiser, he would have bound my wrists together, but he'd allowed me the dexterity to sew. Fortuna had finally smiled on me.

I looked around the room. If I could find something thin enough, I could pick them. My sewing needle was too short and too delicate to do any good. There was nothing in the bed or within arm's reach that could help me. I considered asking Imogen to bring me something from the kitchen or barracks, but I didn't want to involve her in case I was caught. My eyes alighted on the bird on my plate. I said a silent prayer of thanks to its soul before I ripped the carcass apart and went to work with the wishbone. With a bit of luck, by morning, I would be free.

◦◦◦

When the sun rose, my right hand was free but I was still struggling with the lock around my left.

I had gone through all of the smaller bones in the poor bird's body only to snap the last one off in the lock in my weariness and haste. Tears of frustration coursed down my cheeks as I realized my folly. Eventually, exhausted, I had fallen asleep again.

As soon as there was enough light in the room, I studied the jammed mechanism, trying to figure out how to fix it. At first I thought I could remove the bone with my fingernail, but the bone was just big enough to prevent me from getting underneath it.

From the hall, the telltale crunch of boots on rushes signaled someone was approaching. It was likely Imogen, but I put the other shackle around my right wrist, not quite locked, just in case Aine decided to pay me another unanticipated visit.

She had taken it upon herself to check on me last night even though Imogen was asleep on a pallet at my feet. Still awake and hiding my free hand beneath the blankets, I'd glared at Aine as she rounded the bed making sure everything was in proper order. Something in the glint in her eyes told me that had Imogen not been present, we would have come to blows. Ever since the night of her strange ritual, I'd had the sense she wanted my blood and would do whatever it took to get it. But she obviously wasn't keen on doing it in front of her mother. Thank the gods for Imogen.

The door opened, and Imogen waddled in, maneuvering the door with one hand while trying not to drop the tray she balanced on the other. As soon as she was within reach, I whisked the tray away, and she signed her thanks.

Have you made any progress? she asked.

"No. I can't pry the bone loose."

This will help. She pointed at the thin knife sitting next to a hunk of hard cheese on the plate. Aine would beat her at the very least if she knew Imogen had supplied me with a weapon, but still, she'd risked it to help me get free.

I kissed her and swallowed my breakfast as fast as possible.

Once Imogen had removed the dishes and gone to attend to Aine, I went back to work on the lock, trying to free the bone with the point of the knife. I was so engrossed in my work I was surprised to find the sun was high overhead when I looked up. Somewhere in the distance, the rhythmic slap of oars on the water's surface heralded the arrival of a boat, likely the one bearing the fisherman who could answer all our prayers. Slowly, the boat came into view, and equally slowly, I eased the tip of the blade beneath the bone. With an audible crack, the bone gave up its position in the lock and flew out, landing somewhere in the rushes.

It took all I had not to whoop with joy. But I had to restrain myself, for the fisherman was now on the docks, being warmly greeted by Aine and Imogen. He was wearing a hooded cloak, so I could not see his face, but from his build, I surmised he was young and, from Aine's body language, likely handsome. She was doing everything she could to entice him.

But even from this distance it was clear he was embarrassed by her advances. He scratched his chin nervously and shifted his weight from foot to foot. They spoke for a while—I couldn't hear their conversation—then he gestured toward the supply-laden boat. Aine indicated with a wave that she and Imogen would help unload it.

Before taking the first sack from the fisherman, Aine flipped her hair over her shoulder and brushed his hand. He smiled. She grinned back. They disappeared into the house several times, returning for another round of supplies, then eventually they remained in the main hall. Their voices drifted upward, indistinct but a reassuring sign of the stranger's continued presence.

All the while, I worked the lock, desperate to free myself while the man was still here. All my anxiety did was make my brow sweat and my hands grow clammy and slick. Several times I dropped the dagger, nearly missing my big toe once. Cursing and muttering prayers to every god I could think of, I kept jiggling the metal, looking for the sweet spot that would spell an end to my trouble. The release I felt when the lock clicked open was greater than any I'd experienced with a man.

Rubbing my wrist, I stood and pocketed the dagger. I was halfway across the room before I realized the tower had grown eerily silent. I rushed over to the window and breathed a sigh of relief that the boat was still tied to its mooring.

I crept over to the door. Praying it wouldn't squeak, I peered out. The hallway was deserted. So was Malegant's room. I didn't dare open Aine's door, so I crept down the stairs and into the main room. It was deserted as well.

Imogen was slicing parsnips in the kitchen.

"Where is Aine?" I really didn't want an answer, but I had to know before we could reinstate our escape plan.

She rolled her eyes and pointed at the ceiling. Then she made a gesture I'd never seen from a woman before. Apparently Aine was entertaining our guest with the friendship of the thighs, as my mother used to call it.

"Get your things and meet me back here."

Imogen pointed at a bundle at her feet. She was way ahead of me.

"You know what to do then?"

She nodded, signing the word for fire.

I raced back up the stairs on silent priestess feet and uncovered the bundle Imogen and I had made months before on our first escape attempt. I slung the bag over my shoulder and fastened my cloak about my shoulders. With one final deep breath, I said a prayer to Ellen to guide our path, and I stepped into the hall.

I immediately froze. Aine's door was ajar. I could have sworn it had been closed a moment ago when I raced past. I should have headed straight back to the kitchen, but I was compelled to peek inside. Making certain I made no noise, I crept up to the door. No movement disturbed the peace within. Hesitantly, I peered around the door. Aine lay supine on the bed, knees bent, one arm across her body, the other flung above her head. She wasn't moving.

"She's not dead," said a familiar male voice over my shoulder.

I jumped and grasped my thundering heart. It couldn't be who I thought it was. It just couldn't. Slowly, I turned.

Lancelot grinned at me. "She's only unconscious. A blow to the head will do that to a person."

I couldn't speak, only stare at him dumbly. How had he gotten in here?

"I was the fisherman," he explained as though reading my thoughts. "It's a long story, but we have not time for that now. We must get out of here." He reached for my arm.

"Wait. I have to do one thing first." I crept over to Aine's side, still fearful of waking her, and slipped my ring off her finger. I put it back onto mine where it belonged. "Now we can go."

Lancelot dragged me by the hand down the front stairs. Just as we were about to come into view, the main doors burst open.

Malegant strode in, an angry scowl on his face. "Aine! Imogen!"

Lancelot stopped so fast I smashed my nose into his back. We backed up a few steps, just far enough to stay in the shadows but close enough to watch the unexpected turn of events.

The head guardsman rushed in. "My lord, we were not expecting you so soon. Is all well?"

"My horse threw a shoe in the middle of the forest. I had to walk him back to town to have it fixed, but I wouldn't stay in their rat-infested inn for all the gold in Camelot," he said.

Imogen had entered the room now.

"Ah, good. Mother, some ale, please." She turned to fulfill his request, but he stopped her with a touch on the arm. "Why is the fisherman's boat still here?"

Imogen gave him a sly look and repeated the same gesture she had made for me.

Malegant rolled his eyes. "So that is where my sister is then?"

That was Lancelot's cue to turn. "Go! We have only minutes before he finds Aine."

"But Imogen—"

"Knows what she's doing. Come on." He dragged me toward the upper floor. "Change of plans."

Instead of going all the way to the top, where the sleeping rooms were located, he pulled me into a small alcove halfway in-between. I almost screamed. A man who looked passably like a slightly older version of Lancelot was standing there.

"Well met," Lancelot greeted him. "You are right on time."

The man shook Lancelot's hand and headed down the stairs.

"Who is that?" I hissed.

"Listen and learn," he answered with a chuckle.

Lancelot whisked aside a tapestry on the wall and opened a hidden door leading out onto the rickety bridge. I stepped onto the landing, fighting a sudden wave of dizziness. Clouds were quickly filling the sky, and a sharp breeze buffeted the bridge, making it swing precariously. On either side, fog rose off the lake as the cold air hit its warm surface.

"Go on," Lancelot encouraged me.

I took a hesitant step onto the wood beams. Each was about the width of both my feet together, and only four beams made up the bridge, allowing me to easily grasp the ropes on either side.

"Why didn't we take the boat?" I asked, my voice shaking as I tested the next beam.

"The fisherman had to have it back for the ruse to work," Lancelot answered, sliding around me to take the lead. "I convinced him to let me take his place today. I told him if I didn't return in two hours to walk across the bridge and pretend he was the one who had made the delivery so he could get his boat back. It doesn't hurt that we resemble one another."

"And he agreed to that?"

"He agreed to my payment." Lancelot grabbed my right hand, leading me slowly onto the bridge proper.

Behind us, chaos erupted. Voices carried out the windows on the wind.

Aine clomped unsteadily down the stairs. "Who is this?"

"You should know, sweet sister. If rumor is true, you've been riding him all afternoon."

"He's not. . . I didn't. . ." Aine sounded confused.

I smiled, imagining her trying to reconcile the older man before her with the younger one in her memory.

"I'm sure you didn't, just like all the others," Malegant replied dryly. "Now if you don't mind, I am going to spend some time with my wife. We are not to be interrupted. Understood?"

"He's going to find out. We have to run," I pleaded with Lancelot, looking around wildly for a way to steady the bridge.

Lancelot shook his head. "We can't run. The bridge is too unpredictable. Can you calm the winds?"

"I think so." I closed my eyes, sent my consciousness upward into the clouds, and willed the air to be still.

"It's working," Lancelot said.

We took a few steps toward the middle of the bridge, and a primal roar stopped me in my tracks. It was Malegant. He must have found the unoccupied chains.

Below us, the fisherman's boat was a shadow in the mist. It was catching up to us. I could just make out two forms within. That meant Imogen and the fisherman had successfully escaped.

I shoved Lancelot forward. "Go! We have to get across before he cuts the ties and the whole bridge collapses."

Lancelot sniffed the air. "Or notices the fire. I can smell it already."

We walked as fast as the bridge allowed, the boat surpassing us easily. But then I noticed another shadow emerging from the fog. The mist parted and I saw Malegant had followed in his boat with two of his guards, both armed with bows.

Lancelot had noticed them too. He cursed. "I have no shield, so we have nothing to deflect their arrows if they can sight us through the mist."

"Yes, we do. Can you carry me across?"

He looked at me as if I was mad but answered like a dutiful champion, "Yes."

"I can direct the arrows away from us, but I can't walk and do that at the same time."

Without a question, Lancelot picked me up, one hand under my knees and the other at the middle of my back, shielding me with his body. "Do your best. I swear I will get us across."

I closed my eyes again and envisioned the wind curling around us as though we were encased in a protective bubble. Arrows whizzed by, closer than I was comfortable with.

Lancelot set me down. "Climb on my back. I want to have my sword free should we need it."

I did as he asked, but it was enough to break my concentration. An arrow grazed my left shoulder. I cursed.

Lancelot turned to tend to me but was knocked sideways against the ropes as the bridge shook. I fell flat on my face. Turning my head, I realized it wasn't just the bridge shaking. Around us, trees were shedding leaves like rain. Branches fell into the lake like boulders in an avalanche. Waves smashed into the prows of the boats. The entire earth was shaking.

The hairs on the back of my neck stood up, and a chill ran down my spine as a familiar keening filled the air. Aine was fighting back in her own way.

The ground rumbled again, and I struggled to my knees. Imogen's boat was just nearing shore, while Malegant's archers were fighting to keep their boat upright in the choppy waters. We had to make the most of our few moments of freedom.

I crawled toward the end of the bridge, afraid to stand lest another jolt send me tumbling over the edge. Lancelot clung to the ropes, carefully measuring each step.

Aine had to still be in the tower. Stopping for a moment, I closed my eyes and called on Brigid, the goddess of fire.

"Great goddess, protect me from my enemies, those who seek to use the elements against me. Consume them in your great forge," I prayed. I envisioned the flames Imogen had ignited in the storeroom growing stronger and stronger, the fires in the hearths hissing as they grew taller, raging out of their confines. I willed the entire tower to be engulfed.

The rumbling stopped as quickly as it had started. I got to my feet again and raced to the safety of land, Lancelot guarding my rear.

I almost kissed the ground, but a deep creaking behind us stopped me. The ground shook again, but this was more of a rolling thunder than the pervasive rumble from earlier. Across the lake, the entire tower was engulfed in flames and was quickly disintegrating. I could only hope Aine was still inside. As we watched, the upper floor fell inward, forcing the main walls out into the lake. They crashed with such force that a tidal wave carried Malegant's boat toward the shore.

Lancelot pulled my arm so tightly I thought my elbow would dislocate. We dashed into the woods just in time to avoid the crashing surf as the wave slammed into the shore, splintering Malegant's boat while propelling him and his men effortlessly onto dry land.

"It seems the gods wish us to be together. Why, they practically tossed me into your arms," Malegant said to me before drawing his sword and facing Lancelot. "So this is how it ends, is it? Brothers-in-arms in a fight to the death. I could, of course, take you prisoner and let my sister play with you, but watching you die will be so much more satisfying."

At his signal, the two guards, each with a loaded bow, advanced on me, Imogen, and the fisherman. I looked around wildly for some way to defend myself. The taller of the two, a middle-aged man with reddish hair sticking out beneath his helmet, took aim at me. I dove for the trees just as the arrow passed over my head. Scraped and bloody, I was safe for the moment, but hiding was no long-term strategy.

I grabbed the nearest branch I could find to use as a weapon and shot deeper into the woods. Once I stopped, I heard the clang of metal on metal as Malegant and Lancelot fought on the shore. The guards were venturing into the trees, so I had to keep moving. I made a slow arc that would lead me back to the shoreline. Imogen and the fisherman attacked one of the archers, so I made a mad dash in the opposite direction.

I had hardly moved before an arrow bit into my arm. I screamed in agony. It was the same side as the other arrow had hit, only this time it lodged in the muscle of my upper arm, rendering it useless for defense. The archer was already nocking another arrow, so I had no time to break this one off. I ran, trying to ignore the burning pain in my left shoulder, dodging between trees and praying his next bolt would find one of them instead of me.

As I passed a wide oak, I was wrenched sideways. A hand grasped my right arm. For one terrifying moment, I was afraid I had run straight into the archer, but when I looked up, I saw a face I recognized.

"Sobian." I hugged her, scarcely able to believe she was there.

"Lancelot and I found you together. He made me swear to stay here while he got you out, but he didn't say anything about not help-ing you escape." She handed me a sword. "Here, you'll need this. Oh, turn around."

I bit my lower lip, trying to make as little noise as possible as she broke the shaft of the arrow.

Not far away, Malegant and Lancelot battled on, grunting and puffing as they both tired. They were ankle-deep in muddy sand churned into mush by their boots. I was certain that as long as Lancelot didn't make a major mistake, he would prevail. He had more training and a more refined technique than Malegant, who fought as he did everything else—all passion and force with little strategy to back it up.

"Do you trust me?" I asked Sobian.

"Of course, though I doubt you would say the same."

I smiled at her despite myself. "Then don't try to stop me." I swallowed hard, asked the goddess Morrigan for protection, and stepped out into the open. "Malegant! I am here. Stop this battle. It is I you want."

Malegant turned, surprised by the sound of my voice. That was the advantage Lancelot needed. He shoved his sword into Malegant's gut, easily piercing through his armor. Malegant staggered backward and fell, his head landing just shy of the water's edge. Blood pooled in the muck, a trickle escaping his lips as he struggled to hang on to life.

I knelt next to him. His eyes had lost their menace, replaced by fear that revealed the boy he must once have been.

"It is over, Malegant. All of this planning, all of the pain, all of the terror. It is over, and you never truly got what you wanted. I am not your wife, nor ever will I be in any true sense of the word. For every bruise you gave me, for every bone you broke and every time you defiled me, I call upon Ceridwen to take equal vengeance. And not just for myself. In Fiona's name and all of your wives', for every woman you have ever harmed, I curse you. May your soul never find rest."

I could have gone on, but the light went out from behind Malegant's eyes. The hand grasping his wound fell limply to his side. He was dead.

But we were not out of danger yet. I stood, expecting to see joy on Lancelot's face, but instead he held stock-still, frozen by something I hadn't seen. I followed his gaze to see the redheaded guard holding Imogen by the neck. She was weeping for her dead children, heedless of the blade at her throat.

"Let her go," Lancelot called.

"Drop your weapons, and maybe I will."

Lancelot and I both flung our swords to the ground.

"We have done as you asked. Now please, return her to us," Lancelot said.

The guard sneered. "You just killed my lord. He thought that she"—he indicated me with the tip of his dagger—"was worth pursuing. So now I want her for myself—to reap whatever value she brings. That is what I offer. This woman's life for hers."

"I do not know the woman you hold hostage. Her life means nothing to me," Lancelot bluffed. Unseen by the guard, Lancelot was working a dagger loose from the back of his belt.

"So we are at an impasse then."

"It appears so."

I passed behind Lancelot, our heads together in what I hoped the guard took as consultation about his demand.

Lancelot whispered, "I'm going to lunge at him. As soon as I'm clear, aim for his head." He passed the dagger to me.

I flipped the blade around so it was in my palm. "I'm not good at this."

But it didn't matter. Before either of us could move, Sobian and the fisherman tackled the guard and sent him sprawling face-first in the mud, his own dagger sticking out of his back.

Chapter Twelve

For a few moments, none of us moved. In the dying daylight, we stood like statues on a shore ruined by destruction. Leaves and branches littered the shore as though a powerful storm had blown through. The shoreline was in tatters thanks to the tidal wave and Lancelot and Malegant's battle. Three bodies littered the ground. Across the water, the ruins of the tower were smoldering, sending plumes of smoke into the dusky sky. If anyone found this place in the next year or two, they might wonder what had taken place, but they would never guess the devastation was all from the rescue of the queen.

The fisherman stirred. "Please allow me to offer you shelter for the night."

I eyed the man who was so much an older version of Lancelot with suspicion. "How do we know this isn't a trap?"

"Because it isn't," Lancelot stated.

I turned to him. "How do you know?"

"Sobian and I spent many weeks with this man before putting my plan into action. Diarmad is no traitor to the crown."

The fisherman bowed. "My queen."

"You—you know who I am?"

"Indeed. I have pled my case before you many times. I have always found you and the high king to be both fair and wise. When this good knight sought my help in discovering your location, the least I could do was aid him in whatever way I could."

But I wasn't ready to trust him yet. "You are well-spoken for a common fisherman."

"I am anything but common, my lady. But it is a tale best told with a cup in hand in front of a warming fire. Please, will you accept my hospitality?"

Lancelot regarded me pleadingly. "Guinevere, we need to

remove the arrow from your shoulder. Be reasonable."

He was right. My shoulder pulsed with pain, and all of us needed rest.

A short walk later, we approached a small round house fashioned of branches and mud, much like most of our ancestors would have used. From the shadows, a small brown goat bleated.

"That's Ceana. She provides milk and cheese. She's a sweet girl." Diarmad petted the goat as one would a prized hound.

When we stepped inside, my eyes took a moment to adjust, but soon I found we were in a one-room hut with a hard-packed dirt floor. A large fire pit dominated the center of the room. Hanging over it from a long chain was a cauldron of something that smelled divine. On one side was a small oven, likely used for baking bread, while opposite was a small mattress and pillow. A few pegs in the wall held a cloak and three tunics. The only other items in the room were several fishing staffs and nets. He lived as simply as a Druid—or perhaps a Christian hermit.

I couldn't help but wonder how a man of such simple means had found his way to Camelot's court. And more importantly, how he'd become involved in rescuing me. I threw him a sidelong glance. Lancelot may have trusted him, but I didn't.

We need to see to your wound, Imogen signed, as if I could forget the throbbing of an arrow in my shoulder.

"Diarmad, this is Imogen. She cannot speak, but I can understand her hand language and can translate for her."

Diarmad gave Imogen a small bow and touched his thumb to his forehead, lips, and heart. "I know a priestess when I see one. I do not have much, but everything I have is yours."

He laid out four blankets side by side and withdrew so I could undress.

I lay down on one and steeled myself for the painful procedure to come, draining the flagon of mead Diarmad placed by my side. "Lancelot, how did you come to know and trust this man?"

He stood over me. "I suppose that is a good tale to distract you. Brace yourself. This will hurt." He began to draw out the arrow.

I cried out, grasping for something to squeeze. Sobian handed me a wadded-up cloth. I would have rather bitten on leather, but given the circumstances, this would have to do.

"The worst is yet to come, I'm afraid." Something in Lancelot's voice told me he'd done this many times on the battlefield. He knelt beside me.

Nothing could have prepared me for the searing pain that shot from my shoulder straight to my head as the arrow emerged. I screamed but heard my own voice as if from far away, white dots dancing like snowflakes before my eyes. All I wanted was to pass out. Maybe when I woke, the whole business would be over. But no, I was a warrior, a battle queen, some small voice insisted above the shrill ringing in my head. If I couldn't be present for this, I did not deserve to lead others into the same peril.

I was just coming back to full consciousness when my shoulder exploded again, this time accompanied by a splash of something wet. Someone was blowing on the wound in an attempt to allay my pain.

"It's wine," Lancelot explained. "It will clean your wound before Imogen stitches you up."

I was panting like a woman in labor. I turned my head to the side. "That story you were going to use to distract me?"

"Oh yes. It begins many years ago, when I was a young warrior just come from Brittany. I was a lone fighter for hire in those days, anxious to test my blade and build my reputation. I had fought my fair share of battles in order to secure passage to Britain but nothing like those I would face on this isle."

I cried out as Imogen's needle bit into my flesh. Sobian sat next to me and held my hand, while Diarmad busied himself at the cookfire.

"I made my way up north to the land of Angus in the southern Highlands. There I found much work among the warring chieftains. It was there I first met Diarmad."

"You may not expect it, but many a nobleman in Bernicia— where I'm from—has interests up yon way," Diarmad interjected.

"He was recruiting warriors for his army back here. I became one of them."

"Only after you defeated half of the tribes—enough to earn the name Angus. Still hold lands up there, do ye?" Diarmad gestured with his bottle of brew.

I sucked air as Imogen drew the sutures tight. "May I have some of that, please?" I pointed at the bottle.

"Where are my manners?" Diarmad fussed around for another mug.

I gestured to him impatiently, and he came over. I took the

bottle without asking and took one long swallow, then another, and one more for good measure. Wiping my mouth with the back of my hand, I said, "Continue."

Lancelot was so surprised by my unwomanly behavior that it took him a moment to find his train of thought. "After I joined Diarmad in Bernicia, people began noticing the resemblance between us. Quite by accident, we came to realize we were related through my mother's line. I grew up in the sacred grove of the Forest of Broceliande—our version of Avalon—and was raised by the Lady of the Lake, so my parents were but shadows in my memory."

Diarmad picked up the tale. "A woman came to court, claiming to know great things about my past and future. She said I would fall from the heights, never to rise, but that my most trusted man, one of my own blood, would rise higher than I could ever dream. I was intrigued for I knew of no relations still living. This seer wanted a hefty sum for the rest of her knowledge, so I sent her away, but she took a liking to Lancelot and promised him if he did a favor for her, she would reveal to him his true parentage."

Diarmad's voice was coming from far away now. I missed what the nature of the woman's favor was as the pain and drink overtook me simultaneously and I passed out. Apparently neither man noticed, for Lancelot was still talking when I opened my eyes again.

"I followed her most willingly, and she led me to a modest holding where an old woman lay dying. Aoileann was her name, though most called her Eileen or Helen. 'My son,' she said as she embraced me. No one had ever called me that. She told me she was pleased to see me in the employ of my uncle—her brother—and knew I would forever be safe with him. I spent only one evening with her but was able to be present when she passed through the veil." Lancelot cleared his throat then did not continue.

I twisted around and immediately regretted it as my pain flared anew. But I got a glance at the dark green poultice covering my wounded shoulder. "Imogen, what is that? It smells like a midden heap next to a latrine in the heat."

She circled around so I could see her gestures. *Priestess, you know the answer. It will speed your recovery and keep infection away.* She helped me to my feet.

Leaning on her arm, I took a few unsteady steps toward a rug near the fire around which all the others sat.

"Eat," Diarmad insisted, shoving a bowl of fish stew in my direction along with a mug of ale. "This is when the tale takes a dark turn. One day, a young man came to court asking for my strongest warrior. I thought he was going to challenge him to a duel, but he instead relayed a message from King Lot. Lot was planning to challenge Arthur for the throne and desired the strongest and most powerful warriors to join him. This boy here"—he clapped Lancelot's shoulder—"had the sense to refuse. However, I did not. That is how I lost everything."

I looked up from my bowl. That was it. That was why I knew the man's face. I had seen it in my vision while I lay dying in Dyfed. As he explained the repercussions of his actions, my suspicions deepened. If he had committed treachery once, what was to stop him from doing it again, especially now that he had me in his grasp, weakened and nearly alone?

"Arthur condemned me along with Lot and Uriens. I fled Bernicia in shame and settled here because I had built up some measure of respect with Lord Malegant, who always promised he could get me back into court. I suppose he would have had his plans succeeded."

My hackles rose. "So you knew what he was going to do?"

Diarmad was quick to defend his honor. "No, I speak only in hindsight. All I knew was he held this castle in the lake as one of his many fortresses. He mainly used it as a retreat, a place to hide mistresses. I supplied what he needed when he needed it. You see, when I lost my title and my wealth, I still retained many of my connections. I can get anyone just about anything they need."

He cleared his throat noisily. "Last summer, on one of his journeys through the area, he advised me he would be wintering here with a few guests. I assumed he was spending the time with his wife and friends, so I didn't question what he needed. I didn't give the arrangement another thought until these two found me." He gestured at Lancelot and Sobian. "When Lancelot told me his suspicions, my blood went cold. To abduct the queen was most serious indeed, and I was aiding him, albeit unknowingly."

"How did you find each other?" I translated for Imogen, who was held rapt by the story.

Lancelot and Diarmad exchanged glances. "I think that a tale for another time. Our queen is injured and no doubt exhausted, so we should let her sleep."

I hadn't realized it until Lancelot said it, but I was bone weary. At his words, my entire body sagged. I put my half-eaten bowl aside and let Imogen guide me to the pallet. Two moments later, I was in a deep, dreamless sleep.

৶৹৫ ৹৫৹

I woke with a start, uncertain where I was and fearful of reprisal from Malegant. Then, slowly, the events of the previous day returned to me. They were not a dream. The biting pain in my shoulder was proof.

I stood slowly, my legs wobbly from all I had endured. As I moved, every joint hurt, every bruise cried out for attention, but it was nothing compared to what I had endured at Malegant's hand. Imogen, who had been helping Sobian divide up their supplies for the journey home, helped me dress.

Before I could ask where Lancelot had gone, the steady clomp of hooves broke the silence, and I froze, fearing we had been discovered.

Peace, Imogen signed. *'Tis only Lancelot.*

"You're up early," I said by way of greeting as he entered.

"I wanted to be at the village before dawn in case any of Malegant's spies remain. The last thing we need is to alert them of our plans or our method of travel."

"Lancelot, I know you want to use this steed to carry me back to Camelot, but I cannot ask Imogen to walk that distance. I would like her and Sobian to go on ahead of us and be the messengers of good tidings to Arthur. We can follow."

"But there is only one horse. Sobian sold hers in order to be able to stay in town while we formulated a plan to rescue you. You cannot expect to walk all that way. You are wounded and, forgive me, not in your strongest form."

"That has never stopped me before. I will not ride while someone I owe my life to walks."

Not long after, we were saddling the horse and giving Imogen instructions. She didn't want to ride on ahead of us and was still protesting through a series of emphatic gestures, but we insisted.

"Arthur needs to be told we are well," Lancelot insisted. "I set out with Arthur, Merlin, Kay, and Sobian after Merlin told us of his horrifying nightmare. We were split up during a storm, so the others likely don't even know Sobian and I are alive, much less that we found Guinevere. She and I will be traveling slowly and resting frequently. The sooner Arthur can be made aware, the sooner he can send guards to accompany us the rest of the way."

"Take this." I slipped the gold-and-sapphire ring off my finger. "Arthur gave me this and will recognize it. It is my signal to him that I am alive and have truly sent you."

But I cannot speak to him, she signed, her eyes huge with fear and anxiety. *How will I pass on your message?*

"I can understand you," Sobian spoke up.

"You can?"

Sobian grinned. "I understand all manner of hand signals. I was a spy, remember? Do you think I never impersonated a priestess? I had to be authentic or risk being found out."

I stared at her incredulously. Was there no end to this woman's abilities?

"Well then," I said to Imogen, "it sounds like Sobian will be your translator and guide." I hugged her. "I know you are scared, and you have already done more for me than I could ever ask of a dozen people, but I need you to do this one last favor for me. When this is all over, I promise you can retire in any way you like. You are welcome at court if you choose, but if not, name your desire and we will fulfill it."

She nodded. *The journey will give me time to grieve my children in peace. I will do as you wish.*

Lancelot secured her pack, which was loaded with all the provisions she would need should she somehow be separated from Sobian. "You know the directions?"

Imogen nodded.

"Good. May the gods guide your path."

I squeezed Imogen's hand. "Thank you for all you have done."

She smiled. *Don't thank me yet. We both still have a long journey ahead.*

∽❀❀∼

After saying farewell to Diarmad, Lancelot and I headed east, our backs to the progress of the sun. It was about noon on a cold but pleasant day. We would not get far before nightfall, but at least it would put distance between us and the ruined tower. I wanted to be as far from there as quickly as possible.

Our first two days of travel passed without incident, the air growing colder as we neared higher ground. We were fortunate to find shelter in farmsteads, but soon we would not be so lucky. The snow-covered hills of Dartmoor had to be crossed before we reached the safety of the southern terminus of Fosse Way and the road back to Cadbury.

On the third day, we set out to conquer the passes. Had we been on horseback, the journey would only have taken two days at most, but on foot, we faced a trip of at least three times that length.

"What do you feel?" Lancelot asked.

Eyes closed, I searched the energy of the earth and sky. "Nothing. We will have good weather for at least the next two days. Beyond that, I cannot say." I opened my eyes. "This isn't an exact skill, you know."

He laughed. "But a helpful one. I wish I'd had you on my past journeys. You would have saved me many cold, wet nights."

We walked in silence for a while, the ground underfoot sloping steadily upward and the vegetation scarce. Soon there was no path, only wide crags and fissures in the rock, which Lancelot navigated as though he was following a map.

"How do you know this area so well?" I asked.

"I don't. But I traveled it once before, looking for you." He smiled. "Arthur has done everything in his power to try to find you. When you were discovered missing and Gareth was found dead—"

My hand flew to my mouth. "Gareth is dead?"

"Yes. I suppose you would not know. The Samhain revelers said he was stabbed in a fight, right in the middle of the crowd. But it was a mortal wound; no one could have saved him."

"But Gareth was guarding me. There was no fight. Surely I would have known. Unless. . ." The words needed not be spoken. I was certain to the marrow of my bones that Malegant had done this. That was how he'd ensured I was alone and ripe for the picking.

Lancelot cleared his throat. "As soon as we realized you were gone, Arthur launched the biggest search party the country has ever seen. Men and women from all over Britain looked for you in every part of the country. We knew whoever had taken you couldn't have gotten far, but we decided to search everywhere. Merchants and trading caravans had their wagons inspected at every major crossing, and every boat that sailed from our ports was searched before being allowed to weigh anchor. He really did all he could."

I tried to fight the pain welling up inside me. All those resources, all those plans, and yet. . . my mind flashed through months of torment, submission, and pain. Tears overflowed before I could stop them. When I could speak, my voice was strained. "Why was this place so difficult to find? Why did it take so long?"

Why didn't you find me sooner? Why didn't Arthur come for me himself? Those were the questions I really wanted to ask.

Lancelot stopped. He picked up a stick and sketched a crude map in the snow. "Cadbury is that stone over there." He pointed at a rock sticking out of the snow about three arms' lengths away. "This area is open plain, and these are the mountains we are in now." He gestured to each with his stick. "You were here." He drew a circle surrounded by a wavy-lined lake and mountains like spear points. "We were not even aware this area was habitable. That is why no one looked there."

He looked at me, his soft, caring blue eyes seeking forgiveness. I nodded, relieved to be able to genuinely give it.

He took my arm, and we continued walking as he spoke. "It was only after Merlin's dream that we had specific guidance on where to look. He used some kind of crystal to guide us—until the storm. Worst storm I've ever seen, and I've been trapped in many. It was two nights after the eclipse. We had just made it through the narrowest pass in these hills when the sky darkened far too fast for a normal sunset. The air took on the tang of metal, and the wind blew fiercely then suddenly stopped. We knew we had to seek shelter and fast, but there was nowhere to hide. Before we could make a plan, the rain fell in large, heavy drops. We made it to the outskirts of the forest before the hail came too. Lightning flashed all around us, chasing us wherever we went. That's when Sobian and I became separated from the rest."

I thought back. Two days after the eclipse. What exactly had Aine's dark power shown her? Was it possible she could have known? That she could have directed the storm to keep them away? She was certainly in control of powers that should only have belonged to a trained priestess. But if that was the case, then why had Malegant left me alone? Perhaps he had not known help was coming or Aine had not realized her plan was not completely successful.

The path became so slippery with ice Lancelot and I had to hold on to one another to stay upright.

After a while, he looked at the sky. "We should find a place to spend the night."

Eventually, we came upon a cave. After ensuring it wasn't currently occupied by a slumbering bear, Lancelot rousted the bats from its roof. I will never forget their squeaking and the ghostly shiver of their wings as they winged past me to find a new place to haunt. Warrior or no, I cowered in fear until I was certain they were gone. We spent the night slumbering amid our fur-lined cloaks with only a tiny fire to keep us warm. In the still, small hours of the night, Lancelot embraced me in his sleep, his touch igniting the wound in my shoulder. I recoiled, his touch and the sudden pain bringing back vivid memories of Malegant. A small cry escaped my lips as I scrambled to my feet, shaking and desperate to be more than an arm's length away from him.

"What is it?" He looked up, still partially asleep, confused.

I couldn't speak. I tried to catch my breath, which was coming in ragged gasps, but could not. I doubled over. My chest was caving in. I couldn't breathe. It was as though fear was smothering me.

"Guinevere? Are you ill?"

I couldn't stop shaking. My mind kept replaying the same memories—Malegant breaking my fingers, beating me, raping me, tearing my flesh to ribbons. Tears made hot rivers down my cheeks in the cold night air.

I must have looked to him like a feral beast because Lancelot spoke to me in the same soothing tone he used on unbroken colts. "Everything is fine. I mean you no harm. You are safe, Guinevere."

My heart was pounding in my head, but at the sound of my name, the rushing thoughts slowed a little. I could understand where I was but not yet why.

He must have noticed the effect because he tried again. "Guinevere, look at me. No one will harm you."

I met his eyes, and my heart began to slow.

"That's it. It's me, Lancelot—your champion. I am sworn to the Goddess in all her names to protect you, remember? I am here to take you home."

Slowly, my chest muscles relaxed, and I gasped in a few deep breaths. I was beginning to remember who I was, where, and why.

Lancelot reached out his hand. "Come to me, Guinevere. You

will be safe. I swear it."

Hesitantly, I took a small step forward. My arm moved without conscious command to him. When our fingertips touched, I did not flinch but rather relaxed into his warmth.

Lancelot held my hand gently and slowly led me back to where we had bedded down. "I will not hurt you, but we will be warmer if we are close together. If you do not wish to touch, at least let us share our cloaks."

I allowed him to cover us both, our bodies nearly touching. Soon my eyelids grew heavy again, and darkness descended to take all the memories away.

⸙

The next morning, we woke to a light snowfall. After breaking our fast on a brace of squirrels caught in Lancelot's traps, we set out on what we hoped would be the last leg of our journey through the mountains. After that, we should have been able to take the Roman roads back to Cadbury. We walked in tense silence for a while, trying not to slip on the uneven, rocky terrain. Neither of us acknowledged what had taken place last night.

Finally, Lancelot said, "Guinevere, I know this is beyond the bounds of my role as your champion, but what did Male—"

I whirled on him. "Do not say his name. He is dead. It is over."

"But Arthur must be told. Do you wish to tell him yourself what happened, or shall I relay it? Which would be easier for you?"

I stopped. "Why need he know? Is it not bad enough that one of us is haunted by the memories? Why should I so burden him?" I didn't want to tell him anything, say anything. If I voiced my experiences, there would be no denying them. They would be real and irrefutable. I couldn't do it. I just couldn't.

"You need to tell someone. You'll never be free until you do. I swear on all the gods and the Lady of the Lake who raised me that I will repeat what you tell me only to the king."

I fought him for a while, but eventually, as the sky grew lighter and the sun traversed the sky behind a bank of darkening clouds that began to shed tiny flakes, I told him everything, starting with caring for Camille and Llew all the way through learning Imogen's identity and our plans to escape. As much as I wanted to edit my experience and keep the worst from him, I forced the words through my lips. By the time my story was complete, I could barely stand. Reliving it was nearly as bad as going through it the first time.

The snow was falling harder, piling up around our ankles and hampering our progress. On Lancelot's advice, we had each taken a stout stick from a pine tree to use as a walking staff. I was grateful for the support.

We rounded a bend, and I gasped in wonder. Before us, the land plummeted to a deep chasm with only a small ledge hugging the eastern face of the foothills. The hills dropped off sharply to a void of rock and ice, small scrub trees growing defiantly here and there from fissures in its smooth face. Far below, a gray-and-white-capped river flowed, its roaring current only the slightest whisper to our ears. On the far side, the sun was beginning to set behind foothills identical to the ones we had just traversed, where trees promised to lead to level land if one only kept walking long enough. Directly ahead, across the gorge, the ledge widened to accommodate a small stand of fir trees and a tiny cabin.

"There." Lancelot pointed at the house. "That is where we will rest this night."

"Will we have to cross the chasm?" I asked tremulously, memories of the crude bridge at the tower still far too fresh in my mind.

"No, if we keep to the ledge, it should take us there."

"Good." My teeth chattered as much with fear as cold.

Lancelot led the way, testing each step with his staff before making it, clearly uncertain whether or not to trust his sight as to which parts of the snow-packed ground were solid and which were not. We were purposefully silent, knowing what the slightest noise could do at this elevation when the snows were heavy and their pack unreliable.

The cabin was in sight when the rumbling began. Instinctively, we looked up then at each other. We hadn't made a sound. But someone had.

"Someone else is here," I said, spine prickling, ears fully alert like a hound.

It came again—a regular crunch, crunch, crunch—growing steadily closer, but because of the echoes of the gorge, I couldn't tell if it was in front of or behind us. I drew my sword.

The mountain grumbled again, shaking the ground beneath us.

Lancelot picked up a rock and threw it across the path ahead.

It bounced off a tree trunk, clattering to the ground. Not a moment later, an arrow whizzed past us and lodged in the earth where the rock had fallen.

"It's a trap," I whispered.

Lancelot nodded, looking around. "There are likely men behind us, so we cannot turn back, but I don't see a viable way around either."

We charged forward, running at top speed to evade any additional archers, and narrowly missed a rope strung across the pass. Once over it, Lancelot tripped it as we hugged the trees on opposite sides of the trail. A net rose out of the snow, closing over nothing. Lancelot cut it down and slung the mesh over his shoulder.

The sound drew out our attackers. They emerged from the trees—the archer, another man, and a golden-haired woman—confident in their trap. Lancelot was able to dispatch the archer before the others assumed a defensive stance.

My mouth dropped open as I found myself facing Aine—who I'd thought was dead—and more surprisingly, Diarmad.

They took advantage of our shock by charging. Aine came at me as though to tackle me but then shoved me to the right, nearly sending me skittering over the ledge. Thanks be to the goddess Druantia I caught a bowed branch of pine in time to stop my slide. I scrambled to my feet, and Aine swung at my head with her wicked axe. I ducked and weaved so that I was behind her. She turned before I could land a blow, but I was now too close for her massive weapon to be of much use. She turned it and slammed the pole into my ribs, knocking me back, but I was inside her guard again before she could swing.

In my peripheral vision, I saw Lancelot struggling with Diarmad, each knowing the other's fighting techniques, skills, and weaknesses.

I decided to try to distract Aine to break her concentration. "How did you get ahead of us, Aine? Why follow us all this way?"

She panted, "I know these mountains better than your knight. You killed my brother, so I will take your life. But not before ransoming you for all your puny hide is worth."

So she didn't plan to kill me, at least not yet. That certainly changed the tenor of this fight. I relaxed a little, working to disarm her. Out of the corner of my eye, I saw Lancelot bring Diarmad to his knees and ensnare him in the net he had salvaged.

Aine must have seen it too, for she turned and, with a feral war cry, swung at Lancelot. He dove out of the way but not quite in time.

Her axe bit into his thigh. Lancelot crumpled, momentarily defense-less. Struggling to regain his footing, he threw a handful of snow at Aine, hoping to blind her, but she avoided it and raised her axe to deliver the fatal blow.

I screamed and lunged for her, but Diarmad wriggled his way out of the net and came at Lancelot at the same time. In a split-second decision, I changed the arc of my blade and swung at Diarmad instead, ripping a hole in his gut. His blade too made deadly contact, but not with Lancelot. His final act was to save Lancelot by driving his sword into Aine's throat. She gurgled in surprise, dropped her axe, and fell, her blood staining the snow a bright crimson.

Diarmad collapsed into Lancelot's arms. Lancelot could only stare at him, shocked.

I ran to Diarmad's side and knelt next to him. "Oh, Diarmad, I am so sorry. I thought you were going to kill Lancelot."

He smiled ruefully. "I was. But when your blow landed, I knew I could not let that viper live."

I held his wound, watching helplessly as life drained out of him.

Lancelot slowly recovered from his shock. "Why join with her, Diarmad?"

"She traced you to me. Said she would make it worth me turning on you. It was either die by her hand or yours, and after so many years of living on nothing, I'm afraid her promises of riches outweighed my loyalty, even to you." He groaned. "I am so sorry, my friend. . ."

Lancelot bowed his head. "All things are forgiven in the end." He looked at me.

I placed a hand on Diarmad's brow. "May the Lady guide you home, and in her arms may you find rest. Drink from her cauldron and be reborn without sorrow or stain. Go in peace."

Diarmad smiled and covered my hand, red now from his blood, with his own. "Forgive me." He breathed one last time and closed his eyes, still for eternity.

The mountain rumbled again, and Lancelot looked up. "We will get no additional warning. Come. We must hurry or the avalanche will bury us along with our enemies."

◦ৡৣ◦

Cold, bloodied, and limping, we reached the cabin just before sun-down. It must have been a hunting lodge for it was well stocked with preserves, blankets, and a store of firewood. Although what anyone would have hunted up here eluded me. We had seen signs of a few bears but were at too high an elevation for deer or boars. Squirrels and fox were everywhere, but there were easier places to lay traps for them.

But as the sun sank lower, the wolves began to howl, and I understood. I shivered as their mournful cries turned my blood to ice.

"They are the banshees of the animal world," Lancelot said. "That's the one thing I never got used to when traveling on the open roads. I know their habits, but that doesn't stop something inside me from cringing when I hear them. But we'll be safe in here."

Lancelot insisted on examining me before allowing me to tend to him. He sewed a few new stitches in my shoulder blade and pronounced two of my ribs broken from the butt of Aine's axe, but that was the extent of my injures.

Finally he let me see to his thigh, which was still trickling blood. He had removed his breeches out of necessity, and strangely, I was acutely aware that the hem of his tunic was the only thing preserving his modesty. Much to my horror, the thought made my cheeks burn as I bathed the wound. His fingers dug into my shoulders, and I blew on the gash, only too aware of the intimacy of the gesture.

"You never did tell me how you came to find Diarmad on this journey," I prompted. "Perhaps telling me of it will help distract you from the pain." And me from my embarrassment.

"Where did I leave off?" he asked as I repeated the procedure with water, seeking to see just how badly injured he was. "Ah yes, Sobian and I were separated from the rest of the group in unfamiliar land. We headed north because that's what I've always done when I am lost. It's something I remember the Lady of the Lake telling me. 'Whenever you have lost your way, follow the North Star home.'"

He stopped talking and flinched as I probed his wound with my fingers. "It is not nearly as deep as it should be. Your movement must have taken some of the force out of her swing. Don't walk for a while, and there shouldn't be any lasting damage." I met his eyes briefly, seeing relief in them, and poured honey into the wound to clean and bind it before stitching him up.

Lancelot continued through gritted teeth. "After walking for what felt like days, we came upon Diarmad's house, much as you and I came upon this place. At first, he was wary of me. But once

I recognized him and recounted our past history—something no one else could have known—he began to trust me. One day, Sobian returned from town with word of activity in the tower. We watched it for several weeks before we saw you. When Diarmad told us he was due to deliver supplies, Sobian saw our way in. It was her idea to have us switch places. I believe you know the rest."

"She is a master of intrigue," I credited, slathering the stitched skin with a liberal coating of Imogen's stinky salve before I covered it with clean cloth. "This shows no signs of infection. But you need to lay off the heroics," I joked with a wag of my finger.

He grabbed my finger and twisted. "Only if you promise not to get yourself kidnapped again."

I writhed in mock pain and protest. When I looked up, our faces were less than a hand span apart. We froze, staring at one another for a long time. Finally, I dropped my eyes.

"We should sleep," I muttered.

He cleared his throat. "Yes, indeed."

We retired to opposite sides of the bed, backs to one another. I sent my consciousness down into the earth, intent on thanking all the gods who had saved my life today. But I sensed something else, something looming and oppressive. I sat up suddenly.

"Lancelot?"

"Mmmm?" He was already partially asleep.

"We need to stay here. A snowstorm is coming."

⁙

Large flakes fell from the sky for the next three days, and it was three more before we could leave the cabin. I was grateful for the extra time to rest and recover from our injuries.

But soon enough, the sun broke through the clouds, turning the forest into a wonderland of glittering snow and shining ice, a frozen paradise into which we ventured, full of hope that we would soon be home. Our progress was slow. Lancelot was still limping and leaning on a stripped pine branch for support. We took turns carrying the heavy pack of supplies, and I had to stop often to give both him and my shoulder a rest. Another two days passed before we finally came upon the old Roman road leading to Isca. We could follow it for the remainder of our journey.

"There is a village just up ahead," Lancelot said, weariness in every aspect of his demeanor. His shoulders slumped, his eyes were heavy, and his gait was sluggish. "I know this area. We will be safe here."

We must have looked like a couple of outlaws when we stumbled into the village. I combed my fingers through my hair, but it was hopelessly tangled. At least we'd been able to wash in an icy pond earlier in the morning, so I didn't think we smelled worse than anyone else who'd been on the road. But our clothes were dirty and torn from multiple fights, and bruises blossomed all over our bodies.

I pulled the hood of my cloak farther down over my forehead as we passed a small Christian church, uncertain whether someone of my faith would be welcome in this town. I had heard stories of how well the missionaries were doing in the south, and I had no desire to suffer persecution on top of everything else. Just in case, I pulled a few withered juniper berries off a bush as we passed and squeezed them until I had just a few drops of juice on my fingers. I touched my forehead then wiped my fingertips on my skirt. This juice was nearly the same color as the ink in my tattoo, so touching it would enable me "smudge" the tattoo if needed, making it appear to be drawn on rather than permanent. It was a trick all priestesses of Avalon learned in case we ventured into unfriendly territory, but I hoped my precaution would prove unnecessary.

We stopped at the mouth of an alley where two buildings opposed each other and a wooden fence forced a dead end beyond them. The one to our right, if the sour smell was any indication, was a stable—and not a very clean one. To our left was what I could only guess was an inn. Music and raucous laughter flowed out of its open door while men and women played games of chance in the street, shouting over the din from inside. At the far end of the lane, a group of youths used the fence to practice knife throwing, a crude target having been drawn on its surface.

We pushed past patrons in various states of inebriation. All glared in response, but no one was bothered enough to make a scene. The air inside the inn was thick with wood smoke, scents of food—some new, some several days old—and strongest of all, stale ale. Men and women of all ages, shapes, and sizes crowded every table and corner, laughing, joking, or conducting business in hushed conversation. Serving women and children darted in and out of the crowd, providing mugs of thick dark brown ale or golden mead alongside loaves of bread, steaming bowls of stew, or joints of meat. In exchange, coins of all values, from gold and silver to the most meager metal, changed hands—and not just for food. At quite a few tables, men were buying companionship for the evening.

As one of the serving maids passed us, my stomach rumbled audibly. We found an empty place to sit at the end of a long table. The top was laden with burning lumps of candle wax. No one bothered to remove a candle when it burned out—they simply stacked a new one on top of the pool of wax made by the last one. The benches were covered in furs and hides, a welcome comfort after days on the road.

A burley man sidled up to us. "What will it be then?"

"Two mugs of ale and two joints of that boar on the spit. We would also like a room for the evening," Lancelot requested.

The barkeep glared at Lancelot. "One room?" He looked from Lancelot to me. "It's a shame, but our only private room is in use. You'll have to sleep in the common room tonight or seek shelter somewhere else."

He started to walk away, but Lancelot put a firm hand on the man's arm. "Tell me, who is your distinguished guest? Unless it is the high king himself"—Lancelot surveyed the room—"and I doubt he would stay here, you will ask that person to remove himself from those quarters. Unless you would like me to remove him myself."

"Who are you to demand such things?"

"Lancelot du Lac, High King Arthur's Master of the Horse and member of the Combrogi."

The innkeeper snorted. "And I'm the queen."

I turned to him. "Actually, I am."

The innkeeper scowled at me but inspected me closely. Then he roared with laughter. "Tonight the queen, tomorrow the unruly slave girl, isn't that how it goes for your lot?"

I smiled inwardly at his assumption that I was a prostitute playing a role to satisfy the fantasy of my customer. It was probably safer than admitting my true identity as we were still in Malegant's lands. If he wished to believe it, then I would not correct him. Playing along, I merely dropped my eyes to the floor.

The innkeeper cackled again. "Hey, boys, you have to come see this one." He motioned to two young men who were obviously his sons. "And bring them two wet ones and a piece of the piggy."

"Why did you not tell him who you are?" Lancelot whispered to me once the innkeeper had gone.

"We can't have them know who I am, can we?" I looked around, but no one was paying us any heed. "You are safe because everyone knows Arthur's knights go where they please. But the same is not true for me. Until we're back in Cadbury, I trust no one. Neither should you. Pretend to be my customer. They are entertained by it. The more enthralled they are, the less likely they are to be suspicious."

"You are a devious one, you know that?"

I gave him a coy smile. "I've been around Sobian too long."

The innkeeper's boys arrived. They were tall like their father but not yet fully grown. They kept a close watch on us while they set down our trenchers and the rest of our meal.

"Look," the older one said, "she even has the queen's marque." He pointed at my forehead.

"The marque is fake," I said in a sultry whisper only he and his brother could hear, looking up at then through my eyelashes. "This man told me he wanted to be with the queen, so I've done my best to fulfill his wish."

I curled myself around Lancelot, hip touching him suggestively, one arm around him while running my other hand inside the collar of his shirt and playing with his chest hair. I expected the surprised look on his face, but I wasn't prepared for the shock of pleasure that ran up my arm from my fingertips. I did my best to recover by aiming the smoldering I felt Lancelot's way.

"If you say I'm the queen, I am the queen," I purred. "As long as the price is right, I'll be whoever you want me to be."

When I looked back at the boys, both of their mouths were hanging open.

I fixed them with a longing stare, dropping my voice once again. "Are you boys interested in tomorrow night?"

They both stuttered, their words incomprehensible.

The older one recovered first. "But the marque—if it's not real, how did you get it?"

"Like this." I brought my thumb to my lips and licked it seductively, sucking just enough to hold their attention. I brought it to my forehead and down in an arc. The "ink" of my tattoo smeared just as I'd hoped it would. Thank the gods for juniper berry juice.

"Oh." The younger boy sounded disappointed. "Well then, we'll leave you to your meal."

"But I may be back around later to ask about your price," the older added quietly.

I winked at him.

As soon as they were lost in the crowd, I breathed a sigh of relief.

"You know you're going to have to keep up the ruse of being a whore for the rest of the evening, right?"

I gave Lancelot a lingering sidelong glance. "Does that make you uncomfortable, my noble knight?" I couldn't be sure if it was the play of the light from the fire pits or if he blushed.

Before I had a chance to tuck in to my meal, the innkeeper returned. "Your room will be ready shortly, sir."

From somewhere above, a racket rose above the din. It sounded like a herd of bulls were running through the upstairs rooms. A few moments later, the barkeep's sons emerged, each carrying one end of an unruly minor noble. The younger had him under the arms and his brother was fending off kicking feet.

"I will not be treated in this manner. I am a descendant of a Damnonii chieftain as well as a Roman general. I will not stand for this."

"No, but you'll lie down for it," someone in the crowd yelled, garnering raucous laughter.

"If you have a problem with our treatment of you, take it up with the member of the Combrogi who is in our midst."

Lancelot waved at the indignant upstart. He leaned over to me. "Sometimes I'm so glad I accepted this position."

"But not when a crazed noble's half sister is aiming a sword at your gut."

"You jest. That is the best part."

I found myself unable to look away from his smile. Even with the bruises discoloring his right eye and the cut across his other cheek, his looks and charm were enough to make any woman melt. I tore into the hunk of meat in front of me and continued to watch him. "You're enjoying yourself, aren't you?"

He swallowed a mouthful of food. "It's not often I get to spend the evening with a woman of questionable virtue."

"Then you must not spend much time at court."

He laughed. "Point taken."

We finished the rest of our meal while making idle conversation with the patrons around us. A toothless old woman was trying to keep up, but her poor hearing made her repeat nearly every word.

"Cadbury, did you say? Have you met the king's new wife?" she asked a rugged, road-weary man who appeared to be a merchant of some sort. "They say she's a beauty, striking as one of the fey."

My heart froze.

"No. She did not accompany him into town."

The woman's reply was lost in the din of voices.

I grabbed Lancelot's hand to get his attention. "What did she mean 'the king's new wife'? Surely the old crone was mistaken."

Lancelot's face clouded. "I wish she were. This is something best discussed in private. Follow me, and don't forget your role."

"Oh, I haven't," I said, sliding a hand around his waist as he rose. I was surprised at how comfortable I was playing the harlot with him.

Lancelot tossed a handful of coins to the innkeeper as we passed. He acknowledged the largess with a nod to Lancelot and a knowing grin at me. I smiled back and slid my hand down to Lancelot's backside as we ascended the stairs. A few muted hoots floated up from the more observant patrons.

I collapsed on the bed almost immediately once we were alone, exhausted from keeping up the pretense and hollow from the possibility of Arthur's betrayal. New wife? What could that possibly mean? I glanced at Lancelot, both hoping and dreading he would pick up the thread of our conversation, but he was busy rummaging in our bag for the supplies he'd need to clean his leg.

I stood and busied myself by fetching a ewer of water and a basin, which I placed on the floor next to him. I curled up on his other side, tucking my legs into my skirt and hugging them. A cold weight had settled in my chest, like at the onset of catarrh, but this was no illness. It was the weight of betrayal.

"The old woman wasn't wrong," Lancelot said in low voice, as if loath to speak the words. He peeled back his bandage as he continued. "After six moons of searching with only your golden comb to tell us you were taken via the main road into town, the other lords and some of the Combrogi were ready to declare you dead. Arthur did not wish to give up the search, but in the face of your disappearance and the arguments that even if you did return, you would not bear him any heirs, he invoked the ancient laws allowing him to take a second wife. She has no title beyond royal wife and will never be equal to you in stature, but she has already brought him one son, sired before you and he were wed."

I turned around so quickly the stitches in my shoulder pulled. I grimaced. "How does he—how does anyone know the child is his?"

Lancelot chuckled darkly. "One look at him and there is no denying his paternity."

Kneeling, I took the pot of salve from Lancelot, suddenly needing to occupy my hands. "Arthur did mention having another life planned before he became king." My hands trembled as I spread the thick ointment on his thigh. "I suppose now he has everything he ever wanted." Despite my best efforts to breathe and appear calm, my voice betrayed me, shaking with every word.

Lancelot stopped me by placing a hand on mine, which was perilously close to his manhood. "You do not need to continue to act the part here. Not when it is only us. Unless"—his voice grew husky—"unless you wish to do so."

I looked up at him, realizing only then how my hands had transgressed. For a moment, I considered his offer but quickly rejected it. It would be a long time before I could lie with a man after what Malegant had done. Besides, I would not betray Arthur even if he had done so to me.

Laughter bubbled out of me from some deep, hidden place, quickly turning to sobs as the full weight of what Lancelot had said hit me. I laid my head on his knees and wept. With one hand, he stroked my hair as I cried; with the other, he finished bandaging his wound. As soon as he was finished, he slipped an arm under my knees and carried me to the bed.

I clung to him, feeling awash and adrift. He was the rock keeping me from drowning in the darkness. When finally no more tears would come, I curled up in a ball within the warmth of his arms.

"What am I now?" I asked in a voice that sounded small and fragile even to my own ears.

He brushed a stray lock of hair from my face. "You are who you've always been—our queen. She is nothing to you."

"But he has pledged himself to me. What of that?"

"So have I. No matter what, I will not leave you." Lancelot kissed me gently on the forehead, as a mother does her child. It was oddly reassuring. "I cannot lessen the sting of betrayal you must feel, but know this: no one—and I mean no one—will deny you your true role now that you are safe. If they do, they will have to face me."

I smiled into his chest, mood lightened by degrees despite the overwhelming heaviness threatening to engulf me. This man had not only rescued me from my tormentor and defended my life, now he was promising to help me through a terrible transition back to my life with Arthur. Merlin's fears be damned. Choosing Lancelot as my champion was the wisest thing I had ever done.

⁂

The sun was setting two nights later when we approached Cadbury. The fortress could be seen from a long way off, silhouetted against a red sky. After six months of fearing I'd never see home again, I practically ran toward the gatehouse, heedless of the steep climb up the terraced side of the hill. At some point my energy would give out and I would collapse, that much was certain, but right now, all I wanted was to be within its sheltering walls and see Arthur again.

Lancelot struggled to keep pace with me as we ascended the hill. "Guinevere, slow down. You will injure yourself even more."

"I don't care. I'm home. I'm free. It's over!"

"There is one thing you should know before—"

Lancelot never got to finish his sentence. The guards in the towers spotted us and raised the cry, "Lancelot has returned with the queen."

Soon the cry was taken up by the other guards and the townspeople. Before we knew it, we were being ushered inside on a wave of people, some of whom I recognized, others who were strangers, but all were equally joyful. I smiled and waved to them all, so relived to be home, to be safe.

"Make way for the queen," they cried one after another until the doors of the great hall opened.

I was prepared to run into Arthur's arms, but what I saw stopped me cold. Morgan stood next to Arthur, her sly, catlike smile in full effect. Her hands rested on the shoulders of a boy of about four years who was watching me curiously. Arthur was sitting in his usual place, an uncomfortable expression on his face.

"Morgan—I—you are the last person I expected to welcome me home." My voice sounded false even to my own ears.

"Welcome to *our* home," she corrected, looking up at Arthur with affection.

It took me a moment to process this. Morgan was in the place of the queen—in my place. What had Lancelot said? Arthur had married someone he'd known before he met me. But that woman couldn't possibly be Morgan. She had been in Avalon—at least until the incident with the poison... then I remembered the vision I'd had as I looked into Merlin's eyes at Corbenic when he told me of Morgan's fate. It was this exact scene. Morgan had been standing with her hand on her son's—their son's—shoulder.

Arthur finally stood, arms outstretched, and came to meet me. "Guinevere! The gods be praised. I thought we would never see you again."

As he embraced me, I was wooden, unable to return his affection in such an odd situation.

It was Morgan who finally drew us apart. "Nor did I." Her voice was tinged with regret. "We are blessed beyond measure. Is not that right, husband?"

Years of living with her had attuned me to the subtle sarcasm Arthur probably missed. Her use of the word husband, the one which should have been rightfully only mine, stunned me more than if she had delivered a swift blow to my head. Suddenly, it all made sense. He had married Morgan. He had known her before, perhaps during the time she went missing after her banishment from Avalon.

I looked at the boy. It was as Lancelot had said. No one who saw him could deny he was a younger version of the king right down to that particular shade of straw-blond hair and the cleft in his chin. He had Morgan's bright blue eyes, watchful and unnerving. He smiled at me innocently.

My heart and mind shattered. Here in front of me was the life I had always wished to live. Arthur with his heir, a handsome boy who favored him so strongly, but the woman playing the role of wife and mother was my worst enemy. Suddenly I recalled the day in Argante's hut when she had quizzed Morgan and me on elements of the law. *A man takes a second wife,* she had said. She'd known even back then when we were merely girls this day would come to pass. The world tilted. I grabbed Lancelot for support to steady myself.

"Guinevere?" Arthur asked, holding out a hand to me. "Are you unwell?"

I stepped back and began to cry uncontrollably, rage tinting the edges of my vision red. "How dare you ask me that? You have no idea what misery I have felt! Now I return to find you married to *her.*"

"Calm down," Arthur said. "I can explain. I did not know about Mordred"—he indicated the boy—"but Morgan was pregnant before you and I wed."

My whole body was shaking. "Of course. If you had known, you wouldn't have married me." It was a statement, not a question.

In a flash, the sight showed me an alternate life, one in which I thought I was marrying Aggrivane but was given to Malegant instead. One in which Morgan was queen and I lived the life of a slave only to die at Malegant's hand. When my sight cleared, I looked at the family in front of me.

I wheeled on Morgan. "I suppose I am to be grateful to you for consoling my husband in my absence or for saving me from my captor, the murderer who was to be my husband."

Morgan looked at Arthur, forehead wrinkled. "I do not understand what she is saying. Do you?"

Arthur shook his head and took my hand. "You have had a great shock. Perhaps you should lie down, then we can discuss this."

My heartbeat quickened into a deafening pounding, and my eyes clouded over with black and white spots as anger overtook me. "No. I do not want to lie down or be calm." I jerked my hand out of his grasp. "I want to hear you say it, Arthur Pendragon! *I* am your wife, not her. You chose me, remember?"

Arthur regarded me warily, as if I were a beast about to strike. "Yes, you are my wife. But so is Morgan now. I assure you we can sort this all out later."

"I don't want to talk about it later." I flexed my fingers, itching to attack. "You!" I yelled at Morgan. "You are nothing but a manipulative, backstabbing whore. You always do what you can to ruin my happiness. I will kill you for this."

I lunged at her and knocked her to the ground, intent on tearing at her eyes. Morgan fought me, but she was no match for a woman who had been tormented as I had. I was about to punch her in the face when Lancelot pulled me off and wrenched my arms behind me.

Arthur helped a stunned, bleeding Morgan to her feet. "What has happened to make her this way?" he asked Lancelot. "This is not the woman I married."

"She has been through a great deal—" Lancelot began.

"I am your wife," I yelled amid hiccupping tears. "Do not speak of me as though I am not here in front of you. You wish to know what has happened to me? I will tell you. I was kidnapped, raped repeatedly, and beaten nearly to death by one of your men while you faithlessly took this woman to your bed. Lancelot and Sobian saved me. But now I see I may have been better off dying at Malegant's hand."

I wrenched free of Lancelot's grip to scratch wildly at my own skin, which suddenly pricked painfully. I fell to my knees as my sight clouded with memories of Malegant, and my time in his tower mingled with Morgan's triumphant expression at Arthur's side. I held my head and screamed. It was all too much.

From somewhere far away, Arthur called for Grainne and ordered her to take me to Avalon—now.

As Lancelot dragged me from the room, I looked at Arthur through strands of wild, tangled hair. "What did I do to deserve this?" My voice was small now, all the fight gone out of me.

"Nothing," he answered, concerned.

"And everything," Morgan added.

The last thing I remembered was hearing Mordred ask in a small, scared voice, "What is wrong with that lady?"

"She is ill," Arthur answered kindly.

"She is a madwoman," Morgan clarified.

When the darkness came, I welcomed it.

PART THREE

Outlier

Chapter Thirteen

Summar 501

When I opened my eyes, I was in my old priestess's chambers in Avalon. Around me, grayish stone walls gleamed in the summer sunlight. I blinked, taking in the room that was both familiar and foreign. Little had changed even though dozens of women must have called this room home since I was last here. A tall wardrobe stood open against one wall, a handful of blue robes and cloaks visible on pegs inside. A small table with a jug and wash basin, mirror, and comb was on one side of the bed, another table with a tray of bread and a steaming cup of tea on the opposite side.

Warm, sweet breezes wafted in from the eastern window through which I could see the holy Tor, but I had no desire to be out in them. I pulled the fur blanket closer, seeking warmth I feared I would never feel again. I was still shaking, my mind racing with hundreds of terrible thoughts. What if Arthur didn't accept me back at court? Was that the real reason I was here? Would I never return home? What if Morgan was right and I was a madwoman? Would the whole of Britain come to hate me? I curled up in a ball, trying to fight the sensation that my skin was peeling off, that some feral version of me was slowly emerging from it, red and raw and wounded beyond repair.

The only memories I had of the journey were fragmented. The rocking of a cart, Imogen's kind touch reassuring me everything would be well, the bitter taste of some brew I now knew to be drugged, and the darkness of a mind that could take no more pain.

I lay in bed, breathing deeply for a long time, willing the shards of my mind to coalesce, but the harder I tried, the more they fractured.

"You should have stayed with me," Malegant's voice said. "I could have spared you all this."

I sat up, looking around, but I was alone. Malegant and Aine were dead, but they were haunting me, their voices the only disruptions in my waking nightmare.

"You caused this," I said quietly, answering the imaginary voice.

"We did not," Aine responded. "Where is your husband, your mate, your support? Is he not supposed to see you through times like this?"

"Stop!" I yelled, tears springing from my eyes yet again. "Leave me alone!" I pulled at my hair, trying to get the voices to quiet.

Viviane appeared in the doorway, pausing before rushing to my side. "Guinevere, be still. Be at peace. You are in Avalon. You're safe." She sat next to me on the bed, one arm wrapped protectively around me.

"No, I am not. I will never be whole again," I sobbed.

She let me cry and rocked me like a babe, stroking my hair and cooing softly. "May the Lady grant you peace. May she bring you all the love your heart needs, and may you heal in time."

Once my tears dried up, she helped me drink the tea. Normally I would have fought the effects of the herbs, but today I embraced them. Rather than making my eyelids heavy as I'd expected, they washed over me like an ocean wave, leaving an eerie feeling of peace in their wake. I felt like myself again if only for a short time.

◦◦◦

After a few days of the herbs, the voices faded and the shaking stopped. I still felt raw, as if I was walking around without my skin, but at least I could get out of bed. The pain and betrayal were still there, but my mind was clearer now. I could think about my situation more rationally. Grainne took on the role of my personal attendant, and I was grateful for her constant presence.

We were walking through the flourishing herb garden one morning when I asked her, "Do you think Arthur hates me?"

She smiled at me, her golden hair catching the sun. "No. I think you surprised him. He really never thought he'd see you again—even after Imogen showed him your ring and offered him a small shred of hope. Then you showed up like an avenging ghost, all vitriol and fury. They grieved for you, mourned for you, truly." She took my hand. "Lancelot, too. Just when our lives were beginning to feel normal, you came back. It will take time for everyone to adjust."

I stopped and pulled a weed from between two stems of bright green lovage. "He didn't even wait a full year, Grainne."

"He didn't have to," she said gently. "Under the law, he could

Summer 501

have married Morgan at any time, but he never thought her worthy of being the king's wife—she was an orphan, after all. But when you were thought dead, Morgan told him the truth about Mordred."

We stopped on the porch to Viviane's rooms. "But how did he know her? That is one thing I cannot understand."

"That is a conversation you should have with Viviane, not me. She has answers beyond my ken. I only know what Morgan told the rest of court, and that I have relayed to you."

I hugged her. "Thank you for your constant support and friendship."

She smiled at me. "From your first moment in Avalon to our last breath. You know that."

I knocked on Viviane's door as Grainne meandered off to help the others, who were preparing the island for midsummer. Unlike Argante, who as Lady of the Lake had lived in a crude hut fashioned from saplings much like Diarmad's home, Viviane retained the stone quarters she had occupied as Argante's second. These days, that role was filled by her daughter, Ailis, the girl I had rescued from peril in a tree many years before.

I was expecting Ailis to answer the door, but when it opened, I found myself looking at Nimue, the daughter of my maid, Octavia. Nimue had been sent here to escape my father's wrath five years earlier, and though she was only eleven, she was tall and thin, her haunting green eyes betraying an intelligence far beyond her years. "Guinevere, come in."

I watched her as I made my way inside. She was dark haired like her mother but had the pale skin of her father. I had no doubt that beneath the placid surface she so carefully cultivated bubbled the temper she had displayed upon being told she was to leave her mother's home. I looked forward to getting to know her better while I was here. I leaned down so Viviane could embrace me.

"Welcome, daughter." She gestured for me to sit in a wicker chair across from her. "Nimue, you may go."

The girl gave a slight curtsey before bouncing off.

"She shows exceptional promise. Ailis and I have been giving her special lessons. She craves knowledge like no one I've ever known," Viviane explained as she poured hot water into two cups and added different herbs to each one. "But enough about Nimue. How are you today?"

"I am feeling better, thank you." I studied her face, the same blue eyes that had first captivated me when she came to Northgallis after I started showing signs of the sight. They were framed by a few more wrinkles now, but they were no less kind. Her brown hair was pulled back in a complicated knot that left only the locks in the very back trailing down to her waist. She had been Lady of the Lake for many years now, but I would never get used to seeing the triple moon symbol of the high priestess on her brow.

"What troubles you?" She had been studying me too and clearly saw in my expression something she didn't like.

I cleared my throat, trying to summon the courage to ask her the same question I had posed to Grainne. But this was more difficult for I knew Viviane would give me an honest answer. I had to be certain I was prepared to hear what she had to say.

I took several sips of tea and waited for the numbing warmth to flow through my veins before I spoke. "Viviane, I need to know. How did Arthur and Morgan know one another?" I bowed my head and stared deep into my cup as though I could divine the answer from the leaves within.

"You are in an awful hurry to have answers," Viviane noted. "Would it not be better to heal from the abuse you've suffered then face the changes in your home?"

I shook my head. "I want to know it all. That way I can piece it together in my own time."

"You have always been a headstrong girl." Viviane took a deep breath. "Do you remember when the Kingmaker appeared in the sky? Merlin told us it meant a great king would soon assume power. That king was Arthur. He was the Sacred King." She watched me, waiting for her words to sink in.

When they did, it was like a punch in the gut. I stared at Viviane, unbelieving. "You knew all along. You knew and never told me. Do the manipulations of Avalon run so deep?"

I never saw Viviane lash out, but suddenly, there was a crack and my left cheek stung.

"I may be your friend, Guinevere, but I am still Lady of the Lake." Viviane's tone was stern with warning like a disapproving mother's. "I deserve your respect, as does this sacred place. As you well know, Avalon does not mettle in the affairs of kingdoms or people. We joined together whom the gods indicated, and their will took its course. If you wish to be mad at someone, let it be your husband or Morgan. It was not I who betrayed your trust."

Chided, I sank back in my chair, weighing her words. She was right. What was more, Merlin had tried to tell me. Years ago, at Corbenic, he'd told me I had seen the king in Avalon, but I couldn't wrest the memory from my mind. Maybe some part of me had known all along and was just unwilling to admit it. Because if Arthur was the Sacred King... "Morgan was the Virgin Queen. That is how they met."

"Yes." Viviane examined her own cup.

I went through the course of events in my memory. "But Morgan was not with child after Beltane. When was Mordred conceived?"

Viviane looked up. "You should really discuss this with your husband. He can tell you from experience. I can only relate hearsay."

I stood. "I don't care if what you know is third- or fourth-hand. I only want to know the truth."

"Guinevere, sit. I do not appreciate your tone."

I genuflected before her, touching my thumb to my forehead, lips, and heart. "Forgive me, Lady. I forgot my place."

She lifted my chin with her hand and bid me rise. Once I was seated again, she reluctantly continued. "From what we can tell, they reunited after Morgan was banished from the isle. I'm sure you know about that?"

"Yes. Merlin told me."

"The reason we couldn't find her is that she was following Uther's army. Somehow, she had gotten wind that Arthur was a soldier and went in search of him. From what I can tell, once they found each other, they were inseparable. Until—"

"Until Uriens directed Arthur's attention my way," I finished for her. I rubbed my fingers on either side of my nose. "So Arthur gets his first love as well as his queen, and I get nothing. That is fair."

Viviane stroked my leg. "The Goddess never promised to be fair. Only to lead you on the path she sees fit."

"Apparently she plays favorites," I grumbled.

"Perhaps, but she sees the world in its totality. We only see our small part of it." Viviane glanced outside, and I followed her gaze to where Imogen was happily weeding in the garden, speaking in Ogham with the soon-to-be-consecrated girls. "Take Imogen, for example. She has lived a life of power and pain no one here could have predicted. Yet the Goddess chose you to bring her back to us, to give her a few years of happiness in this life. Compared to her, you are the favored one."

I stared into my nearly empty cup, aware Viviane was watching me.

"How would you like to take up your life of priesshood again?" she asked. "It will help you heal."

I nodded. "It would be good to have a purpose while I'm here."

"Good. You can begin by assisting me at the sunset ritual tonight. Tomorrow you can help Imogen with the gardens and perhaps sit in on a lesson. You remember the schedule?"

"Yes. My time here will be part of me always. Thank you, Viviane, for giving me a second chance. I doubt few others would."

Viviane placed a hand on mine. "We all have need of mercy, including Arthur and Morgan. You would do well to remember that."

⁂

Viviane was right. The physical labor did me good, as much, I daresay, as the rhythm of morning and evening ritual. Weeks passed, then months, and my physical wounds healed, yet I found I could not let go of my spiritual demons. Anger, pain, and resentment haunted me, a trinity of oppression I battled every day. I disarmed them by evening only to awaken to them freshly formed in the morning.

As I worked, turning the earth, planting seeds, and tending to growing sprouts, I had much time to think. Merlin had informed me about Morgan at Corbenic, but I was too thick to heed his cautions. He told me the Goddess had warned about division between sisters, and what did I do? Physically attack one of my own. Had Morgan not already been banished from Avalon, I likely would have suffered the same fate for attacking my sworn sister. But instead, I had been granted clemency.

That was what was on my mind as I approached Merlin and a group of young students one early autumn morning. He was seated on the stump of a fallen oak that had been sheared off by lightning during a recent storm, gesticulating grandly as he spun some tale that captivated the girls. They sat at his feet in the grass, some as young as ten, others much closer to legal womanhood. They looked up at him adoringly, lovesick expressions on each face.

As I approached, I heard the end of the story. "So Deirdre, foretold from birth to bring about so much destruction, took her own life by throwing herself out of a chariot and onto the rocks below."

"Her story is so sad," lamented one girl.

"But so romantic," crooned another.

"Too bad she wasn't a priestess. She could have made that terrible Conchobar leave her alone," added a third.

Merlin smiled and nodded in acknowledgement when he caught sight of me, then he returned his attention to the students. "Nimue, what do you think?"

"I feel sorry for her. When she finally finds happiness, Conchobar has to come along and ruin it—to the point where she kills herself rather than face her fate. It's not fair."

Merlin leaned toward her. "No, it is not. But Deirdre isn't all to be pitied. Remember, she manipulated Naoise into eloping with her. If she hadn't interfered, the tragic events would not have happened."

"Is this your way of telling us to mind our own business?" Nimue asked tartly. "Because I doubt that will happen around here."

The girls giggled.

Merlin chuckled, spreading his arms wide. "All right, that is enough for today. You may go."

Some of the girls cheered and scampered away while others hung around in groups, sneaking shy looks at Merlin when they thought he wasn't watching. Nimue hung back, waiting to catch Merlin's attention. I couldn't hear what she said to him, but her adoration was plain. She only stopped talking when another girl elbowed her aside, complaining loudly that Nimue had taken up enough of Merlin's time.

I shook my head. That easily could have been Morgan and me. Some things never changed.

When the girls finally straggled away, I greeted Merlin with a small bow. "She's sweet on you, you know."

Merlin smiled as he watched Nimue walk away. "I do. Jealous too. I daresay poor Branwen will pay for her boldness."

"Merlin, I know it has been many years since you were my teacher, but do you think you could indulge me in one more lesson?"

"Of course. What do you wish to know?" He took me gently by the elbow and led me down to the lake where we could walk among the reeds and grasses as we talked.

"How do you ward against jealousy?"

He smiled, running a hand through his now-short hair, which was still bright orange in the soft light despite a sprinkling of silver. "That is the age-old question, is it not? I assume you speak of Morgan."

I nodded. "I have dealt with my painful memories and am beginning to recover from Malegant's abuse, but in all of my time here, I have yet to find a way to let go of my blinding hatred toward Morgan and Arthur or at least get control of it."

"It is the undoing of many a life, many a nation, and something even I have not yet mastered." Merlin stopped, turning to face me. "If I may be frank, you have always been selfish, Guinevere."

I glowered at him, not wanting to hear this speech yet again.

"You are a woman now, not a child. You must learn that even though you are queen, many things do not concern you at all. When you return to your husband, try to remember he did not intend to hurt you. In fact, his actions were not about you. He was thinking of the future of the realm and of his own heart. What would you have done in his place? Would you have waited for him if you believed him dead and knew Aggrivane could be yours? Be honest."

I studied his eyes for a long time, mulling over the question. "No."

"Then how can you ask the same of him?"

I looked away, defeated. He was right. I was being completely unreasonable. "But it is Morgan," I whined, hanging on him as I had as a child.

He laughed. "I would have been disappointed if that wasn't your response." He placed a gentle hand on my shoulder. "I know the two of you have a natural dislike of one another. It is only because you are so much alike." I started to object, but he silenced me with a look. "You will learn to live together because you must. But it will take time. You will need to look beyond your personal feelings and learn to sacrifice for the good of those you love. That is the true measure of a queen."

Chapter Fourteen

Winter 502

rthur was alone when I found him upon my return to Camelot. I needed to see him, but I was not yet ready to face Morgan. He was sitting in the circular meeting room overlooking the city and staring out the window. He appeared so deep in thought he did not hear me enter.

"Arthur."

It took him a moment to respond, and when he did, he was like one waking from a dream. Slowly, he turned, and a smile like dawn broke on his face. He stood, hurrying to embrace me.

This was the reception I had expected and so badly needed when I first returned to him in Cadbury. I let myself melt into his arms, remembering how safe and secure I had felt there before everything changed. I would not think of Morgan, only of him. Repair my relationship with my husband first, then worry about her.

"Guinevere." He breathed my name the way he had on our wedding night. "It is so good to have you back."

He held me at arm's length, looking me over as though searching for any outward signs I had changed, for anything that might still betoken the crazed woman who had entered his court six moons earlier. My bruises, cuts, and broken bones had healed of course, but if he could have seen within my heart, he would have beheld the interweaving scars and stitches threatening to burst at the slightest tug. Arthur gestured for me to sit with him, which I did, unsure of how to speak with him now.

"Lancelot has told me everything. You need not ever speak of it. If that bastard who hurt you wasn't already dead, I'd kill him myself." He clenched his fist in frustration that he could not avenge me. Then he asked, "How are you?" His sapphire eyes were full of concern.

I dropped my eyes to my lap. "I am better. Thank you. It is . . . strange . . . being back here again with everything so different." I looked at him, wondering if he would acknowledge the living ghost who would forever haunt our love.

"Guinevere," he whispered, shaking his head. "I owe you so much, an explanation words cannot begin to express." He looked down, unable to meet my gaze.

"Why, Arthur? Can we start there?"

When he finally met my gaze, his eyes were shining with unshed tears. "I thought you were dead. No one could find you. We searched everywhere—every fortress, every cave, every seaport—and there was not even a trace. I had my suspicions your disappearance was somehow linked to Malegant—"

I flinched at his name.

"But we couldn't find him, much less connect him to a crime we couldn't prove had been committed. There were whispers you could have abandoned me for another man, gone back to Avalon, or worse, taken your own life."

I gaped at the foolishness of those ideas, and Arthur put a hand on mine.

"You must believe I paid no heed to any of this. But I will not lie to you. As time went on, my hope dimmed. Then those in my council began to speak of remarriage. I didn't think it right, but even the priests said that given the circumstances, God would understand if I wed another."

I was silent for a moment, wondering when Arthur, a devotee of Mithras, had started listening to Christian priests. "What now then? Surely you will not stay married to both of us?" I laced my hands together in my lap to conceal their shaking.

Arthur would not meet my eyes. "Many others have already asked me the same, and Morgan has requested I divorce you. But I will not do it. You are queen. That is an honor that cannot be conferred onto more than one woman at a time, and you have done nothing to cause me to revoke it. The people would be outraged if I put you away."

"Oh, I'm glad to know the people would be upset because you certainly don't look as though you would be."

Arthur shot me a contemptuous look.

I couldn't fight my frustration any longer. "Why can you not divorce her? Why must it be me? After all, as you pointed out, I was married to you first, and I am queen." I sounded like a petulant child, but I didn't care. He had to understand how ridiculous this whole situation was.

"Morgan has brought me a son, a child I never expected. I cannot ignore that."

Pain twisted my heart. Yet again I was being condemned because my children had died and I could bear no more despite my best efforts to encourage life within my womb. Would I ever escape that horrid curse? I swallowed hard, summoning the courage to ask a question I had to voice yet dreaded hearing the answer. "Forget everyone else. What does your heart tell you?"

Arthur's gaze pierced my very soul. "I love you both. I know it isn't what you want to hear, but it is the truth. When I met Morgan in Avalon, she was the Goddess, and I never thought to see her again. I had almost forgotten her when she appeared in camp and told me she had given up everything to be with me. From that moment on, I was hers."

Arthur stood and made a slow circuit of the room as he spoke. "If Uther hadn't died, if I had remained simply Lord Ector's son, we would have wed—and quite happily. No one looks into the lineage of a soldier's wife. But then I found out I was no mere solider but the son of the high king, and everything changed. From being free to marry her, I was now forbidden—all because she couldn't tell me the names of her kin." He shook his head. "It tore my heart in two to know we would never be together."

He stopped in front of me and bent so we were at eye level. "Now, as things have changed and I am free to be with the one I love, I understand what I did to you when I asked you to marry me, that I put you in much the same tragic circumstance, and for that I am sorry. I would not wish such agony on a Saxon."

I smiled at him because it was the right thing, the polite thing, to do, but I was certain it didn't reach my eyes.

"I couldn't leave Morgan to the wiles of fate, so when Uriens expressed interest in her, I realized his would be a safe household for her to be in, one where I could be sure she would not be ill-treated."

"And one that afforded her frequent visits to court."

"Yes, that too." Arthur sounded guilty.

"So where does that leave us?"

Arthur did not answer. Whether he had none or simply chose not to respond, his silence unnerved me more than if he had yelled.

The familiar panic I had felt since leaving Malegant's tower was returning, coiling around my heart. If it squeezed tight, I would lose my composure again.

I stood, seeking air at one of the windows. My eyes fell on the statues surrounding us. In my absence, the stone images depicting Arthur and me as high king and high queen had been installed. "Will she have her own statue too? What a great legacy for future generations. 'Look at King Arthur and his brood of wives,' they'll say. 'He really must have been someone grand.'"

Arthur stood too. "Guinevere, please don't be this way."

"What way is that? Hurt? Outraged? Indignant? How would you have me react?" I ran a fluttering hand through my hair. "Think about how you would have felt if the situation were reversed. What if you had been captured in war with the Saxons, brutally abused, then managed to escape only to return home to find me married to Aggrivane?"

Arthur's jaw tensed, but he said nothing.

"That is how I felt seeing you with Morgan. What's worse is she has given you the one thing I never will—a son. And she can continue providing you heirs. So as much as you may contend that I am and always will be queen, I know she means more to you for that alone."

Arthur seized my shoulders hard. "You are my wife, and I still love you. But Morgan is my wife too, and I love her as well. This is how things are. Unless you wish to divorce me and forfeit your power as queen, you will both have to find a way to accept it." There was no malice in his words, just the starkness of truth.

So this was my new world. Little more than a year ago, we had been celebrating Arthur's latest victory over the Saxons. We had been happy. Now I had to share my life—though it was not of my own choosing, I had fought so hard to build and sustain this life— with the one person I hated more than all others. When would the Goddess stop testing me?

ᴏᴏᴇ ᴏᴇᴏ

Living with Morgan meant more than simply vying for Arthur's attention. The servants, especially the newer ones, had grown used to answering to Morgan while I was away, and they were uncertain which one of us now held sway. Some made their loyalty clear.

Octavia and Sobian, who was still acting the role of my maid, would never take orders from Morgan again, while another small cadre of women were devoted to Morgan. Though their words showed they understood I was queen, their actions proclaimed Morgan their mistress. When we appealed to Arthur, each wishing to have him side with us, he held up his hands and told us to work it out without him, locking us in his study until we came to an agreement.

Glaring at one another across the table, we tried to find a compromise.

Morgan was quick to try to preserve her newfound power. "I have been running this household for more than a year, Guinevere. Why can you not simply let things be?"

I snorted, pacing the length of the small room. "Would you have allowed me to walk into your home with Uriens and take over without a fight? I think not. You have little experience in running a house this large. I have been doing so for five years."

"Four. You were away for the last year, remember?" She arched an eyebrow and took on an imperious tone. "Your time is mostly spent in matters of judgment and diplomacy. The best you can hope for is to employ talented stewards and maids to oversee things for you. You should leave the household matters to me. I have the time to personally oversee such things."

I settled myself on the corner of the table and looked down my nose at her. "What then do you propose would be my duties?"

"Besides being a thorn in my side?"

"I could say the same about you."

"You would oversee your own personal maids, of course," Morgan drawled as though she were doing me a favor. She was quiet for a moment, then she sat up as though she had an idea. "You could handle the guests and their servants as well."

Though I was not happy with that being my only area of power among our hundreds of servants, Morgan was trying, and she had a point about the time I spent with Arthur in my role as queen. "Fine, let's start there."

By spring, however, it became apparent that while Morgan was excellent at getting the servants to do as she pleased and ensuring the quality of their work, she was ill-equipped for the record-keeping and handling of finances that came with being in charge of so many people, especially on a feasting schedule as unpredictable as Camelot's. So we found ourselves back in that same small room negotiating our duties once again.

"Camelot will be broke before the end of summer with you running things." I glanced over a list of supplies and costs for the previous month the head kitchen maid had provided to me. "Though I daresay the merchants will miss you. Who pays this much for oysters? We live on a bay. They should be nearly free, especially to the king. And where are you importing our wine from—Rome? This bill is unacceptable. Gaul gives us a much better rate, and the product is fresh, unlike the bottle of vinegar we served to the Breton ambassador last week."

"You wish to be in charge of the finances? Take them." Morgan spat the words but was unable to completely mask the relief in her voice. "But then let me oversee provisions for our guests. At the moment, their poor maids know not who to listen to for you tell them one thing while I have trained our staff for another, so they get mixed messages. Lady Ettarre has written Arthur to express how shocked she was at the incompetence of our maids." She leveled me with an icy stare. "It's almost as though you are trying to make me look bad."

I rubbed my tired eyes then glared at her. "Yes, Morgan, you've found me out. Are you happy?" I snapped, voice heavily laced with sarcasm. "Do what you like. I have much bigger problems than whether or not Lord Pelles's wife is happy with the way her servants behave while they are here. The Saxons are threatening Bernicia and the Midlands again. Arthur is preparing for battles on both fronts. When will this war be over?" I sighed.

Our domestic squabbles at an end, at least for now—I had no doubt Morgan would continue to push the boundaries of her power as royal wife—I fell into bed, much in need of the surety I could find only in Arthur's arms. He held me for a while, but when he thought I was asleep, he carefully untangled himself from my arms and rose.

He was headed for Morgan's room—that was certain. I didn't bother to try to stop him. He had been playing this game for months now, sometimes even returning to our bed before dawn in the hopes I would think he'd never left. Did the fool really believe I couldn't feel the bed shift when relieved of his weight or hear the creak of the door when he returned?

When I'd first returned, Arthur patiently waited as I found my way back into his arms after Malegant's brutality. For a while, I'd believed I might serve as his wife in every way again. Once we were sharing a bed, it was as though nothing had changed. During those blessed weeks, under the cover of darkness, I was able to convince myself Morgan didn't exist. But then I woke in the middle of the night to find Arthur gone. That was when my ears became attuned to the signs of his departure.

Arthur still spent some nights with me, though they were decreasing steadily in number. I wondered if there was any logic to his choice of companion for the night or if he simply decided on a whim.

One night, I worked up the courage to question him about it. "Tell me, husband, how do you decide between me and Morgan each evening? It must be nice having your choice of women." Admittedly, that wasn't the kindest way of asking, but I wanted him to know I felt slighted by his actions.

Arthur paused in the middle of removing his tunic. For a long moment, he looked at me as though I was daft. "How can you ask me such a thing? It is my duty to act as husband to both of you." He stood and headed for the door. A few paces from it, he looked back over his shoulder. "You are fortunate I respect you, Guinevere. Most men would have beaten you for even inquiring."

So there it was. Our marriage had deteriorated to the point where my husband wanted to hit me for questioning his motives. That was a far cry from the affection and honesty of our early years together. I had gained nothing by my curiosity. In fact, I had practically driven him into Morgan's arms. Now I would never know his reasons. Maybe Morgan didn't ask such questions. Maybe she didn't challenge him at all. Whatever the truth, it was clear she had found a way to satisfy him that I would never match.

Chapter Fifteen

Summary 503

Summer 503

ord reached us of Pellinor's death on a stormy night just after Beltane. The weather prevented us from trying to arrive in time for the funerary rites, but despite all that had happened between us, I wanted to be there for Elaine as she mourned her father's passing. So as soon as the weather cleared and the roads were dry, Arthur, Kay, Lancelot, Sobian, Octavia, and I headed south to the kingdom of Dyfed and Caer Corbenic, where we had first met. As she did not know the family, Morgan remained behind at Camelot to oversee affairs in our absence.

But the pleasant weather was only a tease. For most of the trip, heavy rains hindered our progress, mucking up the horses' hooves and flinging mud onto cloaks and armor. We had to turn back several times when flood waters made the old Roman main roads impassable. The deluge had spotted the flat land with makeshift lakes and ruined entire tracks of grain and vegetables. Occasionally we encountered the victims of nature's wrath: hollow-eyed children and starving men thin as rods. We did what we could to alleviate their suffering, but all the gold in the country would not be enough to repair these shattered lives.

The result of this detour was that we had to keep to the roads that hugged the Saxon border, land long ago conquered and settled by the northern invaders. Sometimes we even crossed over into their territory, putting us in much closer proximity to our enemy than any of us were comfortable being. Signs of their growing influence were everywhere, from their strange round huts to the harsh language spoken in the towns and pale faces with nearly white hair peering at us as we passed.

We were in grave danger if anyone recognized us, so we took precautions. We had stopped flying the royal standard of Pendragon several days prior and had stripped ourselves of all jewels. We sent our valuables on separately to Corbenic for safekeeping. Weapons were hidden with care, and we all dressed simply, hoping to appear as innocuous any other riding party. We simply wished to pass through in peace.

The sun was just beginning to slip below the horizon, coloring the dappled clouds a joyous mixture of peach and gold, when we arrived at a village near the convergence of the former kingdoms of Kent and Sussex. The areas were now one realm ruled through an alliance of two Saxon brothers, Alle and Octha, both kings who our spies told us were allied in dreams of a united Saxon empire. We considered trying to push on through the night to escape into less threatening territory, but it soon became clear both men and horses were exhausted.

We accepted the kindness of a local lord who took pity on our fatigued party and lodged us in the safety of his residence for the night. It was nothing like the fortifications we were used to, but his compound reminded me of my parents' descriptions of their childhood homes. The main building was a large rectangular structure of wood cemented with hardened mud and fortified by a ring of sharp spiked logs sunk into the ground with their points reaching skyward, mortally threatening anyone foolish enough to try to hurdle them. A second spine of points encircled the first and sheltered a set of less important buildings. As we passed through, I spied a storage area, blacksmith, stable, granary, and a handful of other necessities. A wooden gate with heavy iron hinges and a massive bar stood open at the south end of the wall, ready to admit citizens and travelers until nightfall.

Sobian and I had just settled onto our shabby pallets on the floor of the main room, near the central fire with the other women, when a disturbance outside put the servants on alert. Three of them spilled into the courtyard, and I could just make out the silhouette of a hooded woman in the torchlight outside. She was speaking excitedly in the guttural language I had heard as we passed through other towns, urgency apparent in her body language. The servants appeared at a loss to help her, but one slipped back inside and whispered to the lady of the house.

She glided over to us. "Our visitor seeks the services of a midwife. The woman who usually fills this role for us is old and gravely ill. Can any of you be of assistance? She says it is urgent."

I nodded. "I will help her. I have been well trained in the womanly arts."

Sobian made to stop me. "Your husband will never allow you to go unattended, and none of the men will go into the room with you." We had agreed not to refer to Arthur or me by our real names lest we be identified by our enemies. "I am coming with you."

I wanted to protest, but she was right. Delivering a child in danger by myself would be difficult, and I had no way of knowing how capable the Saxon woman would be of helping. "Then you may be my assistant."

We gathered supplies and followed the Saxon woman into the night, trailed by Kay as our guardian. As we moved away from the fortress, down a lonely road in the light of a half moon, I watched the Saxon's round hips swinging in time with the bounce of tight golden curls as she walked, back straight as an iron rod. She appeared to be acting as a maid, but her clothes were not the rags or simple homespun of most servants. I began to wonder what was going on.

She saw me watching her and pursed her full lips in annoyance. "No one knows we are here, and you will keep that secret," she commanded in heavily-accented broken English.

"Of course. May I know the woman's condition?"

"Waters flowed early morning, baby not come. She grows weary. I fear she will die." She fixed me in a piercing blue stare that left no room for argument. "That cannot happen."

"I give you my word as a priestess I will do all I can to keep her and the child alive," I swore, showing her the faint blue tattoo on my brow.

There was no cultural equivalent of my status in her world. She regarded me warily and nodded, but something in her expression told me she was not convinced.

The secluded hovel we approached stood out in sharp contrast to the fine clothing the Saxon woman wore. Even from the outside, I could tell it had only one room. Two tiny unglazed windows, a door, and a smoking chimney provided the only ventilation.

I pieced together the most likely scenario. This woman and likely the other who labored inside were obviously nobility. My best guess was the pregnant one had gotten herself with child by someone she should not have—a lover or perhaps the son of an enemy but certainly not her husband—and they had retreated here for the length of her confinement for her own safety. There was nothing around for miles, no neighbors to witness the woman's shame. It was not the first time such a thing had happened and certainly wouldn't be the last.

The woman's strangled cries reached me even before the brawny Saxon guard opened the door to admit us. He watched warily but backed off at a signal from the woman who had recruited us.

I stopped her before we crossed the threshold. "Wait. What is your name?"

Her body went rigid, and I knew she would not answer me.

"I must be able to call to you with instructions amid the chaos we will encounter inside, so please give me a name. It need not be your real one." I added with a wry smile, "Unless you would rather me call you 'girl.'"

My implied insult had the desired effect. The Saxon woman's face puckered in annoyance. "Udele," she said flatly as she swept through the doorway.

"I am Corinna," I lied, taking my mother's name. It was how everyone outside our party knew me on this journey.

A wave of heat hit me as soon as we entered the room. It was even tinier than it appeared from the outside. A fire blazed in a pit built into one wall, smoke struggling up the narrow chimney. Not four feet away, a small, pale woman who bore a striking resemblance to Udele writhed in her mean bed, two serving women alternating between trying to hold her down and trying to give her strength as the contractions rolled through her body.

Udele rushed over to one side of the bed and held the young woman's hand, speaking quietly to her in their native tongue. The intimacy of the moment confirmed my suspicion they were more than maid and mistress. From their resemblance, I guessed them to be sisters. Sobian set the towels, basin, and bottles of herbs we had brought with us on a small wooden table next to the bed, and I moved to the woman's feet to examine her. As I probed her belly and peered between her thighs, Udele called the girl Mayda, which I assumed had to be her real name. In her weakened, pain-crazed state, no woman would have been able to respond to a false name.

"Mayda," I called to the beautiful young girl in the bed, and Udele shot me a dirty look. I ignored her and continued. "Mayda, your body is ready, but your baby cannot be born as it is. I can try to turn it, but it will be painful for you."

Udele translated what I had said, and the sweat-soaked woman nodded weakly, saying something I did not understand.

"Do what you must," Udele barked.

My training in Avalon took over, and I lost all connection to what was going on around me as I manipulated her womb, inside and out. I was vaguely aware of Sobian at my side mopping up the blood streaming from between Mayda's thighs, Mayda's screams, and Udele's agitation as she tried to keep her sister calm, but they barely registered. All of my attention was focused on the stubborn babe who was determined not to be born. As the hours dragged on and Mayda's strength failed, it seemed increasingly likely she would die too. Finally, I was able to slip my hand around the baby and turn its head toward the birth canal.

I rinsed my arms in the basin and stroked Mayda's head. It was time for her to summon all her strength and push her child into the world. I didn't need to tell her, for now that the baby was in place, her body was eager to be rid of it. Mayda cried out as a spasm rippled through her belly.

Udele and I helped Mayda sit up, and she braced herself against the waiting arms of her servants. As she bore down, barely stopping to take a breath between pushes, the top of the baby's head came into view. Mayda screamed again, and I guided the child out, head, right shoulder, left, then the rest came easily in a rush of viscous fluid.

"You have a son," I told Mayda, and Udele translated.

Sobian took the child, still attached to his mother, and quickly cleaned him. He was a sickly shade of violet but needed no prodding to take his first breath. His throaty wail filled the house just as clearly as his mother's had. I breathed a sigh of relief and glanced at Mayda. She was crying but whether out of happiness, exhaustion, or something else, I did not know. Sobian wrapped the baby in a clean towel and placed him on the table.

"I know who they are," she whispered in my ear, followed by a quick explanation.

I had been trying to place why Mayda's name sounded familiar and understand why this elaborate ruse had been necessary. Sobian put the pieces together for me.

They were royal daughters in their society. The younger of the two southern Saxon rulers, Octha, was engaged to the younger sister of his brother's wife. Mayda's name had been mentioned as Octha's betrothed in our spies' report, as had her sister's, because the union of these two royal families represented a formidable threat to our southeast kingdoms. Arthur would be quite interested to learn how I had chanced upon them under such unusual circumstances.

Once Mayda delivered the afterbirth, Udele picked up her dagger and made for the child, but I stopped her. "Burnish the blade in the fire first so the wound will not get infected," I instructed.

"Matters not," Udele muttered, but she did as I asked anyway.

I helped her cut the cord and turned to lay the now pink baby in his mother's arms, but Mayda was sleeping. "He will need to eat soon, so you will have to wake her."

Udele shrugged and held the gurgling, fidgeting boy as Sobian and I cleaned up. Mostly she regarded it with a look of disdain. I had a cursory knowledge of the language thanks to Arthur, and I thought I heard her tell the child it would have been better had he not been born. A shiver ran down my spine. I remembered Udele's quick move with the knife and wondered if she'd had a more sinister intent than to cut the cord.

When I looked at her, she was watching me intently. "Will she live?" she asked with a jerk of her head toward her sister.

I carefully examined Mayda, trying not to wake her. The blood had ceased flowing, and her body was quickly returning to normal with no signs of infection or complications. "Yes, but she will need much rest."

Udele nodded and gestured to one of the serving women, who handed me a heavy purse of coins. "For your trouble."

It would have been an insult not to accept, so I took the purse, thinking of how we could use the money to help the destitute citizens we encountered on the road, not to mention pay our host for his hospitality. But then another thought occurred to me. "Also for our silence?"

Udele's smile was wicked. "Of course. Now go, Queen Guinevere."

I raised my eyebrows. "You know who I am?"

She shrugged and gestured toward my forehead. "Was guess. Others with mark stay with farmers, not crowned men. They have no slaves." She cocked her head in Sobian's direction.

"Not many Aethelings bear their children in hovels," I countered, praying Sobian's theory was accurate.

Udele—or Elga, as she was truly called—nearly dropped the baby in surprise. "How you know?"

"When you said your sister's name, it triggered a memory," I said carefully, not wanting to reveal Sobian as my source of information, or worse, provoke Elga's wrath. All she needed to do was call her guard, and we would have a bloody fight on our hands. I pressed on before she had a chance to react. "Elga, I mean you no harm. It is in each of our best interests to keep what has transpired tonight a secret. I swear to you I will do so if you will promise the same."

I hoped she would listen to me, knowing we were at a dangerous impasse. On one hand, she knew who I was and where our whole party was staying. If she but breathed my name, we would all be dead before dawn, and her people would have free reign over the country. But on the other, I knew her and her secret. All I needed to do was let it slip to our host where they were housed, and both Octha and Alle would be on their doorstep before they could flee. The brothers would undoubtedly kill their wives, whose family would seek revenge, sparking civil war and weakening them to the point where our forces could overtake them if they weren't killed by their own.

Elga gulped, mouth still open. "Why you help if you knew who we are? We are enemies." Her tone betrayed she truly did not understand. Clearly, she would not have done the same if the roles were reversed.

"I have taken vows to harm no one without cause," I explained. "You gave me no provocation, only asked for my help. So I gave it."

"Now I am indebted to you," she said bitterly, more to herself than to me.

I shook my head. "No. If you keep my presence in the area a secret and let me pass through unharmed, there is no debt. I am not here for political reasons, and I will not harm or disturb a single one of your people. Know that unless you attack us, I am your ally."

The baby began to cry hungrily, and Elga looked at him as though she had forgotten his existence. The familiar hard look returned to her features. "You say nothing of this." Then she cocked an eyebrow and added, "No proof anyhow."

I shivered again, sensing the menace in her words. "It will be as though this night never happened."

"Yes. I swear you not be harmed, Queen Guinevere."

I backed slowly out of the room, listening to the child wail. As soon as Sobian and I were safely on the other side of the door, I breathed a sigh of relief. I signaled to Kay it was time to depart and he shoved off with a final glance at his stone-faced counterpart.

We had walked only a short distance when the crying became an ear-splitting screech, was muffled, then suddenly stopped. That was not the sound of a suckling babe. The silence was too complete. I began to shake and sank to my knees as Elga's warning rang in my ears—"no proof anyhow." I turned and threw the pouch at the closed door, where it exploded in a shower of silver coins. I could not accept money tainted by the shadow of death no matter how noble my intentions for it.

I turned to the side of the path and retched, grieving for the murdered child and the naive mother who had never gotten to hold him.

✽✽✽

I told no one what had transpired with Elga and her sister. It appeared she was true to her word as well for we continued on into Dyfed in peace as though nothing had ever taken place. Now Caer Corbenic stretched out before us like the peak of a mountain on the horizon. It was strange to view it from afar, sprawling on the top of a cliff overlooking the sea. It was so much more imposing now despite the fact that this time, I approached its gates a free woman. Somehow the specter of the past still loomed, surrounding me in a chill as damp and pervasive as the mist and spray of the waves breaking on the rocky shore below.

I took a deep breath, willing this to be a peaceful reunion. The last time I had seen Elaine—six years earlier—was at the feast where Arthur proposed to me rather than to her as we had both expected. For as long as I lived, I would never forget the depth of sorrow etched into her features that night, a macabre combination of disappointment and jealousy. I had what she wanted, and she, in not being chosen, had failed to meet her mother's high expectations yet again. Combined with the heartbreak she had suffered when Isolde fled to Ireland with Elaine's betrothed, a roguish Pict named Galen—an act Elaine wrongly believed I had also played a part in—I feared she would never forgive me.

Elaine was waiting for us at the entrance to the great hall, dressed in black and clearly in mourning for her father. Despite the grief etched into her features, Elaine had grown into a beautiful woman. The intervening years had rounded her once-childish body into womanly curves and transformed the plump plains of her face into soft, delicate features.

No word of a wedding or birth had reached us at Camelot, so I was surprised to see she held the hand of a small boy, maybe five years old, with curly blond hair and eyes so clear and icy blue he looked more fey than human. He was unquestionably hers so closely did he resemble his mother, but the eyes were a gift from someone else.

"Guinevere, thank you for coming," Elaine said before remembering herself and dropping into a low curtsy. "I mean, my queen."

As Elaine repeated her obeisance to Arthur, not daring to look him in the eye, the sparkling emerald she wore at her throat—the gift Arthur had given her at that ill-fated dinner—drooped low, brushing the neckline of her gown.

Arthur touched Elaine's hand and bid her rise. "My lady, I wish our visit were under more joyful circumstances. Your father was a great man, one of the best in the realm. I only regret we could not be present at his funerary rites."

Elaine's smile was tinged with sadness. "I have no doubt he knew of your great respect for him." Only now did she dare meet Arthur's eyes. "My lord, before you retire, may I present to you my son, Galahad. It is my dream he may one day be a member of your Combrogi and be of great service to Camelot."

Arthur bowed with exaggerated formality to the boy. "Galahad, I am pleased to meet you." He laid the hollow of his palm on the boy's forehead. "Remember you carry the blessing of your high king with you always. I look forward to the day I can welcome you to my court."

Elaine blushed like a flower in full bloom at the compliment.

Galahad responded by bowing to his king. "It is my honor, my lord."

Elaine had trained him well.

"I must help Lancelot with horses," Arthur excused himself. "May Lord Galahad accompany me?"

One look at her son's hopeful expression and Elaine consented. Galahad took Arthur's hand and walked to the stables at his side. They reminded me so much of the son I had lost and the father

Arthur was to Mordred—and could have been to my own son—it took all the strength I possessed not to cry.

Sensing my pain, Elaine put an arm around me and led me inside. "I think we both grieve," she said gently as we took seats near the fire.

"Indeed. I mourn your father's loss yet find you blessed with a child."

Elaine's cheeks colored. "Yes, he was quite unexpected." She twisted a large enameled ring on the middle finger of her left hand. "But he is the child my father always knew I would have, the child of the prophecy, and my father lived to see him born and proclaim him his heir." There was a note of pride in her voice.

My lips parted in surprise. "Galahad is your father's heir? What about your older brothers? Will they not contest losing their lands and title to a child?"

Elaine's lips twisted into a cheerless smile. "They can try, but the people of our tribe, I daresay all of Dyfed, are well aware of the prophecy and have voiced their agreement he should be chieftain when he comes of age. Besides, my mother has declared herself ruler until that time, and none of my brothers will dare stand against her."

"I wouldn't either," I muttered, remembering Lyonesse's cruelty all too clearly.

Elaine was silent for a while as if contemplating something. Then she reached behind her and unclasped her necklace. She held it out to me, the large emerald winking in the sunlight.

"What's this?" I asked.

"A peace offering. Arthur should have given it to you that night."

"Elaine, I cannot accept this. It was his gift to you."

Elaine laid her hand over mine and gave it a gentle squeeze, letting the jewel fall into my palm. "Now I am giving it to you. I never apologized for accusing you of being complicit in Galen's betrayal or for not speaking to you all these years. I had no right—"

I slipped my hand out from under hers and held up a finger to silence her. "Elaine, you were heartbroken. I understand why you said what you did, but I've long forgotten it."

"But I—I am truly sorry. I want you to know I bear you no ill will."

I shook my head. "Let us not speak of it. There is nothing to forgive."

Elaine bit her lip as though she doubted my sincerity, but she kept her council.

"Your boy is quite fine, Elaine," I said.

"Thank you." She glanced over her shoulder as if to make certain it was just us in the room. "I was hoping to talk to you about his future."

She looked at me with wide, expectant eyes, the way she had since we were children and she had something to say but wished I could read her mind so she would not have to give it voice.

"What is it, Elaine?"

She dropped her gaze to her lap and twisted her skirt nervously. After a long pause, she spoke, voice shaking as the words spilled over one another. "May I be so bold as to ask to come live at court with you and the king? I—I fear remaining at court with my mother." Elaine rolled up the sleeve of her gown as she spoke, revealing a ring of purple bruises just below her right elbow. "She did not dare touch me while I was pregnant for fear of hurting my child, but now she does as she wills. I know she will never harm him, blessed by heaven as he is, but I am another matter. Normally I would offer my sufferings up to God as I have always done, but I cannot—not anymore."

She finally raised her eyes to meet mine. There was fear behind them mingled with sorrow. I looked closer at the bruises, seeing them clearly now. They were imprints from where Lyonesse's fingers had dug into Elaine's arm as though Lyonesse had pulled on her as she sought to flee.

I swallowed hard, remembering the day Lyonesse had slapped her grieving daughter, blaming her for Galen's misdeeds, and another day when Isolde showed me the crossing welts on her back after a whipping from Lyonesse in retribution for speaking against her.

There was no question in my mind, nor did I need to consult Arthur. "You and your son are always welcome at Camelot. I would be happy to have you as a lady of my court."

"Please do not tell my mother this was my idea."

"Of course not. My invitation was part of my reason for paying you a personal visit." I said it as gravely as I could muster, nodding for emphasis. In that moment, we were once again co-conspirators in a secret plot, just as in our youth, and I could easily let the years slip away and imagine our lives had yet to unfold before us.

Changeable as ever, when Elaine looked at me again, her

expression was somber. "I know you must be wondering who my husband is, but please know I cannot tell you. We are wed in the eyes of God, but though he is a just and upright man, he wishes not to acknowledge me, and my mother has forbidden me to name him on pain of death. Suffice it to say that though he is a nobleman, he has not the lineage my mother would prefer and therefore is not to be mentioned."

I nodded, feeling the long-forgotten, but somehow familiar, twinge of unwanted complicity that came with Corbenic's web of lies and ever-changing ruses. "We shall put it about that your husband is an emissary who spends much of his time abroad. That way no one will ask too many questions."

Elaine bit her lip again. "He is one of Arthur's knights. That much is safe to say."

My stomach dropped. Who? I desperately wanted to ask. Did she mean one of the Combrogi or any of Arthur's fighting men? If so, there were hundreds.

"Oh, Elaine, I do not believe that is a wise thing to say even if it is true. You have no understanding of the perils of life at court. Friendly though they may appear, everyone is looking for an advantage, and if they find one, you will be undone—have no doubt. Court gossip can turn the smallest grain of sand into a valuable pearl. By dangling such a bit of information in front of them, you will be inviting the wolves to your door."

"The Lord commands us not to lie. I will tell the truth to the extent I am able and still uphold my vows to my husband and mother. They are the only ones who know the truth, and I am certain they will not reveal it." She squared her shoulders and looked down her nose at me with an unyielding gaze.

It would have been easier to bid a statue come to life than to sway her now. I just wished she knew the peril she could be creating for herself and her son, especially if his father chose not to acknowledge him too. Selfishly, I was glad the scandalmongers would have a new subject upon our return.

Before I had a chance to reply, a maid poked her head in and curtsied. "Forgive me for interrupting, but Lady Lyonesse is ready to receive you."

"We have been summoned," I muttered. "Some things never change."

I made to follow, but Elaine stopped me with a brief embrace. "Thank you. I cannot speak for my son, but I know your kindness has saved my life."

⁊⁊

Arthur and I decided to hold a pleading day at Corbenic to give the southern people a chance to speak with us without having to traverse the country to reach Camelot. Notices were sent by messenger to the surrounding kingdoms, and a week later, residents from Dyfed, Dyfnaint, and the Summer Country presented their cases to us.

I had forgotten how boring pleading day could be. After doing this for six years, each complaint sounded like the last. One chieftain had raided another's cattle, a merchant had swindled someone in the market, a farmer's daughter had proved herself to be of questionable virtue. I barely heard most of the requests as they came through. Even Arthur was meting out justice by rote. I was ashamed to admit it, but by noontime, I was playing a mental game to see if I could guess the punishment Arthur would give out as soon as the crime was described.

But my boredom was not meant to last. Not long after we resumed our afternoon session, a clamor arose in the hall. A woman was shouting at our men in a guttural tongue that sounded vaguely familiar.

Arthur must have understood them because he chuckled. "Guards, stand down and let the woman enter."

I leaned over and whispered in his ear, "What did she say to them?"

"She called them dogs and told them to let her go or she would personally ensure Freya would remove their testicles and feed them to them."

"A Saxon then?"

Arthur looked up as the doors opened, the woman still struggling to shake off the guards. "Not just any Saxon."

The woman finally wrenched herself free only to trip and land on her knees at our feet, an obsequious posture I doubt she ever intended. It was only when she raised her chin to us that I recognized her.

"Mayda!" I exclaimed.

"Ja."

Arthur arched an eyebrow. "Have you met?"

I realized only then that I had never told him of my encounter with the princesses on our way to the Summer Country.

Mayda saved me from having to explain. "Ja. Your queen provided me a great service. I will be forever in her debt—a deficit I hope to repay in part today."

I was startled by how well she spoke our tongue, much better than her elder sister.

"Mayda, why have you come here? Who else knows you are here?" Arthur asked.

"I come to give you warning. My husband brings an army to overthrow the mountain. He and his brother have allied to win a victory they say will make them dominant forevermore."

Arthur tensed and brought a fist up to his lips. "What mountain?"

"They called it Bay-don."

"Badon." Arthur slammed his fist on his thigh and cursed. "Who sent you here? Why are you telling us?"

Mayda cowered in fear. "They do not know. They cannot know. If they know, if she knows"—Mayda gave me a look that I could only assume meant her sister—"I am dead." Her eyes were wild and scared like a trapped bunny's.

She looked to me for reassurance, but I had none to give. I was still too shocked to be certain whether she was telling the truth or not.

Arthur spoke to me as he considered the frightened girl at his feet. "If she is telling the truth, then they intend to take the fort above Aque Sullis. If they do, they will control the Sabrina Estuary and split the country in two." He turned back to Mayda. "How long do we have?"

She scrunched up her nose as she calculated. "They were still planning when I left them. But they must know I am gone by now. If they suspect, they will move all the faster. I would guess a week, no more."

Arthur gritted his teeth. "Then we have no choice but to trust you and prepare for battle."

⁂

Orders flew like birds as we made ready to depart. The remaining petitioners were politely turned away without even the slightest hint of what was afoot. We couldn't afford to lose the element of surprise.

If the Saxons found out we had been warned, all our efforts could be for naught. They were unlikely to give up their campaign, but Mayda's betrayal would definitely incite them to anger. The last thing we needed them to do was take it out on the countryside, torching farmsteads, murdering peasants, and slaughtering cattle simply because they could. They had done it before under Vortigern, and the whole of the country had taken many years to recover from such devastation. It was for this reason, if not for Mayda's safety, that secrecy was paramount.

As chests were packed and mounts readied, people became aware our party was leaving unexpectedly. To quell the rumors, we loosed a story that Arthur's uncle, Lord Mark, was ill and requested Arthur's presence at his bedside. It just so happened the same route would also naturally take us toward Aque Sullis.

The fastest couriers and most trusted knights awaited Arthur's command, standing shoulder to shoulder with the members of our household who had made the journey with us. To anyone on the outside, it would appear that before taking his unexpected leave, the king desired to honor those most loyal to him during his first years on the throne. But in reality, we were quietly making ready for war.

As Arthur called each man before him, he placed a small purse in the man's palm as though he was bestowing a commendation upon him. But the purse really held only enough coin to supplement rations, refresh mounts on long journeys, and if necessary, tempt the lord to whom the messenger was sent to obey Arthur's royal request.

"Bedivere, take the men and go ahead of us to help prepare the fort. Gather as many provisions as you can behind the innermost walls and secure an unobtrusive supply line. Ask the garrison commander about their defense strategy. They will have a secret way to keep the fort supplied while under siege. Kay, I want you to shore up the defenses. I have not visited this fort before and do not know its state of readiness. Whatever you do, do not raise alarm among the people. I don't want them knowing anything is amiss until it is time to send them away. The less time they have to talk, the better."

Kay and Bedivere bowed to Arthur and returned to their places.

Two boys stepped forward next. The older appeared to be a seasoned rider judging by his muscled physique and sun-darkened skin. The other could have seen no more than fourteen summers. The poor lad was unable to stop smiling nervously and wiping his palms on his breeches.

Arthur addressed the youngest first. "Daniel, I am told you are from Rheged, so you know it and its ruler well, is that right? The freckled boy cleared his throat. "Yes, sire. My cousin is a knight in his army. I know routes traveled only by the deer and can be at Lord Owain's door upon the next sunrise. Well, after the one tomorrow," he babbled.

Arthur's patience held surprisingly firm. "Good. Ride on ahead to ask Lord Owain's assistance in defending the fort and return word to me. Catch us on the road if you can. Do you understand?"

"Yes, sire."

Arthur turned to the other boy. "Owen, they say you know how to cross the country in half the time of other men. Do you swear to me now this is true?"

Owen bowed his head. "Yes, my king. Mountain passes, river roads—I will take whatever courses enable me to best fulfill your command."

"Good. You will have perhaps the longest journey of all. You will go to Pelles in the Summer Country and ask him to join his army to Cadwallion's in the Midlands. Then you will march with them on Mount Badon from the northeast, but do not approach the hill unless you see the signal. If you do well, I will bring you into my court and ensure you are trained as a future Combrogi."

Order after order followed, sending men in all directions, including one to fetch Morgan, for we were sure to be in need of her healing skills. But before Arthur let them leave to fulfill their tasks, he made them swear the same oath of loyalty each of the Combrogi and allied kings and queens had pledged.

He preceded the oath with, "Remember, your word binds you under pain of death. If you do as you are asked, you will be greatly rewarded, but if you betray my trust, your duplicity will resound for generations, and yours will not be the only blood spilled in atonement."

With that threat spurring them to action, the room quickly emptied, leaving me, Arthur, and Mayda, who sat unnoticed, impassively watching the proceedings. I motioned her over to us, and she sat on the step below the dais.

"I am sure you have had plenty of time to contemplate your fate," Arthur said gently.

Her light blue eyes were sincere when she looked at Arthur. "You are a good king. I wish my husband was so, but all he and his brother think of is power and land. All they want is to rule the whole of the island, and they will do what they must to feed their ambition."

She shifted her gaze to me. "I knew what I was doing when I made the decision to come to you today. I knew I was as good as dead no matter the outcome. If they caught me, if I was lucky, I'd only be badly beaten. But more likely, I would be killed outright for I abandoned my husband, betrayed my ruler—my Aetheling—and shamed my family. But after the kindness you showed me when I was in peril, I could not stand by while they destroyed your kingdom. I want to live in Britain as much as anyone, but not if it means doing so at the price of another's blood. A title and a throne are not worth so great a sacrifice."

"You show a compassion not often displayed by your people, especially by one so young," Arthur remarked. "You have nothing to fear from us. Consider whatever obligation you feel paid in full."

"I give you thanks, but it will not be settled until the last of my blood has drained from my body. My sister will be sure of that."

I took both of her hands in mine. "Mayda, you have in effect given up your life, at least as you knew it, to help us. In turn, we wish to help keep you safe. We could provide you with a holding in an obscure village. That is one option, but you would still live in constant fear." I glanced at Arthur. "What we propose instead will require even more sacrifice from you. There is a convent in Bernicia which has taken in women of your race before, those who sought refuge after the battle of York. I can arrange safe passage for you if you are willing to spend the remainder of your days there."

Mayda's mouth was open, but no words came out. She stood and paced from one end of the stair to the other and back again, slowly finding her voice. "I can never leave? Even if those who hunt me are dead? So I am to be imprisoned for my kindness?" She looked at me to confirm her suspicion, left hand fluttering near her mouth.

I chose my words carefully, not wishing to alarm her further. "Think about your options. If you continue running, you will be looking over your shoulder until the day you find a knife buried in your back. Yes, a convent can resemble a prison cell, but you would not be alone there. You would have sisters who speak your language, will teach you a trade, and will help you learn their ways. I cannot offer you much, but this is a guarantee of safety, a home, and warm food to fill your belly."

"But I know nothing of this god. Why would they take such as me?"

"The sisters would rather see those who have no other options slowly come to love their god than die in the streets. They act only out of compassion. I doubt you will get the same offer from your sister."

Mayda shot me an evil look, making her look like a younger version of Elga, but I could see her resolve melting. She knew she had no other choice.

"Ja, ja, I will go," she said at last. "But please make certain no one knows of this, or it will all be for nothing."

"You have our word," Arthur said. "There is a sister at a nearby convent who will accompany you along with one of my guard."

Mayda's eyes grew wide. "What if this sister betrays me?"

"She will do no such thing. She is foresworn not to." Arthur handed her a small roll of paper. "This will guarantee your safe passage. But you cannot be known by your given name lest your true identity be discovered. What name do you wish me to inscribe here?"

"Call me Udele. I know it was what my sister bade you call her before you discovered who we were, but it was my mother's name, and it is the only way I can take my family with me."

Arthur wrote her name as she requested and called for one of the waiting women. "Take this lady to the convent and see she is safely on her way before returning."

ust over a week later, we were standing atop the outer palisade of the fort of Mount Badon, watching as Arthur's men hid a circular ditch around the perimeter of the fort with dried grass and bracken. Alle and Octha were experienced campaign leaders, so we had no hope of fooling them outright with this most rudimentary of defenses, but by felling the grass fifty handspans on either side, we could at least hope to fool them into charging into it. Those unfortunate enough to do so would be greeted by a grave of sharp wooden spikes. Because the ditch was asymmetrical, the remaining troops would be wary of where they placed their tread, leaving them vulnerable to our archers and slingers who would launch their missiles from the wall on which we now stood.

Arthur paced, running a hand through his golden hair as though he was afraid he was forgetting something. "Will you read the stones again?"

"Arthur, I have told you I must see the size and composition of the army to be able to give you a definite outcome. For now, the best I can do is conjecture, and based on that, the stones say the same thing as they have from the beginning. Your strategy of coming at them from all sides will lead us to victory, but only if we ensure the tower is well guarded. The reasons are not clear, but we will need adequate defenses behind the second wall."

"That means they will certainly breech the boundary wall," Arthur mumbled.

"Did you really expect they would not? The best we can hope for is to slow them down long enough for the rest of our plan to be in place. Failing that, we are well supplied, and they are far from home, so there is always the chance we can starve them into submission, pick them off one by one as they forage for food."

Arthur stopped beside me and looked out over the town of

Aque Sullis. "Pray it does not come to that. Even if we succeed in cutting off their shipments, they can always turn to plunder. Even with Gawain and Bedivere's efforts to relocate the people, I am certain most of the populace will stay in their homes. If the Saxons starve, the people are as doomed as fattened calves. Yet if we send in a reserve unit to defend the town, we tip our hand."

I raised his hand and rested my cheek in its warm, calloused hollow. "The Morrigan is with us. I swear she will give us her backing."

For a long time, we stood motionless save for our breathing, watching the setting sun burnish the horizon in brilliant amber. Mark's and Constantine's troops from Dyfneint and Cornwall were already here, as were Pelles's from the Summer Country. Morgan had arrived only a few hours earlier with her guard and the armies from Gwynedd and Dyfed were due to arrive soon. At least we had that in our favor. When those from distant lands would appear was anyone's guess, as was the location of our enemy.

Snatches of conversation crossed the distance to my ears as Lancelot and Bors instructed the men at the gatehouses to watch for any sign of the incoming army.

"They will come at us from the northeast via Fosse Way, which passes right below the fort. By this, they will hope to cut off our food supply and any defenses we may summon from the east," Lancelot said. "Be on your guard for you know not when they will arrive."

As I watched the town of Aque Sullis bolt its doors and shutter its windows to the oncoming war, I thought how odd it was to see such a thriving town so utterly deserted. When Viviane and I traveled from Northgallis to Avalon so many years ago, we had spent the night in this town, taking in the healing waters of the shrine. Nearly a decade later, the cries of the street vendors hawking their wares still rang in my memory and the thought of the warm spiced flatbread we ate caused my mouth to water. But when I made myself look at the town as it was now, the bustle of activity was replaced with the void of uncertainty, its exotic aroma supplanted by the stink of fear.

Thinking of my last time in the area and the new life it had brought to me, my mind drifted to Mayda. I wondered how she was faring on her own journey to a fate she'd never anticipated.

I glanced at Arthur. "You were not so surprised when Mayda interrupted our audience, husband. Tell me, how do you know one of the Saxons' highest-ranking women?"

Arthur's eyes gleamed with mirth despite the gravity we were facing. "I could ask you the same question. I was surprised that she came—that I did not expect. But I recognized her voice. She was there when I fought alongside your father at York. Her younger brother had been taken prisoner, and she begged me to spare his life, a request I daresay we may all regret as he is a powerful leader in the Saxon army. I heard no such tearful pleading from her sister, who I have little doubt would have regarded her brother as a hero had he died by my sword."

"She is cruel. That is for certain," I agreed.

"And what is the service Mayda wished to thank you for?"

I crossed my arms, hugging my shoulders, and turned away from him. "When we were lodging in Saxon territory on our way to Dyfed, Elga came to the door disguised as a peasant, asking for a midwife. I delivered Mayda's baby, a boy who lived only a few hours—much like our own. But unlike our child, Mayda's was murdered, killed by Elga's hand as soon as I was out the door." I shivered at the memory.

To my great disappointment, Arthur did not look appalled or even surprised. "Such is the fate of many an unwanted heir." He saw my expression and hastened to explain. "I may well have suffered the same misfortune without Merlin's wisdom. He alone understood the danger my life posed and so sent me away from my parents. Mayda's son was not so lucky."

I was about to reply when Gawain and Bedivere passed through the gates, shouting a hearty greeting. They were trailed by a cluster of fifty or so men, women, and children, all of whom I presumed chose to seek refuge in the fort rather than flee or take their chances in their own homes.

We met them in the courtyard just as the night fires were being lit. Arthur gave instructions to the families as to where they could stay and take refreshment and where to gather at sunrise so they could be secreted away to safety. It was only when they had departed that I noticed the dozen or so women who remained behind. They were all clad in warrior's breeches and armed from their copper-belted swords to the daggers in their boots and the deadly pins in their hair. It was clear before I even reached Arthur's side that they had come to fight.

I heard Sobian's accented voice before I picked her out in the dancing flames of torchlight. As usual, she was at Arthur's side, joking with him and touching him in a familiar manner that suggested a sordid past between them. Funny how after all we had been through together, her flirting no longer bothered me.

"Did you really believe we would pass up a chance to fight, Arthur Pendragon?" Sobian laughed. "We're women of blood and iron, of that you can be sure. Where else in all the land will you find a group of warriors who have learned from experience to defend themselves in any situation? Land, sea, river"—she gestured around her—"hill fort, it makes no difference. Flesh is cleaved the same way, and blood runs just as quickly. Please, let us provide service to you. After all, it is the least we can do for your kindness in helping set me and my lasses into an honest life."

Bors returned from the wall just in time to hear the last part of Sobian's request. "Arthur, you are not considering this preposterous proposal, are you? Who lets a woman fight? The lot of you should be off at dawn with the others so you will be safe."

Sobian snorted. "Safe from whom? There is no guarantee those who flee this place will make it to safety. For all we know, the Saxons could be out there right now, surrounding us and voiding our best laid plans—"

"'Our'?" Bors mocked. "This is our fight, not yours, woman. Get back to the hearth where you belong."

Sobian had a long dagger at Bors's throat before he'd even finished speaking. "Say aught like that again, I will have not only your head but your stones as well."

"Stop it, you two." I stepped between them, forcing Sobian to lower her weapon. "Save your hatred for the Saxons. We need all the fighters we can get inside the keep, remember? I say let them fight if they wish." I turned to Bors. "As to your question of who lets a woman fight—I do. I will be on the ramparts with you, and there is nothing you can do to stop it. You can thank me once the battle is over."

⁂

Dawn broke a misty gray in the valley below, shrouding the village and road from view. In the courtyard behind the second palisade, a press of women, children, elders, and others who would or could not defend the fort shuffled from foot to foot, waiting on Arthur's orders.

Deep within the hillside ran a system of tunnels which led in and out of the fort through the thick forest behind it. Originally constructed to ferry troops in and out of the garrison, it would now be used to move innocents to safety without alerting the Saxons. Elaine had come with us from Corbenic for this very purpose.

At the center of the throng, Elaine wrung her hands, fretting. "Guinevere, I do not think I can do this alone. I am not familiar with the area. What if I get us all lost or killed?"

I placed my hands on her shoulders, forcing her to stand still. "We are not sending you off without a guard, you goose. If you fear losing your way, let one of the locals guide you out. It is only a little more than a day's hike from here to Cardiff. Once you emerge from the caves, just follow Fosse Way northwest, and you will eventually see the port. All you need do is stay strong for them until you can get them safe housing across the estuary in Dyfed. And if anyone can do that, it is you. It is your land, after all. I have faith in you."

Elaine smiled softly and took a deep breath. "If you believe I can do it, then I know I can."

I squeezed her shoulders and signaled to Arthur, who handed Elaine a green flag raised high on a pole.

He raised his voice above the din. "Everyone who is leaving should follow the Lady Elaine and her green banner. She will lead you to safety across the channel."

The line moved slowly, inching single file through the doors of the keep and down into the darkness of the underground passages. When most of the crowd had disappeared, Arthur approached a score of women who stood, unmoving, near the gate. Octavia was among them.

"You should hurry if you wish to keep up with the others," he urged.

"We're not going," said a black-haired woman wearing the apron and cap of a baker or cook. She crossed her massive arms, which could have rivalled most of the Combrogi's and, I had a feeling, wielded a deadly iron pan. "If they get to stay and defend this fort"—she rolled her eyes at Sobian and her band of female pirates—"so do we. I have cooked for these men for twenty years. I am not going to abandon them now. Besides, who do you think will tend the soup pot and change bandages while you are giving orders? Mouths don't fill themselves, and you've got no camp women to assist you here."

Arthur could not argue with her, so the women stayed behind

under Morgan's command, tending to the necessities of the fort while the rest of us waited on the ramparts, watching the fog slowly thin. I was grateful Elaine and her party would have some natural camouflage to bring good fortune to the beginning of their journey.

❦

It was nearly midmorning when shouts arose from the watchtowers. The valley below was becoming clear, but I had to rub my eyes at what I saw. Peeking out of the mists were the tips of hundreds of tents, smoke from the cook fires competing with the fog to obscure the enemy army from sight. Their temporary camp stretched as far as I could see, eventually melting into the trees on the horizon.

There had to be nearly a thousand men camped in front of us—more than twice our number. How could they have made camp since nightfall without arousing any suspicion? Men could be ordered to be silent, but no matter how well-trained the animals, they whinnied and stamped as they willed, yet the guards who watched swore they'd heard nary a sound. It was as though they were phantoms from a previous war, there to reenact a battle long since decided. I shivered, wondering what magic they could have wrought to go unnoticed.

The warriors looked so small from my vantage point, as though I was a god looking down upon the earth and could crush them under my thumb. But it would not be nearly so easy—that much I knew. As the view became clearer, I watched those closest to the outer palisade as they went about their business, clearly preparing for their first maneuver. Bushy-bearded men mended leather armor and sharpened spears of varying lengths while boys with long poles poked at the piles of grass and bracken, trying to determine the boundaries of the trenches. Several armored women were practicing attack and defense. On the outskirts of the camp, the ring of axes signaled the felling of trees for firewood and, I feared, the building of siege weapons.

Not wanting to waste precious time, I took up my board of Holy Stones and arranged an accurate ratio of their troops to ours, accounting for the spears, swords, and stone hurlers I had seen plus the handful of archers they likely kept well out of view.

I closed my eyes and tried to imagine the scene from their perspective. Even without the sight, it was not difficult to imagine how impressive the fortress must appear to an army used to battle in open fields. Directly before them was the span of broken grass, trampled as though under a hundred hooves. Beyond lay a ring of bright green grass, a seemingly innocent lot that put any fortunate enough to cross the chasm directly in the sights of our archers atop a long wall of sharp, thick wooden stakes that stuck out of the ground like hundreds of angry styluses. Three gatehouses flanked the main entry, with two more at intervals on either side to guard the indirect approaches. Beyond, the massive triangular hill dominated the landscape, its steep grassy slopes a formidable challenge for even the most experienced of climbers. From this vantage point, the thin silhouette of the fort itself rose like a rearing horse, surrounded by yet another ring of spiked timber.

I left the stones on our side alone, indicating we would not change tack, and waited to see their response. Finally, I opened my eyes.

"We still have a few days," I told Arthur and Lancelot, who stood in the main gatehouse, sizing up their opponents. "They need to locate and fill in the ditch wide enough to get their men across then make their way through the outer fence. By then, our archers and slingers should have depleted their front ranks to almost nothing. The stones say it will buy us enough time for the outer flanks to be in place. . .but just barely."

"How did the Saxons get here so quickly?" asked Arthur.

It was Lancelot who responded, pointing at the edge of the camp where some of the horses were being turned loose. "They traveled on horseback and carried provisions in wagons, but they do not intend to fight mounted. Those are tough-bred pack animals only. It appears the Saxons have no intention of leaving with them, so you can be certain they will fight to the death."

"But they will certainly die. There is no way an army on foot can take a fort such as this. That is why it was built. To even try is suicide," I protested.

Lancelot shook his head. "I have seen enough of war to know there is nothing stronger than a force determined their cause is in the right. And according to Mayda, they believe this victory is their destiny, so they will fight all the harder. We must prepare for a long, bloody fight."

"No, not yet," Arthur said. "I may be able to buy us some

additional time. Is there one bridge left intact?"

Lancelot wrinkled his brow. "Oui, the western gate." He indicated it with his finger.

Arthur stormed off in that direction with me following closely at his heels.

"Arthur, please, no. Why sacrifice yourself when we can wait?" I grasped at his arm.

He shook me off. "Did you not hear me? I can weaken their leaders and stall them through a single action. All of their work will have to cease until the matter is settled. I indulge you in most things, but I will not in this. Kay!" he called, then added to me, "Either come with me or stay behind, but I will challenge them either way."

 споре ероs

The gates creaked, and we rode single file across the bridge, Arthur in the lead. Kay and I followed, Lancelot bringing up the rear. Morgan had chosen to stay within the safety of the walls, preparing for any wounds that would need to be tended once the fighting began. We each bore a sprig of mistletoe, a sign of truce to Briton and Saxon alike, which hung in the rafters of every fort throughout the island for healing and as a signal of peace. Above us, on the wall, our warriors gathered to watch, their weapons lowered according to Arthur's command.

We stopped about thirty paces past where the grass had been trampled down. A clamor arose from the edges of the encampment as the warriors noticed our approach. As Arthur had predicted, all work ceased, and those at the forges and saws gathered in their tribal camps to gawk.

"Alle, Octha!" Arthur bellowed. "Come forth. We bear Freya's sign of peace, so I swear no harm will come to you."

The front line of Saxons picked up their spears and round shields, forming a defensive wall against any treachery we might attempt. They muttered and jeered in their own tongue, sure we could not understand them, but I needed no translator to know they were calling for our deaths. Slaying us would have been easy enough for them, but I wagered they feared the wrath of their gods, especially since Arthur had invoked their goddess of war. From somewhere in the crowd, a rhythmic banging erupted, and as those in front took up the motion, someone began chanting. Soon the whole of the camp was likely to surge and engulf us.

Then a low horn broke through the clamor, followed by total silence. The crowd slowly parted, and two men emerged followed by Elga and a man who had to be her champion.

The two men were brothers, both tall, nearly the same height as Arthur. They had muscular arms and broad frames that made it clear they could give a threatened buck a challenge before felling him. Alle, clearly the elder by several years, had a mane of white-gold hair twisted in odd knots and braids reaching nearly to the center of his back. His beard was decorated with golden baubles and twisted into a series of spikes that made him appear more demon than human. Octha, on the other hand, was shorter. His long flaxen hair, worn loose at his shoulders, nearly matched the hide armor protecting his chest from ribcage to clavicle. His skin was smoother and less weather-worn than his brother's save a jagged scar winding from his left temple to his nose, just skirting his eye socket.

Alle stepped to the front and addressed us in his language, which Arthur translated for the rest of us.

"You come here, to our camp, bearing a token of peace. Are we to take it as your surrender?"

Arthur chuckled darkly. "No. I come to challenge you by right of honor, as Aethelings, to single combat to the death. You cannot refuse without disgracing yourselves—that much I know."

"You mock our gods by wearing their tokens of truce yet demanding violence!" Octha yelled.

"I do no such thing," Arthur countered. "I bear the seed of peace only as a signal I mean no treachery. I seek to avoid the clash of armies and the loss of countless lives. How much bloodshed follows is in your hands."

Octha growled, but Alle remained impassive. The brothers conferred in hushed tones that were more like a series of grunts.

Alle turned back to us. "We accept, but as there are two of us and only one of you, I will fight you alone with my brother as witness. Name your terms."

"We fight now, on the grass with its edge and the hidden ditch as our bounds. Two spears and a shield for each. As I have challenged you, you may strike first. The victor claims the fort but must swear he will not harm the others here present."

Elga eyed me suspiciously as Alle weighed Arthur's stated terms.

I doubted she liked these odds any more than I did.

"Agreed."

Arthur dismounted and removed his mail armor, leaving only the leather undersheath so the two would be evenly matched. According to tradition, I had the right to inspect Alle for any weapons or hidden trickery that did not abide by the terms of the agreement. Elga did the same for Arthur, making a show of running her hands across his body and checking under his armor and in his boots.

"Kay, why are we letting him do this?" I whispered, biting my thumbnail.

Kay placed a reassuring hand on my shoulder. "His choice of weapons was no accident. He knows what he is doing. I promise you he will live."

The two kings took their places on the grass, careful to keep the invisible gorge at their sides. Arthur chose to begin with a single spear and shield, while Alle took up spears in both hands, shield slung over his left arm.

The banging and chanting began again as the two faced off. Alle circled Arthur, testing him, trying to force him to turn his back on the fort. He struck with one spear at Arthur's shield and hooked his other behind it, yanking forward to try to dislodge the defense. Arthur leaned back, narrowly avoiding the second blade, and pushed outward, using Alle's own motion to unbalance him. The Saxon stumbled back, and Arthur swung his own weapon, piercing Alle's thigh.

The crowd grumbled and redoubled their clanging.

Alle snarled and came at Arthur again, this time using his shield as a battering ram to force Arthur back. Arthur dug in his heels, trying not to slip, but his boots skidded along the grass against his will. Alle was pushing Arthur nearer to the center of the field, and Arthur could not attack since all of his effort was put into halting the assault. But without warning, Arthur bent double, sending Alle tumbling over his back.

I expected the Saxon to sprawl onto the ground, but he was a better trained warrior than I'd anticipated. He recovered by rolling to a halt, spears held close to his body to keep them in hand. His shield had shattered as he hit the ground, and Arthur stabbed down at him, but Alle evaded and was quickly back on his feet. He punched his spear toward Arthur's shield, aiming for a vulnerable area at the base of his armor, but Arthur anticipated him and raised his shield at the last moment so the tip of the spear lodged in the boss at its center. With a wrenching motion, Arthur relieved him of his now useless weapon.

Arthur retrieved his unused spear from Kay so that he now held two and turned once again to face Alle. Alle twirled his remaining spear expertly, deflecting Arthur's jabs with movements similar to a swordsman. Only once did he breech Arthur's defense and slice his side, right beneath where his armor ended. Had Arthur retained the chain mail, he would have been uninjured.

Arthur hissed and instinctively stepped back, going on the defensive until the pain, writ clear on his face, abated.

The two were perilously close to the ditch now, avoiding its edges by sheer luck. Alle changed tack, turning his spear sideways to use the pole like a staff. Arthur mirrored him, holding his spears double to provide extra strength. Their dance reminded me oddly of the battle between the Oak King and the Holly King on Beltane, only this quest for power was very real. They were tiring, both bleeding, arms dropping lower and lower as the strain of the long battle fatigued them. Once, Arthur's foot slipped as he found the edge of the ditch, but he was able to save himself and step away. But that gave him an advantage Alle did not have. Rallying, Arthur guided Alle to where the ground gave way and forced him onto his back, pinning both his shoulders to the earth with his spears. Alle's screams silenced the chants of his followers.

Arthur kicked aside Alle's remaining weapon and turned to Octha. "I will let him live if you will retreat this instant, never to harass my people again."

Octha's face split into a menacing grin. "You know I will do no such thing."

In stony silence, Arthur removed his spears from Alle's limp arms and rolled him into the pit. Alle's screams echoed up and over the field as his body was impaled on the stakes. While Octha stood motionless, Arthur limped over to his horse, and Kay gave him a boost into the saddle.

"It is done. And you have lost. Return to your home," Arthur panted.

"By right of blood vengeance, we shall vindicate my brother and slay you all!" Octha called after us as Elga's guard gave chase.

"Burn the bridge!" Arthur yelled to the guards as we crossed.

A shower of oil followed in our wake, then with the tickle of a torch, the whole thing was ablaze.

"Now what do we do?" Kay asked.

Arthur passed a hand across his fatigued face. "Pray the gods speed Owain and the others to our aid."

Chapter Seventeen

It was no use telling Arthur he had made the Saxons' hostility worse. That he realized as much was evident by his silence as Morgan cleaned and dressed his wounds.

Spurred on by rage and grief, by nightfall, the Saxons had the trench revealed and a wide swath of it filled. Our archers rained down arrows and hurled stones on those who crossed, but Octha's army was so large it felt as though for every man we killed, two more appeared.

It took little battle training to know they would set the gatehouse and outer palisade ablaze at the first opportunity. So while Arthur slept, I slipped away to the first unoccupied place I could find—a deserted granary at the base of the keep. It was dark and still inside, the only light seeping in between slats in the wooden walls. I sat where the gap was largest—the only place I had a clear view of the stars—and prayed.

I rarely used the gifts afforded to me as a priestess, but Arthur needed to sleep and to heal, and we needed more time to allow our backup troops to take their positions.

Lady Morrigan, hear me, I prayed silently. My husband, a devotee of the soldiers' god Mithras, has been rash, and I could not stop him. I fear our pride will cost us not only this fort but our very lives and the future of this isle you hold so dear. Do not abandon us, Great Mother, but hear my desperate cries for aid. I ask you to give us the time we need to turn this enemy from your shores. Aid me now, Great Lady, by bringing the elements under my command.

I sent my consciousness down into the earth, closed my eyes, and raised my arms high. The wind whistled in response. Concentrating on the blackness behind my eyelids, I waved my arms, willing storm clouds toward me, pulling them on the howling wind until the stars were blotted out. Channeling all my guilt and rage, I twitched my finger and imagined a spark rising upward to charge the clouds. I brought my arms down hard, and rain pelted the roof, followed by a bolt of lightning and the answering peal of thunder.

I had done what I could. The Saxons would be unable to set anything alight tonight, and no one would dare battle in the muck and mire quickly taking shape in the grass below the hill. I started to rise, but a wave of dizziness forced me back to my knees. It had been so long since I'd done anything of the kind I had forgotten what a toll it took. I lay down on my forearms as another wave hit me, and I closed my eyes in a vain attempt to steady the spinning room.

The crack of thunder woke me from what I'd thought was a dreamless sleep. I stood cautiously, testing my legs. Finding them steady, I rushed back to Arthur's side, images emerging from the fog of sleep with every step.

In the dream, which was beginning to feel more like a vision, I'd stood at the entrance to the subterranean passage leading out of the fort. At first I saw the dark, uneven walls of the tunnel that had swallowed Elaine and the residents of Aque Sullis only hours before. Then there were figures within, only shadows, but instead of moving away, they were coming toward me. We had made arrangements to have food and supplies ferried in through the passage if the siege was drawn out, but it had been only a day since the Saxons made camp, so why anyone would be using the tunnels to get into the castle made no sense. Unless—yes. As they came toward me, I saw the glint of steel in the low light.

"Arthur, Arthur!" I shook his shoulder, but he did not wake. Damn that sleeping draught Morgan had given him.

I spun around, trying to remember where Lancelot or Kay were lodging. I knew not, so I wandered the empty halls searching for someone, anyone, who would listen to my fears. In the dining hall, I found Octavia curled up by the fire, and I gently roused her.

"Octavia, we have to find some of the men. I believe we are in danger here."

When she'd gathered Kay and Gawain, they listened to my story with somber expressions. While others would have laughed at the imaginings of a silly, frightened woman, these men had enough respect for the sight to take me seriously.

When I was finished, Kay sighed. "It is possible. Similar things have been done in Rome and other places, though I would hardly credit these barbarians with being cunning enough to conceive such a plan."

"You saw them today. Alle and Octha are hardly backward fools. There is strategy behind all they do, and that makes them a double threat."

"We should take a look just to be certain," Gawain decided.

The rain had slowed to a drizzle by the time they reemerged from the tunnel.

"We have been halfway down and saw no signs of recent occupation, but it is hard to tell what footprints were made by those fleeing yesterday," Kay said. "If you have any reason for concern, we should seal it up. But we don't want to wake the entire barracks with our hammering. I will stand guard until the morning."

I went back to Arthur's room and climbed into bed next to him, wondering as I listened to his breath if I was a fool. The tunnel was our only method of escape if things went badly. Tearing down a wall would only slow our egress. But if I was right. . . I shuddered and drew closer to Arthur, willing sleep to carry away my fears, founded or no.

☙❧

The rain had done its job. Three days later, we were still at an impasse, the Saxons prowling impatiently outside the castle, our guards trading shifts with equal unease behind the safety of the wall.

Not only were the timbers soaked and the ground turned to mud, the ditch had filled with water during the storm, washing away much of the debris the Saxons had used to fill it.

So as dawn broke on the first clear day, I rejoiced that I had not only bought us time but set them back a bit as well. Or so I thought.

By midmorning, knots of Saxons were placing long, wide pallets of tightly nailed planks over the gorge. Though they tried to defend with their shields, our arrows and stones found targets while men and women emerged from their protective cover to cross the bridge. But the number of Saxons successful was still small compared to their total.

From the gatehouse, Arthur yelled, "What are you waiting for, you fools? Burn them down."

But his command went unheeded as a second Saxon battalion split down the middle and a great rumbling like an earthquake shook the ground. The sound of grating wheels and creaking wood reached us before the thing emerged from cover, but Arthur knew well enough what it was.

"Fall back!" he commanded, and all but those expressly required to stay with the gate retreated up the hill to the safety of the second palisade.

I caught only a glimpse of the battering ram before Arthur grabbed my hand and pulled me along to safety. It was little more than a pointed tree trunk suspended by rope over a wheeled base, much like the bottom of a cart. A crude roof had been built over the top and covered in hides, ostensibly to protect it from fire.

It crashed into the gate before I'd reached the base of the hill, and its reverberating boom knocked me off my feet. Again it came, but this time I was ready. By the time I reached the second palisade, the archers had killed most of the warriors keeping its pendulum in motion, and as the second group took up position, the archers let fall a cauldron of oil, which quickly caught fire and killed everyone around it. But it was not enough to save the wall, for what damage the ram had begun, the fire finished, incinerating the guards who had sought to stop the Saxons' progress.

"Light the signal fires!" Arthur commanded.

As Saxons streamed across the trench into the courtyard at the base of the hill, archers fanned out along the last remaining wall. Some fired on the advancing Saxons while others let fly a volley of flaming arrows, one group toward Lansdown Hill to the west and the other toward Dean Hill in the south. At the summit of each hill, large bonfires flared to life in response.

"Now we must pray the kings will do as we have asked," Arthur said to himself.

I scanned the countryside for signs of hope. At first there was nothing, but then I saw them, small as ants—the northern troops riding at full speed to cut off the Saxons' left flank.

"Arthur, they're coming!" I shouted, but my voice was drowned out by screams within the keep.

I raced inside, sword drawn, to find the tower in chaos. People were running through the halls, some bleeding, some seeking to escape injury. Others lay dead, crumpled where they had stood. How was that possible? The Saxons hadn't yet gained the terraces. How could our people already be fighting for their lives? I fought my way through the fleeing servants to find Sobian battling a Saxon woman wielding a war hammer. That was when I understood. I had been right. They had been here all along.

"There are about fifty of them," Sobian said between slashes. "Hid in the cellar, as far as I can tell."

Together, we dispatched the woman, and I took her armor, not having had time to don any. We followed sounds of distress to the kitchen, where a pair of Saxons were menacing three of the servants. It was a cramped space, but one servant was holding her own with a frying pan while another made do with the spit from the fire and the third wielded a knife resembling a small sword. Taking a cue from one of the maids, I grabbed a wooden serving tray and tossed it to Sobian to use as a shield.

Amid the maids' clamor, the Saxons failed to hear us approach. Sobian had one's throat cut before the other could react, and as soon as he dropped his defense, I ran him through.

One of the maids whimpered.

"Will you be all right?" I asked, and she nodded, obviously horrified by the violence she had witnessed.

The keep was once again quiet by the time Sobian and I made it to the ground floor, doing our best not to look at the corpses we passed and praying they were no one we knew.

But near the front door, Sobian stopped short. Sprawled on the floor was one of her girls, a long slash down the front of her chest. Sobian knelt next to her and cradled her head.

"I will find the bastard who did this to you, Bonnie, and rip out his entrails. I swear it to you." She kissed the younger girl's forehead and stepped over her body, determined to continue.

Outside, the tumult was deafening. Some of the Saxons had gained the hill and were using makeshift ladders to try to scale the walls surrounding the keep while stones and arrows flew in every direction. Sobian darted off, and I ducked into a gatehouse for safety. Leaning against the wall to catch my breath, I had an unobstructed view of the fighting far below. The Saxon numbers were dwindling. Owain's army had nearly dispatched a third of them, and Pelles's contingent was pushing the remainder ever closer to the foot of the hill. Soon there would be nowhere for them to run.

I needed to find Arthur. He was still weak from the duel with Alle and no doubt by now had undone any healing that had taken place. I had to get to him before he injured himself beyond saving. I searched from one gatehouse to another to no avail. I would have to enter the fray.

I descended into the open courtyard. Immediately I found myself trapped in the middle of a melee in which weapons were being wielded indiscriminately. The Saxon in front of me stank of burning flesh, his right arm raw with oozing blisters. Unfortunately, he appeared to be left-handed. We grappled, parrying and thrusting like the dozens of fighters around us. Try as I might, I could not disarm him while hemmed in by bodies. He pushed me back, and I stumbled, saved from falling only by the back of the warrior behind me. The Saxon's sword came within a hairsbreadth of my head, slicing off a hunk of my hair and part of my ear before I could bat it away. Ignoring the pain, I aimed a blow at his ribcage, but I needn't have bothered. A large stone whizzed over my shoulder and hit him square in the forehead. The Saxon's eyes widened, and he fell backward, dead.

Stunned, I turned to see Octavia holding a sling, another stone at the ready.

"Your mother always said I was a good shot," she yelled triumphantly.

I started to laugh, but then the warrior behind her raised his arm. I understood what he intended to do and flung myself at Octavia as the bearded bastard let his weapon fly. I was too slow. His javelin caught Octavia in the lower back as I pulled her down—one moment too late.

I gasped in horror as my heart broke into a thousand pieces and the war around me faded away. Amid all the screaming and bloodshed, I no longer cared if I lived or died. Yet again, I was holding someone who meant everything to me as she slipped away.

I'd never thought of Octavia as a servant but as a second mother. Now I was watching the light slowly drain from her eyes. She was there in my earliest memories, holding me on her knee in the warm spring sunlight, helping me struggle into my first set of armor, weeping as I left for Avalon, comforting me after my mother's death, and soothing my uncertain heart during my first days of marriage. Whether I'd prattled on about a new toy, a pretty dress, my infatuation with Aggrivane, or complained about my husband, she was always there with a kind word and a patient ear. She was listening, always listening, but soon her ears would hear no more.

I wanted desperately for the last thing she heard to be my love for her, but I could not form the words. Horror constricted my throat, and she was in too much pain to speak, so I simply interlaced my fingers with hers and lay with her in silence on the hard dusty ground as her life drained away, our eyes betraying emotions our tongues could not express.

I found my voice only after she had gone, and I recited the traditional prayer for those who died in battle. "May the Goddess grant you rest, daughter who has died in her service. Her blessing be forever on you."

With shaking hands, I closed Octavia's eyes and laid my head on her silent chest. Cold slowly seeped from the earth into my bones, leaving me numb and hollow and wishing for death myself.

◈◈◈

I could not recall what happened after or how the battle finally ended. I was told Sobian guarded me as Octavia died and Lancelot avenged Octavia's loss, two acts for which I would be forever grateful.

My next memory was of walking among the dead. There were so many, more than I could have imagined in my worst nightmares, all bloody and broken from all manner of injuries. It was not uncommon to see limbs hacked off or twisted in grotesque contortions or men holding in their own guts from gaping wounds. Others were severely burned and howling in pain. I helped those I could to the infirmary, where Morgan quickly took over. But for those less fortunate, whose wounds had not killed them but would not heal, the only thing I could do was whisper a blessing, obtain permission with a nod, grunt, or whisper, and give them the Goddess's final mercy— a quick death.

Numb with shock, I carried out my duty as a priestess by saying a final prayer over each of the bodies I encountered, Saxon and Briton alike. With the help of the other women, I washed and dressed them in makeshift shrouds with equal dignity for whether friend or foe, all were children of the same great gods. We burned the bodies of the Saxons, as was their custom, and buried our men on the site of the battle, their bones an eternal reminder of the horrors that had taken place here. After we departed, this fort would never be used again.

After two sleepless days, priestesses from Avalon arrived to continue the rites of the dead, relieving me to tend to Octavia. I could not bring myself to bury her with the fallen warriors, much less dump her body into the ditch with the nameless dead once we ran out of burial space.

Nearly faint with exhaustion, I walked down to Aque Sullis to secure permission from the priests to bury her in their cemetery just outside of town. As she was a Roman and this was as close to Roman soil as we could be, they were more than happy to oblige my request. I doubted my title and the sizable donation I made to their shrine hurt our cause.

In the following days, news trickled in from returning Combrogi who had pursued the fleeing Saxons. All told, fewer than one hundred Saxons escaped alive, Octha and Elga among them. Although they were now well within their territory and likely so shaken by their losses it would be a long time before they raised a sword against us again, I could not help but remember the fury on the *Aethelings'* faces as Arthur and I fled into the sanctuary of the hill fort. I feared we would yet pay for the wounds inflicted on their pride.

Chapter Eighteen

Autumn 503

One month passed, then two as we recovered at Cadbury. Slowly, bones mended and wounds healed, at least those that could be seen. Those inside our minds and hearts would take longer to cure. I took small comfort in knowing that mine were not the only haunted eyes ringed with shadows. Sleep eluded us all, and when it deigned to appear, it was accompanied by vivid nightmares that forced us to relive our strife. I wondered often how Arthur lived with the memories of more than a dozen battles.

Our court tarried at Cadbury in this convalescent state until we could wait no longer, seeking a normality I doubted would ever come. Soon the snows would begin to fall. We needed to make ready for Camelot if our slow-moving party was going to make the long journey back home before the roads became impassable.

But Arthur felt we could not leave without honoring those who had made our victory over the Saxons possible. So he declared a weeklong feast to mark our triumph. He sent a sizeable donation to Aque Sullis so the townspeople, who were not untouched by the battle, could join in the celebration as well.

"Are you certain we can afford to be so generous after so costly a war?" I asked, not wishing to imply ingratitude but also mindful of practical matters.

Arthur shrugged off my concerns. "A few years of peace and bountiful harvests will more than recoup our losses."

"But bountiful harvests are not guaranteed."

"No, but the goodwill of our people goes a long way toward making them possible. Trust me."

So I did. Kings and lords, nobles of every clan and rank, Druids, priestesses, Christians, warriors and their families all descended upon Cadbury with the speed of a flock in flight—or a plague of locusts, as our fretful host referred to them.

The first two days honored those who had given their lives in service to their king and country as well as those who had acted heroically in battle. The Combrogi met for the affair in Cadbury's cavernous great hall, which was decorated with the standards of kingdoms and tribes who had contributed men or funds to the battle of Mount Badon. Rather than sitting in the far end of the room, Arthur had asked that a platform be built in the center of the room so everyone present would be able to see us and we them.

So as the festivities began, Arthur, Morgan, and I were surrounded by the Combrogi, their wives and children, and our own families, as well as Merlin and Viviane, who led an ancient prayer for the dead.

"Hail spirits of our ancestors, those of blood, bone, and spirit. We invoke you from beyond the seventh wave. Join with our fallen brothers and sisters who wait just beyond the veil. Be their guardians and protectors as they make their final journey to lands of golden sun, perfumed breezes, calm seas, and verdant meadows. May peace and joy be upon them for they died noble deaths. May those whom Ceridwen chooses rise again from her cauldron hale and whole to be reborn and defend our children's children and maintain the peace bought with their blood in this lifetime."

Grieving families were invited to come forward and receive our royal condolences. Each family brought with them a small token of the one who had passed—many times a ring, a dagger, or some other personal possession. We collected them in baskets that would later be taken in solemn procession to a nearby sacred pond and offered to the gods with prayers for mercy upon the departed. In exchange, we gave them their soldiers' pensions, and to the poor, we gave a set amount of additional funds to help them weather the financial strain of their loss.

Some wives, now completely bereft of income, begged us to help them find work lest they turn to crime to feed their families. Arthur found each of them positions in the sculleries, dining halls, or sleeping chambers of Camelot or one of the noble houses. Those who expressed an interest in or talent for a trade were employed in shops. Regardless of their status in society, no one would scorn a war widow, for to do so was to call down the ire of the gods.

Before they departed, we asked the names of their preferred tribal and personal gods and blessed each of them in those names.

"Be at peace. For though you grieve, your loved one lives on. A long draught from Ceridwen's cauldron heals all infirmities and makes all men new. In due time, they will be reborn. You who grieve suffer far more than they. In the holy names of your gods, we bless you and pray you will come to know that this is but one turn in the cycle of life."

Of all of them—widows, families, and in a few cases, even orphans—the ones who will remain with me forever are Nimue and Peredur, Octavia's children, now orphans. I had seen Nimue only a year before, but now her ethereal green eyes shed silent tears onto the blue robes of a priestess. She held the hand of her brother, who stood beside her like a statue, the image of stoic grief.

Even though he had been at court since the tournament where Arthur and I met, Peredur would always be to me the boy who had shed no tears as I bid him farewell before leaving for Avalon. I still remembered the sweet smell of his hair—like fresh clover—as he pressed his wooden dog into my hand, telling me the creature was magic. I never saw Peredur's father again after I departed for Avalon. He had been killed in service to Uther's army by the Saxons. And now Peredur was here, mourning the loss of his other parent at their merciless hands.

It was Peredur who roused me from my reflections. With great solemnity, he presented us with Octavia's memorial, a necklace of coins from her native Rome.

"My mother wore this around her neck when she fled from Rome. It was all she had in the world when she joined your family," Peredur whispered. "It is only right she should have it on her journey to the next life."

I took the necklace, not pausing to examine the coins. I didn't want to think about her life before I knew her, how she must have suffered as a lone woman, hardly more than a child, traveling any way she could—by caravan, boat, or on foot—to put as much distance as possible between herself and her native land, where her whole family had been killed by the invading Visigoths. She had told me the story many times, but in the naïveté of my youth, I thought it a tale of grand adventure rather than grim reality.

I took Peredur's hand. "Your mother was so much more than a servant to me. She was my nursemaid, my teacher, and my closest confidante. Losing her was like losing my mother all over again. My heart will never heal from that wound. There is little I can do to comfort you now except tell you this—she died peacefully." I tried to choke back my emotions, but the tears broke free anyway, and my voice faltered. "In—in my arms. She did not speak, but her eyes said volumes. They shined with love, love for both of you, for the life she was leaving. She spent her entire life caring for me, and she died defending me. You should be proud."

Nimue's head snapped up.

I was startled to see not grief in her haunting eyes but pure, cold hatred.

"Proud? We should be proud she died doing her duty—defending her mistress? She never had a choice to follow you. She did as she was bid and died in bondage."

"What are you saying?" I stammered.

Her green eyes narrowed, hard as chips of ice. "Do you really not know? My mother was a slave." She scoffed at my shocked reaction. "Yes, a slave. Your father didn't welcome her with open arms out of some sense of charity. He bought her on the docks. She may not have told you, but the boat that brought her to Gwynedd was a slave ship. She was captured in Gaul. The friendship you hold so dear was nothing more than duty, pure and simple."

"Nimue," Arthur said gently but firmly, "I saw Octavia's love for Guinevere firsthand. It was no sense of duty. Who told you such lies? Surely she did not admit this to you herself. No mother would debase herself so to her children."

"The Lady herself told me, and she speaks the truth."

Arthur shook his head. "Even the Lady of the Lake can be mistaken."

Nimue's gaze flickered between Arthur, Peredur, and me as she weighed the plausibility of Arthur's words.

Peredur squeezed his sister's hand. "Does it really matter, little rose? Our mother is dead either way. We are here to mourn her with our friends, and I for one would rather the focus of her legacy be on the good she has done."

"She died a hero and a free woman. As high queen, I declare that here and now. Whatever the truth, I release Octavia from all bondage. If not for her bravery, you would be mourning me at this moment. I will forever be in her debt and therefore in yours. Name your price. What is it I can do to help ease your loss?"

Peredur and Nimue looked at one another. I doubted they

would ask for monetary compensation for they both had fruitful lives, he as part of Arthur's army and a Combrogi-in-training and she as a daughter of Avalon.

"Erect a memorial stone here and at Camelot in her honor," Peredur declared. "They will ensure she is remembered as she should be. That is all we ask of you."

"It will be done," Arthur and I said in unison.

Peredur and Nimue melted back into the crowd, though I caught Nimue watching Merlin closely as he sang a eulogy for the dead. Having their song proclaimed at the royal court by the Archdruid and chief bard of Britain was the highest honor that could be bestowed upon any subject. His song would be taught to all other bards and repeated in halls and hovels throughout the kingdom so the legacy of those heroes would remain as long as memory prevailed. No one would forget those who had fallen in the battle of Mount Badon.

⁂

The following day, we gathered in the great hall with the members of the Combrogi and Mount Badon's remaining men. We formed a smaller group, more intimate than the grieving rite, because Arthur wanted to bestow his honors on those who'd experienced the battle away from the prying eyes of courtiers and others intent only on spreading gossip.

Clustered among the sea of men were Sobian and her remaining women. As usual, though they certainly didn't blend in, they were right at home. Also as usual, Gawain was flirting with Sobian, who looked on the verge of punching him. Fortunately, before things could escalate any further, Arthur began his speech from the same dais we had occupied the day before.

"I would have preferred to hold these honors in our council chambers at Camelot, in the sight of my ancestors, but under the circumstances, this is the best alternative." His smile was a beam of light warming the entire room. "First, I would like to thank all of you for your service to your king and country. As we noted yesterday, there is no greater sacrifice than to give one's life for one's country. But you, all of you, risked your lives and survived to fight another day. And for that, I will hold you forever in my heart."

He reached down to me, and I grasped his hand. He pulled me

up next to him as though I weighed no more than a feather. "First, I wish to acknowledge my wife, the first battle queen in several generations to lead her people in times of conflict. If not for her bravery and skill, the fight would have been over before it had begun." He took my hand and kissed it. "My love, you have my eternal gratitude and, I daresay, the respect of everyone in this room."

Morgan glared at me—a sure sign I'd gained no respect from her—but the Combrogi's cheer was deafening. Arthur spun me around, and they smiled at me. Lancelot jumped up and placed a ring of leaves on my head.

"They aren't laurel, but this was the best I could do this time of year," he whispered before kissing my cheek and hopping back down. I prayed no one else could see the blush his act had produced.

"Gentlemen, gentlemen, calm down. There's more celebration yet to be had. The second person I wish to honor is Aggrivane." He sought out my former lover in the crowd. "Please come forth and receive your due."

Aggrivane hesitated only a moment before being propelled forward by the shouting men. He scrambled onto the dais with surprising grace.

"My friend," Arthur addressed him with the ease of a comrade-in-arms, "I really should arrest you for treason for you disobeyed a direct order. But you are Lot's son, so I should not be surprised."

A low chuckle rumbled through the assembly.

"If not for your wisdom, hundreds of Saxons would have escaped," Arthur added. "Tell me, how did you think of pursuing the ships before the overland riders?"

"Call it learning from past mistakes." He gave Sobian a barely perceptible nod. "There have been other battles where I was not as well advised, nor our men as fortunate. Luckily, the gods gave me a second chance."

"Indeed!" Arthur boomed. "For your creative tactics, you may take your place with your father, reporting directly to him. I name you now Second Council of Strategy."

The men erupted into cheers again as Aggrivane expressed his thanks.

"Settle down," Arthur chided. "There are many others among you who deserve our praise. Sobian, known formerly as the Scourge of the Sidhe, please come forth."

Sobian wound through the throng of men followed by the five other women who had survived through Badon with her.

Despite my initial misgivings about her and her place at court, she had saved my life twice now—first in rescuing me from Malegant and again in this battle—and over time I had grown to care for her. "Thank you," I whispered in her chestnut hair as we embraced. "I owe you my life."

She pulled back as if stung. "You owe me nothing. I swore my allegiance to you. I did nothing more than any of these men would do in similar circumstances."

Arthur had listened to our exchange, though I was fairly certain the rest of the room had not heard it. "Oh, but you did. Your actions were anything but commonplace. These men here"—he gestured to the room at large—"are paid to use their bravery and skill against any enemies to the crown. You and your fellow female warriors are different. You volunteered to be in harm's way. You offered your swords, spears, and lives when you saw a need. If that isn't the true definition of bravery, I don't know what is."

Sobian nodded, standing even taller now.

Arthur continued. "As if that were not enough, your battalion took on all comers. Some of your women are not here to celebrate with us, but we honor them the same. I am told that among the dozen of you, you killed nearly thirty Saxons. Is that true?"

"Well, I didn't stop to count them," she said with a sly smile and glittering black eyes. "If I had, you'd be talking to a corpse."

I laughed along with several of the men. That was the fiery spirit I had come to admire in this pirate-spy-turned-heroine.

"Indeed, you are right," Arthur admitted. "But that was not your only service to the crown. You stood guard over the queen as she nursed a dying friend. You are the reason we are here today rather than mourning her. As we all know now, you are more than the maid you appeared to be. There is little I can do to repay such a service, but I will try. I offer you a boon. Name what it is you wish, and it shall be granted."

A few gasps broke the silence, but no one seemed to know what to say. For a king to offer a boon was almost unheard of except for in legend.

Sobian, normally so cool and collected, was clearly stunned. She stood perfectly still, oblivious to the waiting crowd. Her lips were parted as though she intended to speak, but no words formed. Then she blinked, and her face took on a quizzical expression as though she were weighing her options, deciding if her request was likely to be granted. The crowd shifted, waiting impatiently to hear what she demanded.

Finally, Sobian fixed Arthur in a resolute gaze. "I wish to become a member of the Combrogi."

The room went completely silent. Sobian's girls looked between one another in utter shock. Then the yelling began.

"A woman cannot be part of the Combrogi!" asserted a deep voice I thought I recognized as Bors's.

"Indeed," another agreed. "Does the word not mean 'fellow country*men*?'"

"You're going to quibble over the word's origin?" Lancelot challenged. "Does your name not mean 'exotic'? Then why are you Bor-ing?" He chuckled at his own quip, which infuriated Bors all the more.

"It *cannot* be done! It shall not be done, not while I live," Bors roared, emerging from the crowd and jamming his dagger into the wood at Sobian's feet with a violence that made the dais visibly shake.

Sobian did not even flinch. In one fluid movement, she grasped the dagger and jumped down, knocking Bors onto his back. She landed in a crouch on his chest, dagger at his throat. "Shall I kill you now so I can claim what is mine?"

Arthur motioned for her to stand down. "There is no need for that. Sobian has made her request, and under the terms I freely laid forth, I must grant it. If any of you"—he narrowed his gaze on Bors—"feel so strongly against this, you are welcome to relinquish your position." He turned to Sobian. "You. Up here. Kneel."

She obeyed.

"Repeat after me. 'I, Sobian of—where *are* you from?—do swear now—"

"I know the rest." She returned his smile and took one of our hands in each of hers. When she touched Arthur, something passed between them I couldn't quite read. "I, Sobian, daughter of Grendel the Dark One of Ulster, do swear now special allegiance to my king, queen, and country. I swear also to uphold my fellow Combrogi, to defend and honor them in all things, and to keep close to my heart the confidence of my lord and lady. Should I fail them or break these vows, may the wrath of the gods be visited upon me."

Arthur helped her to her feet, and we embraced her in turn. "Welcome, fellow countrywoman."

⚬⚭⚬

Slowly, families began to depart from Cadbury, returning at long last to their homes to enjoy our newly won peace. We said our farewells to those not accompanying us to Camelot and packed our own caravan for the long journey home. At the last minute, I noticed Merlin was not in his customary position next to Arthur. I found him and my husband with Viviane, Nimue, Morgan, and the other priestesses.

I placed a hand on his forearm. "Merlin, why are you not with our party? We are nearly ready to depart."

Merlin turned, expression just the slightest bit wistful. "As I have just told Arthur and Morgan, I am not coming with you."

"What? I—"

He held up a hand to silence me. "Badon was my final battle as Arthur's advisor. I have seen what may yet come, and I wish no part in it. I have seen too much death in my years as counselor to kings." He slid his arm around Nimue's waist and pulled her to him. "Now that peace has come at long last, I wish to devote my remaining days to teaching and being with those I love. Arthur has already given his consent."

Over his shoulder, Viviane flinched, her gaze resting jealously on Nimue. Inwardly, I sighed. If even the Lady of the Lake could be supplanted, I couldn't feel too bad about Arthur's affection for Morgan.

I hugged him. "If that is what you wish, far be it from me to oppose you. We will miss you though. Who will keep us out of trouble?"

Merlin laughed, running a hand through his graying hair. "One is coming who will more than make up for my absence, I assure you." He bent down, lips grazing my cheek. To everyone else, it probably looked as though he was kissing me farewell, but his voice was stern in my ear. "Have a care whom you take into your confidence. Not everyone at court wishes to see your star continue to ascend. Remember the prophecy."

I remembered it all too well. The first part had already come true when Arthur took the throne. The second appeared to be happening now with Viviane in power in Avalon as Lady of the Lake. I repeated the third and final part to myself silently. The day will come when sister shall oppose sister, both in this sacred place and without. Loyalties will be tested and betrayed, so heed my warning. That which is birthed in jealousy shall not give life but infect all who draw near. Therefore, act with love and not out of spite. Only then shall you escape the fate the stars foretell.

I shivered. Merlin was right. I must keep my own counsel and keep careful watch over my actions lest those words come to pass.

PART FOUR

Traitor

Chapter Nineteen

Spring 504

Elaine was driving me mad. She paced constantly, running her hands through her hair, fiddling with her dress, unable to concentrate on her sewing or even sit still for a meal.

She'd been this way all winter. Then, I'd thought it was the effects of being cooped up inside with little to occupy her mind, but now the sun was bright, the breezes cool, and we were supposed to be enjoying simply being alive.

"Dear heart, what troubles you so?" I asked from my blanket beneath a pink dogwood. "Elaine, did you hear me?"

A little ways away, Elaine was picking at her fingernails as though determined to rid them of their cuticles once and for all. She looked at me, perplexed. "What do you mean?"

"This." I put a hand over hers to stop her from peeling off more skin. "Your agitation must have a source. Out with it so the rest of us can live in peace."

She searched my eyes as if trying to decide whether or not to trust me, then she glanced away. "I shouldn't say."

I knelt behind her, took her hair in my hands, and began twisting it into a golden braid just as I had done when we were children. "Of course you should." I adopted a mock stern tone. "Your queen commands it."

She sighed and nodded toward the training yard where roughly twenty of Arthur's men were sparring in pairs and small groups. "I thought I would enjoy being closer to my husband at court, but now I find it brings me nothing but distress. During the day I try to think of ways to be pleasing to him, to get him to pay attention to me, while at night I watch him dazzle all manner of women, talking with them, flirting with them, even with you. I am not certain it is all frivolous either." She turned to look at me, her long tresses slipping out of my hands. "If that was not enough, I dream of him at night.

Being at court is best for my son, and I would rather be here with his father than anywhere else in the world, but I cannot stand it."

I couldn't help but feel sympathy for her. "Sweet girl, you deserve none of this. Why do you not ask him for a divorce?"

Elaine twisted around. "It doesn't work that way in my faith. Our marriage was consummated—everyone knows that because of Galahad. I would not trade his life for anything, but as a result, I am bound to my husband whether he admits it or no. To leave him now would be a mortal sin, though I doubt there is a greater hell than to love someone whose heart will forever belong to others. How do you do it, Guinevere—live with Morgan and Arthur, especially with Mordred always under foot?"

I bit my lower lip. That was a good question. How did I manage? Oddly, Mordred had never been sore spot for me. Even though he was a reminder of my failing as a wife and mother, I could not bear him any ill will, innocent as he was in the machinations of his parents. In fact, I enjoyed helping to raise him, showering him with all the affection I could never give to my own deceased children. Now, as he grew, he came to me for advice often, which was balm to my heart.

His mother was a different story. She tolerated my tenderness to her son as long as he followed the rules she laid out and behaved as she taught him, but she made no effort to hide her disdain for me. Because of that, when I first returned from Avalon, I had expected constant discord between us, and there was for a time, but we'd learned to tolerate one another. I had accepted Arthur's preference for Morgan's bed over mine, though a small part of me resented her for it.

Finally, I answered, "I have no idea. Some days I want to kill her just as much as I did in Avalon. We still hate each other, but we've developed a sort of truce. I still loathe sharing Arthur with her, but I have no choice."

Elaine gave a small, wry laugh. "Neither do I. I see my husband with other women every day. I know he is in love with someone else. I can see it in his whole demeanor. He looks upon others with a soft-ness I will never know." She choked back hurt and rage-filled tears, clenching her hands at her sides. "I am determined to find out who his mistress is—if for no other reason than to relish the look on her face when I tell her he is already mine."

I twisted to face her. In that moment, she looked so much like Lyonesse it was frightening. "Why will you not tell me who he is? I will tell no one. I promise. But at least I could counsel him to be more discreet. Or perhaps I can convince Arthur to send him somewhere on a diplomatic mission. Then you could live here in peace."

She shook her head. "I must take that secret to my grave. But mark my words, she *will* regret crossing me."

Without knowing why, I shivered. Something in the tone of Elaine's threat cut to my very core. I never wanted to be on the receiving end of her wrath.

I placed gentle hands on her shoulders, looking her squarely in the eye. "You cannot go on like this. If you will not allow me to spirit him away, then we must find something for you to do—something to distract you from him. What makes you happiest?"

She answered almost instantly. "Drawing and prayer. You know that."

I nodded. "Well then, you shall be Galahad and Mordred's tutor. It will give you a chance to spend more time with your son. You can teach them each day after they go to the stable yard for their lessons. Art lessons will be a nice addition to what they already learn from the Ollamh Arthur employs."

"Do you really think they will want to learn art? Aren't boys more interested in swords and punching each other?"

I laughed. "Yes, but they are of an age you can convince them to do anything if you put it to them in terms of their future career as knights. I'll remind them that scouting will be an essential part of their training and tell them the story of Tristan and how his accurate maps won the battle of Caledon Wood for us."

Elaine grasped my hand. "Thank you, Guinevere. You've always known just what I needed even before I did."

I smiled at her, pleased to see her mood lifted. "Well, there is one more thing, something I wasn't going to mention yet, but I could use your help. You must swear you will keep it secret at least for now."

Elaine placed a finger to her lips and leaned in close. "I swear it. Tell me."

I took a deep breath. Just because I was not happy with it did not change the facts. "Arthur is thinking of becoming a Christian."

Elaine squealed in delight. "Oh, do you know what this means?" She clasped her hands at her breast and looked up to the sky as if in prayer. "A Christian king of Britain. I never thought I'd see the day. God be praised."

I lowered her hands to her sides. "Do not get too excited yet. He is just exploring the idea. He says the war changed him, and he's met with Father Dafydd a few times. But you know how priests are. Arthur could use someone to help him understand what being a Christian really means, how it is lived out in daily affairs."

Elaine's eyes widened like the gibbous moon. "Truly? You wish me to counsel the king?"

"Given your love for Christ and your Church, I can think of no one better to guide him."

Elaine threw her arms around me. "You will never know what a gift you have given me this day."

❧

Elaine's new position tutoring the boys turned out to be a boon for me as well because it gave me a chance to see Lancelot every day when he brought Galahad and Mordred to her chambers. In the aftermath of the war, I had found myself craving his companionship. Arthur was distant, seeking comfort of his own in Morgan's arms and leaving me to deal with my own trauma all alone.

As he had promised that night in the inn, Lancelot was there for me no matter when I needed him. At first, he'd merely listened as I confided my fears, holding me when the panic was overwhelming and letting me cry when the guilt surfaced. Sometimes I fell asleep in his arms. When I woke in terror in the dark of night, it was not Arthur I sought but my champion.

One night, months after we had returned to Camelot, I slipped into Lancelot's doorway, breathless and sweating, heart still pounding from the vivid nightmare in which Elga had succeeded in killing both of us at Badon. I was so happy we were both alive I didn't even greet him. I ran over to where he lay drenched in moonlight and kissed him, waking him from a sound sleep. He never tried to push me away, merely smiled into my kiss and drew me to him. Peeling away my sticky shift, I bit his neck, letting him know I no longer wished our relationship to be chaste. He responded by tangling a hand in the hair at the nape of my neck and pulling me on top of him. His face was buried in my breasts as I moved against him, welcoming his touch as though I was starving without him. And maybe I was. It had been ages since Arthur had touched me.

When we had finally sated our hunger, he laced his fingers in mine and smiled. "I knew you cared for me. Finally, so do you."

That was how it had begun, but that certainly wasn't the last of it. Every day, Lancelot sought me out once the boys were safely in Elaine's care. Arthur and Morgan, who claimed she wanted to convert with her husband—I didn't believe that for a moment—were taking their catechism lessons at that time, so we had no fear of being caught, which often made us reckless. Once, he didn't even pull me into a room—he grabbed my hand as I came around the corner, pushed me up against the wall, and took me right there in the hallway.

We grew bolder as time wore on, and no one gave indication of suspecting our forbidden trysts. On Beltane, I found him waiting in my chambers after dinner. It wasn't long before we were intertwined on the bed, gasping as we searched each other's bodies. Forgetting myself, I cried out under his probing tongue.

Lancelot clasped a hand over my mouth. "I am flattered, but do you wish all of Camelot to know what we're up to?"

I felt my face, already pink from exertion, flush. "Many couples will do the same tonight. Perhaps I was not heard?"

But Lady Fortuna was not with us. Not long after, Arthur called my name from the other side of the door. "Guinevere, are you unwell?"

Damn. Of all the people to be nearby. Admonishing Lancelot to hide, I hastened to don my tunic.

Bracing myself for what may come, I opened the door and placed a hand on my middle back. I prayed my moan could have been mistaken for pain. "There is no need to worry. I simply wrenched my back."

Arthur grimaced in sympathy. "Do you need any help?"

I shook my head. "I will manage. Thank you."

"At least allow me to massage your back."

Seeing no way around it, I opened the door farther so he could pass through, and I scanned the room. Lancelot was nowhere in sight.

"Where does it pain you?" Arthur asked once I was facedown on the bed.

I indicated a muscle below my right shoulder blade that had a history of giving me trouble.

"Ah, that one again." He kneaded my back with long, soothing motions.

It wasn't long before I realized he had intentions beyond relieving my sore muscle. His breathing grew ragged, his arousal evident.

I could not do this with the possibility of Lancelot somewhere in the same room. Carefully, I turned onto my side. "Arthur, I do not think that is wise. What if we make the muscle worse?"

"A bit of loosening up may be just what you need." He kissed my neck, trailing his tongue across my shoulders.

I pretended to give in, trying desperately to think of ways to resist without offending him.

There was a knock at the door.

"Go away," Arthur muttered but went to answer it anyway.

It was Lancelot. He must have escaped out the window or crept out while Arthur's attention was on me. "My lord, I am sorry to call on you at this late hour, but you were seen entering this room, and Morgan is looking for you."

"Can't it wait?" Arthur asked through gritted teeth.

"I think not."

Arthur paused, and I sensed him soften. *Thank the gods. Tonight was one night I wanted you to choose Morgan over me.*

"Of course." Arthur gestured to me over his shoulder. "The queen has injured her back. See she wants for nothing."

Lancelot bit back a smile, bowed to Arthur, and stepped into the room.

"How did you escape?" I asked, incredulous, as soon as the door was closed again.

He grinned and nodded toward the window. "Magic. Now, where were we?"

CHAPTER TWENTY

Summer 507

pleasant breeze blew in off the bay as we sat in Camelot's council chambers. Gawain and Peredur were debating how best to use the Combrogi's skill in peacetime. Peredur was arguing that since each kingdom was represented on the council by a lord and a knight, they should establish a school to train future members who may not be able to afford to travel to Camelot to serve Arthur directly. Gawain, on the other hand, felt their skills would be best used as a traveling band of soldiers policing the countryside in cooperation with the local kings and lords.

"We have here two intriguing yet contrasting proposals. What say the rest of you?" Arthur inquired of the group.

"If we bring Peredur's vision to life, I would like to travel to each school to ensure they have adequate horsemen to train the cavalry steeds as well as inspect their methods," Lancelot requested.

"What about women?" Constantine jested. "We already have one here. Why not recruit more?"

Sobian faced him down, picking at her fingernails with her dagger. "Afraid I have bigger berries than you? Oh wait, I saw yours just last week." She made a clucking sound with her tongue. "I'm afraid my twig is longer too."

"Enough," Arthur called. "Gawain, I am intrigued by the potential of your plan to keep the Combrogi going through future generations. But it comes at a large financial cost. How would you recommend paying for it? Am I to ask the kings of each territory to shoulder the burden, which means raising taxes, or do you have another source of funding in mind?"

"We amassed considerable fortune from the Saxons—" Gawain began.

But I didn't hear the rest of what he said for in the courtyard below, a ruckus was brewing. I stood and went over to the window, straining to see what interruption awaited us.

"Make way," a young deacon called. "This man of God is here to see the king."

Around them, the crowd of people parted, a few dropping to their knees and crossing themselves as a priest blessed them.

"It is so good to see how the true faith has spread," the priest mused loudly.

I shivered. I knew that voice. Father Marius had returned at long last from his sojourn in Rome. This could mean only one thing—trouble was sure to follow.

I slipped silently around to Arthur's side and whispered, "We have visitors."

Arthur cocked an eyebrow.

"Father Marius has returned. He and his followers are asking after you."

Arthur nodded almost imperceptibly, never taking his eyes from Gawain. "You make a valid point, Gawain," he said as though I hadn't spoken.

A few moments later the priest in question made his entrance. All discussion ceased immediately, and half the room got to its feet, some with weapons drawn to defend us against whoever threatened our peace.

"My king, I am so pleased to hear about your conversion," Father Marius said by way of greeting. "The Bishop of Rome sends his blessings." He extended his arms as though he would embrace Arthur.

"Father Marius," Arthur acknowledged coolly.

"Bishop," he corrected. "His Holiness saw fit to elevate this humble servant of God." He held out his hand as though he expected Arthur to show deference.

To his credit, Arthur didn't move.

At least that explained why I hadn't immediately recognized Marius. Gone was the shoulder-length golden hair shaved in the Celtic style. Instead he wore his hair short and cropped into a circular tonsure that left the top of his head completely bald. He also wore a short hooded mantle over his signature crimson robes.

"Bishop Marius," Arthur amended, "I thank you for your kind words. I will gladly speak with you later, once our meeting has adjourned. Will you and your"—he looked the deacon up and down, unsure what to make of him—"boy take some refreshments until then? Kay, will you please escort our guests to the audience chamber and see they are comfortable?"

Kay obeyed, trying his best to usher the two men out of the room, but Marius would not be swayed. "My lord, I mean no disrespect, but I think it fitting that I stay."

His appearance may have changed, but his personality certainly had not.

Arthur pressed his lips together and took a deep breath before answering, fighting to keep calm in front of his men. "And why is that?"

Bishop Marius was itching to take a seat. "I bring news from across the Continent that may well influence your decision-making."

Constantine spoke up. "We have had a long day and are no closer to reaching a decision, my lord. Perhaps we should break for a while so you can speak with your guests. We can resume tonight after the evening meal if you are in a hurry to decide."

I wanted to hit him for speaking up. The last thing I wanted was a private audience with this hateful man who had apparently only prospered as the years passed.

"You are a wise man. We shall all meet back here after we have supped. You may go," Arthur dismissed the group.

Kay and Lancelot lingered behind in their role as our protectors, but once the rest of the Combrogi dispersed, we gathered in the small antechamber off the round meeting room. At an order from Arthur, servants set out goblets of wine and the platters of breads and cheese intended for the Combrogi. Bishop Marius seated himself with royal flair on a stool near the window, a location which guaranteed all eyes would be on him. Arthur and I stood around him, uncertain how to proceed.

Arthur was not afraid to speak first. "Please tell me, Father—or what should I call you now?"

"'Your Excellency' is the proper term, but as we are no strangers, you may call me Bishop Marius if you like," he answered with a smug smile while his deacon hurried like a frightened slave to pour him some wine.

"Your Excellency, what news is so important that you saw fit to interrupt an official gathering of the council?" The slight twitch in Arthur's jaw as he ground his teeth did not escape my notice.

"Must we rush our time together?" Bishop Marius said languidly, picking up the goblet and swirling it in lazy circles. "I have not even been introduced to this lad"—he indicated Lancelot—"or had a chance to greet your lovely wife." His voice was as sweet as nectar, but the way he narrowed his eyes at me left no illusions that his views on me had softened over time.

"I would say it is wonderful to see you, Your Excellency, but it is a sin to lie to a priest, is it not?"

Arthur shot me a look that would have chided me to tears had I been a child. But I was not, and I had not forgotten that this man was the main reason why I had been torn away from the love of my life and kicked out of my father's house, something for which I would never forgive him.

Father Marius clucked his tongue. "Such temper, my queen. Do you remember what happened when last you loosed your wicked tongue on me?"

"Do you remember what you said when last we met?" I countered. "You said I was cursed and compared me to Lilith, the mother of all demons, if I remember correctly."

"You exaggerate, my dear." He looked at Arthur. "I was merely trying to explain a possible reason she had not yet borne you an heir."

Arthur wasn't buying his story. "You forget, Your Excellency, that I know what transpired between you and my wife before we met."

"Are you certain? Who is to say she is telling you the truth?" Bishop Marius asked before he sipped his wine, his manner as blithe as though we were on a summer outing.

I opened my mouth to respond, but Arthur was faster. "I trust my wife."

"At least one of them," Marius said disapprovingly.

Arthur refused to acknowledge the dig. "Guinevere has given me a thousand reasons to believe every word she says. You, however, are relatively unknown to me and have yet to gain my trust. I do not care what rank or title you hold over me in the eyes of the Church. In this world, I am still high king, and you are my subject, so I suggest you remember that."

Marius appeared not to have heard Arthur's threat. He smiled. "Well then, perhaps now is the time to begin earning your trust. That news I mentioned? I thought you would be interested to know that Clovis of the Franks is winning his war against the Visigoths in southern Gaul."

"What has this to do with us?" I asked.

"Patience, my queen. Clovis won the support of the Gallo-Romanic aristocracy by virtue of his choice to embrace the Christian faith. It is their money funding his war and their men who are sacrificing their lives to rid the Continent of the savage unbelievers."

Arthur was watching Marius with keen interest. "So you are saying my new faith could have political advantages as well?"

Marius took another swig of wine. "Certainly. The Romans and the Franks—Clovis's group at least—now consider you a strategic ally, provided of course you don't make any bold moves against them. I am willing to bet you have quite a few Gallic supporters as well, although they tend to be a quieter lot."

I wrinkled my brow. "You are a man of God, so how are you getting your intelligence?" I was trying to ascertain if his words were all lies to gain favor in Arthur's eyes or if his information was genuine.

He smiled, apparently guessing my motive. "During my time in Rome, I met many dignitaries. As a result, I now have friends in monasteries and palaces from Byzantium to Gaul. You could do worse than to have someone in my position at your side."

"I already have a strategic advisor, Bishop Marius. I have no need for another," Arthur said, but I could see he was chewing on the idea that damned priest had just fed him. "And I do not seek to usurp him. I am simply giving you the benefit of what I know. My greatest concern is and always will be in spiritual matters."

"I already have a spiritual advisor as well."

"Oh, that is right. I have heard of this young priest. What is his name?" The bishop feigned ignorance.

"Father Dafydd," I supplied.

Marius snapped his fingers. "Yes! His reputation has reached even the ears of Rome." He turned to his deacon. "Timothy, would you be so kind as to fetch Father Dafydd? I would like to meet him and express my gratitude for all he has done."

I stopped listening as Marius and my husband debated some matter of the Christian faith, something about a heretic called Pelagius and whether or not perfection was possible without grace from their god. They held opposing views, which each expressed passionately. They were giving me a headache.

I was grateful when Timothy returned with Father Dafydd in

his wake.

Arthur greeted Dafydd with a warm smile and a manly embrace. Then he turned to the bishop. "Bishop Marius, may I present to you Father Dafydd of Dyfed, personal confessor to myself and certain members of my court. His humble example is much of what attracted me to Christianity."

Father Dafydd bowed, eyes wide and cheeks flushed, as though astonished to have someone of Marius's rank in his presence.

Marius bid him to rise. "Word of your excellent care of our king reached me even in Rome. I wish to thank you for carefully shepherding him into the fold."

Father Dafydd looked down humbly. "I only answered his questions and guided him as he sought me out. The rest was the work of God."

"Ah, but it has found a willing instrument in you."

"You are too kind."

"Not at all. In fact, I must confess I have an ulterior motive for calling you here. His Holiness has expressed a deep desire to see this land converted." Bishop Marius looked at me pointedly before returning his attention to Father Dafydd. "You did so well with our king that he wishes to see your work continue in other parts of the isle."

"But who will fill my role with the king, Lady Morgan, and Lady Elaine?"

"I am sure we will find someone."

Someone like you?

"Wait." Arthur put out a hand to halt the conversation. "You cannot simply replace Father Dafydd. If I wish him to remain, he will do so."

"I'm afraid he can. He is my superior, and I am answerable first to him," Father Dafydd said.

Arthur spluttered, unused to anyone contradicting his will.

"Where will you send me?" Father Dafydd asked with more calm than I felt.

I narrowed my eyes at the bishop. Something wasn't right with this situation. Marius did nothing without personal gain, so wherever he was assigning our beloved priest would surely benefit him. I hoped he was sincere in his compliments and the younger priest would be rewarded accordingly, but past experience encouraged doubt to gnaw at my stomach. No doubt Bishop Marius was also aware Father Dafydd had not insisted I convert along with my husband and was, therefore, a failure in his eyes.

Bishop Marius stroked his chin where the shadow of whiskers had begun to appear with the advancing day. "I was thinking you would be perfect to preach to the Highlanders."

My mouth fell open. The Highlanders were notorious for their intolerance for missionaries. Sending Father Dafydd into their lands was akin to a death sentence. "Not even you could be so cruel!"

"Cruel? No, I am giving this man the greatest opportunity a Christian can have—the chance to preach to a pagan people. If he can successfully convert them, it will cement his place in history, like our revered Patrick. If not and he loses his life in the process, he will achieve the crown of martyrdom, which is the ultimate goal of all Christian souls. There is no greater sacrifice than to lay down one's life for one's faith."

"Nothing we can say will change your mind, will it?" I said, finally understanding the strategy of Marius's visit. He meant to take over as Arthur's advisor. The man was brilliant—evil but brilliant.

"I am afraid not."

Father Dafydd bowed his head humbly. "When do I depart, Your Excellency?"

"I think it best for the transition to happen quickly. You will have tomorrow to say your good-byes."

I looked at Father Dafydd, unable to believe this kind man would soon be gone forever, likely to be replaced by Bishop Marius. Tears filled my eyes, and I blinked them back, determined not to let that vile man see how deeply he had affected me.

"Would that all men had your grace, your tolerance, and your fortitude," I said to Father Dafydd quietly as I escorted him from the room.

"But if they did, there would be no need for people like you and me," he answered with a soft smile. "Every wife has a duty to guide her husband to the side of right. I am afraid you are doubly pressed in this regard as a priestess and as a queen living amid religious turmoil. Promise me one thing."

"Anything."

"Do not allow Bishop Marius to gain control of the king. Remember that you are as powerful as he, and do not let him intimidate either of you. I must listen to him, but you are under no such obligation."

I nodded. "I swear I will do everything in my power to do as you have asked." I paused, trying to decide whether or not to ask the question weighing on my mind. "Are you frightened of your new assignment?"

Father Dafydd smiled once more, lit from within. "'The Lord is my shepherd, and so I shall not fear.' When I became a priest, I made a vow to do whatever God willed of me, just as you did when you became a priestess. We may not always like what they say to us, but we must follow where they lead." He placed a hand on my shoulder. "May your gods bless you and give you strength."

I bowed my head to hide the tears seeping from my eyes. "The same to you."

He squeezed my hand once and disappeared around the corner.

I never saw him again.

<h1 style="text-align:center">CHAPTER TWENTY-ONE</h1>

Spring 514

rthur shook me awake. "Guinevere!"

"What?" I mumbled, refusing to open my eyes or shift from my comfortable position.

"I have had the most incredible dream! Wake up! I must tell you about it."

"Go tell Morgan about it. She's your favorite wife, is she not?" I grumbled.

"You don't understand. Please, just listen."

Arthur's voice was so animated I couldn't ignore it, as much as I wanted to. I rolled onto my back and opened my eyes. It was still dark, probably a few hours before dawn. The room around us was quiet save for Arthur's ragged breathing. I said a silent prayer of gratitude, invoking the goddess Arianrhod, who watched over all couples engaged in lusty affairs, that this was one of the rare nights Lancelot wasn't with me.

I turned toward Arthur. His eyes were more alive than I'd seen them in ages, sparkling in the moonlight like faceted jewels. I couldn't resist teasing him. "What? Did you dream that Marius allowed you to keep us both?"

If he heard me, he didn't react. "I have seen her, Guinevere!"

"Who?" I propped my head on one arm so I could regard him closely.

"The Blessed Virgin. She came to me in a dream." His eyes unfocused as he recalled the vision he had seen. "She wishes me to undertake a quest."

I wrinkled my forehead, suspicious of his dream. "What kind of quest?"

Arthur drew me upright, palms on both of my shoulders, and looked me straight in the eye. "She wishes me to find the Holy Grail, the cup which touched the holy lips of Jesus Christ and held His

Precious Blood." Arthur's whole expression was alight with fervor. "This is why I came to you first. You, too, have dreamed of it."

I tried to keep my face neutral, though I had little doubt Arthur's fertile imagination had something to do with this. He had spent too much time with Bishop Marius lately, who, with Merlin and Father Dafydd gone, had become his advisor in all things. "Arthur, slow down. Tell me exactly what you dreamed."

His eyes took on that dreamy expression again. "The Virgin Mary appeared to me. She was dressed all in blue, like the robes I've seen you wear. Her long brown hair was loose and uncovered, spilling over her shoulders, and she was suffused with light. It should have blinded me, but it did not. Behind her, the world was split in two, ringed in a circle, onto which her crucified Son was bound. In the top half of the circle, there was happiness and light. Camelot prospered, and the land was fertile. She touched the circle, and it spun so that Our Lord was crushed beneath it. There below, storm clouds raged and lightning flashed. Sickness, death, and decay were everywhere. Camelot lay in ruins at the hands of our enemies."

I recognized the image Arthur described. She was not the Virgin Mary but the goddess Fortuna with her wheel of fate. She directed all things, positive and negative, and her whims determined whether we prospered or fell to ruin. But now was not the time to contradict him. "Go on."

"The Blessed Mother held out a cup—at least I think it was a cup. It could have been a bowl or cauldron too. The light coming from it was so bright it was difficult to gaze upon it for too long or look directly at it. Above the cup was a shining white host, the symbol of our Lord here on earth."

Host or full moon? The Grail—holy to Christians and Druids alike—was, for my faith, the repository of all inspiration as well as the tool the goddess Ceridwen used to bestow rebirth upon those destined to live again. Its shifting appearance was no surprise to me for, as Arthur accurately recalled, I had seen it in my dreams since I was a child. Once it was a golden chalice. Then a drinking horn. The next time an iron or bronze cauldron. Once, it was even a stone. We could argue all day over the identity of the woman, but one thing was for certain—Arthur had indeed seen the Grail.

"Did the woman say anything to you?"

He nodded. "Once I had taken in the scene, she regarded me

placidly and said, 'My son, you have served me well, but now I have a greater request of you. You are to seek out this holy object, not for yourself or for a select few but for all. It is a gift for all my people and a sign of my heavenly blessing. With it, you shall know peace and everlasting contentment. But take care not to betray the promises you have made to me, for doing so will cause this gift to vanish and your reign of peace to come to an end.' Then she held the cup to my lips, and I drank of it. It was at once the sweetest and most bitter liquid I have ever tasted. It was as though blood and starlight had combined."

I knew the taste well. Once imbibed, it could never be forgotten. The night in Avalon when I found out about Mona's dreams and Morgan's lack of lineage, I had dreamed I drank from the Grail. The shock of bitterness awoke me, and from that moment on, my life changed. I wondered if the same would now be true for Arthur.

"When she drew the cup away, I felt an acute sense of loss, like some vital part of me went with it. I knew in my heart I would not be at peace until the Grail is found. She left me with these parting words, 'Go now, son of the high dragon, and do as I have commanded. I am with you always.'

Arthur grasped my shoulders, his blazing blue eyes locked on mine. "Do you see, Guinevere? This is my destiny. All the battles and trials that have come before, even my conversion, were preparation to make me ready for this heavenly quest. Turning away the Saxons may have been the first step on the road to peace, but finding the Grail will cement it for all time. My legacy to this land, our legacy to this land, is to retrieve the Grail and preserve the peace in Camelot forever." He fell silent then, most likely contemplating his dream once again.

I blinked, trying to comprehend this sudden obsession that had overtaken my husband. Was he drunk or ill? He had been sober when I retired for the night, and it was not like him to drink once supper was ended unless there was a great feast. I felt his forehead. Though his cheeks were rosy with excitement, he showed no signs of fever. Maybe he was in his right mind. If Fortuna had truly come to him, I was not one to stand in her way.

"Grainne recently returned from Avalon with rumors that the Grail Maidens have abandoned their post beneath the Tor and moved their holy treasure somewhere in our land. I didn't think anything of it when she told me because Avalon is full of such whisperings, born of moon madness or too many nights of fasting, but what you say confirms her report."

He embraced me. "You believe me?"

"I cannot confirm if it is your destiny, but yes, I believe you are under divine orders to find the Grail." I was so grateful he had come to me first rather than Morgan or that damned bishop, either of whom might have manipulated his experience to suit their own needs.

Arthur kissed me deeply. "Then you will support me as I raise the quest?"

I shifted my position so I was sitting in his lap, legs wrapped around him. "I will do you one better—I will help you. We ride together, side by side, just as we swore to one another we would be in all things."

⁂

Arthur sent for the Combrogi before dawn colored the eastern sky, and soon Camelot was abuzz with rumors of the unprecedented voyage to come. The kitchens were set to full staff to prepare rations for the men. Only the stables, forges, and armory buzzed with more activity as horses were shod and groomed and men prepared for unknown battles by mending shields and armor and sharpening blades. I spent most of my time in the armory, directing the flow of weapons and men, while Lancelot held sway in the stables. As my champion, he normally would not have left my side, but Arthur had agreed to allow him to join them on the quest since he was the most widely traveled and might be of assistance.

Mordred, newly returned from his five-year fostership with Lot, had been asking every day for the last week to accompany his father, little dismayed even though Arthur always forbade it. Mordred was not quite seventeen, the age at which he would qualify, but I doubted Arthur would have let him go—and put his only heir in danger—at any age.

Morgan, Grainne, and I were preparing poultices, draughts, and other herbal remedies the men may need on their quest when Arthur burst in.

He grabbed my hands. "The Combrogi are nearly all here. I need to know where to begin looking. My dream told me nothing. The

Grail could be in the north country or Brittany or just around the bend for all I know."

I looked at him, wondering what he wanted from me, as I kept one eye on the bubbling brownish-green concoction simmering at my side.

Arthur huffed, impatience rising along with the color in his face. "You have the sight. Isn't there anything you can tell me?"

I snorted, slightly offended. "Arthur, I'm not your personal oracle. Besides, I cannot foretell the future. I can only see what is happening at this very moment. If you want the future, ask your other wife."

Morgan looked up then. "What does he want?"

I regarded her over my shoulder. "For us to tell him where to find the Grail."

Morgan went back to the herbs she was grinding with her pestle. "I'd suggest starting in Avalon."

Arthur threw up his hands and stomped out of the room, muttering something about women being no help. Morgan and I laughed in a rare moment of camaraderie that reminded me of our better days in Avalon.

"You know," Grainne said, "I think there is something we can do to help the Combrogi."

I strained the simmering liquid into a vial and set it on a shelf to cool. "What is that?"

"Tomorrow is the time of equal day and night. If the three of us join forces, I am willing to bet the gods will enlighten us. Our gifts may be different, but if this truly is Fortuna's command, she cannot ignore our invocations."

"Yes," Morgan said. "I like this idea very much."

I stared at her, weighing Grainne's idea. "But you are Christian now. Isn't such a thing against your faith?"

"Normally, yes, but it is the Grail we seek, holy to both faiths. I'm sure God wouldn't mind me breaking one little rule in this special circumstance."

"Even so, we do not know the exact time of balance. We would need that information to tap into the magic of the day," I said.

Morgan's smile was sly. "Ah, but we know someone who can tell us."

"Who? Merlin is not here, and Marius is not versed in the stars," I noted.

"No, you witless woman. Your beloved, Aggrivane."

I glared at her, crossing my arms defensively. "He is not my lover."

"Not anymore, but that doesn't mean he cannot be of use."

I mulled over the options in my head, trying to decide how best to approach Aggrivane. We had barely spoken since I returned from Avalon years ago because his son had died from the fever he'd contracted just before Malegant kidnapped me. But on the other hand, when Aggrivane found out the nature of the mission Arthur was sending us on, he would be eager to help. Aggrivane had always dreamed of finding one of the thirteen holy hallows of Britain, and the Grail superseded them all. No doubt his Christian wife would urge him on even more.

"I will ask him. If you are right, then the Combrogi will leave as soon as Arthur tells them what we've found." I put down the wooden spoon I was using to stir a thick burgundy gooseberry paste. "Grainne, can you take over here? I must be sure to be packed before our ritual."

"You need not rush. You will not be going with them," said Morgan as I removed the apron covering my tunic.

My head snapped up. "How do you know?"

She tapped the center of her forehead, indicating she'd seen it with second sight. "Trust me."

Her laughter trailed behind me as I ran into the night, intent on finding Aggrivane.

⚬⚭⚬ ⚭⚬⚭

The appointed day and hour had come.

Thin shafts of sunlight occasionally pierced through the low, milky clouds as we picked our way through the moss-covered rocks where the earth met the sea far below Camelot. Only a few hours before, high tide had submerged this whole area in shoulder-deep saltwater all the way to the base of the cliff on which the fortress rested. But now it had retreated, leaving behind gleaming tide pools in the pockmarked stone. Waves still lapped at the outer banks, so we stayed farther inland, but we ventured out far enough that the hiss and gurgle of the surf could be easily heard.

"Here," Grainne called our small party to a halt. "This is the place."

We sat on the soft moss in a loose semicircle, three small pools between us. We joined hands, eyes closed and breathing deeply to attune ourselves to the energy around us. That was more difficult than it seemed in this place of shifting sea and land, both grasping and conceding power with each roll of the waves. Add to that the warring of day and night in the sky above us, and it took us some time to find the place of calm deep within where all acts of magic have their origin.

"Lady Danu, Lord Lir, rulers of this sacred place, we do you homage. We come in peace to implore your aid. The Lady Fortuna has commanded our king to seek the hallowed Grail, one of the treasures of Avalon. In this time of equilibrium, we ask you to help us, your priestesses, as we seek the location of this sacred vessel so that he may fulfill her holy will."

The wind rose in response, whispering in its secret tongue, lifting the sleeves and collars of our blue robes. Along with the sweep of the water and the cries of the gulls, the wind lulled me into a trance. Everything went silent as though the entire world had ceased to exist. For a few splendid moments, all the elements, night and day, summer and winter, were in balance.

Morgan, Grainne, and I blinked at each other in wonder.

When a ray of light spilled its glimmering liquid gold onto the pool in front of me, I knew it was time. Squeezing my sisters' hands, I leaned forward to gaze into the water. A starfish clung to one side, scarcely noticing a small crab scuttling over him to reach the safety of shore. Rings of green algae floated on the surface, and if I stared past them, the stones and shells at the base of the pool became visible.

But then a white-gray mist clouded the surface, and I lost all sense of the mortal world. I was flying on the brown and white wings of an osprey, viewing a far-off landscape through its masked eyes. Below, a procession of women wound through a narrow valley between two dense thickets of wood, following a thin ribbon of silver water as it sought the faraway sea.

Their blue crescents marked them as priestesses, and their silver-gray robes and belts of dangling silver charms singled them out as keepers of the Grail. They chanted as they walked, eyes closed, feet effortlessly skirting rocks, fallen branches, and even the delicate buds of lavender snow flowers.

At the head of the nine women, one carried a thurible of glass and copper that glowed as if with its own light, providing amber illumination and scenting the air with a heady smoke through holes in its spiraling metal finial. Behind her followed two women acting as guards, each carrying a fearsome silver sickle. Next came my childhood friend, Rowena, her long dark hair caught in twin braids that bounced as she walked. She carried a tall silver amphora that I instinctively understood contained waters from the red-and-white spring. Two more guards came after her, then a veiled woman swathed in golden robes. She could be none other than the Grail Maiden. Her sacred charge also was veiled, so I could not see what form the Grail took within her hands. Another pair of guards brought up the rear.

Magic radiated from them like a shield, preventing me from drawing too near. I cried out, hoping to catch Rowena's attention, but she paid me no heed. They were following a voice only they could hear and gave no indication of their destination.

Frustrated, I soared high, trying to use my avian senses to tell me where we might be and in what direction they were headed. The air currents were a tailwind pushing me along. This time of year, they usually came from the south and east. The women were walking against the flow of the river, so that must mean they were traveling north.

But to where? Banking upward again, I scanned the horizon for some familiar landmark. After following them for what felt like hours, I saw it—a wide circle of tall thin monoliths surrounded by a white chalk ditch. Inside the large circle were two smaller ones. That had to be the ancient Sanctuary of the Stars. I expected them to head toward it and camp there, but they passed it by.

By then, I was losing my connection with the bird, slowly regaining my human consciousness. I had learned all I was going to know. I opened my eyes to find Morgan and Grainne blinking at me as if they too had just awoken from a dream.

We thanked the God and Goddess in turn but did not share our experiences. Those were for Arthur alone to know.

"Shall we tell him?" Morgan asked.

Grainne and I nodded. "Let's go then."

❧❧ ❧❧

We found Arthur assembled with the Combrogi in the meeting chamber. He was standing atop the table to be better heard over the clamoring crowd. He must have just told them what the quest was to be for they were cheering and whistling, pagan and Christian alike, as we wound through the throng to his side. Lancelot helped me climb onto the table, where I came face to face with a beaming Bishop Marius.

Not one to lose the opportunity to pontificate in front of a crowd, Bishop Marius held out his arms as though welcoming the adulation of the crowd until they finally quieted. "My brothers and sisters, we have been blessed by God to not only have a Christian couple to lead our land"—he nodded at Arthur and Morgan, ignoring me completely—"but now our king has been favored by heaven to be the instrument of the greatest miracle of our age. As you embark upon this perilous journey, I beg you to consider the well-being of your souls and shrive yourself of any sins before you depart. Only in that way will any and all of you be worthy to behold such a sight as the Holy Grail. Were it in my power, I would accompany you myself. But as my duties keep me here, go forth with my blessing and that of the Father, Son,"—he made the sign of the cross over the gathered soldiers—"and Holy Ghost."

Some of the men crossed themselves while others made the sign of Avalon and a few stared awkwardly at the ground.

"Thank you, bishop. We go with joy in our hearts knowing we have your benediction," Arthur said to Marius with a pleased smile. He turned back to the assembly. "Some of you may have noticed I have yet to mention where we are going. That is because I do not know myself. But I have asked three of our strongest seeresses for their guidance—"

"I must strenuously object," Marius interrupted. "It is highly improper to consult pagan oracles when you have been entrusted with a Christian mission."

"Jealous they have knowledge you do not?" came a female voice from deep within the crowd. It was one of Sobian's girls.

"Yes," someone else agreed. "Let them speak."

Morgan and Grainne looked at me hesitantly before joining us atop the table.

I cleared my throat. "Know that what we see is not writ in stone but shifts with the actions of men. The most we can do is advise you as best we know."

"See?" Marius yelled. "Even they admit their information is fickle at best."

I ignored him. "The Grail has indeed left Avalon. I have seen its procession. Earlier today, they passed the Sanctuary of the Stars on the great chalk plain. Head south, and you shall meet them. But beware. They are heavily armed, so if you desire the Grail for yourself or have any ill intent, better you stay behind than face their blades."

"Indeed," Grainne continued, "not all who undertake this journey will return. For some of you, this will be your final task—I have seen your souls march to the Otherworld. But fear not, for all who set out do so under the aegis of the Goddess."

Morgan stepped forward. "Of you, only three shall find the vessel. One will prove unworthy and return before glimpsing its glory. But when it is brought to Camelot, all those honored by the great King Arthur shall behold it. So have I seen, and so shall it be."

The crowd was silent, stunned as though the threefold Goddess had appeared before them and spoken words of prophecy. Even Marius was speechless, contemplating the implications of our words.

Arthur was the first to find his voice. "Choose your groups and your destinations. Stay out of Saxon lands for we do not wish to start a war on this mission of peace. Eat, drink, and say your farewells for we leave at dawn."

Once the four of us climbed off the table, everyone began talking at once, making it nearly impossible to hear any one person, but Morgan's voice still found me. "Arthur, be careful. Not just for my sake but for your son's."

"Mordred is nearly a man. He will be fine."

Morgan rubbed her belly. "Not Mordred. Your new son." Her smile was more luminous than I'd ever seen it.

"You are with child?"

"I am. You will have another heir by midwinter. Hurry home." She kissed Arthur softly.

Arthur hugged her tightly. "This is the best possible news you could have sent me off with. I will return with the Grail for our son—or daughter."

"Benedictio Dei," Marius blessed them with a joyful grin. He apparently approved of this second marriage even more now that it had been graced with new life.

Arthur caught sight of me, and his expression changed. He was unable to hide the flash of pity that came before his joy transformed into sobriety. Anger, hurt, and jealousy warred within me. After all this time, he still felt pity for me. I had finally accepted I would never bear him another child, but now Morgan was going to publicly prove once and for all that it was I who was barren, not Arthur.

"This changes everything," Arthur said.

I took a deep breath, willing myself to be calm and collected before answering. "Indeed it does. A baby will turn the whole castle upside down." I forced a smile.

Arthur's face clouded over. "No, I mean you cannot accompany me on the quest. Morgan will need a midwife. You must stay here and look after her."

"No." I would not let Morgan take away yet another opportunity. "Grainne is just as qualified as I am. That is no cause for concern." Every muscle in my body tensed as I fought for control over myself, my voice growing more strained.

Arthur took my hand and patted it. I was sure he meant the gesture to be comforting, but in my current mood, it was patronizing.

"I know Grainne is your friend, but after how badly your childbirth ended, I cannot trust her with the life of Morgan and my child. Plus, someone must see to Camelot while I am away. You are my queen—only you"—he looked me deep in the eyes to ensure I understood his double meaning—"have the authority to pass judgment in my absence. You are the only one I trust with this power."

I nodded, understanding what he was trying to convey. Morgan may have been his royal wife and mother to his child—soon to be children—but I was queen. That was something Morgan could never take away from me.

"Camelot will be safe in my keeping. This do I swear to you. Return to me hale and whole, husband." I kissed him then looked at Morgan, who was reveling in the well wishes of those who had heard her announcement. "For you have more to live for than ever before."

CHAPTER TWENTY-TWO

Summer 514

Arthur wrote to Morgan and me as often as he could, keeping us abreast of their progress and obstacles in finding the Grail. By the time they reached the Sanctuary of the Stars, the Grail maidens had long since moved on, and they were having trouble tracking their movements.

Arthur wrote, *"Despite the setbacks we encounter, I have great faith that the Holy Ghost will direct us to the Grail in the end. As each moment of our lives has led us to this point, each step we take brings us closer to our destined prize. Its acquisition will assure Camelot's safety and prosperity as well as fix our legacy in the annals of time. Have no fear for me, for my passion for this great quest does not wane with time but rather grows as I see signs of God's divine hand all around us. I beg you to keep me, the Combrogi, and this divine mission in your prayers. I send my love to both of you and to my son."*

When I read the letter aloud to Morgan and Mordred, he grumbled, "As his son, I should be by his side, not here with the women."

But as much as he complained, Mordred was making good use of his time stuck in Camelot. He'd proclaimed himself Lord of Camelot in his father's absence and my champion while Lancelot was away. He more than proved himself worthy of the jobs, displaying a subtle cunning he could have learned only from Lot and—despite his age and general attitude of superiority—a wisdom no doubt born of Ana's influence.

Elaine was as taken with his progress as though he were her own son, which I supposed was only natural given that Galahad was off with Arthur and his men. Now that the boys were too old for her art lessons, she clung to me like spider silk, and her constant vacillations in mood grated on my nerves. Between Morgan's gloating over her advancing pregnancy and Elaine's ever-shifting joy at her son's good fortune and despair that he would never return, I was surrounded by madwomen. I was liable to lock Elaine in the dungeon if I couldn't find something useful for her to do.

One sticky summer afternoon when the clouds hung low in the sky, teasing us with the prospect of a storm, the Irish emissary and I were discussing the finer points of a new treaty with King Illan mac Dúnlainge of Leinster. I was trying to convince him that a proposal of marriage between Mordred and his lord's daughter was only one option to securing peace in our lands when one of Arthur's scouts was announced.

"Forgive me," I said to the emissary, who, to my great annoyance, appeared relieved to be given leave of my argument. "Send him in."

The scout was still breathing hard when he sank to one knee before me. "My lady, I come in advance of a party in need of your help. Lancelot and several others were most grievously wounded in Rheged battling a man who called himself the Grail Sentinel. I beg you make ready for their party."

My hand flew to my mouth. For a moment, I could not speak. Fear coursed through me, panic riding in its wake. Lancelot, the man who had saved me countless times, the one whom I considered invincible, was wounded, and badly enough to be transported here. What of Arthur? Had they been together? My knees shook. But then, just as quickly, my experience on the fields of battle and my training as a priestess overrode my emotions.

"The king? How many injured? What is the extent of their wounds?" I found myself asking when all I wanted to do was collapse and cry.

"The king is well, I assure you. He is off in another land, following a lead in pursuit of the holy relic. Eight wounded in all. Most are in need of stitches and bone-setting, but I fear Lancelot suffered the worst. He took a blade in the side, and we cannot fully staunch the bleeding."

"How much time before they arrive?"

The scout thought for a moment. "A day at most."

"Thank you for giving us time to prepare." I asked for Mordred to be sent to me. Once he arrived, I said, "See that our guest is well attended. Also, please find your mother. I have need of her assistance." I nearly choked on the last sentence.

Mordred's face lit up at his new responsibility. "Yes, my lady." He turned to the scout. "Come, sir. Follow me."

I found Elaine in the chapel, on her knees. "Elaine, raise your prayers to God as you work. We must prepare the barracks to receive a number of wounded."

By nightfall, we had converted the barracks into an infirmary, just in time for the soldiers to arrive. Morgan set up a station for mixing herbs and dressing wounds while Elaine ensured supplies were at the ready and water was boiling in the cauldron over the fire. Grainne and I prepared a room in the castle, which was warmer and drier, for those requiring our constant attention.

The carts pulled into the gates of Camelot in the small hours of night, desperate shouts and whinnying of horses breaking the silence of the slumbering castle. Mordred stumbled from the entrance hall and began seeing to the horses without being asked, relieving the men to carry the wounded into the barracks.

The cart bearing Lancelot was in the middle of the pack. Before I even saw his face, I knew he was near to dying. His clothes and the sacks beneath him were pools of black, and even from a distance, the stench of infection made bile rise in my throat. Next to him in the cart were the spoils of his hard-won victory—the armor and head of the knight he had killed.

I wrinkled my nose at the rotting head and told the nearest guard, "Spike that up with the others and take his mail to the armory to see what we can learn from its construction. You two"—I gestured to Gareth and Owain, his guards on the journey here—"get him into the castle. Morgan will show you where to go."

I watched them go, conflicted about whether to attend to him immediately or assess the others first.

"Go, be with him," Grainne said as if reading my thoughts, as if she knew exactly what we were to each other. She squeezed my arm. "You and Morgan are his best hope. I have Elaine to help with the others. Go." She shoved me gently toward the doors.

Morgan was already removing Lancelot's clothing when I arrived. I grabbed a rag and soaked in it hot water, then I applied it to an area around his wound where his clothing adhered to his skin.

"It's a wonder he has not died of blood loss," Morgan said.

Lancelot looked to have been beaten within an inch of his life. His eyes were swollen, painted with purple and black bruises. His lower lip was split and puffy, a long gash running from the left side up an inflamed cheekbone. As my eyes traveled lower, his injuries only worsened. His skin was pale and clammy, a sure sign of inflection if the stench from the wound between his ribs wasn't indication enough. One shoulder stuck out at an odd angle, and he appeared to have taken several crushing blows to the chest. But those would have to wait.

The cloth around his wound finally gave way, and we were able to see the full extent of the damage. The skin around it had already begun to fester, the sickly yellow-green bile the source of the stench. The men had done their best to pack the wound with moss and spider silk, and it was likely the reason why he was still alive now, but it was also the source of the infection.

"We're going to have to cut this skin away," Morgan said. "We need to cleanse the wound first though. Give him some poppy juice to ensure he feels nothing and does not wake."

While she doused his wound with vinegar, I forced Lancelot's mouth open and poured in a carefully measured dose of ruby syrup. Too little and he could stir, crazed with hallucinations. Too much and he might die.

"Be strong, my champion. For me. For the Goddess who raised you and the one who chose you as her own," I whispered in his ear.

We set about the gruesome task of cleaning and debriding the wound. I was thankful for my years of training in Avalon, and even what I had seen at Caledon Wood and Badon, for without it, I surely would not have made it through the surgery. Once we could see the wound clearly, we found the source of the bleeding.

"It looks like he received the bite of an axe. We will have to close it off with heat," Morgan said. "Take that poker out of the fire and bring it to me."

I looked at her uncertainly. I'd never heard of such a method except in conjunction with amputation, which was external, not internal.

"Do you wish him to live or no?" She snapped her fingers at me. "The Greeks did this with much success. I learned it from the healer of Uther's army, a Saracen woman. Have no fear."

She placed the glowing tip of the poker into Lancelot's wound. His flesh sizzled, giving off a smell not unlike meat over a spit. Morgan rinsed the wound once again—this time with boiled, cooled sea water—and inspected it.

"That should stop it." She handed the poker back to me and

motioned for a second one, which she placed on the external wound. With a puff of smoke and another sickening whiff of burning flesh, it closed. "If he was likely not to move this area, I would dress the wound as is, but given he will likely tear it open again, I think it best to reinforce it with stitches. Would you like to do the honors?"

I knelt at Lancelot's side and carefully sewed his wound. "Where did you learn all of this? It goes well beyond our training in Avalon."

"One does not spend years as a camp woman without learning a thing or two." Her smile was wry. "Or did you believe I spent all of my time whoring? Of course you did. A battleground where the injured are from multiple lands is the best school a healer could ever ask for, if not the toughest."

After I finished sewing and bandaging Lancelot's wound, we set his broken bones and cleansed his remaining wounds.

Muttering as she worked, Morgan gave vent to her innermost feelings about her profession. "I've told Arthur a thousand times to bring a priestess with him on every mission for we could save lives if they were tended earlier, but he does not listen."

Finally, we lifted the calfskin shades to let in fresh air and cleaned up the space so it resembled more a sick room than a surgery tent. I placed sweet-smelling herbs in vases and on hot coals and cool cloths on Lancelot's forehead and neck to bring his fever down.

"Do you remember how to make a healing beer?" Morgan asked me.

"Yes."

"When he is conscious and can tolerate water from the sacred springs, give him a thick beer of honey, mugwart, oats, and nettles. He will not like the taste, but he has lost a lot of blood, and it will do wonders to help him regain his strength. Then, and only then, allow him to try some bread. We don't need him suffering stomach ills on top of everything else."

I nodded, relieved to see her go. I began the process of brewing the ale, and once it could be left unattended, I sank to the floor next to Lancelot's unconscious form and prayed. My mind could scarcely form words, but I trusted that my patrons, Rhiannon and Lugh, as well as the Morrigan, patroness of those wounded in battle, and Brigid, the great healer, would know the cries of my heart without words.

Sometime in the midst of my prayers, I must have fallen asleep for I walked in the land between worlds with Lancelot, battling a giant dressed in black, the man whose cruel eyes had stared at me from Lancelot's side in the cart. I saw how hard Lancelot had fought and how he received every wound we'd tended, but what I did not know was why.

The knight had just sliced into Lancelot's side with a fierce-looking axe on a long pole when I awoke with a start to a soft rapping on the door. I grunted something that was supposed to resemble "enter," and Elaine peeked around the door. I sat up, motioning for her to come in.

She handed me a cup of wine, which I gratefully drained. "I thought you could use some relief. I have already slept a little. Morgan is abed, and Grainne is watching over those in the barracks. Get some sleep. I will stand vigil." Elaine's eyes misted over, and her face became wistful.

Her expression reminded me of her youthful crush on Lancelot and her fancy that he would become her husband. Oh, how our lives had taken paths we could never have foreseen.

I stood and kissed her cheek. "He is in the hands of his gods. We have done all we can."

Elaine smiled sadly and fingered the enameled ring on her left hand. "Indeed. I will pray for him."

I returned her joyless smile. "That is all we can do. If he wakes, please come find me. Oh!" I suddenly remembered the beginnings of the beer. I covered it tightly. "Be sure no one disturbs this."

Elaine nodded, sitting on a stool at Lancelot's side.

As I slipped out, Elaine took Lancelot's hand and kissed it. Silent tears rolled down her cheeks. Was it possible? Could Elaine still harbor feelings for Lancelot? Surely he could not be her mysterious husband—or could he? I shook my head. No, he certainly would not have engaged in an affair with me were that the case. Yet the memory of Elaine's grief lingered in my mind, as did the seed of doubt.

⚬⚬⚬

One week passed, then two. Lancelot did not improve. I began to fear he would never wake. My days were spent in constant vigil at his side, trading off with Morgan or Elaine only to sleep or perform necessary duties. By the time the full moon came around, we were all at our wits' end.

Morgan wanted to give him wolfsbane to try to draw his spirit back, but I was hesitant.

She wheeled on me when I expressed my concern. "So it was all right for Isolde to use the same drug on you when you were far less injured, but you take issue with me using it to save a dying man?"

I couldn't answer her because she was right in calling out my hypocrisy. But I couldn't let go of the story Merlin had told me about her poisoning Rowena so long ago in Avalon.

"How do you know you won't kill him?" I asked.

She glared at me. "You know I do not know. I am only doing as we were both trained. And as I have far more experience in these dire situations than you, I do not think you are in a place to judge."

I decided to lay my fears on the table. "What about Rowena? You made a mistake once, and she nearly died."

"You"—she pointed at me—"were not there. How dare you judge me based on what you did not see for yourself?" She shook her head. "Is that it? Are you afraid I will poison him on purpose? To what end? I have nothing to gain if Lancelot dies. He is Arthur's dearest friend. I would do nothing to hurt him. Why do you always insist on finding me guilty before even asking my side? I may not like you, but I am not out to destroy everyone I meet."

She was right. "What did happen that day?" I asked in a small voice.

Morgan gave a sarcastic laugh. "Twenty years on and now you wish to know." She turned away from me as she prepared the elixir. "I will tell you this—it was not I who added the offending herb to my brew but another who wished to take my place as second. I will not name her, as I have never found proof, but if I ever do, I will kill her with my bare hands in public for all to see. That is the real reason why I left Avalon. I could not remain there knowing there was one willing to kill to take my place."

She gave Lancelot the wolfsbane, and we continued our cycle of vigil, tending wounds, and sleep.

A few days later, as I was trudging back from a particularly difficult pleading day, during which I'd lost my patience with the petitioners more than once, Owain and I crossed paths.

"You look like death visited you then changed her mind," he joked.

I glared at him but said nothing.

"Are you hungry?" He was already steering me toward the kitchens.

"Famished," I answered as I sank down on a bench.

He set a cut of meat in front of me on a thick trencher of bread along with a mug of heady ale.

We chewed in silence before I finally asked him, "What happened to Lancelot?"

Owain looked up. "I was wondering when someone was going to ask. Nasty situation that. We were heading into a valley near the border of Rheged and Powys when we encountered him." Owain gestured out the window to where the knight's head now decayed on a pike. "Did you know the villagers are calling him the Black Knight since his entire armor was dark? Anyway, he called himself the Grail Sentinel and declared that anyone who sought it must defeat him first. None of us know if he had any official position or was simply a local loon capitalizing on the quest, but we had to face him in case he was really the final guardian." Owain took a long draught from his cup. "Whoever he was, he was well trained. He insisted on challenging each of us to single combat. You've seen what he did to Lancelot. The others in the infirmary are the ones who managed to escape. Some were not so lucky."

I stared into my cup. "I wish I had known how all would suffer." I looked at him. "I had the chance to stop this, to talk Arthur out of this madness, and I did not."

Owain scrutinized me. "Who said this would be easy? A quest commanded by a god or goddess never is. Think about the old tales. These situations are sent to test our strength and our faith. If we pass, the rewards will be great."

"If" was the word ringing in my head as I finished my meal. I was just about to thank Owain for his company and insight when Elaine found us. Her eyes were red-rimmed, and tear stains marred her face. My heart stopped. Surely she was here to tell us Lancelot was dead. I placed shaking hands on her shoulders, looking deep into her eyes.

"Lancelot is awake," she whispered.

"Oh, thank the gods." I hugged Elaine.

I started to release her, but she stopped me by holding up two small vials. She must have taken them from the store in Lancelot's room.

"May I borrow these?" she asked. "If I am correct, they are chamomile and comfrey. I would like to use them on my nervous stomach and sore knees."

I squinted at them, making sure she had properly identified them. "Yes, but be certain not to ingest the comfrey. It is poisonous."

Leaving Elaine, I rushed to the sick room. I was so relieved to see Lancelot conscious that I fell to my knees at his side.

"How do you feel?" I asked, grasping his hands. It took all my willpower not to kiss him lest someone walk in at the wrong moment.

"I'm in pain. A lot of it. And I'm having trouble recalling how I came to be in Camelot. I remember the knight and his armor, but that is all. I don't remember drawing my sword or being attacked." Lancelot looked down at his mending body. "But obviously I was." Looking at me, he added. "Thank you for saving me, Guinevere."

I put a hand on his shoulder. "You remember who you are, where you are, and who I am, so you will be well. It will just take time." I handed him a cup of healing beer.

He started to shrug then winced. "If you believe so, it must be true." His tone was slightly flirtatious, so I knew he would be just fine.

"I will stay here with you as long as you like. But when you feel up to getting out of bed, let me know. Morgan has given me detailed instructions on how to continue your treatment."

He puffed out a small laugh, all his broken ribs would allow. "Follow it or face the consequences, yes?"

"Something like that." I chuckled. "Finish your beer."

◦◦◦

Again the moon waxed and waned, and we had no word from Arthur nor any of the other questing knights. Lancelot was improving, eating a steady diet of liver and whatever greens we could find to help him regain his strength. Each day, we walked with him around the grounds, going a little farther each time.

By spring, Mordred's seventeenth year was drawing near, the time he would be considered a man according to his father's tribe. But Arthur had not yet returned, so Lot stood in at Mordred's manhood ritual. Morgan, as his mother, was not allowed to witness the ritual for it symbolized Mordred breaking free of his need of her and coming into his own. However, as priestesses, Grainne and I watched over him as he meditated deep in the woods the night before he was set loose to kill or be killed by whatever beast the Hag decreed.

In silence, we approached him, Grainne dressed all in white

with flowers entwined in her hair, acting as the Virgin Goddess who armed him for the hunt. She gave him a spear and a sling with a single stone. I was the Mother Goddess. My red dress reflected the blood with which I now painted him, blood kept from the stag Arthur had killed in Avalon, reconstituted for this very purpose. His absent mother represented the Crone and the wisdom he had gained at her skirts. Together, we handed him off to Lot and the other men, who would council him until nightfall, when his hunt would commence.

The following day, we haunted the forest, trying to sneak a look at the young warrior and making noise to throw off his senses. It was great fun for adults but, I was sure, not amusing to Mordred, who could not return to this camp until he had proof of his kill.

Lancelot and I walked and talked as we usually did but were so engrossed in our conversation we failed to notice when we became separated from the others.

Thunder rumbled in the distance. It was the first thing that drew our attention away from each other.

"A storm is coming," I said stupidly as heavy drops of rain began to fall.

We raced back toward the castle, but the rain was coming down so hard we both knew we would not make it before the storm broke in earnest. With a deafening crack, lightning struck a tree not one hundred paces in front of us. I screamed and practically jumped into Lancelot's arms.

Once my heart had slowed to its normal rhythm, I looked around to get my bearings. Even through the rainy haze, I knew where we were. I grabbed Lancelot's arm and tugged.

"Come on," I yelled over the rolling thunder. "I know where we can take shelter."

I led him to a small hut deep in the woods. It was made of bent saplings, just as Diarmad's had been, but this made his house look like a castle. I pushed on a clump of branches, and they gave way, allowing us entry into the tiny dwelling.

The hut was a single room, barely wider than Lancelot was tall. The floor was bare earth, and a circle of rocks served as a fire pit. Overhead, a few ancient clumps of herbs hung from the roof, long past their prime.

Lancelot immediately went to the only furniture in the room—a small chest. He pulled out a moth-eaten blanket and threw it at me playfully. I caught it and dried my hair while he kindled a small fire.

"It's a hunter's cabin, meant to be a retreat while they wait for game or need a place to spend the night," I said by way of apology for the mean surroundings, dumping my wet cloak in one corner. "Not nearly as nice as the one we found in the mountains."

Outside, lightning lit up the sky, and thunder shook the ground.

"It is fine, I assure you," Lancelot said. "I've bedded down in worse places."

I peered through the branches. "I hope Mordred won his hunt already. I cannot imagine fighting a wild animal in weather like this."

Lancelot stood behind me. "He is fine. The animals have better senses than we do. They would have disappeared into their dens, burrows, and caves long before the storm rolled in."

I felt simpleminded in the wake of such a logical explanation. "You know this from experience, I suspect?" I turned, not realizing until it was too late that I was now trapped in the cage of his arms.

Lancelot's face was only inches from mine. "I have spent quite a bit of time in the wild." He backed up, turning away. "Some of it with you," he added with a small laugh.

I sat next to the fire and traced random patterns in the dirt to distract myself from his nearness, his smell, and the heat beginning to course through my veins. He wasn't ready yet, I told myself. He still needed time to heal.

Lancelot sat down opposite me, the small orange flames between us. For a while, we simply listened to the storm. Eventually he pulled off his wet shirt and discarded it next to my soaked cloak.

He said my name between booms of thunder. "Can I tell you something?"

I had to move closer to hear him. "Anything."

"Sometimes—" He swallowed and tried again. "Sometimes I feel like I will be forever haunted by a memory I do not have. Of the Black Knight who almost stole my life."

I gazed at him, unused to a man being so open about his feelings. Perhaps it was his Breton ancestry that made him be so candid with me. I gave him a small half smile. "I understand, in a way. I too was haunted—but by what I did remember. If Avalon taught me one thing, it is that until you admit what you've experienced, you cannot move on."

Lancelot stoked the fire and added more wood until it was a

respectable size. "But how can I if I cannot remember it?"

"I can help you."

"How?"

"We have a ritual of remembrance in Avalon. I went through it myself before I returned to Camelot. All you have to do is trust me." I stood.

He took my hands. "I have pledged my life to you. Say the word, and it is done."

I plucked a handful of herbs from the clusters above. Sage and wild lettuce. They were dusty and bone dry, but they would do. I rearranged the stones so that, when placed on top of them, the herbs would smoke but not be consumed by the flames until they had given off their full fragrance.

"Do you have a water skin?"

Lancelot unhooked it from his belt. We each took a drink, then I poured a generous amount on the fire. I inhaled deeply. It was hickory wood. This was a good start.

I cast the herbs into the steam and fire. "Move over."

He moved against one wall so I could sit in front of him, water skin in my lap.

"Now breathe deeply."

We both inhaled.

"Close your eyes. Listen the rhythm of the rain." Once his breathing slowed, I took his hand and placed it on my chest. His breath caught, but I ignored it. "Now concentrate on matching your heartbeat to mine."

I poured another handful of water over the stones, and they hissed, sending hot white smoke into the air.

"Open your eyes and look into the steam. Tell me what you see."

His heartbeat increased along with his breathing. "The Black Knight is coming at me, swinging his terrible axe. I am defending myself but only just. He slams into me, knocking me to the ground. But that is not enough for him. He bangs my head into the ground, punching me about the face and chest while I am immobile. But I rally, pushing him off, struggling to my feet. I slash out with my sword, getting in a few good blows before he is on me again. I force him back, knocking off his helmet, and he stares at me with those crazed black eyes." Lancelot's voice caught.

His body trembled against my back. I poured more water onto

the rocks.

"Then what? What happens next?" I prompted.

"He wraps his hands around my neck, trying to suffocate me. I'm choking, but then I get a grip on his hair and yank his head back. Turning my head, I bite his fingers, forcing him to release me. We come at each other again, breathing heavily. He swings his axe, catching me in the side. I am down, done for. But my companions are not. They rush the knight and finally bring him down as I fade in and out of consciousness. They help me up and put a sword in my hand, holding down the dying knight.

"'Take your honor for this victory is yours,' they say to me. Suddenly, I am full of strength. I know what I must do. I raise the blade and bring it down through the flesh and corded muscle of his neck, through the bone and nerves, until it rolls to the side in a river of blood and he is no more.'"

"Good, now there is one more thing you must do so this new knowledge does not haunt you." I patiently recounted the steps of closing one's mind to a memory, the very same steps Viviane had taught me so many years before when I first arrived in Avalon.

Silence descended on us, comforting as a blanket. We sat in it until a peal of thunder startled us out of our reverie. I glanced over my shoulder at Lancelot. His skin was covered in sweat, face pale as chalk, eyes still haunted. I started to get up, but he held me fast.

"Thank you." His voice was husky, as though he'd just awoken from a deep sleep. "You truly are a goddess."

I ducked my head, embarrassed, and plucked at my tunic, which was clinging to my skin in the heat from the rainwater, fire, and steam. "I am not. I am a priestess, and it is my sworn duty to use what I know to give relief to those who are suffering whenever I can."

Lancelot brushed a piece of hair from my cheek. "There is something else, something I haven't told you." He shifted so I could face him. "After the battle, when I was unconscious, I saw the place where the Grail is kept. I was allowed to venture inside but only so far. When I tried to move forward, it was as though an invisible barrier held me back. But I could see beyond. There, on a pedestal, was the Grail. But it was veiled. Nearby was a beautiful woman with eyes like leaves after the rain and ink-black hair. She had your face."

I gasped.

Lancelot put a finger to my lips. "I heard her voice, or rather your voice, in my head. 'Son of the Lake, your soul is torn. You cannot serve the Grail and the queen, for she is Sovereignty, singularly demanding of your attention. You must make a choice.'"

He leaned into me, his breath warm on my lips. "I chose you. I will never behold the Grail in its true form because of that, but I am at peace. I have been yours from the moment I set eyes on you at the tournament."

I learned in and kissed him, my fingers tangling in his black curls, tightening, pulling, wanting. Needing. Our tongues touched, seeking the deepest recesses of one another.

I gently pushed him onto his back, mindful of his still-mending wounds, and pulled off my tunic, baring my breasts in the firelight. Leaning over him, I ran my tongue over his chest and stomach, stopping only when his trousers got in the way. Running my fingers slowly up his thighs, I groaned when I felt his arousal. He lifted his hips, and I peeled off his trousers. I'd intended to take him into my mouth, but he guided my hips over his. I closed my eyes and brought him into me.

I raised my arms and brought the energy of the storm into my body, every nerve tingling as I moved against him, grinding my hips in time with the vibration of the thunder all around us.

Lancelot sat up and lowered his head to my breasts, tongue flicking, tantalizing, teasing. I arched my back, crying out as pleasure built in my limbs. I moved my hips faster, seeking release. He moaned and kissed my neck, gripping my shoulders as his breathing grew ragged. I closed my eyes and grasped his shoulder blades. Waves of pleasure washed through me, and I dug my nails into his back and tossed my head back with a primal scream. Moments later, Lancelot groaned, and a spasm shook him as a surge of warmth filled my loins.

We collapsed in a heap next to the fire, panting, slowly returning to our senses.

I gazed at him, amazed at how happy I felt. This man was once again my lover, and I had no shame in it. For what felt like hours, we lay in each other's arms, caught up in our own thoughts, his fingertips tracing lazy circles on my upper arms.

"We should probably go," Lancelot finally murmured. "The worst of the storm has ended, and the others will be wondering what happened to us."

"Mmm. . . hmm," I replied but made no move to get up. Then I remembered Mordred and my duty to him.

After hastily donning our clothes, we stepped out into the rain. It was still coming down hard, but I relished it, letting it wash the sweat and smell of desire off of me.

Lot and Grainne were waiting beneath the canopy of an ash tree when we reached the place Mordred had departed the morning before.

"We were caught in the storm. Found a hunter's hut," I explained before anyone could ask.

"We were too," Lot said, holding up his dripping sleeve as proof. "But we were not so lucky. This is the best cover we could find."

"It helps to know these woods." I rubbed my hands together. "Any sign of Mordred?"

"Not yet."

The rain slowly dissipated, then the sun broke through, giving the remaining drops an Otherworldly quality, like golden showers of faerie dust. I laughed and ducked out from beneath the leaves, spinning in the rain like a giddy young girl. It wasn't long before Grainne joined me. We held hands and skipped in circles, reveling in the joy of the moment.

"Look!" Lancelot cried, pointing toward the west.

At first I thought he was directing our attention to the vivid rainbow stretching across the sky, but then a figure caught my eye. Mordred stood at the edge of the wood, scratched and bloody, a large boar slung over his shoulders. He flung his burden to the ground and flashed a triumphant grin.

Lot was the first to reach him. "Congratulations, son. You are now a man of the tribe."

Mordred wrenched a tusk from the boar and used it to slit open the beast's belly. I painted Mordred's face and chest with the blood, confirming the veracity of his kill.

Then, while Lancelot and Lot spoke words of welcome into the tribe of men, Grainne and I removed the beast's entrails, seeking to divine Mordred's future in them. I plunged my hands into the hot, steaming mess, and my sight clouded over. Mordred was before me, fully grown. His face was painted in wild symbols with woad and chalk, hair limed for battle. Behind him was a vast army of Picts, Irish, and Saxons, and next to him stood Elga in all her ferocious glory. I could not see whom he opposed, but whoever it was stood little chance of victory over this army.

I came back to myself with a start and looked at the proud boy being kindly harassed by Lot and Lancelot. What was to come to turn him into such a hardened warrior? I shook my head, seeking to clear it, and washed my hands and arms clean.

"The gods have foretold you will be a great warrior," I told Mordred, keeping the particulars to myself. There was no need to burden him at such a young age with knowledge that may or may not come to pass. "Receive the blessing of Sovereignty." I kissed his forehead, lips, and heart.

Grainne took up his spear and sling along with a sword specially commissioned by Arthur for this occasion. "Be armed by the Goddess and live to uphold her ways."

Lancelot and Lot cheered, lifting Mordred onto their shoulders.

"Now, son. . ." Lot chuckled. "Let's find you a woman and finish making you man!"

Chapter Twenty-Three

Winter 515

The Grail party was secreted into the castle under cover of darkness and heavy guard. We couldn't let everyone know they had found the Grail until we knew for certain. It wasn't that I didn't believe what I had seen or that the mysterious object really was the Grail, but if word leaked out uncontrolled or, the gods forbid it, if we were duped, there would be chaos in Camelot. We could not afford to take that chance.

The next morning, in the silent moments before dawn, the Combrogi gathered in the secret labyrinth at the center of the castle. No one spoke or even shuffled their feet. We were all waiting, holding our breath for what was to come. In the shadows and bushes around us, crickets sang their hymns to the dawn, and a warm, briny breeze blew in off the ocean.

Arthur arranged us carefully in the center of the labyrinth around the apple tree from Avalon. He was at the northernmost point with Galahad. Morgan and I were on either side of them, then Marius next to Morgan, Peredur next to me, and the rest of the questing knights around the circle. Lancelot chose the southern point, opposite Arthur, and Elaine stood behind Galahad, beaming. The Grail women stood on either side of our circle, the ones with the intimidating scythes guarding the only door against uninvited guests.

As golden dawn crested the horizon, Arthur spoke. "We are here to witness an event not only of our generation but of an epoch. This treasure has been hidden from human eyes for over five hundred years save to a chosen trained few." He nodded to the Grail guardians, who inclined their heads as one in acknowledgement. "For the first time, secular eyes will fall upon a sacred vessel some believe was an ancient gift from the gods, others the cup touched by Christ Himself before His death. Whatever the truth, we know it is a holy relic deserving of our respect and veneration." He let his words sink in then stepped aside, allowing me to take his place at the fore. "As the representative of Sovereignty herself, our queen has the honor of unveiling it to you."

To my left, Bishop Marius cleared his throat loudly. We'd had quite a row the night before over who would oversee the Grail ritual. He believed that as a consecrated representative of Christ on earth, he should be the one to preside. I'd reminded Marius that I too was consecrated, which he refused to acknowledge as valid. The argument grew heated, the entire Grail party taking sides and no one knowing for certain how to settle the argument. Peredur and Galahad were firmly in Marius's camp, while the Grail women sided with me. To my astonishment, Morgan made no move to assert her own authority and actually sided with me.

Finally, it was put to the Grail Maiden to decide for she was the only one among us who knew the true nature of the vessel. She took my hands and read the lines on my palms before doing the same with Marius, who was loathe to hold still for such a pagan practice.

She looked up and made her proclamation. "Ours is the final generation in which men and women will seek the Grail with equality. It will pass through the hearts, minds, and hands of many men in years to come. Therefore, it is only right that Sovereignty herself reveal it to the world. This has been our queen's destiny from the moment she was born. The dreams she had as a child are realized in this very moment."

I stepped forward, quite unsure how to begin. There was no precedence for this, no well-taught ritual of Avalon. But as the fates would have it, the Grail guardians knew what to do, or at the very least, they were excellent at making up pageantry on the spot.

The Grail Maiden stood in front of me, her back to the crowd. She held the Grail out to me, and I took it with shaking hands. She reached up and removed her veil. I gasped, recognizing Mona's deep black eyes immediately. Her hair was gray now, but there was no mistaking her face. So her dreams, though they were of the ancient past, had led her to the Grail too.

She touched my forehead, lips, and heart, in effect transferring her power to me. We bowed to each other, then she slid the veil from her shoulders and placed it over my hair. Immediately, silver light and comforting warmth filled me as they had the day I chose my champion. I was no longer the queen but the Goddess.

Mona backed away, melting into the throng of maidens, while a blonde-haired woman glided toward me with the thurible. She walked sunwise around me and my precious charge three times, enveloping us in haze of sweet smoke that reminded me of honeysuckle. She then circled the knights, purifying all present.

Rowena approached and poured ice-cold water over my hands. She then dipped an evergreen sprig into the pitcher and used it to shower all present. She waved her hand over the water, and it shimmered, changing before my eyes. Stepping to one side, she motioned for me to remove the golden cloth from over the Grail.

I took a deep breath, remembering the many forms it had taken in my dreams. Slowly, I drew the cloth away.

A gasp went up from the crowd, but no one spoke.

I looked down. In my hands was a bronze cauldron about the size of a large winter squash. It was decorated with intricate scrollwork, much like the pattern on the robes worn by the Lady of the Lake. As I gazed at it, I found I could read it, but it shifted as soon as I understood its meaning. It was not something I would ever be able to put into words, for it was the wisdom of the ages, meant to be held only in the soul, not transmitted through human senses.

On the sides of the vessel were four golden seals, each representing one of the elements. I turned it in my hands so I could see each in turn. Nearest to me was the seal of earth, depicting mountains, trees, and a pointed buck. As I looked at it, I was enveloped by the scent of pine and freshly turned earth. The next was air, an ethereal design that brought to mind clouds and invisible summer breezes. As I watched, it ruffled the edge of my veil. Next was the seal of fire, which glowed a rose-colored hue and was hot to the touch. Finally, a seal depicting waves and streams. It was cold, like melting snow, and smelled of briny seas.

Rowena poured water from her vessel into the Grail. She then took my free hand and one of Marius's and joined them together over the Grail. Even in my altered state, my stomach clenched at his touch. He scowled at me as we each silently blessed the vessel and its contents in our own way before releasing our grasp.

An inner voice told me to drink, so I did. A sweet honeyed mead filled my mouth, more pleasant than anything I had ever tasted. It had to have been the drink of the gods, the potion of Ceridwen that gave new life to the dead. It coursed through my veins, warming and healing every part of me. My once-broken fingers reset without pain and old battle wounds mended, though their scars remained. Even my womb glowed with warmth, and I knew that had I consumed this drink when I was younger, I could have borne children again. But alas, I was growing too old for such things.

As the tingling subsided, I was granted a single vision—a blond woman of the north, a Votadini from the tattoo on her left shoulder blade, sneered in the heat of battle. But she was not my enemy. I knew not her name but was certain that she, and perhaps her people, were part of the life I had yet to live.

All of this took place in the space of a breath, a single heartbeat. Looking up, I passed the Grail to Morgan, who also appeared surprised when she drank. For a moment, her eyes clouded over, then she handed the cauldron to Marius, a wrinkle in her brow indicating she was contemplating her own vision.

As Marius touched it, the Grail changed. It became a chalice of finely wrought gold, more perfect and beautiful than any of our goldsmiths could have created. Marius drank from it, tilted his head up as though seeing something no one else could, then reluctantly passed the cup on.

As it moved down the line, the Grail changed back to the cauldron or became a bone drinking horn or a plain pottery cup depending on who held it. Only for Peredur, Galahad, Arthur, Elaine, and Camille did it take the form it had for Marius. Based on the serenity or puzzlement on each face as the cup passed on, I surmised everyone was granted some sort of insight upon drinking.

Only when it reached Lancelot did the pattern change. The Grail again became veiled. Just as he'd predicted, he could not see it, nor did he drink from it. All because he'd chosen me. He met my eyes with a soft smile as he passed it on untouched.

Once all had drunk from it, the Grail returned to Mona's possession.

"You are a blessed few, the only people who shall consume from this vessel. Now it must be held in a sacred place where all can venerate it but none can touch it. My sisters and I shall continue to stand guard for as long as the Lady wills it, but it needs a lifelong protector and champion. Who shall fill this role?" she asked the assembly.

Galahad stepped forward. "I shall. God has told me it is His will."

"And I." Peredur stood next to Galahad, smiling at him. "You will need an attendant."

As one, they knelt before Marius.

"Bishop, we ask you to take us into holy orders straight away and instruct us in the ways of Holy Mother Church," Galahad said.

Marius's face lit up. "As God wills it, my children." He made the sign of cross over them both. "I am humbled by such a task."

I highly doubted it.

"There is one more among you who has been called by the Grail," Mona stated.

Everyone looked around, mumbling.

Finally, Camille squeezed Aggrivane's hand and went to Marius. She fell on her knees before him, face nearly touching the ground. "Your Excellency, when I drank from the cup, I felt the same urge that came upon me many years ago when I first received the body and blood of Christ. For many years, I longed to become a bride of Christ, but that path was denied me by my family. Instead, on pain of death, I married a kind, loving man." She glanced over her shoulder at Aggrivane, who stood in stunned silence, pain chiseled into every feature. "I bore him a son and heir who died many years ago. I have done my duty to him and to my husband."

She mouthed "I'm sorry" to Aggrivane before continuing. "I ask you to release me from my marriage vows that I may take the veil and become the first Christian woman in charge of the Grail's protection."

The courtyard erupted in a melee of voices, some praising her, others filled with derision. A few vowed to defend the insult to Aggrivane's honor. I said nothing, as stunned as Aggrivane, who still hadn't moved.

"Silence. Let the bishop speak," Arthur shouted.

Marius regarded Camille curiously. "What you ask of me is no small task, my child. It is true you have fulfilled your duties to your child, but what of those to your husband? They continue on even though your womb bears no more fruit."

Camille shook her head. "I bore the one child only. Before then, and since, my husband has allowed me to live as a bride of Christ as I have asked of him. He is away in foreign lands much of the time, so I am not denying my duties to him in asking such a thing."

Marius didn't appear to know what to make of this. "Are you saying you no longer have relations with your husband?"

I winced. This was not a conversation they should have been having in the company of others, even the Combrogi. Before Camille even answered, I was mortified for Aggrivane. I had to do something to stop this madwoman from bringing further embarrassment upon her husband and her house.

I put out a hand. "Please, let us continue this conversation in private where such delicate matters can be discussed openly without fear of what may come of them." I motioned Lot to take his son back inside.

Camille turned on me, still on her knees but looking for all the world as though she would bite me. "No! I have sinned before God in breaking a private pledge of virginity by marrying and bearing a child, and I will confess it before the whole court."

"Your sin is one thing, but do you not care for the ruin you bring upon your husband in the process?"

Camille stood, coming nose to nose with me. "You would care more about saving face for Aggrivane than what is right before God, you who never stopped loving my husband." She pulled the dagger out of my belt.

On all sides, Combrogi drew their swords in my defense.

Camille backed up, blade raised in her gloved hands to show she meant no one harm. She turned back to Marius and began sawing off locks of her hair. "No, Your Excellency, I have not had relations with my husband these fifteen years. I am a privately sworn holy woman now. See?" She held up a chunk of her hair. "This is proof of my devotion to Christ and to the cup which bore His blood. Whether you accept me or no, I am His slave. I am only asking you to make it official before all."

Marius was silent, clearly thinking as he watched the impassioned woman hack off her hair. "There is precedent for what you ask, though it is rarely used. If you were, as you claim, vowed to Christ in your heart before you married and did not wish to enter into such a union, then I doubt your marriage was ever valid in the eyes of God. The better question then is to ask this—does your husband give consent?"

All eyes turned to Aggrivane, who was nearly at the door, his father dragging him by the shoulder. Aggrivane faced the assembly, skin pale and clammy, clearly uncertain as to what to say. He cleared his throat. "Camille, if you wish to devote the remainder of your life to God, I grant you permission."

The crowd buzzed again, but Bishop Marius silenced them by raising his hand. He took the dagger from Camille and returned it to me. He spoke to Camille. "That being so, I declare your marriage dissolved in the eyes of God. You may enter the order whom I council. But be forewarned. Any more rash acts such as this"—he gestured to her shorn hair—"no matter how piously intended or induced, will result in disciplinary action. A servant of God, especially one who wishes to guard the Grail, must be meek and mild, not given to flights of recklessness."

"Thank you, Your Excellency." Camille kissed his hand then the hem of his robe.

"It is decided then," the Grail Maiden declared.

Elaine stepped out of the crowd in the silence that followed. "I—I have something to confess." Her voice was timid at first but gained confidence with every word. "I know I shall not attain heaven with this secret on my soul, so I wish all of you to bear witness to my shriving." She walked over to her son and clasped his hands. She swallowed hard before continuing. "Galahad, all your life you have asked me who your father is, and I have refused to answer you. Today, as you prepare to enter the service of the Church, I tell you to look upon him." She pointed at Lancelot. "He is the most honored of the king's knights, his master of the horse and the queen's champion, Lancelot du Lac."

I grasped Arthur's arm, legs suddenly weak, head buzzing. Lancelot was married. My mind whirled. That meant we were doubly complicit in our affair, each betraying not only a spouse but a dear friend.

After a few moments of stunned silence, Galahad went to Lancelot and kneeled before him. "Father." He looked up at Lancelot, all the years of wondering plain in his eyes along with his admiration. "Do you claim me as your son?"

Lancelot raised his son to his feet and embraced him. "I always have. It is I who ensured that you have had all you desire. Go with my blessing into a life of service to your god." He turned a steely gaze on Elaine. "You, however, I do not accept. I have never loved you, nor will I ever. You lured me into your bed then into marriage by trickery. I never agreed to be your husband, nor do I call myself that now. Here and now, with public witness, I disavow all knowledge of you, woman."

Elaine crumpled in pain, face contorting as tears streamed down her face. She wailed as the crowd broke anew into a confused buzz of conversation, some condemning Lancelot, others Elaine. I rushed to Elaine and put my arms around her, holding her up as she shook in the deepest of heartache.

"You are my husband!" Elaine shrieked.

"Actually, if he indeed entered marriage against his will, then just as with Camille, the marriage is not valid," Marius interrupted, quieting the whole room. "However, it also means our Grail champion was not conceived within the bounds of a sanctified marriage." He paused, holding Galahad's future, all of our futures, in the balance. "But that is the sin of his parents, no transgression of his. If God is willing to look beyond and bless him with the Grail, then none among us may judge."

Galahad breathed a visible sigh of relief.

Arthur took hold of the situation then, before anyone else could make more proclamations, inspired by the Grail or not. "We have all had an unforgettable morning. I beg you please do not start rumors about what has taken place here today. I do not swear you to secrecy but beg you be truthful and discreet in what you choose to disclose. Go now and return to your lives, forever changed by your encounter with the Grail."

Elaine was still wailing as I dragged her away from the labyrinth.

◦◦◦

"Her husband?" I rounded on Lancelot later that night when he found me in one of the deserted towers. "All these years and you couldn't have told me you were married?"

Lancelot reached out to me. "But I am not, not in any meaningful way. You heard the bishop."

I sat on the floor then, face buried in my hands. "How did this happen?"

Lancelot sat next to me. He took a few deep breaths before replying. "When Arthur left Corbenic to marry you, he needed someone to guard against Isolde's wrath and the revenge of the Irish. He found me and offered me the position." He brushed the hair out of my face. "I accepted only because I knew you to be from that house and thought I would see you again. I did not yet know you were engaged to Arthur.

My first night there, Pellinor feasted me until I was deep in my cups. That is when his daughter came to me in the dark of night. Inebriated, I thought her to be you. So Galahad was conceived. It was only the next morning I discovered my mistake and Elaine told me of your upcoming wedding.

"The following month, she learned she was with child. I told her I wanted nothing to do with the child but would pay for its rearing until adulthood. That was not good enough for her pious family, who sought to undo her sin. Under pain of exposing me to Arthur—and thus to you—as a philanderer worthy of neither trust nor honor, much less the king's esteem, they forced us to the church, where we were wed. I never told anyone because to me, there was no marriage. I do not believe in her god, nor did I vow myself to her. You are the only woman to whom I have ever pledged my heart or soul."

I looked at him then. "Truly?"

"Truly." He tried to slip an arm around me, but I shrugged him off.

"I need time to think, Lancelot. I cannot simply rush back into your arms after a revelation such as this."

He bowed his head. "As you wish, my queen."

Chapter Twenty-Four

Summer 515

Construction began on a chapel to house the Grail almost immediately after our ritual. Galahad, being its champion, selected an island just off the coast, within sight of Camelot on clear days. Arthur, to my surprise, had architectural ambitions like his father, so when Galahad was free from his priestly studies, the two spent most of their time closeted away, working on designs. Marius even contacted some of his friends in Rome and paid for safe passage for two of them to Britain so Arthur's dream could be executed with the latest advances in Roman engineering.

I had seen Arthur's final plans. They called for an inner sanctuary with a gleaming red cupola supported by six tall stone pillars. A walled chapel and living area would surround this sanctuary, with a defensive wall three times taller than a man encircling that. The outer wall wasn't just protection against would-be thieves. It was also defense against the crashing waves, especially during storms. The whole structure would be accessible only by a narrow causeway created by natural rock and sand deposits. At high tide, it would be completely inaccessible, except by boat, making it the perfect place to house such a treasure.

With my husband occupied and my champion at least temporarily disgraced, I returned to Avalon with Mona and Rowena. I needed time and space to sort out the tangled knot of my life, and I could think of nowhere better.

I invited Morgan to accompany us, if only to make amends with Viviane, but she just laughed, saying, "Avalon abandoned me. Why should I return, especially now? I am a Christian woman, remember?"

"You are as Christian as the Saxons," I scoffed. "We both know you put on a show only to assure Arthur's continuing affection. And perhaps to gain favor with Bishop Marius."

"What I do is my business alone, Guinevere. Go back to the isle if you must. But I will remain here with my husband. You can tell Viviane I will never return."

But when we reached Avalon, I could tell Viviane nothing. She lay ill in her chamber, growing weaker by the day, according to Ailis, who was acting as her guard. She allowed me to see Viviane only because of our long friendship.

Viviane's skin was gray, her lips and fingers tinted lavender. Her eyes were closed as if in deep slumber, but the rise and fall of her chest was barely perceptible. A small vein slowly pulsing in her neck was the only other sign she still lived.

"She is unconscious now but had quite a time before. She started feeling ill just after the new moon, and at first we thought she had a normal illness. But then about a week ago, the convulsions began. Slowly, she became paralyzed and now. . ." Ailis's voice shook, "I believe she is nearing the veil."

"Poisoning?"

Ailis nodded. "That is what we suspect. But we have checked her belongings, and Nimue personally tests her food, so we cannot find a source."

I tossed and turned in my bed for the next two nights, turning Ailis's account of Viviane's mysterious illness over and over in my mind. There had to be something we were all missing. We were a community of trained healers, after all. But then again, we were trained to give life; only a rare few knew how to take it.

Restless, I finally decided to get up and walk the labyrinth, as I often did at home when wrestling with weighty issues. Around and around I trod, allowing my feet to trace the pathways of their own accord, freeing my mind to think on Viviane, Morgan, Lancelot, and Elaine—all of the distractions I had come here to escape. So deep was I in my thoughts I barely noticed when I reached the top of the Tor. Only Merlin's distraught voice made me pause before I was seen.

"Surely the Goddess will release her soon. Viviane has served her well. Why prolong her sojourn here?"

"Is there anything we can do bring her peace?" a female voice asked.

"Are you suggesting we hasten her death?" Merlin's voice was sharp.

"No." The woman laughed nervously. "I simply wish to see her death be as painless as possible. Provided we cannot find a cure, that is," she hastily added.

I shifted my position behind the stone separating us. If I angled my body just the right way, I had a slightly obstructed view of the couple. Long dark hair came into view first, then blue priestess robes. Finally, the lone candle flickering between them illuminated bright green eyes. It was Nimue.

Merlin sighed and laid a hand on her shoulder. "Perhaps it will be my time soon as well. I have taught you everything I know, my daughters are grown, and Arthur has no need of me anymore. With Viviane dead, what will be left for me?"

Daughters? I had long suspected Ailis but was not aware of any other children of the Archdruid.

Nimue seized Merlin's chin, forcing him to face her. Her eyes were hard with malice. "You should know the answer. Me." She kissed him hard, letting her lips reflect her anger at his neglect to factor her into his life's worth.

I backed away slowly. Something in Nimue's disposition frightened me, but it also inspired a thought. Racing back down the Tor, I prayed that for Viviane's sake, I was right.

When I reached Viviane's chambers, I woke Ailis with a shake.

"What is it?" She raised herself onto one arm and squinted at the window. "It is not even dawn yet. Go back to sleep."

"Ailis." I shook her again to make sure she didn't go back to sleep. "Who prepares Viviane's meals?"

"Nimue. Why?"

I tugged on her arm. "Come with me."

I lit a candle and dragged her out into the night. We paused on the threshold to Nimue's room, just long enough to ensure it was still unoccupied. I began throwing open chests and drawers.

"What are you looking for?" Ailis asked, shocked at my actions.

"Proof of Nimue's guilt. I have heard a secret conversation tonight that leads me to suspect her." But there was nothing to be found. "The kitchens."

Ailis likely thought me mad as she followed me, but when I opened a small bag of rye hidden deep in the pantry, we were assaulted by the stench of fish.

"Oh," Ailis exclaimed. "This is ergot. Rotten rye. Deadly. Such a thing should be destroyed." She looked at me as her thoughts fell in line with mine. "You don't think. . ."

I nodded.

One of the young acolytes, a girl of perhaps ten summers, appeared to begin the day's baking. If she was surprised by our presence, she said nothing, merely knelt and made the sign of Avalon in deference to Ailis, who was acting Lady during Viviane's illness.

"Does Nimue prepare the Lady's bread with this?" She held up the offending bag.

"Yes, Lady," the girl replied. "She says it is special but not to touch it. She threatened to curse me and anyone who ate of it if I did."

Ailis looked at me. "We must find Nimue."

But we were too late. By the time Nimue was dragged, kicking and screaming, from the forest, even graver news than the likelihood of Nimue's guilt reached us.

"Merlin is dead," one of the young priestesses told us, her hand fluttering around her mouth. "They say his body is still warm. Nimue is covered in his blood."

◦◦◉◦◉◦◦

Viviane slowly recovered as the ergot left her system, but she was likely to have lasting damage to her nerves. Two weeks later, she was well enough to be carried to the Tor. Rowena, Ailis, and I trudged up the labyrinth behind her, just as I had done so many times in my years as a priestess in Avalon, but tonight our purpose was far grimmer than any ritual. Tonight we would see justice done for Merlin's murderess.

Nimue knelt before the altar stone, barefoot, hands bound, and head lowered as if to shield herself from the intense heat of the fire burning on the other side of the stone.

Slowly, Druids and priestesses formed a circle of alternating white and blue robes around her. I stood to Nimue's left, unable to read her face thanks to a thick strand of raven hair that had fallen loose of its knot during her struggle with those who had brought her here.

Viviane and the new Archdruid, who took the title Myrdin—an imposing man of middle years with a full beard as white as clouds—stood before her.

"Nimue, priestess of Avalon, you stand accused of murder, a most unholy crime on this isle and across this land," Myrdin declared in his deep baritone. "It is said you killed the Archdruid of Britain by bloody means in the hopes of gaining his power. Also, you are accused of conspiring to kill the Lady of the Lake and take her office. What say you to these charges?"

Nimue raised her head, her hard eyes glinting like fresh-cut emeralds. "I did as you say, and I would do so again."

"You admit your wrongdoing then," Myrdin said. "When Merlin's body was found, he was pierced through the wrists with wooden stakes, had suffered a blow to the head, and his throat was slashed. You said as you were apprehended that you were defending yourself. Tell us, what manner of crime requires such lengths?"

"I arranged to meet him as we have been doing for many years. It is no secret we were lovers." She cast a gloating glance toward Viviane. Then she pointed at me. "If you wish to know what we talked about, ask her. After all, she was there."

"You knew I could hear you? How?"

Nimue tapped her tattooed brow. "But what you don't know is what happened after you left." Her eyes filled with tears, and her voice quavered. "Merlin turned on me, and I feared he would do me harm, so I picked up a stone and swung it at him to deter him. I caught him on the head."

"But he was not found on the Tor, and that does not account for the way his arms were pinioned or his cut throat," I reminded her.

She turned her malice on me. "Ah, the queen speaks. Tell me, am I being tried in Avalon's or Camelot's court?"

"Both." The steel in my voice surprised even me. "You will answer us."

Nimue laughed, a strange, unhinged sound. "And if I don't? You will kill me anyway. Why not let Merlin's death remain a mystery? It is more exciting this way."

One of the Druids approached Nimue. She raised her arms, and thunder and lightning filled the sky. The Druid jumped back, much to Nimue's delight.

She cackled madly. "Do you see? I have his power within me! All that he was, I am now!"

Viviane stopped the show in the heavens with a wave. "You know nothing more than that which I taught you, which any woman here can do. You are not as powerful as you think."

"No? I breathed in his last breath, and have consumed his blood. I can do all he could and more!" Nimue was crazed now, eyes wide, practically foaming at the mouth as she struggled against her bonds.

"So that is why you killed him," Myrdin said. "In that case, I think we can safely assume you pinioned his arms to keep him still while you slit his throat, a quick but intimate death."

"As you say." Nimue rocked back and forth, consumed by what she saw as her own genius.

"And as to your attempt to poison me?" Viviane asked.

"I tried to wait, but you wouldn't die. Why wouldn't you just die?" Tears sprang to Nimue's eyes and rolled down her cheeks. "Then we could have been together, and I wouldn't have had to do this."

Myrdin cleared his throat. "You have confessed to crimes against the Archdruid and Lady of the Lake. Now you must face the consequences."

Viviane spoke. "Your actions are an affront to the Goddess and God and a betrayal of your vows. As such, you shall suffer the three-fold death, never to rejoin our community. Do you understand?"

Nimue did not reply but held Viviane's gaze. Two priestesses helped Nimue to her feet and stripped her of her blue robes until she stood shivering in only her shift.

Viviane slowly approached the fire and withdrew an iron poker tipped with a small flat square. She carried it to over to Nimue, hands shaking.

"I would not do this for anything in the world," she said with a ragged breath. "But you have dishonored this holy mark and no longer deserve to bear it. Do you understand?"

Two Druids stepped forward, each bracing one of Nimue's arms. She held herself defiantly tall and proud, glaring at Viviane. "Do what you must," she answered, voice devoid of all emotion.

"So be it then," Viviane said quietly, raising the brand.

I looked away, unable to watch. The white-hot metal met Nimue's forehead with an audible hiss. When I looked back, tiny tendrils of smoke danced skyward as the crescent was burned off her brow. To her credit, Nimue did not cry out, though her eyes streamed with tears and her face contorted in silent agony. When the Druids released her, Nimue fell to the ground, clutching her head and making animalistic grunting sounds. For a long while, she lay on the ground, dazed.

When she finally stirred and climbed unsteadily back to her knees, the Archdruid approached her. When he stood next to Viviane, they drew blades simultaneously and pointed them at her.

"The blade is naked against her. Never again shall she be one of ours," they said in unison.

Slowly, each member of the circle came forward, touched their blade to her throat, and repeated the words. When they returned to their place in the circle, they turned their back toward her, signifying her excommunication.

I was the last to do so because as queen, I had one final duty to perform. I placed my hand on Nimue's shoulder, forcing myself to look at the angry red and black weeping wound between her eyes. I took a deep breath, remembering the willful young girl who had grown up in my father's hall.

"I am so glad your mother did not live to see this. Under other circumstances, you would face your temporal punishment outside the mists, on unhallowed ground, like other criminals, but you have committed no ordinary crime. You have spilt blood consecrated to the gods in a holy place. Therefore, to maintain balance, like must happen to you.

"I will show you one final act of mercy. I will allow you to choose the manner of your death. But it will be a death which you approach willingly in recompense for your actions, not one wrought by human hands. Should you refuse, wild beasts will be unleashed to tear you to pieces. If you do not wish this fate, you may choose to be buried alive in a cairn, submerge yourself in the mist and marshes, walk willingly into the flames on the next holy day, or cast yourself from the top of Chalice Hill, but know if you survive, we will leave you for dead. You have the night to think it over. We will return for you at dawn."

I drew my dagger and repeated the ritual of excommunication, but instead of sheathing it, I laid it on the ground before her. "You have one other choice. You may take your own life this night."

I looked into Nimue's haunting eyes to make sure she understood. What I saw was not the fear I had witnessed in the eyes of countless criminals condemned to death nor the contrition of one afraid to meet death. It was the stark, shocking lucidity of the truly insane, the ones who have given themselves over to the dark forces that tempt them away from everyday life.

Just when I thought I would get no reaction from her, she smiled. A wicked grin split her marred features, and she laughed, a manic, high-pitched cackle.

"You have no idea what you have begun this day. My blood will haunt this land forever. Never again will you know peace."

It was a curse, one proving how truly dangerous Nimue was. Around me, the priestesses and Druids chanted as those left to guard her took up their positions.

ⲟⲅⲇ ⲇⲅⲟ

At dawn, I returned with Viviane and Myrdin. Nimue had made her choice—but not without struggle with whatever dark forces possessed her. Her fragile body, covered with self-inflicted scratches trailing the length of her arms, legs, and chest, lay in a pool of blood. Deep gashes marred her wrists and elbows.

As a criminal and an oath breaker, she would have no funeral. Her body was loaded onto a stretcher and placed in a boat bound for the outside world. We committed her body to the bogs on the other side of the mists just as had been done to outlaws in ages past.

Chapter Twenty-Five

Summer 518

Outside the mists, the Grail was true to its promise of peace until our own men began to turn on us. The rumors began with rumblings from the countryside of bands of marauders terrorizing farmers and herders, destroying crops and livestock. Then one of Arthur's men was brought before us, accused of inciting a riot in a village by killing the local lord's heirs and carrying off his eldest daughter to become his wife.

I would never forget the intensity in his eyes as he strove to justify his actions, pupils dilated, blue-green irises burning with the passion of the depraved.

"What would you have me do, sit around and whittle figurines out of wood? I am a fighter. I know nothing else. When the opportunity for combat doesn't arise naturally, I make one." He pointed a stubby finger at Arthur. "You made me this way. I am only doing what you've trained me to do."

The warrior's words hit Arthur hard. He sent the man to work in the gold mines of Gwynedd, hoping a sense of purpose would rehabilitate him.

That night, Arthur ran a hand over his tired face and through his graying hair. "I wish Merlin was here to tell me what to do. He was wise. He would know how to handle this."

I wanted to remind him that he was the one who had told Merlin he could go and replaced him with Bishop Marius, but I did not. I stroked his shoulders instead. "You too are wise. You learned from him. You have his wisdom inside you."

My words calmed Arthur for a while, but there was one thing we weren't prepared for—a charge against Arthur's own kin.

The next full moon, only three days after Beltane, we heard cases as we did every month, but there was something different about this gathering. The crowd was agitated, restless as if they were waiting for something. Many of them didn't come forward, so I began to wonder why they were there, what it was they were present to witness. I didn't have to wait long.

One of Arthur's underlords from Strathclyde, a man called Ceredig, approached our thrones with a hooded woman at his side. He bowed before us, expression somber.

"My king and queen, Lady Morgan, I am sorry to have to lay this before you, but I must do my daughter justice. I charge your son, Lord Mordred, with the rape of my daughter, Caitlin."

I inhaled sharply. That was a most grievous charge. If Mordred was found guilty, the official penalty would only involve a fine, but it would also make legal any retribution the girl's family wished to make against Mordred, including murder.

I looked at Mordred, who appeared as stunned as I was. He was holding onto Morgan's arm as though he would fall without her support, and his mouth was open in silent horror.

Arthur's whole body was taut, but he responded as he would have if the person in question were a stranger. "What grounds have you for this charge?"

"Three days ago, on Beltane eve, my daughter attended the fires with her friends. Your son and his companions met them late in the night, when they were already deep in their cups. Your son took a particular liking to my daughter. They danced together, and soon he took her off to a secluded area. I have several witnesses who will testify to this. After that—" Lord Ceredig became flustered, apparently not wishing to speak of sexual details about his daughter.

Arthur held up a hand. "Let us hear from your daughter."

Caitlin lowered her hood, revealing two bruised eyes, several scratches, and what appeared to be a bite mark on her cheek. When she lifted her arms, there were bruises on both wrists, and the longer I looked, I realized they matched the ones on her neck. This woman had definitely been abused. The question was, by whom?

"We went off into the woods, as all couples do on Beltane," she spoke in a small, shaky voice. "Mordred kissed me and touched my body, to which I had no objection, but when he began to remove his trousers, I knew what he intended was different from what I wanted. I told him no, but he wouldn't listen. He tried to hold me down, and I fought against him, scratching at his hands and face, screaming with all my might, but he was too strong. It was then he—he over-powered me." She looked down, clearly ashamed.

I grasped the arms of my chair, digging my nails into the wood and fighting the panic that followed her testimony. It was so much like my own experience with Malegant that the memories, so long ago locked away, threatened to come rushing back.

"What did you do then?" Arthur asked in his most tender voice.

"Eventually, I stopped struggling." She looked up, eyes plead-ing. "I just wanted it to be over. When it was, he stumbled away as though nothing had happened. I lay on the ground, sobbing. That is how one of my friends found me."

"Is your friend here?"

Caitlin nodded and pointed at a plain girl with hair the color of dirty dishwater. She was standing with two others of the same age who must have been their other companions.

Arthur motioned the girl forward. "You may return to your father," he said to Caitlin.

Caitlin's friend curtsied awkwardly in front of us.

"What is your name?"

"Ellen."

"Ellen, what is your account of that night?"

"What Caitlin says is true. We met the boys and danced, and she went away. Not long after, we heard screaming, but it took us a while to find her. By then, the deed was done. I found the poor thing crying and shivering. She was bleeding, especially from—" She motioned to the place between her thighs.

Arthur turned his attention to the other two girls. "Do you sup-port her testimony?"

"We do, my lord," they answered in near unison.

"Thank you, Ellen." Arthur motioned Mordred forward, his face stricken. "What say you to these charges?"

Mordred looked as though he had no idea what to say. "I didn't rape her if that is what you are asking. What she said is accurate up to the point of me leading her into the forest."

"What happened then?"

"I—" He looked at Caitlin. "I don't remember. The next thing I recall is meeting up with my friends at a dockside tavern."

"You lie!" Lord Ceredig yelled.

Caitlin clung to her father as though her life depended on it.

"Son, if you cannot recall, how can you be certain you did not do what you are accused of?" Arthur asked.

"Because I would never do that!" Mordred's voice cracked. He looked at his mother. "You raised me better than that." He turned back to Arthur. "I have sworn a vow to you to respect all of your people. I couldn't, wouldn't do this." He was desperately pleading now.

"Are any of your friends from that night here?"

Mordred looked around. "Yes, Naill."

Arthur gestured for him. "What say you?"

Naill stood confidently before Arthur. "They are all correct about the attraction and going off. What happened then, I cannot say. I was with a girl of my own—consensually, mind you. We had agreed to meet at the Paps of Anu—that was the tavern—if we split up. Mordred came in shortly after I did."

"Did he say anything that would lead you to believe he'd forced himself on that girl?"

"No, sire. He said he had lain with a girl, but it sounded like she was agreeable."

"Did he have any marks on him indicating he had been in a fight?"

"No, only those consistent with the heat of passion." Naill grinned.

Caitlin found her voice and used it to shout at Mordred. "Then what are those scrapes on his knuckles? I gave him those."

Mordred held up his left hand. "These are from archery practice yesterday. Ask Lancelot. He was there."

Arthur and I inspected his hand.

"He is telling the truth," I said. "His wounds are too recent to have been received on Beltane."

"He could have reinjured himself!" Caitlin's father yelled.

"Silence, all of you! I've heard enough. Does anyone else have anything else to add?" Arthur asked.

The room became eerily silent.

"My wife and I will discuss this in private and return with our judgment. Lancelot, guard Mordred. Kay, Bedivere, Bors, make sure the crowd remains peaceful."

He and I went to a small antechamber reserved for this and other private matters.

Arthur leaned heavily against the closed door. "You were trained as a judge. What do you think?" Even though we were alone, his voice was barely a whisper.

"I don't know. I want to believe Mordred, but because he cannot remember, either one of them could be telling the truth. It's clear she was abused and probably even raped, but the question is was Mordred the perpetrator? Her family could just be accusing him to try to extort money from us."

"On the other hand, even if he is innocent, if we let him go without punishment, it will appear the law does not apply to him because he is my son."

"Arthur, we cannot punish an innocent man."

"I know, Guinevere. I know." He banged his fist against the wall. "Three decades on the throne, and this is the most difficult decision I've ever had to make."

When we returned to the great hall, the crowd was growing restless. All eyes were on us as we took our seats. Arthur spoke. "We cannot determine whether or not a crime has been committed by the man accused. However, since it is possible, Mordred, you will pay this family the full body price and honor price as prescribed by law."

"This is outrageous!" Caitlin's father roared. "The crown is simply going to pay away his offenses? I demand stronger punishment."

"Lord Ceredig, we have ruled. You cannot bring suit again," I reminded him. I chose not to remind him there were now other legal ways for him to exact revenge.

"However, given the shame this charge has brought upon the throne, I hereby strip Lord Mordred of his membership in the Combrogi, and all the rights and privileges that accompany it, for a year and a day. At that time, we will consider reinstatement," Arthur added.

"What?" Mordred attempted to surge toward us, but Lancelot held him fast. "This is ridiculous! You are practically disowning me over a crime I did not commit." He pointed at both of us. "You will pay for this! Mark my words."

"Lancelot, Kay, lock him up until he regains his senses." Arthur addressed the crowd now. "This pleading day has ended. If you have concerns that have not been addressed, please take them up with your local lord or return next month."

ഒരു ഈ

Mordred didn't speak to any of us unless he had to, which was to be expected. What I hadn't anticipated was Morgan's added hostility toward us. If it had only been me, I wouldn't have been as surprised, but her anger at Arthur was unprecedented. Granted, Mordred was her son, but what else could we have done?

After Mordred's threats, Lancelot and I decided it was best we end our relationship. Though we had reconciled after my return from Avalon, things were never the same between us again. Couple that with the possibility of Elaine, unstable ever since she had been publicly humiliated by Lancelot, finding out, and there was no sense in continuing.

In Lancelot's mind, that meant leaving Camelot. A few weeks after Mordred's censure, he was packed and prepared to be away. We met at the edge of a swampy clearing leading away from Camelot. It was nearly midnight—Lancelot wished to leave under cover of darkness to avoid questions from the Combrogi, whom he was abandoning.

"Where will you go?" I asked.

"I'm not sure. Maybe back to Brittany, perhaps to the Goddodin. I still have some lands there."

I vaguely remembered Malegant or Diarmad making reference to that. "So this is good-bye then."

He smiled in the way that broke hearts every time he neared a woman. "Not yet. We still have a few moments more." He leaned toward me.

I put up a hand. "Lancelot, you know my position on that—"

"That's not what I'm suggesting." He put his arms around my waist and pulled me to him. "I simply want to hold you one last time."

I sank into his warmth, my head on his chest, and listened to his heartbeat. Around us, the forest continued its chirps and clicks, oblivious to our presence. We hugged each other closer, loathe to part. But finally the moment came.

Lancelot was the first to pull back. "You know I have loved you from the moment I saw you at the tournament, and I will always love you, simply from afar."

Tears welled in my eyes. "I love you too. It may have taken me longer to realize it, but I do. I do not know how I would have survived these years with Morgan were it not for you. You will be in my heart always."

I rose onto my tiptoes and kissed him, long and deep.

That was when I heard a crack in the trees. I started to step away but was too slow. We were still in each other's arms when Mordred and Aggrivane leapt into view, weapons drawn. Instinctively, Lancelot pushed me behind him and drew his own blade.

Elaine emerged from behind Mordred and Aggrivane, clapping slowly. "Isn't that touching? You're still defending the trollop after all these years. And those declarations of love? Almost as good as a bard's song." She pretended to wipe her eyes.

"Elaine, what are you talking about? Did you follow us?" I squinted at her in the moonlight.

"Oh, yes. He's been following you for some time now." She indicated Aggrivane and circled us as she spoke. "You know, I've suspected for years that my husband—do not bother to protest, Lancelot—was unfaithful to me. Then Mordred mentioned he thought Guinevere to be unfaithful as well. I couldn't imagine the two of you together, but it was worth investigating. Turns out I was right."

I turned my attention to Aggrivane. "And what are you doing here?"

"Having my worst nightmare confirmed. Not that I haven't known for years what was going on." The dejection in his voice and disappointment in his eyes tore my heart in two. They asked the question, "Why him instead of me?"

I had no answer.

Mordred cleared his throat. "We are not here for a reunion. Let's get on with it." He leveled his sword at us. "In the name of High King Arthur, you are both under arrest on suspicion of adultery and treason."

As Mordred approached me, Lancelot slashed at him, tearing into his arm. Three guards appeared from the trees. I had no weapon nor any will to resist, so I allowed one to bind my hands while the others assisted in capturing Lancelot. He laid one low before Aggrivane finally disarmed him. Lancelot continued to struggle as he was bound.

Aggrivane's expression was full of disdain. "Believe me, I take much pleasure in doing this." He brought the butt of his sword down on Lancelot's head, knocking him out. "Carry him," he ordered the two Combrogi who remained unharmed.

They each grabbed him under an armpit and dragged him forward, feet scraping the ground, head lolling to one side.

"Elaine, take care of our injured friend," Mordred called as he led the way into the woods.

"Where are you taking us?" I demanded, finally terrified.

Mordred looked back over his shoulder. "He is going to the prison. You are going to face the king."

A week later, Kay led me, bound in iron shackles, before Arthur in his council chambers. I had been in here countless times over the years, but this was the first time I'd ever felt threatened in this room.

Around the table stood my friends, the Combrogi. But today their faces were anything but welcoming. Bors, Accolon, and Gawain regarded me with disgust, while Bedivere, Sobian, and Lot gave me looks of pity and concern. Even the statues of Arthur's ancestors seemed to scowl at me from their stone perches. With a start, I noticed someone had covered my statue with a black cloth. That was the true measure of the trouble I was in.

A special area had been set up at the head of the table. Arthur sat in his usual place, with Marius on his left and Morgan on his right. The empty chair on the other side was presumably reserved for Kay. Three additional chairs off to the left were occupied by my accusers: Elaine, Mordred, and Aggrivane. I looked around, searching for my place, but there was none. I was to stand then, as one already condemned.

"Where is Lancelot?" I asked Kay in a whisper.

"He is being held in a safe place."

I barely had time to comprehend his words before the court scribe read out the charges against me.

"Guinevere, Queen of Camelot, you stand accused of treason by way of an adulterous affair with your champion, Lancelot du Lac. What say you?"

I looked at them each in turn, amazed that people I knew so well could so quickly become strangers.

"I am guilty of no crime," I said in a loud, clear voice so the entire assembly would be sure to hear.

"How can you say such a thing when we have witnesses who

have already attested to seeing you in his embrace?" Marius asked, his voice as full of disgust as the day he condemned me before my father.

"So the witnesses have already spoken? Am I not to be part of my own trial? Is this how Camelot is governed now?"

"You were there," Marius spit. "You know what they have told us."

"Do I? For all I know, they may have told you they caught me fornicating with the devil himself. Would you like to hear my side, or have you already sent the headsman to sharpen his axe?"

"Guinevere, that is enough." Arthur addressed me for the first time. "Tell me what happened. And if anyone interrupts"—his cold stare threw daggers at Marius—"I will have him or her removed from this room."

I swallowed, fighting to control the panic and nerves at war within me. "Badon changed me, as I'm sure it changed many of you." I looked into each face in turn, seeing a few nods, a few expressions of agreement. "Before then, I was able to live with Morgan being my husband's second wife. When he abandoned me for her after the war, I had no one. So I sought out companionship." I fixed Marius in a cold stare. "But not in the way you would imply. A few days ago, when we were 'discovered,' as you say, we were saying our farewells, queen to champion. Nothing improper took place."

"Maybe not that night," Mordred interjected. "But it had on plenty of previous occasions."

"What proof have you of this?" Arthur asked.

Aggrivane spoke up. "I saw the two of you once, many years ago, in the stairwell outside Elaine's chambers. Lancelot had just given charge of his students to her. You were kissing, your hands all over one another. When I realized you were not aware of my presence, I followed you. I did not stay long, but I saw enough to know you had carnal knowledge of one another up against the wall."

I tried hard not to react, at least not visibly, but my whole body began to shake. I heard my heartbeat drumming in my ears. I remembered that day well. It was our most reckless moment, and now it was being used to condemn us. I stared at Aggrivane, wanting to ask why he had kept it a secret for so long. But I dared not.

"Do you still claim innocence?" Marius asked.

I forced myself to hold my head high and remain defiant in the face of this farce. "I never claimed innocence, only that I am guilty of no crime, and that I maintain."

Marius rested his elbows on the arms of his chair and steepled his hands at his lips. "How do you reason that?"

"The law allows a man to take more than one wife—this we know. It used to allow a woman the privilege, too."

"But that no longer applies due to questions of paternity."

"Exactly. Given that I cannot bear children, that law does not pertain to me."

"You are saying you should be allowed to have an affair simply because no issue can come from it?" Marius scoffed.

"In these circumstances, yes." I turned to Arthur. "You put me away mentally and emotionally long ago, just as the nobles had advised you to do when it became clear I was barren. But I stayed with you. I prayed. I begged the gods to prove them wrong. But they did not hear my prayers. Then when I came back from being held by Malegant, I found you had indeed replaced me. You forced me to learn to live with Morgan as my near equal and constant competitor for your affection. Even this I did in fidelity until you abandoned me in my darkest hours after the war. Only then did I waver."

"So you are blaming your sin on him?" Marius laughed. "You are even more a fool than I anticipated."

I ignored him, focusing all of my attention on making Arthur understand my plight. "What else was I to do but love the man who offered me everything you denied me? I have not the resolve or the fear of the gods to keep me pure like your Christian nuns. You must have suspected something. By your silence, you gave your permission, Arthur Pendragon, but now in my hour of need, you remove it. Merciful and just ruler indeed!"

Arthur's eyes flashed dangerously, but there was a softness in his expression that told me my words had done their work. "I will not deny I am partially to blame for the situation we find ourselves in today. But I will not allow your offense to go unpunished either. You are a judge. You know the fines your kin must pay for this offense. I also banish you from Camelot. You are hereby stripped of your title of queen and sent back to Northgallis to live out the remainder of your days."

My stomach seized at his pronouncement, and I feared I would vomit in front of the whole court. My head swam as the Combrogi erupted into deafening argument around me, shouting at Arthur, Marius, and me. I fought to steady myself, having nothing to brace my body against.

Kay started to rise to escort me out, but Marius stopped him by placing himself between Kay and Arthur.

"High King of Camelot," he said in his best sermon voice so it would carry over the uproar.

Arthur rose to meet Marius's challenge.

"You have addressed the charge of adultery, but what of treason? By betraying you, she betrayed the crown. Surely you will not let that go unpunished? In order to keep your Combrogi together"—with a sweep of his hand, Marius took in the entire room—"you must show you govern the land by one law, not a separate rule for yourself and another for your people, just as you showed them with your son. They need to know that the supreme law which governs your heart is the law of Christ, which forbids adultery—here the method of her treason— under pain of death."

The Combrogi erupted again, several rising from their seats.

"Sit down and be silent, or I will throw you out!" Arthur bellowed.

"Think of her eternal soul, Arthur," Marius continued, unaffected by the outburst. "She is already in the depths of sin by her pagan profession. Would you damn her soul to eternal fire by letting her treachery go unpunished as well?"

"This is ridiculous," Aggrivane shouted. "No one wishes for her death."

"He goes too far," Mordred said at the same time.

The clamor started up again, with Combrogi lining up to take sides with either Marius or me. As ludicrous as the whole situation was, it was oddly comforting to know most of the knights stood behind me, even those who were party to bringing me here.

Arthur huffed, weighing his options.

"There are alternatives, my lord," Kay reminded him. "She could be tested by fire or water."

Morgan snorted. "She's a priestess. She could cheat that even with the king's blood fresh on her hands." She sneered at me, clearly enjoying the opportunity to be rid of me once and for all.

"A better option would be judicial combat," Aggrivane offered. "It is used only as a last resort, and I would say we are there."

"She is a battle queen," Constantine reminded him. "She will win that as well. It does nothing to serve justice."

"Are you trying to kill me?" I cried, fighting through the ringing in my head. I tried to remain stoic but was rapidly losing control. "Bishop Marius, you claim that in your faith, adultery is punishable by death, but did your Christ not stay the hand that would have stoned the Magdalene? Why do you not show me the same mercy?"

All eyes turned to Marius, awaiting his response.

"The Magdalene was a repentant prostitute. I see no signs of repentance in you." A sly smile split his face. "If, however, you are willing to publicly confess your sins—all of them—convert to Christianity, and live out your days in a convent, I think you could be allowed to live."

So that was it then. Just as in my father's court, it came down to my faith. Marius hated the Avalonian priestesshood so much he was willing to make my life the price of his agenda.

I took a deep breath. "I made vows many years ago that I have no intention of breaking"—I looked at Morgan—"unlike some. I do not see what my faith and the charge of treason have to do with one another, but under no circumstances will I break the oaths I've made to my gods."

"They relate," Marius sneered back, "because your king, whom you offend with your treason, is a Christian man. By adopting his religion, you show faith in him and make slight recompense for your offenses. I will give you one more chance to change your mind."

I stood still and silent, willing the power of priestesshood to flow through me.

"Very well then. Arthur, her fate is in your hands. How would you treat any other traitor to your crown?"

"I need time to think this through. Kay, take her to the prison and be sure she is well guarded. I will rule at dawn."

Lot rushed forward to kneel before Arthur. "Once, you spared my life when I was far more deserving of your vengeance than she. I venture to say you've never once regretted it. Please, show her the same mercy. If you must have some outlet for your wrath, take my life instead. It is yours to do with as you please."

My heart broke at Lot's selfless gesture. He would have been my father-in-law had I married Aggrivane. I knew he wished that was how things had turned out, but I'd had no idea the depths of his affection for me.

"Thank you," was all I had a chance to say as I was led away by Kay and two guards.

☙ ❧

I was imprisoned in one of Camelot's cellars that had been converted to hold criminals awaiting trial or those considered too dangerous to house in normal rooms. I shivered as I tried to keep my mind off the deliberation going on upstairs and keep some small shred of control over my sanity.

When the door to my cell opened the next morning, I was certain they had come to lead me to my death. But it was Sobian, not Kay, who greeted me. One look at her horrified face told me something was very, very wrong.

"What is it? What has happened?"

She shook her head, unlocking my shackles in silence. "See for yourself."

I expected her to lead me back into the castle, but instead we walked across the grounds to the edge of the river, not far from where it emptied into the bay. A small knot of people stood on the bank, their backs toward us.

"Arthur?" I asked tentatively.

He turned, holding out an arm as though asking me to pass beside him.

As I approached, the crowd parted, and I caught sight of a small boat that had been dragged onto shore beneath a willow. When I was close enough to see there was a body within, I dropped to my knees in the sand.

"Oh, no. No, no, no, no," I cried, tears choking me.

Inside lay Elaine, clad in a white dress with a garland of flowers in her hair and her head resting against a small pillow, surrounded by all of her favorite flowers: lilies, daisies, roses, and buttercups. She was pale, and her eyes were open, staring forever at the heaven she'd always longed for.

The men lifted her ashore, but I already knew it was too late to save her. I had seen enough dead bodies to know when the soul was gone. When they put her in my arms, her skin was ice cold.

"Oh, Elaine, dear heart, what have you done?" I asked her as I gently closed her eyes.

"These were in her hands," Sobian said, holding out a roll of parchment and a spike-shaped flower with clusters of purple bells.

The flower was comfrey, but it was untouched. It was merely a symbol. She wanted us to know, even before we opened the missive, she had taken her own life. From out of the depths of my memory, I recalled the day she had borrowed the vial of comfrey from the room Lancelot was being treated in. I had told her not to ingest it because it was poisonous. Vaguely, I wondered if that was when she'd first gotten the idea.

I rocked her in my arms like a baby. "Sweet girl, why?"

"Guilt," Arthur said. He handed the small parchment to me.

I wanted to ask him to read it to me, but I could not speak.

"Sobian, will you stay with Guinevere while we take Elaine up to the castle? We will lay her out in the council room along with the contents of the boat. If this is how she wanted to die, then this is how she will be buried—and in holy ground. I care not how her life ended. She is still a child of Christ."

Numbly, I trudged behind Arthur back to the castle. I couldn't feel my feet nor even the rest of my body. All I could do was weep and wonder why my oldest friend had chosen to take her life and if Arthur was right. Please, Goddess, do not let this be over me.

They wouldn't let me stay with her body, but Sobian was allowed to sit in my cell with me while I read Elaine's final words.

> *I go to meet my Maker without the Sacraments but not without making my final confession. I do so publicly so those involved may know the heaviness of my heart. Maybe because of this they will not judge me for what I have done but let me go in peace.*

> *They say "I love you" is supposed to be a blessing, but for me, it has been nothing short of a curse. The ones I love the most are the ones who have hurt me the deepest. I, in turn, have done nothing but hurt them.*

> *Guinevere, I never meant for your life to be in danger when I condemned you in front of Arthur. I simply wished to have revenge for the betrayal I felt. As I cannot have your death on my conscience, I will cause my own, praying that Arthur will consider your wrongs avenged. Our Lord said, "There is no*

greater love than to lay down one's life for one's friends." This I
do for you out of deepest love.

By the time you read this, I will be at peace, and I wish the
same for you.

Pray for my tormented soul.

Elaine of Corbenic,
Daughter of Pellinor and Lyonesse, wife of Lancelot du Lac,
mother of Galahad—chosen one of the Grail

I handed the note to Sobian without a word and motioned for her to leave me.

"Arthur said he will take another night to consider your case in light of Elaine's death," Sobian said.

I nodded, but I didn't really hear her. I was too numb, too broken to care about my own fate.

With nowhere to sit but on the earthen floor, I picked a corner and hunched my knees up in front of me. A single thought chased itself around my mind—I was indirectly responsible for Elaine's death.

Images of her flashed through my mind, like the portraits she'd so loved to draw. Elaine as a young girl, picking daisies under the summer sun; covered in mud when we returned from exploring the moors; her joy upon hearing one of Isolde's fanciful Irish stories— dear, long-departed Isolde, who had also taken her own life, I recalled with deep sadness—Elaine's love-struck expression when she first saw Galen; the single tear dripping down her cheek when Arthur proposed to me; her face shining with pride over Galahad; and finally, her stricken expression when Marius suggested I should die for my crimes.

The dam within me broke, and I wept for my friend. Somewhere in midst of the pain, a thought struck me—depending on Arthur's decision, our separation might be brief.

◈◈◈

Once I had cried myself dry and the shock of Elaine's suicide started to wear off, I was once again acutely aware of my own situation.

Arthur is merciful. You've seen him judge hundreds of people.

He is nothing if not reasonable. He won't harm you. You have nothing to fear. That was what I told myself. But the more I tried to pray and remain calm, the more panic shot through my veins.

You are going to die. You have betrayed your king and country. Your affair caused your best friend to die. You will meet the Goddess on the morn, and she will not be merciful. Those thoughts were much louder than my feeble attempts to calm myself.

My breathing grew shallow and short until I was hyperventilating. In this state, I understood Nimue's insane rantings in a whole new light. I understood why she'd rocked back and forth because I was doing the same. This was ten times worse than the fear I had felt in the cave with Lancelot or even while in the grip of Malegant's torture. At least in those situations, I'd had some small means of fighting back. Now I was completely helpless. My fate was in the hands of someone whom I had hurt badly.

I bit my knuckles to keep from screaming.

That was how Aggrivane found me, weeping on the floor like a child and making small whimpering noises around my fist. At first, I didn't even recognize him. Of all things, it was his scent, clean like the woods after a rain, that brought me back to my senses.

He was sitting next to me and holding my head against his chest, which spasmed occasionally. I realized he was crying. No, not crying—bawling. I touched a hesitant finger to his neck and found rivers of tears.

"Aggrivane?"

"I never wanted it to be this way, Guinevere." He hiccupped. "I never thought it would come to this. Oh, what have I done?"

My tears answered his in silence. Neither of us spoke until he had regained control over himself.

"When Mordred told me what he suspected, I was irate. More than anything, I wanted to prove him wrong. Then when the signs began to suggest he was right, all I wanted was to get back at you for choosing Lancelot over me. It should have been me. That is all. Not this. Never this."

I took a deep breath, somehow, even after all these years, still finding my center in him. "Even if you had refused to help, told Mordred and Elaine they were mad, they would have found a way. This is not your fault." I wiped my eyes. "Elaine wanted revenge on any other woman Lancelot loved. As for Mordred, when Arthur and I ruled against him on the rape accusation, he promised revenge—and now he's taken it."

Aggrivane kissed the top of my head. "No matter what happens, I will stay with you. I will be with you to the very end."

I snuggled into his chest, finding enough peace there to sleep. I only knew I slept because I dreamed. I was in the Grail castle, but it was as though I could see everywhere at once. Arthur knelt before the Grail, praying so fervently sweat ran down his face. In a nearby room, Bishop Marius blessed the sacramental bread and wine. He added a drop of water from a cruet and a drop of something else from a small vial.

After muttering a few more prayers, Marius interrupted Arthur by placing the host on his tongue with the words, "Corpus Christi." Then he gave him the chalice to drink from with the words, "Sangue Christi," to which Arthur responded, "Amen."

"Go back to the castle and get some sleep, my son. I am sure the Holy Ghost will illumine your dreams with wisdom," Marius urged.

Arthur did as he was bid.

While Marius busied himself cleaning the chalice Arthur had used, a hooded woman approached him from behind.

"Father," her voice was tinged with a familiar lilt, "I trust all went well."

Marius turned, passing something into the woman's waiting hand. He folded his hands before him in an attitude of prayer. "God's will be done." He chuckled darkly.

The woman turned, and I caught a glimpse of her face. It was Morgan.

Before I could see more, the door to my cell squeaked open, and I was jolted awake. I scrambled to my feet.

Mordred stepped in first, trailed by Bishop Marius. Mordred saw Aggrivane and grimaced. "Why am I not surprised to find you here?"

Only then did Marius realize who Mordred was speaking to. "Ah, together again. It ends how it began. Poetic, isn't it?"

"Ends?" I asked, scarcely able to breathe.

Marius looked at me as though it was obvious. "Why yes, our king has made his decision."

Two women entered, carrying one of my gowns and my cloak along with a few pieces of my jewelry. They helped me put on all of it.

When they were done, Marius simply commanded, "Follow me."

I looked at Aggrivane, confused. Did this mean I was free or not?

"But what is my sentence?" I yelled after Marius.

He said nothing, only motioned for me to come along.

I started to follow, but Aggrivane grabbed my arm. "Please. Tell me one last thing. Do you forgive me?"

"Yes. And part of me has never stopped loving you. Whether I meet freedom or death outside these doors, I can be at peace knowing you know."

I thought I heard him whisper his love to me as I stepped into the blinding light of morning, but I couldn't be sure.

⁂

Death had come for me.

But she was not an old woman as I had always imagined but a young man, barely more than a boy, sent to accompany me on my final walk.

When my eyes adjusted to the light, he was waiting for me with Bishop Marius. The bishop could hardly contain his glee as he said, "The high king asks me to pass his sentence on to you. On the charge of high treason, you are sentenced to death at the stake. His Majesty asks your forgiveness."

The world tipped, but the boy caught me before I fell. My stomach cramped, and my bowels threatened to empty right there in the street. Terror, more pure than anything I have ever felt, filled me from head to toe. I shook so violently my teeth clicked together.

"I forgive him," I managed to say amid waves of nausea.

They led me to the mouth of the street known as the bloody lane because it was a popular location for duels, revenge killings, and the occasional public execution. My final destination was within sight. Where the road opened to a square, a pyre stacked high with wood was the focal point. Never had a short road seemed so long.

Somehow, word had gotten out already about what was to happen. The street was so packed with spectators that a burly man had to be recruited from the crowd to push the gawkers out of our path. But first, Marius removed my jewelry—save for the sapphire ring Arthur had given me that I managed to hide—and tossed it into the crowd, who fought over it like starving dogs. Punches were thrown and blood spilt, and that was before one of the guards tore my cloak from my shoulders and hurled it at them too. Finally, it came time for my dress, which I opted to remove myself. I would go to my death with no possessions, clad only in a shift for modesty.

As I walked the gauntlet, stumbling and unsteady in my panic, the people shouted all sorts of taunts, curses, and filthy words at me. The same people I had vowed to give my life to protect were now gladly cheering on my death. Garbage and all manner of rotten things were hurled at me. Just when I thought the indignity couldn't get any worse, from somewhere above, someone emptied a bucket of water on me. Well, I'd thought it was water. It turned out to have been a chamber pot.

We finally reached the scaffold. The boy had to help me mount the stairs because I was paralyzed with fear.

"Where is my lord? Where is the king?" I asked as they lashed my wrists to the pole. "Is he not supposed to witness such an act?"

"He was detained. But that is why I am here in his stead, to make sure the job is done." Marius inspected my bindings. "Have you any last words, priestess?"

Priestess. The word was like a trigger in my brain reminding me who I was. I was not some helpless whore but a woman dedicated to the gods. This was not how I would meet my end, not at least without a fight. With that, the panic subsided, and my mind became full of clarity.

"Yes. You can go to hell. And all your kin with you." I spat in his face.

He took the burning torch and touched it to the kindling at my feet. "You first."

The kindling caught in a whoosh of smoke and heat. If I was to have any chance of escape, I had to act fast. Coughing and spluttering, I tried to find a grip for my feet on the uneven, splintery wood. It was not easy, but I soon found a position I could hold for some time.

While the crowd jeered and cried around me, I closed my eyes and concentrated on sending my consciousness down into the earth and forming a shield around me, just as I had done during my priestess trials in Avalon. I imagined the flames staying at least an arm's length away from me, and I pushed back the heat and smoke with every exhalation.

It was not long before the sight took over. I could see through the flames, into Arthur's bedchamber, where he'd woken just moments ago, desperate to get to me and commute my sentence. He tried the doors, but they were locked. Weak, unsteady, and retching, he fell to the floor. Still determined to stop this madness, he crawled to the windowsill, body partially paralyzed by that wicked drop in his communion wine.

He called my name, but over the crowd, no one could hear him. He continued crying, "Stop! Stop! This must stop. I am the king!" until his throat was raw.

When I came back to myself, I was still struggling with my bindings. My strength was beginning to wane. The heat crept closer as my shield slipped. Just as the blackness was about to take over, I heard the familiar clanging of swords and whinnying of horses. I raised my head and forced my eyes open. Riders—Bedivere, Sobian, and Gawain among them—were deep within the crowd, fighting to reach me.

Then the bonds around my hands slackened. I turned to find Mordred hacking away at the ropes. His clothes were drenched to stave off the flames, and he had a cloth over his nose and mouth so he could breathe.

"Promise me you will not seek the throne while I live," he said.

Astounded, I could barely respond. "Yes. I swear."

"Then go. Lancelot waits for you. Go and live."

I looked to where he indicated just in time to see Lancelot ride toward the pyre at full gallop on a massive black horse, trampling people underfoot. Mordred ducked as Lancelot reached through the fire to swing me up onto his horse. My hair and clothing caught as I vaulted through the flames, skin blistering, but I barely felt the pain.

I clung to Lancelot with the last of my remaining strength, coughing out smoke as the horse's hooves beat a steady rhythm on the hard ground. Only once did I chance a glance back over my burned shoulder. We were not being followed. Sobian and our allies were doing their jobs.

We rode until Camelot was a mere speck on the horizon. Smoke from the pyre was still visible, but the dwindling thread at its center indicated the fire had been doused.

Lancelot turned to me and examined my arms, face, and the burned crisp that used to be my hair. "You are injured. We must find you treatment, or you will grow ill. I did not rescue you only to have you die of your wounds."

I nodded, still numb to the pain, but I knew that when it came, it would be excruciating. I needed a safe place to recuperate. "We cannot stay on the open road long. No matter how long Kay and the others hold off the chase, they are sure to send more soldiers after us."

"Where do you wish to go?"

That was a good question. I was free. I could go anywhere. But I was no longer queen, no longer Arthur's wife. What did that mean for me? Where would I be safe? I could not be guaranteed anyone, even my own kin, would not betray me. Avalon was too far away. I knew of only one place where we could be safe, at least for the time it would take me to heal and reevaluate my life without Arthur.

"We ride to Lothian."

MISTRESS OF LEGEND

BOOK THREE OF GUINEVERE'S TALE

HIGHLAND PICTS
LOWLAND PICTS
DALRIADA
STIRLING
FIRTH OF FORTH
DIN EIDYN
(EDINBURGH)
ANTONINE WALL
VOTADINI
LOTHIAN
DAMNONII
FIRTH OF CLYDE
STRATHCLYDE
SELGOVAE
HADRIAN'S WALL
DÚN BREATANN
(DUMBARTON)
DIN GUAYRDI
(BAMBURGH)
NOVANTE
CARLISLE
BERNICIA
ISLE OF WINDS
SOLWAY FIRTH
CAMELOT
DIN GEFRON
(YEAVERING BELL)
RHEGED
YORK
ANGLO~SAXON TERRITORY
MIDLANDS
NORTHGALLIS
GWYNEDD
POWYS

PART ONE

The Broken Crown

Chapter One

Summer 518

rthur's men caught up to us before we reached Lothian. I thank the gods they did. Otherwise I would be dead.

Lancelot and I were camped in the woods less than a two-day ride from Camelot when they found us. No doubt they spotted our fire, but we could not be without one, for I lay on the ground, wrapped in Lancelot's cloak and shaking with fever. The burns on my left side that ran from above my hairline down to my foot stung with the fury of a whole nest of hornets and my skin glistened with sweat, yet nothing could warm me. We had had no choice but to stop, for I could no longer sit a horse.

Only days before, Arthur had tried to have me burned at the stake after Lancelot and I were accused of infidelity and treason as a result of our extramarital affair. Initially banished from Camelot, Lancelot returned just in time to rescue me from death, though I suffered severe burns in my escape. We had intended to flee to my mother's homeland in the Votadini territory, but my injuries proved too severe for so long a journey.

Now, a group of Arthur's most loyal knights—the Combrogi—approached on horseback, no doubt to drag us to back to face the justice we had fled. Lancelot was doubly condemned as both a traitor for his affair with me and for interrupting my death sentence, so he had even more to fear than I.

Lancelot drew his sword, ready to defend me. I stumbled to my feet, holding onto him for support. Each movement was fresh agony, pulling at my inflamed skin and taxing the damaged muscle underneath. But I was a warrior. No matter how ill I was, I would not cower on the ground while they dragged me away like the spoils of the hunt. Repositioning Lancelot's cloak to give me greater freedom of movement, I took up his dagger, prepared to use it if I had to.

As they approached, Aggrivane, Bedivere, and Kay held up their hands, still on the reins, to show they wielded no weapons against us.

"We come in peace," Bedivere called.

They would have to forgive us for not believing that.

My heart stuttered and squeezed at the site of Aggrivane, unsure whether to love or hate him. In our youth, he had been my lover. We'd planned to marry, but my father made a contract with Arthur before we could tell him, which trumped our plans. Then less than two months ago, Aggrivane was among those who betrayed Lancelot and me to Arthur, though Aggrivane later repented of his actions.

They dismounted, hands still raised.

"We are not here to arrest you," Kay said. "Arthur ordered us to bring you back to Camelot. He wishes to grant Guinevere a full pardon. He never intended to have her killed. That was the work of his bishop, who now awaits his trial in prison."

"How do we know you speak the truth and are not simply trying to get us to come along peacefully?" Lancelot retorted.

"If we had ill intent, would we warn you to flee, Lancelot?" Aggrivane asked. "Arthur may be merciful to his former wife, but he has not spoken of you. As far as we know, you are still exiled, still a subject to death upon your return."

Aggrivane was right. Arthur may once have been a king of justice and mercy, but with the events just passed, it was impossible to know if that still held. After all, if he could order his wife's death, what worse did he have in store for the man who'd cuckolded him? Even if they were telling the truth about him not wishing me dead, Arthur was still a wronged man who had a right to revenge.

I turned to Lancelot, his blue eyes frightened and conflicted. "You cannot return to Camelot, but I will not go without you. Let us carry on as we had planned."

Bedivere cautiously approached me. When I didn't lunge at him with the dagger, he put out a tentative hand, carefully examining my charred skin and weeping, red blisters. If he noticed how my teeth knocked together despite my clenched jaw, he didn't show it. "If you remain on the road, you will die. Only a priestess can heal these wounds, which I'm certain you know, seeing as you are one." He gently brushed a finger over the blue crescent moon tattoo on my brow—a mark that all priestesses of Avalon wore—as though to remind me.

Lancelot turned to me. "You must go with them, Guinevere. I

will go on to Brittany. Send word when you are well, and I will make sure a boat awaits you in Camelot's harbor."

I made to grasp his tunic but stumbled as a wave of dizziness overtook me. Lancelot steadied me. "No. We will not be separated again. You are Arthur's best knight. Surely he will pardon you too."

Kay joined the two men at my side. "Arthur has reason to forgive you, Guinevere, especially in light of all you have suffered. But Lancelot defied him twice. He will not be inclined to be merciful, lest he set a precedent of weakness with the other Combrogi that could lead to his ouster. The people are not pleased with him after what he did to you." Kay turned to Lancelot. "You can take the risk if you'd like, but I do not advise it."

Lancelot growled in frustration, looking at the stars as though they could advise him. After a period of thought, his gaze returned to me, cataloging my injuries. To the Combrogi, he said, "She will get worse the longer she goes without aid. I will not sacrifice her life to save mine. Let me come with you as far as the edge of town. If I can see she is well received, then I can bear the guilt of knowing I abandoned her and that she suffers without me."

⚬◐ ◑⚬

They carried me to Camelot on a stretcher. While it was not quite the indignity of being transported in a prisoner's cart or forced to walk behind the Combrogi in chains, it certainly was not the entrance any soon-to-be-redeemed queen wished to make. But I did not really care, for my wounds turned even breathing and blinking into torture. They throbbed and burned, rubbed even rawer against the fabric of the stretcher with every jolt. My fever came and went, plunging me into nightmarish visons where I relived my failed execution and created far worse fates for myself, only to be brought back to reality with startling clarity when the heat relaxed its grip.

I was between bouts of delirium when Camelot came into view. The castle loomed large on the hillside above as we trod the hidden track to a private entrance, rather than the wide thoroughfare used by noble guests, merchants, and all manner of visitors. The people need not know I had returned. There was no need to stir up a mob now, especially when I needed peace and quiet to heal. They would have plenty of time to voice their joy or displeasure later.

Seeing this place, this dream begun by Arthur's father and

fulfilled in our reign, through fresh eyes was strange. When I'd first seen it as a new bride so many years ago, it was to me a place of wonder and majesty, a place of light and welcome. Now, its shadows held dominance, swallowing up the comfort I used to find within its walls, daring me to attempt to find solace here.

Kay and Aggrivane had just carried me into my old bedroom when Arthur met us. Grainne and Morgan—Arthur's second wife and my lifelong enemy—trailed in his wake, their blue robes of priesthood covered by thick off-white aprons that signaled their readiness to see to my wounds as soon as I was released into their care. Arthur dashed to my side, his eyes widening as he took in my scarred face and neck, all that was currently visible from beneath my clothing.

"Guinevere! Sweet Mother of God, what have I done?" Arthur brought a hand to his blond beard, covering his mouth.

"You've nearly killed her, that's what you've done," Grainne shot back, already examining me.

Morgan moved in to help transfer me to the bed, but Arthur stepped in front of her. Her eyes widened in offense. If I was not in so much pain, I would have laughed.

Arthur leaned down to me, his blue eyes softened with tenderness and grief. "I did not intend to kill you, please know that. I gave no order, despite what you may have been told. You must believe me."

"Arthur, move away and let us work," Morgan snapped, elbowing past her husband. She dripped a few drops of a bitter liquid onto my lips, and I instinctively licked them away before recognizing my error.

"No. I will not let you poison me too," I yelled, flailing my right arm at her and trying to sit up. A wave of nausea pushed me back to the pillows.

Grainne held me down with muscles honed from years of birthing babies and wrestling recalcitrant patients like me. "Stop fighting us. No one is trying to poison you. It is only a small dose of poppy juice, just enough to make you sleep. You do not want to be awake to experience what is to come."

"Why did she accuse you of poisoning her?" Arthur asked Morgan. When she ignored him, slicing into my dress with a dagger to expose the extent of my injuries, he turned to me. "What did you mean, Guinevere? You said 'too.' Who has she poisoned?"

I attempted to answer, but my lips felt swollen and my tongue wouldn't obey my commands. Snorting out a breath, I balled my fists and tried again, but the effort was too great. Blackness tugged at my eyelids, making them feel as though they were made of wet sand.

Finally, I managed to slur, "You," before I slipped into unconsciousness.

Chapter Two

Winter 519

The next month was a blur, lived in flashes that were more like visions than solid reality. First the world was black, then searing light pierced my eyes and the left side of my body was consumed by fire, burning, skin crackling and peeling back, leaving tender flesh and muscle exposed. Strong arms held me down when I tried to fight the sting of water and wine. By the time the sweet scent of honey and herbs reached my nose, I was worn out, numb, spent from the pain.

I slipped in and out of fever dreams that were no more pleasant for my mind and soul than the treatment my body was undergoing. In one, Arthur embraced me at Camelot's gates, only to sink a sharp blade into my side again and again. This blade did not kill me, but rather it gave him a place to begin peeling away my skin, which came off in searing strips until my flayed flesh was gone completely. Sometimes this was intermingled with Morgan or Grainne's voice and the now-familiar scent of their healing salve.

Other times I dreamed that Bishop Marius had his boney arms around me, pressing his poisoned Communion chalice to my lips, only to wake and find one of the priestesses holding a mug of warm, earthy liquid to my lips and commanding me to drink.

Long stretches of blackness followed, interspersed with periods of agony. Had I an axe, I would have happily cleaved myself in two, if only to stop the sharp, burning pain. Many times in the past I had burned myself while cooking, on a candle flame, or practicing manipulating the element of fire in Avalon. Then, I'd thought I would die from a wound no bigger than my little finger. Now, with half of my body flayed, skin pulling and pinching as it tried to recover from the deadly kiss of the flames, I begged the Goddess for relief. *Deliver me, Mother, and I swear that from this moment forth, I will suffer small injuries in silence, without complaint. Deliver me, please. But* most of the time I could not form rational thought. All I could do was scream, and when my throat grew raw, my screams were silent.

◦◦◦

In the cold gray days between the winter solstice and Imbolc, I woke to find the pain, while still present, was much more manageable. Grainne was sitting by my side, holding a cool, wet cloth to my forehead, her gray eyes as full of love and concern as a mother's for her child.

"Praise Brigid, you are with us once again." The relief in her voice was so great, I wondered how close I had come to dying. I tried to sit up, but Grainne placed a firm hand on me. "Do not move. Your wounds are exposed. I was just about to cover them when I felt you stirring."

My eyes were drawn to find the source of my pain. From my shoulder, down my left arm, to my hip, knee, and part of my left shin were pockets of angry red rivulets where blisters had once bubbled and burst. Around them, the skin was twisted, blackened, and tough. Slathered on top was a layer of the honey herb mixture I had smelled in my dreams. I had seen my share of battlefield burns and knew enough of healing to understand how badly I was injured.

I searched Grainne's gray eyes for some sign I was wrong. "These will scar, won't they?"

She pressed her lips together. "I'm afraid so. But at least you are past the risk of blood poisoning."

She relayed the events of the last few months as she wound me tightly in white cloth to keep my wounds clean. Arthur still held Marius in the jail. Morgan had brushed off my comment about her poisoning someone as a mistake of the fever, and rumor had it Lancelot was involved in a civil war with his brothers in Brittany, but Arthur still hadn't offered to pardon him.

I was only partially listening, having raised my healthy hand to my left cheek. The skin was leathery, pulled tight over my cheekbone. What was worse, I could not feel the touch of my fingertips. I moved my hand to my ear with the same result. Snapping my fingers, I was relieved to be able to hear the sharp sound with as much clarity as before. But when I brushed my hand through my hair, it came out in dry, straw-like black clumps.

I stared at it for a moment before the tears fell. "What have I become?"

She held me close and rocked me as I cried. "You are still you, a queen—regardless of what Arthur says—and a strong, courageous woman. You only need time to heal. By summer, you will be back to your old self. You'll see."

A knock on the door interrupted any further conversation. I wiped my eyes so that whoever it was couldn't see that I had been crying.

Grainne went to the door. From the bed, I could not see who was on the other side, but I heard her tell my guest I was awake.

She turned back to me. "It is Arthur. Do you feel well enough to see him?"

I scowled, tempted to say no, but reluctantly agreed. I couldn't avoid facing him forever.

Grainne slipped out as Arthur entered, leaving us alone.

Even nearing forty summers, Arthur's height and brawn were fearsome to behold. Where other men responded to the passage of years by curling in on themselves like the fronds of a fern, Arthur held his head high, shoulders squared, every inch the High King. Even his skin, which was crossed with deep wrinkles and battle scars, appeared chiseled rather than wizened. Had he not betrayed me so, I would have been proud to be married to such a handsome warrior.

Arthur made to embrace me, but seeing my bandages, he stopped himself. "Oh, praise God. I will offer a thousand Masses of thanksgiving that you are well."

I smiled, knowing it was expected of me, even though the gesture meant nothing since I did not share Arthur's faith. "I am alive," I corrected him. "But I have a long way to go before I can be called well."

I shifted in the bed, unsure of how to act but unable to flee. How does one interact with their former husband who might or might not be guilty of trying to have one killed? I supposed one could pretend everything was fine, but that was not in my nature. I desperately wanted to ask how Morgan had deflected his curiosity about the poison, but leading with that was likely not a good idea.

Arthur cleared his throat. "If you don't mind, I would like to explain what happened that night. I want you to know."

"Go on," I said cautiously.

He sat on the edge of the bed. "You may recall that at Bishop Marius's suggestion, I received Holy Communion and retired to bed after being unable to come to a verdict in your case. A night of prayer showed me how wrong Bishop Marius was in demanding your death. Upon reflection, I realized he was not in the least concerned with your affair with Lancelot, which was my reason for putting you on trial. He claimed to be concerned with your treasonous betrayal of me, but he was really acting out of his own selfish concerns—all because you do not share my Christian faith. You were unfaithful to me, yes, but as you said, I was equally disloyal to you. The whole trial became much more than anyone, Aggrivane and Mordred included, ever intended. They have told me how sorry they are."

I eyed him warily, pulling the blankets tighter to my breast like a shield. "They have shown me their regret by aiding in my rescue and healing. But what of you? I know you were unable to stop the burning. I saw it in a vision as I fought back the fire that raged around me."

Arthur's face lit up with hope. "If you had a vision, then you know I was ill, incapacitated." His words came faster now, as he sought to make me understand. "I have been over and over that night in my mind, trying to determine why I was so ill. It was no ordinary sickness, so I must suspect poison. The only thing I consumed that no one else did was Holy Communion, so I am holding Bishop Marius under suspicion."

In my mind's eye, I once again saw the bishop tip a tiny drop into the Communion chalice. He turned and handed the vial to a woman in a dark hood. Her face was obscured, but a strand of copper hair peeked out, betraying her identity. "He did not act alone. You likely will not believe me when I name his accomplice, but I must."

Arthur studied my eyes and squeezed his own shut. He pinched the bridge of his nose as though his thoughts pained him. "Please do not say it was Morgan."

"Why do you suspect her?"

"I don't, but the bishop has named her as an accomplice."

"He tells the truth, at least in that regard. That is why I refused to let her near me with those anesthetizing drops. She heard me say she poisoned you. It is not so far a stretch to think she might not want someone who knows her secret to live."

Arthur scowled at me. "Morgan could never kill anyone, least of all you. You have known each other since you were girls in Avalon together."

"I would not be so sure." I told Arthur about my vision of him crying out that the burning should be stopped. He was alone, so no one heard, and he was so ill he could not stand to go to anyone and give them word that he did not condone what was happening in the courtyard below.

"Yes, that was exactly what happened." He bowed his head, hunching forward, elbows on his knees, encumbered by the burden of guilt he carried. "I don't know what exactly took place that day, but I aim to find out." He looked at me as though struck by a sudden inspiration. "Would you be willing to be the judge when Marius has his trial? I cannot act as judge in the case because I am its victim and certainly not impartial—"

"And you think *I* am?" I chuckled mirthlessly. "Do you realize you are giving me the chance to exact revenge on a person who has done nothing but antagonize me for years? Arthur, you are mad. If it is a judge you seek, ask any priestess. We are all trained in the same manner."

"No. It must to be you. And for now, leave Morgan out of this. I cannot bring charges against her until I know for certain—"

"What more proof could you need? Marius admits that she aided him, and I have told you of my vision. You have a claim and someone to corroborate it. That is enough for you to find them both guilty. I will testify if needs be, but I do not understand why you need me to act as judge."

Arthur rubbed the back of his neck. "I can try the bishop, but I cannot sentence him, not with the whole of the country watching. If I find him innocent, my soul will not rest easy, for justice will not be done. But if I find him guilty... well, he has powerful allies, so you know what that could mean. Open rebellion." Arthur's bloodshot eyes were pleading. "I am trying to save Camelot."

"So what you are saying is that if I don't act as judge in your place, you fear you will be viewed as unjust and someone may try to overthrow you." I made a disbelieving sound. "Who have you become, Arthur? You used to be a just man whom I respected. Now you are just as concerned with your reputation as every other noble I've ever known. Personally, I think that is exactly what you deserve. What you did to me, even putting Morgan and Marius's involvement aside, is unforgiveable. Yet you dare ask me for help."

"Is there nothing I can do to change your mind?" Arthur's voice was pleading.

I may not have been as conniving as Morgan, but this was an

opportunity I could not let pass me by. This was my chance to set my life straight and I was going to take it. "Pardon Lancelot in open court and ensure his safe passage back to Britain. If you personally guarantee no harm will come to either of us, I will assent to your request."

A range of emotions flickered across Arthur's face—incredulity, pain, serious deliberation, and finally, acceptance. "It will be done. I swear it on both my God and yours. As soon as you are well, you will get your pardon, I will recall Lancelot, and we will have a trial for the bishop. I am more than ready to put this all behind us."

I squirmed, my wounds flaring up again. One day these events would be but a distant memory for him, but I would have to live with the consequences every day for the rest of my life. If he wanted me to act as judge, I would. But he should not expect the Mother's mercy. Too much had happened, too many trusts shattered, too many hearts broken. No, so much pain could only summon the wrath of the Crone.

Chapter Three

The Combrogi leaked word that I had returned under Arthur's guard as though it was secret information intended only for a select few. They let it "slip" through tongues seemingly loosened by liquor in the taverns, traded it as currency in dim back alleyways, and passed it to servants during illicit relations. As expected, the news slithered from ear to ear faster than a flea-born disease.

When the proclamation went out that Arthur wished for all of his subjects to assemble in Camelot's courtyard, they eagerly complied. Some camped out overnight, wrapped in thick blankets and cloaks, leaning against buildings or sleeping on the cold stone pavers. Others straggled in near dawn, staking out their places with wooden crates or dirty quilts. Enterprising merchants set up booths and sold spiced wine, hot cider, roasted nuts, and fresh bread to the crowds as though this were a festival.

The pale winter sun had just crested the horizon when Sobian stepped into my chambers, stomping her feet from the chill. "They are riled up. Some are speculating this will be a hanging, while others hope you will be reinstalled as queen. They are taking bets as to whether by the end of the day, your head will sport a crown or end up in a basket."

I swallowed hard. "That's comforting."

"Don't worry. The Combrogi will guard you. Arthur will not let anything happen to you, not now."

By mid-morning, the courtyard was full to bursting with people sitting on every stall roof, leaning out of windows, and lining the walls. Those not as lucky were forced to wait in the frigid shadow of the gates or make do with a patch of open land on the road leading to the castle. By noon, they were packed in so tightly, no room remained for even a rat to scurry over the feet of the assembled people.

Arthur led me out onto a balcony overlooking the throng. As Sobian promised, the Combrogi lined the rail, shields at the ready to defect any rocks or arrows aimed at hastening the king's justice. Behind me, to my right, Morgan sat on a throne, her copper hair plated into a thick braid that wound around her head like the crown she was denied as only being named royal wife, rather than queen—a title I had held until Arthur stripped me of it during my trial. Her face was set into an impassive mask, despite the fact it must have been killing her to have me within Camelot's walls again. This was my first time laying eyes on her, outside of when she nursed me, so my heart was thrilled to see her misery. After what she had done, she deserved so much more.

I was glad, however, that her four-year-old daughter, Helene, was not here to see her father and mother pitted against one another. As I had spent time in Lyonesse's household, so was Helene being fostered in the House of Rheged with the family of Morgan's first husband, Uriens. She would return here when she was older to assist Arthur and Morgan in running Camelot until she was betrothed.

Morgan's partner in their crimes against Arthur, Bishop Marius, stood to my left, wrists and ankles shackled, flanked on either side by Arthur's guards. His red tunic—which he claimed to wear as a symbol of the blood of Christ, but I'd long suspected he favored because it brought attention to him—hung off a thinner frame than I remembered, but he appeared otherwise well treated.

Mordred, Arthur's son by Morgan long before they married, rounded out our party, standing in his father's shadow. Surveying his people, he looked every inch the heir in his golden tunic and cloak, his thick necklaces glinting in the sunlight.

I leaned over to him. "I haven't had a chance to thank you yet for helping set me free."

He gave me a boyish smile. "It was the least I could do. I'm hoping now that you are here—"

The Combrogi ringing the balcony struck the butts of their spears on the floor to quiet the crowd. The resulting boom drowned out the rest of what Mordred said.

Arthur stepped forward, and two of the guard parted to let him through. "My people, I have long governed this land with the intention of being as just and as fair as possible. That means admitting when I have done wrong. I have committed a grievous error against a woman I should have honored above all.

"Hear me, people of Camelot. I was wrong to condemn Guinevere and even more in error when I considered ending her life as a fitting punishment to assuage my thirst for vengeance. I never intended her death; she never should have been sent to the stake. I was ill-guided but do not fall upon that as an excuse. I ask you here and now to witness my apology to the woman whom I wronged."

He fell to his knees before me, hands clasped as though in prayer, appearing more like a penitent at the feet of a priest than a High King addressing his former wife. "Guinevere, there are no words I can offer to make things right, but I can assure you of my deep repentance for the sin I have committed against you. I am truly sorry. Can you ever find it in your heart to forgive me?"

I let the silence settle like so much dust underfoot as I debated how to respond. For a king, much less the High King, to humble himself so publicly was rare indeed. On one hand, mere words meant little—were I not trained to manipulate the elements, I would have succumbed to the deadly flames. But on the other, his repentance was sincere. Around us, people shifted from foot to foot, hardly daring to breathe as they awaited my answer. Deep within, the nudge of the Goddess—as we collectively referred to all goddesses in Avalon—urged me to swallow my considerable pride and grant him clemency.

"I can, and I do," I said, allowing my voice to carry over the crowd, who cheered and applauded in response.

Arthur stood and embraced me. Then backing up a few steps, he removed his sword—one of the treasures of Avalon—from its scabbard and held it aloft. "In the sight of the citizens of Camelot, I hereby pardon you of all charges leveled against you, especially and including the charge of high treason and the accusation of heresy. You are allowed to practice whatever faith you see fit. Return to your life as a free and innocent woman in the sight of all."

Most of the crowd yelled encouragement and whistled, but their joy was countered by a not insignificant number of boos and hisses from those who had noticed Arthur had failed to directly address the charge of adultery.

"Heretic!" someone yelled.

"Whore!" called another.

I bristled at the insults but made no move to defend myself.

Arthur raised his hand for silence, and at his signal, guards elbowed through the crowd to remove those causing the most agitation before they could spark a riot.

Arthur said, "Bishop Marius stands accused of grievous wrongdoing in connection with these events. He will be tried at my convenience. While she no longer holds the title of queen, I have asked Guinevere to serve as judge."

Marius's eyes widened so far and so fast, they nearly popped out of his head. "I object most strenuously."

Arthur carried on speaking, either not hearing or ignoring his prisoner's protests. "You have seen her dispense justice and mercy in equal measure for more than twenty years, and I have every reason to believe she will render impartial judgment in this case as well."

Marius broke free of the steadying hold his guards had on him and rushed Arthur. "If I am to be subject to a farce of justice, then she should be charged as well." He gestured to Morgan with his bound hands. "Your beloved wife helped to incapacitate you. Arrest her for the traitor she is."

The rowdy crowd stilled, suddenly silent.

I looked over my shoulder at Morgan. She gripped the arms of the throne so hard her knuckles were white. Her face had paled like curdled milk, her blue eyes hard as flint and her jaw taut as though she was fighting to resist spewing forth rage.

She stood, graceful and silent, regarding the assembled people. Finally, she took three steps forward. "I am innocent, but if our king wishes to try me, so be it. I trust that justice shall prevail." She held out her arms to Arthur, offering them for binding like a prisoner.

Arthur faced her, still and solemn as a statue. To most, he likely appeared impassive, but I had spent enough time with him to be able to detect the warring emotions flickering across his features. He wanted to believe Morgan was innocent; that much was clear from his directive to not involve her in Marius's trial. But now that Marius had publicly accused her, Arthur could not ignore the charges. To do so would be proving the very point he was trying to invalidate—that he practiced favoritism with those close to him.

Arthur motioned to her. "Morgan, royal wife to the king, you stand accused of conspiring with the bishop to interfere in my justice toward Guinevere and Lancelot. You will stand trial immediately following that of the bishop. In the meantime, I will not remit you to the prison, but know you are free only at my mercy."

It did not escape my notice, nor that of the grumbling people, that Arthur had reduced Morgan's crime from high treason in the form of attempted assassination to conspiracy to impede justice. While some cheered to see her publicly accused and humiliated, many others rallied to her defense, loudly reminding Arthur that she was his wife and deserving of his respect. Some even called for her to be named queen in my stead, while others demanded he divorce her on the spot as he had done with me.

In the back of my mind, a memory tingled, vying for my attention like an itch. More than thirty years prior, under a full moon in Avalon, the Goddess had predicted this moment. *"The day will come when sister shall oppose sister, both in this sacred place and without. Loyalties will be tested and betrayed, so heed my warning."*

The goddess of war would face the goddess of the moon, wife would turn against wife, two priestesses locked in a cosmic battle. We had come so close to this before, but always something had stopped us from engaging one another. It was still not our time. But the shadows were retreating, making room for us to stand in opposition. The culmination was not far off, and when it came, it would be to the death. The question was which of us would be left standing.

"I know you asked that Lancelot be pardoned before we try Marius and Morgan," Arthur said to me one night several weeks later, "but I am beginning to wonder if I will be able to wrest him from his duties in Brittany."

I turned from watching out the window as the bitter wind drove leaden storm clouds pregnant with snow toward Camelot's spires to glance at Mordred, who was with us in Arthur's private study. He was pointedly ignoring our conversation, intent on his book. "Why is that?"

"Lancelot has pledged his service to the house of Dorngwenn. Their king is dead and the four heirs are engaged in civil war with each other and their sister. It is a terrible situation, one I fear becoming too involved in, lest they see my interest as an act of aggression against them. I have not forgotten my promise to you, but circumstances tie my hands."

I wrinkled my brow. "Did you say Dorngwenn, the family of the White Hands? Is that not Yseult's family? I thought Lancelot was fighting with his brothers? Why would he be at war with those responsible for Tristan and Isolde's deaths?"

"The war between the brothers ended shortly after you recovered, then he took up arms against Dorngwenn." Arthur shrugged. "As for why, that is for him to explain. Sometimes that man is too loyal and virtuous for his own good."

I glowered at Arthur, wishing he would at least hazard a guess. "Lancelot is nothing if not loyal." *If only he would be as loyal to me.* I was surprised by my own bitterness. I wanted Lancelot home, or at very least, to receive word from him. It was time for this farce in Camelot to end. But instead of saying that, I toyed with the open book on my lap. "How will you proceed?"

"I do not know yet. I've tried letters and emissaries, but the

Bretons are determined to hold on to Lancelot until their war comes to an end."

"But that could be years!"

"I know. I may be his king in this country, but in Brittany, they are his lords."

Arthur might be content to bide his time, but I was not. Fortunately, a plan was already forming in my mind. "They do not know you intend to absolve him, correct?"

Arthur raised an eyebrow. "No. Why?"

"They have no doubt heard he deserted his duty to you and escaped imprisonment. You have every right to have him returned to you to face punishment, no matter what other duty he has promised. His first loyalty is to you. If you go to Brittany with a small contingent of the Combrogi, no one can accuse you of inciting a war because you won't have enough manpower. But you will have enough force to bring him home."

He hesitated. "Perhaps, but I would like to leave that as a last resort."

I turned on him, unable to stand his detached manner any longer. "Is this all a game to you? I will go over there myself and fetch him if you will not act. This is my life, my future you are gambling with, and I'll not have you make a sport of my happiness simply because you no longer have the power you once did."

Arthur stood, his chair scraping loudly across the stone floor. "Watch your tongue, woman. You may no longer be my wife, but I am still your king. I demand respect from you."

I rose, refusing to let his attempt at intimidation cow me. "You speak of respect, but the very reason we are here, together, is for me to adjudicate the result of your utter disregard for me. If anyone in this room should be demanding respect, it is I! Forget not that I am here as a favor to you."

"If that is the way you feel, then leave. I can handle the trial without you."

I gave a small, mirthless laugh. "Truly you are mad. Blind and mad. There is so much more at play here than your petty little trial, Arthur. If you wished, you could have sentenced Bishop Marius and Morgan without my aid. But no, you came to me because you are too weak to make a decision. People are beginning to sense that.

"Camelot is falling to ruin around you. Just this morning,

Sobian returned from the quay with tales from the merchants that two of the Combrogi were injured in putting down a demonstration against you in Cornwall. It seems Constantine is actively speaking against you, seeking to leverage his claim as your heir." I placed both hands on the table and leaned forward, trying to make Arthur hear me. "Your people are turning against you, yet here you are, fixated on justice for your wife. Open your eyes, Arthur!"

Mordred shut the book he had been reading with great force, as though to remind us of his presence. "Those incidents are becoming more and more common. Yesterday, I heard Kay and Bedivere speaking of a similar event in Carlisle. They claimed the people there want to see you deposed in favor of me and demanded to have the charges against my mother dropped. It seems she has supporters even outside of Camelot."

"They don't trust you, Arthur." I rounded the small table so that I stood in front of him. "You ruined much more than our relationship when you let that priest lead me down the Bloody Lane in shame. You showed yourself to be an unfeeling despot who was willing to shed blood over petty jealousy instead of the wise, temperate ruler they thought they knew. You allowed them to see a future for which they will not stand."

"I didn't *allow* anyone to do anything! That is my whole point. That is what the outcome of this trial will establish. The bishop used me for his own ends."

"What will that do, Arthur? Yes, justice will be done, but half the people will disagree no matter what ruling I give. It will not solve the bigger problem."

"I think you underestimate your influence," Mordred said. "As judge, you are acting in the Goddesses' stead since you are still sovereignty personified, regardless of whether or not my father wishes to acknowledge you as queen. It is an honor that cannot be reversed by mortal man. Those who follow the old ways know this. That is why some of the people are demanding you for their queen instead of submitting to my father."

My eyes grew wide and my mouth fell open as I struggled to voice my shock.

Mordred chuckled. "Sobian did not tell you?" He clucked his tongue. "The country is not only divided in allegiance between the High King and his two heirs, one of blood and the other of declaration. No, there are many who back you. You have been their mother-figure for more than two decades and they trust you. This is why the role my father has set for you is so important. It will not only show that the High King follows the same rules he enforces, but it will shore up the people's flagging faith in Camelot once again."

Arthur seized on his son's logic. "He is right, you know. You can turn the people's thoughts back to loyalty to our cause and end the brewing unrest before it blossoms into something worse."

I sat back down, stunned at the sharp turn this conversation had taken. I had come to Camelot to heal and do a favor for Arthur, and now the fate of the kingdom rested in my hands. I closed my eyes and inwardly groaned. Long ago, I swore as a priestess of Avalon to enforce the ways of might and right. Then on the day I was crowned queen, Arthur's subjects became my children, unruly and taciturn though they may be. I owed it to myself and to them to once again shoulder the twin weights of priestesshood and queenship, no matter how distasteful I found them.

But even more than that, Arthur and Mordred needed me. I may have had every right to be angry with Arthur, but he was still the man I'd once loved and my heart tugged me back in his direction. Mordred may have been Morgan's blood, but I'd acted as a second mother to him, watching him grow from a boy into the man who would be king. Mordred was as much son to me as the twins I had long ago given into the arms of the Goddess. I could not abandon father or son simply because doing so was easier. That was a coward's response, and I was not one to shirk my duty. The quick escape into a peaceful life with Lancelot I had envisioned would have to wait.

⚬⚬

After waiting another three weeks for word from Lancelot, but not enacting my suggested solution, Arthur chose to move forward with the trials. He gathered those concerned in his circular chamber, the one in which I had been tried and found wanting months before. Only this time, it was not I who was to plead for my life; Fortuna's wheel had turned, and rather than being crushed beneath its weight, I rode it to its apex as judge.

I sat alone at the front of the room in the throne I'd always occupied when we met in council in this room. Unlike previously, Arthur did not sit beside me, choosing instead to stand off to the side where he could pace nervously. On my right and left, Morgan and Marius waited in the chairs previously occupied by Arthur's most trusted knights. Morgan's expression was serene, as attentive and composed as though she was going to lead a council session and nothing was amiss. Marius, on the other hand, fiddled with the chains binding his wrists. His uneven beard and wrinkled, dirty tunic indicated he had been plucked straight from Arthur's dungeon. He may have been gaunt from his travails, but that did nothing to extinguish the fiery loathing he threw my direction with every glance.

The remaining chairs were occupied by the top Combrogi. Others clustered behind them arranged based on allegiance—Accolon leading Gawain, Bors, and the others who supported Morgan and Arthur, while Aggrivane sat at the head of Bedivere, Sobian, and those who favored Mordred and myself. There was little difference from the groups that had formed at my own trial, showing loyalties only slightly shifted in my favor. Those eager to oppose me needed more than attempted murder to change their allegiances.

They shifted nervously, many refusing to meet my eyes. Now that I was the one in control, they knew I might exact revenge and so feared me. The temptation was strong. But my role as judge had its origin in the power of the Goddess herself, and so I tried to keep my pride and personal feelings in check. My role was to be as neutral as possible until the moment I was asked to render a verdict. Still, it would be easier if I could call the Goddess down into me as I had on the day I chose my champion. But this was not a ceremony or ritual; it was a judicial matter among mortals, and as such, I had only my instincts and conscience through which to hear the guidance of the gods.

Thankfully, Arthur had chosen the most secluded area of Camelot to hold this trial. Had we been in the great hall—or really anywhere else in the castle—the buzz and chant of the crowds likely would have been audible during the proceedings. Word had gotten out, and throngs of people waited outside, some of whom were shouting their support for Morgan or the bishop, while others made it clear they were already reserving their seats for an execution.

Arthur approached me and turned to face the assembly. Even though he was the victim as well as a witness, it was his duty as king to open the proceedings since the Archdruid was not here to do so. "As you all know, we are gathered here today to determine what really occurred last autumn when Queen Guinevere was erroneously sentenced to death by fire. She is serving as judge in my stead at my request, and she has intimate knowledge of the events from two perspectives, which she will share. But first, I invoke my right as the wronged party to tell my own tale."

He paced again, head bowed in concentration and hands clasped behind his back. "After listening to all assembled at Guinevere's trial, I retreated to the Grail Castle to be alone with my thoughts and pray. When night fell, Bishop Marius suggested I retire and ask God's guidance in my dreams. I was bone weary, so after taking Holy Communion, I did as he suggested. That night I slept fitfully, waking often to the sensation I had consumed far too much drink, even though I had not had any.

"By daybreak, I was retching and so dizzy I was unable to stand. I heard the crowds below and became concerned, but I was not yet alarmed. I'd given no order, so I never imagined what was taking place. However, when the wind shifted and blew the smoke to me, I knew something was very wrong. I tried to stand but fell to the floor. I needed to know what was happening, so I crawled to the casement and threw myself upon it. That was when I saw that the fire had been lit. Again, I tried to stand, but to no avail. All I could do was cry out my dissent, hoping someone would hear me and stop what was taking place below.

"Eventually, I must have lost consciousness because when I next opened my eyes, I was in Morgan's arms. She was rocking me and telling me I had become ill, but all would be well." He stopped and faced me. "It was only later that I heard about Lancelot's intervention and that you were alive." He looked over his shoulder at Mordred. "I wish to publicly thank my son for his part in setting you free. And when we finally locate Lancelot, he will have my gratitude and pardon as well. Please know that I would never have ordered you to be executed."

With that, Arthur ceded the floor to me and I was free to question him. His testimony matched up to what I had seen in my vision, but I still had a few questions. "Did you ever determine what made you ill?"

"No. There was no way to do so."

I didn't expect so. If only I could have gotten my hands on that communion chalice before the damn priest washed it. Even smelling the dregs or tasting the residue on my finger might have helped. I put that aside and turned to my next concern. "What was Morgan's reason for being in your chamber?"

Morgan answered instead. "Perhaps you would like to address that question to me rather than asking Arthur to guess?"

I fought the urge to roll my eyes. "Fine. But you have to wait your turn. I would like to hear from Bishop Marius first. And I suggest you remember that I hold your fate in my hands and address me with the respect I deserve." I eyed Marius. "That goes for both of you. Bishop, you may speak."

Marius cleared his throat and stood. "I stand here today an innocent in chains, much like our Lord and Savior before Pilate. But unlike him, I know my judge has already found me guilty and I have not the virtue to remain silent."

I took a deep breath, willing myself to remain calm. I should have expected a performance from this man. He never could resist an audience.

"I do not deny placing a drop of some liquid in the king's communion wine."

An astonished rumble went through the Combrogi. Marius raised a hand to silence them.

"But it was not poison, as everyone was so quick to assume. I would never do such a thing to my king." He fell silent and did not seem inclined to continue.

"What was it then?" I prompted.

Victory glittered in his eyes. "I do not know. I was only following the orders of Arthur's wife"—he gestured toward Morgan—"whom I assumed had his best interests at heart. She is a healer and so could have given him any number of remedies for any number of conditions. I am but a humble priest who knows nothing of such things." He touched his breast and bowed his head slightly in a gesture of humility that made me want to gag.

"Now, as I have explained the only charge against me, I suggest you question her"—he nodded in Morgan's direction—"about the exact nature of the substance."

Arthur stood before Marius in three long strides, a finger poking the bishop's chest before I could even speak, his pent-up anger on full display. "That is not the only charge against you, you pompous traitor. How do you explain giving the order to kill Guinevere? I never offered my final judgment."

Marius looked at me as if to inquire whether I would allow Arthur to question him in my place.

I smiled coldly. "I was just about to ask the same question." I sat back, awaiting his response.

Marius's eyes shifted back to Arthur as a wolf-like grin spread across his face. "Oh, but you did. Perhaps you do not remember because you were so ill. You looked at me and clearly said 'guilty.'"

Arthur grabbed the priest by the collar of his tunic. "I said no such—"

Marius continued as though Arthur had done nothing. "The point is, I was still carrying out the king's will."

"No. You. Were. Not." Arthur ground out each word between clenched teeth.

"Morgan, you were there when Arthur was ill. Did he say anything of the sort?"

Morgan shook her head. "No. Marius told me before I saw Arthur that he had spoken to the king in private and he had passed his verdict. He said he was headed to help Guinevere meet her fate, but never elaborated."

"There you have it." I fought back a smile. "Two people say no and one, with a very strong motivation for self-preservation, disagrees. Plus, we have testimony stating you spoke of Arthur's will before anyone saw him that day." Given this evidence, there was no need for me to mention my vision. "It seems to me there is nothing left to be said. I am ready to render my verdict."

This was one sentence I did not have to deliberate upon. I had been waiting twenty-five years to avenge the wrongs this man had done to me—separating me from my first love and my family, turning Arthur away from Avalon, installing Morgan in my place, and trying to have me killed—and now I could do so in full knowledge it would be justice.

I finally allowed my grin free rein. "Bishop Marius, through the power granted to me by High King Arthur Pendragon, you are hereby found guilty of the crime of high treason for the attempted murder of a royal person, the punishment for which is death by the method of the king's choosing."

Marius's mouth hung open in shock.

"Take him back where he came from," Arthur ordered Gawain and Bedivere.

Each man took one of Bishop Marius's shoulders and dragged him toward the door.

"I protest! I am not guilty. I protest!" he yelled. "You cannot do this to me. The Bishop of Rome will hear about this! Arthur, think what having the blood of a priest on your soul will mean when you go before God."

Arthur shuddered involuntarily, which made me wonder if he had the stones to go through with the punishment demanded by law, especially since he was giving that damn priest time to frame himself as a martyr. I would have executed him on the spot.

Putting away such dark thoughts, I turned to Morgan, whose face had gone white, as though she only now realized this was not some silly play we were enacting; I truly held over her the power of life and death. "It is your turn to speak."

Slowly, she rose, regarding each person in the room before finding her voice. "I am guilty of no crime except caring for my husband. Each of you remembers what that day was like. By the time Arthur left this room, his nerves were frayed and he still had an enormous decision to make. I cannot imagine what he must have been feeling, but I knew he needed the clear mind that would come with rest. That is why I suggested the bishop add a drop of valerian to his cup. Arthur had already refused dinner and I knew he would argue with me if I suggested to him that he take it. I only meant to ease his nerves and help him sleep." Her eyes welled with tears.

Once again, I fought the urge to make a face. I had seen Morgan's false tears before and they did not move me. "You know as well as I that valerian doesn't make people violently ill."

"Not usually, no. But we also know that many things can change how an herb works. It may not have even been the valerian that made Arthur sick. It could have been anything."

For the first time all morning, Aggrivane spoke. "Is that the same excuse you offered Viviane when Rowena nearly died during the testing to determine the next Lady of the Lake?"

That Aggrivane remembered the incident was a surprise. But he had been close with us during our time in Avalon and understood what a puzzle that event had been to everyone who knew Morgan. She had always maintained her innocence, and no one had ever conclusively proven Rowena's poisoning was Morgan's fault. However, the rumor of her guilt dogged her, lending her a reputation for being talented with poisons, deserved or not.

Morgan's eyes narrowed and her cheeks flamed. "How dare you! Did Guinevere prompt you to say that? My life is on the line and the two of you are dredging up the past because it might help justify your hatred of me. Perhaps the bishop was right and we were both condemned in your eyes from the start." She was crying in earnest now, tears dripping onto her freckled cheeks.

"Oh, this is bullocks," Sobian muttered, just loud enough for those around her to hear.

"I have a question," Arthur interjected, perhaps to allay further argument. "Morgan, how did you come to find me that morning? I never had the chance to ask."

Morgan wiped the area beneath her eyes, giving Arthur a soft, sorrowful smile. "I couldn't stand to watch when the bishop went to get Guinevere. Something about his manner made me believe he was leading her to death, and despite all that has passed between us, that I could not bear. I went to your room when you were not outside with the crowds, nor in the great hall. I was worried something might have happened to you, especially in light of your uncharacteristic verdict."

"Something might have happened to me?" Arthur raised an eyebrow. "Like what?"

Morgan shrugged. "I don't know. I was scared you might have been taken by an ill humor and could be a danger to yourself. You were so upset the day before. Frankly, you hadn't been yourself since you removed our son from the Combrogi because of that woman's false accusation against him. Then there was poor Elaine's death, and then Guinevere betrayed you." She took Arthur's hands. "I couldn't leave you alone if you were still in pain."

Arthur looked at her with such tenderness, I thought I was going to vomit. I cleared my throat to break the spell between them. "Do you still have the bottle?"

Morgan blinked. "The what?"

"The bottle of valerian. I'd like you to take me to it so I might examine it myself." Morgan had no way of knowing I had seen the bottle in my vision and this was my way of testing her.

She blinked a few more times, as though considering my odd request. "If you wish."

She led Arthur, Gawain, Bedivere, and me through the halls

to her chamber. A cheer went up when we passed the great hall. Through the cacophony, my ears discerned a few cheers of joy that Morgan was still with our party and two particularly loud shouts of protest over Marius's verdict from his acolytes Galahad and Peredur, who vowed the wrath of God upon our heads if we carried out his sentence.

When we reached Morgan's room, she knelt and unlocked a large chest sitting near the fireplace. She withdrew a small wooden box from within and lifted its lid. Inside stood a dozen small dark glass vials, each identical.

Morgan held two bottles up to the light before finding the one she desired and holding it out to me. "This is it."

It matched the vial in my vision, but so did all of the others in the box. "How do you know it is the right one? I don't see any markings on it." It was possible Morgan could have mixed up the vials and inadvertently given Arthur the wrong liquid.

She looked at me as if I was a child in Avalon once again. "I don't want untrained people pawing through my medicinal store and mistaking a poisonous herb for something innocent, so I use a special ink made from the milk of goat's lettuce that is only visible when you apply ash over it." She displayed a sooty thumb I hadn't even seen her dip into the cinders. "Once the milk is dry, it won't rub off, but the ashes will, so the bottles are unrecognizable to anyone else."

I took the bottle and examined it. Now that she pointed it out, tiny letters near the neck designated it as valerian. While I had hoped this test would clearly proclaim Morgan's guilt or innocence, all it had done was show that her case was not as cut-and-dried as that of Bishop Marius. I needed time to think. As much as I hated her, as much as I wanted to use this as an excuse for revenge, I could not do so out of hand, because everything Morgan said was plausible.

I handed the bottle back to her. "I was hoping that would provide us with a clear answer. But it has not." I rubbed my head. "Let us adjourn for today. I may speak with each of you tomorrow if more questions arise."

⁓◦❧ ❧◦⁓

I left the council chambers and was on my way to the labyrinth at the center of Camelot, a courtyard garden made by Arthur for me as a wedding gift and meant as a place of refuge when I needed to clear my mind, when Arthur bellowed Aggrivane's name.

I raced toward the sound, only to find Arthur leaning over a letter in the great hall, a messenger at his side. The midday light revealed his anger, his eyes flashing as they skimmed over the ink, cheeks enflamed, golden hair standing at attention like stalks of barley.

"My lord?" Aggrivane stepped as close to Arthur as he dared, wisely well out of arm's reach.

Arthur looked up, seeming for a moment to have forgotten he'd called for Aggrivane. "I need as many fighting men as you can muster. Bring them to the barracks yard within the hour. I will survey them then." He turned to me. "Guinevere, I need you to find the Combrogi and call back as many as you can."

When Arthur made for the door, I grabbed his arm, stopping him before he could make it into the hall. "What is it? What is happening?"

"They—the house of Dorngwenn"—he stabbed the parchment—"have taken Kay hostage. I mean to get him back."

"Isn't there any other way? You said yourself you were loath to start a war."

Arthur glared at me. "It is this or receive my brother's body in pieces. They were very clear about that."

"Then let me come with you. You know what an asset I can be in battle. You can leave me there with Lancelot once everything is over."

Arthur studied me, considering my words. "No. I will not draw you into yet another war. Besides, your job here is not finished."

He turned away, but I stopped him, forcing him to face me. "Then I will tell you my judgment now and you can act upon it whenever you will. *Please*, Arthur. Let us call an end to this."

"No. I need someone here to ensure Morgan and Marius do not escape."

"So I am their jailor now?" I asked, aghast.

"Be reasonable," Arthur all but yelled. "Mordred will be concerned with affairs of state and I will be taking most of the Combrogi with me. I am entrusting them to your care because I know you will do what is right."

"And you aren't willing to be rid of me," I said under my breath, but Arthur did not hear over his own summons to Mordred.

Mordred trotted to Arthur's side before the echo of his name had faded. "Yes, Father?"

Arthur removed the torc from around his neck and placed it around his son's. "I turn control of Camelot over to you. I must go to Brittany as soon as possible and likely will not return for some time. Do not carry out the sentence against Bishop Marius or pass judgment on your mother until I return." He clasped his son's shoulder. "See that peace is maintained in my absence and watch over Guinevere."

Mordred beamed. "Of course, Father."

The exchange should have been innocent, but when Mordred looked at me, something in his smile chilled my bones. An ambitious and well-trained heir, he had been waiting for just such an opportunity. Only time would tell how much Arthur would come to regret this choice.

CHAPTER FIVE

Summer 519

As summer's heat slowly took hold, it became clear that Camelot was changing under Mordred's rule. With most of the Combrogi off fighting at Arthur's side, he enjoyed nearly absolute power, something to be feared in one so young and rash.

I was not the only one to take note, and that meant our people, already distrustful, became increasingly nervous. It began with rumblings in the countryside. The lowly men and women who came to Camelot on pleading day—a custom Mordred tolerated but delegated to me because it tried his patience—all told tales of the Picts massing as though for some great council. According to one woman, the northern tribes—the Damnonii, Novantae, Selgovae, and Votadini—were growing restless as well, no doubt spooked by the sudden activity of the Picts.

Next came whisperings in the marketplace, brought back by Sobian's ever-observant ears. "Some of the women say the townsfolk are quietly taking sides. The whores at the Boar's Head say their patrons argue nightly. Some of the merchants' wives say their husbands have been discussing it too."

I stopped the spinning wheel in front of me, relaxed the arm holding the yarn, and looked at Sobian. "You cannot truly believe Mordred is planning an insurrection, can you?"

She leveled me with her most serious look. "I can, and I do. And I do not believe he will do it alone. He aims to unite the Picts and the Saxons against Arthur. The northern tribes too, if they'll take him. I think that's the real reason why he's keeping you here."

"Keeping me here?"

"Yes. Mordred easily could have sent you to Brittany with Arthur or put you on a ship following in his wake, but he needs you. You are Mordred's greatest asset, and also a threat. Regardless of what

Arthur said that day in front of the Combrogi, you are still our consecrated queen. Arthur cannot undo that. He can renounce you all he wants, but only death can unmake a queen. We all know how the ancient law works. For another to become king, the power of sovereignty must pass through you. He needs your cooperation, if not your blessing, to fulfill his plans."

I considered her words. "I have already told Mordred I will not seek the throne, so I am no threat to him. How else could I be of help to him?"

Sobian fixed me with a hard stare. "Are you daft or in denial? He could marry you, for one. Do not tell me it never crossed your mind. He needs a strong wife to cement his power, and you have more than proven your skill. It is either you or one of the Saxons or Picts. He already knows and loves you. It is not so big a leap."

"But I am like a mother to him!" I swallowed hard to contain the bile that soured the back of my throat.

"Still, you are not his kin, so nothing is stopping him if he is of a mind to do it. All I am saying is to be wary."

Thanks to this exchange, that night at dinner, we both had our hackles up, especially given the extravagant meal. The largess was unusual and could not be without meaning. Who was Mordred trying to impress and why? I couldn't help but watch every move he and Morgan made, my eyes narrowing as I calculated the nuances behind the idle conversation as we slowly demolished the fully dressed swan and several additional courses.

The pageantry had to be for his mother's new champion, Accolon, the second son of the house of Rheged. I had never trusted that man, not since the day he'd tried so hard to catch his cousin Aggrivane and I in the act of a dalliance under Pellinor's roof. He certainly shouldn't be privy to the intimate conversations of our private meals.

For such dynamics to be at play, more had to be going on in Mordred's court than simply holding power in Arthur's stead. Waiting any longer to find out if the rumors were true, if Mordred was angling to make his temporary power into something more, would be dangerous. However, I couldn't simply ask him outright; I needed to use a question that would appear innocent to outsiders, yet test the limits of Mordred's willingness to confide in me.

Picking at my pudding with feigned disinterest, I asked, "The barracks and smithy were quite busy when Sobian and I passed them earlier today. You have given them some special assignment?"

"Only ensuring our standing army stays in practice and our weapons are at the ready in our king's absence," he answered.

"That does not explain the Saxon spears and Pictish swords I saw cooling on the racks," Sobian said, one eyebrow raised in subtle challenge.

Mordred shrugged. "Just because Arthur refuses to adopt the weapons of our enemies does not mean I will be as narrow-minded." He turned to me. "You were a battle queen. Do you not agree that we should have every useful weapon at our disposal?"

I ran a finger around the rim of my cup, considering his words. He did have a point. If his words were true, then my suspicions were nothing more than a case of mistaken purpose. Maybe the rest of the rumors were the same. The Pictish gathering everyone was so concerned about could have been planned long before Arthur left for Brittany. As for the villagers taking sides, wasn't it natural to compare the son to his father? It could all come down to a matter of interpretation. Having known Mordred for so long, I desperately wanted to believe it, to trust him.

"I do. In fact, I wonder that we did not think of it before."

Mordred smiled. "It is understandable. You had more pressing matters to attend to, such as securing the peace we now enjoy. But I wish to be prepared, for our enemies will only stay quiet for so long. We will be ready when they decide to move."

Satisfied with his answer, at least about the smithy, I settled back into my chair, casting a glance at Sobian to gauge her reaction. She was observing Mordred through lowered lashes, pretending—for I had learned many of her schemes in the last nineteen years—to be overcome by the generous food and drink. That she was employing such an act meant only one thing—she didn't believe him.

Though I accepted his answer about the weapons, I still harbored misgivings about his overall plan. Did Mordred know a strong contingent of his people were suspicious of his motives? He deserved to know what was being whispered behind his back. "I fear your good intentions may have been misunderstood."

Mordred wrinkled his brow and fixed me with a questioning look.

"Surely you have heard what the people are saying about you?"

"I have not," he said slowly, leaning forward over his plate, elbows on the table, intensely interested now.

I cleared my throat, unsettled by how much he looked like Arthur in that pose. "They say you are planning rebellion. They tell tales that you are allying with the Picts and trying to convince the four northern tribes to overthrow Arthur while he is in Brittany."

As quickly as they'd materialized, the similarities between father and son melted away. Whereas Arthur would have gone quiet at that news, blue eyes pensive with concern, Mordred merely nodded, a slight smile tugging at the corners of his lips.

"This news cannot possibly please you," I said, aghast.

"Of course it can," Mordred answered over the rim of his cup. "What did the old philosopher say? 'The enemy of my enemy is my friend'?"

Mordred's calm unnerved me more than if he had screamed his outrage. I narrowed my eyes at him as I ripped off a hunk of bread, needing something to do with my hands. "But the northern tribes are our allies. Whose enemy does that make them? The Saxons?"

"For one," Mordred replied around a mouthful of spiced plums.

I narrowed my eyes at him. "What exactly are you planning?"

It was Morgan who answered. "That is for us to know." She gave me an indulgent smile that reeked of triumph and stroked Accolon's hand as though he were a prized pet. "While we're talking about enemies, I have it on good authority that Mark's nephew, Constantine, may be our next threat."

"Is he still waving his sword around?" Accolon asked, more amused than concerned. "He is fairly impotent as long as Arthur and Mordred live."

"What about Helene? Does she not factor into the line of succession?" I asked, glancing at Morgan.

"No one would accept a woman as High Queen alone, much less a mere girl who has not yet lost her milk teeth," Accolon scoffed. "But as Arthur's daughter she will be quite a prize as she grows." He turned to Morgan. "You would do well to guard her against men like me."

She glared back at him, but said nothing.

Returning to his original point, Accolon added, "No, Constantine is not a real threat. His claim to Camelot rests only in that Arthur favored him before he knew about his son, so he can do nothing until the throne is vacant."

"Tell that to the people of the Summer Country," Morgan retorted. "I hear that he is working his way north and has his sights set next on Venta Belgarum. The people there are either fleeing into the hillfort or trying to outrun his army to safety."

Mordred's expression clouded. "Why did I not know of this?" His tone was sharp, a mixture of anger and accusation aimed at his mother.

"I only received word yesterday." Morgan placed her hand over her son's as though to placate him. "I have friends in the south who report he is showing signs of having taken after his uncle in ambition. They say he now demands his household function like a Roman villa. His confidants say he wishes to restore Britain to its former Imperial glory."

Mordred adopted Arthur's pensive look, staring across the room into nothingness.

"That is troubling." It was the only thing I could think to say.

"Indeed," Mordred mumbled, still deep in thought.

Morgan looked at us as though we were daft and threw up her hands. "Am I the only one who sees the opportunity here? Son, you need to act decisively against Constantine without delay. The people need a reason to trust you—perhaps even fear you. If you can secure Venta Belgarum, you will be a hero to the largest kingdom in Britain and you will demonstrate your might to the kingdom of Bernicia and anyone else who might oppose you."

Sobian leaned over and whispered in my ear, shielding her mouth from view with one hand, "She is acting like Mordred is king in fact as well as name, as though Arthur is dead."

I shivered involuntarily. "Perhaps to her, he is. He abandoned her without a ruling, and no one knows what will happen when he returns. If she doesn't act now, she may miss her only chance."

"Meaning?"

I shook my head, glancing at Mordred. "Not here. I'll tell you tonight." I sighed, watching Morgan quietly explained her idea to Mordred. Accolon nodded along like a devoted hound. "I don't like that she can so easily manipulate Accolon. He and Owain are a formidable force, and popular as well. If she can control them, Arthur may not have a throne to return to."

"Guinevere," Mordred called, breaking up our side conversation, "do you still have your set of Holy Stones? Bring them out."

"What? Why?" Despite my confusion, I rose, already obeying his command.

Why would he make such a request? Holy Stones, considered by some to be merely a game but taught to all priestesses as part of our training, was a method of divination long used by the Druids to advise chieftains in battle. Each stone represented a different type of solider, each triangle an opposing army led by a red queen. When combined with the sight and proper training, a Druid or priestess could use them to divine the outcome of a battle, thus ensuring the safest course of action for their ruler. It was normally only used in times of war or uncertainty.

Ah, that was it. Mordred was weighing the wisdom of his mother's plan and wanted to know what the gods predicted. Since Morgan's conversion to Christianity, she had forsworn such acts of divination. But lucky for Mordred, I had not and I had a different gift. Whereas she could see the future, I could see what was presently happening at a distance, which would give Mordred the chance to head off any future that his mother had already foreseen.

My stomach churned as I traced the halls to my chambers and back, a small round board under my arm and a bag of stones in hand. My feet moved by long habit, mind absorbed in the ramifications of what I was about to do. I had little choice but to read the stones for Mordred; while he did not hold me there against my will, I had nowhere to go if he tired of me or turned me out. Plus, angering him was dangerous; there were sufficient people who wished to finish what the bishop had started that I was best under Mordred's protection until Arthur could pardon Lancelot and see me safely to Brittany.

When I returned, they had all arranged themselves in front of the fire, leaving an empty place to Mordred's right for me. I set up the board with two sets of opposing stones, the clear quartz representing Mordred's army, the red jasper Constantine's, just as we had been taught in Avalon. But something was not right. Every time I looked at the board, I saw shadows to my left and right. There were more parties involved.

"Morgan, do you still have your set? I need more stones. They are telling me there is more at play."

She scowled at me but silently got to her feet and left the room.

While she was away, Mordred drew me off to one side, out of Accolon's hearing.

"I heard you and Sobian speaking earlier."

"And?" I tried to keep my voice light, but my embarrassment at being caught burned in my cheeks. How much had he heard?

He leaned in so that our noses almost touched, an oddly intimate gesture. "What is your ruling? Would you kill my mother along with the priest?"

I swallowed, not wishing to divulge my thoughts to him, especially without Arthur as witness. Although, since Mordred was acting king, he had just as much right to that information as his father. I took a deep breath.

"No," I answered slowly, forcing myself to look Mordred in the eye. "Just as when you were accused of raping that girl, I cannot determine her guilt or innocence with any certainty. She could be lying or she could be speaking the truth. As much as I want to punish her for what she has done to me and to Arthur, I cannot condemn a fellow priestess without irrefutable proof."

"So you would allow her to go free?" His warm breath brushed my cheek.

"Not exactly. I will recommend to Arthur that he set Morgan up in comfort in a remote estate of her choosing so she will be less prone to trouble. I wouldn't advise keeping her at court, lest she interfere again. And I don't recommend you condone whatever plan she and Accolon have concocted. Chances are good it benefits them more than you."

Morgan returned then, and we jumped apart like two children caught in the act of stealing a cooling bread roll from the windowsill. Morgan didn't seem to notice, holding out a bag to me. Her icy glare conveyed that if anyone outside this room ever heard that she still possessed a set of Holy Stones, she would make me regret it.

I tipped the bag into my palm and picked out the lapis, placing it on my left, before setting the malachite on my right. I breathed deeply, allowing the quiet rhythm of four people breathing and the soft crackle of the fire to lull me into that place between worlds where the voices of the gods could be heard.

The sight took over and I was no longer in the room with them. Flying above the field of battle and seeing through the eyes of the Morrigan's crows, I learned this skirmish was meaningless. Yes, it would stop Constantine from advancing—for now—but it was but a small thread in the tapestry the gods were weaving with our lives.

My fingers manipulated the pieces on and off the board until no more quartz or jasper remained. This war was not about the red and clear stones—Constantine and Mordred—at all. It was about those who were left, the blue—Morgan, the child raised in Avalon—and the green—me, the daughter of the Votadini. In the center, all alone, save for our two queens at the head of our armies, was the quartz king. But it wasn't Mordred or Arthur; it was both. The stones were saying that in the end, the fate of Camelot would not rest in the hands of other lords or even foreigners; it depended on those of us in this room and our absent king.

I came back to myself with a start. Mordred and Accolon were staring at me, but my attention was drawn to Morgan, who was gripping the edges of her chair, her eyes glassy and far away. She may no longer court the sight, but it clearly had a hold of her now. Her visions may well augment or explain what I had just experienced.

I rushed to her side. "What do you see?"

She did not respond immediately. Her eyes whipped back and forth, like those of a dreamer, watching something only she could perceive. "Arthur. He will never again set foot in Camelot."

Blood drained from my face and I grabbed her hand, seeking to steady myself on the arm of her chair. "He will die in Brittany?"

"No. Not death, not yet." Her eyes darted again as another vision overtook her. She paled and her eyes grew wide with horror, her mouth gaping, chin trembling as though she would cry.

"What is it? Please tell me."

She was back to herself in the space of a breath, but her face still bore the etchings of worry and fear caused by her vision. She refused to meet my gaze, caught somewhere between this world and the next.

"Morgan?"

She did not answer, only shook her head slowly, gazing past me at her son.

I squatted in front of her so that I was at her eye level, breaking her line of sight to Mordred. "I know you bear no love for me, but you need to unburden yourself. We both know the pain will only grow if you do not confide your fear. What did you see?"

Her attention whipped back to me and her blue eyes fastened

on mine. "I do not fear that which I can yet control." She rose, back perfectly straight and shoulders set. "We can yet avoid calamity." She took in Mordred and Accolon, who regarded her with a combination of curiosity and fear. "Arm yourselves, my loves. You have a battle to prepare for, one that will do much to cement your futures as leaders of Camelot. Guinevere can tell you more based on what she has seen. I have other matters to attend to if we are going to avoid the fate the gods have shown." With no more explanation, she stalked toward the door, muttering, "Goddess help me, I will not allow them to make fools of us all."

Who exactly were *they* and how did her visions fit with mine? What role did she and I play in the coming war and how—and why—did Arthur and Mordred stand between us? The stones had told us that the gods knew the answer, but they were not yet ready to make us party to their plans.

he next morning, I woke from a dreamless sleep before dawn, certainty like a block of ice in my stomach. Morgan had gone to see Marius after we read the stones. Why hadn't I seen that before? Or at least understood it last night? I had been so caught up in my own visions and interpretations of them that it had taken the blackness of sleep to wash away the distractions.

Marius, Morgan's only ally in Camelot—outside of her son— was currently locked in Camelot's cellar, awaiting Arthur's return and his final punishment. In truth, it shocked me that Mordred had kept him imprisoned after freeing Morgan, but then again, Mordred bore no love for the bishop and at least this way he could keep him under close watch.

The opportunity for duplicity had been there all along, and now Morgan would see him as a willing pawn in whatever game she was concocting to stave off the darkness of her mysterious vision. As mother to the acting king, anything the prisoner desired was in her power, so striking an accord with Marius would not be too difficult for her. Knowing Morgan, she would do anything Marius wanted if it ensured the future she feared would not come to pass.

As I neared the cells, my skin prickled with panic and cold sweat dampened my neck. I would never again be able to go near this place without being taken back to my time here, when this very prisoner was plotting my death.

Taking a fortifying breath, I motioned for the guard to unlock the stout cell door. For a moment, darkness overwhelmed me, but soon my eyes adjusted. In front of me was an empty cell devoid of anything save a fresh coat of rushes under a small pallet. Marius was not kneeling in prayer or huddled against a wall or even mocking me for taking so long to visit him. He was gone.

I cursed. Depending on how long he had been missing, Marius

could be halfway to Rome by now. Seething, I turned on the guard, drawing a long, thin dagger from my belt. "Where is he?"

The guard stood frozen and unresponsive, fear etched into his features.

Gritting my teeth, I tried again. "Where is the prisoner? Tell me, man, or it will be your blood upon these stones." I prodded him with the tip of the blade.

The guard swallowed hard, the motion making him wince as his Adam's apple grazed the steel. "He was released a few hours ago. The Lady Morgan—"

"Where did they go?"

His eyes bulged in fear. "I do not know. I only did as she commanded."

I sheathed my dagger. I didn't need to hear any more. Once Morgan had someone's allegiance, she didn't easily let it go, which was why many of the guards and servants still took orders from her. Damn Mordred for releasing her. Whether he knew it or not, he was slowly undoing all the justice Arthur had managed to impart before he left for Brittany.

Emerging into the dawn, I shielded my eyes, trying to uncover where they would have gone. Slowly, I turned in a circle, taking in the familiar landscape as if I could reveal their footprints by sheer force of will. Camelot's great fortress surrounded me on three sides, while the Bloody Lane branched off of the other. The castle's exterior doors were barred to intruders, so unless Morgan had made a deal with the guards inside, there was no shelter for them within. That meant they had to have taken the Bloody Lane into the village.

I had no choice but to set foot on the road that had once nearly led to my death. My stomach was in my throat by the time I reached the midpoint of the path. Homes, shops, and inns lined both sides, but few people were about at this early hour. I considered asking a woman loaded with sodden washing if she had seen a red-haired woman and a priest on her walk back from the river, but before I could approach her, I spied a small path leading between two buildings.

Narrow and nearly hidden by vines, it could be easily missed. Walls taller than a man cast deep shadows, plunging the path into perpetual gloom. This must be the Smugglers' Path where Sobian heard so much of her information.

I palmed my dagger, following the prodding of my instincts, which warned me this was not a safe place for a lone woman. But I was here and I had to see this through.

Stepping into the shadows, I recoiled at the sour stench of urine. At my feet, a beggar lay sleeping, covered in filthy rags. I gingerly stepped around him. The alleyway was not long; already, sunlight beckoned from the far end. For an area no wider than my outstretched arms, it saw a fair amount of activity. Against one wall, a prostitute plied her trade, the girth of joined bodies nearly blocking my passage. As I squeezed past, back toward them to show I took no interest in their activities, two thieves bartered with a third over the value of a purloined bracelet and a little boy begged for coins and scraps. *Thank you, Lady, for calling me to a station above this.* Though my role as a disgraced queen was not the life I'd chosen, at least I need not make my living here.

"Going somewhere, love?" The whore's patron gripped my bottom with a grimy hand, his other arm coming around my neck.

I ducked and tried to pull away from his grasp, but he was too strong. Abandoning his conquest for the moment, he pulled me against him, his naked prick rubbing against my back. My heart pounded. Memories of being raped and tortured by Malegant, one of the Combrogi, came rushing back as though they had happened just yesterday. They would not, could not happen again. I would not let it.

"Why not join us?" the woman called, revealing several missing teeth. "'Tis always more fun with two." She laughed salaciously.

"I prefer to leave you to it," I answered, slamming my elbow into my captor's gut.

The air whooshed out of him in a grunt and he stumbled back, pinning the woman to the wall. I started to run, but he grabbed a fistful of my hair, pulling me back.

Despite my prickling scalp, I whirled on him. "I was trying to be nice, but you are making that impossible." I slashed out with my dagger, pinning his free hand to the wattle-and-daub wall.

Instinctively, he released my hair. His howl of pain followed me down the alleyway as I fled. Men with contraband items scattered before me like rats, the beggar boy clearing the way by raising the cry of "intruder."

I stumbled into the adjoining street and my foot found a rut made by a wagon wheel, ankle twisting. I sucked in a sharp breath at the burning wrench, but I did not stop. A safe distance away, I stopped, bending double, hands on my thighs as I fought to catch my breath and ease the stitch in my side.

Where was I? I had been so intent on escaping danger that I hadn't paid attention to where I was going. Before me, a low stone wall protected travelers from plunging into the churning ocean as they made their way to and from the port below to the village. In the sea beyond lay the Grail Castle, its red-gold copula gleaming in the rising sun. The tide was just beginning to ebb, uncovering the narrow causeway connecting it to the mainland.

I shielded my eyes from the brightness of the rising sun. On the near side of the island, a small boat bobbed in the current. Someone had journeyed there while the land passage was underwater—a risky maneuver in the best of times, but even more so in the twilight before dawn. Rocks and sandbars could easily wreck a vessel if one did not know where to steer, and though the castle was not far from shore, the water was deep and rough enough to drown even an experienced swimmer. Few people knew the area well enough to have navigated it safely. As bishop and one of the guardians of the Grail, Marius was one of them.

⁓ഉ ൦⁓

The massive stones linking island to land were still slick as I raced across them, praying to catch up to Marius. If I did not, I likely would never find him again.

I rushed through the exterior gate, past the small cells lining the outer ring of rooms, only to be stopped by a knot of pilgrims waiting to be admitted to the inner sanctuary where the Grail was housed.

"What is this? Why are the doors closed?" They were never supposed to be closed. The Grail was always available to all, night or day.

"The bishop asked for some time to pray alone," answered a small woman who held a sleeping babe in one arm.

"Did he?" No doubt for some nefarious purpose.

I hurried down the circular corridor. What the pilgrims did not know was there was more than one entrance into the main chamber. Arthur had designed this building and could not talk about it enough during its long construction. As a result, I had its plans forever seared into my mind.

The maze of corridors led me to a small antechamber where the priests and deacons of the Grail prepared themselves to celebrate its sacred rites. As I'd suspected, the cabinets were thrown open, their contents askew, sacred linens rumpled in half-open drawers. Marius had likely pilfered the finest, intent on either selling them to finance his flight or at least provide a basis of riches to establish his life outside of Camelot.

"Going somewhere?" I demanded, bursting into the silent main chamber.

Bishop Marius blinked at me like a mole newly emerged from underground. He was on his knees in front of the Grail, a large pack belching gold patens and a small book with jewel-encrusted binding at his feet.

"How dare you disturb my prayer?" he exclaimed, his voice as sharp and cold as a newly honed knife blade. "I could have you arrested for disobeying my direct order of privacy."

"Why should I start listening to your commands now?" I countered, moving closer to him with each word. "You have no power over me. You never have. That is why you fear me."

Bishop Marius snorted. "If I feared you, I would not be here. I would still be locked away." The bravado in his voice did not reach his eyes.

"It *is* convenient to have friends who are willing to do you favors when it suits them, is it not? Morgan would not have released you if it did not suit her. What deal did you strike with her?"

Marius glanced at the Grail. "That is none of your concern."

"Then call your guards. Have me arrested as you say."

Marius's gaze flicked back to the cup raised high on a pillar for all to see.

"No? Then you must not wish to draw attention to yourself either. What is your plan? Steal the Grail, then support Mordred's rebellion from afar?"

"I would never condone that pagan whelp as king," he said, his voice dripping with disdain. "My aims lie across the sea."

His destination had to be Gaul or Brittany. Morgan did say Arthur and Lancelot were in trouble. Surely she would not move against her beloved Arthur, no matter what her son may or may not be planning. So he had to be supporting Arthur in his current battle. Marius had mentioned once that he had friends among the Bretons and Gauls.

"How does this plan benefit you?" I narrowed my eyes, trying to position myself between him and the Grail.

"Let us just say I will have the gratitude of the king if I can bring this war to an end." Marius picked up his sack, its rich contents clanking loudly. "Now, if you will excuse me. It is time for me to depart." He moved toward the Grail.

"So that's it then. You pay off the Breton nobles and move the Grail where it will bring them unending revenue. How do you expect to spirit it away without everyone chasing you?"

Marius's smile was wicked. "Haven't you heard? Galahad dreamed that God wished it to be moved to Brittany, for they have held the faith much stronger than here. Or at least that is what we will tell everyone. Morgan has the ability to convince even Galahad it is true—and in many ways, it is. Arthur proved unworthy by placing power in his pagan son's hands instead of trusting in his closest advisor." He touched his own heart.

"You tried to have him killed with that drugged wine, remember? Why would he ever trust you?"

"Once he sees my role in ending the war and assuring his continuance as king, I will have his unending gratitude, even if I had to use the Grail to bring it about. It will wipe away all of my past sins and secure my position in his esteem."

"You were counting on his devotion to his faith to save you all along, weren't you? Arthur could never bring himself to kill a priest, no matter what he's done."

Marius gloated. "I know." He reached for the Grail. "And neither could you or you'd have done it by now."

A low chuckle made us both turn.

Mordred was standing in the entry, his arms crossed, with Mona, the Grail Maiden, at his side. "Then it's a shame for you his son does not share his faith. I have no such compunction."

Marius's face filled with dread.

"If you touch the Grail, I will kill you myself." Mona held up a large silver sickle, the weapon all Grail guardians wore at their sides. "You have proven yourself unworthy."

"You. How did you know?" Marius stuttered.

Mona lightly touched the crescent moon at her brow. "We guardians always know when our sacred charge is in peril. We

are bound to it. Now I must demand justice on its behalf."
Mordred grabbed Bishop Marius by the cowl and dragged him
toward the Grail Maiden. "By your leave, Lady, I fear your punishment too swift for the likes of him. I have something else in mind
that I assure you will satisfy both spiritual and temporal law."

❧❧

"Is he dead?" I asked Mordred when more than a week had passed
with no sign of Bishop Marius.

Mordred squinted at me, wrinkling his nose. "I'm not sure. We
could go together to find out." He held out an arm, as though offering to escort me to the fair.

I looked at him sharply. "What have you done to him?"

"Come with me and see." He motioned for me to rise.

Pulling my shawl close around me against a chill that could have
no natural origin, I followed Mordred. Past the cellar where Marius
had been kept, past the place of public execution, through Camelot's
gates, and into the forest, we trod. At the crossroads where two
smaller Roman roads met to join the main road to Camelot, we
stopped.

I peered around, searching the empty dirt road and the thick
underbrush on either side. The only thing I found was a pile of offal,
the reeking, viscous remains of some animal's recent kill. Other
than that, we were utterly alone. I turned to Mordred, seeking an
explanation.

"Look up," he said, pointing into the trees.

I did as he instructed. Suspended high above me was a pen
made of saplings, its crisscrossing bars and domed roof resembling a
bird cage. But inside it was no bird; it could barely be called human.
Marius lay naked on his belly, arms and ankles bound behind him at
unnatural angles like a freshly trussed boar. Blood was slowly dripping from his wounds onto the leaves at my feet. A low moaning
scream escaped my lips.

As we watched, a carrion crow hopped from a nearby branch
and landed on one of the bars. It cocked its head to one side, as
though considering a thought, then craned its neck to peck something. Marius cried out in pain and the bird jerked away, launching
itself into the air and taking with it a bit of Marius's flesh.

Marius moaned, his head on the bottom of the cage. He saw

me, and his moans shaped into something resembling my name. Drawn as if by a spell, I moved closer until I was directly beneath him. I looked up, meeting his gaze. One of his eyes was obscured in shadow. No, it was missing altogether. One clear blue eye and one scabbed socket stared at me as he whimpered. I didn't dare look down or move in case his eye was decaying at my feet.

I twisted so I was facing Mordred, catching a glimpse of what I had taken for carrion earlier. No, not carrion. It was bits of Marius's blood and skin and muscle torn away by animals. I took a few unsteady steps toward the hedge and vomited. When I turned back to Mordred, he was standing tall and proud, hands on his hips like some triumphant king returned from battle.

"What is this?" was all I could think to say.

"A gibbet," he answered as though I'd asked what manner of animal we'd treed. "Our ancestors used them often. They provide the guilty with plenty of time to think about their crimes, while sending a strong message to anyone else who might be fool enough to cross the local leader. They say even Boudicca used them when she terrorized the Romans." His voice reflected pride in being in such esteemed company.

"This is not the way of Camelot. This is not our justice. This is"—I searched for the right word—"barbarous." I scrutinized him, looking for any sign of the sweet boy I once knew. "I suppose you are the local leader with the message. Exactly what message would you send with this display of cruelty?" I gestured toward the dying priest.

"Camelot has a new leader now. One who will not stand idly by while guilty men get away with attempted murder and treachery. The gods demand justice for his actions, and that he shall get."

"You," I said slowly, "are a monster." I wheeled around and pulled out the dagger I always wore at my side. Trying to avoid looking at Marius, who was now opening and closing his mouth like a fish out of water, I followed the line of rope securing the cage in place to the base of a nearby tree and sawed at the knot.

"What are you doing?" Mordred demanded.

"No one should end their life this way," I answered as the first cord snapped and the cage swayed. "No matter what they have done."

"You cannot free him. He will die anyway."

"Perhaps." I grabbed the rope as the second cord snapped and sent the cage tilting wildly, then I fought for control as I lowered it to the ground. It hit the earth with a thud and Marius groaned. "I may not be able to save his life, nor in truth do I wish to, but I can offer him the quality that has always united Camelot and Avalon—mercy."

Mordred did not move to stop me as I pried open the door of the cage. Marius's wounds were far worse than I'd anticipated. Infected lash marks covered his back, indicating Mordred had had him tortured before throwing him in the gibbet. His skin was pocked where the birds had plucked out divots of flesh. I untied his bindings and slowly turned him over. Entrails protruded through gaps where the birds had had prolonged exposure to his body.

Marius was beyond sense now, trying to form words that would not come.

I placed a gentle hand on his forehead, willing him to focus on me. "Be still. Be calm. Your suffering is at an end." Despite all of my years of hating him, my eyes welled with tears and my heart bled pity for the broken man. "I may not know your god, but I know he would not condone this. The only thing I can do for you is assure you are quickly united with him. Do you understand?"

Marius's eye locked on mine and he whimpered. As I had on more battlefields than I could count, I took that for agreement.

"May your god be merciful to you. Leave this world in peace." I drew my blade swiftly across his throat, a trickle of red following in its wake.

He was so weakened, it took but a moment for Marius to breathe his last.

I wiped the blade on the grass, finding no vindication in his death, only a growing hatred of Arthur's son. "Do what you will with his body, but know this. If you string him up again, you honor his soul by allowing his bones to be picked clean and bleached by the sun, rather than rotting in a grave. *That* is the tradition of our ancestors."

⁕

The bishop's death only added to the rising anxiety of Camelot's people. Christian and pagan alike condemned the brutality with which he was treated, while fearing succumbing to the same fate under Mordred's increasingly brutal reign. Mordred was denounced from the pulpits of the Christian churches, and his name became anathema to those of the new faith. In Camelot and across Britain, priests urged Christian citizens to rise up against the usurper who'd martyred a man of the cloth.

I paid little heed to the clamor at first, believing it to be merely the rhetoric of rage that flares bright and hot but burns out just as quickly. We had seen such demonstrations of moral outrage before—such as when Arthur refused to either divorce me or denounce his marriage to Morgan, choosing instead to live with both of us—but they were usually words without much follow-through.

The first sign that this time was different came on a day in early autumn, a few weeks after Lughnasa. Earlier in the day, the Combrogi had arrested a handful of men for speaking out against Mordred in the market square, and six others had been detained for blocking the path of a party of Saxons come to meet with Mordred. But now as that meeting took place, all was calm.

I swatted a fly buzzing around my right ear, trying to pay attention to what Ida, King of the Saxons, was debating with Bors and Mordred, when a commotion in the courtyard caught my attention.

A man pointed to the west and gave the cry we all dreaded, "Fire!"

His voice carried clearly into the room, which erupted into chaos after a moment of stunned silence. Men and women jostled one another, some seeking immediate escape, while others crowded around the windows to try to ascertain the location of the fire.

I ran outside, dismayed to find smoke billowing from the western tower. By the time I'd crossed the massive courtyard and made my way to the foot of the tower, fire had consumed the upper floors. A bucket brigade tried in vain to douse the blaze, but it was slow, no match for the inferno raging above.

The hiss of flames set my palms sweating and my heart pounding. It was too soon since my own encounter with deadly flame. I fought the urge to cover my ears and cower as memories rushed at me from every side. My wrists raw from fighting the rope that bound them. The soles of my feet burning as the wood beneath them began to catch. The sulfurous odor of my hair catching fire as I leapt onto Lancelot's horse. I shook my head to clear it. This was not the time to give into fear. Someone could be hurt or dying and as a priestess I had a better chance of reaching them unharmed than anyone else.

"Is anyone inside?" I yelled to the people racing around me.

Either they did not hear or chose to ignore me.

I tried again, asking the same question of the man directing the line of volunteers snaking inside and up into the tower. "We don't believe so."

But they don't know for sure and I can't take the chance. Dropping my cape to the ground, I raced inside the tower, shoving aside well-meaning men who tried to stop me. They had forgotten I could control the elements and so could shield myself from the flames. I called upon Brigid as I raced up the stairs, seeking the source.

When the heat and smoke became too much, I mentally pushed outward, creating a pocket of clean air around me in every direction. I checked each room until I reached the end of the top floor. Only my chambers and Arthur's lay ahead, with his library above, connected by a short staircase only accessible from this room. I started to open Arthur's door but stopped, sensing the pulsing heart of the fire within. Even with my training, entering while the fire raged unchecked would be dangerous.

I took a deep breath and sent my senses outward, searching for the nearest clouds. They were some distance out to sea, so I had to use the breeze to coax them in this direction, but that was easily accomplished. When they appeared on the horizon, I brought them together and drew them toward me. The sky darkened rapidly, wind whipping the flames into a frenzy. I raised my arms and brought them down swiftly, unleashing a torrent of rain. The fire hissed and sputtered as it fought the water, but it eventually gave in, curling in on itself only to expire in tendrils of steam.

Once the walls around me were no longer alight, I kicked in the charred remains of Arthur's door. Mordred had changed the room little since moving in when he ascended power. Here and there he had made it his own—the tusk of the boar he'd killed on the day he became a man hung on one wall, and the remains of his tunics dripped from their place inside a ruined wardrobe—but for the most part, it was as I remembered.

I ventured farther in, turning, seeking anything out of place. My gaze swept over the far side of the room, and I started. A large, black, man-shaped figure loomed from the shadows, and I swallowed down a rush of bile. If the perpetrator had been caught in here, he wouldn't have made it out alive. I took a few cautious steps closer and breathed a sigh of relief. The bulbous shape I had taken for a head was only the charred remains of a sheep's bladder attached to a wooden sparring dummy. I squinted. Around its neck was Arthur's torc, now melted into the wood, and the fabric draped over the form was the tattered remains of the ceremonial cape Morgan had gifted to Mordred when Arthur acknowledged him as his son.

My hand flew to my mouth. This thing had been dressed as Mordred and set ablaze. The fire was no accident then. This was a deliberate move against the acting king. Mordred's life was in danger. He had to be notified.

I stumbled down the stairs, drained from the shock and the effort of calling the rain. My shield from the fire had slowly slipped away, but I was out of danger.

When I emerged, a furious Mordred greeted me, water pouring from his cloak. "Are you mad? Who runs into a raging fire? What were you thinking?"

I smiled at him tiredly, leaning against one wall of the archway. "I am a priestess. I was in no danger."

"Are you sure?" Mordred brushed soot off of one of my cheeks and held up a burned strand of my hair. "Gods, Guinevere, I've already saved you from one fire."

I gestured to the scars on my face, arm, and leg. "Which is why I was unafraid of this one."

Mordred sighed heavily. "Sometimes I question the logic of Avalon in teaching you those tricks." He shook his head. "But I guess I should be grateful. It appears the worst is over." He gestured around us at the rain. "Will you please make this stop?"

I closed my eyes and thanked the gods and the elements for their aid. Then I commanded the rain to cease and swept my arms out in front of me, willing the clouds to disperse. The sky cleared.

"Mordred, you need to know something about the fire." He looked at me expectantly, so I hurried on. "It was not an accident. I found—I found an effigy of you in your quarters. It appears to be the source of the blaze."

Mordred stared at me, dumbfounded. "You're saying someone went through the trouble of building my likeness and setting it on fire in the very room where I sleep?" His voice rose in volume and tightness with each word.

I hadn't had time to consider the intimacy of the location. It meant that the person who did this was no stranger, but rather someone who had access to our innermost circle. Memories coursed through me of another time at Camelot, when someone had left a series of increasingly threatening notes addressed to me in private places, forcing me to live in fear. I fought back a wave of dizziness and nausea. This was different, but the feeling of violation was the same.

"Yes," I answered, putting a hand on his shoulder. "I am so sorry. But I thought you should be warned to be on your guard."

We left the volunteers to keep watch for any smoldering areas, and Mordred returned to the hall where nobles and other dignitaries were once again assembled. I slipped past, taking one of the side halls into the garden. When the door shut behind me, I breathed a sigh of relief before dashing to the stone bench beneath the apple tree at the center of the labyrinth. I collapsed upon it, finally letting go of the fear, tension, and anger that had fueled my fight against the flames.

Though my body gave in to exhaustion within the silent lullaby of this sacred place, my mind whirled, thoughts tripping over one another like water rushing over rapids. That had been far too close a call. Someone could have been hurt or even killed. Was that the point? Was this an assassination attempt gone awry? It certainly wouldn't be the first I had experienced, though I prayed it was the last. We were lucky that no one had been in that part of the tower when the fire began. Or had it been planned that way? It was no secret we were meeting with the Saxon leaders today. Perhaps this was more of a warning. Otherwise wouldn't they have attacked the hall?

Soon my spiraling thoughts eased, melted into oblivion by the morning light that filtered through the leaves of the apple tree, warming my face and slowly replenishing the well of strength within me. I dozed beneath its strong branches, grateful once again for Arthur's thoughtful gift of a protected place where I could gather myself in times such as these.

As I slipped in and out of sleep, I was vaguely aware of the birdsong around me. Perhaps that was why I dreamed a crow and a dove were fighting on the windowsill outside my room. But it was not the larger crow who was the aggressor. The cooing mourning dove aggressively raced at the crow, pecking at its chest, feet, anywhere it could reach. The crow cried out and I woke with a start.

I sat up from my slumped position and looked around. Something wasn't right. At first I thought I must still be dreaming, because the air around me was silent. Far too silent. Even the birds, whose coos and caws I had been enjoying only moments before, now refused to sing. I rubbed my arms as the tiny hairs stood at attention. Slowly, I scanned the space in front of me, ears attuned to even the slightest sound. I peered through branches and into shadows, but as far as I could tell, I was alone.

A shiver ran through me from neck to feet. It was time to return to the hall.

I had just emerged from beneath the canopy of the tree when a shadow moved on the outer wall. Someone was there. I could make out the silhouette of a man but did not dare move closer for a better look. A brief spark of light illuminated his face. It was one of the deacons from the Grail Castle. Before I could call out to him, he threw something toward me. It landed with the crash of shattering clay within the boughs of the apple tree. The upper branches burst into flames. Stifling a scream, I raced for the door leading into the castle.

"Run! There is another fire in the garden," I called to those inside. Following them toward the main entrance, I met up with Sobian. "Find Grainne and Morgan. I am too weak yet to douse this fire myself. They will be able to help."

She nodded and scurried off, but help never came. Eventually, word reached me that Grainne was still in Carlisle and no one could locate Morgan. By the time they did, it was too late. We had prevented the fire from spreading, but the labyrinth and gardens were destroyed.

As dusk fell, Mordred took me out on the walls to watch as a group of people in chains were herded into the courtyard below.

"Who are they?" I asked.

"Those responsible for today's fires."

"How do you know?"

"They admitted as much when my men found them. Christians to a one, they rejoiced, shouting that Camelot's last bastion of hell— your pagan labyrinth—was destroyed." He reached into a pouch at his waist and produced a broken piece of clay that looked like the neck of a bottle. "We found this among the ashes. It appears to be part of a bottle that was filled with oil. They stoppered it with an alcohol-soaked rag, which was lit on fire. When it broke against the trunk of the tree, it spread flaming oil everywhere."

From below, voices raised in protest as the guards led the

perpetrators into the cells.

"You cannot arrest us for doing the Lord's work," yelled a bearded man I assumed was the rabble's leader. "We act in the name of King Arthur!"

"How can they claim to be working for Arthur when they have destroyed part of his capital and his home?" I asked.

Mordred rubbed the back of his neck. "They are also, apparently, organized against me. They don't like that I am a pagan. If they are the same group that burned that dummy, they don't like that I live either."

As if on cue, a woman yelled, "For Saint Marius!"

"Pray for us, patron saint of Britain," answered a man behind her.

So that was what Camelot had come to—arson, incendiary weapons, and canonizing a monster. *Please, Goddess, let Arthur return to us soon.*

అలో అాల

We had little time to grieve our losses or even to rescue the remnants from the ashes before the fighting escalated. The following night, Mordred's supporters struck back, burning homes and buildings owned by known supporters of the absent king. But they didn't stop there. Fanning out into the countryside, they torched farms, slaughtered livestock, and destroyed crops, heedless of the consequences their depravity would have on all of Camelot's citizens. Come winter, we would all pay for their madness with shriveled bellies.

By dawn, the survivors were on our doorstep, their need turning the partially burned castle into a makeshift hostel. We set up beds in the great hall and sent the kitchens into festival-level day and night shifts of cooking. I split my time between helping Mordred and Morgan manage the chaos and providing healing to those injured in the attacks, as well as to others who normally did not have access to a healer. They were eager to tell their stories, to unburden their minds and hearts of the horrors of that night, telling detailed tales of cruelty and hatred directed against Arthur and his supporters.

"They will go any lengths to prevent him from ever sitting on his throne again," one man told me.

Outside, the whole town was buzzing, mobs forming in the sodden, blackened streets. The fortress guards had their hands full trying to contain the crowds and keep violence from breaking out among rival factions. Their chants and demands reached us in Camelot's council chambers, where we were trying to sort through the mess Arthur's capital had become.

"This is not the way of Camelot," I said to the assembly. "Arthur and I founded this town on the ideas of peace and mercy, uniting our tribes, not fighting amongst ourselves." Though I was no longer officially part of the council, Mordred had asked me to join him in this meeting.

"Pretty words. But what do you propose we do to stop them?" Bors asked.

I glared at him but directed my words to Mordred. "Arthur left you king in his stead. You must make a public statement. The people riot because they are wondering whether the rumors are true. You must tell them once and for all whether or not you seek the throne."

"It is not a wise move, my lord, to turn against Arthur," Owain said. "I am told whatever message or bribery the bishop sent to Brittany before his death did its job. The war there is ending. Your father, the king, will return soon."

"Then we make our announcement now, gather what strength we can while Arthur is across the sea. That way we will be ready for him when he comes," Accolon said with conviction.

"*Are* you seeking the throne?" I asked Mordred. He had never been clear on that, preferring to let speculation play out.

Mordred was seated in Arthur's place of honor. Morgan sat in the throne of High Queen, a title which she had not been awarded, but she wore the mantle of power all the same.

"I have made certain alliances my father would deem foolish," Mordred said, choosing his words carefully. "We have at our disposal the armies of two powerful factions, should we choose to use them."

So he had allied with the Saxons and Picts. Mordred had previously admitted to learning from them, but he had given no sign how deep his diplomacy with them ran. Exactly what had he and Ida discussed in private when he was here? What negotiations had we not been privy to? Anything he would keep from the council had to be either illegal or unethical.

Bors must have been thinking along the same lines. "Tread carefully, my lord. Let us not forget what trusting the Saxons meant for the old tyrant Vortigern." He made a slicing motion across his neck. "Besides, I'll not fight alongside their filthy armies with their brutish women. Women are meant for the home, not the battlefield." He threw a poignant look at Sobian.

"Is that so? Well then, the next time I have the opportunity to rescue you, I'll pass you by. I've already saved you twice. That is enough," Sobian spat. "But Bors is right. The Saxons have been our enemies for sixty years. There is no reason to believe that if we ally with them now, they won't simply betray us like they did Vortigern."

"Ah, but we do have a reason to trust them," Mordred countered.

"And what is that?" I asked.

Mordred signaled to Accolon to open the doors. Elga stood on the threshold, her dark eyes shining with a powerful secret. A collective gasp went up from the crowd as warriors recognized their enemy from the battle of Mount Badon.

"What is *she* doing here?" Owain asked.

"She should have been killed on sight. An oversight that can be quickly remedied," Aggrivane said. He hand went to his side where his sword usually hung, as though he had forgotten all weapons were surrendered before each council meeting.

Mordred placed himself between them, but it was Elga who spoke, slithering past Mordred's shielding shoulder with a cruel grace Morgan would have envied. "You are still upset I evaded your pursuit after the war, I see. No matter. I would have killed you had we engaged, so it is better this way for us both." Her accent was still thick, but her mastery of our tongue was much improved.

Mordred turned to me, continuing our interrupted conversation. "I suppose it is time all of you knew the extent of my plans. My accord with the Saxons goes deeper than mere words. You see, Elga is my wife. We were handfast according to the traditions of both our peoples. The gods willing, we will soon be bound by blood." He patted her belly softly.

The silence that followed was so absolute that had it not been for the chanting of the protestors below, I would have thought myself back in that limbo between life and death. I stared at Elga, whose whole being radiated power. She was likely twice Mordred's age, but for all those years, she was still beautiful and could reasonably produce a few more heirs before her breeding time ended.

Aggrivane was the first to find his voice. "Is she to be High Queen then? We have never had a foreigner hold that title. You must know how upsetting it will be to the people."

"I am no foreigner," Elga countered. "I may have Saxon blood, but I was born on British soil. I would see my people rise to power, yes, but alongside yours. Badon taught me much, as I am sure it did you. The biggest lesson was that my first husband was wrong to try to annihilate you. My people are not ever returning to our ancestral lands and I know the fierceness with which you defend your homes, so we are at an impasse. We must learn to live side by side if we are to survive."

More pretty words. Elga couldn't be trusted any more now than the day I met her, the day she took the life of her newborn nephew. "How can we be sure the words you speak are not just lies aimed at softening our underbellies?"

Elga regarded me appraisingly. "You are wise to ask this, Queen Guinevere. I call you by your title for you still hold it according to our old ways. I will not ask you to pass it to me until after we have ascended to power. Only by my actions will you know my words are true."

Her actions? Which ones? Aiding in Mordred's rebellion? Engaging Arthur in another battle? "You are saying that by killing the king, you will prove to me you are not a traitor to Britain?"

Elga looked down, unconsciously fingering the blades hanging at her waist. "I hope it does not come to that. I would much rather live in peace with my husband's father."

"He will never accept you," Aggrivane sneered. "And neither do I." He rose, confronting Mordred. "No matter Arthur's trust in you, I cannot continue to serve a man who allies with Saxons. I will rejoin Arthur's army when he returns."

"Watch your back until then," Bors warned Aggrivane. "For you have just declared yourself an enemy of Mordred's crown."

"Indeed I have. But if you wanted to kill me, you would have done so years ago. You've had ample opportunity." He was in Bors's face now, pointing a threatening finger at his former brother-in-arms. "But if you wish, I will face you in single combat. I do not brook cowards, so don't even consider a sneak attack. We are all witnesses to your declaration, and I swear to you, if anything happens to me, there are men here who will hunt you down."

As if in agreement, Gawain and two of his friends drew their eating daggers, making a show of cleaning them on their tunics.

Owain bolted to his feet. "Stand down, all of you! We have

enough factions at war outside. We do not need to create dissension among our ranks as well. I am not happy about Mordred's choice of wife, but I wish to hear him out. There is one question he has yet to answer. What about the Picts? How will you secure their loyalty?"

"Thank you, Owain. I have nothing so solid as a marriage to offer you with the Picts, only a traditional alliance. We have been discussing how the borders of the ancient imperial walls hold no value in a world without Rome. Our agreement is based on the mutual understanding that when I become king, all the people of this island—Britons, Picts, and the tribes in between—will be one. I seek to expand north what my father started."

It was Sobian's turn to stand. "But first there must be a mighty battle to determine who is indeed king." She scoffed, disgust writ large in her features. "Neither you nor Arthur will have my sword. My girls and I will go seek our fortunes in Eire, where at least some bit of reason remains."

She signaled to her women scattered about the room, who detached themselves from the rest of the crowd. Without a word, they all headed for the door.

Sobian paused before me. "You are welcome to join us, but I know your heart lies across another sea. Call if you ever need me and I will return." She kissed my cheek and was gone.

My stomach lurched. As bleak as life in Camelot now was, if Mordred followed through on his plans, the future would be even darker. For all his playing at power, he was still relatively untested and idealistic, and so failed to grasp the repercussions of his bid for power.

"Mordred, have you fully considered the impact of your actions? Your intent is noble and it sounds reasonable in theory, but as soon as you let the Picts south of Antontine Wall, they will invade the Selgovae, Damnonii, and Votadini, who will then flee into Lothian, Bernicia, and on to Strathclyde. Do you really want them overrunning Camelot? Because it will happen. Look at the people who now call Camelot home after one night of insurrection. Can you imagine how much worse it will be when they are pursued by the Picts? Before you know it, you will be overrun with refugees and will have civil war on your hands, thanks to the prejudices against those living north of Hadrian's Wall."

Mordred sighed. "You are correct, but you are also thinking

within old tribal rivalries. All of that will be gone under my reign."

I shook my head. "You are young and naïve. Do you really believe people will drop tribal allegiances they've held for thousands of years simply because you tell them to? You are merely giving them an excuse to harass each other in ways they've only dreamed of until now. Please, at least consider my words. I was High Queen for twenty years. I understand how our people think."

Mordred's expression softened. "I know that, and I respect your experience. It is one of the reasons why I keep you in close council. We have time yet before such things will take place. We can discuss them more later. But now"—he took Elga's hand and rose to stand beside her—"I have a populous to address."

As he strode onto the balcony, I slipped from the room with Aggrivane at my heels. I could not stay and listen to Mordred and Elga speak. The reaction of the crowd would be too painful, and it would be a betrayal of all I stood for to silently witness the shattering of the dream Arthur and I had created. But even the thick walls of Camelot could not shield my ears from the competing cheers and jeers that rose like an angry sea in the aftermath of Mordred's words.

Like it or not, we were in full-on rebellion.

CHAPTER SEVEN

Spring 520

Time was running out.

The inevitable clash between father and son was drawing near. According to my latest communication with Pelles, Arthur and his troops were even now at sea, heading toward home. By the next full moon, they would no doubt be matched in pitched battle.

I set aside Pelles's letter with a sigh and looked out the window across the burned-out shell of the western tower, down to the village below, wondering if Arthur would even recognize his home when he returned. Though this day appeared no different from any other, with tradesmen, fishermen, servants, and soldiers all going about their daily lives, there was an undercurrent of tension in the air, as though we were under constant threat of a storm about to break. If we could feel it even here in the castle, how much more keenly must the villagers perceive it?

In the streets, clashes between warring factions were now the norm, even as Mordred's men struggled to keep order. Their exhaustion fed short tempers, causing Camelot's men to seek any release they could find. The barkeeps welcomed them with flowing ale and whores loved the uptick in business, but when the barrels ran dry and the women were all occupied, even the noblest of men resorted to beating his neighbor to a bloody pulp.

In the castle, things were little better. Aggrivane had already left to meet Arthur's party when they docked on the Lothian coast. If Owain could not make Mordred see sense, he was likely to follow. Bors spent his time whipping Mordred's followers into a froth by harping on the injustices done by Arthur and his men—some real, some spun out of whole cloth. Amid this tension, Morgan was strangely quiet, deeply withdrawn into herself, refusing to take sides between her husband and her son.

I was all but forgotten, which suited me fine. I had my own decision to make regarding the coming war. On one hand, Arthur was king and I his queen. But on the other, he had divorced me and declared my power void before seriously considering ending my life over my affair with Lancelot. Part of me still hated him. The other part could not bear to see our shared dream laid to waste.

I understood Mordred's ambition. After Arthur's role in my near-burning, many thought him unfit to rule, even if he was the victim of Morgan and Marius's machinations. Why should Mordred not step in? He could wait for Arthur to die, but Arthur's weakness and absence gave him the perfect opportunity to ascend while his father still lived. As he'd pointed out last time we spoke, he had been born for the throne, even before he knew he was Arthur's son. He had been raised by Uriens, King of Rheged, blessed with Morgan's cunning, learned statecraft from Owen, skills of the blade from Accolon, and was fostered by Lot, the realm's greatest strategist. Those things, combined with more than a decade at Arthur's side, made him a capable ruler.

Yet I could not offer my support to him either. For all his diplomacy and strategy, he was still a rash young man whose ambition could quickly get the better of him. He was so focused on becoming king, I doubted he ever gave a thought to what would happen once he was officially king and the ruler upon whom all of our lives depended.

A knock brought me back to the present. Mordred stepped into the room, a round board under one arm. "I hope I am not disturbing you."

"No, not at all. I was just thinking."

Mordred took a seat near me. "About the future, I am certain. It is on all minds these days."

I nodded.

When I did not elaborate, Mordred let the silence stretch between us. Finally, he pulled over a small table and set his circular board on it before arranging stones from a pouch at his waist into two triangles facing off across a field of wood. He sat forward, taking my hand. "I know it cannot be easy for you, being trapped between Arthur and me. You know I need your support for the people to accept me. You are Sovereignty herself. Those of the old faith will only back me with your blessing. But I know you also feel some measure of devotion to my father, in spite of all you've been through. It is my hope that these stones will show us where your loyalty should lie."

The same thought had crossed my mind, but I didn't want him to know that. "Then why not let me do it in private? What do you hope to gain from asking me to read these with you?"

"I simply wish to run the battle twice, once with your support and once without it. That will tell us if you are as important a factor as I believe you are." Mordred's attempts to sway me without being cruel or unjust were admirable. In that way, as in so many others, he really was his father's son.

"But you will also get a glimpse of how prepared Arthur is," I added.

"I did not say there would not be other benefits," he teased.

I exhaled a deep breath through my nose, looking at him, reluctant to succumb to his charm. "Only this once, and only because I see benefit in it as well. When I make my decision, you will stand by it, no matter what."

Mordred placed a hand over his heart. "On my honor, I do so swear."

I took a deep breath and closed my eyes, willing my whirling thoughts to still. Sending my being down deep, I sought the heartbeat of the earth. Focusing on my breathing, which settled to an even rhythm under such close scrutiny, I let all things go. Soon, there were no crying gulls circling outside, and even Mordred's presence became a memory.

I opened my eyes, focusing on the pieces, seeing in their place troops of men. Arthur and Mordred faced off in a grassy field bisected by a shallow river of quick-flowing, dark water. In the space of a heartbeat, the battle began, father against son, Saxon against Briton, Pict cutting down Combrogi. My hands directed the stones without my knowledge. The battle was fierce and bloody. In the end, not a single stone remained on the board.

Blinking away the trance that had overtaken me, I found Mordred staring at my cupped palms.

"Guinevere," he said slowly, reverently, "look at your hands."

I opened my palms to find the two red queens joined as though glued together. I forced them apart, examining the stones closer. They were red lodestone. That was why they were connected. They were naturally drawn together by their magnetic cores.

"This is not our battle," I said quietly to myself. "No matter who Morgan and I choose, the queens are set apart. Even should all fall in battle, we will survive." I set the two stones on the board, trembling in anticipation as they wavered, seeking to find one another again. Part of me knew what I was uttering was more than my human senses could perceive, but I was as powerless to stop it as the tides are to resist the moon. The two pieces snapped together again. "We are joined, in life, in death, in infamy."

"Is this my wife?" Mordred asked, indicating the queen stone that belonged with his army.

"Or your mother. Both. We three have a fate beyond your own, one only we can fulfill."

We were silent for a time, both wrapped in private contemplation. Finally, whatever prophetic spirit had filled me fled, leaving me to piece together its meaning with a throbbing head and shaking body.

"So what is your answer?" Mordred asked, his voice clipped.

"I—I—what?" My thick tongue would not form words.

"Given what you have seen, do you support me or him?" Mordred's face was red, a vein in his forehead pulsing, just like Arthur's did when he was upset.

"How can you ask me that? You saw the outcome. It does not matter."

He brought his fist down on the board, making the pieces jump. "But it does. It means everything." He upended the board, bellowing, "Choose!"

I shrank back, more afraid of him in that moment than I had ever been, even when his cruelty toward Marius was revealed. *Be calm. This is nothing more than a display of temper. It will pass.* I breathed deeply. *He is a spoiled child who fears he may be denied his favorite toy, nothing more.*

I inhaled again then stood, looking him straight in the eye. "Long ago, before you were more than a seed in your mother's belly, I made a promise. I swore to watch over my people and guard them from all harm. That was my first vow. Those I made to Arthur, and any loyalty I may feel toward you as his son, are secondary. As you remind me, I am queen, a woman above and apart. I cannot choose between the two of you any more than your own mother could. Fight your battles as you will, but with the gods as my witness, I wish no part in them." I turned on my heel, focused on the door.

"Where will you go?" he called after me, and I looked over my shoulder. "You have no one to take you in if I denounce you." He crossed to me in long, quick steps. "My father was merciful to you, and following his example, so was I. But once I become king, all of that can change. I will have the power to do with you as I will. I could sell you to the Picts as a slave, end your life with the snap of my fingers." His eyes brightened and he moved closer, his breath warm on my cheek. "Better yet, I know a certain Saxon woman who would take great pleasure in torturing you for the rest of your days." His words were directly in my ear now. "Think on that, my queen. I will give you one more chance. I want your answer by midnight."

❧❦❧

Mordred's threats still rang in my ears hours later when I looked up from staring into the fire and found myself facing Elga. How long had she been standing there watching me? A shiver ran down my spine and I forced myself not to flinch. I would never show fear in her presence.

"I heard what my husband said to you earlier," she said by way of greeting. "He knows nothing. You were right. This is not your battle."

I stood, not wishing to give her the satisfaction of towering over me. Little good it did, for she was still two heads taller, but at least we were both on even ground. "You were spying on us?"

She shrugged, completely unapologetic. "I do what I must to know my husband's heart."

"You said this is not my battle. You wish me to side with Arthur then? Is that what you are saying?"

"Matters not."

A wave of nausea rolled through my stomach and I swallowed hard. Those were the exact same words she'd used years ago when we first met, just before she killed an innocent child. Despite my best efforts to hold it back, I shivered.

Elga perked up, as if sensing my discomfort, and sauntered over to the window, her movement making the silver tubes holding her blond curls rattle like wind chimes. "You are a powerful woman, but your time has passed, so who you back in the coming storm matters little. My husband says no one will accept us without your blessing, but he knows better. He would not have married me if he didn't." She turned to face me. "You see, I already have the loyalty of my people, and in the coming days, many of our enemies will fall by our swords. Those who remain can be controlled with or without you." She toyed with the line of daggers hanging from her belt, as if trying to decide which to select. "So we have no need of you."

"What then do you plan to do with me?" I asked. She could kill me on the spot if she so intended.

Elga's answering grin chilled my heart. "My husband was right that I would enjoy torturing you"—she removed a thin knife from her belt and inspected it, holding it up so it caught the slanting rays of late afternoon light—"but I am in no mood today." She pointed the blade at me. "You and I will do battle, mark my words, but this is not the time. You do not belong in Camelot anymore. You knew that when you ran to Lothian. So today I offer you a gift."

"And what is that?" I asked slowly, never taking my eyes from her knife in case I needed to evade its bite.

"Safe haven. Somewhere you will be protected until this battle is over."

"Why would you do that?"

"Have you not been listening? You are a liability to me. As long as you are here, some part of my husband will rely on you as queen. His devotion should be completely *mine*." She shoved the weapon back into its leather sheath with greater force than necessary to punctuate her point. "I will allow you to escape if you promise me one thing."

"What is that?"

"No matter the outcome, you will not seek to alter its course. You will let me rule in whatever way I see fit."

"If I refuse?"

"I kill you." Her voice was cold but even. This was a matter of political gain to Elga, not a personal one.

I stared at her a long time, weighing my options. If I stayed in Camelot and Arthur was victorious, would he believe I was innocent or that I'd backed Mordred? If he thought me guilty, I would be once again branded a traitor and he would seek my death. On the other hand, if Mordred won the war, he might keep me around until Elga was crowned. But after that, I was of no value, only a figurehead of a regime that no longer existed. Worse yet, I could be seen as an excuse for rebellion against him. Either way, my life was in danger. If he didn't end it, Elga certainly would. How had I gotten myself into this mess? Seeing no other alternative, I nodded.

Elga smiled. "Good. You may seek refuge at the convent of St. Peter. The abbess owes me a favor."

My eyes widened, cold sweat springing to my neck and back. Had I been duped? "But the abbess is—"

Elga's grin widened until it was more of a snarl. "My sister. You thought you were so clever, hiding her away like a precious jewel. It did not take me long to find her. But when I did, I realized she was of more use to me alive. And so she remains."

"Of use to you how?"

Elga shrugged. "All you need know is you both will be safe. You have my word."

What was that worth, the word of a Saxon who wanted to kill me? I could well be walking into a trap. But as she said, I had little choice. From holding all the power in the realm to being at her mercy, my descent had been swift.

"I am to journey alone, then? Is that not dangerous? Why not simply kill me now?"

Elga regarded me as though I was a simpleton. "My men will keep an eye on you from afar, but they cannot be seen escorting you from town. Too many questions. I have sworn my protection and that you will have. Now go. You leave tonight."

My jaw dropped. "Now? It is nearly sundown."

Elga flexed her hands at her sides, clearly growing agitated. "Have you forgotten you promised to share your allegiance with my husband by midnight? There is a place not far outside the city where you will spend the night. There you will at least be safely out of his grasp."

I had forgotten. "What will you tell him?"

"Leave my husband to me. Now, pack your things and be gone."

My feet automatically carried me out into the hall while my mind reeled with this sudden change of events.

"Oh, Guinevere," Elga called after me. "Do not forget. This is not farewell. We will meet again."

When I glanced at her over my shoulder, she was fingering one of her knives again. I swallowed. That was a promise—a threat—she fully intended to keep.

Chapter Eight

Sleet stung my skin as I approached the convent grounds, a small tract of land on the banks of the river Ouse. From behind a wooden fence, a small chapel rose with a forlorn frozen garden on one side, its long-dormant plants unresponsive to the gray light of dawn. Opposite, a long building attached itself to the church like a barnacle. Some distance behind, smoke rose from the open chimney of a kitchen.

The haunting melody of chanted prayer greeted me as the porter opened the gate in response to my ringing the guest bell. Without a word, the bent old woman motioned me inside and I followed her to the church door, the nuns' song growing louder with each step. Shielding my face from the biting wind, I gratefully stepped inside the nave.

Where I had expected darkness to rival the dreary day outside, I was greeted by light. Though the church wasn't large—five pairs of small pews each held three gray-clad sisters—and had only two small windows, one set high in each long wall, iron pillars filled with slender beeswax candles illumined each corner, filling the room with the subtle, sweet scent of honey. All attention was focused on the altar, which held a length of switch, its ruby thorns glowing bloody in the soft light, and a small equal-armed stone cross. Two fat candles held vigil on either side.

It was Lent, the Christian season for repentance. This austerity likely was symbolic of the shriving of sins and the penance each sister undertook this time of year. I had seen Arthur undertake the privations of Lent many times.

Though I did not share their faith, the beauty of their ritual stirred my heart. It had been a long time since my prayers were made out of anything other than desperation and fear. But here, with my body safe and warm, my spirit cried out for nourishment. As the sisters sang, I sank to my knees on the cold, hard floor, adopting the posture of submissive prayer used on Avalon, arms crossed over my heart, head bowed to the ground. Abandoning my bag of provisions at my side, I touched my right thumb to my forehead, lips, and heart, and prayed.

My thoughts were no better than a jumble of yarn, tying itself ever tighter with each passing thought. I had to start over several times before my mind produced anything intelligible. But I was able to offer a quick word of thanks to the goddess Ellen for a safe journey and a supplication that Morrigan would keep Arthur and Lancelot safe before my mind went galloping off again.

Nevertheless, the Goddess seemed to understand my heart, and as if in response to my prayers, a vision flashed before my eyes. Arthur and Lancelot were safely back in Britain. But Arthur was not in Lothian, nor was he heading for Camelot. He stood in the courtyard of Cadbury, watching Lancelot train a group of men on how to use the saddle with the stirrup in the nearby stables. That could only mean Arthur intended to mass his supporters at Cadbury and lead a march on Mordred.

Gods, preserve us from an attack on Camelot. Do not allow this foolish quarrel over power to further destroy what we worked so hard to build.

I raised my head only when the chanting came to an end. The sisters, their faces obscured by heavy black veils, filed solemnly out a side door and soon, only one woman remained. Even before she turned, her plump shape and the strands of curly blond hair peeking out from the bottom of her veil gave away her identity.

The years had been kind to Mayda, revealing her to be a beautiful woman who would always retain a hint of her childhood innocence. Her face, covered in Lenten ashes, was still round, but it had gained sleek angles from simple living, along with the ghost of lines at the corners of her eyes and mouth. Away from the cares of her tribe and dedicated to God in a place of safety, she now appeared far younger and healthier than her battle-worn sister. Clad in the black robes of the abbess, she radiated gentle power and confidence, much like the Lady of the Lake.

I rushed to embrace her. "Mayda! The gods be praised you are well."

Forewarned I would be arriving, she was not surprised but radiated joy at our reunion. She clasped me with great affection.

"Thanks to you and your husband. You gave me a great gift the day you assigned me here. I only wish I could have seen it at the time."

I pulled back, regarding her from head to toe but not letting go of her shoulders. "How are you? I see you have done much with your time here." I gestured to her robes.

Her smile was as radiant as I remembered. "I took your advice to heart. When I was young, my family tirelessly reminded Elga and me that we were meant to lead. They thought we would oversee our husbands' tribes, but here I have found a different kind of family to lead. It can be difficult, but it is all worth it when done in His service." She flicked her gaze meaningfully to the cross on the altar. "Truly, you and Arthur gave me the most loving, loyal spouse I could ever ask for. He may be invisible, but He treats me much better than any earthly man ever would."

Having seen the brutality of the Saxons, especially those who clawed their way into power, it wasn't difficult to believe she was right.

Mayda put an arm around my shoulders, directing me toward the altar. "Come, let me show you our dearest treasure." When we stood directly in front of the altar, she lifted the stone cross off its base. Only then did I see the center was adorned with a shield of glass. Behind it, small yellowed bits of what appeared to be bone and hair rattled with her movements. "These are the bones of the blessed St. Peter and the hair of the missionaries who died protecting them. We hold them in our prayers every day, asking that their blood make us stronger in our faith." Her eyes gleamed with pride.

Bishop Marius had told us of the veneration which Christians paid to the bodily remains and sometimes possessions of their saints, especially those who'd given their lives for their faith. It was a popular practice on the Continent, but I had no idea it had spread here.

"How did you come upon these? Did not your St. Peter die in Rome? If so, they are far from their home."

Mayda's cheeks colored under the soot. "You are correct. They were a gift." She studied the rushes at her feet. "From my sister." Then looking at me, she continued. "The missionaries who brought these here from Rome had the misfortune of setting foot in our kingdom. This was only a short time after Badon. Our people were hungry to exact revenge, so they took it out on those who sought to change their ways. Relics such as these mean nothing to my people. But Elga was well aware of why the Christians so vigorously defended them.

She saw an opportunity to gain sway over the convent and took it. After stripping the relics from their gold container, Elga sent these to us as a sign so I would know she was aware of my fate. She is now considered a great patroness, a protector, because they are a source of income from pilgrims, in addition to providing spiritual grace."

I wrinkled my brow, trying to piece together her story. "How did Elga know you were here? We were so very careful." Apology lay heavy in my voice, making it unsteady.

Mayda shook her head. "It was nothing you did. Elga is far more intelligent than anyone would think. A convent known to take in Saxon women was certainly not the first place she looked for me, but it was not low on her list either. How she figured it out matters little. When I was elected abbess, I think she believed she could control the convent, and with us, the whole of York. I told her I would rather meet the same fate as the martyrs she'd created than help her gain control of the country, even just this small part. We pose no threat to her, so for now, she does nothing, lest she appear as a tyrant." Mayda took a deep breath. "I have no doubt the day will come when she is queen and I will fall to her blade, just as she always intended, but at least now it will be for a greater cause. I will be defending my faith and my home and I will be certain the others are safe. I have made my peace with my fate."

I swallowed hard, my throat constricting with guilt. All Arthur and I had wanted to do was keep her safe, yet it looked as though we'd inadvertently condemned her to a martyr's death. "I pray it does not come to that."

She smiled. "So do I. But until that day, it is my duty to keep my sisters safe and help them grow in faith." She glanced over her shoulder toward the side door. "Speaking of which, we should probably join them in the refectory. No one may begin eating until the abbess is present."

I followed her into the gloom, already missing the brightness of the church. A handful of sisters were standing around the frozen well, chipping at the surface with a rock. When Mayda approached, they backed away respectfully to allow her access. She dipped her hands into the cold water and splashed it on her face, washing away the ashes, before drying her face with the hem of her gown. I did the same, starting at the shock of cold but relieved to remove some of the grime of the road, even if it meant my cheeks went numb in the process.

Inside the refectory, the sisters had removed their veils. The ashes were gone too, having served their ritual purpose. Mayda led me to the head of a long table, where she sat with great ceremony. She whispered to one of the sisters at her side, who promptly offered me her seat. There were no others open, so she sat on the floor.

"Please," I said to the sister, "that is not necessary—"

Mayda silenced me with a look. "They know who you are and welcome the humility of giving up what they can to the queen."

The sisters spoke little during the simple meal of bread, cheese, and thin broth, and when they did, it was in their native language. The mulled wine served to me by Mayda and the elder sisters warmed my heart and spread through my veins, leaving me feeling fuzzy and more loved than I had in months. The younger ones, who I guessed from the color of their habits were still in training, much as we had been in Avalon, had to make do with watered ale. Many of the sisters glanced at me curiously, and I smiled in response. To a one, they dropped their eyes to their plates.

Mayda noticed and whispered to me, "They will protect you in any way needed. Have no fear."

After the meal finished and they recited a Latin prayer, a small bell chimed. Chairs scraped noisily as the sisters hurried to their various duties.

Mayda took my hand. "Come, I will show you to your room." She gestured to the sister who had given up her seat. "Sister Magdalena will serve you. Do not hesitate to tell her of anything you may need."

I glanced from sister to abbess. "That is not necessary. I can fend for myself."

"Nonsense," Mayda replied, her tone indicating the subject was closed.

Sister Magdalena bowed. "It is my great honor, my queen, Mother Abbess."

I leaned in close to Mayda. "Am I to address you as such? I wish to pay you due respect."

"No, you may call me Mother Mayda. You are under no vows and need not make obeisance to me."

From the refectory, which was attached to the kitchen, we trudged through the increasing sleet, careful not to slip on the ice forming underfoot. Once inside the long building attached to the chapel, Mayda led us down a long main hallway to a room near the main church.

"These are our guest rooms," she said. "They are far enough away we should not disturb you with our routine, but close enough should you wish to join us."

When we entered the room to which I was assigned, Sister Magdalena watched me expectantly, eyeing the small pack of belongings I set on the bed.

I smiled softly at her. "I can see to my own things. I wish to rest a while, so you may go about your normal duties."

Mayda nodded. "Sister Magdalena will fetch you when it is time for our late meal, if that is agreeable."

With my assent, both women turned to leave.

"Mother Mayda?" I called. "Is it safe to correspond from here? I would like to be in touch with those who might give me a better idea of what is taking place in the rest of the kingdom."

Her smile was benevolent. "Of course. I will have my messengers on standby should you need to send communication urgently. Though I would advise not to use your true name. Is there another by which those whom you address would know you?" Before I could answer, she laughed. "Oh, I remember now. Corinna. Is that right?"

I squeezed her hands. "It is. It appears the situation is reversed. I am now in your care."

She returned the gesture. "As it should be. God always gives us the opportunity to repay a kindness. May He, by whatever name you call Him, bless you. Rest now."

✦

Mayda's way of life was not very different from the one I'd lived for four years in Avalon, which surprised me greatly. It had its own rhythm and rituals but provided the same comfort and stability I'd found so soothing during my formative years.

While exploring my room that first afternoon, I'd come across a tiny door in one wall, no bigger than my hands held side-by-side. When I pulled cautiously on its curled handle, it revealed itself to be the shutter to a small barred window overlooking the church. If I knelt, it was even with my head, affording me a bird's-eye view of all that took place below.

When I asked Mayda about it that evening, she told me it had been installed before she arrived for a holy woman who was often ill but still wished to attend Mass. The height was measured so that she could only view the service if she was in the proper posture for prayer. Mayda said although I could not attend their rituals, I was more than welcome to observe from there. After the saintly sister died, when Mayda was still new to the convent, she spent much time in that room, and it was those hours of quiet contemplation that led her to embrace the Christian faith.

Through that same window, I was able to observe the rites of Lent during the fortnight of Passiontide, a solemn time leading up to Easter, the holiest of days for Christians. All of the sisters arose at dawn and dressed in simple white robes. Even though the air was cold and the ground covered in heavy frost, they processed around the church barefoot, each holding a single yew branch, singing Hosanna, before entering and taking their places around the perimeter of the room.

In many ways, they resembled our Candlemas procession so many years before. Grief tugged at my heart as I recalled that day—Isolde's joyous smile on her favorite feast day and Elaine's humble expression as she took up the role of the bride. They were both gone now, victims of fates too cruel for their few years, too awful for hearts so in need of love.

My eyes stung with tears, but soon it was not the ritual nor the faces of my remembered friends that passed through my mind. Instead, I felt the dizzying sensation that meant the sight was upon me. I tried to fight it, but it would not relent. Long ago, the Lady of the Lake had warned me the sight would be out of my control when one whom I loved was in danger. It was a cruel trick of the Goddess, to show me that which I was powerless to control, but I had long ago made my peace with it.

Arthur was alone on the ramparts of Cadbury, his expression set in grim lines as he watched a shadow wash over the horizon, heading straight for the castle. The wave of soldiers did not slow or part, showing determination to engage their king, and leading the way was Mordred.

"All the while I loved you, I also feared you, cursed as you are with your mother's lust for power," Arthur said to his son, who was barely distinguishable from the nearing horde. "I prayed this day would never come, but God did not heed me. My only prayer now is we can turn you away while your heart still beats." His eyes welled, but he did not allow the tears to fall.

Lancelot approached Arthur from behind, and I gasped, unaware he had returned to Britain.

Arthur must have sensed his approach, for he cleared his throat and turned before Lancelot could speak a word of greeting. "You have no business in this battle. Go to Camelot. Find Guinevere and show her I am a man who keeps his word, no matter what she may believe. I will deal with my traitorous son."

They bickered for some time, Lancelot insisting on offering his sword in repayment for the offences he'd committed against Arthur, but Arthur's insistence prevailed.

"You have more than repaid your debt by your valor on the fields of Brittany. I promised Guinevere a new life with you and that I shall deliver, even if it is my final gift to her. Go now. Send Kay to me."

Reluctantly, Lancelot departed. Kay appeared soon after.

This time, Arthur did not turn. "I have no desire to mar this fort by placing it at the center of a war. We will meet them on the banks of the river, press in before they expect us to engage. In that way, we can hope to throw them off."

"Our troops can be ready within a few hours. Mordred will not have gained the river by then."

"Good. I wish them to know their rightful king was expecting them."

With those words, my eyes grew dim and the sight left me.

⁊⁊

At dawn, I helped the lower-ranking sisters scrub the floors of the church after morning prayer, our bare feet freezing on the cold, wet stones. While we did this, Mayda and the sisters of higher rank stripped the altar of its beautiful cloths and lovingly washed it, preparing it for the rituals to come.

Later, they gathered in the church for Mass and I watched from my room above. Their priest blessed a vial of healing oil then invited the poor of the area to come forth. The sisters humbly washed their feet in imitation of a gesture performed by their Christ before his death. Mayda followed on her knees, kissing the feet of each man and woman before giving them a loaf of bread, flagon of wine, and bag of coins.

Years earlier, when I was a ward in the house of Corbenic, its lord, Pellinor, had performed similar service to the poor of his lands on Candlemas. Looking back, I missed that time and those people. Though often infuriating and perplexing, in retrospect, my years with him, Lyonesse, Isolde, and Elaine were a blessing, shielding me from the struggles of the outside world. Yes, Lyonesse could be cruel, but that was little enough sacrifice in the face of what we would experience in the years to come.

Bowing my head, I prayed. *Thank you, God and Goddess for everything that family taught me. Please bless those of their line who still live and may those who have died be at peace.*

Eyes closed, the sight came upon me again.

True to his word, Arthur's army stood in wait as Mordred's troops poured out from wooded tracts into the open fields sloping down toward the River Cam. The unexpected sight of the opposing wall of warriors slowed their progress, eventually forcing them to halt.

The curving river, with its steep banks, was the only thing separating father and son. Slowly, as if each trying to each decide their own strategy, Arthur and Mordred picked their way through their men until they were facing one another across the narrow waterway.

Arthur made the first move. "I have offered you my hand in peace time and again since returning from Brittany, only to find you with an army raised against me. One final time, I do so again. I do not wish to move against you, son, but make no mistake, I will if you press on. Greater men than you have resisted my requests for peace and lost their lives for their folly. I would hate to see the same happen to you."

A puff of warm, disbelieving breath in the frigid air was Mordred's first response, followed by a haughty, "It will not, for I have in my employ forces stronger than you have ever faced, men who believe you have wronged this land, abandoned it in the wake of your own selfish missteps. We will not bow to you when a new king is needed, one who will rule this land for all its inhabitants, not just those of native blood."

Behind him, the Saxons and Picts cheered, taking up a steady tattoo with their cudgels and shields.

Arthur ignored them, unfazed by their attempts at intimidation after so many battles. He walked down river to a place where the water narrowed, banks nearly hugging one another, and Mordred followed like a mirror image. "You may believe you fight for something bigger, but this battle is between you and me. As you will not back down, I will offer you one more opportunity to spare the lives of your men and mine. We fight now in single combat, King Stag and rutting buck. Let the gods and our skills determine the outcome."

Mordred studied his father with cold blue eyes, appearing to turn the option over in his mind. Then he laughed. "Do you truly believe that would solve anything? My death would only mean further incitement of my army, whereas yours would mean the crumbling of a nation, and for what? You cannot stop this, Arthur Pendragon. A new era has begun."

For a moment, Arthur's face betrayed his disappointment, but then he bowed his head, muttering a prayer too quiet for anyone else to hear. When he raised his face again, it bore the hard lines of a seasoned warrior. "May the gods have mercy on us all."

The armies slammed into one another with a series of deafening cracks as shields split and spears found their targets, breaking through bone to lodge in the soft tissue beneath. The carrion birds alighted in treetops and amid the trampled grass as bodies fell, turning the river into a mass grave. Soon, soldiers used the bodies of their fallen comrades to cross the breech and face their attackers in units, rather than one by one.

But when the fighting was at its thickest, Mordred did something unexpected. He turned and ran, leading his troops north toward the Midlands. Arthur was not long in catching on, pulling the greater part of his troops from the fray to give chase.

Suddenly, I was back to myself again, lying on the floor of my small room in the convent, panting and covered in sweat from the exertion of my visions. I lay on my back, staring at the wood support beams overhead, trying to understand what I had seen. The rebellion had begun. But why did Mordred not finish it there? Why run? He was obviously not retreating. His movements were too orderly, too planned. It seemed there had been a prearranged signal, some sign that told certain contingents when it was time to follow him away from the battle. But why?

I sat up, fighting a wave of dizziness. I pulled myself to the ewer of wash water and poured some into the basin, willing it to cleanse me of my fear and anxiety as I removed the layer of sweat from my skin and struggled to regain my senses.

For a while, I watched the convent's ritual, thankful for the distraction from my visions. The sisters' voices floated up as they celebrated the Mass, their songs joyful in the triumph of their Savior, yet tinged with sadness, for the worst was yet to come—for their God and for Arthur.

When Mass ended, all the candles in the church were extinguished, save one many-armed candelabra, plunging the congregation into near total darkness. I pinched out the wick of my candle as well, wishing to experience the ritual as they did. The sisters' songs turned to mournful dirges as the priest recited a story about their Lord being betrayed by his closest friend and handed over to the authorities to be tortured and condemned. One by one, the remaining candles were extinguished, until only a lone flame remained.

The church was silent, the crowd seemingly holding its breath in expectation. I scooted closer to my small window, trying to take in everything with heightened senses.

The clear voice of a young boy rang out from the north, intoning "Kyrie Eleison," a plea to their God for mercy. Then the bell-like voice of a sister responded from the south, "Christe Eleison," which meant much the same. The blending of their voices into a mournful chant raised goose pimples on my arms as they repeated the invocation.

Swept up in the chant, my prayers turned to pleas of mercy. *May the gods of war grant us mercy. Protect our king and his heir from all harm and help them see the senselessness of their battle. May they find a path to peace and spare our people the pain and privations of war.*

With two kings pitting the armies of three nations against each other, we needed any help the heavens were willing to provide. Were I there with Arthur, following Mordred's army north, perhaps I could advise him, but here in this convent, so many miles north and east of them, I could do nothing. Well, not nothing. I could pray, just as I was doing. But it felt like so little. I could not defend Arthur with my sword, or try to make them both see sense. I was powerless, for even my magic could not help them. I could not help Arthur strategize or even read the stones for him. He and Mordred were beyond my reach. All I could do was watch through eyes cursed with the sight as it all played out.

Below, in the chapel, the single flame was extinguished. From the west, the deep rich bass of a man's voice sang, "Christ is dead," three times. I shivered, certain to my core that soon a similar elegy would be sung for either the High King or his son.

⁂

The rituals did not end each night, but rather they faded into silence before picking up again at the prescribed time, as they would each day until Easter. In the time between, the sisters communicated only as necessary through a series of hand signals similar to those we used during our period of silence just before being consecrated as priestesses in Avalon.

The familiarity made me long for my days on that blessed isle, for the kinship and sisterhood these nuns clearly felt and that I had once known. Though I was surrounded by women, my heart ached with the hollow void of loneliness. I wished I had someone here in whom I could confide about my visions, who would understand the frustration, the utter helplessness of watching something tragic and pointless you could not change. But if I told them, the sisters would surely think me as demonic as that damn bishop Marius had.

The snow and ice prevented me from worshiping outdoors and I could not face being alone in my tiny cell, so on the night of the new moon, I slipped into the back of the chapel, intent on performing my own rituals while the sisters sang and adored the bare cross placed before their altar. I searched the shadows for a place I would go unnoticed. To my right was a small alcove with a statue of the Lady Mary. Normally serene and welcoming, tonight she was an ominous specter with her black shroud.

I could not believe I was even considering confiding in her, the mother of a god in whom I had no faith. But yet, how different was she from the myriad of goddesses to whom I had prayed before? Wasn't she the same woman, called by a different name? Was she a being like Deichtine, Cú Chulainn's mother, who, while incarnate on this earth, was singled out by her god for a special purpose?

It was not as if goddesses giving birth to heroes was a new idea, or even one confined to the Christians. Taliau was the mother of Lugh; Dôn had given birth to Arianrhod and Gwydion, all of whom I worshiped, so why could I not pray to Mary? I had no interest in the redemption offered by her son, so I was in no danger of abandoning my faith. I was simply adding another goddess to my pantheon, something my forebears had been doing for hundreds of years.

The previous night at dinner, after the sisters had covered the statues with a thick black cloth—a tradition of their faith I found rather odd—I had asked Mayda about the statue and the woman it represented. "How does she relate to your people's faith? Did you have trouble accepting her when you were new here?"

Mayda had answered through a mouthful of hard bread, the only daily sustenance until Easter. "No, not really. She is much like our goddess Ostara, who gives fertility to the land and its people. Her feast day is usually close to Easter." She scooted a little closer to me in her seat. "We would never tell the bishop, but the flowers we lay at her feet on Easter are less to gladden her heart at the resurrection of her son than they are to honor her. We still hold our families' traditions in our own ways."

Mayda's honesty warmed my heart, a comfort I carried with me now as I contemplated Arthur's conversion to Christianity, and then Morgan's. Had she found this goddess and accepted her as one and the same as those we'd worshiped as part of the rites of Avalon? Early during my time in Pellinor's house, I had noted the similarities between his faith—with its Host that so resembled the full moon and its rituals that invoked the elements in incense, water, candles, and bread and wine—and my own. Even some of this Christ's teachings were like those of the Druids. And now there was this Mother goddess. Had Morgan been able to look beyond the names and see enough of Avalon in this new faith?

If so, she was indeed a wiser woman than I, for there were aspects of this Christian world I could not accept. No matter what Mayda and her sisters may believe in secret, their faith still forbade the ancient gods, who were in so many ways our tie to the land and to our ancestors. Pious bastards like Marius made certain women had little place in or influence on the faith—and that they would never be worshiped in any proper way. Plus, I would never be able to believe we needed to be saved, much less that the death of one man could achieve such a monumental task. I believed in right and wrong and had seen both tremendous good and horrific evil, but the idea that one man's sin, brought about by a woman—of course—so long ago could be the reason why we did wrong today was hard enough to believe and then to tell me that the torture of one man, god or not, undid all of that and made it tolerable for me to do wrong, so long as I asked forgiveness for it, was simply too much. Father Dyfadd and

I had had many rounds of debate on these points when I sought to understand Arthur's faith, but to no avail.

I gently removed the material that covered the statue, setting it aside so I could recover it before any of the sisters knew of my transgression. There she stood in blue robes so much like my own as a priestess, beckoning me to know her as another Lady of Avalon. I lit a candle with the flint and fire steel I'd brought from my room. Setting the candle before the statue, I gave the sign of Avalon and looked into the Lady's hollow stone eyes.

"Great Mother, called by many names, hear this priestess who requests your aid. Safeguard our king, he whom my heart holds so dear—" My words stopped as the sight took over.

I was riding with Arthur, Kay, and the Combrogi at a hard pace, still giving chase to Mordred. The land there was flat, grazing pastures and farmland as far as the eye could see. We were about a day or two's ride from Cadbury, in the heart of Salisbury. We rode for what felt like hours and the land subtly changed, sprouting trees at intervals, until we were once again in forested land. Somewhere nearby, a river or brook trickled.

"We need to rest the mounts soon, or they will falter," Kay advised.

"Agreed. I wish I'd known that little cur was going to lead us on a hunting expedition. I could have sent word to Powys to prepare new mounts, extra soldiers, anything." Frustration colored Arthur's voice over the pounding of the hooves.

Where was Mordred leading them and why?

"We'll find him, Arthur, and when we do—" Bedivere never got to finish his thought, because he was slammed sideways off his horse.

"Ambush!"

The cry went up from the head of the line and was quickly echoed to those at the rear, but not before Mordred's army descended, larger and more heavily Saxon this time, if the weaponry was any indication.

Arthur hacked a line through the onslaught, laying low man and woman alike. I didn't need the sight to know he was on a mission to get to his son and end the violence once and for all. But if Mordred was in the fray, he was well hidden. No doubt this attack had been orchestrated to inflict maximum damage on Arthur's army while keeping Mordred at a safe distance. For all anyone on the battlefield knew, Mordred had already retreated to some hideaway and was watching the battle unfold through his mother's second sight, just as I was doing now.

One member of the Combrogi fell, then another. Owain was badly wounded, but fighting on. Gareth and Garheis were not so fortunate, brothers to the bitter end. Gareth perished defending his younger sibling, their limbs tangled in death, eyes glassy and staring, their souls fleeing to the safety of the Otherworld.

As blood spurted from hacked away limbs and the agony of death throes filled the air, I had a moment of lucidity where I was grateful to be only witnessing this horror. Yet my hand involuntarily reached for the sword that slept on the cold floor beneath my pallet in my room above, my warrior's instinct aiming to protect those I held dear.

For several moments, the chanting sisters filled my ears with the lamentations of their God. *"I led you out of Egypt, from slavery to freedom, but you led your Savior to the cross."*

And then the visions and sorrowful voices mixed.

My attention was drawn not to Arthur but to Aggrivane, who was battling a large Saxon wielding a spear and a sword simultaneously. Aggrivane was on the defensive, backing away as the Saxon poked his spear at Aggrivane's guard, then sought an opening with his sword. Even without a shield, the Saxon evaded all of Aggrivane's attempts to wound him, only snarling in pain when a Combrogi saw the situation and stabbed the Saxon's sword arm from behind, severing the main muscle in his shoulder.

"For forty years, I led you safely through the desert. I fed you with manna from heaven, and brought you to a land of plenty; but you led your Savior to the cross."

Aggrivane took advantage of the Saxon's pain to slash out, tearing the Saxon's leather chest plate, but otherwise inflicting no damage. If he could repeat the move, the Saxon would be dead. Aggrivane circled around, seeking another moment of inattention as he and his ally took on the ox of a man now snorting like a raging bull. Aggrivane lunged, burying his sword in the soft part of the Saxon's side, just above his hip bone.

But he was too late. The Saxon had seen an opening too.

"What more could I have done for you? I planted you as my fairest vine, but you yielded only bitterness: when I was thirsty you gave me vinegar to drink, and you pierced your Savior with a lance."

Aggrivane's eyes went wide and his mouth twisted into a wicked grimace. The Saxon's spear had caught him low, probably in the belly, and the wound forced him to the muddy ground. Men blocked my view, so I only saw flashes of his face as he grimaced and twitched in pain, hands wrapped around the shaft of the spear as his lifeblood poured onto the unforgiving ground. The next time I caught sight of him, his head had lolled to the side and his hands were slack, chest no longer heaving.

"I raised you to the height of majesty, but you have raised me high on a cross. My people, what have I done to you? How have I offended you? Answer me!"

My scream ripped through the worlds, and for a moment, the battle ceased. Each soldier stood frozen, heads and eyes turning to locate the source of the unearthly sound. Some crossed themselves, while others made the sign of Avalon, and a few ran away in terror. For three breaths, everyone was silent and motionless, paying respect to a pain that rattled through the core of each man. Then the battle began again as though nothing untoward had taken place.

Back in the chapel, my body crumpled, reacting to the trauma of what I had seen before my fragile mind caught up. I clawed at the statue's feet as though she could save him, as though by hanging on to her, I could will Aggrivane back to life.

Her serene face was the last thing I saw before my sight shattered into a blinding field of stars, their white heat painful to behold in the blackness that sought to consume me. I grasped my head, unable to see, crippled by the pain turning my blood to ice. I was crying, I had to be, for the neck of my sleeping gown was wet and my chest muscles were spasming in time with my heart. How it still beat, I did not know. I could barely draw breath.

Mayda's strong arms gripped me beneath the shoulders as she and Sister Magdalena lifted me from the floor and carried me past the faces of startled sisters. I gave into the pain, senseless.

I woke in my cell, retching before I was even fully conscious, but Mayda was there, holding a bowl beneath my mouth, supporting my shoulders and holding back my hair. When I was finished, stomach muscles cramping, too weak even to lift my head, she placed a cool cloth on my forehead and squeezed my hand. That small gesture was all that kept me from giving up completely. I wanted to sleep and never wake, to join Aggrivane in the Otherworld. I had been there once; the transition was easy. All I had to do was will it. But the warm reassurance of her hand was like a cord tying me to this world.

Weary, I looked at her. Mayda's lips moved in whispered prayer.

When she noticed I was awake, she smiled. "I will be with you as long as you need me. No matter how long it takes for the pain to stop." She wrapped me in her arms, holding me like a child.

"How did you know I would need you?" I asked weakly.

"Do you think the Britons are the only ones gifted with the sight?"

I had never considered the possibility of Saxon women having it too.

"I do not have the gift, but I have seen it many times, so I knew what to expect. I know you are tired, so I will not trouble you with questions, save one. The rest you can tell me when you are ready." Her gaze met my eyes, which hadn't stopped pouring since the visions ended, making certain I understood her. "Does our king live?"

I nodded weakly.

She breathed a sigh of relief. "Good. Then we will redouble our prayers. Our good Lord cannot fail to hear us in this holy season."

I envied her confidence, her faith. My Goddess had abandoned me, never to return, or so said the impenetrable cloud in my heart. I knew little of Mayda's god, but if he made Arthur's victory possible, I would seriously consider following him.

⁓ⓔ ⓔ⁓

Two days later, thanks to Mayda's expert ministrations, I was strong enough to be on my feet, though I did not leave my cell. Mayda had been called away to the visitor's parlor for a meeting with King Cuncar, ruler over York since its capture by the Saxons decades before, and his archbishop. Why were they here? Could they possibly know Elga had sent me here? When I'd voiced my concerns to Mayda, she assured me they simply wished to make certain everything was in place for the town's celebration of the Holy Week, in which the convent played a large role.

With Mayda occupied and the other sisters wrapped up in preparations for the upcoming solemnity, I had a stretch of much-needed time to myself to think through all that had happened. I sat on the small bed, elbows on my knees, head in my hands. What had happened to Arthur after my visions ended? Surely he could not be dead. If the Goddess had chosen to show me Aggrivane's last moments, she likely would have done the same for Arthur, so he had to be alive. If he had been defeated, Mayda would know by now. Surely word would have come and the Saxons would be rejoicing.

I sighed, flopping back on the bed, eyes on the sloping timber ceiling, willing myself to think through the situation as I had been trained. There had been heavy losses on Arthur's side. That much was certain. Many of his best men had died. I forced the image of Aggrivane lying still amid the carnage out of my mind. Those who had survived would have taken shelter somewhere nearby—wherever that was.

Would Morgan have chosen Arthur or backed her son? How does one make such a choice? I shook my head. I'd been down that line of thought before, and it had no clear answer. Only she could say where her loyalties truly lay. Even without her, chances were good the army had picked up some camp women. Hopefully some of them were priestesses and could help aid the wounded.

And what of Mordred? Surely his army had suffered losses as well. But then how had they gained in number since their attack near Cadbury? Mordred had to have back-up units supplying fresh men and horses. That meant he wasn't fleeing from Arthur; he was leading him on a predefined course, one he knew he could reach before his father and set the next phase of his plan in motion.

Damn Morgan and her influence on her son. She was never one for battle strategy, but that wouldn't have stopped her from teaching Mordred to think through every possibility, to turn every situation to his greatest advantage, just as she had been doing her whole life. Damn Lot for teaching his fosterling battle strategy. He'd thought he was preparing the heir to the kingdom. Little did he know he was arming a tyrant.

My blood went cold. Damn me too. I had taught him to read the Holy Stones, the one weapon of war neither Lot nor Morgan could or would pass on. I had armed him with a conduit to the gods. Damn my ignorance.

I tapped my thumb against my leg, turning a thought over in my mind. Two could play at that game, and I had more experience. No one was likely to have a set of stones in a house of the Christian god, but that never stopped the poor children on the streets who thought it only a game to be played with whatever pebbles littered the ground.

Standing, I touched the wall, fighting a wave of dizziness as my mind leapt ahead of my body. Most of the things I needed would be easy enough to procure. I still had the platter from my dinner; it would do as a board. While the sisters were attending to their prayers tonight, I could read the stones. But where would I get the stones themselves? Several feet of snow on the ground outside made it unlikely I could simply pluck them from the garden. Plus, I needed stones of pure quality to ensure the accuracy of my visions. Thanks to my hasty departure from Camelot, the only stones of any value I had with me were set in the ring Arthur had given me. I was not about to take it apart, but it gave me an idea.

Quietly opening my door, I peered down the hall, finding it deserted. I made my way toward the sisters' work area. They embroidered and affixed jewels to robes for the bishop in one of these rooms, or so Mayda had told me when she gave me a tour. I didn't expect them to leave such valuables out in the open, but I was willing to bet they'd be easy enough to find.

As I neared the end of the hall, a small, clear bell tolled twice, calling the sisters to prayer. I stopped, flattening myself against the wall as they passed. Some of them smiled in greeting, while others ignored me. A few looked at me askance, no doubt wondering why I was in their hallway when no one had seen me since I fainted in the chapel, but no one could question me as they were currently under the commandment of silence.

Once they had all passed out of sight and the soft murmur of their prayers filled the air, I slipped in and out of small workrooms until I found the one I was seeking. Light filtered in from a bank of windows on the west wall, illuminating two spinning wheels, three looms, and a few benches laden with silks and delicate thread in a rainbow of colors. I approached the latter, hoping to find a stole or other garment I could take and rip out the jewels—I could always sew them back in later. But after rummaging through all of them, I found Fortuna was not with me.

Mayda must have kept the jewels in her office. My skin prickled at the thought of invading her private space. That would be wrong. I did not want to betray her trust, but this was something I needed to do. Surely she would understand, and she needn't know if I returned them quickly.

I skittered down the long hall lined with rows of cells until I came to the largest. I tried the handle, but the door was locked. No matter. I had borrowed a long needle and thin metal implement used in affixing jewels to fabric from the workroom. They would work to spring this lock, as well as any that secured the stones. With a snick, I was inside.

Mayda's room was comprised of an outer office and what I guessed was her bedroom beyond a closed door. The office was only slightly bigger than my cell, so it didn't take long to locate a small wooden box with a heavy iron lock inside one of the chests behind her desk. This had to be it.

I carried the box over to the light. Pausing for a heartbeat, I closed my eyes and said a prayer of thanks to Isolde for teaching me this forbidden skill. When the lock popped open, I turned over the box, letting its contents fall into my palm like raindrops. I counted the glittering jewels. Exactly forty waited at my command, enough to represent both armies. But I was still missing the queens.

After running back to my room, box ill-concealed beneath the folds of my robe, I dove under the bed and withdrew my pack. Rummaging through its contents, my fingertips touched brooches, parchment, a bone comb, and an old wooden dog figurine I carried for protection. The stones were not there. Running my hands over the gowns hanging on pegs on the wall, tears pricked at my eyes as I traced one empty skirt after another. Just when I was about to give up, my fingertips met a reassuring lump in the seam of one hem. Reaching in, I retrieved the two red stones Isolde and I had won, lost, and won back again so many times over the years.

After kissing the queens, I arranged the stones in their proper formations, snuffed out all the candles save one, and took up my place before the board. Closing my eyes, I chased away all thoughts and concentrated on my breathing. With the first dizzying tingle of weightlessness, I opened my eyes.

This time was different than those that had come before. It was not a battle the gods were communicating, but something else. I stared past the stones I had so precariously procured until the knots and grain of the wood platter formed pictures, just as the clouds had when I would watch them as a child from the hillsides around Northgallis.

I saw Mordred pacing the halls of Camelot like a caged wolf waiting to be let out. Then I saw him barring the gate and filling the walls to the brim with archers. A rain of arrows fell on Arthur's army, forcing them to choose retreat or die trying to scale the impregnable walls of Camelot.

The visions ended, leaving me with a chilling certainty. Mordred was leading them into a trap they could not possibly escape. He knew it and Arthur soon would too. I had no way of getting word to him, but I could warn those who would help him, and perhaps provide him with some fresh reinforcements too.

Slowly, my hands moved the stones until I had twice played out the likely outcome, once with Arthur's current army, and again if I was able to help him. Both situations were dire, and oddly, each ended in a stalemate where the two queens and their kings remained, but there was no way for either side to claim victory.

The outcome vexed me so much my bowels rumbled, but there was nothing more I could do, at least not with the divination tool before me. I used the glowing taper to relight the others with shaking hands and hid the plate and stones so Mayda would not find anything amiss upon her return and suspect my very unchristian activity. With trembling fingers, I took up the stylus and composed a letter to Owain's wife, who was loyal to Arthur and the only one within range to augment Arthur's army while her husband fought at his side.

Not long after I sealed the letter, a knock broke my concentration and Mayda appeared in my doorway. I looked up, trying to appear as though nothing had changed from when she left me.

"How was your visit?" I asked brightly.

"It went well, thank you." Mayda's face grew solemn. "They brought news of Arthur."

I bit my lip and smoothed my skirt, trying to delay the inevitable news in case what I had seen was wrong, a product of wishful thinking. When I looked at her, my face was passive, though it took all my might to school it so. "And?"

"He lives. What is left of his army continues north, but to where we do not know."

"I may." I glanced at the letter on the desk. "How quickly can your messengers deliver this?"

Mayda picked it up. "Two days, four at most." Her expression betrayed concern and not a little apprehension, but she asked no questions.

"That will have to be fast enough. Please see that it is on its way as soon as possible."

I may not have been able to fight next to Arthur in the clash that was to come, but I could do everything in my power to assure he was as prepared as possible.

A week later, the church was dark and silent, black-veiled sisters watching in vigil like wraiths at a tomb. In many ways, the day's rituals were more arcane than our native rites of Samhain. Both feasts mourned the death of a god who would come again, but this Christian tradition focused on the brutality of his death. Long Friday, as they called it, was the most solemn day of the year, with rites beginning in the middle of the night and lasting half the day.

Mayda came forward, crowned in thorns in imitation of her Savior. She and Sister Magdalena, her attendant, veiled the empty altar in black cloth. Mayda then held up a skull, to which all present genuflected. The archbishop said a brief prayer in Latin, and the sisters chanted as Mayda gently placed the skull on the altar. Two sisters set heavy wooden chests on either side of the altar. Mayda had explained earlier that they contained bones of the sisters who had passed away since the convent was founded so that all might be present at this most solemn vigil.

The Latin chant was intoned so low that I could not make out the words, but the haunting melody seemed to transcend time and space, opening the veil between worlds so that the souls of those who witnessed this man-god's crucifixion could rise from their graves to recount the deeds of that terrible day, lest it ever be forgotten.

The sisters swayed as the chant lulled them into a trance, and I found myself slipping into the Otherworld with them. Mayda and the bishop prostrated themselves before the altar, and my vision blurred. For a few frightening moments, blackness engulfed me. Then the clang of metal and grunts of exertion and pain reached my ears.

My sight cleared and I found myself in a mist-filled valley near one of the forts on Emperor Hadrian's wall, a place called Camlann I had been many times with Arthur, looking for any signs that the lowland tribes were stirring. Now the fort was crumbling, a shell of its former greatness.

Around me, battle raged, Briton against Briton, Saxon and Pict allied against them all. Owain's men were among the warriors, so my letter had made it to its destination in time to help Arthur. Thanks to the extra troops, this battle was less of a slaughter than the previous two had been, both sides holding their own in a tiring stalemate.

Mordred stood well back from the main engagement, watching and issuing commands from atop the wall. He didn't seem to notice as Arthur approached him from behind, flanked by Kay and Bedivere.

But before Arthur could attack, Mordred whirled, blade drawn, ready to strike. "I took you for many things, Father, but a coward is not among them. Would you really stab your own son in the back?"

Accolon and Bors stepped out of the mist, holding Arthur's companions at bay several steps behind.

"It is only what you deserve after setting upon me and my army unawares." Arthur raised his own blade. "But this does not concern them. It has always been *our* fight. Our time has come."

Mordred smiled darkly. "Indeed it has. If you are of the mind to die, lay on."

Arthur struck out, and their blades met with a deafening clash.

The force of the strike vibrated through me as though my own weapon had been hit. Dizzy, my sight faltered, pulling me into an in-between world where the keening of the sisters' chant made the hair on the back of my neck stand up, but I was not fully in my body either. Vaguely, I heard the priest intone the words of Jesus, who had descended into hell to condemn the devil and liberate the souls therein, including the first man and woman. To Adam, he commanded, "Repent of your sin and be freed by my blood."

Instead of an answer, Arthur's grunt of pain reached me as Mordred swung his shield, connecting squarely with Arthur's left cheek. Arthur stumbled back on the rocky, wet ground, doubled over, but he managed to block Mordred's stab, swatting away Mordred's sword before spitting a mouthful of blood onto the stones.

When Arthur stood upright again, he was less steady, turning his whole head to locate his opponent, which made me think he'd lost the sight in his left eye. He recovered quickly and lunged at Mordred. Despite the sucking mire underfoot, they parried and thrust with exhausting speed, as though they were in a hurry to kill one another.

Mordred lost his weapon first. He took one of Arthur's blows on the edge rather than the flat of the blade, and it broke, making

Mordred lose his grip. The remnants of his sword sank in the mud. Momentarily stunned, Mordred left himself open to Arthur's fury but managed to avoid injury. He grabbed a low-hanging branch from a silver birch, partially broken in a storm, and wrenched it free, wielding it alternately like a club and a staff. Arthur advanced with confidence but never took the killing blow. I suspected he was trying to tire Mordred, to force him to yield the fight, and hence, the kingship.

But his son was too persistent and too clever for that. Fighting with the tough branch, he resembled the Oak King seeking to overthrow the Holly King. Mordred held his own, eventually disarming Arthur with a crack to the wrist of his sword arm that made my teeth twinge, even in the spirit world.

Soon the two were locked in a skirmish that more resembled the brute force contention of horned goats than the engagement of two highly trained warriors. They wrestled one another to the sodden ground, Arthur's bulk easily overpowering his lithe son.

"Call a halt," Arthur demanded as battle raged all around them.

"Never," Mordred declared.

Arthur fumbled at his belt. "I will give you one more chance," he said, holding a dagger to his son's stomach. "If you yield to me, you will live."

Arthur was so busy watching his son's reaction, he couldn't see Mordred's right hand creeping along the ground toward his broken sword.

"And if not?" Mordred's hand closed around the jagged blade, freeing it from the mud.

"Then I am afraid I will have to kill you."

"Please, Father. Don't."

His pleading gave Arthur pause, just long enough for Mordred to raise the sword and smash the hilt into Arthur's head. The force of his blow hammered Arthur's body downward. Mordred yelled, his eyes going wide. He scrabbled backward like a crab. As Arthur's unconscious body fell away from Mordred, it revealed Arthur's dagger protruding from Mordred's stomach.

Time stood still.

Or at least that was how it felt. Realization hit me with the force of a gale sweeping down a canyon face, pulling me inexorably to my own death.

A bloodcurdling scream fell from my lips, echoed by another that held even more pain.

Morgan.

As my spirit body pushed through the thick of battle toward my husband, she dashed to her son's side, flying across the field like a banshee. Of course. She would have been having visions of her own while nearby with the other camp women.

"Get them out of here! Get them to safety," Kay yelled as he, Bedivere, and some of the others fought through the crushing mass of bodies to shelter their king and his heir from further harm.

They took them into the remains of the fort, its skeletal walls casting odd shadows in the half light and affording us some measure of dryness and privacy.

In this odd place between worlds, I could touch them. I sank to the floor at Arthur's side and cradled his head in my lap, begging him to open his eyes. His pulse was faint and fluttering under my fingertips, so he lived—for now.

I inspected his wound even as Kay tried to bind it to stop the copious bleeding. Mordred's blow had been powerful, smashing Arthur's helmet and rending the side of his head with a deep, angry gash. At the rate his blood coated my hands, I feared a small artery had ruptured on impact. Even if that were not the case, the blow would cause severe swelling that could lead to host of problems, should he survive long enough to experience them. He needed help beyond what battlefield medics could provide.

Morgan gathered her son's body onto her lap, weeping so hard she could find no voice. He stroked her cheek. "Mother."

"Stay strong, my son," she answered as though hope still remained.

But the only outcome for him was death. No other ending could be read in the pool of blood gathering black around him.

His gaze flicked to me. "Guinevere." He smiled. "I am so sorry."

I swallowed hard, trying not to choke on the tears streaming down my face. That he could see my spirit-self meant he was close to passing through the veil. "All is forgiven, Mordred. The Goddess knows. She will have mercy."

His features smoothed as his breathing slowed, the lines of hatred and anger that had marred them over the last year disappearing until he resembled the boy who had welcomed me upon my return to Camelot from captivity, rather than the bitter monster he had recently become.

In my lap, Arthur groaned. His eyelashes fluttered and he opened his good eye, squinting at me. "I knew you'd come."

"I would be nowhere else." I squeezed his hand, ignoring the twinge in my gut that told me his seeing me meant he was near death as well. "Arthur, I love you. If you remember nothing else, let it be those words."

He shifted, turning his head to have a better view of me. "And I you." He caught sight of his son, slumped in Morgan's arms. "Son?" His voice was thick with confusion.

He did not know what he had done. Mordred's blow must have rendered him unconscious before his blade pierced his son's flesh. Now was not the time to tell him.

At least Morgan seemed to feel the same. Still crying, she grasped Arthur's other hand. "He died in battle. Is that not what you have always wished for him?"

Arthur gave a small bark of a laugh. "A hero? Yes. Death? No." He drawled the last word like a drunkard. The darkness was about to claim him.

I patted his cheeks, gently at first then harder when he did not respond. "Arthur, do you not wish to say farewell to your son?"

"My boy," was all Arthur managed before he fell into unconsciousness again.

I shook his shoulders. "Arthur! Arthur, no!"

As his breathing slowed, I sobbed harder, glancing over his shoulder at Morgan. She was weeping so hard her whole body shook as she clasped her son to her breast, his hands flapping limply at his side, the bloody dagger at her feet. Her skin was as pale as moonlight, her red lips twisted into a silent scream of anguish.

Kay stood, shaking his head while tears rolled silently down his cheeks.

Mordred was dead. For all intents and purposes, so was Arthur. That was the news Kay emerged from the fort to tell their men. I lay Arthur gently on the floor and went to the window to watch the armies react. As word spread, men ceased fighting and turned to face the fort. To a one, every Briton fell to one knee in honor of their fallen leaders.

Only the gods knew how things would have been different if

everyone on the battlefield had shared their allegiance. While most saw the ceasing of hostility as a sign of respect, others used it to their advantage. The rumbling of horse's hooves shattered the silence as a Pict on horseback raced through the crowd. Swinging his axe like a scythe, he removed the heads of eight kneeling Britons before anyone could react. The Saxons followed suit, stabbing another dozen with their javelins as they mourned their kings.

"Raise your arms, men. Defend your fallen kings with your life. This is your final tribute to them," Kay yelled before disappearing into the fray with Bedivere.

Morgan and I were alone with the bodies of our beloved men. She reluctantly laid Mordred on the floor, passing her hand over his eyes. She crossed his arms over his breast, hands forever laced with the pommel of his damaged sword, before she bent over him.

"Goodbye, my son," she whispered and kissed his forehead.

Arthur's heart beat lightly beneath my hand, the sensation carrying with it a thousand memories—the first time his gaze met mine at the tournament, his expression of adoration when I told him I was pregnant, even his grief when he thought me dead, his joy at my return after my exile with Malegant, the wonder and regret in his eyes as he traced my scarred face when we met again after the fire. All those things and more tumbled over one another in my mind as I contemplated what must come next.

I knelt, pressing his hand to my lips, grateful for this last moment with him, for I knew it for what it was. "For all that we were, all that we dared to dream, I love you. In this life and the next." I turned to Morgan. "He's yours."

She was still staring at the lifeless body of her son. She'd barely heard me. "What?"

I walked over to her and took her shoulders, forcing her unfocused eyes to me. With exaggerated volume, I repeated myself. "I said, 'He's yours.'"

She blinked at me as though I spoke a foreign language.

"Arthur is not dead, not yet, and I know the only place that can heal him." I shook her lightly to get her attention. "Morgan, listen to me. You are the only one who can help Arthur now. I concede the last of his life to you. Get him to Avalon and summon Helene in case she needs to say goodbye to her father. She will be safer there than with Owain and Accolon in the days to come."

The mention of her daughter's name brought Morgan out of her grief-stricken trance. She blinked at me again, shook her head, then came to life. "You are not really here. But I am. I can save him." A wicked grin spread across her face. She stuck her head out of the back of the fort. "You!" she called to a woman standing nearby. "Find Grainne and Mona and tell them to bring the Grail." She turned to the man guarding Arthur. "Get him to a horse. We must away to Avalon."

"Not a horse, lady. It will be faster to take him by water," one of the women said. "I will take you." She was one of Sobian's girls, one of a handful who'd stayed to fight with Arthur even when their leader refused. She would do everything she could to ensure he made it in time to be healed.

They took him from my arms, and all of my strength bled out as though I were the one with a mortal wound. Arthur was in the hands of the Goddess now, and those of Morgan as her representative and his wife. My vision blurred. Gray tendrils of smoke rolled in from its edges until I could see nothing more. I was vaguely aware of rejoining my body in my cold, small cell. But I did not care. I embraced the darkness with all the passion of a lover.

After twenty-four years, it was over. Camelot was no more.

⊰ഛ ☙⊱

I woke to the bright light of Easter morning and the joyful song of "Alleluia" wafting in from the open window overlooking the chapel. For a few moments, I floated on this optimism, my spirit buoyant and free, my mind clear of all but the light and song.

But when I sat up, my head throbbed and memories returned in flashes—Aggrivane fallen among his brethren; then Arthur senseless on the ground, a bloody gash to his head; Mordred clutching his abdomen; the grief-stricken face of Morgan. Her voice rang in my head, "We must away to Avalon."

Was I meant to follow her? For the third time in less than two years, I had nowhere to go. Avalon was a logical choice. I would be safe and welcome there. But yet, as comforting as that idea was, it didn't feel quite right. There was something else I was yet meant to do, and Avalon wasn't where it would happen.

I shuffled mindlessly as I gathered my few belongings, rolling robes and cloaks into a pack for my departure. I may not have a destination, but I could not stay here. I had troubled the poor sisters enough. They had shown me more kindness than I could ever ask. I could not turn around and ask them to harbor me in what would likely be dark days ahead.

Now that Arthur was at the very least severely incapacitated and his heir dead, there would be a fight for the throne of High King. Just as in the days following Uther's death, men with any claim and none at all would turn against one another in the quest for power. If my whereabouts were known, I would be a target for everything from assassination attempts—lest I make my own bid for the throne, which I had no intention of doing—to insurrections in my name, or even yet another abduction by one who sought to use my sovereignty to bolster his claim. I would be a danger to everyone I came in contact with.

That didn't even factor in the Saxons and the Picts, who, even if the last of the Combrogi managed to contain them, would likely be making their own bids for expanded land. I had a feeling Elga still lived, and if I was correct, she would come here to seek my blood. I would not let Mayda pay for her sister's twisted sense of vengeance. Plus, even if the Picts chose to turn tail and return to their homelands, they would no doubt wreak havoc on their way, and sooner or later, they would resume their centuries-old war with the tribes of the north. With no strong Briton leadership to stop them, they would press as far south as they could.

No, this was not the time for me to retreat into the mists. Let those who will believe I died in a convent, but I would complete my life as I had started it—as a warrior's daughter. There was only one place for that—my mother's homeland and its capital of Din Eidyn.

I knelt one last time, squinting through the small window to ensure the sisters would be at Mass a while longer. My gaze traveled over the white-robed women, hair covered in light lace veils and crowns of lilies, and alighted on Mayda. She was at the head of the group of older sisters, nearest to the priest, her face suffused with joy at the resurrection of her god. I would miss her terribly. I couldn't predict what her sister would do when she showed up here and found me missing, but at least Elga would have no reason to harm her. That was the best repayment I could give—for now.

I smoothed out the bedspread and turned in a circle one last time, making sure I hadn't left anything. On impulse, I swept a hand under the bed, and it brushed against something hard. I withdrew the box of jewels. I opened it, tempted to take one to safeguard my passage north. But I could not. It would be wrong to use my hosts that way.

I closed the box and set off to return it to Mayda's office. On the way, I passed the kitchens, silent save two young maids, one turning the spit and the other minding a bubbling cauldron, both of which would be served at the feast after Mass. They were so intent on their duties, it was not hard to slip past them and into the small larder. As I would not be around for the morning meal, I did not feel guilty about taking some bread, cheese, a bit of smoked fish, and a skin of wine for my journey.

Provisions packed, I unlocked Mayda's door and placed the box back where I had found it. The light caught on Arthur's ring in its customary place on my right hand, and I realized I had the means to fund my journey after all. I could easily pawn it in town. No one would recognize me, and it was doubtful any enterprising man would turn down a rare piece of gold and jewels. It was also fitting, I supposed, that I leave my last vestige of Arthur behind, as I was leaving behind my life as queen.

I stepped out into the bright light of the courtyard with a heart weighed down by sorrow. No one was around to witness my leaving, not even the porter. She too was attending Mass. But that also meant there was no one to witness my grief. As I closed the latch of the convent gate, I didn't even bother wiping the tears away or trying to stave off the throbbing of my thrice-broken heart. Facing the open road and an uncertain future, I gave in to my loneliness and misery, praying that at my journey's end, I might find some measure of peace.

People Of The North

Chapter Nine

Summer 520

On my way north, I detoured to Traprain Law to express my condolences to Lot and Anna over the loss of their sons.

Not long after I arrived, word reached us from Avalon that Arthur was dead; even the ministrations of nine priestesses hadn't been enough to save our king.

Anna and Lot shared my loss and understood my relationships with Arthur and Aggrivane better than anyone, so they allowed me to fall to pieces in ways few others would have tolerated. I did not sleep and refused to eat, taking only a little bread and water and only after Anna practically forced it down my throat.

I had lost my husband—estranged though we were—and the man I considered a son even though we were not related by blood. Mordred's death brought back the stinging pain of losing my own children in childbed, redoubling the bitterness that lingered in the cockles of my heart. I mourned Mordred's unfulfilled potential, for what could have been had he not been corrupted by the lust for power that poisoned his blood, a curse inherited from his mother. He had been a brilliant man, perfectly suited to carry on Arthur's legacy, but somehow he had gone astray, forming loyalties that may have destroyed our country had he lived to overthrow his father.

I railed at the gods for the loss of Arthur. Despite all we had been through, he was my husband and I still loved him. I grieved the man that only Morgan and I truly knew, the humorous, tender soul behind the gruff, noble exterior. The man who built the labyrinth and garden at the center of Camelot out of concern for my welfare, who laid his newborn children to rest alone when I was too ill to attend their funeral, who accepted a madwoman back into his heart and made room for me beside the woman he truly loved instead of consigning me to the whims of fate, as was his right.

I had been so focused on hating Arthur for his missteps over the last two years that it took his death to make me remember what a truly remarkable man he was. I shed tears over my shortsightedness and mourned the loss of any chance of reconciliation. I would have relished watching him grow old from afar, passing Camelot on to Mordred and enjoying his twilight years in peace. But such is not the fate of a warrior, much less a king, and somewhere deep down, I knew his soul gloried at having died in battle, even if it was against his own son. Perhaps they were even now making peace in the Otherworld.

Then there was Aggrivane. Of all the losses I had faced in my life—my mother, father, Arthur, Octavia, countless friends and warriors dead in war—this pain was the most bitter. Aggrivane was my first love, and with his death, I grieved the end of the hopes I still held from our youth. He had been my first great mistake, but one I would make again if given the chance. A man I betrayed in my efforts to safeguard both our hearts and our reputations; he had betrayed me too, but he had also been there for me in the darkest moments before what, by all rights, should have been my death. To say good-bye to him was to bid farewell to so much of who I had been, to dreams buried deep, to a love that could never be.

In his death and the end to all I held on to from my youth, I had to accept my own aging and mortality. I was no mere girl, nor even the thriving queen who had once overseen the whole of the country; I was now an old woman, a crone, who had seen forty summers. Tangled with my mourning was a loss of self unlike any I had ever known. Even as a young girl facing my reflection before stepping onto the boat to Avalon, I had been secure in the knowledge I was the daughter of the king and queen of Gwynedd. I may not have known whether I was fated to become a priestess or rule a kingdom—or both, as the years later revealed—but I was certain of my roots. I had a foundation on which to build my budding personhood.

Now, all I had was a pile of discarded identities—lover, wife, queen, mother—none of which fit anymore. I didn't even know what had become of Lancelot. Had he tried to find me in Camelot? What fears had plagued him when I was not there? Was he still searching for me? Until I was settled and could send a message of inquiry, I had no way of finding out. The only thing that was certain was that I was still a priestess, for that honor was etched into my very soul. That was the only comfort I could wrap around my cold, shaking shoulders.

None of this made any sense. In Avalon, the Lady of the Lake had taught us to trust in the gods and follow their voices, but in my grief and uncertainty, all I could do was question their wisdom. They had taken not only Camelot's future, but its leader as well. Why? What was the purpose? Yes, Arthur had fallen on hard times, but I had to believe that, given time, he could have earned back the trust of the people, especially if he had separated from Morgan and dedicated himself to securing peace once again. Did the Goddess wish us to fall into foreign hands? What a strange and unknowable future that would be.

What was my role in this? Why could Lancelot and I not have lived our intended life in Brittany? What was my purpose in this land? All of the other times I had questioned the will of the Goddess—when I arrived in Avalon, when my mother's death forced me to return to Northgallis, when Father Marius's hatred forced me to live in Dyfedd, when I unwillingly became queen, at the death of my children, during my captivity and its aftermath, and when Arthur and the bishop nearly had me killed—the Goddess had been preparing me for a new role.

What could possibly be her will now?

♦♦♦

While I was struggling to find my place, Anna showed remarkable strength, continuing to direct and protect her kingdom in an increasingly unstable country, with Lot by her side. I stood in awe of her. She had lost three sons in the last two years—only Gawain remained of the four—yet she carried on as though her bones were made of stone and her blood fueled by her private tears. Surely she had the same questions as me, but she never showed her doubts in public, remaining stoic until we were alone, with only the deepened wrinkles around her eyes and on her brow and her chalky complexion betraying her pain. Lot showed his sadness more readily, retreating into himself and conducting a fast borne of grief until he became a hollow shell, more ghost than man. He stood sentinel at his wife's side, but he was not really present.

Together, she and I watched from afar, like nesting eagles looking down upon the forest, as Britain reverted to its native state and warring tribes and ambitious men fought for the throne Arthur had left empty. Some, like an uprising in Powys, were easily quashed, while others, like Constantine, rose with each kingdom that fell to his sword. Constantine's closest competition was the joint forces of the sons of Rheged, Owain and Accolon, who were known to all as loyal members of Arthur's Combrogi and had the support of Morgan, the former royal wife and mother of Arthur's only living child. If I knew her, she was really supporting them to give her daughter a chance at the throne. If they defeated Constantine, she could declare Helene queen and rule as regent until she came of age. Together, they dominated the northern part of the country and protected Camelot, while Constantine ate up the south and central kingdoms. The confrontation of those two forces was inevitable, and when it came, it would change the course of our country utterly.

In many ways, it was like watching a game of Holy Stones play out, only these consequences were immediate and often devastating. Borders were redrawn with such speed that the cartographers gave up trying to accurately reflect the changes. In the cities and towns, workers supplied the armies with weapons, and able-bodied men—and a few women—enlisted to support the noble of their choice, while in the countryside, people moved animals to safer pasture and hid valuables and food against marauders and defeated armies. The Irish, smelling the blood running from the battlefields, attacked our western coast with a vengeance not seen since my childhood. To the north, the Picts rumbled, forcing the tribes between the walls into high alert. Only the Saxons remained silent, watching and biding their time just as we did, which chilled my blood more than if they had shown up on our doorstep demanding vengeance.

Soon, Lot and Anna would have to travel to Din Eidyn to pledge their allegiance to the Votadini, for they had no desire to be involved in Britain's war. Though Lot and Anna had been loyal to Arthur, their kingdom was historically an annex of the Votadini tribe, and now Anna desired once again to bring her people under the protection of the Votad and Votadess, as their leaders were known, trusting them more than any of her former countrymen. I was to accompany them in order to claim my ancestral lands inherited from my mother, the only choice left to me as a throneless, homeless former queen with no living relations.

Our departure was delayed when, near midsummer, Lot was felled by a mysterious ailment that caused his blood to boil and consumed him with fever and sweat. That he succumbed to the illness was of little surprise to those of us who had watched his grief eat away at him, but the speed and ferocity of his decline frightened us all.

Lot lay abed, walking between the worlds in fever dreams that made him cry out to his dead sons, offering them apologies for offenses both real and imagined and declaring his eternal love for them. He even spoke with Arthur in a conversation so seemingly lucid that I could make out what Arthur was saying to him. Not long after, Lot reached out into the open air, eyes focused on something I could not see.

"My ancestors call to me." He turned his head, and a smile like the dawn lit his face. "Ah, Gareth, Garheis, my boys, come to see your father home, have you? I am ready."

After Lot breathed his last, Anna closed his eyes with silent sobs and a gentle kiss. I rested my head on his shoulder. I had few tears left with which to bathe him, but my heart contracted all the same. In its bitter consequences, the Battle of Camlann had taken one final life and one of the last remaining shards of my heart in the man who should have been my father by marriage.

Now it was my duty to help Anna settle into the role of widow. Then I would continue to Din Eidyn as planned. Lot would not see the new kingdoms that would sprout from his body and those of so many others fallen in battle, but I would, and I needed allies if I were to survive. Drying my eyes and calling on the last dregs of my resolve, I faced north. It was time to go home, even if I had to face my new life alone.

Chapter Ten

Autumn 520

nna chose to cede control of Lothian to Gawain, so after Lot's funerary rites, she and I set off for Din Eidyn, riding through hills and mountains resplendent with autumn color. All around us, fiery oaks competed for attention with rust-colored rowan, while elders offered their juicy purple berries as a final harvest before winter. Birches provided a splash of sunlight even on days of driving rain, especially when set against emerald pine and green alders that refused to give up their summer foliage. On the banks of mountain streams, willows and birch gilt the water's course with showers of golden leaves, and in the mountains, fields of fragrant heather defiantly bloomed pink, even as the mornings took on a slight chill.

Only a few days remained until Samhain when we arrived, and lines of travelers clogged the roads into the fortress both overland and leading up from the harbor. Anna explained that it was tradition that those who sought employment or married into other lands return to their tribal capital to honor their dead on Samhain.

As Arthur's sister, she would commend him, Lot, and her sons to the Votadini tribal gods during the Samhain rituals. After, she would become part of my household as an advisor and lady's maid. Having given Lothian to Gawain, Anna wanted nothing of power or war, only to live out her days in peace. In that, as in so many things, she and I were a good match.

We pushed through packed streets thundering with the guttural tongues of many tribes. Imprinted on the forearms of men and shoulder blades of women were tribal markings declaring the birth tribe of each person: the Votadini horse, the Selgovae raven, and even a few Novantae stags. Noticeably sparse was the Damnonii wolf. Above the din, blacksmiths' hammers rang as they mended wheels for those transporting goods from the countryside and sharpened swords for the Votad's army, and merchants hawked their wares, tables heavy with apples, nuts, and meat freshly slaughtered for the coming winter. With the boisterous exchange of goods for what currency remained, Din Eidyn was thriving despite the chaos looming to the south.

Compared to Camelot, the castle itself was small, cramped, and dark, but from the outside, it presented a formidable façade, blending the intimidating strength of a fortress and the opulence of a castle into the black mountainside. Inside, men and women jockeyed for position in the great hall, eager to present themselves and their needs to their rulers. Anna had explained that here, they only held pleadings four times a year—for the three days before, during, and after the full moon nearest the major feast days—so their subjects were even more desperate for attention than ours had been. On top of that, there was no orderly system of presentation such as we had had; petitioners were seen in the order they could rush forward and fall to their knees before the throne.

Anna stood to my left, whispering advice and commentary to help me understand the rules and players at this court. On my right and to my back stood strangers covered in woolen tunics and fur coats reeking of sweat, eyes attentive to an opportunity to move forward. My line of sight, however, was blocked by the fur cloak in front of me. Not for the first time, I cursed my short stature. Because Anna could see over most of the crowd, we agreed that if she saw an opening, she would shove me forward so I could plead my case and she would follow immediately after.

Being on the other side of the throne, praying to be noticed instead of being the one to listen and dispense solutions, was humbling, a stark reminder of all I had lost and that I was once again dependent on someone else for my welfare. A choking insecurity bore into my chest at the thought that the Votad and Votadess, Mynyddog Mwynfawr and his wife, Evina, held the power to grant my request and secure my future or cast me out into the mud to fend for myself. With the hindsight of age, I wished I had had this perspective before taking my own throne; it would have made me a more sympathetic and patient ruler.

After several hours, my feet tingled and my muscles were locking in place, but at least the Votad was clearly in my line of sight now. As the crowd shifted, preparing to spit out its next supplicant, I turned my shoulders to the side and stepped forward, determined to push between the human barrel in front of me and the gaunt woman next to him. As I took a breath to wedge myself between them, hands grasped my shoulders and pushed. I fell forward, knocking the couple to either side. My right knee hit the stone floor with an impact that rattled my teeth, and I narrowly missed scraping my chin on the paver in front of me. Gracefully or not, I had made it before the throne.

Cheeks flaming with embarrassment, I dared to look at the Votadess. She so closely resembled my mother that, for a moment, I could not speak. Her hair was a bit lighter, closer to brown than the black I'd inherited, but her glittering green eyes and the pout of her lips were nearly the same. Even now, years after my mother died, it took my breath away.

"Surely this is one of your kin, eh, Evina? She could be your double," the Votad said, his voice holding more than a hint of amazement.

"Indeed," was all she said as her eyes roamed my face, skipping over the scars that marred its left side and taking in every unblemished feature. Her cool tone did not match the openness with which she regarded me. Was it merely surprise that dampened her welcome, or did she not relish having one of her blood appear at her court? Perhaps both.

Unlike his wife, the Votad was delighted by this turn of events. "Tell us your name and purpose here, kinswoman."

As was tradition, I recited my ancestry, which was the best form of identification a man or woman could produce. "My lord and lady, I am Guinevere, born in Northgallis, but Votadini by blood through my mother, Corinna, whose father was Cunedda, who defended Britain against the Irish and established a safe haven for our people in Gwynedd. He then arranged for my mother to marry Leodgrance of Gwynedd, thus securing an alliance of peace for both tribes. You may have known me as High Queen of Britain, but I am now only one of your humble subjects. I have come to ask for the inheritance which is my right by blood, the lands belonging to my mother north of Stirling."

The petitioners murmured sounds of surprise and disbelief. In the front of the room, the small crowd of men surrounding the royal couple stirred, and an older man with a graying blond beard whispered something in the Votad's ear. He nodded and signaled to one of his men, who quickly departed to fulfil his master's command.

"How do we know you are whom you claim to be? Have you anyone to speak for you?" Evina asked, though she didn't sound suspicious, just rightly wary.

As Arthur had discovered when I was taken by Malegant, frauds and pretendants to the throne were many, and some of them were convincing. The Votad and Votadess could not be too careful, especially with lands as strategically important as Stirling at stake.

"I will." Anna stepped out of the crowd before bowing to both rulers. "I am Anna of Lothian, sister to the former High King of Britain, Arthur Pendragon, and wife of the recently deceased King Lot. Surely you remember me and will take my word that what she says is true."

Mynyddog nodded to Anna. "We do. Please allow me to offer my condolences on the deaths of your husband and sons." The regret in his voice was sincere.

Anna bowed her head again. "Thank you, Votad. I wish you to know that it was my husband's intention to accompany me on this journey and pledge his sword in your service. But the gods did not allow it. I pray that you will treat my son, Gawain, with the same esteem as his father, as he is now ruler of Lothian and wishes to be brought under your protection."

"Of course," Mynyddog responded. "I will send one of my sons to Traprain Law within the week to welcome him as a member of the Votadini tribe and confer his blessing. He has been marked, has he not?"

"Yes, sire. My husband marked each of his sons when they came of age. Though he followed Arthur, he always considered himself a Votadini at heart and bore both the horse and dragon—symbols of your tribe and his—on his arm."

Evina had been chewing her lower lip as she listened, as though mulling over thoughts heavy with meaning. She sat forward and addressed me. "If you are whom you claim to be, you will also be marked. If you will, please show us."

I swallowed hard and shook my head. "I do not have a mark, Votadess. I was away in Avalon when my mother died, and there has been no one since to mark me."

Evina threw her husband a suspicious glance. "Is that so?"

"It is. She speaks the truth," came a silky French accent from the back of the room.

All heads turned. Waves of shock and soaring joy threatened to overwhelm me when I recognized Lancelot. I had to grab Anna's arm to steady myself. Lancelot was here. He was safe. Thanks be to the gods. But why? How? What a silly question. Finally, one thing in my life had turned out for the good; the details didn't matter.

The crowd parted to allow Lancelot to approach the throne, and it took all of my willpower not to run to him and throw my arms around him. As he approached, the silver in his black hair caught the light, as did a new scar on his left cheek. Two years and a war had taken their toll on him, but he was handsome as ever.

"I have served Guinevere for the better part of my life," he said when he reached my side. "She is my queen, and I am her champion. She is also my beloved. Please accept my words on pain of honor as they are the truth."

Evina gave him a dazzling smile and raised him from his bow by the hand as though asking him to dance. "Of course, Angus. If you say she is true, then she is true."

The years of war had not dampened Lancelot's natural charisma, for Evina was as taken with him as every other woman. But why had she called him Angus?

Evina's gaze slipped to me, her smile fading a bit. "We will still need to have you marked. You cannot rule in our lands without being fully brought into our tribe." She thought for a moment. "If Corinna was your mother, then I am your cousin, so it falls to me. Three days hence at dawn, you will officially become a Votadini woman.

"As for your claim to the lands north of Stirling, I will have to consult with our records keepers, but I believe it is legitimate. The only complication is that Rohan, cousin to Morcant, leader of the Damnonii and conqueror of Bernicia, currently rules those lands, so to oust him will cause tension between our tribes."

"You mean it will *increase* tension between our tribes," her husband corrected dryly. "There has been tension between us for generations. Rohan will take some convincing."

"With respect, you misunderstand me," I said before Evina could reply. "I have no desire to rule another kingdom. All I ask is to take possession of my lands and be given the freedom to live on them. Nothing more. I have no wish to upset the current way of things."

Evina arched an eyebrow at me as though she could not

fathom why anyone would wish for such an arrangement. She and Mynyddog exchanged a look that said they were unsure if I was a fool or simply insane. "If that is what you will, then it will be done."

In the corner of my eye, I saw a shadow detach itself from the wall and slip out. A spy, no doubt, on his or her way to inform Rohan of the new claimant to his lands in Stirling.

Pushing those implications to the back of my mind, I curtsied to Evina. "Many thanks for your generosity, my lady. I do not know what form your court's oath takes, but please know that I honor and respect your position of authority over me and do swear my loyalty to you. In the names of my ancestors, I pray for a long life for both of you and promise to do all in my power to defend you in word and deed."

It was Mynyddog's turn to raise me from my curtsy. "Your oath is hereby acknowledged, and we bestow upon you our blessing."

"Now that the business is concluded, may I see these ladies to a guest room, for I think they have nowhere to stay," Lancelot said, looking from Anna to me for confirmation.

"Of course," Mynyddog said. "You are our most honored guests. Take them to Sorcha. She will know where we have vacant rooms." He motioned for us to depart.

Turning from the throne, I let out a deep breath. That had gone much better than I'd expected. Perhaps too well. The Votad and Votadess may have been agreeable, but there may still be repercussions for interrupting the established order of things. This was only the beginning. The people would spread the news of my return across the four tribes. By morning, everyone from Hadrian's Wall to north of Soloway Firth would know the former queen has returned to her native land.

It did not surprise me to hear cries of "This will not stand!" and "Rohan will tame her before the next full moon," before the doors closed behind us. But the most chilling prediction was not proclaimed across the hall, merely whispered as we passed. "Gods be praised. The rightful Votadess has come home."

◈◈◈

That night, Lancelot and I lay together in the moonlight for the first time since before Mordred's lies ruined our lives. I had not seen him in any meaningful way since before the Grail's spell of peace broke and Camelot began to crumble. After that, we were estranged, and once Mordred betrayed us, Arthur's guards kept us apart.

Now, two long years later, his arms felt like a heaven I had finally earned. At last there was no more guilt, no more lies and deception shadowing our love. We were free to give fully of ourselves and receive in return. He was no longer Arthur's knight and I Arthur's wife; we were one another's chosen lovers, belonging to no one else.

I breathed in his scent, so like the heather on the hillside that it made my heart soar. "I haven't had the chance to thank you." I burrowed deeper into his arms and nestled my head against his chest, as if the heat of his body could heal me.

"For what?"

"For saving me—again. For coming back when everyone else had abandoned me. For not believing what the bishop said and leaving me to die"

"Do you not remember?" He angled his body so I had to look up at him. "I am sworn to you until my dying breath. I have been yours since I thought you gave me that flower at the tournament. I chose you over the Grail. Why do you think I would abandon you when you need me the most? I love you and I always will."

Emotion welled up in me and tears pricked at my eyes, an overwhelming combination of happiness and fear. "Even with this?" I turned my head so he had a clear view of the part of my neck and cheek that would forever be withered.

He stroked the side of my head, where my permanently ravaged hairline met my face. "Beauty fades. Had the fire not damaged your skin, time would have eventually. You are still beautiful to me, even more so for your scars. You are a warrior woman. You earned your scars just as truly as if you had received them in battle. When I look at you, I see a woman who triumphed over the strongest adversity and lives to glory in her victory. Even more than that, you have your sight, your hearing, and your mobility. You still have a bright future ahead of you."

His hand slipped down my neck, tracing my scars to my arm and across my left breast. "Those flames may have marred your skin, but they did no serious damage, and they certainly did not touch your spirit. *That* is why I really love you. I love your ability to come back from every attempt of your enemies stronger and braver for it. That is what will always make you Sovereignty herself, title or no."

I kissed him, letting myself be swept away by the softness of his lips and the warmth of his skin against mine. He followed the line of my scars with his tongue, sending a shiver across my ribs. His hands gripped my hips, and he kissed my navel before continuing downward. As he pleasured me, my hands explored his back and shoulders, finding new ridges and scars where there had previously been only hard muscle and sinew. When his lips next met mine, I wrapped my legs around him, forcing him onto his back and taking my fill of him.

After, we lay in each other's arms, listening to the night orchestra of crickets, cicadas, and other insects.

"Why *do* they call you Angus?" I asked, turning onto my stomach so I could look up at him.

He kissed my forehead. "To answer that, I have to mention a man I know you would like to forget." The concern in his eyes was so deep that it could only be one person.

I shuddered. "Go on."

"Do you recall Malegant mentioning that he had a Votadini wife?"

I murmured my assent, breathing deeply to ward off the tension that turned my muscles to stone every time I remembered those horrible months of captivity in Malegant' s hidden island tower. Nearly twenty years had passed, but panic still surged through my veins at his name.

"As you can imagine, he treated her very poorly," Lancelot continued. "Her father hired me to put an end to her suffering by killing Malegant. Obviously I failed, but when Malegant tired of her and tried to take her family's land by force, I was there to defend it. My men and I gave him a beating he nursed for many years."

"No wonder he was so angry when you rescued me. You were taking his prey from him for the second time." A whole new respect for Lancelot blossomed within me. This man who had been a blessing from the gods for me on so many occasions had also been one for many people before I knew him.

"Not only that, but I had replaced him as your personal guard. He was not going to let me have you again. That was why he was so determined to kill me on that beach. He wanted to end our feud once and for all. But I killed him instead." Lancelot squeezed his eyes tight then opened them wide, as if trying to rid himself of the memory of Malegant's body on the shores of the lake. "In return for my service to the Votadini, Evina's father gave me the land of Angus, a title I still hold. I always thought of it as a failsafe, a place to retreat to if ever I needed a home. As the war in Brittany proved, that was a wise decision. When I could not find you in Camelot, I went there, hoping to hear word of your whereabouts. I did not know you'd come to Din Eidyn. I was only at court today because Evina wished me to evaluate candidates for her weapons master."

"It is fortunate you were. I'm not sure if Anna's endorsement of me would have been enough to sway Evina. I could have spent this night on the dusty floor of an inn had you not arrived when you did."

He smiled, wrapping an arm around my neck and pulling me even closer. "It was not luck; you of all people should recognize the hand of the Goddess when you see it. It is she who reunited us."

"And she who gave us a home. I cannot wait to spend the rest of my life with you."

"And I you. Will you marry me and make me your husband in truth? Now that Arthur is gone and we have secured our future, I see no reason for us not to wed." His eyes lit with hope, reflecting the youthful enthusiasm he would always possess, no matter how many years passed.

I pulled away, unable to give him the answer he desired. How could I explain that marriage had become abhorrent to me, that I had no desire to wed again, without hurting him? He had been nothing but loyal to me for decades. He deserved more than my selfish rejection, but to marry him when I felt this way would be unfair to us both.

I met his eyes and shook my head. "I cannot. Please do not be offended. I love you and wish to spend my remaining days by your side, but I cannot, will not, bind myself to another man ever again. Look where it has gotten me, all it has cost. Surely you of all people can understand." My last words were both a plea and a question.

Though he tried to hide it, his face fell. He cleared his throat, swallowing his disappointment. "Of course. What is marriage anyway but a contract, and you and I need no document or witnesses to prove our love true." He forced a smile. "I believe we did that for all time in the Bloody Lane when you leapt onto my horse's back."

"And will do so again at Stirling. Anyone who sees us will not be able to mistake our fidelity."

Three days later, in the bluish-gray pre-dawn light of Samhain, Evina led me down a sloping path to the base of the rocky hill, then out into the heather and across a broad plain edged by low hills on either side. Soon a lone quiot rose ahead, white and stark against the overcast sky. The ancient tomb was formed by three vertical megaliths, a horizontal capstone lying on top. The last was so wide as to form a roof tall enough for a man to stand under without stooping.

Nearby were three women, all pale, with hair as black as midnight. One of them saw me, and for a moment when her eyes fixed on me, I thought my mother had been raised from the dead. But then she moved, squinting in the bright sunlight, and lines formed around her mouth and eyes and I could see she only resembled my mother. Another relative.

Evina linked hands with the others. "For generations, the women of our tribe have gathered to witness their daughters become women. For you, that transition occurred long ago, but without the rite that is your due. As your mother has passed through the veil, Calliac, our high priestess, will be the one to mark you. Yet you will not be without kinswomen in your time of joy. I have called together our closest living relations through your mother's bloodline. This is my sister, Maracail."

Maracail, the one who so closely resembled my mother, stepped toward me. "Greetings, Guinevere. I am your cousin, and these are my daughters, Gavina and Fia."

The two younger girls raised their hands in greeting.

I embraced each in turn. After so long only having one blood relative, my cousin Bran, who was a relation through my father's line, meeting four in a matter of days was astonishing. "It is an honor to meet all of you."

Calliac was the first to pass beneath the dolmen, followed by Evina and then me, as our relatives brought up the rear. Evina's guards stood sentry at the entrance, ensuring we remained undisturbed. We did not stop in the area beneath the stones but continued into an earthen cave not visible from the surface. Once inside, Calliac struck a flint, and a spark of light glimmered, caught in her torch, and soon was reflected in several lanterns placed around the chamber.

As my eyes adjusted to the light, images appeared, painted on the rock walls and carved into stones that sealed niches. They were ancient and crude, done by inexperienced hands, but their meaning was clear. In one, a woman danced in a field of heather, surrounded by six children, while the one next to it depicted a warrior with a bloody spear on the field of battle.

Calliac spread a blanket on the ground, then removed the stone showing a woman presenting her young daughter with a horse. She withdrew a clay beaker, long ago stoppered with wax or some sort of gummy sap, and placed it on the ground at one end of the blanket.

"This," she said, pointing at the beaker, "is the remains of your grandmother—Corinna's mother—last of your line to die in our lands. It is only fitting she should bear witness to this rite. All around us are the bones of your ancestors. Were it in my power, I would bring your mother to rest here too, but it is best to leave her where she is. Perhaps one day you too will lie in eternal sleep here, once your spirit has moved on. But that is not for me to say."

She built a small peat fire in the center of the room and cast upon it a handful of herbs that perfumed the air with a rich, sweet scent. Then Calliac held out a small offering dish. In it was a tiny white stone, small chunk of bread, a bit of wine, and a thistle blossom.

My mother had set up similar shrines on Samhain in Northgallis. For her, the objects represented the relatives whose bones she could not venerate. Today, they stood in place of her bones, which were buried in Northgallis.

I took the bowl from Calliac and laid it carefully in front of the beaker. Kneeling back on my heels, I made the sign of Avalon and closed my eyes. "Mother, had circumstances been different, I know you would have rejoiced in this rite and in the woman I have become. I wish with everything in me that you could be here today, but I am confident you will watch over this gathering of women of your blood. Receive these my offerings with love. May you be at peace, may you never hunger, may you never thirst, and may you always find beauty, even between the worlds."

I touched the beaker. "Grandmother, though our eyes never met, your blood flows in my veins and I am certain our spirits know one another. I rejoice in finding my family and in finding you. Matriarch of my line, please bless this rite and welcome me as a woman into our family."

At Calliac's gesture, I discarded my tunic and lay flat on my stomach on the blanket. This was the opposite of the ritual that had marked my entrance into womanhood, the day I became a priestess and received the crescent upon my brow. Then, I lay face up on a stone beneath the rising sun, surrounded by priestesses. Today, I lay with my forehead to the ground, deep within the cool earth, among the bones of my ancestors and guarded by women who share my blood.

Calliac struck a small gong, and the others gathered around us. "Daughter of the Votadini, hear now the tale of your making, the knitting of blood and bone through the generations that resulted in your life," she intoned as her instrument bit into my tender flesh, leaving behind the first mark.

Maracail took up the tale. "In the days of old, we were of two hearts, the people of this land. We came from wanderers, the people of continent who knew no fixed home but followed the land and its seasons, living not off the earth but from their flocks, paying homage to the oldest of gods through blood and stone, living and dying according to their will. They were short and dark, the children of the ancient ones."

"But we were fair and sinewy, a brave, adventurous people who traveled out of the wilds of the mainland to found great cities. By their blades, whole tribes rose and fell. Their fires forged great beauty from bronze and weapons of iron," Gavina continued, her songlike voice dulling the teeth of the needle and lulling me, along with the heat and heady aroma of the incense.

Soon, the story became real and I walked with the shades of my ancestors, traveling through time with them, age after age.

Fia added her voice to the rhythm of the story. "They thought themselves unstoppable until one day, they woke in the shadow of the eagle. Bearing her talons, she chased them into the sea, where the god Lir and his son Manannan took pity on them, setting them down in the verdant lands we now call Britain. Never ones to be content, they explored that land, eventually meeting up with our darker half."

By the time the story came back to Maracail, I was barely conscious of the needle's sting. "When they came together, first it was with fire in the head and the fierceness of battle fury. There was much bloodshed as the old ones sought to protect their lands from the newcomers, each trying to hold sway over the other. But soon, they saw this was only decimating their population, so they drank of the horn of peace. They intermarried, their children a mix of light and dark, just as you are today. Over time, the newcomers' knowledge of the land allowed our people to live in one place, and they formed kingdoms and tribes, which they jealously guarded."

"Just when it seemed peace would prevail, the eagle, their long ago enemy, returned, seeking to destroy their new home," Gavina said. "But this time, the people were ready, having learned from their history. They fought when they must, but they also bartered with the eagle, for the comingling of the two people had produced many talents. They agreed to live under her protection from those who lingered in the north, an insular people who thought their mixing with the light ones from the mainland an abomination."

Fia paced as she spoke. "Trapped as we were between two people, we were always on our guard, training our women as well as our men so we would have as many warriors as possible should the need ever arise to defend ourselves. In your grandfather's generation, a great hero of our people journeyed south to answer the call of a king and, in so doing, gave our people a place of refuge in the new land. To secure this alliance, your mother was given as a bride, and the old and the new joined once again, giving birth to you, a great warrior queen like the women of old."

"Though from your loins no living children spring, your influence will forever change this tribe, as does every generation that tells this tale. This is the story of the Votadini, of our people, of which you are now officially one," Evina concluded. As I sat up, she embraced me, careful not to touch my enflamed shoulder blade.

I shook my head to clear it. My mind was fuzzy, as though I was waking from meditation or a powerful dream that still threatened to pull me back into the depths of sleep. The sight danced around the edges of my mind, tempting me with visions that flickered and flamed out before I could grasp their meaning.

They seemed to be coming to an end when one burst to life in violent color. In it, two armies were fighting over an island—not Avalon or Mona, but like them, it radiated a holy air, one of asceticism and peace. Before the conflict was over, the shoreline was tinged pink with blood. A man's image rose before my eyes—light red hair and beard, near my age. He wore the strangest cloak, embroidered with a green wolf on his left side and a blue bird of prey with a particularly large, sharp beak on the right. The same symbols and colors were painted on his shield. On a desolate plain beneath a midnight sky flashing with heat lightning, he met a woman with golden curls. Elga. She smiled wickedly, then the vision splintered apart.

Still blinded by the sight, I turned toward where Evina had last been standing. "Votadess, you should be wary the red king, for he will turn his loyalties and betray our people. He is in collusion with the Saxons."

Her strong hands gripped my shoulders, shaking me a little, as though she could will me out of the grip of the sight. "Who? Who is this man?"

I shook my head. "I do not know his name, but even now he meets with her, forming an alliance that will affect us all." I closed my eyes and opened them. The visions had stopped. "I am sorry. That is all I know."

Evina turned away, pacing while I recovered myself.

When I indicated that I was ready, she stood before me, holding two feathers, one black as night, the other creamy white. "There is yet one more step to formally welcoming you into our tribe. As the scars on your shoulder attest, you long ago won your sword. This day I invest you with the feathers of your clan, one for being a warrior and the other denoting your family's status." She affixed the feathers to my braid. "Wear them when we gather and no one will dare question if you belong here, for you are now one of us as truly as if you had taken your first breath among the heather."

❧❦❧

Within a week, we were on the road to Stirling, the land growing steeper as we traveled northwest. Here, the trees had shed their autumn colors, surrendering to dormancy in shades of tan and gray. A light kiss of frost each dawn marked the footsteps of the winter hag as she descended from the mountains, trailing winter in her wake.

By mid-morning of our second day on the road, we passed the hillfort of Stirling, where the army was garrisoned and from which Rohan ruled the countryside. Our destination was still several hours off, a castle nestled in the valley between the Ochil Hills and Strathern Mountains.

The sun shone high in the sky when we approached my new home, casting the mountains in the distance into deep purple shadow and making the river below sparkle as though it were made of jewels. The fortress itself was gray stone likely mined from the surrounding hills, which gave it the quality of having sprung straight out of the land like a hardy flower turning its face toward the light.

Inside, the great hall was clean and bright, lit by large windows that let in pine-scented breezes, while two large fireplaces chased away the sharp wind. The full staff—a bevy of cooks, bakers, maids, and pages—was assembled to greet us. As soon as they were dismissed, they scurried away to their duties, all but Kennon, a balding man of average height whose thick arms made him look more captain of the guard than steward of the house. He solemnly handed me the keys and pulled me aside.

"Evina instructed me to give you a gift," he said in a conspiratorial tone, glancing over his shoulder to be sure the others didn't hear.

"She did? She said nothing of it to me."

"I think it was meant to be a surprise. She said you would know what to do with him."

Him? Had she given me a horse or a hound? Or perhaps a bull in the field? What else could Kennon possibly mean?

He whistled, and the main door opened. One of the guards entered, leading by the arm a man shackled at the wrist, a metal slave collar around his neck. He gave the man a nudge in my direction.

"Meet your new mistress," he said without warmth before turning on his heel and slipping back out the door.

The man kept his head down, long black hair obscuring his face. He was shirtless—I supposed so I could assess his physique and worthiness for any task I might desire. I could not fail to notice the angry scars that twisted up his right arm from wrist to elbow, for they were much like my own, the result of skin warring with flame. Yet they were darker somehow, as though the skin beneath had once held a tribal tattoo. Their location was too precise to have been the result of an accident; he had been intentionally burned and the sign of his tribe removed.

A pinprick of recognition tickled my spine, though I could not quite place him. Something about him brought to mind the memory of a white rose, a wooden cross, and a fresh purple thistle. The items were clear in my mind's eye, but I couldn't quite give them context. *It couldn't be—could it?*

I crossed the room to get a closer look at the man who was now my slave, whether I wanted him or not. As I drew closer, my heartbeat sped and the niggling sense of knowing grew stronger until my pulse was pounding in my ears. It *was* him.

"Galen," I whispered as I used my index finger to raise his chin to force him to look at me. I expected to find fear in his eyes, or maybe even anger—we hadn't parted on the best of terms—but all their blue depths reflected was my own surprise.

"Hello, lass. I dinna expect to be seeing you again."

"Nor I you. How, why—"

"How did I become a slave?" Galen hadn't lost his knack for reading my mind. "'Tis a long story."

"One that I wish to hear. Come, sit." I led him to a bench near the window. I fumbled with the chatelaine at my waist, searching for the key to release his bonds. "You may be indentured, but you are no danger to me, that much I know."

None of the keys seemed to fit. I desperately wished I had something to offer him, even a meager cup of broth. I called to Kennon, instructing him to have the kitchens bring a light midday meal. Leading Galen by the forearm, I crossed to the rest of our party, who warmed themselves by the fire, trying to pretend they hadn't noticed the intruder. When I introduced Lancelot and Anna to Galen, the slave shivered despite the warmth.

"Do they allow you no tunic?" I removed my cloak and draped it around his shoulders.

His dimples appeared, along with a wry smile. "Aye, they do, but not on first introduction. I suppose they wish you to see I am indeed enslaved." He lifted his arms, displaying the grotesque scars on his right arm. "They burned my tribal markings away and gave me this." He lifted his chin so I could see the marking on the side of his neck. It was a crude tattoo, handwritten: *daor*—slave. "They put it there, over one of the major veins, so that it cannot be removed without endangering my life. So as you can see, though I live within Votadini lands, I am no longer one of them."

"That's terrible." I picked up the cord around his neck. At the end was a key that must fit his shackles.

He bowed his head, allowing me to remove it. For the briefest of moments, we were close enough to kiss. Butterflies tickled my belly at the thought. After all these years, I still desired his touch. I prayed Lancelot had not seen the slight frisson of attraction.

My cheeks flamed as I pulled away, breaking the spell. "Please, tell us your story."

Galen shrugged, looking at each of us in turn. "There's not so much to tell. Isolde took me with her to Ireland, and I ended up here as part of a bargain she orchestrated. It was my own people who condemned me." The manacles clicked open, and he rubbed his wrists. "Serves me right. I could not expect mercy after bringing shame on so many families." He looked at me. "I owe you a great deal, even more so to Elaine and Isolde. Tell me, how do they fare?"

I turned away, unable to face him when I answered. "They are both dead." I wiped at the tear rolling down my cheek. "So you have no one to apologize to."

He took my hand. "I am afraid I do. I am sorry for leading you on, for getting you involved in my affairs."

I pulled my hand away, not wishing to forge any bond that would be inappropriate in my new home. "It was a long time ago. All is forgiven. We need only look forward, not back." I looked him straight in the eye now.

"Of course," he said quietly. "What will you do now?"

"Right this moment?"

"No, I mean now that you are here."

"I was just asking myself the same question." I shrugged. "I would like some time to simply be. That is why I am allowing Rohan to continue to rule in my stead."

"A generosity you will no doubt regret," he muttered. "You have as much claim to rule this tribe as he does, if not more."

Seeing my puzzled expression, he hastened to explain. "You still do not understand your lineage, do you? Evina is your cousin. She rules because she is doubly royal through her grandfathers of Cunneda's line. But you"—he traced his fingertips gently down the scars on my arm—"are his direct descendant. I doubt Evina has figured that out yet, but when she does, she will rue allowing you to stay, and more so granting you lands that are of such great strategic importance. You'd best be on your guard."

Lancelot scoffed. "That is ridiculous. Why would Guinevere approach her as she did if it was her intention to challenge Evina's authority?"

"People have done stranger things."

"But I have no desire to rule a people I know nothing of." I paced the large room that was closing in on me. I worked my fingers into the folds of my gown, twisting the material. "I cannot even tell you at what hour dinner is served or where, much less what is best for this land and its people."

"But you are well known for your wisdom and diplomacy," Lancelot said, grasping my hands as I passed him. "The ambassadors sang your praises during your reign with Arthur. Once word gets out, there will no doubt be those who will support your cause."

"Even if I do not raise it?"

"Especially then. Those who oppose Rohan or Evina will grasp at anything to bring someone else to power," Galen said.

I ran a hand through my hair. "I do not want this. Let me be clear. I have had more than enough of ruling and intrigue to last a lifetime. I came here to find a home, not a crown."

"'Tis not I you need to convince." Galen looked at me wonderingly. "Have you ever been anyone's subject before? Besides Lyonesse, I mean." He chuckled darkly.

I punched him in the arm good-naturedly. "Of course. I was Arthur's subject long before I was his wife, and I obeyed his father before him, but you have a point. I do have much to learn about this court." Decades earlier, when I was first introduced to the house of Corbenic, Isolde warned me that in order to survive in a new household, one had to understand the players. It was time to heed her advice. "We know Rohan and Evina will mistrust me once they figure out I could be a threat. What else do I need to know about them?"

Galen's face lit up. "That's the woman I remember. I am afraid our affairs are not much more stable than the ones you recently escaped in Britain. It seems the time for peace is at an end across the isle, I'm afraid." He took a deep breath, seemingly trying to decide where to begin. "Evina always knew she would be Votadess. She was raised to marry whomever became Votad after Cunedda's successor. Unfortunately, as these things often go, the line of succession was not so simple in flesh and blood as it was on parchment. The throne changed hands many times and Evina was shuffled around with it. Finally, the tribal leaders gathered and agreed to dispense with all previous plans and go back to the old way of electing the Votad from among their number. Mynyddog, brother of the Cunedda's successor, Clydno Eitin, was chosen. Evina married him, and I believe you know the rest."

"What is her goal?" Lancelot asked. "I have yet to meet a ruler who does not have a motive beyond staying alive and keeping the peace."

Galen grinned. "Wise man. I like the way you think. It seems to be that that she has two main intentions. One is to keep the Picts at bay. They have been harassing this area since Camelot fell. I believe they are testing their boundaries. It is Mynyddog's responsibility to keep them within their ancient bounds. Evina is also focused on overthrowing Alt Clut so she can rule all four tribes. She studied Arthur's reign closely, and I think she aims to emulate it here."

"But the Damnonii of Alt Clut and Votadini she rules are only half of the tribes. What of the others?"

"I am afraid they are weakening by the day. The Selgovae and Novantae haven't produced a capable ruler in nearly fifty years and are slowly being absorbed by the two more powerful tribes. I predict that within a generation, they will cease to exist."

A somber pall fell over the room. For a long while, no one spoke, each envisioning a future in which whole peoples could disappear in a matter of years. In many ways, it seemed far-fetched, but with battalions of men dying every day in the service of power mongers, it wouldn't take long for women to outnumber men and birth rates to plummet. With fewer babies born to each tribe and the possibility of conquest, the Votadini and Damnonii might well be the only ones left.

My thoughts drifted back to my experience at court. Despite her kindness during the ritual of marking, I couldn't shake Evina's initial coldness toward me. "Evina seemed suspicious of me when I presented myself to her. Why should she worry about me?"

"You know as well as anyone that a ruler's crown is never secure." Galen gave me a sardonic look. "The rules governing us and our relationships with the other tribes, even the nature of our boundaries, are much more fluid than you are used to. Though we have a Votad and Votadess, they are not High King and High Queen with absolute authority like you enjoyed with Arthur. Evina is our ruler only so long as she can prove herself worthy—a battle she fights every single day. There are many who would hasten her fall. All they need do is expose a single weakness and raise another candidate in her stead." He looked at me, expression concerned. "But I fear I have overwhelmed you. That was not my intent."

"No, not at all. We need to know this. Thank you." I smiled at him, regretting my suspicions of long ago. "I am sorry for the unkindness I showed you in the past. It's ironic that I used to mistrust you and now you are the only one in my new household I am certain I can trust."

Before Galen could reply, a deep, commanding voice reached us from the back of the room. "I hope I will quickly earn your trust."

All heads turned toward the sound. We had been so absorbed in Galen's tale that none of us had heard the guards admit a guest. I would have to speak to the head of security in the morning about increasing the layers of admittance. From the look of him—thick, fur-lined cloak of royal blue over a well-made burgundy tunic—this man was not an assassin, but then again, I wouldn't have guessed Sobian to be one either.

Lancelot must have been thinking the same thing, for he shot to his feet, blocking my body with his own. "Who are you and what is your purpose here?"

The man bowed, showing a shock of orange-red hair held back by a circlet not dissimilar to the one Mynyddog had worn. "Forgive me. I did not mean to startle you. I am Rohan of Alt Clut, and this is my home. Or it was, until recently." Despite our guarded reception, his tone held no animosity and his green eyes sparkled with capricious mirth. "Consider it well prepared for you." He bowed again with the sweep of an arm.

What type of man thought it appropriate to barge into someone else's home unannounced? He seemed kind enough, but his presumption grated. His former role as master of the house would explain why no one thought to make a fuss or question his presence, as they were likely used to seeing him come and go, but it was still disconcerting. Best to be wary until we learned more.

When no one spoke, Rohan continued, looking from face to face as though trying to ascertain who would be his most likely ally. "Please forgive the breech of protocol, but I could not wait to meet you and see how you were settling in." He stepped toward me, and Lancelot tensed.

I stepped to the side so I could see around him. "I appreciate your enthusiasm, my lord. I too look forward to getting to know you. I have just called for the midday meal. Would you care to join us?"

ﻌﻌ

By the time the roasted chicken was but a pile of bones, Rohan had charmed us all with his quick wit and even sharper tongue. He was a pleasure to listen to, partly because of his intelligence, but also because his voice was attractive—smoky and rich, yet smooth as ice. It put me in mind of the spirit they drank in these lands, the one with the spicy tail that had gotten Arthur so spectacularly drunk on our wedding night.

Rohan insisted on giving us a tour of our new home, taking special pride in the size of the town—which, unlike Camelot, was not clustered around the castle but spread out for miles in every direction—the fact that the blacksmith produced the strongest swords in the area, and that the farrier could shoe a horse with a new set in under an hour, something he assured me would prove useful when the next attack came. He was certain it was only a matter of time.

When we reached the tiltyard, talk naturally turned to Lancelot's many victories in the ring, including the one over Aggrivane that had brought him to Arthur's attention when we were all much younger.

"I was there that day," Rohan recalled, a boyish look of wonder spreading across his face. "I was not yet a man, but I'd earned myself a place at court, one I sadly had to give up after a year when my father was wounded defending Alt Clut from the Picts." His gaze became distant as his mind traveled back in time. "You were spectacular. I have always envied your ability to disarm and subdue a man without harming him. I tend to favor a more… direct approach. I wonder if you could help me refine my technique."

"Certainly. I believe mastery of the sword begins with mastery of the mind. Any brute can hack and swing and stab and kill, but a man who can link his brain and his blade has a better chance of escaping a duel unharmed."

Rohan gave me an impish look. "I wonder how Guinevere would have fared against you. I hear my lady is quite the swordswoman. Have the two of you ever sparred?"

"We have, many times." Lancelot put an arm around me. "I daresay she taught me as much I have taught her."

"I had the advantage of my mother's training," I demurred, knowing that would win me points in her homeland.

"Indeed, she was legendary." Rohan looked away, pressing his hands to his lips as though praying in the Christian manner. "I wonder… would it be impertinent of me to ask you for a demonstration?"

"You want me to duel with you?" That was not a question I

ever expected to hear, much less from someone I hardly knew. Was it meant as a compliment, or was he testing me to find out if the rumors were true? Either way, it was yet another large presumption from a stranger. "Or am I to perform like a tamed wolf?"

A predatory grin spread across his features. He bared his right forearm, showing off his mark. "They are my clan's animal, so if anyone should be able to tame a she-wolf, it is I."

Lancelot jumped in, pushing Rohan back with a light touch to the chest. "Mind your tongue, else you do battle with me."

I pressed my lips together to hide the smile that threatened to betray me. Two powerful, handsome men fighting over me was quite a compliment for an aging queen. "Gentlemen, please. There is no need for a real duel today. Lord Rohan, yes, I will spar with you, but only briefly as I am well out of practice and have no desire to make a spectacle of myself so early in my time here."

Once in the ring, Anna picked out two blunted practice swords for us and we faced off across the dusty field.

"No blood. First contact is the winner," I stated.

He nodded. "Lay on."

We didn't circle one another for long. Though he was nearly three hands taller than me, it took only a moment of footwork before I spotted his weakness. He relied on the length of his arm to protect him, so in order to defeat him, I needed to bind up his sword. Instead of advancing on him, I drew him toward me with a series of fake attacks that enabled me to push his sword aside and get past the range of his blade. He, meanwhile, tried to push me back. Finally, I was able to strike his wrist, ending the fight.

He shook out his arm. "I find myself regretting agreeing to allow you to live here but not rule. You would be a boon to our army, even in training if you no longer wish to fight."

I opened my mouth to retort that it was rude to allude to a lady's age, but then I froze. Something in the way he turned his head, the glint of the sunlight off his reddish-blond hair, forced a memory from the depths of my mind. My blood went cold. This was the man in my vision, the one who would betray us all to Elga.

He bent over, palms on his knees, catching his breath, oblivious to my dark thoughts.

I shouldn't let on that I knew, should I? Or would it be best to confront him, try to stop this disaster before it went any further? He was already in league with Elga, so I had to be careful. It could all go south too quickly if he knew what I suspected. Isolde always told me knowledge was power, so for now, I would do nothing but smile and pretend nothing had changed. As far as he was concerned, nothing had. But as soon as he went back to the fortress, I had to investigate him. Luckily, I knew just the person for the job.

Chapter Eleven

The following morning, I woke to find word had spread not only of my presence, but also of my encounter with Rohan.

A line of men, women, boys, and girls waited patiently for me in the courtyard, as though I was still queen and it was pleading day.

The low hum of their conversation reached me through the walls and windows as I went about my morning ablutions. Though they waited with uncommon patience and civility, my palms grew damp and my hands shook as I fumbled with the buttons of my gown.

"What do they want?" I asked Galen when he seated me at breakfast. I eyed the offerings warily, my queasy stomach urging me to choose something bland.

"Why, to see you, of course," he answered with a knowing smile.

I rolled my eyes at him, tearing off a hunk of bread and passing the remainder to him.

"Clearly. But why?" I popped a piece into my mouth, savoring the still-warm sweetness of its honey glaze.

"You'll have to ask them. But if you want my best guess"—he swallowed a mouthful of spicy ale—"they want to see if it is true that Corinna of the Votadini has returned from the dead."

I stopped chewing. "Tell me you jest."

He grinned around a hunk of half-chewed bread. "'Tis the story I heard on my way to the kitchens."

My shoulders sagged and I muttered to myself, "How do these tales get started? Now I must contend with my mother's shade as well." Louder, I said to Galen, "I suppose they will all be disappointed to find me of flesh and blood without a trace of Otherworldly essence."

"You have more than a trace, lass, as you proved to Evina," he said, referring to the prophecy about Rohan, which I'd told him about the night before. "I reckon she'll nae like the attention you're attracting."

"Best to disperse them quickly then." I rose, smoothing my skirt. "Are you going to open the door for me, or must I dismiss you for incompetence, slave?"

Galen chuckled at my lighthearted reminder of his position and rose to do my bidding. "Are you certain you wish to meet them out in the courtyard?"

"Of course. That way everyone can see I have not called them here in rebellion and have nothing to hide. I'm sure there are at least one or two of her spies among them."

The chatter ceased as the door opened. Every eye turned to me. I smiled self-consciously, at a loss for where to begin, how to address these curious onlookers who were within my new realm but not my subjects. I was saved by a rugged man with dark hair and dark eyes, who detached himself from the crowd and approached me. His face was familiar, yet I could not call up his name or how I knew him.

"Lady Guinevere." He inclined his head to me. "I am Nachton the Huntsman. You may remember me from my visits to your husband's court."

I took his hands and squeezed them fondly. "Of course I do. You were close friends with Lord Tristan. I still maintain we would not have survived Caledon Wood without the two of you."

Nachton's cheeks reddened. "It was my honor to serve you and the Lord of Lothian. Now it is also my honor to welcome you to Stirling. We"—he swept his arm wide, taking in the whole of the crowd—"mean you no disrespect by gathering here and will leave if you wish."

I took in the assembly, counting no more than two dozen souls—far too few to be suspected of a riot. "No, please stay. I know no one in these parts, save for those who traveled with me and my new steward. If I am to live here, I would like to get to know my neighbors."

For the next several hours, as the sun rose higher, I talked with them about all manner of things. Many inquired about my scars and asked if Arthur's death had been confirmed. Still more—some of them relatives both distant and near in relation—wished to hear of my mother and father and why I had returned.

A few of the young women asked me to use my sight to tell them the name of their one true love, which my gifts did not allow, but I was able to confirm to one that her love was planning to ask for her hand, while I assured another that her beloved sought to make his true feelings known.

A gaggle of young men had heard of my tussle with Rohan and wished me to show them the sequence that had brought him down.

"No one has ever seen his face in the mud before," one noted.

"We want to learn how to make it happen again," another said with vehemence unusual for one of his age. What had Rohan done to carve such a groove in a young heart?

I eyed them, taking in skinny limbs and fledgling muscles attempting to make the transition from boy to man. They were clearly used to hard labor and exercise, but it was unwise to instruct them in such an advanced maneuver when I hadn't assessed their skill level. Best to begin by demonstrating the two moves that were the basis of the complex string of footwork and blade skills.

"It is easier if I show you first. Then I will explain it as we go." Picking up two fallen sticks, I handed one to the most inquisitive of the boys. I motioned him toward me. "Come at me with great force."

After a moment's hesitation, he lunged. I sidestepped his branch, pivoting on the balls of my feet and bringing my own fake weapon under his with a crack. To his credit, the boy kept his hold, spinning away from my grip then pushing me back, forcing me into defense position.

"Very good, Cinon," a husky female voice called from over his left shoulder.

I looked up, surprised to see a tall blond woman approaching.

"Well met, Master Kiara," my opponent greeted her with interlaced fingers touched to his bowed forehead in a gesture of deep respect.

One by one, the boys fell into a straight line. Each made the same gesture.

"Master Kiara?" I asked when she reached me.

"I am one of the weapons masters for the Votad and Votadess, recently appointed to Stirling to help Rohan with the new students."

I took her measure, from the soles of her thick hide boots to the deep brown braccae tucked in at the knee, and her gray tunic hung loose and unbelted, as though in readiness for movement. She exuded confidence but not a single trace of malice. "I am sorry if my instruction gave you offense."

She waved away my concern. "On the contrary, I was hoping to see you in action. Please, continue."

Now that I had an audience, especially one who would note every misstep in my teaching, I second-guessed everything I had known for years. My plan for instructing the boys completely fled my mind. "Let's do it again."

As we moved through the familiar—at least to me—motions, I relaxed, losing my concern over Kiara. Who was she to me? My mother had taught me, and there was no way she would have let me persist if my technique was weak.

When we reached the end of the first movement, I showed them the second and then demonstrated the connecting footwork, which I in no way expected them to learn yet. "Now split off into pairs and practice what I have shown you. Your master and I will be here if you have questions."

The boys did as instructed, the sharp cracks of their practice blows punctuating my conversation with Kiara. I twisted to one side then the other, seeking to relieve aching muscles as I watched her. I wasn't as young as I used to be, so fighting was no longer as easy as breathing.

"I must admit that when I first heard Corinna's daughter was in Votadini lands, I did not believe it," she said. "But even if you did not so strongly resemble your mother, your skill proves it, just as Evina says."

Kiara's implied knowledge of my mother was suspicious. She was likely half my age, so she couldn't have known her. "Did you know my mother?"

Kiara shook her head. "I am Selgovae by birth, Votadini only through marriage. But my family knew yours. In fact, we are pledged to your service for the next three generations." She paused, observing the boys' progress. "Kian, you're dropping your right shoulder. Hold it steady and you'll be less vulnerable." Turning back to me, she resumed her line of thought. "But that is not why I came to see you."

"No?"

"No. I wanted to see your skills for myself. I could use some help training our wee ones." She held up a finger, staving off my objection. "Before you plead old age, know you don't fool me. Anyone who can execute a dancing dragon with no preparation is more than capable of taking anything these lads and lasses can toss at you. Besides, I only ask you to help the youngest, those still learning to hold their weapons."

I stared past her at the walls of the fortress, where the guards were changing position, some slinking off to sleep or drown their sorrows in drink, while others steeled themselves for a long afternoon of attentiveness. In my mind's eye, I saw myself with the Votadini and Damnonii children, helping them learn to balance their blunted blades and heft spears. That was one of many things I missed about not raising children of my own. In Camelot, we'd had others to see to the boys' training. At least here I could do it myself and—as Kiara implied—I would be teaching girls as well as boys, so I could pass on my mother's knowledge, even it was to those not of my own blood.

I swallowed a lump in my throat and blinked back unbidden tears. "I accept."

Kiara grinned. "Tonight I will tell Rohan of our agreement. If he does not object—and he won't, I will be sure—you can meet the rest of the youngin's on the morn."

We sat in companionable silence for a while, every so often shouting correction or praise as the boys went over and over their drills. By the end of the hour, Cinon had picked up the whole sequence, including the footwork, and was correcting the technique of the others.

"He is remarkable," I said.

"Cinon? He is. His father was one of our greatest warriors. I only wish he could have seen his son complete his testing. Would you like to bear witness? It is your right twice over as one of royal blood and a warrior yourself."

My shoulders relaxed and my heart lightened at the prospect. My palm already itched to hold a sword again. This was what I had been trained to do, not sit on a throne. Plus, Kiara's offer would give me the chance to see the trial of a Votadini warrior first-hand. My mother had hinted at the arduous test over the years, but because I was never able witness it or complete my own, it captivated me even now. "I would. Thank you."

"It will take place at the next full moon."

◈◈◈

A few weeks later, in pale hours of a crisp, cool morning, I mounted my horse and took off in the direction of the closest village, Galen at my side. The people who had gathered at the castle had helped me to understand that in spite of Rohan being their ruler, most citizens were in need of someone to be attentive to their needs. That was not to say Rohan was a bad king; he collected taxes, judged disputes, and protected the surrounding countryside with his army, but he didn't seem to understand that was only part of the duties of a ruler. From what they'd told me, despite his charm, he had none of the interpersonal skills that would appeal to the people.

When I suggested to Galen that perhaps this was because Rohan didn't have a wife to tend to them, he burst out laughing. "You have the measure of him already, I see. Watch your back, else he aim to put you in that position." I opened my mouth to protest, but Galen voiced my thoughts first. "Don't go thinking Lancelot is any bit a deterrent to him. I ken he fancies wooing you away from Lancelot as a challenge."

What good would it do Rohan to try to charm me? He was already ruler of the area and had previously lived on my lands. Unless that was it. Perhaps he wanted to formally return my lands into his control through me. But no, that didn't seem likely enough, even if he was genuinely attracted to me, especially with the prospect of having to best Lancelot for my affections. There had to be a greater plan at play that I wasn't seeing.

As we rode through winter-dimmed valleys of moss and dying grasses hugged by rocky, mist-shrouded mountains and forests of deep green pine, I imagined a map of the area, trying to tease out Rohan's strategy. This was a strategic area connecting the Damnonii to the west, Votadini to the south and east, and holding the Picts at bay to the north. If it were an independent kingdom, I could see the Damnonii and Votadini fighting over it, but it was clearly in Votadini control. Perhaps Rohan was scheming to wrest it from Evina. If he held sway over the border with the Picts, he may be able to use the threat of invasion to bring her to heel.

The more I thought about it, the more sense it made. Just as Evina harbored ambitions to rule all of the lands north of Hadrian's Wall, so might Rohan. If that were the case, I was merely a pawn in their scheming—a perilous place to be. I had to learn more—and for that I needed Sobian, wherever she was.

We slowed our mounts as we approached a village that seemed to have sprung up in the shadow of a Christian church, like violets in the shade of an oak. A few curious faces popped out at the sound of hooves, and I greeted them, inquiring after their welfare.

A man of middle years emerged from one house, crossed his arms and scowled at me. "Why are you here? Ain't no one ever cared about us before." He raised his chin in the direction of Stirling. "All them kind want is taxes and men to bleed in war. Most of them battles don't affect us none, 'cept in making widows and orphans. Now you 'spect me to think you don't have no reason for being here other than kindness. What are you—a gruagach?" He chuckled at his joke.

Inwardly, I groaned at the insult. It was not the first time I had been compared to a benevolent household spirit, especially with my short stature and dark coloring. Now, with my scars, I probably resembled one of the wrinkled fae more than ever. I wanted to hit the man upside the head and yell that I was only trying to help him, but his wariness of outsiders was understandable, especially ones that came bearing gifts and asking nothing in return.

Instead, I said, "If you wish to think of me that way, then so be it. Regardless, I am here with your welfare in mind."

While we were talking, a woman who had slipped out of a small house across the street sidled up to us. "Never mind him. John is still sore about his time in Rohan's army." She raised a hand in greeting, as friendly as he was cold. "I'm Gin. I know everything that goes on in this town, so I can probably help you."

For the rest of the morning, we followed Gin from house to hut to hovel. Gin's familiar face eased the introductions. Galen noted needs and made plans to send food and supplies upon our return to the castle, while I offered employment in my household when I could for those willing to relocate, and did my best to heal the sick.

One household, recently quarantined from the pox, wanted nothing to do with me as a priestess. They were proud Christians, the woman of the house told me, faithfully attending the church we had seen on our approach to the village. Covered in ruptured scabs that indicated she was only recently recovered, she would let me no closer than the door, despite my assurances I could not be infected.

"I understand. Shall I arrange a visit from the priest? Surely he will bring you comfort," I asked through the slightly cracked door.

She snorted. "He never sets foot outside the church. Ain't no holy man who's paid us mind since ol' Ringan told us 'bout Christ and then moved on." She gestured over her shoulder to her husband

and three children who lay, unable to move, on mats on the floor. "As you can see, we can't go to him."

I balled my fists at my side. Yet another Christian priest shirking his duty to his people. Father Dafydd, whom Marius had exiled to this part of the world in a bid for control over Arthur, was not like that. Why couldn't there be more like him? Combined with Rohan's inattentiveness, it was no wonder John was wary.

"I will speak with him." I glanced at the sickest of the children, whose tiny body was riddled with pustules so close together as to be nearly indistinguishable from one another. He cried, his mouth and tongue so covered that he likely couldn't eat and had little hope of recovery. I did not wish to raise the possibility with his mother, but they had to be prepared. "May I ask, if the worst happens, do you have sufficient funds to see that your loved ones are properly buried?"

Her eyes flared with anger. "Look around. Do we look like we kin afford a shovel, much less to have that priest say his fancy words over our dead bodies?" She threw me a look so full of disgust, I involuntarily stepped back. "Begone! Away with you!"

I hurried back down the lane behind Gin, Galen bringing up the rear. Once we had put three blocks between us and the sick house, I stopped Gin with a hand to her forearm and held out a small purse of coins. "Will you hold these for me? I would like them to be used in the event anyone from that family dies. If they all recover, have a Mass of thanksgiving said in their honor."

Gin looked at the coin purse, then back at me, her eyes full of wonder. "How generous of you, my lady, especially given the way she treated you."

She stowed the purse in a pouch beneath her tunic as we headed back toward the church, where the priest assured me he would visit the house, but only once everyone was recovered. I closed my eyes, fighting to remain calm. His timing would be too late to offer them any comfort, which was what they so desperately needed.

"How were you able to speak with that family?" Gin asked as we departed for the stables. "Even the priest isn't brave enough to go to them, and he has the power of Christ on his side. Most of us would have given the house a wide berth, yet you gave them food and counsel. Are priestesses unaffected by the pox?"

I smiled. "No. But there was an outbreak when I was a young girl."

Snippets of those dark days flashed in my memory—my mother pressing a cold cloth to my forehead, her face dotted with red marks; my father hacking away at half-frozen ground to bury my little brother; Octavia sacrificing mourning doves to her old Roman gods to keep the worst of the pestilence at bay. We eventually recovered, but some, like Arthur's kinsman King Mark, were permanently scarred. Hundreds died.

Gods preserve us from another summer like that one. "From what we were taught in Avalon, a person cannot be afflicted twice. I am blessed that my family only suffered a mild case. Many others were not so fortunate."

We stopped in front of the stable. John, the suspicious man we'd encountered at the start of our venture, blocked the way.

He stood tall and stepped aside as we drew near. "Beg pardon, my lady, but I wanted to say thank you for what you've done fer us today. Many of them people is sayin' you're the rightful queen o' the Gododdin, and I ken they're on ta somethin'. You've been more a queen to us today than anyone in a crow's age. If you ever have need of us, ask an' it's yours."

❦

The next several weeks passed in a blur of parchment and ink, as I called in every contact I had to try to find Sobian. Lancelot did the same. But the information that made its way to us wasn't usually about our favorite spy; rather, it carried news of the current political climate, which had slipped my mind since arriving in Din Eidyn. Now, between the two of us, we were getting a pretty good idea of how fractured Britain had become.

"Accolon says that Mordred's fellows have disbanded and returned to their own tribes," Lancelot said.

I looked up from the letter I was reading. "The Saxons have not. Elga is still intent on ruling as much of the country as she can. Owain reports that she is allying herself with whoever has the most power at the moment and is considering marriage again—no doubt to increase her own standing."

"Then she should next fix her gaze on Constantine." Lancelot flicked a page toward me. "Read this."

I picked up the letter. It was from Bran. As I read, my stomach twisted. This was a detailed account of kingdoms falling under the boots of Constantine's army. First Dyfnaint and the parts of the Midlands not already under Saxon control. He skipped the Summer Country because it was already under Elga's rule. Cornwall was resisting, and Gwynedd too. But Powys had surrendered. He was even putting it about that Helene was his top choice for a wife, once she grew to marriageable age, an idea Morgan vehemently opposed.

"He aims to be High King," I said, shocked at how much progress Constantine had made since we left Traprain Law. The lands we had once roamed so freely were now under the control of a man with great ambition. But then again, that was not much different than what Arthur had done to become king.

At least on the surface. The more I read, the more troublesome the clash of thrones became. As they pressed north, Constantine's gigantic army ruined the harvest, descending like a plague of locusts, eating or confiscating bales of wheat, bushels of fruit, and robbing families of livestock they were depending on to see them through the winter. In their footprints lay acres of stubbled fields, naked trees, and bloodied earth from the slaughter of animals—normal sights in autumn to be sure, but now whole towns starved even before the first snowfall and despaired what would become of them in the cold, shadowy days ahead.

Oblivious to my concerns, Lancelot asked, "Would it be so bad if Constantine prevailed? He has a blood claim through his relation to Iggraine, and Arthur always liked him."

"He did. I suppose what is happening is only natural. Are we really getting so old as to begrudge a new generation their successes? I have lost my taste for the intrigues of courtly life."

"Then what are we doing here?" Lancelot mused.

I put his letter aside and picked up another. "This is what really worries me. Morgan and Accolon have made an alliance aimed at holding the north from Constantine's advances and retaking some of their ancestral lands in Bernicia. For some reason, they are focused on the Isle of Winds. I don't see why they would be interested in a small island north of Catraeth."

"That is a key strategic point for blocking any Pictish attack by water. Whoever holds it controls whether or not the Picts can access Britain via the Firth of Forth."

"How do you know that?"

"My time in Din Eidyn and Angus has taught me a great amount about politics and strategy in this land."

I looked back at the letter. "It says here Morcant hired a group of Saxons to patrol the waters." I shivered. Tragedy had resulted from a similar offer made by Vortigern decades before I was born. The result was the Saxon presence on our eastern shore. "That must be why Owain and Accolon are interested in the area. I would be concerned if I were them."

"It certainly makes taking back their lands that much harder." He shook his head. "One of these days, perhaps your people will learn not to trust those back-stabbing bastards."

We lapsed into silence, each studying the map of Britain before us.

"I wonder if we will ever experience peace again," I whispered, more to myself than to Lancelot.

"There is one way to know for sure," he replied.

I looked up, intrigued. "What's that?"

"Be the one to bring about peace." Lancelot's gaze on me was intense. "I know you said you wanted nothing more of politics, but I also know you are not one to sit idly by and let others suffer. If you were, you wouldn't have ridden through the villages. You would have let them rot under Rohan's neglect." He leaned toward me and grasped my hands. "I think you should consider it—making a bid for the throne, I mean. The time is ripe, and the people would willingly rally behind you."

I cleared my throat, fighting a sudden constriction. "How can you even ask me that? I have seen enough bloodshed, feuds, and petty fighting to fill three lifetimes. While I was queen, I was kidnapped and almost killed twice. You know the dangers I faced better than anyone."

"But the people are crying out for a strong ruler. These letters"—Lancelot tapped his index finger on the pile, as if trying to illustrate his point—"tell us that. They have no love for people who march into their lands with hordes of soldiers and declare themselves rulers, be they Saxon or Briton. You would have no need to do such a thing. You earned their trust long ago."

I fled to the open window with its tranquil view of the river. I breathed in deeply, desperate to be physically away from him and the argument he was spinning. He was appealing to my need to protect Britain's people, the very reason why I'd assented to be queen in the first place. The dutiful part of my mind said I owed them my protection as long as I was strong enough to give it. But I could not, would not take up the mantle of power again. It had cost me too much. Lancelot knew that. Why was he pressing this?

"Some of them may trust me, but not all. You saw how quickly our friends turned against me during my trial. And what of those who supported Morgan as Arthur's rightful wife? He divorced me, took away my title as queen. To them, I am not fit to lead. Then there are those who never liked me in the first place. You were not there in the Bloody Lane. You did not witness the jeers and taunts, how they relished degrading me in the broad light of day. I would still have to win over their fickle hearts, which just as likely now would support a Saxon over a woman whose weaknesses have been on display."

"Surely they are in the minority. Anyone who seeks the throne will have some enemies."

"That may be, but I am no young queen anymore. Plus, all my detractors would have to do is point at my scars. The most ancient laws forbid a maimed person from being king or queen out of fear their imperfection will ruin the land. That's why Bedivere was doomed to live in Kay's shadow. He would never be whole, and neither will I." I sighed then finally looked back at him. "Do you wish to be king? Is that why you are making this argument?"

Lancelot scowled. "You know it is not. I only wish for you to be sure in your heart, so you do not look back on this time and wonder if there was something else you could have done."

"I know my heart, as do you. Do you not remember what we said to one another when we were reunited in Din Eidyn? I wish to live out my days in peace."

"I am afraid peace is not something the gods are willing to grant us for a while."

"I have to agree." My gaze drifted to the ships on the river below.

Was Sobian even now on a ship like those, perhaps somewhere far out at sea? Was that why we couldn't locate her? But surely the current political instability was rife with opportunity for one with her skills. She had to at least be keeping an eye on the situation.

As a crew unloaded their boat, I recalled how quickly rumor spread among the shipyard workers. With people coming and going from a multitude of kingdoms each day, information was, in many ways, more valuable than the cargo contained in the ships. "Lancelot,

I think we have been seeking information in the wrong place. If you were Sobian, would you not maintain your illicit connections?"

He followed my gaze to the boats bobbing in the harbor. "I suppose so. Do you think they know where she is?"

I was already headed toward the door. "There is only one way to find out."

✿❦❦✿

Sobian's laughter reached us before she appeared at the top of the gang plank, a bird perched on one arm and a long rectangular box about the length of my arm in their other. She was followed by two men carrying chests and other luggage. For a woman who had lived on the river when she first came into our lives, Sobian certainly had grown accustomed to the lifestyle of being one of Arthur's highest ranking officials, his head spy. Wherever she had been since before Camlann hadn't damaged her lifestyle any.

She met us at the bottom of the ramp. "You lured me out here by appealing to my basest instincts. You knew I would not be able to resist solving one more mystery with you." She took off her leather gloves and handed the hooded falcon to Lancelot as though he was in charge of keeping hunting birds.

"Do you always travel with such creatures?" he asked, struggling to use one of her gloves to shield his wrist from the bird's talons.

"Only when I feel they might add something to my ability to track the person I seek. You would be surprised what they can be taught. As it does not sound as though I will have time to train one here, I brought one already accustomed to my will." She placed the box vertically on a stack of crates and opened a door set into one side, revealing a perch made of rope. Carefully, with the tenderness of a mother, she guided the bird from Lancelot's arm onto the perch, removed its hood, and shut the door.

She held out the box to me, but I motioned to Galen. "This is Galen. He is my"—I still struggled with calling him my slave—"servant. He will see to your needs as well while you are here."

Sobian looked him up and down in the same appraising manner she had first used on Arthur. A small smile played on her lips as she took in his dark hair, shimmering with silver at his temples and on his chin. His bright blue eyes met hers not with deference, but with equal challenge and equal lust. "I shall enjoy getting to know him."

The attraction between them was instantaneous and palpable. I leaned over to Lancelot, voice low so that only he could hear. "This will either be the strongest love affair anyone has ever seen or combust in a matter of days."

"Either way, I think we have just witnessed a meeting of equals."

I held my arm out to her. "Shall we go back to the castle? I am sure you wish to rest after so long a journey."

Sobian fell into step next to me, Lancelot following. "No. I feel suddenly invigorated. I would like to hear how you came here and what happened for you to call on me. I hear the sight was involved?" She tapped her forehead.

"It was. But I would prefer not to discuss it in so public a place."

Sobian entertained us with tales of sailing the Irish Sea until it turned into the North Sea. There she clashed with a fleet of Norse pirates and faced off against the Witch of Orkney, who prophesied she would lose her heart to a man whose father was murdered by a god.

By the time we were settled by the fire and all that remained of the midday meal were crumbs and sticky fingertips, I was beginning to doubt the validity of Sobian's tales—lying *was* part of her job after all. But knowing Sobian, every word was probably true. Only she could find such fantastic situations, yet live to brag about them. That was exactly why I needed her. If anyone could uncover Rohan's motives in time to preserve the peace, it was her.

As though she could hear my thoughts—and I often suspected she could—Sobian said, "So tell me about this prophecy of yours."

When I had finished recounting the day of my marking, all I knew about Rohan, and that I needed someone to get close to him, Sobian stretched and slowly gave into a languorous grin. "This sounds like your most fun assignment yet. I accept. Do you think he'd take me for training at the fort?"

"No. Our approach can't be so direct." I stirred the fire with a poker until it hissed sparks. "We need him to accept you into his confidence, to trust you. He would never spill his secrets to one of his men—even if she was a woman."

"Sounds like I'll be playing a prostitute again." She considered the idea, watching the newly stoked flames.

"Actually, infiltrating a brothel not far from the barracks wouldn't be difficult," Lancelot said. "One hears all sorts of rumors in a house like that…."

Sobian sighed. "You may work wonders with horses, Lancelot—and please do not be insulted by this—but for a renowned warrior, you know so little about so many things. That is too obvious. Plus, a man like Rohan doesn't need an average whore. I need to be irresistible, someone whose position and beauty are useful to him."

"You already have the beauty part down," Galen observed.

Was it my imagination, or did Sobian blush? I had never seen her flush once the whole time I'd known her.

"Let's step back for a moment," I said. "If we're right and Rohan wishes to overthrow Evina, he first has to best Morcant and me. He needs power, wealth, and position to do that. He can either gain those through war or marriage, and we know he favors the latter because he has been trying to woo me. What if we give him a more attractive option?"

All eyes fell on Sobian.

She raised an eyebrow. "You mean I get to play a noble this time, instead of your lady's maid?" She made a gesture of happiness.

"Not just any noble," Lancelot said, picking up on my line of thinking. "You need to be a relative of Morcant, one who promises to enrich her husband greatly."

"His kingdom is so close to the Pictish border that I have no doubt he has some woad-covered by-blow. Why can't you be one?" I winked at Sobian. "I know Morcant from his visits to Camelot. I think I can get him to agree. After all, if it means unmasking a traitor in his midst and possibly strengthening his alliance with Evina, he has nothing to lose."

Galen cleared his throat and caught my eye. "If I may interject?"

"Galen was not always a servant," I explained, having forgotten Sobian didn't know the sordid tale of how we had known one another. I would have to fill her in soon, but now was not the time. "He was once a noble who was very good at getting others to believe exactly what he wished them to." I narrowed my eyes at him and twisted my lips, remembering how deep his subterfuge had gone. "Then he crossed the wrong person. A life of slavery is his punishment." I turned back to Galen. "Go on."

He cleared his throat again, more anxious at addressing Sobian than I'd ever seen him. "Forgive me, kind lady, but you are not from here and are unfamiliar with our customs. If you are to do as you say, you will need a translator at the very least, and a guard at the most. I hear tell you can defend yourself, but Rohan will not know that. If you will allow me, I can provide a cover for you." He looked up at me, as if just remembering he would need my permission. "That is, if Guinevere will allow it."

I nodded.

Sobian eyed him again, brow wrinkling and lips pursing as she considered her options. "I usually prefer to work alone, but you make a valid point."

"You don't happen to speak the Pictish tongue, do you?"

Sobian proceeded to ask him in their language how he thought she'd faced down the Witch of Orkney if she could neither understand nor speak to her.

"Don't underestimate her skill with languages. She's like one of those rare birds that can imitate any of its kin," I said. "Galen, I suppose you speak it as well?"

"I do, lass. I knew a bit of it when we were young, but when Isolde sold me back to my people, I was forced to learn it while working in a mine in Dalriada. But that's a story for another day."

I looked at Sobian. "Well, then. Now all we have to do is create your new identity and arrange to have you visit your 'father.'"

"And paint her skin with woad," Galen added, a task his prurient grin hinted he would gladly volunteer to take from me.

PART THREE

The False Queen

Chapter Twelve

Spring 521

My name was being whispered in the wind. It tickled my hair, brushed my skin like a feather, and sometimes, it woke me in the night, pressing into my mind like a probing lover. Sobian was still in Morcant's capital of Dùn Breatann, but I didn't need her network of fishermen and sailors to know my name slithered through the waterways too. My name was attached to a word that could condemn as easily as it could seduce—insurrection.

Treason found me on an ordinary spring morning, shortly after Beltane, sparring with Kiara and our students in the Stirling barracks south of my holding. Like a dog whose scent I thought I'd lost back in Camelot, it came bounding through the gates in the person of Nachton the Huntsman. My conflicted heart did not know whether to leap at seeing a friendly face or dread hearing the news he brought from the surrounding countryside. Since my arrival in Stirling, Nachton had become my favorite and most trusted informant.

He bowed low before us, but would not meet my eyes. He kept his gaze on his shoes while fidgeting with his cap. "My lady, I dare to interrupt your instruction only because I bear news of great import."

Kiara and I exchanged a worried glace. Without a word from me, she rounded up the children and led them inside.

Once we were alone, I said, "You look like you ate a bowl of worms. Your news cannot be that dire unless someone is dead. Spit it out."

His words tumbled over one another in a rush as though he could contain them no longer. "A contingent of Selgovae, Votadini, and Venicones have banded together in your name west of Din Eidyn, near Velvniate. They seek to overthrow Rohan and install you as ruler of both Stirling and Alt Clut."

"What?" His image winked in and out of view as I blinked

rapidly, trying to make sense of what he said.

Nachton nodded so vigorously, he nearly bowed. "'Tis true, my lady. They took over the fort in your name. My brother in Carriden confirmed the movement has spread to this side of the wall. He predicts that within a fortnight, insurgents will be proclaiming you Votadess from here to Dùn Breatann."

"What?" I said again, still stupefied.

I shook my head, eyeing Nachton closely, certain this was a prank, an elaborate jest I failed to appreciate. It had to be. We'd long known the people favored my rule over Rohan, but short of John's jest that he would join my army any day and occasional prodding from Lancelot, no one had dared openly suggest I raise my station, much less engage in open sedition.

Kiara returned to my side. "Who is calling you Votadess?" Her voice was as light and inconsequential as though she were speaking of the direction of the wind rather than high treason.

I held up a hand, forestalling Nachton's answer. On the tail of a deep breath, I explained. "Nachton is under the delusion that a rebellion is taking place in my name to the south."

Kiara studied him, running a finger across the braids holding back her golden hair. She pursed her lips and cocked her head. "It's possible." Her eyes went distant with thought, then she snapped her fingers. "I know who may be able to tell us."

She disappeared into the fort commander's quarters.

"You can answer this easily, though the only question is in your own mind," Nachton said. At my puzzled expression, he added, "What use is the sight if you don't employ it?"

I narrowed my eyes at him. I never liked using my gifts except under absolute necessity. It wasn't that we were forbidden from using them—Morgan did every chance she got before she converted to Christianity—but it had always felt to me as though I was taking advantage of the gods. However, given that Evina would have my head if what Nachton said was true, perhaps it was wise to make an exception.

Tossing aside the practice sword I still held, I sank onto a hay bale and closed my eyes. At first, the whistling of the wind through the pines was all I perceived, but as I willed my inner vision southward, the whistling became a snapping and I saw a rough blue flag with a crudely drawn crowned white horse at its center flying high above the fort. They were flying my standard.

Willing myself free of the sight, I struggled to breathe, each gasp too fast and too shallow. There was no going back now. I was involved in a war of the people, like it or not. My hands shook. I buried them in my skirts, but it was too late to hide my distress.

Kiara returned. "The commander says he has heard the same. We had a messenger this morning from Caimlan who told him of the unrest."

I sighed, all the strength draining from my limbs. "That means Evina will know soon as well." Her steely glare flashed before my eyes, turning my stomach to lead. Even from several days' distance, I could feel her wrath. I stood and motioned for them to follow me. "Come, come, we must discuss this with Lancelot and Anna. We must devise a solution before this becomes unmanageable."

"If it is not already," Nachton whispered ominously.

⁘

Longing for Avalon and the labyrinth Arthur had built for me at Camelot, I carved out for myself at the center of my new home a sanctuary of another sort, a small room in which I could meet privately with Lancelot and dear advisors of my choosing. The room itself was small, dimly lit by a single window that faced the rushing river below and a dozen or more flickering candles. There was no fire, so as the sun dipped below the purple mountains, turning the river to liquid bronze, we hugged our cloaks about us.

It was there that Galen, Lancelot, Anna, and I discussed what could not be spoken anywhere else in the kingdom, lest we find our heads on pikes outside Din Eidyn. My younger self would have focused on the why, wondering why I was being used this way yet again and wailing at the injustice of it all. In my mind, I snickered at her, knowing now the only question that mattered was what we were going to do about those who sought change in my name.

I took a deep breath, pacing the circumference of the small room. "I will not kill the rebels to silence them, so we can forget that option straight away. I suppose I must choose whether to try to tamp them down and convince them to pledge allegiance where it should be—to Rohan and Evina—or to be the beacon they seek." The weight of such a decision threatened to bow me once and for all. I sank into a chair.

"Here is how I see it," Lancelot said, rubbing his cheek wearily. "After Camlann left a gaping void in the succession, the world as we knew it ended. All the rules were erased, gone with the souls of the wise rulers who died that day. Now we are living in a world where young fools reign, in their hubris thinking themselves wise." He sipped a tankard of ale Kennon had supplied us with before retiring for the night. "I'm not saying we always know best, but at least we have the wisdom and experience to know right from wrong. I asked around today, and most of the people who back you are the sons and daughters of your generation, those who look up to you as their only remaining mother."

I shivered. Not long after my babies died, I'd vowed to be a mother to my people. Now they were asking me to lead them. Who was I to say no simply because I was tired? When did my mother ever ignore a single one of my cries, even when she could barely open her eyes long enough to tend to me? My people needed me, and I had a responsibility to scoop them up, dry their tears, and do what I could to make everything better once again.

"There is good reason they feel that way," Anna added with a small tut of disapproval at those currently ripping the country apart in their quest for power. "And I say this as one of the ruling class. But I am also a Votadini, and I have seen the results of my peers' actions. We nobles have abused our power for too long, and it is the country that suffered. I fear Evina and Mynyddog will be no better. Our country has gone from a patchwork of tribes to cowering under Roman rule, only to be abandoned then split asunder by more rulers in more formations than can be counted. Arthur attempted to stitch us back together. You can continue his work. We need someone who can call upon the power of the elements, upon the earth herself, to make us whole again. Rohan, Evina, and Mynyddog fear you because they know you can lead us and that your collective power is greater than all their commands ever will be."

I had to admire Anna. Logic like that was why Arthur was wise to put his sister in charge of Lothian so many years ago, after her husband had attempted to overthrow him. Anna was a born statesman with a strong knowledge of history and a gift for flattering words. Many times she had advised me over the years like the mother she should have been, had I married Aggrivane. But this time, I could not allow myself to capitulate to her words so easily, not without serious reflection.

"Anna, I don't think—"

"I know you don't want to listen to me, but please at least hear me with an open mind. What you do beyond that is on your soul. Balance needs to be restored. We need someone to be the sutures binding us back together or we may bleed to death. You can do that. You are both them and us, the old and the new, the threshold. The people are scared, but so are the rulers. They fear that one day the people will rise up against them. Well, that day has come. That is why the people are asking you to lead."

I sat back in the chair, rubbing my temples. "I hear you. I understand your argument." I let out a forceful breath. "I simply do not know if I can do this again. I was a younger woman, full of drive and ambition, the first time around. Now… now, I just want peace."

Galen smirked. "No doubt you meant for yourself, but you just admitted you share the same goal as the people who call upon you to lead them. All they want is peace. If they thought the current Votad and Votadess could give them that, they would not have left their fields and their planting." Galen patted my hand. "You may fancy yourself helpless, but you are nae. You nae'ver have been. You have options, more than you realize."

I gave a sarcastic huff. "Like what?"

"This island is at war on at least four fronts, and you could lead any of them, save the Saxons. I dare say they'd slit your throat if you tried. But look here." He stabbed the map on the table in front of me with a narrow finger. "I may only be a slave, but I have eyes and ears and I used to rule a sizable part of this land. I know as much as those at court. As you say, you could join this foolhardy quest to overthrow Mynyddog and Evina. The easiest way to do that is either to ally with Rohan or kill him. Depends if you want Mynyddog as your enemy or your ally."

"I vote for ally," Lancelot put in.

"Or you could take back Camelot's throne." He ticked off a second option on his fingers. "Constantine would bow to you and the people would back you." I opened my mouth to protest, but he cut me off. "I know, I know, you don't want it. You've made yourself abundantly clear on that score. I didna say you had to keep it. You could hold it long enough to end this bloody civil war. Then you can pass the crown on to Constantine or Helene or whomever you wish.

My point is that in that role, you could put pressure on our enemies to get anything you will."

I shot him an unconvinced look.

"If that doesn't please you, you could back Owen and Accolon in their fight against the Saxons," Lancelot said, warming to Galen's line of thinking. "But in order to be of value, you'd have to have an army behind you, which necessitates being queen of some kingdom—which puts us back where we began."

Anna and Galen nodded.

"Why does it always come back to power and a throne?" I threw up my hands, wishing I could punch something to relive the growing frustration within me.

Galen smirked. "Have you nae been paying attention? It's your destiny. You were born to rule, to lead this country, this land through times of great uncertainty. That much was plain to me the first time I laid eyes on you as a lass, which is why I knew I could never woo you as I did Isolde, nor break your heart like I did with Elaine. You had too much of a role to play for me to muck it up simply for my own amusement." His eyes were shining with pride.

I dropped my gaze to the floor, no longer able to look at him directly. To think, so many years before, while I was second-guessing his every move and pouting that he chose Isolde over me, Galen had already foreseen the heights to which I would rise. My throat tightened and tears pricked the back of my eyes. I could not speak now even if I wanted to.

Galen gently took my hand. "Let me ask you this. What would you do if you were not in power? Go back to Avalon and spin your magic until you die?"

I shook my head. I had already considered that upon leaving Mayda's convent. As much as I loved Avalon, the life of a resident priestess felt too… contained. Deep down, my spirit told me there was still something I needed to do before I retired to a life of solace on the holy isle.

"Good. We've eliminated that possibility. Despite all your protestations to the contrary, I certainly do nae see you settling down with Lancelot to live a quiet life." He shot Lancelot an apologetic look. "If you had wanted that, your inclination would have been to flee to Brittany after Arthur died, not come here. No. You came here because you wanted to reconnect with your kin, with your blood.

And that means accepting your power."

Galen was right, but if I did what he was proposing, what they all were proposing, I would be mirroring the actions for which I'd criticized Mordred so harshly. For was I not moving against my own kin? But then again, my name was being used without my consent, so I was linked to this evil even if I never acted. Would Evina believe me innocent? Not likely. If my reputation was already in tatters, what did I have to lose?

I looked to Lancelot for advice. He had been so quiet, so unusually reserved, I feared he objected to what I was considering.

He breathed out forcefully through his nose, snorting like a bull. "I can't say I relish another war, and I never thought I would challenge my sovereign lords, but what must be done, must be done. I will stand with you against Evina, if that is what you choose." He entwined his fingers in mine across the table. "I am yours in all things, be assured of that."

I nodded, buoyed by his support, and blew out a breath to calm my jangled nerves and jittery stomach. "Then I suppose it is decided. But we must remain silent until we are certain this revolution has teeth. As far as anyone else is concerned, this is nothing but a silly rumor."

CHAPTER THIRTEEN

Spring 522

A year passed without a whisper of my role in the ongoing clashes between the people and lords who supported me, and the Votad and Votadess. Thanks to Sobian's network of spies, I had an easy way to funnel money, food, and weapons to those fighting for my cause—all without a single link to my name. The only person who knew I was the source was Sobian, and I was confident she would tell no one.

While I was acting as ghost benefactor, Sobian was playing her part as Eithne, daughter of Morcant. She had done such a good job slithering her way into Rohan's affections that she was now living with him in Dùn Breatann. He expected to marry her at Lughnasa, so we had only a few months to conclude her role and send Eithne back to the Picts.

I invited the two to stay with me for a while in the hopes I could help move along the ruse. Morcant was supposed to arrive from Bernicia two days before them, ostensibly to discuss how we could deal with the revolutionaries spouting my name at every turn, but so far we had no word from him.

We had been hunting earlier in the day and were now taking a much-needed break from the chase. Sobian and I waited by the riverside for Rohan and Lancelot to return from field dressing our kill and seeing to their horses, which both men insisted on doing personally, though an abundance of capable grooms flocked around them. I suspected Rohan went along with it only because it was Lancelot's way and he didn't wish to be seen as inferior or lazy in comparison.

I had already laid out our cloaks, which were no longer needed as the day grew warmer, along with a small feast of bread, cheese, fruit, and a flagon of ale. Sobian trailed behind me as I plucked leaves, flowers, and roots from the edible or medicinal plants that grew along the bank.

"Rohan's father wasn't killed by a god, was he? Otherwise you may be fated to stay with him beyond Lughnasa," I teased, referring to the Witch of Orkney's prediction.

Her answering laugh was a tinkle that never failed to lighten my heart. She turned to face me, and for a moment, my breath caught. Though I had seen her a few times since she began this ruse, I was still astounded by how thoroughly she had changed her appearance. She looked a decade younger, hair tinted slightly red with a dye given to her by a Greek merchant's wife, and the whorling lines of woad around her eyes and on her cheeks masked the age lines that could have betrayed her deception.

"I think not. But I'm a betting woman, so I'll take that wager. Besides, it's not like much would change if we did marry. Let the deception play out in its own good time."

"How does it not make you nervous living two lives?" I asked quietly, after reassuring myself no one was near enough to hear.

She shrugged. "I've been doing it for so long it comes as second nature." She stopped me with a touch to my wrist. The weight of her fingers said something serious was on her mind. "Do you not find it strange that Morcant is delayed? Should he not send a rider on to let us know of illness or other problems on the journey? It doesn't feel right."

"One would think, but I'm sure there is a very good reason," I said, trying to assuage both of us. But the tingling in my brow had already begun. A few more steps and I sank to my knees, unable to resist it.

Once again, I was flying on the wings of a bird, soaring above a sky tinged with smoke curling from the remains of a badly scarred hillfort atop a double-peaked mountain that stood out from the Cheviot Hills like a woman's breast. We circled the area, borne on warm air currents, moving closer and closer to the smoking walls with each pass. To the north, the white-capped North Sea endured the abuses of men's boots and boat hulls as hulking Saxon ships overtook British curraghs in the narrow waters between the mainland and the Isle of Winds. Below us, tiny and insignificant as ants, men, women, and children scurried over the fragrant heather, panic and fear etched into their faces alongside tear tracks, clutching what few belongings they could hold, seeking sanctuary they would not be granted by the invaders who had destroyed their town. Finally, we lit on a crumbling stone fence that had protected the fort and its occupants for centuries, but today failed miserably. One look inside the central keep revealed Yeavering Bell was now in the hands of our enemies. Ida, king of the Saxons, sat in Morcant's place.

My vision ended before I could tell whether or not Morcant lived, but it was enough. Cold to the bone with shock, I leaned on Sobian as we stumbled back to the castle to assemble an army and depart to support our ally and overlord. While Lancelot and Rohan saw to the muster, Anna prepared for a hasty departure to aid her son, should the Saxons press north into Lothian. I gathered our fastest messengers to send word to Owain and Accolon. They likely already knew of the coup, but more than that, they needed to know we would stand with them in the inevitable clash at their eastern border.

"I told those fools years ago that paying the Saxons to hold the Isle of Winds would come back to haunt them," Sobian raged, pacing my study while I wrote. "Morcant summoned me to help organize their naval defenses, but he would not listen to me in any other capacity. Arrogant dog." She punched the windowsill before stalking back toward me. "Just you wait—he will come crying to me for help. I should refuse him, but we both know I can't resist the call of a sea battle."

"I'm glad you will be there. If Owain and Accolon attempt to retake the isle, which I believe they will, we will need your help. Rohan and I can lead the ground troops across the causeway and onto the island, but the last thing we need is them surrounding us in those sea-serpents they call ships."

"I will put the call out for my girls to meet us in Din Guayrdi."

My eyes widened with a chilling thought. "How will you handle Rohan?"

In all the chaos, I had forgotten he still thought her to be a Pict. She would travel with us, and him, and once we reached Din Guayrdi, she would fight by his side. He may even recognize her. That would ruin everything.

Sobian gave me an impish smile that so reminded me of Isolde, my heart squeezed in pain. "I've already got that planned. Tonight when Rohan returns to our rooms from overseeing the last of the troop details, I will tell him I think it best that I, or rather, Eithne, should return home. The Picts will be anxiously watching the outcome in Bernicia, because the fight over the Isle may give them an opportunity to slip in and take control of the waterway. If they do, Lothian and Bernicia are done for. Eithne will want to be sure her troops are prepared." Her face darkened, and she stuck out her lower lip in mock sorrow. "Of course, it will be a very tearful departure for the lovers, with many promises of fidelity and love." She cackled an evil laugh.

⁘⊙⊘⊘⊙⁘

Given that Lord Morcant was nowhere to be seen in my vision, I suspected he was already on the run and would arrive here soon—if he indeed had escaped the Saxon's wrath—but I was not prepared for what greeted us a week later when the guards called out that a large number of visitors were requesting admittance just after nightfall. I had been expecting a small party of Morcant and his guards, perhaps a few attendants, not the remnants of his whole household with horses, furniture, and other trappings in tow. Their bedraggled state indicated they had fled in the same panicked state as their people.

"Lord Morcant. Thank the gods you are alive and hale," I greeted the young, dark-haired man in the courtyard with a curtsy. Behind me, Lancelot, Rohan, and Sobian did the same.

Instead of the slight incline of the head I expected, one of his men stepped forward. "By order of the king of the Damnonii, Morcant Bulc, by whose benevolence you hold these lands, you are hereby ordered to vacate this fortress by daybreak. He invokes his right to seize any assets at will."

Stunned, I could only stare at Morcant, whose impassive face betrayed not a hint of embarrassment or guilt at making such a request. Rather, he was simply doing as needed.

Finally, Morcant stirred atop his stallion. "I am sorry to impose upon you this way, but as you no doubt know, I am in need of a new capital. You and yours may occupy the smaller holding at Dùn Bhlàthain. I have sent word that its keepers are to prepare it for you."

My mind swirled with thoughts and protests, but every time one slipped to the front of my mouth, I had to swallow it down by reminding myself he had every right to do as he wished. I was no longer queen, but his subject, directed by his will in all things.

"Dùn Bhlàthain is not a castle. It's a ruined fort not fit for a pack of wild dogs," Lancelot spat under his breath. When I glanced over my shoulder at him, he stepped forward and squeezed my hand. "Do not worry," he said into my ear. "We can always stay on my lands in Angus if we need to. I will not let you go homeless."

Rohan stepped forward, smirking. He obviously saw the irony in this situation, as I had not long ago run him out of his home, the very same fortress Lord Morcant was now demanding I vacate. I steeled myself for a sarcastic quip, but he showed concern instead. "My lord, will you not give her time to prepare? Or take my holdings in Both an Uillt instead. Surely they are more to your liking."

Lord Morcant turned a stare on Rohan that may as well have pinioned him to the wall. "If I wanted your holdings, Lord Rohan, I would have seized them." His gaze flicked to the castle around us, then south to the fort in the distance. "No. Now that the Saxons hold Bernicia, all of Alt Clut is vulnerable to attack. I wish to direct my forces from the fort of Stirling, not far away in the Vale of Leven." He turned his dark gaze on me, jaw taut with irritation. "Besides, perhaps when they see you humbled, my people won't be so eager to proclaim you their new queen."

Ah, so that was what this was really about. It was no mere coincidence that Morcant needed a home and chose to take mine. This was a punishment for the insurrection. He was stripping me of what little power and resources I had. Still, his reprimand stung, just as he'd intended.

"Am I to understand that you intend to join Lord Owain in his fight to reclaim his island from the Saxons?" he asked me.

"Indeed. Although since you have taken my lands, it is really your army to command. Shall we lead them under your banner?"

Morcant grunted noncommittally, looking from me to Rohan and back again. "It is a fool's errand, don't you see that? As long as the Saxons hold Din Guarie, even if Owain is victorious, he will have to keep fighting to hold the isle. All the Saxons have to do is send out yet another contingent of men. Eventually they will overwhelm Owain's forces." He flicked his fingers dismissively at me. "Go if you will, but you will go alone. I will not have you move in my name with my army. You no longer speak for the people of this land. Is that clear?"

⋘⊙⋙

"It was generous of you to offer your lands to Lord Morcant," I said to Rohan as our party—down from nearly a hundred to only Lancelot,

Rohan, Galen and me—rode southeast the following day.

In the hills around us, gorse bloomed a vibrant yellow and scented our path with its distinctive nutty aroma. Lapwings and crossbills whirled and dipped overhead, chattering in their tongue as we conversed in ours.

Rohan grimaced. "What he has done to you is deplorable. Those lands are yours by right of blood. After this battle is decided, you must appeal to Evina. He cannot take from you what she has granted."

I gave a small, sarcastic laugh. "I think it is best to stay below Evina's attention at the moment. The last thing I need is to remind her that some people think I should have her title."

"When this is done, we will go north," Lancelot said decisively. "All of us. We do not need any of them."

"What if I wish to come along as well?" Rohan said in mock pout.

"You have a kingdom to lead," I responded.

He took my hand. "But I will miss you so very much."

Lancelot rolled his eyes. "You will get used to it."

I eyed him with a half-smile. He was even more attractive when he was jealous.

In Din Eidyn, we met up with Sobian, the addition of her cadre of girls making us finally look more like an army than a small group of pilgrims. She wore her hair loose, and I noted she had darkened the red with coal ash and maybe some ink; it was slightly darker than her natural dark brown.

"I don't like this lack of wind," she said with a frown. "It will make using our boats under sail nigh impossible in the narrow waters between land and isle. This stillness will make it difficult to maneuver."

"Ah, but a priestess should be able to raise them, should she not?" Rohan gave me a wide smile.

I glared at his presumption. "I can, but we have to think through if that is the strategy we want to employ. If these winds becalm your ships," I said to Sobian, "they will force the Saxon fleet to stay near land as well. Your girls can fight on land just as well as at sea, but we don't know how well-trained the Saxon navy is for a land battle. It could turn out that they would be easier to defeat at sea. I am of a mind to leave the weather as it is and only challenge nature when we must."

Rohan reined in his horse so he rode alongside mine. "You think of everything, don't you? Are you sure you want to run off to Angus with him if this battle goes against us?" He hooked a thumb in Lancelot's direction. "I think you could make a much bigger impact at my side."

I raised an eyebrow at him. Was he really so presumptuous as to blatantly flirt with me in front of Lancelot? He was either astonishingly arrogant or incredibly foolish.

"Think about how great you and I could be together. No one would deny your right to Stirling if you were my bride."

I looked at him askance. "Aren't you engaged to Eithne?"

"Yes, but that can easily be changed. She is beautiful and valuable, but you…you are so much more. If we were wed, you and I could control the western half of the tribes. Why, Morcant would be a mere figurehead. Then if you really did want to depose Evina, we could make a run at her. Imagine being Votadess." He smirked, suppressing a chuckle. "On the other hand, you could run away with Lancelot and… do what? Fade into obscurity? We both know you are meant for greater things."

I halted my horse, forcing the rest of our party to a stop as well. In that moment, Rohan reminded me so much of the power-crazed, overly confident version of Mordred I'd left behind that my stomach knotted and I swallowed down bile. I gave him my haughtiest look. "Not. On. Your. Life. Giving you the power of Votad would be signing the death warrant of this land. I would rather die nameless under Evina's rule than be remembered as your wife."

Rohan flinched, his jaw and fists tightening as though he wanted to hit me. Part of me wished he would so that Lancelot and I could wallop him. Perhaps with his pride wounded, he would turn tail and run for home.

"If the only reason you came on this journey was to try to turn my head, you better go back now. I am here to fight for my friends and allies, not to plot another revolution." I spurred my horse on and took up the lead, motioning for Lancelot to join me.

Instead, it was Sobian who rode by my side. "While I admire you for putting him in his place, I don't know that insulting him so badly was wise." She glanced over her shoulder at Rohan. "We still need him in this battle."

"He is driven by power, so it is in his best interest to aid Owain and Accolon. Have no fear. I know him, and I know how danger-ous it would be to make him think, even for a moment, that I might really consider treason with him. This way if he chooses to go behind my back and act in my name, I have witnesses who can testify I pub-licly stated in no uncertain terms that I would not ally with him."

"That is wise. But I still think you should set things to rights with him before we engage the Saxons. I've lived with Rohan for the last year and have seen how volatile he can be, especially when he feels betrayed. You never know what he may do."

᎗᎗

I would much rather our basecamp have been situated in the hillfort of Din Guarie, where we would have had spectacular views of the Isle of Winds, than in a cramped, camouflaged tent on the shore, but the fort was Ida's realm. He was also the reason we had to remain hidden; on this campaign, surprise was of the utmost importance.

I would also much rather not have had Morgan with us. I had not seen her since my mystical journey to Camlann, the site of Arthur and Mordred's deaths. When we met up in Traprain Law with her, Owain, and Accolon, she had been shy and tentative, if not a little embarrassed at me having seen her at her most vulnerable. Though my reflex was still to treat her poorly, I fought it and summoned kindness instead. Camlann had changed us both; we may never be friends, but in our shared pain, we had learned to put aside our youthful pettiness and work together for the greater good.

Inside the tent, Lancelot, Sobian, Rohan, and I collaborated with Owain, Accolon, and Morgan, and their generals to determine our best method of attack. The isle was guarded by a small hillfort at its center, but it was not well maintained. Owain had sent spies disguised as Saxon recruits days before to scout out what we would be facing. Two still remained, charged with opening the gates from the inside when we gave the signal.

Tidal waters controlled access to the island, so we only had a few opportunities each day to transport our troops to the island, other-wise we would be either trapped on the mainland with no way to get to the isle other than by boat, or be swept away by the waters. Despite Sobian and her girls standing by on their ships, attack by boat wasn't really an option since the sight of the boats slowly cross-ing the channel would likely cause the Saxons on the isle to shoot arrows and rocks at us, not to mention alert those in Din Guarie to our activities.

No, this fight would have to be conducted entirely on foot by infantry. There was no room for horses, and the best our boats could do was defend against reinforcements from Din Guarie and any use of Saxon boats against us by those on the isle.

"We must time this perfectly," I said. "There is a period in the middle of the night when the causeway is clear. We should be ready to move as soon as it is safe. Once across, we need to move quickly to build our siege camp inland so that we can be in place before dawn. By then, we will be trapped on the island until the tide goes down in early morning."

"I think we can help with that," Morgan said. "Together, you and I should be strong enough to hold back the waters in case we need extra time on the exposed causeway."

"Good," Owain said. "That will be valuable, should our plans go awry. Now, when we charge the fort, my men will help by opening the gates, but we will still have to fight our way in. Some of my men are prepared with ladders and grappling hooks so we won't face a bottleneck at the gate. But no matter how hard we plan, I fear this will be a bloodbath."

৩৫০ ৩৫০

We faced the causeway with only the light of the moon to guide us, glimmering on the water and turning the sandbars into ghostly pathways. Any light we would use, no matter how small, would be seen by the Saxon guards in the towers of the fort. Taking careful steps on the slippery rocks and packed sand that was likely to give way with each step, our progress was slow. Occasionally a cloud blotted out the light of the moon, plunging us into precipitous darkness, and we had to freeze until Morgan or I could force it to move along.

Despite the cool night temperatures, sweat trickled down my back and beaded on my brow as I concentrated on each step. As we neared land, one of the Saxon guards in a watchtower cried out, and we all stopped to put our shields over our heads like the Romans did for protection. A few of our men peeled off at a run to dispatch the guard before she could alert anyone else of whatever had alarmed her. My heart pounded so loudly in my ears, it blocked out the rhythm of the surf and should have acted as a beacon to all in the fort above. Oh, how I longed for the familiarity of two armies facing off across a field at midday.

When we finally gained land, we stayed to the shadows as much as possible, working our way to the northern side of the isle, where it would be safest to make camp. The last few men in our caravan were in charge of sweeping away our footprints so no evidence would alert the enemy or lead them to our camp. The sand hampered our pace, especially through the dunes, though rabbits darted across them, mocking our slow progress, but we eventually reached a small patch of grassland protected by the dunes.

By the time we had quietly erected our tents and prepared for the battle to come, the eastern sky was lightening to a grayish-blue. Our full force needed to be in front of the main gates—which thankfully faced west and so would be in darkness a bit longer—before the first rays of sun lit the sky if we were going to take the Saxons unawares.

Morgan and I thickened the shadows as long as we could. We had just settled into formation when the sun's power broke our hold and the guards on the walls stirred. Rohan whistled like a swallow. Within the fort, someone tweeted a response, followed by raised voices as the guard changed shift.

With the first crack of firelight visible through the gates, we charged with a deafening cry. Shields up over our heads, we ran, swords, spears, and elbows at the ready to push aside or kill all who stood in our way. An arrow lodged in my shield with a jolt that sent me to my knees. I sprang up as fast as I could. To remain in one place for more than a moment was to die.

As soon as we approached the walls, my world narrowed into mad whirl of leather, steel, and blood as I attacked and defended, slowly hacking through all who stood in my path. By now, we had lost the element of surprise and the garrison had emptied. We were trapped without hope of retreat until nightfall. A second wave of support was due to arrive any time on Sobian's boat, but chances were good the Saxons would launch their ships as well, cutting off our reinforcements.

Day turned to night in a haze of blood, until finally we retreated to our camp in the gloaming. There we met the second unit, who were happily staking the heads of a few dozen Saxons onto pikes around the perimeter of our base.

"They tried to bring us down," a flaxen-haired soldier reported, "but as you can see, we held firm."

I sighed wearily. "We cannot thank you enough. You have paid a good service to your tribe and to your Votad this day."

After eating a hasty dinner, Lancelot and I retired to our tent. We took turns cleaning one another's wounds, which thankfully were all minor, as we had so many times before. Then we prepared for the following day's battle.

I looked up from cleaning my sword. "Do you ever wish you had married a docile, meek woman who would stay at home and pray while you went off to war instead of pledging yourself to a trouble-some warrior like me?"

Lancelot looked up from mending a tear in his leather chest plate. "You mean like Elaine? I *was* married to her. It was torture." He kissed me on the lips. "I would take your troublesome self over her any day. I am a warrior, and no woman could make me happier. Do you ever wish you had married a lord with no taste for war?"

I let out a small "ha" of incredulity. "Does such a man exist?"

"Fair point." Lancelot put down his armor and pulled me onto the bed, taking my sword from me and setting it aside. "Enough for tonight. Let us rest."

Part of me wanted to kiss him, to wrap my arms around him and show him how much I loved him, but as soon as I lay down, fatigue overwhelmed me. Tonight, falling asleep in his arms would have to be intimacy enough.

⁘⁙⁘

Roaring waves, shouts, and snapping wood heralded the dawn as Sobian's crew clashed with a Saxon vessel trying to stop her from ferrying additional troops to shore. At Rohan's command, scouts ran back and forth across the causeway when it was clear, bringing news of the unexpected naval battles.

Because of this development, Morgan and I stayed behind to offer our aid to those at sea while the rest of our army attempted to gain the fort. We sat concealed in a fold in the cliff face, controlling wind and water as needed, trying desperately to help Sobian while not hampering the efforts of our men on land. It was a delicate bal-ance, one so difficult to achieve I had never dared to try it before. But with Morgan by my side, I felt our combined powers might be worth the risk.

Neither side seemed eager to destroy their own boat by ramming it into the other, but still they harried one another, attempting to board the enemy ship and destroy her crew. When that did not work, they resorted to hurling flaming projectiles at one another until one boat finally sank in a haze of smoke and ash.

But as soon as the cheers from the victor's boat died down, another launched, until our meager fleet was surrounded and hope waned. I prayed that no matter what happened, Sobian and her girls would survive to fight again.

"Why don't we just call a storm and make the waves so choppy, they are forced to cease fighting to keep their boats from capsizing?" Morgan asked, her voice indicating she had no concept of the repercussions of such an action.

"Because if we do, we will turn the sand beneath our soldiers' feet to a clinging, slippery mush and endanger them all. You were there at Mount Badon. Do you recall how both sides waited out the storm I called then? There was a reason."

She glared at me then turned her back on me, sulking.

By nightfall, Owain's army had made headway on land, but Sobian's fleet was destroyed. The last scout reported that she and most of her crew—they had lost two, one to fire and the other when she was swept overboard—lived, though they were in hiding somewhere up the coast until they could procure additional vessels from nearby berths or repair what remained of their own.

"Rohan predicts we will take the fort tomorrow," Lancelot said as he returned from the cook fire with two plates of dinner. He held one out to me.

A heavy sigh escaped my lips as I took it, sniffing at it warily. Dinner was some type of fish, likely caught today while we fought, and the ubiquitous grain-based mush, a staple at every meal while on campaign. "Good. I don't know that I can take much more of this." I rubbed my eyes. "I hate to admit it, but I am feeling my age. The constant physical and emotional toll of battle was easier borne before my bones ached and my vision dimmed."

Lancelot smirked around a mouthful of fish. "Tell me about it. Earlier today I was fighting a spearman, and when I moved to strike, pain flared in my back so strongly I feared it, not the Saxon's weapon, would bring me down."

I nodded. "This is it. After this battle is won, I will hang up my sword."

"And I mine. I would gladly trade it for my remaining years with you." He wrapped me in a tight embrace.

"Promise me something."

"Anything."

"Whether we win or lose, we will not return to Din Eidyn. Evina has soured my heart for the homeland I once so desperately longed for. If we die, then it is done. If we are victorious, we send the army back without us. We can always use the truth—that some will have to stay behind to secure those taken captive—as our reason for not accompanying them. If we lose and still have our skin, we run—far way, to Brittany, where she cannot touch us without starting a war."

"Her assassins know my homeland. They could always find us."

I smiled. "Ah, but we have the best in our employ. We get a message to Sobian, written in Ogham so others cannot read it. She will take care of the lot of them."

"Brittany it is then. The life we wanted before Arthur threw our plans to the wind." He kissed my hair. "Now we have something worth fighting for."

"We certainly have nothing left to lose. That makes us more dangerous than the Votad could ever dream. Plus, it gives me an idea how to incite the troops even more." I turned over so that I was facing him and let my breasts brush against his naked chest. "This is our last night here, and certainly our last alone until all is said and done."

He didn't need me to say any more. His lips met mine with all the fury he hadn't spent in battle, and I responded in kind, kissing him hard, deep, and rough. My hands sought the most sensitive parts of his flesh, eager to stoke his arousal. His teeth grazed my neck while his fingertips dug into the soft flesh between my thighs. Soon we were joined in a feverish embrace. This was not the pretty love making of Beltane, the languorous celebration of life, but the wild rutting of animals who sensed the approach of winter's deadly chill.

⚬◍ ◍⚬

Just after midday, the Saxon resistance faltered. Their attacks at the wall became halfhearted, and when we breeched the fort, the remaining warriors showed themselves to be either too aggressive and desperate in their tactics or lackluster at best, as if they wished as much as we did for this whole affair to be over.

Our army easily cut through them, allowing us access into the keep, where we found Theodric and Osmere, Ida's two oldest sons and those who were leading the campaign, surrounded by a cadre of guards.

But where was Elga? In her unending quest to rule Britain, she had married Osmere not long after Mordred died. She would not allow her husband to go into battle without her, so she had to be there. I turned and surveyed the room, trying to ascertain possible points of ambush or trickery. I would put nothing past her.

Owain faced the brothers, sword drawn and ready but not posing an immediate threat. "My lords, you can come with us peacefully, or we can fight to the death here. The choice is yours."

Osmere sneered at Owain. "Your High King once did us the honor of allowing single combat to decide the outcome of a war. Will you not offer the same mark of respect?"

Owain replied, "I was there at Mount Badon and I remember quite clearly. Your people immediately betrayed the outcome of that combat because it was not in your favor. How can we be assured you will not do the same now?"

Theodric gave a mirthless laugh and threw his arms wide, as if to encompass the whole room. "Look around. We are the only opponents you have left. Surely you are not threatened by less than a dozen men?"

Owain stood his ground. "I am when those men have thousands of reinforcements waiting across the channel. All you would need to do is give a signal and your ships would set sail, treeing us on this isle like a pack of hunting hounds with their quarry. Plus"—he made a show of looking around—"not all of your troops are in this room. Your wife is missing, is she not? Let me guess, she lies in wait to finish us off while we crow in victory?"

"Enough chatter. Let's be done with this," Rohan broke in.

Osmere stood, ignoring Rohan. "Leave my wife out of this. This battle is down to you and me. The victor takes the fort and the whole of the island. I will even allow you to choose the location of our duel."

"I know the perfect place," Rohan declared.

Owain led the men out of the fort, following Rohan around to the back side of the island to a flat jut of land in the shadow of a thick woodland of alder, hazel, birch, and willow. Beyond the sandy beach, the ground was packed and even enough to ensure a fair fight. It was the perfect location. The duel could take place in full view of our camp and the Saxons we had taken prisoner, but out of sight of those on the mainland who may try to provide assistance.

The half-dozen Saxon ships that bobbed offshore, however, raised my suspicions. From my first view of the isle, I'd recognized it as the place in my vision and had been keeping an eye on Rohan, lest he try anything untoward. Now with these ships placed so conveniently close to our battleground, I had to make sure nothing was amiss.

Most of the boats appeared to have sustained enough damage in yesterday's skirmishes to keep them from being seaworthy. Climbing aboard one after the other, I checked their hulls and cargo holds for stowaway Saxons. All were empty, save one, where I found Elga ostensibly making repairs but more likely preparing for escape.

She hissed and cursed at me in her native tongue as I dragged her onto shore by the arm.

"Oh, stop it," I spat. "I'm not going to hurt you. But I do wish you to witness the single combat that will bring your reign here to an end." I pushed her onto the sand and she responded with a hand gesture that was likely some sort of curse.

Her husband and Owain faced off, each with his brother as second. Osmere struck first, but Owain parried, stepping into a series of complicated blade and footwork moves that even I had trouble keeping up with. He pushed hard on Osmere, never giving him a chance to recover. Osmere, to his credit, fought hard, always on the defensive, pushing Owain's blade back with little opportunity to strike.

The battle was over before it had really begun. Owain tore his blade across Osmere's chest from right shoulder to left hip bone, and Osmere crumpled like a discarded scrap of parchment, trying to hold in his entrails to little avail.

Back at the fort, cheers erupted from our men as the flag of the house of Rheged was raised. On the beach, Elga screamed, rushing toward her husband and brandishing her sword at anyone foolish enough to get in her way. At the same time, Rohan grabbed Owain by his tunic before he could even register his victory, much less celebrate it, and Theodric turned on Accolon, his blade at our leader's neck.

For a long moment, the three couples stood in deadly embrace, each contemplating their varied futures that were dependent on their next actions. As a spectator, there was little I could do but watch. Elga held her husband's body, rocking much like I had when Arthur fell at Camlann. Rohan twisted Owain's neck, killing him instantly. Accolon lunged toward his brother, trying to stop Rohan's traitorous act, but Theodric's blade held him immobile.

Suddenly, the beach was red with blood. I ran to Accolon, trying to help him escape, but Theodric slammed his fist into my head, sending me reeling. I fell back upon the sand with a thud that robbed me of breath. While I shook off the sparks of light that littered my vision and struggled to stand, Sobian barreled into Theodric, planting her sword in his thigh and immobilizing him. Like the trained assassin she was, she flipped him over and tied his hands behind his back, her knee digging into his shoulder blades. In the same instant, Lancelot tackled Rohan.

Only Elga remained free, and she used the chaos to her advantage, seizing Accolon as he moved toward Owain's lifeless body. She tackled him, slamming his head into the ground and dragging him backward toward the ship I had pulled her out of.

"Move away, all of you, or he dies!" she commanded, using her sword to punctuate each word as she backed him onto the ship. She motioned for a few of her crew to join her, and soon they were drifting offshore. From the deck, she pointed at Morgan. "You killed my husband, so I will take your lover in exchange."

Morgan responded by raising her arms and summoning a storm that threatened to capsize the boat. But Elga's crew were skilled enough to ride it out, somehow sensing that Morgan's power didn't carry as far out to sea as she would have others believe. Morgan howled as her grip on the waves waned. I ran to her side, mingling my power with hers, but still it lasted only a few moments more. Spent, we both collapsed onto the sand, surveying the wreckage around us.

Owain's body lay abandoned on the earth beyond the beach, rivulets of blood seeping toward the sea as though his essence sought its maker. Not far off, Sobian knelt atop Theodric's prone form, frantically signaling her girls to bring a ship around to this side of the isle. Near the trees, Lancelot held Rohan, whispering what I could only guess were graphic threats in his ear.

When I had recovered, I strode over to Rohan, tears in my eyes for my dead compatriot and friend. "Why, Rohan?" I glanced at the piteous form at my feet. "Why did you turn on him? He trusted you. We all did."

Rohan smirked. "What is trust in time of war? My allegiance is with the victors, so when I saw an opportunity to change the outcome, I did."

"But we took the island. *We* were victorious. Shouldn't your allegiance be with us?"

Rohan gave a short bark of a laugh. "This skirmish was a pittance compared to what is yet to come. I don't think in terms of battles; I think about the whole war. We won this tussle, but as Morcant said, what good will it do in the long run? We will just keep defending an outpost we are destined to lose. If not today, someday, and then the Saxons will have free rein into the north. I want to be their ally when that day comes."

"So why even fight with us then?" Lancelot asked.

"I didn't know which way the outcome would go. If they won, I wanted to be here to celebrate with them. As they did not, I rid them of a powerful enemy. Owain would have died either way. Now that they have Accolon in their possession, the house of Rheged is no longer a threat."

"Meaning Evina is their next target," I said.

He tipped his head noncommittally. "Perhaps. Her or you. Both of you are obstacles to their goal."

"Is that why you wanted to marry me, to rid yourself of an obstacle to greater power?"

"Yes, and I wanted your lands back. Nothing I have said to you has been untrue."

"Yet everything has. You and Elga planned this ahead of time, didn't you?"

Rohan smirked. "Of course we did. Why did you think I was in such a hurry for Owain and Osmere to stop their pointless arguing? How do you think I knew right where to lead them? I knew Elga was on that boat, but I have to admit I thought our plans were lost when you dragged her to shore. But the gods were smiling on us after all."

My palms itched to punch the self-satisfied smirk off his face, but I restrained myself. Out of the corner of my eye, I saw that two of Sobian's ships loomed just off the coast. "Well, it won't be long now until you face justice."

We clumsily loaded Theodric and Rohan onto one boat, and Sobian set it on course for the port of Dunbar, just east of Din Eidyn. Since traveling by sea was much faster than by land, we expected to reach our destination by morning. The rest of our army followed in a second ship with Morgan, who was tending the wounded with the aid of the other camp women.

In the small hours of the night, most of us managed to steal a few hours of rest, but not Sobian. In addition to captaining the boat, she took it upon herself to act as Rohan's guard. Once he was chained in the back of the boat, she approached him, taunting him. Even though I advised her to keep her own council about the subterfuge of the last several months, her resolve broke as we neared Dunbar.

She held her hair back from her face in a rough braid. "Do you recognize this face?" She said something in Pictish I could not understand, but from her tone, it translated roughly to "you piece of shite bastard."

When Rohan failed to respond, she poured a mug of water over her head, washing out the coal dust to reveal the lingering red in her hair. His eyes widened.

"Yes, you sorry sod," she said in the Briton tongue. "I was your 'lover,' Eithne. All these months I pretended to be close to you, to care about you, and all I was really trying to do was prove your treason. Yet now you have demonstrated it before a full party of witnesses, Votadini and foreigner alike." She moved right next to him, her breath stirring the fine hairs on his cheek. "Tell me, was vengeance against Owain worth what Evina will do to you?" She turned her back to him, leaning her shoulders against his like a lover. "I can't imagine much that would be worth sacrificing my stones for, much less my very life."

"I did what needed doing," he said gravely, turning his face away from her. "I ask mercy from no one."

"Good. I doubt you will find much from them." She pointed toward the port.

My gaze swung in the direction she indicated. At the mouth of the pier, Evina and Mynyddog waited, arrayed in their finery. Sobian must have sent a messenger ahead to make the Votad and Votadess aware of the prisoners we held on board.

As soon as we stepped off the boat, guards met us to take Rohan and Theodric into custody. I started to make my way to the second boat to see if Morgan needed any help transferring the wounded, but after a few steps, my path was blocked by two guards. They motioned for me to turn my back and surrender my wrists to them.

"What? What is this?" I looked to Evina and Mynyddog for an explanation. "Have I not regained the Isle of Winds from our enemies? By what charge do you arrest me?"

As if he had been waiting for such a cue, one of the guards recited, "Guinevere of the Votadini, late of Stirling and the lands surrounding, you are hereby reprimanded into the mercy of the Votad and Votadess on the charge of high treason. You stand accused of inciting rebellion and causing the people to rise up against their rightful rulers in your name."

Chapter Fourteen

Summer 522

Thick, stale air threatened to choke my waking breath before I could even draw it. Bright sunlight blinded me as I sat up in my tiny cell, its touch causing sweat to pool beneath my skirts and in my armpits. Judging from the position of the sun, it was just past midday. I pulled my linen shift away from sticky skin, seeking some relief from the unbearably hot room. Though the air outside was likely warm and refreshing, I had no such hope in here, for the prison was in the path of runoff heat from the kitchen fires. With so little time between the break of fast and the second meal, even in winter the air did not have time to cool. Perhaps that was by design to torture the prisoners, or maybe the gaol was placed there because no one would live in such conditions voluntarily.

I must have fallen asleep, something that happened frightfully often since being taken captive some weeks before—I'd lost count of how much time had passed. Between the heat and boredom, a drowsy stupor was my normal state. Little of what went on outside the walls reached my prison cell, only snatches of conversation when the guards conferred at shift change. Early this morning they had whispered about their strange orders for the summer solstice ritual tonight, so something important was afoot.

The clink of metal on metal at my door interrupted my thoughts. With a grunt, one of Evina's guards heaved open the heavy wooden door far enough to poke his head in, as though I wasn't worthy of moving his entire body. "Lady Guinevere, you have been summoned by the Votadess. You are to wear your best gown and bring any personal possessions with you, as you will not be returning to your cell. I will wait outside to escort you."

For a few dreadful moments after the door boomed shut behind him, I sat in my bed, shivering despite the heat, certain I was being called to my death. What had I done to warrant Evina's wrath after she had looked the other way for so many months? Which of my actions on the isle had tipped the balance? Something had to have. According to the guards, my supporters had been lying low since word spread of my containment, but rumblings still rolled across the countryside like seeds of thistle in the summer wind. Until they were silenced, I remained a threat, so perhaps there had been a riot I was unaware of.

Slowly, as though I was moving underwater, I braided my hair into a rough plat and donned the midnight-blue tunic I had been lent to substitute for my dirt-stained, bloody battle gear. It may not have been a royal gown, but it was a fine enough garment to lose my life in. I tipped water over my hands from an ewer and rubbed my cheeks, invoking the Goddess as though I washed with Beltane dew.

"Mother, guide me. Give me strength. If this is the day I am to meet you, I am ready. All my life I have followed your voice and tried to do your will. When I breathe my last, may your judgment be swift and merciful."

With a deep breath, I rapped on the door, offered my hands to be bound, and followed the guard out to meet my fate.

⚬෨෩ ෨෩⚬

I stumbled down the slopes of Din Eidyn into the darkening fields where a great crowd had gathered. They parted like summer barley in the breeze as we approached, revealing a wooden platform on which stood Evina, Mynyddog, and Calliac, the high priestess, surrounded by guards and attendants. Lancelot and Sobian waited nearby, under guard but unfettered, but I didn't see Morgan anywhere. Unlike the rest of us, she seemed to have escaped Evina's wrath unscathed.

To my left, more soldiers ringed a large wooden pen taller than a man, the like of which a farmer might keep cattle or horses in at market, but it was not open to the air. It was covered by a thatched roof like a house. When I tried to peer into the darkness within, the guards crossed their spears to prevent it. On my other side, the crowd laughed and talked, while a few jeered or cheered as I passed. Thankfully, they were much too distracted by the free-flowing ale and the men jumping bonfires or rolling flaming sunwheels down the hill to pay much attention to me.

When we reached the dais, the guard halted me with a hand to my shoulder. He nodded to Evina, and at her signal, the rhythmic pounding of drums began, followed by the jangle of horse tack as mounted men and women ringed us on every side. What was this? No ritual I had ever witnessed required so many armed men, much less a ring of cavalry. Perhaps the purpose of this gathering was much more dire than it appeared. My heart hammered, fear of the unknown replacing my earlier detachment. I swallowed. Perhaps I would indeed die tonight.

Calliac stepped forward, bowing her head so all could see the equine skull she wore as a crown over her long silver hair, then she raised and dipped her arms in gestures of supplication and praise, her voice lost in the din. As Calliac turned, she drew nearer, the rough surface of her horsehair cloak catching the light. The brown strands woven into the cloak were not ribbons, as I had thought, but rather the thick hairs from a horse's mane or tail. She was the embodiment of our tribal goddess, Rhiannon.

Four priestesses adorned with feathers and antlers stepped forward and bowed before her. She placed a hand on the crown of each one's head before entrusting her with a pottery bottle and sending her off into the dark. As we watched, the priestesses went from rider to rider, sprinkling them with the contents of the jars and giving them each a torch. The last rider blessed by each priestess took possession of her jar, and when the benediction was done, the four singled out gathered at the crossroads directly behind the dais. The other riders surrounded them in a circle.

When all had assembled, Calliac raised her staff, topped with the skull of a pony, and cried out in a language I did not know. The Otherworldly sound raised the hairs on my arms and forced a shiver down my spine. Whatever she was doing summoned great power, the like of which I had only seen twice before: in Avalon, and on the night Aine raised the dark spirits in Malegant's tower. With a scream like a banshee, she struck the earth with her staff and the skull burst into flames. She used it to light the torch of the rider nearest to her, and within moments, the circle was alight.

Calliac ceded the dais to Evina, who with her hair pulled back in complex braids and soot staining the skin around her eyes, resembled a wraith raised from the dead. Her eyes gleamed with a feverish intensity as she looked over the crowd, silent now in anticipation, and perhaps a little fear.

"My people," Evina's voice carried across the fields, "as you know, our homes are threatened on three fronts. To the north, our old enemies, the Picts, are stirring."

A few men in the crowd called curses upon on all sons of the Highlands.

Evina moved with feral grace, stretching her limbs like a dancer each time she changed direction. "To the west, we keep vigil against treachery from our own people, which some have recently enacted."

A loud hooting and booing rose from the crowd when a guard forced Rohan up onto the platform. Like me, he was bound at the wrists, but he wore no finery. His chest was bare, exposing the bruises and gashes of torture. Cries of "traitor" and "kill him" burst forth. If they so easily called for his death, was the same spectacle planned for me?

Evina gestured for the crowd to quiet, which they did by slow degrees. "And to our south, the Saxons roam our borders, looking for even the smallest crack through which to pass and harry us all."

The crowd was shouting, working themselves into a frenzy of bloodlust and hate. Outraged faces circled me on all sides, jostling and shoving. A young woman with shorn red hair pushed between my guard and me, and for one disconnected moment, I thought I was back in the courtyard of Cadbury on the night Malegant abducted me. Panic rose in my throat so fast I thought I would retch. I doubled over, breathing rapidly, a cold sweat weighing me down. I coughed and heaved, but my body produced nothing.

When I straightened again, Lancelot was beside me, having broken from his guard. I threw my bound hands over his head and hugged him tightly.

"Praise to the gods that you are here. I don't know how I would have faced this alone." I looked around. "Whatever this is."

Lancelot ducked out of my grasp and held my shoulders firmly, staring deep into my eyes. "No matter what may come, I am here. Know that they will have to kill me before they harm a hair on your head. So even if you die, I will precede you and clear the way to glory."

I made to respond, but Evina's powerful voice interrupted, forcing our attention back to her.

"We are not helpless, even in the face of such formidable foes," Evina declared. "Oh no, far from it. That is why tonight, we invoke the goddess Rhiannon, she who is also called Epona and Macha, patroness of our tribe and of our bloodlines. By the strength of her horses and with their speed, she will protect us and bring us peace."

She turned so that her back was toward us as she faced the circle of riders. The sun had dipped below the horizon and was losing its battle against the onslaught of night, bleeding into the sky in vivid streaks of burgundy, burnt umber, and ocher. Against such a backdrop Evina resembled a goddess herself, one who represented retribution and rage.

"You, my beloved ones, have been specially chosen to act in her stead this night. Go now! Go forth and trace the borders of our kingdom, sealing them by Rhiannon's power to keep our enemies at bay and protect our land. May she speed you on your journey."

With a collective whoop, they scattered to the four winds, torches like beacons in the night.

When the riders were no longer visible, Evina turned back to her subjects. "You, my people, have been false." She wagged a finger at the crowd like a remonstrative mother. "You have laid aside your vows to me to raise up a false queen. And why? Have I been so terrible to you? Have I ignored or abused you? Tell me now, why have you turned against me?" She signaled to the guards ringing the pen. "Bring them out."

The four guards nearest to the door of the pen stepped aside. Two disappeared inside, only to emerge holding the arms of two bound captives. I didn't know either face, but I was willing to wager they were Sobian's contacts, the leaders of the insurrection in my name.

The strong hands of my guard shoved me forward and I tripped, the ground rising fast. My hands hit the grass, and searing pain erupted in my knee as it met the hard earth. Before I could catch my breath, I was lifted, face to sky, on the hands of the priestesses, who cooed oddly soothing words in my ears as they raised me to the platform.

Once I was standing next to Rohan, Evina put her hands on her hips. "Well? Tell us why. Why did you back this usurper?"

The two captives stood erect as statues, impassive and empty expressions on their bruised faces. She would have no answer from them. Likewise, I could give no explanation that would satisfy her. I hadn't sought the throne, nor did I believe she had proof that I was in any way involved. But it was my name they proclaimed, and that was crime enough.

"Does it matter?" Rohan asked. "In our eyes, you were unfit to rule. Or at best not the most worthy of the throne. We proclaimed the one who was. So has it been since our ancestors first divided into tribes and so shall it be into our children's children's time. It is the way of things."

"You do not have the right to give testimony before me, traitor," Evina spat. "*You* have committed the worst crime of all. Moving against me is one thing, but to move against your country, your tribe, *and* your people is inexcusable." She looked around, taking in the mass of people. "Those who ally with the enemy have moved beyond the bounds of justice, beyond our codicils of fines and laws. There is but one punishment for traitors." Evina unsheathed her sword and held it up. There was no mistaking her meaning.

My heart sank to my feet, and I struggled to swallow the oversized lump in my throat as my earlier fear was confirmed.

Evina stalked around Rohan at arm's length like a wolf circling prey. "But do not fear," she said with a cold laugh. "You will not die alone."

I expected her manic gaze to fall upon me, but instead, she faced the pen again. One guard whistled, and two lines of people—men, women, and a few boys just barely of marrying age—stepped out, blinking at the torches like moles in the sunlight.

"These are your people, those who rose with you, are they not?" Evina asked the man and woman. Without waiting for an answer, she shoved them off the platform toward the lines of prisoners. "Let this be a lesson to all of you. Those who incite others against their rulers die alongside them." To the soldiers, she added, "Take them away."

While the lines were herded back inside the pen, a few men and young boys shoving against their captors in a futile bid to escape, Evina stood in front of me, staring into my eyes. So much of my mother was there, but this woman lacked her warmth. After tonight, I believed she lacked a heart—and possibly a soul—as well. I swallowed and willed my shaking knees and hands to be still. Keeping the image of my mother before my eyes, I held Evina's gaze, queen to queen, one granddaughter of Cunedda's line to another. This madwoman would not see how much she frightened me.

Finally she turned away from me, swinging her sword in a showy arc, before kneeling at her husband's feet and presenting the blade to him with bowed head. He took it and approached us, the determined, stoic expression of a warrior writ across his features. He raised his blade, and I closed my eyes, steeling myself for pain. Rohan grunted next to me, and a whoosh of cool air rushed over me. I opened my eyes. His headless body had collapsed next to me, a patch of blood already forming at my feet. I exhaled loudly and stumbled backward, shock and relief warring in my veins.

A slow grin spread across Evina's face. "No. Not you. Not now. I have other plans for you."

As Rohan's blood stained the boards and seeped between the cracks to the earth below, Mynyddog squatted and drew his fingers through spreading pool. He rose and painted his wife's face in streaks of crimson so that she appeared ready for battle.

"The traitor is dead. But the scales remain unbalanced. Just as a mother punishes a child who goes beyond the bounds of her law, so as your Votadess am I honor bound to give correction to my people. Unfortunately, the offense committed here goes beyond fines and the making of outlaws. I will not tolerate insubordination." She raised her arms to the sky, face turned toward the starry heavens. "As I am strengthened by the blood of my enemies, may the goddess Epona accept the sacrifice we offer this night. May our land be protected and forever blessed."

Before I could comprehend what was happening, the guards surrounding the pen wound thick lengths of chain around it and secured the door with a padlock before resuming their places. From the inside came a few shouts and whines of protest. Below us, the crowd stirred in response, shifting uneasily from foot to foot, heads turned toward neighbors in question.

"This is the summer solstice, the longest night. We celebrate the power of the sun and beg it not to leave us behind for its winter home, encouraging its potency through fire and flame." Evina nodded toward the pen. "For ages, our people have lit a bonfire representing the spirit of the Votadini people and kept watch over it through the night. Usually the honor of starting the fire belongs to my husband or me." She turned to me. "However, since you so desperately wanted to become Votadess, I will allow you to light the fire."

Shock reverberated through me as though I had been struck by lightning. This was no ordinary ceremony, and she was no ordinary woman. The Votadess was asking me to be responsible for the deaths of dozens of her people, my people, whose only crime had been trusting me. I squeezed my eyes shut. This went against everything I had ever been taught or thought I stood for. I had taken lives before, but those were lives lost to war and the gods understood that. This was far different, the murder of innocents to assuage one insecure woman's overblown sense of justice. I could not, would not comply, come what may.

I opened my eyes. Evina and Mynyddog were staring at me.

"You are a priestess, are you not?" Evina gestured toward the pen. "Light the flame."

I looked for a proffered torch, but none was being held out to me. Everyone around me stood in silent expectation. Then I understood. Evina was asking me to use my skills as a priestess to execute those she had deemed guilty. *No. No. I cannot! This goes against every single precept of Avalon, every rule governing the use of my skills. I cannot. I will not!*

"Unless you wish to join them, you'd better make it look as though you are trying to comply," an authoritative female voice threaded its way into my mind.

I turned my head, trying to find the source of the sound. Most were still waiting for me to do something, but Calliac caught my eye and shook her head almost imperceptibly, silently commanding me not to let my face reflect what was happening.

I narrowed my eyes and focused on the pen. I had to make it look as though I was willing the fire from the guards' torches to fly to the thatched roof.

Calliac glided toward me, stopping at my side. "My lady," she addressed Evina. "Fear blunts our abilities. No doubt you have frightened this woman with your awesome display of justice and authority. Perhaps you will allow me to aid her power?"

Evina considered this. "Do you mean like adding more spark to the kindling?"

Calliac nodded. "Just so."

"Proceed."

Calliac took my hand. Again her voice rang in my head. "You need do nothing. I will start the fire so your conscience may remain clear." She squeezed my hand. Smoke wound skyward from the roof. "My form of magic is different from yours," she silently explained. "Though the taking of a life in ritual is usually frowned upon, it is permitted in certain circumstances, so I am doing nothing against my own faith. You bear no guilt upon your soul for what is about to happen."

With a pop, the roof ignited, followed shortly thereafter by one of the walls. Soon the whole structure was aflame.

Around me, the crowd dispersed, some fleeing the heat and horror, others throwing themselves against the guards, seeking to save the people inside, while a handful ran to the well and tried to organize a bucket line to staunch the flames. But all their efforts were in vain, for no mortal could be faster than the wind that whipped up from the west, spreading the conflagration with elemental speed.

For the rest of my life, the screams and cries of those trapped and dying souls would ring in my ears. I would wake from dreams reliving this night, imagined blood on my hands and very real blame on my soul. With each beat of my heart, I would see their shades in the shadows and hear their accusing voices. But at the moment, all I could do was stand in mute horror, tears pouring down my face as their bodies blackened and charred like so much overcooked meat, paralyzed, unable to defend or to rescue them. For all my wealth, my powers, and my wisdom, I was helpless in the face of such tragedy.

⁂

With her immediate enemies vanquished and me publicly brought to heel, Evina resumed her duties as though nothing unusual had happened. She even allowed me to take a room in the main castle and for Lancelot and Sobian to be housed nearby. Our accommodations were nothing grand, but anything beat the sweltering gaol. I should have been grateful for her generosity—the fact that all of us still had our lives was nothing short of a miracle—but I couldn't help being suspicious of Evina's motives.

My fear of her revenge made every waking moment torture. There was no way Evina was ready to call my punishment complete, so I expected her vengeance around every corner. Sleep came in short, fitful bursts, just enough to keep me from getting ill or losing my mind, but not nearly enough to allay my constant state of alert anticipation and humming nerves. Each meal was torture, since I suspected each cup or bowl set in front of me was laced with poison. Sobian grudgingly began sampling a spoonful or sip of each part of my meal so that I wouldn't starve to death. Anytime we left the safety of our rooms, I insisted Lancelot walk before me and Sobian guard my back. Evina said nothing but watched me with shrewd eyes that were constantly plotting, calculating, feeding my troubled mind a steady diet of fear and doubt.

A fortnight after the solstice, Evina summoned Lancelot, Sobian, and me to her private chambers, and my stomach dipped in agitated anticipation. This was the moment I had been dreading, the reckoning I had been waiting for.

Evina and Mynyddog sat in throne-like chairs, surrounded by assorted sycophants and friends. Mynyddog slouched in his seat, relaxed, drinking ale and laughing. Slave women weaved between guests, bearing trays of meat and cheeses, fruit and delicacies, as though serving at a feast for close friends. Did they always dine this way? Or had we interrupted something?

As soon as Evina saw us, she snapped her fingers and everyone stopped what they were doing and departed. When we were alone, she did not offer us seats but required us to stand before her.

She toyed with the rim of her leather cup, looking at us through her eyelashes. "I have a proposal for you, one that you may refuse, but know that the other option is death."

I eyed Lancelot. So much for free will.

"You are too valuable for me to kill, which I suppose you have surmised by now. You have skill and experience that cannot be replicated. It pains me to need you, but each of you are necessary to the future of this kingdom. Lancelot, we need your skill with the sword and your ability with horses. Sobian, you are a master of intrigue with a network that rivals my own. Guinevere, your knowledge of strategy and of the hearts of the players on Britain's field of battle are second to none. Plus, you wield the power of Avalon. All of these skills combined will position us to be supreme rulers of the four ancient tribes. So I am asking you…" She cocked an eyebrow and gave us an all-knowing twist of her lips, her eyes gleaming menacingly. "No, I'm telling you, that you will remain by my side as my advisors in the coming war. And it will come to that, have no doubt."

I did not doubt it, even for a moment.

Evina stood, coming to rest before Lancelot. She placed a hand on his shoulder, a gesture that seemed to encircle him far more than her physical connection with him would allow. "To ensure your loyalty, Guinevere, I will take Lancelot's life as my own. Know that if you disobey me, even in one small matter, he will pay the price."

I swallowed hard, understanding the severity of the situation, for it was nearly an identical position to the one Lot had found himself in after his own failed coup against Arthur. Would that I had learned from him; perhaps then we'd all still be living in peace in Stirling. But that was not the case, and I had to deal with the here and now, not what could have been.

I bowed to Evina, so low that my head nearly brushed the floor. "As you say, Votadess. I am yours to command."

"As am I," Lancelot and Sobian echoed.

She smiled. "Good. Now we can get down to business."

Evina finally invited us to sit. When we were settled, she continued. "You likely have noticed that thanks to the Saxon war, Morcant's relocation to Stirling, and the Pictish threat, my army now has three fronts to patrol, which means fewer and fewer men in each regiment. I can afford to stretch my northern army thin, but I certainly don't wish to underestimate Morcant's ambition—if he senses weakness, he could rebel as well—nor can I afford to skimp on troops guarding the border to Bernicia." She pinched her mouth with her thumb and forefinger and pulled downward, as if doing so would relieve the strain such words placed upon her. "Therefore, I feel that the only way forward is to conscript soldiers from the people, which I know that they will hate, especially since harvest time is nearly upon us and all hands are needed in the fields."

I shook my head before she'd even finished speaking. "No. That is not the strategy you should pursue. Unless further rebellion is what you desire, then by all means, continue."

"What do you recommend as an alternative?" Mynyddog asked, speaking for the first time since we answered his wife's summons.

Lancelot looked at me as well, as though curious as to where I would take this line of thinking.

"After the battle of Badon, when the Saxons were quelled and the Holy Grail had granted us peace, we needed something to do with the soldiers and brigands who usually occupied their time fighting for the king. Several suggestions were put forth by the Combrogi. One man thought we should establish a school to train future members who may not be able to afford to travel to Camelot to serve Arthur directly. Another thought their skills would be best used as a traveling band of soldiers policing the countryside in cooperation with the local kings and lords. I think the best solution for our present situation might be a combination of the two."

I rose, standing directly before them to better impart my point. "I believe we should bring the remaining Combrogi to Din Eidyn to help train the young and encourage people to volunteer so it doesn't come to conscription. They are well-known, and their names alone will attract people to your cause."

Mynyddog leaned forward, interest plain upon his face. "Tell me more."

"Well, we have lost many of our greatest knights, but you have the two best here in this room. Put it about that Lancelot will offer personal lessons in horsemanship and blade work, and you will attract a certain contingent of young men." I turned to Sobian. "This lady here has a storied past that will no doubt attract women to your cause. Add to that Gawain, whom I am sure could be persuaded to lend his skills in exchange for a fortifying army at Traprain Law, and I know I can convince Bedivere and maybe even Kay to travel north." I turned to Sobian. "You can track them down, yes?"

She looked up as though I had interrupted more important thoughts. "Of course."

Evina sat up straighter. "And you? Will you teach your magic to our people?"

"No. That I cannot do. I can only train those who have a genuine calling to priesesshood and even then my skills are limited. But I can work with Kiara to help the others in training."

Evina nodded. "Yes, I like this plan. Let us see how many people volunteer for our army before Lughnasa." She looked at Mynyddog. "Have it put forth that we are reconvening Arthur's Combrogi in order to defend against the Saxon hordes. Let us see who shows up before we resort to conscription." Evina stood, towering over me. "Guinevere, I hereby charge you, Lancelot, and Sobian with building the greatest army the Votadini have ever seen. You will report to us when the tribes are gathered for Lughnasa."

Lughnasa was only six weeks away. To get the word out in that time would require a spectacular feat of communication, the like of which this isle had never seen. I looked at Sobian, who grinned at me, clearly up for the challenge in spite of having lost two of her best informants to Evina's revenge on the summer solstice. Not to mention we needed a place to house the influx of troops and a plan to condense years of study and practice into weeks, even days, to meet Evina's timeline.

"You can count on me," Lancelot said, once again reading my thoughts.

"Right then," I said to Mynyddog and Evina. I would work with Kiara and whoever else she recommended to produce a training plan for the students I prayed would materialize. "Send word to the people of the four tribes that you require their attendance at the Lughnasa festivities."

Chapter Fifteen

Autumn 522

Looking out from Evina's royal tent over the gathered tribes playing at games of sport and betting on the horse races, it was difficult to believe that it was on this day so many years ago I first met Arthur and Lancelot. I still felt like that girl, though my hair was now shot through with gray and my hips thickened with age. Part of me said I should be one of the lasses dancing 'round the hallowed first sheaf of the harvest. Or at the very least I should be one of the young women being handfast today, as Evina's daughter was being bound to one of Morcant's descendants to ensure peace with the Picts and Mynyddog's youngest brother was pledged to a widowed woman with ties to Bernicia.

But there was I, an old woman lost in the folly of nostalgia of bygone days. It was on that same Lughnasa that Galen disappeared with Isolde, abandoning Elaine to her broken heart and the wrath of her indignant mother. Yet we were together again, Galen waiting patiently behind me to attend to my every whim. Years ago I could not earn his attention no matter what I did; now he was duty-bound to give it to me. In so many ways, life had brought us full circle. I sighed.

Lancelot must have heard the note of wistfulness in it, because he came to my side and slipped an arm around me. "What troubles you, my love?"

I looked up at him, my heart warming every bit as much as it did that first time I had met his gaze at the tournament. "Oh, nothing. I'm just feeling my age, I suppose," I answered with forced lightheartedness.

"Why is that a problem?" he asked with a smile. "I personally find you more beautiful and wise with each passing day." He followed my gaze to the festivities. "Shall I accompany you to the fair? It would be my honor and will take your mind off your troubles." He held out his arm.

I smiled and looped my arm through his. Yet again, Lancelot knew what I needed before I did. I could not have chosen a better champion and lover.

As soon as we stepped inside the maze of tents and stalls, all the aches and pains of age, all the wrinkles and age spots disappeared. I allowed the girl within to take over as we passed from vendor to vendor, nibbling on sweet rolls and admiring acrobats and jugglers. We cheered as Sobian bested Galen in a horserace, and we held hands in anticipatory horror as Kiara performed hair-raising tricks with knives and swords for the amusement of the crowd.

At one stall, Lancelot braided a fine red ribbon into my hair and placed a chaplet of poppies, dried wheat, and cowslip onto my head. We wandered over to one of the many bands providing music for the crowd—this one composed of drum, fiddle, flute, and lyre—and listened appreciatively, sipping cups of sweet heather ale and keeping time by tapping our toes and lightly patting our hands on our thighs. Soon, the music was in our blood—or perhaps it was the ale—and we took hold of one another, dancing bravely into the crowd. We turned and whirled, speeding with the tempo of the music, the world around us blurring until the only sight in my focus was Lancelot's beautiful blue eyes.

"Marry me," he said into my ear.

Lost in the trance of the dance, I shook my head. Surely he could not have said what I thought I heard. "Come again?"

He grinned. "You heard me. Let me take you to wife. After all these years, do you not think it is time?"

We stopped our twirling at the edge of the crowd.

"Do you mean it?" I asked incredulously.

"Of course. You know I do not jest about matters of love. We could be handfast before sunset." He tossed his head back, indicating behind him, where couples nervously stood outside a stone circle, waiting for their turn before the Druid who would bind them for a year and a day. "You have previously said you have no desire to wed again, but I thought since we have escaped death together a second time, it might be wise not to tempt fate. What say you?"

He looked at me with such love, gentleness, and caring, my heart melted and pooled at my feet. Seized by a streak of impetuousness, I nodded. "Oh, why not!"

Lancelot took my hand, and we raced downhill to the small circle of stones, stopping behind a tow-headed couple young enough to be our children.

My heart pounded as we inched closer to the entrance of the circle. Several Druids and priestesses were performing the rites, each positioned at one of the cardinal points within the circle. At the center was Calliac. Gone were her skulls and fierce markings, replaced by feathers and flowers and three blue dots in the shape of a triangle on her brow, where the crescent was set into my own. In place of her horse-hair cloak was a simple white gown cinched by three red cords in varying shades.

She beamed at us. "What a happy occasion to see the two of you here. I assume you wish to be wed?"

Lancelot and I looked at one another shyly, grinning like adolescents in the first throes of love.

"We do," he answered.

Calliac nodded to me. "Do you love this man?"

"I do," I answered without hesitation. "He has been for me a balm in some of my darkest moments."

She faced Lancelot. "And you love this woman?"

"More than anything."

"Do you wish to be bound to one another in spirit as well as flesh?"

In this ancient wedding rite, blessed by the Druids long before the days of Rome and their written contracts, when a couple pledged their love and declared themselves spirit-bound, they were tied to one another until death.

Looking into Lancelot's eyes, I said, "I would like nothing more."

"I am hers and she is mine," Lancelot answered.

Calliac took my right hand, joining it to Lancelot's, and wound around our wrists a thick gold and red ribbon embroidered with intricate Ogham symbols for fertility, love, peace, and prosperity. She then presented each of us with an end of the ribbon. "To show your mutual consent and dedication to this union, your hands alone will tie the knot that binds you."

With nerve-slicked palms and shaking fingers, we wound our ribbons together, at first stumbling over how to interlace them to form a knot. But our second attempt succeeded. We pulled and the knot held fast.

"By sun and moon, light and dark, night and day, you are bound. May the gods bless you and bring you long life and peace, along with every grace and blessing." She placed a hand over our intertwined palms.

The priestesses surrounding the circle sent up a cheer then chanted in a language I did not understand.

"They are thanking the gods and asking their blessing on us in their native tongue, far older than the one we use now," Lancelot explained, leaning down to me.

I placed a hand on the back of his neck, drawing him even closer to me. "Then perhaps we should seal our union." Without waiting for a response, I pulled him in and kissed him deeply, the way I had so long wished to do at Camelot, free of fear and secure in our love.

⚬๑ℰ ℊ๑⚬

On the fourth day of the festival, our revelry was blighted by word of war. The Saxons had taken Catraeth, a strategic town south of York that controlled the fork of Dere Street where it branched off into the main trade routes to Corbridge and Carlisle. I cringed inwardly at the news. Elga and her ilk now had a direct line to Camelot, should they choose to try to defeat Constantine. Even though he'd taken Cadbury for his capital, the symbolic importance of Camelot remained deeply embedded in the hearts and minds of generations of Britons. Whoever controlled it, ruled them.

Upon hearing the news, Evina withdrew from the festivities, dragging Lancelot and me with her, leaving Sobian and Galen to entertain and serve her husband. Privately, I questioned the wisdom of that decision. Mynyddog had taken quite a shine to Sobian as of late, something the besotted Galen surely would not appreciate. On the other hand, if Sobian's feelings weren't as strong as I believed, she might well break Galen's heart. She had no compunction about trysting with a married man if it benefited her, and being in the Votad's bed certainly would. Either way, this likely would end in disaster.

"I have sent messengers to try to ascertain whether the House of Rheged intends to try to march on Catraeth," Evina announced as soon as the door to her private chambers clicked shut behind us.

Oh, they would. With Owain dead and Accolon captured, the family, if not the people as well, would want revenge. Catraeth, though not geographically connected to the kingdom of Rheged, was part of Accolon's ancestral holdings, just like the Isle of Winds. If pride did not motivate them, the town's importance would, for it could prove a convenient staging ground for Elga and Theodric to push west into the fertile lands of Rheged.

"Are you thinking of joining them?" I asked.

Evina chewed her lower lip, eyes faraway with thought. "Perhaps." She sighed. "We have to do something. If we don't oppose the Saxons before they march north, they may be too strong to defeat by the time they arrive here. If anything, the loss of the Isle of Winds made them more determined."

"So why don't we use their methods against them?" Lancelot suggested. At my quizzical expression, he explained. "Look what they did at Camlann. They didn't have enough men to come at us alone, so they joined with Mordred and the Picts. We already have Accolon's army, so if we do the same and ally with the Picts, we should outnumber them." He looked to Evina for encouragement. "Do you think that is something your daughter might be able to arrange through Morcant?"

Evina considered the proposition. "Perhaps." She blinked as if rousing herself from a great stupor. "Guinevere, what do you think?"

I shook my head. "I don't like it. What is to stop the Picts from pillaging Bernicia or Rheged once they get there? Or going back on their word and staying here to fight you? There are too many ways they could use this proposed alliance as an excuse to get a foothold in our lands."

"*My* lands. *You* have no lands," Evina reminded me spitefully.

I closed my eyes and swallowed down a retort to her pettiness. "Regardless, they have shown they are not to be trusted."

"Then why did the Votadess bother to marry her daughter into their line?" Lancelot countered. "If we are not going to begin to trust one another, what is the point?" He turned to Evina. "I have fought in many battles with people from many lands. I can tell you this, nothing unites disparate men like a common enemy. If we can show them the Saxons are as big a threat to them as they are to us, we need not fear treachery."

Evina narrowed her eyes at him, probably thinking through how this might play out. "How do we do that? The Saxons would have to eat up all of our lands before they ever reached the Picts. There is nothing to say their ambition stretches so far that they would pass into such inhospitable land."

"I agree," I said. "I understand your way of thinking, Lancelot, but I don't think it will work. However, we could find a compromise, something that still invites the Highlanders who wish to fight to our table, but does not require anything of those who do not."

Evina's eyes brightened at the suggestion. "Yes. When we make the announcement at the closing feast that we are recruiting warriors from all lands, we can be sure to emphasize that those from the north are invited to join. I want to be certain that—"

Before she could finish her sentence, the door burst open. Mynyddog's personal slave knelt low, head to the floor before Evina.

She jumped to her feet. "Speak, man." Her tone said more about her fear for her husband than words ever could.

"Forgive me, Lady Votadess, but you are needed."

We followed him to the main tent, where Mynyddog sat, clutching his nose. His eyes spoke of murder.

"I want that man publicly flogged," he commanded, pointing at Galen. I could barely make out his words through the wad of fabric he held to his bloody nose.

Evina knelt next to him to examine his wounds. "What happened here?" She looked from Mynyddog to Galen and back to me, as though I would know.

Sobian stepped forward from where she'd been hidden in the shadows. "Galen was only defending my honor," she said, looking at him with great admiration.

Galen, in turn, looked as though he would reach out to her from his place kneeling on the ground, but his wrists were bound behind his back.

"Guinevere's slave punched the Votad," Mynyddog's slave explained.

Evina set her steely glare upon me, as though as his mistress, I was responsible for his actions even though I hadn't been present. "He dared lay a hand on his ruler?" Her tone was incredulous.

The slave bowed. "Yes, Lady."

She whirled on Sobian. "What did you do to provoke this?"

Sobian stared her down, never one to bow to authority, real or imagined. "Why are you so certain the guilt lies with me? Your husband is the one with wandering hands. Ask him." She crossed her arms as though the gesture put an end to the matter.

Evina shook her head. "Take him away," she ordered the man keeping Galen in check. "Toss him in the gaol. I will deal with him later." She stalked toward me, finger pointing into my face. "He is your property, and as such, you are responsible for him. Do you wish to take his flogging, or should I add this to the list of offenses for which you are still in my debt? I would levy a massive fine on you, but everything you have is thanks to my mercy."

As she went on about my responsibility, I questioned her sanity. How was I to be held responsible for another person's actions? Galen was a slave, but he still had free will. Surely she did not think I had broken him entirely. It was foolish for Galen to have struck Mynyddog, but it was not worth all of this.

As she raged, the look in her eyes became familiar, for I had once borne it as well. She felt threatened by her husband's interest in Sobian, just as I had by Arthur's interest in Morgan. Nothing I could say or do would change her mind. All I could do was apologize and offer to make amends, as though such a thing were really possible.

"I assure you no one meant any harm. I will speak with Galen and ensure he understands the gravity of his crime." Even to my own ears, I sounded like a mother making excuses for a recalcitrant child. "I will also ensure he submits himself to the required punishment. After that, if the Votad would like to have use of him until his debt is paid, he has my blessing." I said the words, but it was a lie. I didn't want Galen anywhere near that man, but I had no choice.

"I suppose that is sufficient," she said, sulking. "But know the day is coming when your debts to me will come due. Prepare yourself."

⋅ઝૅ ৩৯⋅

On the last evening of the Lughnasa festival, Evina and Mynyddog gathered all the young men and women in training at forts across the four tribes for a friendly competition. The overall victors of the nine challenges would be responsible for helping Kiara and me train the volunteers who came to Din Eidyn to join our army over the next ten months. The events they competed in today would be the exact same training they would administer to those who wished to endure the grueling challenge of condensing years of training into three seasons, a remarkable test of endurance, fortitude, and will.

Before the competition began, Kiara explained to me the tradition behind the way the warriors of the four tribes trained. "For centuries we have been caught between two competing peoples who each want our land, so our strength as warriors is our primary asset against our foes. The ancient tribes trained this way to ensure their land would not be taken by another tribe. Now we do so in order that it not be stolen by invaders."

For the young people, this day was deadly serious, comparable to the day they tested to first become warriors. Just as in actual battle, they painted their skin and limed their hair, drinking henbane and winding themselves up into bloodlust with battle cries, chants, and banging on shields.

For the adults, it was a time of fun, sporting bets, and nostalgia for their own youth. As Kiara and I walked the perimeter of the competition field, I heard more than one lord and lady reminiscing about their own testing or telling tales of battles long since won or lost.

Some of the judges—like Mynyddog, who was off in the forest monitoring those completing the evasion test; Evina, who led the hunt; Sobian, who ran the stealth course; and Lancelot, who was evaluating the competitors' handling of horses—were stationed at specific events. Others, like Kiara and me, were general judges. We had a responsibility to view each competitor at least once in each of the five remaining events.

We had already seen all manner of blade dexterity, from showy sword juggling and spear dancing to more basic skills like knife throwing and general sparring. My ears were still ringing from the voice test, in which each warrior demonstrated his or her ability to strike fear in the heart of the enemy with a fearsome battle cry.

Up next was the spear vault, a famous move I had heard of in tales of old but had never witnessed, not even by my mother. It had been the most common way for warriors to mount a horse before the coming of the Romans, but was rarely used anymore. Those who knew it kept its secret, as it was advantageous in quickly evading the enemy in times of war.

Two men led a small, stocky pony into the center of the clearing. Cinon took up a shorter spear and stood facing the pony as though he was staring down the enemy. Lancelot often adopted that look when he was concentrating. Then without warning, the boy took off at a sprint, racing toward the animal, spear held high. For a moment, it seemed he would impale the beast, but at the last second, he rammed the spear into the ground and leapt like a stag, using the handle to vault himself onto the horse's back.

Kiara and I cheered for his spectacular agility and grace.

At the next station, a girl of perhaps fifteen, face still rounded with the fat of youth, prepared to make the salmon leap. She stood before a stack of wood reaching higher than her head, expression stony with concentration. Rocking back and forth on her heels, she flung her arms above her head and leapt straight to the top, a feat doubly impressive given that she was a little slip of a thing.

Jumping down again, she headed for a thick felled tree trunk at least twice her height. Before she could reach it, a little girl of perhaps seven summers, painted with a single horizontal strip of blue across the bridge of her nose, ran onto the field, begging to be allowed to join in. Bending, the competitor scooped the girl in her arms—the resemblance was so strong, they had to be sisters—and whispered something to her. The girl relaxed and allowed her sister to carry her back to their family, who stood watching from the sidelines.

In a flash of memory, I saw myself as a seven-year-old girl. I had just graduated from a wooden training sword to my first sharpened blade. I was so proud, so certain I was the toughest female warrior of my bloodline—save my mother of course—and I strutted around just like that little girl. That was the same summer I began to boss around Elaine and came into my own as a future ruler. It was also the same year I began having visions and talk of Avalon was first mentioned. That was the age that changed everything for a Votadini girl, and here she was facing a war that even her family couldn't shield her from. But I could. No matter what happened, I would keep that girl safe and see her grow to womanhood.

Her sister sorted, the warrior took a deep breath to regain her focus, bent low, and took a firm grip of the tree trunk. She hugged it near the base before lifting it nearly onto her shoulder. Muscles straining, she took a few uneven steps before letting it fly. The log landed several feet in front of her. It was a good toss—sure to be beaten by the men in the competition, but fair enough to keep her in the running. A grin lit up her face, and suddenly she was no longer the hardened warrior I had seen before, but an uncertain adolescent girl seeking approval from the elders and peers that swarmed around her, offering their congratulations.

As the competitors finished their turns, I calculated their scores in my head. Some were clear standouts for me, but it wouldn't be easy to honor only three. The tribes had many great warriors, a sign I hoped heralded good fortune in the war to come.

⚬⚬⚬

Mynyddog stood atop a tree stump so he was visible to all the assembled warriors and spectators, his swollen, bruised nose contributing to his image as a fierce warrior, as though he had earned his injury in the competition, rather than at Galen's hand. "The judges have met and determined our winners. I am pleased to announce that the leaders of our new army are Cinon, son of Clydno Eityn, who once held the office of Votad; Corag, son of Fergus called Quickshanks; and Ailith, daughter of Davina the Strong."

Ailith. That was the name of the willowy girl who had charmed me with her tenderness toward her unruly sister. I would have to watch her over the next several months, for I was still seeking a commander of infantry, and with a little training and maturity, she could be a viable candidate.

The winners had one final stop before they could celebrate with friends and family. I followed them to a tent on the outskirts of field, away from the noise and activity of the competition. There they would meet with Calliac, who represented the Death Mother. She was charged with ensuring each warrior understood that for those who make their living by the sword, everything ends in death—for those killed, if not for the warrior personally. She also had the responsibility of determining if they could handle the guilt and pain that sometimes came with taking life, and if not, she was to let the judges know so another could be selected.

Inside, at the far end of the tent, Calliac sat draped in black fabric, swathed in deep shadows broken only by three candles: one on her right, one on her left, and another directly before her. The two boys and girl hesitantly approached her, and I followed suit, though I kept to the shadows so as not to disturb them. At first, Calliac's veil obscured her face from view, but when she raised her head and the candlelight touched it, it faded from opaque to translucent like dissipating smoke. A ring of human skulls circled her brow, and charcoal painted around her eyes and over her nose gave her an uncanny resemblance to them.

"Welcome, chosen brothers and sister," she hissed in a voice like stones grinding under wagon wheels. She raised a hand, palm up, indicating they were to sit.

To a one, they chose to kneel instead, sensing the power of the one who spoke through Calliac.

"Some of you know me, for I have taken your brothers and sisters, your mothers and fathers unto my breast. I have visited your homes in plague and accidents and have stolen life from the childbed." Her eyes roamed over each of them in turn. "None of you has escaped my shadow, nor will you avoid my touch in the end."

The three glanced at one another nervously.

"Know that in training others for war, you do my bidding, for war has no end but death, no purpose but destruction. You may think your aims noble, but in the end, you are but my scythes, harvesting the souls whom I call to reckoning. Guilt and innocence concern me not; I leave those to Cerridwen, for they are her purview. My only desire is to close the eyes of those who have used up their time on earth." She watched them, as though evaluating each.

Then she treated Cinon to a rictus grin devoid of all warmth. "Know now the gift you bestow upon all you kill and all who kill in your name."

She reached out a bony finger and touched Cinon right over his heart. His face went pale as though he was in a faint, and he choked. The moment she removed her finger, he caught a breath.

She turned to Corag, who made to scoot away from her touch, but she grabbed his wrist. He shook as though touched by lightning. Only when she let go did his body calm.

The Death Mother reached out to Ailith. Unlike the boys, she did not cower, so the goddess lowered her hand and pressed her cold, colorless lips to Ailith's brow. She did not shake or spasm but simply closed her eyes and exhaled, as though resigned to her fate. When the goddess pulled back, she drew another breath.

"You have all experienced the agony of my touch and lived. Therefore, you are bearers of my lethal gift. I ask you now to take it and spread among your enemies. Can you do that?"

The three were silent for a moment, eyes closed in contemplation.

Reverence for their culture washed over me. From the outside, they appeared brutish and brutal, but they treated death with great respect. It was a higher calling among their people, a mindset others would do well to share. Years ago, Aggrivane had told me that Lot had sent him to study the ways of the Druids before he could go to war, in order to help teach him responsibility and respect. Perhaps this was something like what he'd learned. If all were taught the same, maybe, just maybe, we would have less senseless killing.

Ailith answered first. "Yes."

The others echoed her.

"Then so be it. Your names will be immortalized in song for your great deeds done in war, and down through the ages, warriors will toast to your honor."

Her head snapped up, as though I had made a sound that alerted her to my presence. "But you"—she pointed at me, eyes boring into my own—"you will lead these innocents to the grave."

Chapter Sixteen

Winter 523

By the time the snows began, Evina's army had nearly doubled, with nearly three hundred new recruits in training.

As their teachers, we—the remaining Combrogi, Lancelot, Kiara, Sobian and I—had a responsibility to see their training continued through the cold winter months. Though there would be no campaigns until spring, they could still spar and learn basic knowledge. We divided them into classes of approximately thirty students—though twenty would have been preferable—and devised a learning schedule similar to the one used in Avalon so they could study multiple skills at once.

On a leaden day about three weeks before midwinter, we took them north, into the mountains above of the Firth of Forth. Though chances were good we would not campaign in winter, we chose to test the students' endurance and fealty to the commitment they had made by exposing them to the elements.

During our three-day excursion, the warriors learned how to walk with heavy packs, maneuver horses in the snow, and fight on a variety of surfaces, from ice and snow to steep mountain passes. They were also required to swim in a freezing lake and practice rescue and healing skills. They learned to find a defensible position, build shelter with and without usable timber, how to light a fire under a variety of conditions, and how to find fresh water, even when all appeared frozen. Their final lesson was one Lancelot and I had learned by nearly losing our lives when fleeing Malegant's mountain fortress— sound carries differently in the cold and snow and forgetting that can be deadly.

By dawn on the fourth day, we were all ready to head back to Din Eidyn, even though it was snowing. We had just left our campsite— Sobian and Kay in the front, recruits in the middle, and Lancelot and I bringing up the rear—when I noticed Lancelot's horse lagging behind.

"What's wrong?"

Lancelot bent over his horse's neck. "He's not stepping correctly on his left foot."

I pulled up next to him and we both dismounted.

Lancelot took the horse's hoof in his hand and turned it over to examine the underside. He cursed. "An ice ball. I just inspected his hooves earlier. How could one have formed so fast?"

I peered at it. "In these conditions, anything is possible." I picked at the ice ball with my fingers, hoping it would dislodge easily, but it didn't budge.

Lancelot dug at the mound of ice with his dagger, but with the same results. He squinted at me. "It is going to take some time to remove this without hurting him. Go on without me. I will catch up with you."

I was loathe to leave him behind, especially knowing the snow would get worse as the day went on; I sensed it.

When I made to follow him back to the remains of our campsite, Lancelot waved me away. "I'm going to have to rebuild the fire and heat the hoof pick to try to get this out. It almost looks like someone jammed ice in his hoof, then melted it so it would cling to the shoe. The wrath of the winter gods never ceases to amaze me."

"Are you sure you will be all right out here alone?"

"Of course. How many winters did I survive alone on the road before I met you?" He flashed a heart-melting grin. "Besides, I have the remains of this morning's kill with me and I know where you are headed. I'll meet you at the next campsite."

I kissed him quickly and mounted my horse. "Be careful."

༄ঌেঌ৾

Day turned to night and Lancelot still had not joined us. The evening star replaced the morning star a second time, and I panicked. So many things could have befallen my husband—bears, wolves, snowdrifts, thin ice, cold, hunger. If there was even a chance he was injured or in need of help, I couldn't sit idly by and do nothing.

One day out from Din Eidyn, I broke from our party, leaving the students in the care of the former Combrogi while Sobian and I retraced our route. We found our former campsite, but nothing appeared amiss. However, a short distance away, we found Lancelot's horse, his ears frostbitten and hoof still impacted with ice, but otherwise healthy.

"Where is your master?" I asked, looking deep into his eyes as though I had Lancelot's talent for speaking with horses.

His eyes rolled as though recalling some unspeakable horror.

With a jolt, the sight came upon me and my mind was transported south. Lancelot was bound and gagged, kneeling at the feet of Elga and Ira. The Saxon said something to him and Lancelot shook his head. A guard drew his sword, then the vision vanished.

"No," I shouted. "No!" Violent spasms racked my frame.

Sobian dismounted and put her arms around me. "Guinevere, shush. Shhh," she hissed in my ear. "We must be quiet or risk triggering an avalanche. Remember what we taught the students?" She took my face in her hands as my wails increased in volume and violence. "Remember? Look at me, Guinevere. Look at me."

I complied, blinking away frozen tears.

"Good," she soothed. "Come now, we must be away from here. You can tell me what has you so upset when we are in a safer place."

In the shelter of the pine forest, I poured out my heart to her.

"I will get my girls on it. If anyone can find him, we can," she assured me with a squeeze of my hand.

"But he is with that unholy witch of a woman," I cried. "She swore to me someday she would have her revenge. What if this is it?"

"Then we will have to kill her before she can do any permanent damage. She should have died at Badon and has been living on borrowed time ever since."

When we were finally back in Din Eidyn, Lancelot's horse safely in the stable, I fell asleep in Sobian's arms, exhausted and unable to find comfort anywhere else.

I was just beginning to dream when Sobian gently shook me awake. "Guinevere, you have a visitor."

My sleep-addled mind leapt to Lancelot, expecting to see him when Galen opened the door. But instead, Morgan stood on the threshold.

She rushed toward me and fell at my feet. "Oh, Guinevere, I am so sorry. I never thought… I never intended…"

Morgan apologizing? Surely I was still sleeping. This had to be a dream; she had never once apologized to me in all the years I had known her. But if I was dreaming, why would Sobian have had to wake me? No. As improbable as it was, this was very real.

I raised Morgan to her feet, holding her at arm's length. Her red hair was disheveled under her black hood, eyes bloodshot, cheeks stained with tears. Her lips quivered as though she was about to let loose a fresh torrent of tears.

"What is it Morgan? What have you to apologize for?"

She looked at me in consternation, some of her old defiance returning. "Lancelot's disappearance, you daft cow."

"What?" I could not believe she'd had anything to do with it. How could she have known where we would be? I hadn't even seen her since we returned from the Isle of Winds. I must have misheard her.

I was about to question her further, when the complaint of a wooden chair groaning under weight drew my attention across the room to Accolon, sunken-cheeked and missing an eye, but very much alive. Maybe I *was* dreaming. The last time I had seen him, Elga was dragging his unconscious body aboard one of their ships at the Isle of Winds. How had he escaped her and when? And if he was here and Morgan was apologizing for Lancelot's disappearance, that meant—

"Elga offered me a trade," Morgan explained as though she could not keep the words inside any longer. "Lancelot's whereabouts for the return of Accolon." She looked at me, eyes pleading. "You must believe that I never expected she would take him. Now... now..." She reached inside her gown and removed a roll of parchment. It shook as she held it out to me.

I handed it to Sobian, not trusting my own eyes to read it.

"She is demanding your life and the allegiance of the Votad and Votadess in exchange for Lancelot."

❧ ❧

Less than an hour later, a small crowd gathered inside the smoky council room for an emergency meeting in the wake of Morgan's revelation. Evina and Mynyddog poured over correspondence and maps while a handful of counselors whispered advice and suggestions out of our hearing.

They had been silent for so long, I feared they had forgotten my presence. "We must rescue him," I pleaded for what felt like the thousandth time.

Mynyddog raised a hand as though he could shield himself from my panic and outrage with a gesture. "I understand your need for action. I am troubled by this situation as well, but we cannot simply take up arms without thinking through all eventualities."

Mynyddog's words—no, it was more the surprising compassion in his tone—surprised and soothed me. Deep down, I knew he was not reacting out of any fondness for me, but out of concern for Elga's terms. My life was one thing; he would turn me over to the Saxons in a heartbeat. But asking them to bow before foreign rule was another matter altogether.

"It would be tantamount to murder to send our men on campaign in the middle of winter," Evina pointed out.

"Which I'm sure the Saxons took into consideration," Sobian said, more to herself than to anyone else.

Mynyddog nodded, tapping his balled fist against his lips, eyes distant with thought. "They need time for whatever they are planning. That's why they did this in winter. They want to be ready when we come to them."

"But where will we engage with them? We don't even know where they are," I said.

"Let me try to find them," Morgan suggested, tapping her forehead.

I crooked an eyebrow at her. *I* was the one with an emotional connection to Lancelot. *I* was the one with the ability to see events at a distance. She could only… see the future. She would be able to see where they *would* be when our forces were ready to move, which was much more valuable than knowing where they presently stood. Inwardly, I scoffed at myself. My petty, jealous pride had nearly blinded me to Morgan's wisdom. If I hadn't exorcised my demons where she was concerned by now, would I ever?

Morgan sank down gracefully before the fire, tucking her feet beneath her and smoothing her gown over them. She breathed deeply a few times, but instead of closing her eyes as I would have done, she stared deep into the fire, letting her vision unfocus. To my left, Accolon tapped a steady beat on the wall with his palms to encourage Morgan's trance. Galen soon joined in.

Morgan's eyes moved, darting back and forth like a dreamer's as she beheld a scene invisible to the rest of us.

"Morgan, what do you see?" I coaxed.

"A hillfort. To the south. It's…" Her brow wrinkled. "It's farther inland than the rest of the Saxon holdings. In Accolon's lands." She turned toward her husband, eyes still blank with trance. "They have taken him to Catraeth and are preparing for a siege. They want us to come." She raised a hand to her head, seemed for a moment to regain herself, then collapsed in Accolon's arms. He quickly carried her from the room.

Evina, who had been listening attentively, ran a finger along one of the maps in front of her. "This is dire news indeed. If they have time to enforce the boundaries around Catraeth, they can cut us off from Rheged and Strathclyde, effectively blocking any reinforcements or aid from the south."

Mynyddog grunted, his brow wrinkled. "We would be penned in like hogs, ripe for slaughter."

Evina leaned over and said something into her husband's ear. Soon, two of the counselors were blocking them from view.

I eyed Sobian, not liking the enthusiasm with which Evina was conversing with the men.

When she turned back to us, Evina's eyes were sparkling.

My stomach knotted in response.

"Leave us," Evina commanded the room. I turned to follow the others, but Evina stopped me. "Not you, Guinevere."

Slowly, I faced her, unsure why they would wish to speak to me in private. Evina waved me toward the throne. I dutifully stepped forward and knelt at their feet.

"Do you remember that I once told you the day would come when I would call in your debts to be paid?" Without waiting for an answer, she continued. "That day has come."

I looked at her, confused. "What is it you wish of me?"

Mynyddog glanced at his wife, then addressed me. "You will lead our army to Catraeth in spring."

"Me? But why would you wish me to command in your name? I thought that was the very thing you forbid."

"Lancelot is your husband, is he not?" Evina asked.

"Yes." I still didn't understand. "But surely there are leaders among your sons or within your army whom you trust more."

They did not respond, simply continued to watch me, waiting.

Slowly, understanding dawned. They had others they trusted and valued more, but they didn't wish to waste them on this expedition. I, on the other hand, was expendable.

"You are not confident of victory." It was a statement, not a question. I marveled at Evina's capacity for revenge as the pieces fell into place in my mind. "You wish me to lead them in case we fail."

Evina smiled cruelly, an expression I had only ever seen on Morgan. "I expect you to fail. We cannot let the Saxon bid for Catraeth go unanswered, but knowing they anticipate us and with our army split as it is, we have little chance of defeating them. I must keep my best troops in reserve here for what may come. I already have a contingent in Lothian and another guarding the Picts in the north, so I can only give this cause so many men." She shrugged.

"Then why send me at all? What is to stop me from beginning the journey to placate you and abandoning them and you for another court, say that of Accolon or Constantine?"

Evina laughed. "Do you think I do not know you at all? You are too loyal, too concerned for the fate of the people. You would never abandon an army to certain death, even if your husband's life wasn't at stake." She leaned forward. "Make no mistake, your troops are not welcome back here without you, and you are not welcome back if you fail. Victory or death are your only choices."

So that was it. After so many months of toying with me and using me, Evina had finally delivered my death sentence. She would not put me to the sword or hang me in front of a crowd, but I was being executed for treason all the same. She would rather a Saxon blade do the work for her.

I looked at them. "And if I refuse?"

"I will send word to Catraeth that we have refused their terms and Lancelot dies."

PART FOUR

Y Goddodin

CHAPTER SEVENTEEN

Spring 524

At Din Eidyn, war was as much of a ritual as the turning of the year was to those who worked the fields. In the smithy, weapons were prepared and stored. The kitchens stockpiled rations of dried meat, salted fish, cheese, and other nonperishable food items that would sustain us on the long journey to Catraeth and into the siege beyond.

By the time the winter melted into spring, Din Eidyn was home to a motley band of approximately five hundred trained warriors from Evina, Accolon, and Constantine's armies and another three hundred aspiring soldiers. We had lost a small band of less than fifty boys a few weeks prior when they decided to go off alone in pursuit of the Saxons who had taken Lancelot. Their bodies were found a week later, skewered on pikes in the Pentland Hills, but their heads were never recovered.

When I had told my warriors we had been assigned a dual mission to rescue Lancelot and take back Catraeth, some were eager to begin spilling blood, out of revenge for our lost youths, hatred of the Saxons, and loyalty to Accolon. But others were more reticent.

"This is an ambush!" Bors, who had reluctantly joined us at Constantine's bidding, yelled.

"Yes, it is," I answered. "The Saxons are using Lancelot to lure us to our deaths. But you were once a member of the Combrogi. Can you honestly tell me you could leave him to die simply because of a trap?"

Bors looked down, muttering under his breath. It was as close to agreement as I would get from him.

I turned, taking in my other troops. "Many of you came from Stirling and the lands surrounding it. Once you and your neighbors begged me to lead you as your Votadess. I may not bear that title, but I am asking you to trust me now as if I did. Allow me to lead you into battle. Whether we claim victory or shed our blood in vain, we are fighting for our lands and our families, that they may live in peace in the tradition of our ancestors, rather than under the Saxon's boots."

"Aye," Cinon shouted. "We are the warriors of a people fed from the breast on battle. If we did not wish to risk our lives, we should have chosen to be bakers or blacksmiths or tailors. This is our duty to our families and to ourselves. There is no question of fear of death. We are meant to die in battle, so let's do as we are commanded."

"We have no honor if we don't at least try to take back one of our own," Corag added, watching me. "Angus may be from across the sea, but he has helped so many people, my da included, that he *is* one of us, blood or no." He turned on Bors. "So if you think we are going to back down, you're wrong and you'd better start running. This lot"—he made a gesture meant to encircle the barracks—"does not take kindly to cowards or traitors, and if you are against us, you are both."

৵৹৫ ৯৶৹

In preparation for our journey south, Evina called a great three-day feast, insisting we celebrate like the warriors of old. No expense was spared, no animal left unslaughtered, or cask of heather ale or honey mead untapped. She knew we may not return, and so gave us a feast to either herald our coming victory or guide our souls to the Otherworld.

On the first night, the great hall was full to brimming with warriors from all the tribes. Votadini made up the majority, but there were also Novantae, Selgovae, and Damnonii, plus a handful of Picts and Britons sympathetic to our cause. Among these were Bedivere and Kay, who had not yet apparently seen their fill of battle.

"It is an honor to fight alongside you one last time," Kay said with a small bow when I encountered him among the throng of bodies inside the hall.

"It may be the last time for you, but I intend to live to see another day," Bedivere joked.

There was no missing the tension and fear underlying their words, so I laughed to try to dispel it. "I do not think even the gods could kill the two of you tough old sods unless you were ready. We have seen much. This is just the next in a long line."

"Before we retire, yes?" Bedivere joked.

"Not me. I plan to die in the saddle, as should you lot," I said.

Kay touched his mug to mine in response. "I'll drink to that."

"To victory!"

As the night progressed, we ate, drank, and danced, trying our best to forget the reason for our gathering, even while listening to the tales of past victories and heroes long dead sung by the bards. Even Calliac participated, singing a particularly moving tale of a husband and wife who died together on the battlefield. Their deaths assured their progeny back home could live, resulting in Mynyddog's bloodline.

On the second night, the mood was decidedly more somber, as the reality of what was to come manifested. The bards sang songs of bitter doom and called curses down on our enemies. The seers made a spectacle of reading the entrails of slaughtered animals, holding them aloft for all to see. But because they foresaw nothing but victory for us and death for our enemy, they were hardly to be believed. No battle, in my experience, was so one-sided.

Around the great hall, warriors huddled in groups or pairs, engaging in some kind of pre-battle ritual. They would speak a few words to one another, draw blood from their finger, palm, or forearm, then touch the wounds together, clapping one another on the back proudly before licking their wounds clean.

"Do they have blood bonds where you are from?" Kiara asked when she noticed me watching them.

"No. Many of our men are close and would gladly die to save the other, but we have no formal way to seal our loyalty."

"You do now. Come on."

She dragged me by the hand to the central hearth fire, where Kay and Bedivere were facing one another like a couple about to be wed. The cheer of another group drowned out most of what they said, and when I looked back, they were hand in hand as though ready to arm wrestle one another.

"In the names of all our gods, I do so swear to bind my life with yours. I will defend you with all my power. If you be cut down while I still live—" Kay said.

"I'll hunt the bastard down and feed him his own prick," Bedivere finished for him before pulling him into a tight embrace.

Kiara turned to me. "In our tradition, you cannot bond with your champion or spouse, as you already have ties to those people which might interfere in battle. Only another warrior is deserving of your solemn oath." She held out her hand to me. "Will you do me the honor?"

Without waiting for me to reply, she took out her dagger and made a slash on the inside of her forearm, where it would not pain her in the heat of battle. For a moment, I could only stare, watching the crimson line form on her arm. Then I looked into Kiara's clear blue eyes. This was the woman who had taken me under her wing when I was new to Stirling and knew no one. In asking for my help training her young warriors, she'd given an old woman back her youth and endowed me with a purpose beyond being a prize for anyone seeking the power. Now, she and I were about to lead the mission to rescue Lancelot and save our people from the Saxons. There was no one else I would rather fight to the death for.

Without a word, I took the dagger from her, sucking in air as I made a similar gash on my arm. I took her hand, entwining our arms until our blood mingled. "Kiara, battle maid of both the Votadini and Selgovae, I hereby pledge my life to you. In victory or defeat, may our bodies and souls be bound."

"In life and in death, I will watch over you and see you victorious or revenged. This do I swear in the sight of all my gods," she finished.

We hugged one another tightly.

"We'll destroy those bastards," she promised before licking her arm.

Our blood was bitter on my tongue as I did the same. "Each and every one."

⁂

The last night was for saying farewell. Kiara, Morgan, and Accolon would be coming with us, so I had few people to address, unlike many of the men and women who were saying goodbye to spouses, children, and sometimes many generations of family. But there were remarkably few tears and many expressions of love and encouragement. This was a culture of war, and this was the moment many of them had trained for their whole lives.

There was one last ritual before we could say our farewells in private. We took our place in a long line of men and women, each with the same dazed, introspective expression. Before us on the right was a large pile of flat rocks. As each person passed, he or she took one, then placed it on top of a stack on the left to form a cairn, the final resting place of the dead who would perish in the coming battle. Those who returned would retrieve a stone, leaving the remainder as a memorial.

I shivered as the stack grew higher and higher, reaching toward the heavens. *Bless us in battle, great Morrigan, and protect us, so that many of these stones may be removed, discarded, and forgotten. May they find their way into walls or roads, rather than remain standing as a symbol of slaughter for generations to come.* Feeling strangely hollow, I placed my own stone on top of the one Evina had designated for Lancelot.

To Kiara, I said, "Let's get out of here. I need to remember why we live for as long as I can, rather than dance among those already dead."

We headed back to our quarters, passing scores of couples who defiantly refused to let one another go. It wasn't long before we found Sobian and Galen, heads bent together, whispered endearments becoming tiny puffs of steam in the chill night air. She was prepared for battle, but he would stay behind in the service of Evina and Mynyddog, so these were their last moments together.

The separation of lovers as one turned their face toward battle was never easy, nor was it fair, but these two were especially unfortunate. They had waited so long to find one another and were so well-suited. As a slave, Galen could not fight unless he was conscripted, but Sobian went voluntarily. She was not of our tribes or bound to our loyalties or laws, yet she willingly faced death out of friendship for me. That had to count for something.

It would. I would make it so. *I may not be able to tell my own fate or those of anyone around us, but I can save two lives and ensure some happiness comes out of this.*

I ran over to Galen and Sobian, smiling amid the tears streaming down my cheeks. "Sobian, take back your stone. You are not going with us."

Her face crumpled. "I'm not? I don't understand. Have I done something to offend?"

"No, no, this is something much better." I grinned. "The affection the two of you have for one another is no secret to anyone, try as you may to hide it." I took Galen's hand. "That is why I release you from your bondage. From this day forth, you are a free man, absolved of all your past transgressions. Take this naughty lass and begin a new life with her."

Galen stared at me, obviously mystified. "But is not Evina the one to release me? Her father *was* the one who condemned me, after all."

I shook my head. "She gave you to me. I may not be able to restore your tribal mark, but I can grant your freedom." I slipped the key from around my neck and opened his collar, and he rubbed his neck in great relief. "Tell Calliac what I have done. She will be able to cover your mark of slavery."

Sobian still looked concerned, her brow wrinkled. "But where are we to go? I have no permanent home, and Galen cannot purchase land."

"But it can be gifted to him for his service. Galen, Lancelot owns land in Angus. He and I were planning to give it to you when your service was over and you had earned your freedom. Tell them you come in his name and give them this." I slipped a bracelet off my arm before holding it out to Galen. "The whole of the town knows the story behind this gift, which was given to Lancelot in exchange for his service. He wanted me to keep it in case something ever happened to him and I needed to flee. Now it is yours. The people of Angus will treat you like the chieftain's son you were born to be. Plus, you will be safe there from any fighting that may result from our march south."

"I—I cannot accept this. What about you? Where will you live when you return?"

I shook my head. "The gods do not promise that I will live. They make that promise to no man. But when this is over, Lancelot and I will return to Brittany. He has ancestral lands there. Have no fear for our welfare." I placed Galen's hand over the bracelet. "Give me one less worry on the battlefield. Say yes and be happy."

Galen looked at Sobian. "I do not wish to force you into anything you are not prepared to accept."

She grabbed him by the shirt collar. "I have been waiting for you the whole of my life. You are my match in all things. I will not let you go." She kissed him, long and deep. When she finally pulled away, she asked, "Your father wasn't murdered by a god, was he?"

Galen looked at her quizzically. "No. He died in battle on Beltane. He was accidently killed in what was supposed to only be a mock dual between the Oak King and the Holly King."

I gasped. "Then he *was* murdered by a god. Each of them is portraying an aspect of the god during that ritual. One is the god of winter and the other the god of summer. It seems your Witch of Orkney was right after all." I clapped Sobian on the shoulder. "Go, pack your things and leave before first light. You will be long gone before anyone notices."

Galen hugged me tightly, his eyes welling with tears. "Truly, you are a good woman. I wish there was some way I could repay you."

I looked away. "Be happy. That is the best repayment there is."

As they retreated into the darkness, my heart fluttered with joy. I may have mistrusted Galen in the beginning, but his years of captivity had changed him for the better. He was worthy of a woman like Sobian now. I may not have been able to save Arthur, but I was sure that wherever his soul was now, he was smiling, grateful to know at least one of his old friends, a pirate-turned-assassin-turned-heroine with more lives than a cat, had emerged from this strife unscathed.

⁕

After a grueling week-long journey south, our army, some nearly nine hundred strong, including an equal number of horses for the cavalry that made up a third of our army, finally spotted the fortress of Catraeth. It loomed high above us like a mountain grown out of the edge of the peat-covered Cheviot Hills, where they gave way to the fertile plane of the Tweed Valley. Between us and our target lay fields of bracken, sweet heather, and bilberry, all of which would both help and hinder an army on foot.

Just after midday, when we were still a ways off from the fortress but within range of where we should set up our siege camp, they appeared on the horizon—an awaiting army meant either for ambush or simply to whittle down our numbers before we reached the fortress.

I signaled for the long train of men, women, and supply carts to halt. Had the Saxons seen us? If not, it was possible we could double back and come at them from a different route. They had no camp, so they must have been confident they could either finish us off by nightfall or they were close enough to make an easy retreat within the walls of the fort. Their army had nearly double the manpower of ours, and no doubt their scouts were now scampering back to the fort to report our presence.

There was no way around confronting them head-on. This was my least favorite type of battle, but one we could not avoid. I gave the signal for us to continue, sticking to the original plan. At least now we knew the terrain and general configuration of the army we would be fighting. It was little comfort, but we would take what we could get.

We had come prepared to take a hill fort, no easy task, and now we were faced with a pitched battle too. We needed time to change tactics and prepare before engaging. Accolon sighted a location suitable for our camp and set about creating a home base for ourselves. I saw to the large tent that would house our operations and strategy, while Morgan took charge of the camp women and healers who would stay behind to help while the soldiers fought. Accolon took responsibility for the barracks, smithy, and stables, and the captains organized their men. Accolon also assigned groups of men to surround the fort and cut off any food or other supply lines.

By nightfall, we were ready. The siege itself could last for weeks while we waited for the supplies of food and water inside the fort to diminish. We would attack the fort at the same time, attempting to weaken their defenses and kill as many of the enemy as possible. But first we had to defeat the battalion waiting for us.

At dawn, we would charge, and there would be no turning back. How I missed Lancelot and wished I could hold him one last time before the battle that might end my life. Knowing he was so close— just inside that prison of a fortress—yet so far away and with an army between us was torture. As I lay between Morgan and Kiara in my tent, trying desperately to get some sleep, I told myself that the next time I opened my eyes, I would be mere hours from seeing Lancelot again.

The sky was still dark, moon riding low in the sky, stars sparkling, when my eyes popped open. I would sleep no more this night. I sat up, watching Morgan and Kiara slumber on, and recalled a night so many years before in Avalon when I woke to find Mona crying and comforted her with the wooden toy dog Peredur had given me.

Peredur. I hadn't thought of him in years. Nor his half-crazed sister, Nimue, who had ended up murdering Merlin before taking her own life. I shivered, recalling the night we cast her out of the priestesshood of Avalon, leaving her alone on the Tor to decide her own manner of death. Was my remembering them a sign? Worse yet, an omen of ill fate? One would think with the gift of sight, fear of the future and of omens and portents would be pointless. Perhaps that was the case with Morgan's gift, but mine provided no such comfort.

I rummaged in my bag of personal possessions, trying to find both Peredur's toy dog, which I considered a token of good fortune, and my set of Holy Stones. I had to know what my memory of them meant. Plus, it was time to conduct my first divining for the battle to come.

I must have made more noise than I'd intended, because when I looked up again, Morgan was staring at me.

"Why are you awake?" She sat up, rubbing her eyes. "Better question, why are you keeping me awake?"

"I am doing no such thing. Go back to sleep."

"What *are* you doing?" She eyed me curiously.

"I was looking for a few items to help with my pre-battle rituals." I lifted the little wooden toy and pouch of stones so she could see them. "Do you have any rituals of your own?"

Rather than answering my question, she reached for the dog. "I haven't seen him in years. What was his name? Bricriu?" She gazed at the little dog lovingly. "The last time I recall holding him was that winter night when we were in the House of Nine." A soft smile played on her lips.

"Yes. I'm surprised you remember."

She looked at me, hurt in her eyes. "Please don't think me so heartless. Despite what has passed between us, I treasure our time in Avalon, especially that night." Morgan gestured for me to sit on the bed. "We were, what? Ten? Eleven, maybe? Do you remember I asked Mona if she would try to see into my past?"

I looked away, not wanting to meet her eyes on such a sensitive subject. "Yes. You were hoping to learn the identity of your parents. Was she able to tell you?" I found the courage to face her then, wanting to be able to look into her eyes if she claimed to know her parentage. I wanted to see if she told the truth or if there was any hint of falsehood shadowing them.

Morgan toyed with the top of her brown wool blanket. "No. She was never able to see much clearly for me." Her eyes met mine, and they were shining. "But I do know who they are… or should I say were." She leaned forward so that barely a breath of space remained between us, and her voice dropped to confidential tone. "The Grail revealed their identities to me that night we first drank from it. Viviane is my mother. Merlin is my father. I was a child of the Beltane fires. That is why they chose me over you to be the Virgin Queen. It had nothing to do with our childish competition, or who was really the best among us. They thought I would be more likely to conceive the Sacred King's child because I came from the same type of union."

I sat back, stunned. All these years, Morgan and I had hated one another, vied for attention and recognition and pride of place in Argante's eyes and then in Arthur's, and for what? It was never about us, but about who would continue Arthur's line. If we had only known, we could have avoided decades of animosity and bitterness, and avoided so much pain. If only...

"I suppose they were right, just wrong about the timing," she continued. "As it turned out, I did bear his children." Her voice trailed off, and I imagined she was lost in memories of her dead son and the daughter she barely knew.

Morgan had been chosen by the Goddess because of her bloodline, and Arthur fell in love with her that night. If my father hadn't intervened and proposed my hand to Arthur in repayment of his debt, then Morgan would have been queen in my place. And I would have been wed to Aggrivane. *No,* I corrected myself. *That is not right. I would have been wed to Malegant.* I shuddered. What a living hell that would have been. I found myself grateful—for the first time in my life—for Morgan's interference in my plans, however unwitting.

"I owe you a debt of gratitude, it seems."

Morgan startled out of her reverie. "What?"

"I said 'Thank you.'"

She looked at me warily, as though I had transformed into a rabid beast. "For what?"

I shrugged. "For everything." I did not want to try to explain my reasons to her. "I just felt like it was something I should say, especially given we don't know if we will see tomorrow. I suppose I should say I'm sorry as well—for all that I have done over the years. I'm sure you have kept a mental list." I certainly had.

Morgan continued to stare at me, her eyes growing damp.

I glanced at the opening of the tent, where a small crack of light showed dawn was near to breaking. "I should get on with my divination." I shook the bag, lifted the board, and stood.

"Wait." Morgan grabbed my wrist.

I turned.

"You forgot this." She held out Bricriu in her other palm.

"Thanks."

"I'm sorry too." She squeezed my arm.

⚜

The stones predicted a short period of harrying the Saxon army before the siege would begin in earnest, but they would not yet show me the final outcome. It was blurred, playing out one time in our favor, portending mass causalities the next. I had never encountered a battle where the stones were so indecisive; it was as though some factor I had yet to account for could change everything. All I could do was set them aside and hope I would have time to consult them again before we gained the fort.

The camp rose when the eastern sky was just beginning to pale. Instead of breaking our fast with porridge or stale bread, we gathered around the cook fires for a ritual of a different sort. Warriors broke into their fighting ranks and passed around buckets of slaked quicklime, which had been allowed to cool overnight. Each man and woman worked it into his or her hair so that it stood up and out as much as possible. When it dried, our hair would be stiff and paler than usual, giving us a spectral appearance.

Next we passed around pots of woad to paint one another's skin. Many of the men simply slapped on stripes with their fingertips, but Kiara and I were more artistic, drawing spirals and knots and adding a few sigils for protection and courage.

Then we dressed for battle in the garb of our tribal animals—the horse, the wolf, the raven, and the stag—tunics and braccae made of their skins, their fur slung around our shoulders, skulls attached to our heads as helmets, and teeth and bones worn as jewelry.

Finally, we moved single-file past a large cauldron, into which Morgan and some of the other camp women were dipping wooden mugs. Each man took a cup and retreated to a place of his choosing to consume the sacred drink. When I was but three people from the front of the line, the henbane's noxious scent assaulted me, bringing stinging tears to my eyes and forcing bile into my throat. I coughed a few times before my body adjusted to the acrid, smoky, leather-like scent.

Kiara and I sat next to one another and stared at the viscous liquid in our cups.

"I suppose you have consumed this before?"

"Only twice. We don't drink it regularly because too much can be poisonous." She looked at the contents of her cup again and sniffed. "I think they mixed it with goat's milk to make it more palatable." She grimaced, then looked at me. "What you have heard about its effects is true. It will slowly take you over until you have the undeniable urge to kill, a true thirst for blood. Be prepared."

With one last glance into the cup, I touched my mug to hers then brought it to my lips. The thick, clammy liquid slid down my throat with little effort on my part, leaving a bitter trail in its wake.

"Ugh. I feel like I swallowed a slug!" I grimaced, trying to keep from looking like a total fool.

Kiara laughed. "That would have tasted better."

Her chuckle was the last joyful sound our camp would hear. Slowly, our warriors grew subdued, laughter and boastful shouts replaced by a menacing silence, akin to the calm before a storm. Then slowly, one by one, the soldiers began to fidget, to pace, to glare suspiciously at one another through dilated pupils.

I felt it too—the restlessness. My whole body grew warm and my vision narrowed. I could no longer see to either side, but everything in front of me appeared crystal clear, sharper, more focused than ever before. Then my leg twitched, bouncing up and down without my conscious command. All of my muscles grew taut, ready to spring, poised on the edge of action. I could no longer sit still. I had the aggression of a thousand angry bulls charging through my veins. I wanted—no, *needed* to move. I was strong. I was invincible, and I was ready to attack.

I prowled around the camp like a wildcat until somewhere behind me, a group of warriors pounded on their shields with spear shafts and sword pommels. My heartbeat sped up to match.

"Form up!" I yelled.

The command echoed from man to woman to man across the camp until we were arranged by unit, spearmen and swordsmen at the front lines, archers and slingers at the rear, everyone surrounded by our cavalry.

Kiara took her place at my side. At my signal, the pounding ceased, replaced by several heartbeats of deafening silence. Then as one man, we screamed, charging forth.

The war had begun.

Chapter Eighteen

The heads were the first things I saw, rotted away on poles surrounding the base of the fort like discarded fruit in the summer sun. What was left of our lost group of young would-be heroes barely looked human, their decomposition made even more by violent by the henbane flowing through my veins. Worms crawled out of sockets where eyes had once been. Jowls hung, torn and desiccated like badly butchered meat. Ravens pecked at hair, at tongues or skin, leaving deep divots into which flies gratefully buzzed.

Then their jaws shook as though the skulls would speak.

"Save us," one screeched.

I whirled around, seeking the source of the voice.

Just as quickly, another echoed, "Save yourself."

"No, save him!"

"Who?" I turned again and ran smack into Kiara. "Save who?"

She grabbed my shoulders to steady me. "Guinevere." She shook me slightly. "Guinevere!"

"They want me to save him," I said frantically. I blinked hard a few times, trying to focus my eyes. When I opened them, I was staring into Kiara's face.

She smiled. "You're fine. It's only the henbane. Sometimes it can make you see things that aren't really there, especially when you aren't used to it."

"But they said—"

Before I could finish, Accolon called for a halt. He pointed up at the wall, where figures jostled about, followed by unintelligible growling and a few curses. Some kind of struggle ensued above us, and men were knocked down, only to rise once again. Finally, a familiar head of blond curls appeared. All the other figures stepped back, ceding the primary position to her.

"Yield to us or he dies," Elga commanded, nodding at the man she held by the hair, a sharp blade pressed into his throat.

Lancelot. The henbane evaporated from my blood, my stomach cramping and my bowels threatening to turn to water.

He was bound with his hands behind his back, forced to kneel in front of Elga. Given the way she was dragging him around, his feet were lashed together too. Behind Lancelot stood three large men, weapons trained on him, should he attempt to free himself. There was no way he would escape unharmed unless I did as she wished.

I laid down my sword. "You have asked me to yield, and so I do. But I cannot swear for the actions of others, only myself. Now please, return him to us. He has done nothing against you."

Elga smirked. "Perhaps not in this war, but his blade has meant death for many of my countrymen." She twisted Lancelot's head so he could see the scarred area of flesh above her left clavicle. "You gave me this." She clucked her tongue. "So close to ending my life, yet so far away. Perhaps I should show you how it is done." She pressed the blade into his flesh, eliciting a grunt of pain from Lancelot and producing a rivulet of blood that wound slowly down his neck.

"No. Stop!" I cried. "Spare his life and I will do anything you ask." I made sure the men around me could see that my fingers were making a cursing formation behind my back.

She laughed. "Kneel before me."

I did.

"Will you disown your kin and country, forsake your quest to defeat us? Will you finally admit that I've beaten you?"

"Yes, anything. You have won."

She cocked her head at me. "I do not believe you." She glanced at Lancelot. "Pity." In a flash, she ripped the knife across his throat. As blood bubbled from his neck, she leaned down and kissed him, long and deep, taking in his dying breath. When she looked up again, her mouth was covered in his blood. "Now, kill them all," she commanded her troops.

Primal fury propelled a scream from my lips, a sound more terrible than the war cry of the greatest warrior queen, more chilling than a banshee. Perhaps it was the remnants of henbane, but no grief weighed me down in that moment, only pure hatred. The desire for revenge turned my nerves to iron, my blood to fire. I was on my feet in an instant, lunging toward Elga, who had melted into the sea of bodies within the fort. *Even if we fail to take it, I will get inside and kill her, or the Goddess strike me dead.*

A torrent of troops surged past me as the two armies engaged. From some distant place, I was aware of fending off blows and delivering deadly strikes with my sword in one hand and a spear in the other. I was acting on a warrior's instinct, born of years of training. As my body reacted to defend against threats, my mind had but one goal—find Elga.

As I drew closer to the gates, it became harder to distinguish ally from enemy. The world around me was a dizzying sea of colors and whirling bodies. When I heard my name or recognized a face, I gave aid, but otherwise I did not involve myself in others' strife.

Day passed into night that way, with only a brief respite to tend to wounds, bury the dead, and fall into dreamless, exhausted sleep. Soon we were on our blistered, aching feet again, swords in hand, shields at the ready.

The Saxons kept coming. While our numbers dwindled, theirs seemed only to increase. Kiara had ridden out last night and checked on our second unit, the ones preventing supplies from reaching the fort, and they reported no one had crossed their lines. It was impossible they really were multiplying, but that didn't make them any easier to fend off.

As the sun set on the sixth day, our morale was flagging. There simply were not enough soldiers left. We had already recalled the second unit into battle. Tonight we would have to break camp and press into service anyone who could hold a weapon, whether they were trained or not. The following day would be our last push, an offensive that would determine whether we went down in history as heroes who'd saved our tribe or were eulogized as brave warriors who'd perished in defeat.

I called all of our remaining troops together just after Accolon sounded the retreat for the night. Looking over the tired faces and broken bodies, I summoned all the courage I had left. "I was not going to tell you this, but given that tomorrow we will make our last stand, you deserve to know." I made sure all eyes and ears were on me. "There is no home for any of us to return to, should the battle consume us. Before we left Din Eidyn, our Votadess made it clear that should we fail, we were no longer welcome there or anywhere else within Votadini lands."

Grumbling rose and fell like an ocean wave as the troops took in this news.

"I tell you this not to upset you but to light a fire within you. We may be outnumbered, but we are not without hope. We can take the anger and betrayal we feel toward our leaders and use it to propel our javelins and sharpen our swords. We can show the Saxons what offended Britons look like, especially when their homes are threatened."

Before me, heads nodded.

"And once the Saxons are dead, we will overthrow the Votad and Votadess and install you in their place," someone shouted.

"Aye!" The word rang through the crowd like a tolling funeral bell.

Inwardly, I cringed. I would never accept that title, but they didn't need to know that. Let them believe it if the idea of making me Votadess would give them extra courage to fight. "One step at a time. Now, say your prayers and make your peace with whatever gods you believe in. Tomorrow, we fight!"

☙ ❧

The next morning, a deep, pervasive calm filled my body and mind as I took a final walk through what was left of our camp, checking for deserters or anyone left behind and making sure cook fires were properly doused. The last thing we needed was a fire at our backs preventing retreat, should the day come to that. If we had learned nothing else from Boudicca's disastrous final battle, it was make sure our troops always had a way out.

Near the rear of the troops, I found Morgan with a group of women armored in the discards of the dead, reluctance writ large on their faces.

"You can run, you know," I said to them gently. "You do not have to fight."

"Yes, we do," said a stately dark-skinned woman who towered above me. "The cravens among us ran already under cover of darkness. The rest of us are here to do our part. We're just scared."

I gently pushed my way into their circle and took her hand. "I understand. I was only fifteen the first time I faced down an army in battle, only nine the first time I defended myself against attack. Nothing I can say will make it easier. Please know you are doing the right thing."

"My husband died in this battle three days ago," a young woman clutching a spear told me. "I want to see his soul avenged, even if it means meeting him soon after."

"I promised my little sister I would protect her, and I cannot do that by running," said Ailith, who had come up behind me. "It would be my honor to lead you into battle. Will you follow me?"

The women nodded. Ailith led them to Accolon, who directed them with hand gestures and words I could not hear.

Once they had all moved off, I was left alone with Morgan. She turned her sword over and over as though she had never seen one before, though I knew full well she had had lessons from both Arthur and Accolon on how to use it.

"I never thought my life would come to this," she said, not taking her eyes from the blade in her hands. "I am a priestess vowed to peace, not a soldier. What do I know of war?"

"You have been married to three kings," I reminded her. "You know more than most of the men here."

She snickered and tossed the sword at my feet. "I don't need one of these to be dangerous. If these bastards want to see what happens when they cross a child of Avalon, they better be prepared." She raised her arms, and a brisk southwest wind stirred our hair. "I will fight in my own manner."

I handed her back the sword. "Please take this. Your powers are no good if you get pinned between two Saxon blades. Even the Lady of the Lake carried a dagger for that very reason, and the Grail Maidens are armed as well."

She sheathed the sword with sarcastic smile. "You still always have to be right, don't you?"

Her words took me back to a day on Avalon when we were but children and were both assigned to clean the sanctuary stairs as punishment for our roles in two mishaps the day before. Then, she had been lording her place as favorite acolyte over me. Now, she may have used the same taunting tone, but all the venom was gone from it.

"Only where you are concerned," I shot back with smile.

"May the God and Goddess of Avalon watch over and protect you," she called over her shoulder as she melted into the waiting troops.

"May your god bless you as well," I shouted after her.

⁕

On the front lines, Kay and Bedivere were forming a schiltron, or pike block, to try to take out the heart of the defending mass. I slipped underneath the shoulders of some of the taller men to take my place in the second rank of spearmen. We would throw our weapons while those in front of us, armed with swords and shields, would defend us from the volley of javelins likely to be launched in return. Flanking us on all sides was a mass of cavalry ready to charge through the enemy and do their own damage.

At a signal from Kay, each spearman raised his or her shield, forming an overhead and side armor for our crew. A steady beat of sword on shield was taken up by one of the cavalrymen. Its sole purpose was to help us keep in time as we progressed, so that no one fell and was trampled, which would make the whole unit dissolve into chaos. On Kay's command, we surged forward, keeping our steps in time with the reverberation echoing in our ribcages. It was hot beneath the veil of shields and my hand grew slick around the shaft of the spear, but when a volley of projectiles thudded into our shields a few moments later, I was grateful for the protection. A few breeched our defenses, and we parted momentarily to avoid stepping on our fallen comrades, but then it was our turn to attack. On the command, we lowered our shields in unison, standing long enough to throw our weapons before ducking behind our shields once again.

The cavalry surged forward, breaking any formation the defenders hoped to keep. The swordsmen plunged into their depths while another volley of spears came from behind. I unleashed my own sword, hacking down as many Picts, Saxons, and attacking Britons as I could.

"Guinevere!" Kiara screamed above the tumult.

I turned, searching for her. In my quest to locate Elga, I had completely forgotten I was supposed to stay by her side. Now she needed me.

I spotted her a good distance away, near the wall. As I ran toward her, I sized up the situation. She was defending against an oddly matched pair of Saxons wearing full-face masks that made them look like creatures out of a nightmare. One, who was about the size of an ancient yew, wielded a large battle axe, while his much smaller and more spindly companion jabbed at her with a dagger or short sword. The strategy, if there was one, seemed to be keeping her attention divided between the constant small threat of the dagger and the looming slice of the axe.

Kiara was doing a fine job keeping them at bay, only once being stabbed by the gnat with the dagger. But there was no way she could keep up her position for long and they knew it. I launched myself at the little one, colliding with him from the side and knocking us both painfully into the ox with the axe. As we struggled to right ourselves, he stumbled sideways, giving Kiara an opening in which to attack.

By the time I had the smaller one pinioned to the ground, my sword through his chest, she was advancing on her opponent, finally able to get under his guard. He hadn't yet noticed I was free of his friend, so I greeted him with a sharp slice to his weapon arm. As he howled in pain and dropped his axe, Kiara sank her blade into the tender flesh of his belly, giving him a swift kick so that he landed on his back with a thud.

When we were sure he was dead, she took his weapon, sheathed her sword, and clasped my arm. "Thank you, sister."

"You're welcome. Now, let's get inside." I started back toward the remnants of the schiltron, but Kiara grabbed my arm.

"I think I know a quicker way we can get in, but we'll have to be fast." She pointed at a portion of the wooden wall where the majority of our schiltron's spears had stuck in the timbers. "We climb. It's the only way in until they breech the gates."

I looked at her, slack jawed. "Are you mad? We will be completely exposed."

"That is why I said we will have to be fast." She looked at the battle around us while securing the axe to a strap running across her back. "I hate to say it, but I think the war is turning against us."

I followed her gaze to where more and more of our men were falling, their bodies piling up several deep where the fighting was the strongest. She was right. It was now or never. "Will they not attack us from the walls?"

She grinned. "Not if we distract them. I forged a plan with Cinon in case anyone needed a bit of cover." She whistled sharply three times.

A dozen heads whipped around on the battlefield, and several men emerged from the trees with ladders, which they raced to prop against the walls. Cinon handed us each a length of rope with a grappling hook attached.

As soon as we had the ropes secured at our waists, he yelled, "Now!"

We sprinted toward the wall, relatively unnoticed once we had dispatched the few warriors in our way.

"Couldn't we have used one of those?" I asked, pining for the surety of a ladder as I tossed the hook to the top of the wall, where it bit into the stone.

Kiara was already part way up the wall and using the shaft of a spear to help her stretch down to pull me up. "Only if you want to remain on this side. They will never succeed." Kiara contemplated her next handhold. "They are only meant to draw attention away from us."

A spear whizzed by my head, jamming itself with an audible thwack into the wall above me. I tightened my grip on the rope and redoubled my efforts to climb.

Kiara cursed as an arrow narrowly missed her leg and wood exploded into splinters above her head. Startled by the noise, she looked up just in time to get a face full of sawdust. Coughing and half blinded, she groped hand over hand, pulling herself up.

By the grace of the gods, somehow we made it to the top and over the other side of the wall, near an abandoned tower that led down into the courtyard.

In the streets below, nothing moved—no smoke spiraled from the chimneys, no animals snuffed or clucked, not even a rat slunk along the alleyways. The barracks stood empty, doors shut tight, the stables seemingly abandoned. Even the smith was silent. There had to be reserves waiting for the command to bombard our men, but none were visible.

The hairs on the back of my neck stood on end as I scanned the outbuildings for any signs of life. "Why do I feel like we've walked into their trap?"

"Because we have."

We were headed toward the main keep when the scrabbling of feet on stone reached us. The sound was too deep, too heavy to belong to animals. It had to be people. I signaled to Kiara to follow me, and we headed deeper into the fort. It was darker on this side, the sun not having risen high enough yet to penetrate the shadows cast by the keep. Kiara touched my shoulder and pointed toward the east. Elga and two of her masked guards were scurrying down a narrow alley, heading toward the anterior gate. With our troops closer to infiltrating the fort, they were whisking their leader away to safety. We followed them, careful not to draw their attention until we were ready.

After ensuring none of them were carrying bows or spears that could be directed at us, I called, "You are many things, Elga, but a coward isn't among them."

All three froze. Elga turned first.

I smiled at her, weapon at the ready. "Where are you going? The battle isn't over yet. Please, stay so we can end this."

She regarded me for a moment, her gaze calculating. "Yes. Our time has come."

With a snarl, she pushed aside the guard who stood between us and came at me with frightening speed. I met her attack with vengeance of my own, leaving Kiara to fend off the other two men. Our swords clashed, the bite of metal on metal vibrating down our arms. In the moment it took for Elga to recover, I knocked aside her helmet and slammed her up against the wall. Her head hit with a sickening crack, but instead of disorienting her, it enraged her more. She pushed back with a primal grunt, driving me into the middle of the passageway. While parrying her blows, I turned so that my back was toward the mouth of the passage, not wishing to be trapped as poor Kiara was, should the fight turn against me.

Elga advanced, pushing me into the open courtyard. One of her guards followed, but Kiara was hot on his heels, having already dispatched his friend. Their movement was enough to distract me, giving Elga the opportunity to change the arc of her blade, a move I didn't see coming quite fast enough. I leapt to the side, trying to avoid her swing, but it caught the outside of my wrist, tearing a gash up to my elbow. Pain exploded before my arm went slack, useless. Reliant now on my sword arm, I kept fighting, trying to find a way to get under Elga's guard before I tired. I stabbed at her, but she was quick, so the tip of my blade barely pierced her leather armor. I had to stop her advance. Otherwise I was likely to trip over something or simply falter from fatigue.

A deafening crash sounded behind us, followed by a boom so loud it shook the ground. The main gates of the fort collapsed inward in a cloud of dust and dirt. Our soldiers rushed in—Accolon, Kay, Cinon, and Morgan among the sea of faces—only to be met by Saxons pouring out of every door and window, emerging from barracks and the keep to engulf our much smaller force. From the direction of stables, a chilling howl rang out, followed by a chorus of growls and snarls as a pack of man-sized wolfhounds were set loose. Within moments, they were tearing into flesh and ripping bones from sockets while their Saxon masters stabbed and sliced their way to victory.

Evina's army would not survive this. But they would die with blood on their swords and courage in their hearts. If the gods were kind, that was the memory that would pass down through the song of the bards when this day was recalled.

I could do nothing to aid any of them, so I turned back to Elga, whose attention was still riveted on the battle at the gates. She was smiling, which only inflamed my anger. I took a deep breath, imagined Lancelot's smiling face, and thrust forward, determined to finish this Saxon whore for good.

Elga blocked my thrust, flicking my weapon aside as easily as if it had been made of grass. Before I even realized what was happening, her boot connected with my ankles and I was knocked off my feet, sword clattering to the ground as I dropped it so I wouldn't impale myself in the fall. I hit the stones, trying to brace myself with my uninjured arm, but it crumpled with a snap as the bone broke. My hip was the next to make contact, sending pain radiating in every direction. I struggled to push myself onto my knees, but my arms were too wounded to be of much use. Elga stood over me, her tall form in silhouette against the blazing sun.

So this was how I would end my days, cut down by a woman I'd made the mistake of trying to aid, who had been my sworn enemy for so long. Like a trapped animal, I searched for Kiara, praying she would come to my rescue and deliver me, but then I spotted her body in the alley, her opponent headed in our direction, no doubt to finish me off if Elga could not. *Please, Mother, be with me,* I prayed, refusing to avert my eyes as Elga raised her sword to deliver my death blow.

But it did not come. Instead, the earth rumbled again. Elga stumbled, her swing thrown off course. A flash of copper hair filled my vison as Morgan threw herself between Elga's blade and me. She landed on top of me, blocking Elga from view.

As I scrambled out from beneath Morgan's unconscious and bleeding body, I saw Morgan's sword protruding from Elga's torso.

For one long, frightening moment, she remained standing, staring in shock at the hilt sticking out of her gut. Then she collapsed.

Stunned, I could not move, even as the guard advanced on me. When he was close enough to kick, I lashed out, connecting my foot with his shin, knowing he would kill me.

"Be still, woman. I will not harm you," he barked from behind a full-face helmet, hopping in my direction.

I obeyed, my stomach twisting. There was something familiar about his voice.

"Can you stand?"

My heart lost its rhythm and my spine tingled as he grasped my shoulders and hauled me to my feet. My body recognized him even if my mind did not. I took a deep breath to steady myself, but the scent I inhaled nearly made me swoon. Oak and apple wood. But it was not possible. It could not be. I'd seen him die with my own eyes. Perhaps I had hit my head in my fight with Elga and was simply imagining things.

He pulled me away from the carnage, but I dug in my heels. "I will not leave her," I said, nodding toward Morgan.

"If she is still alive, people are coming who can tend to her better than we can. If not, she does not need our aid. We have to get out of here."

"Why are you helping me?" I asked, my voice tremulous.

Ignoring my question and my protests, my rescuer picked me up and dashed toward Kiara, who was beginning to stir. He kicked her weapon to her. "Get up. We must go or face what is left of Theodric's army."

Holding her head with one hand and her side with the other, she obeyed. They took off at run, darting through the postern gate and into the surrounding wood as fast as their legs would carry them. My weight was no doubt slowing them down, but if I were put down, I would collapse on the spot. This was the best we could do.

A series of shouts went up inside the fort. I could only assume the Saxon horde had found their leader dead.

"Elga had horses tethered down by the stream," the guard said between ragged breaths. "We must hope we get there before someone comes searching for us."

A shiver coursed through me as a hound bayed. It was not one of the war hounds. That was a tracking dog, and it had caught our scent.

Likely, I had left a trail of blood that would lead them right to us.

I was shaking uncontrollably by the time we reached the horses. Kiara had to hold me upright while my rescuer mounted his steed. Then she passed me up to him like a sack of grain. When he reached for me, the sleeve of his grimy tunic inched back and I saw a pattern of blue swirling up his arm. Suddenly dry-mouthed, I looked again. Covering his right arm was a dragon, the sign of the house of Lothian. But the men of that line were all dead, except for Gawain, and he was back at Traprain Law. Wasn't he?

The baying was getting closer. Before my thoughts could go any further, we were off, galloping as fast as Elga's steeds would carry us. I clung to the horse's mane as well as I could with my better arm, praying my rescuer's grip on my waist would be enough to keep me seated.

We had been riding for quite some time when he yelled for Kiara to slow her horse. We pulled up beside her and she helped me down, keeping one steadying arm around me.

My rescuer removed his helmet, rubbing his face with both hands.

When he dropped them, I stared into brown eyes I thought I'd only see again in the Otherworld. My lips parted in an astounded breath as I struggled to reconcile what I was seeing with what I knew to be possible. Perhaps I *had* died at Elga's hand after all. It was the only explanation for how I found myself staring into Aggrivane's face.

Chapter Nineteen

hen I next opened my eyes, I was facing the peaked roof of a cloth tent. Where was I? How had I gotten here? I breathed deeply, surveying the pains in my body. Nearly every part of me ached, but especially my hips and my arms. Glancing down, I found my left arm was splinted with a tree branch and immobilized in a sling, and my right arm was heavily bandaged. Slowly, carefully, I sat up, putting as little pressure on my bandaged arm as possible.

Fighting off a wave of lightheadedness, I took in my surroundings. Four canvas walls, one of which was split in the middle to make a door that rippled in the soft breeze. A small fire burned not far away. Hesitantly, I swung my left leg off the pile of blankets that served as a bed and tried to stand. My right hip was bound tightly to restrict its range of motion, but I guessed it was not broken. As long as I didn't put my full weight on my right leg, I could remain upright. Walking might prove to be a different matter, however.

I took tiny, halting steps toward the door flap as pain flared in my limbs. Memories of the previous day returned in a rush, as though carried back to me on a gale. In flashes, I remembered scaling the wall, relived Elga's attack and knowing I was going to die. Morgan's intervention still puzzled me. I owed her my life. *Please, Mother Goddess, let her live. She deserves a few years of solace after what she did for me.* In a flash, I remembered Aggrivane, but I pushed that thought out of my mind. It was too much; I would think about him after I learned where I was and how the rest of our troops fared.

By the time I reached the door, I had to grasp onto the material to stay upright. Sweat drenched my brow, yet my teeth chattered. But I willed myself onward. I had to find out where I was and what was happening.

Before I could venture outside, voices caught my attention—a man and a woman, not far away. They weren't exactly arguing, but speaking intensely.

"I must return to finish what I started," Kiara said. "Our warriors deserve better than to remain exposed, food for the carrion birds. We must burn their bodies and take word of our defeat back to Evina."

"If the carnage is as bad as you say, then you will need my help," the man insisted.

My heart stopped. It really was Aggrivane.

"No. You stay here with Guinevere. There are other Votadini who can help. When you can, flee. Do not return to Din Eidyn. Go anywhere else you will be safe. Just keep Guinevere out of Evina's reach. I will calm her wrath as best I can."

I could not stand to be in the shadows any longer. I limped out of the tent toward their voices. "Was it really so bad? Were we so roundly defeated?"

They looked up, startled by the sound of my voice.

Kiara rushed to my side, allowing me to lean on her. "I am afraid so. I just returned from what is left of our camp. By my count, less than fifty of our men and women remain, though some may have already fled north. We were slaughtered. Corag and Ailith are among the dead."

My shoulders sagged. "It is all my fault. I led us here. Calliac warned us I would bring about their deaths, but I did not listen. I should have died alongside my men."

Aggrivane handed me a stout branch. "Use this to balance your weight. It is not your fault. I was there. I saw what you did to try to save Lancelot. Be assured Elga was going to kill him even if you had taken your own life before her eyes. Both of you were but pawns in her game. For weeks, she talked of nothing but wiping out the Votadini. She may not have succeeded, but she dealt us a fearsome blow."

"May each of the dead be a curse upon her spirit," Kiara spat. "But even though she is dead, her people will try again. I may not have your gift of sight, but I know in my bones this is the first of many battles. Accolon still lives, and the men of Rheged will not stop until they bring the Saxons to their knees. Luckily for us, I am alive and so is Cinon. If I can convince Evina that she needs us to rebuild her army so that we can fight another day, we may yet live to see victory."

We were silent for a while, the sounds of forest animals and birds a calming backdrop to our sobering thoughts. Finally, I broke the quiet. "You said they were going to burn the bodies. Can I not return to see Lancelot is properly attended to?"

Kiara swallowed hard. "I am afraid they have not recovered his body, nor Morgan's. We fear the Saxons took them as prizes to celebrate their victory."

Aggrivane put his arm around me, no doubt intending to comfort me, but I shrugged him off. The fury I hadn't even realized had been building inside me unleashed like a broken dam.

"Will I never get to say goodbye to anyone I love?" I shouted, tears streaming down my face. "Why is that finality always denied to me? My mother, Arthur, you." I looked at Aggrivane. "Now Lancelot. Everyone I love dies, and I never get the chance to bid them farewell." Sobs racked my body, rendering me mute. Kiara reached out to me, but I shrank away, lowering myself painfully into a ball on the ground.

"I will make sure a memorial stone is erected for him in our homeland," Kiara said. "He was much loved by our people and died defending them. They would never let anything less stand. It is not much, I know, but at least he will be remembered."

She was right. So many of our best had gone home to our ancestors with nothing to mark that they'd ever lived.

I wiped my tears. "Thank you. I'm sorry for my outburst."

Aggrivane helped me to stand. "I'm surprised it didn't happen sooner. You have more strength than me. I would have broken down the moment I remembered yesterday's events."

Kiara glanced at the sun. "I am sorry to leave you, but I must be getting back to camp."

I hobbled over to her and embraced her with my one good arm. I knew I would never see her again. "Thank you for everything. You were my first true friend in that land, and I will never forget the kindness you have shown me. Will you do me one last favor?"

"Name it."

"On the night Cinon, Corag, and Ailith were chosen as our battle leaders, I promised myself I would protect Ailith's little sister. Since I cannot return to watch over her, will you take special care of her and do your best to see her grow into a strong woman?"

Kiara nodded solemnly. "Of course. I will make it my goal to foster her whole generation in Ailith's memory."

I hugged her one more time, squeezing tight. "You are truly a blessing. Watch yourself around Evina. She is likely to take out her wrath on you since I will not be there to abuse."

Kiara waved away my concerns. "I can handle her. I thank you as well for your friendship. We are blood bonded, remember? We will always be in one another's hearts." She nodded to Aggrivane. "Take care of her."

"I will."

Kiara mounted and set off toward Catraeth. As she faded from sight, all the strength left my body, as though she was taking it with her.

Holding on to Aggrivane with my good arm, I staggered toward the tent. "You are limping. Are you injured as well?"

"No. Just the remnant of my brush with death that I will nurse for the rest of my days," he said with a wry smile.

"What happened? I saw you die. How is it that you are here?"

Aggrivane helped me onto the blanket bed. "That is a story for another time. You need to rest. We should be safe here for a few days." He kissed the top of my head. "Sleep now."

⚬⚬⚬

I lay in my bed, staring at the tip of the tent, completely hollow, for several days. I had no concept of the passage of time, only of the pain in my heart and of what I had lost. My mind kept replaying Lancelot's final moments, guilt goading that I could have done more to save him. I cried so hard my abdomen ached and the tears coursing down my cheeks formed chapped lines that stung with every fresh wave of grief. I recreated my encounter with Lancelot from every vantage, even trying to put myself in Elga's place—what would I have done if I could have abducted her husband?—but no matter now I turned it around, the outcome was the same. Aggrivane was right; Elga would have killed Lancelot no matter what I did. Now I had to learn to live with his loss.

For his part, Aggrivane let me be, interrupting my mourning only to change my bandages or to feed me soup. I was nearly as incapacitated as I had been when Malegant broke all ten of my fingers. I wanted to believe Aggrivane's ministrations were genuine, but the part of me that was still deeply wounded by his betrayal of Lancelot and me to Arthur expected him to deliver me to the Saxons at any moment. After all, he *had* been posing as one of Elga's guards. It wasn't so great a stretch of the imagination to think he could still be working for their side.

The rational part of my mind knew that was ridiculous. He had helped me escape capture by the Saxons. That should have put an end to all of my suspicions, but in my grief, I needed someone to take the blame for Lancelot's death. Elga was dead, so I couldn't rail at her; Aggrivane made for a convenient substitute. I was grateful to him, yes. Without his intervention, I would be dead. But that didn't mean I had to trust him.

I startled awake in the gray hours before dawn, unsure of what had woken me. I strained to make out any movement in the pitiful light cast by the embers. Nothing seemed out of place, so I stilled myself and listened. Above the sound of Aggrivane's breathing came the forlorn howl of a dog. I froze, every muscle on tense alert. Could it be one of Theodoric's hounds, finally caught up to us? Or was it merely the vocalization of one owned by a nearby farmer?

I gently shook Aggrivane. "Wake up. Wake up."

He came alert slowly, rubbing his face with the heel of his hand. "What is it?"

"I hear a dog. I think the Saxons may have found us."

Wait. What if that was why Aggrivane had insisted we stay here? What if he was waiting for the Saxons to catch up? We couldn't be too far from Catraeth. I felt the color drain from my face.

Aggrivane sat up, ears perking to pick up the sound. "Are you unwell? You are pale as a bone." He listened for a long time. The dog called twice more, then was silent. "We should pack up and move. You need the services of a true healer."

"What I need is time," I protested. Nothing could be done for my broken arm or my hip except wait for them to heal. As for my other arm and the relatively minor cuts and abrasions on the rest of my body, those were nothing that could not be solved with a mixture of yarrow and other herbs. Even with a sore arm, I could make such a poultice. But more than that, I needed time to trust him again and time for my shattered heart to knit.

Aggrivane dipped a rag into the last of the wash water and cleaned my face. "Time is something we may have none of or all we wish, depending on what we do next. Hold still." He grabbed my chin with his thumb and forefinger to keep me from fidgeting.

"I may not be able to lift a spoon, but I am capable of cleaning myself, in case you hadn't noticed."

"Not without difficulty," he pointed out. "Besides, I miss touching you."

My heart warmed, but I turned away. "Aggrivane…"

He turned my face back toward him and continued stroking my skin. "I know. This is all very sudden for you. I am not suggesting anything. It was simply a statement."

I glared at him. "It was more than that. Please, be patient. I have not yet grieved my last love, much less come to terms with your return."

He plunged his hands into the bucket before splashing water over his face and hair. "Fair enough. I will treat you only as a friend until you tell me otherwise." He puttered around the small tent, gathering up the few supplies. "So where should we go now?"

It was a good question. The world as we had known it when last we were together had completely changed. As Kiara had said, heading north was not an option. "What about going to Lothian?"

Aggrivane shook his head. "Gawain and my mother do not know I still live, and I fear the shock would kill her. I wish them to live out their days in peace. Besides, Evina knows you came to her from Traprain Law. She would think to look for you there."

He had a point. But how was I to know where she would and would not search for me? Or even if she would make the effort? Was that to be my destiny then, always on the run, always shrinking from shadows, too scared to settle down? I hadn't stopped running since Elga let me leave Camelot, and I was fed up. If all the future held for me was looking over my shoulder, then I would have been better off if Morgan hadn't taken the blow meant for me.

Aggrivane packed up our meager belongings and saw to the horses while I sat, useless and restless, as we discussed our options. We could not journey south, as that would take us into the heart of Saxon territory. Constantine controlled much of the land beyond that, and we were uncertain whether he would consider us friend or foe.

"We could always appeal to his mercy. He may be kind to us if you renounce your role as queen," Aggrivane said.

"The last thing I want to do is take that chance. I am tired of being the prize in the constant quest for power. I do not think he would allow us to live in peace."

There was a small chance we could return to Gwynedd, but neither of us knew who held power in Northgallis now. Since my cousin Bran had died in the last battle with Constantine, I did not even know if Northgallis was an autonomous kingdom or part of Constantine's burgeoning empire. Anywhere farther south was out because that was his base. But there was one place even Evina couldn't find.

The next time Aggrivane came into the tent, I took his hand and gave it a gentle squeeze. "Are you ready to go home?"

He looked at me, confused.

"To Avalon. It is the only safe place left."

"Are you certain they will allow me to enter?"

"They allowed you to cross their borders once. Why not now, after you have spent your life defending one of their own? You are still loyal to the old ways, are you not?"

Aggrivane nodded.

I fought a sudden, unexpected, and perplexing urge to kiss him. "Then they will allow you in." We lapsed into silence until a thought flashed through my mind. "What ever happened to the Grail?"

Morgan had called for it in the chaos after Camlann. Had it been used to try to heal Arthur? No. If it had, he would have lived.

Aggrivane blinked at me, having trouble following my change of topic. "I truly do not know. I think it is still there in its castle. Why?"

"If the last few years have taught me anything, it is that this land and its people are no longer worthy of it. We need to return it to Avalon."

"I don't know if returning to Camelot is wise," he protested.

"Why not? Everyone who wished us harm is dead."

"But it has surely decayed. Are you sure you do not wish to preserve your memories of it?"

I smiled without warmth. "My memories of that place are of my trial and burning. They are nothing a little ruin will harm."

Aggrivane sighed. "Surely there are others, brighter memories." He tied the last bag onto his horse's saddle. "But I have known you long enough to know when to yield. Camelot it is."

⁓⊙⊙⁓

The journey across Britain was slow. We were careful to avoid the main cities unless Aggrivane knew for certain someone he could trust was living there. Otherwise, we begged charity from farmers and shepherds, often sleeping in their barns, in the tent, or under the stars, as the weather allowed. In many places, we were welcomed warmly by virtue of my priestess mark, but in others, it was best to keep it hidden under the folds of my veil. We told no one our real names. Yet again, I posed as Corinna, and Aggrivane adopted the name of Declan, a tradition in his family as well.

One night, as we were lying in a grassy field, gazing at the stars, our bellies full of stew made from the hare Aggrivane trapped and the vegetables I saved from the last housewife's generosity, I found the courage to ask Aggrivane the question that had been niggling at me since I first saw his face. "I saw you die on the battlefield at Camlann. How is it possible you are here?"

He turned his head to look at me and took my hand. "I will never get used to that sight of yours. I did die, or at least I thought I did. When I closed my eyes on that plain, I thought my next sight would be of my ancestors in the Otherworld. But the next thing I knew, there was a hard boot in my side. The Saxons and their allies were checking to be sure we were all dead. Those who were not were either captured or killed, depending on how useful they assessed us to be."

"You were captured?"

"No." His eyes took on a faraway look as he yielded to his memories. "They passed me by, thinking I was dead. But Morgan was also on the battlefield, administering help and mercy where she could. She saw that I had opened my eyes. Once the Saxons were gone, she dragged me off the battlefield and took me to a safe place to recover.

"I had no memory of who I was or what had happened for months. Yet every morning she was there, encouraging me to try, saying that 'there will come a day when she will need you.' I can only assume she had foreseen your near-death by Elga's blade and that I would rescue you."

That startled me. How long had she known? If she had foreseen before we met on the battlefield of Camlann that I would one day rely on Aggrivane for my life, why had she not told me he was alive? How long had she known she would suffer Elga's blade—and possibly give up her life—for me?

Great Goddess, protector of the priestesses of Avalon, send your protection to Morgan, daughter of the Lady of the Lake and the Archdruid. If she is still in the land of the living, minimize her pain and give her the strength and fortitude to heal. If her soul has passed beyond the veil, please grant her peace and richly reward her for her sacrifice.

I shook my head to clear it and forced my mind back to Aggrivane's story. "Morgan nursed you back to health?"

Aggrivane nodded. "And then some. My injuries were so bad, I had to learn how to eat all over again. How to walk. It was more than a year before I held a sword, much less re-learned what to do with it. You've seen my limp. Without Morgan, it would be the least of my worries." He shook his head. "I can honestly say I would be dead without her."

"So can I." I paused, lost in thought again. "How did you come to fight on the side of the Saxons?"

He looked away. "You have always said Morgan was a woman of two faces. I had grown used to regarding her as a kind healer, but after the Isle of Winds, she changed, revealing the cunning woman behind the mask. You see, Accolon's capture nearly broke her. So when she heard Accolon had offered me to the Saxons as potentially of more use than he was, she jumped at the chance to turn me over to them, hoping they would return him.

"In Din Gefron, Accolon took charge of me personally and spent the next several weeks explaining to me why it would be best to go along with what Elga wanted, as he was doing. The day he asked for my support was the most difficult of my life. By then, I knew Arthur and Mordred were dead, but I had heard nothing of you. I longed to know your fate and thought the best way of obtaining information would be to ally with a powerful ruler. As I had no in with Constantine and I knew my mother did not desire to be a power player in this latest struggle, I agreed, at least verbally, to change my alliance."

"But you said your mother did not know you were alive. How, why did Accolon go along with keeping your identity a secret?"

Aggrivane grimaced. "He believed that Lothian would be easier to overthrow if my parents were weakened with grief. If all of their sons were dead—and the future of their kingdom with them—then they would be more likely to cede their lands peacefully."

"But they did not. Gawain lived, and Anna supported our side at Catraeth."

"Indeed. I fear Lothian would have been Elga's next target, had she succeeded in killing you. As it stands, I do not know if they will attack now or simply wait for my mother to die. I pray it is the latter."

"That explains how you infiltrated the Saxons, but how did you get so close to Elga?"

"That was much easier than I expected. Word soon came of your role at Din Eidyn and then in Stirling. Elga knew I had betrayed you to Arthur and decided to use me as a spy to gain information on you. I told her only what would have been common knowledge to anyone watching the Votadini camps prepare, but it was enough. I have a feeling she intended to bait you using me, but when she realized Lancelot was your greater weakness, she changed tack."

My heart thudded, anticipating where his story was headed. I covered my face with my hands. "Please tell me you had nothing to do with his capture."

"I led them to the location of your camp, but I did nothing to aid in the act itself, I swear to you. Elga lured him by making it look as though we were scouts who would help him and his horse. I did not know what they were planning to do."

"Did Lancelot see you?"

"Yes. It was unavoidable. I think he died believing I'd betrayed him." Doubt must have shown on my face, for Aggrivane continued. "You will have to take me at my word. No proof exists that I can offer. I hope you know my heart well enough to understand that no matter what had passed between us before, I was grateful to Lancelot for rescuing you and taking care of you. In my sickbed, I had no way of knowing if you and I would see each other again. Why would I deny you his love when I could not guarantee I would be there to give you my own?"

Crickets sang their soothing lullaby in the silence that followed as we each mulled over his story. This night, with its beautiful weather and secret confessions, was so much like that of our first kiss in Avalon. Remembering that young man with his dreams of glory and peace, I had to believe in Aggrivane's innocence, no matter what misgivings my jaded heart might now possess.

"And Elga? You were helping her escape when Kiara and I found you?"

He looked away. "Yes. She wanted me out on the battlefield but did not trust that I would not turn coat when faced with my former compatriots. So she kept me behind with her. I was grateful, because it would have been hard to avoid killing or being killed when no one else knew I was not who I appeared to be."

Aggrivane was looking at the stars, as if reading his own story in them. "Elga knew she was in danger, regardless of the outcome of the battle. There was no question you would pursue her to your final breath for what she had done to Lancelot. Even if you fell before reaching her, there was a chance your men would still hunt her in your name. All I had to do was drive home that point, and her survival instincts overrode her considerable pride. The plan was to take the horses to a nearby Saxon convent until the skirmish was over."

I gasped. That was Mayda's convent, the one where I had sought refuge during Mordred's revolt. I explained to him about Mayda's fate after she'd tipped us off about Badon, my time at the convent, and how I came to Din Eidyn. "Elga may well have taken out her anger at me on her sister. It was something Mayda feared, and rightly."

"Well, now I am especially grateful you foiled our plan. You helped us avoid bloodshed no one knew was coming."

"So am I. How did you manage to continue your ruse when Kiara and I appeared?"

Aggrivane shrugged. "It was not that difficult, really. You and Elga were so intent on one another that your attention was not on me. All I had to do was play at taking on Kiara while my partner did all the real work. Once she dispatched him, I could already see the battle turning against you. I had to knock Kiara out, lest she think I was joining in the attack against you. She has a hard head, that one. As it was, I was too slow to stop Morgan. I was barely able to get to you in time…"

It was my turn to squeeze his hand. "But you did. That is what matters." I scooted toward him, allowing him to hold me for the first time since our reunion. "Things may never be as they once were between us, but there is no one else yet living I would rather spend the rest of my days with."

Aggrivane stiffened at the qualification in my statement. "I know I have much to make amends for. I will take whatever measure of affection you are willing to give."

The once gleaming, impregnable fortress of Camelot was a shell of its former glory. Judging from the trickle of people coming and going, it was still occupied, probably by Constantine's men who were keeping it warm for the day he conquered the entire island. I could only imagine the havoc wreaked inside, the toppled statues of the Pendragon dynasty in the council chambers, the burned-out labyrinth dedicated to gods in whom Constantine did not believe.

We avoided the main roads, not wishing to revisit the places that lived on in our memories or chance being recognized. Instead, we trod the winding coastal roads that led to the harbor. Few people were about, and many of the houses we passed were derelict, feral dogs, cats, and vermin coming and going from their open doors and windows in place of the merchants and tradesmen who used to live there. Rotten shutters hung haphazardly from windows. Thatched roofs went unmended, gaping holes letting in all sorts of weather and rendering whole buildings uninhabitable.

Here and there, there were still signs of life. A stubborn baker cooked his fragrant wares, and a steady tink-tink-tink announced the garrison was keeping the smithy busy, but it was more a sight for sore eyes in the abandoned capital than an expected part of daily life.

When we turned down one street, we were greeted by an unexpected view of the sea. A whole swath of buildings, an entire neighborhood it seemed, had burned to ash, the blackened hulls staring at us like the unseeing eyes of the dead.

Aggrivane whistled. "So it is true. Huh. I thought it was just a tale spun by the victors."

I stopped, facing him. "What was?"

He pointed at the remnants of the street in front of us. "It was said that after Camlann, those loyal to Arthur and Mordred joined forces to try to destroy Camelot so that no one else could ever use it as their seat of power. Tales of the city burning circulated for days, telling of an inferno unlike anything that had been seen for generations. Ultimately, the arsonists did not succeed in burning down the city, but the story of their attempt was lauded as nothing short of heroic."

I tried to orient myself and recall what had once stood here. Though I did not know every inch of the city by heart, I prided myself on knowing most of it. "This was a residential area." I recalled the home of a tailor on the corner of one street. I had helped his daughter give birth to twins. "Over there is where Sobian lived for a while with her girls." I nodded toward a square patch of land that had once held a fine two-story home. "But what I don't understand is if they truly wanted to do damage, why did they not set the castle on fire too?"

Aggrivane pointed. "I think they tried."

I followed his direction to one of the massive square turrets that had not been visible from the main road. It too bore the indelible stain of soot, but that was from the destruction before Camlann. Down further, one entire section of the wall was gone. Judging from the pattern of scattered stones on the hillside below, it had likely exploded from the heat. Those that remained were unmended, as though forgotten and unloved.

Tears filled my eyes as I surveyed the damage done to my beloved home, to the city on which two generations of High Kings had placed their hopes and dreams, their vision for a unified country, the dream I had shared with them through many years and against many dangers, from invaders to corrupt hearts. A dream that was not to be.

"It really is over, isn't it?" I asked.

Aggrivane placed a consoling arm around me as I wept. "I am afraid so. The world around us is changing, giving way to a new power structure, one in which our ideals no longer have meaning."

I looked at him, my heart cleaved by despair. "Then why did we bother? What was it all for?"

"You bothered because you believed you could make our country and our people better, and you did, for many years. You and Arthur allowed generations of Britons to live in peace. You turned away the Saxons and preserved our ways. What you did is so much more than most people ever dare to imagine doing. You acted out of the urgings of your heart, following the will of the gods as you saw it. But all ages come to an end. It is the way of things."

We walked to the water's edge in silence, each wrapped in our own thoughts. Aggrivane was right; returning here had been a mistake. Everywhere I looked, I saw Camelot as it used to be for a split second before my mind registered the change.

The tide was out, and Aggrivane calculated we had about an hour before it would return, so it was safe to cross the causeway leading to the Grail Castle on foot. As we picked our way across the slimy stones, I looked for signs that it too had been looted or suffered abuse at the hands of angry mobs or those eager to get their hands on its precious treasure. But from the outside, it appeared not to have suffered as the town and fortress had. Perhaps the people had been too respectful or too superstitious to harm the castle.

Then again, perhaps I was wrong. I stopped inside the outer gate. Where once there had been a garden and outbuildings for the upkeep of the castle and those who lived within, now there was a graveyard, at least a dozen headstones marking mounded graves.

"What evil has been done here?" I asked, flitting from stone to stone, seeking to know how so many had died in such a holy place in such a short period of time.

"I did not hear of a plague," Aggrivane mused as he scanned the names memorialized in stone. "Such news usually travels far and wide."

I fell to my knees at the foot of the graves with the two tallest monument stones. "Oh no. No, no, no!"

The names Galahad and Peredur inscribed on them. Both bore an image of the Grail and recounted how the two men had found the Grail, heroically defeated those who rose against them, and brought their sacred charge back to Camelot. Thereafter, they became priests and guarded it with their lives.

"So that is it. They died protecting the Grail. No doubt they are in heaven with their god." Aggrivane's voice came from right behind me, but I paid him no heed.

Just when I thought I had no one, save Aggrivane, left to lose, no more tears to cry, this happened. I looked at him. "I do not know how much more of this I can bear." I felt like a towel long ago wrung threadbare, with only the slightest, thinnest of stitching holding me together.

"Do not grieve for them," came a female voice a few paces away.

"Rejoice. They are the martyrs of the Grail, men who shed their blood for the good of the land, just as their Christ gave his life to save others."

I recognized the voice before I looked up. It was Mona.

I stood, embracing her at once. "And you, how do you yet live?" I stepped back, eyes drinking in her silver hair and dancing eyes. Her face was wrinkled in all the usual places, but she maintained the tranquility of a priestess.

"I could ask you the same." Her smile was as radiant as my first day on Avalon. "The Goddess willed it. That is all I can say. It is not for me to question."

I hugged her tightly. "How have you borne it all these years? You spent your childhood dreaming repeatedly of death and destruction on the isle for which you were named, only to witness equal depravity here."

Her smile was tender now. "It was my fate. Long ago, Argante warned me that my dreams had purpose, even though they seemed nothing more than a cruel joke of the gods at the time. Do you remember that winter night by the fire when we were young and I repeated Argante's advice that to know the past was to be able to change the future?"

I nodded, recalling how we'd sat in front of the fire in the House of Nine in the dark of night while snow fell outside the window. She was in my arms, weeping, terrified from yet another nightmare of the pillage of the isle of Mona. She said Argante had recently told her that her dreams marked her as special, as powerful.

"Later, during my initiation, I had an experience that revealed to me my vocation as the Grail Maiden. I have known from that moment that it was connected to my dreams. It was not until the fall of Arthur and destruction of Camelot that I understood why. I cannot tell you the pain it caused me to know that all these good men"— she gestured, indicating the dead around us—"innocent men, would lose their lives just like the Druids and priestesses on the holy isle of Mona, and for the same reason—the desire for power and control. When the time came, I did what I could to defend them, somehow knowing I would escape unharmed, as would the Grail, for I was its sworn protector. I was as helpless to stop the bloodshed here as I was in my dreams, doomed to be a spectator once again. But I tell you this. These men fulfilled the fate laid out for them with more courage and valor than I have seen in any knight. They are truly worthy of the title of heroes."

I gazed around again, seeing not a drab place of mourning but a hall of heroes, a fellowship united in faith and purpose. Tears once again sprang to my eyes, but this time, they were of pride and joy in having known such courageous men. I sat back down, remembering the first time I saw Galahad in Elaine's arms, grateful I had had the opportunity to watch him grow into a virtuous young man, then a fine priest at Camelot.

I recalled Peredur as a young boy at our home in Northgallis, remembering with startling clarity the moment he gave me his favorite toy, a carved wooden dog—the one Mona and I had shared to ward off our personal fears as acolytes on Avalon.

I dug around in the pouch at my waist and removed the toy dog.

"Bricriu!" Mona cried with joy. "Oh, you truly are one of Ellen's own." Her eyes welled with tears as she stroked the wood, worn smooth with time and the attention of many fingertips.

I looked at her, feeling once again like a girl on Avalon. "I think he has done his service, do you agree?"

"I do," she answered in a tremulous voice.

"Then he should rest here with Peredur, who was, after all, his master."

Mona took from her belt the silver scythe that all Grail maidens carried and held it out to Aggrivane, who wiped his eyes and took it. As he hacked a small hole into the ground at the base of Peredur's memorial stone, I realized that Aggrivane was also grieving the loss of two of his fellow soldiers, members of the Combrogi with whom he had fought in battle and with whom he'd celebrated in times of peace. My stomach clenched. I had been so selfish, I had not been able to see his pain.

I took his hand. "Aggrivane, I am so sorry. I was so wrapped up in my own grief that I failed to recognize yours. Please forgive me."

He squeezed my hand. "There is nothing to forgive. I prefer to pay my respects in private anyway."

Mona joined her hand with mine, and together we knelt to bury Bricriu.

"Thank you, Peredur, for such a special gift. At an age far before reason, you followed the prompting of the gods to bestow this gift upon us. Throughout your life, you continued to follow that same divine urging, which ultimately led you to the Grail and to this place. Your life was one of love and service, to your king and to your god. Please know you are loved and your sacrifice does not go unremembered," I said.

After a few moments of silence, Mona stood. "You have come for the Grail, yes? I will accompany it and you back to Avalon." Seeing my astonishment, she tapped the faded crescent between her brows. "I knew you were coming."

⁓ᴏᴈ ᴊᴏ⁓

Inside the Grail Castle, all was quiet and still, seemingly undisturbed by the violence that beat at its walls and had taken so many lives. I had to stop and hold on to one of the stone pillars to catch my balance because the sense of repeating this moment was so strong. Only the last time I was there, I had been in pursuit of Bishop Maris, who intended to steal the Grail and sell it to the highest bidder in Brittany. Now, we were about to return it to its home in Avalon.

Mona approached the pedestal with great reverence. Kneeling, she touched her right thumb to her forehead, lips, and heart. Then she prostrated herself completely before her sacred charge. Feeling the solemnity of the moment, I knelt, bowing my head. Out of the corner of my eye, I saw Aggrivane do the same.

Mona whispered a few words of quiet prayer not meant for my ears. What must it be like for her, knowing her time as Grail Maiden was coming to an end, that she had fulfilled her vocation? It must be mixture of joy at a job well done, grief for mistakes made that could not be undone, fear of the unknown, and excitement at the anticipation of what was yet to come. I understood because it was exactly what I was feeling. Just as we had been scared initiates together, we were facing the culmination of our duties as priestesses together as well. *Thank you, God and Goddess, for giving me a lifelong companion to experience such things alongside.*

When I opened my eyes, Mona was holding the Grail. In one hand, she held the same shimmering golden cloth in which it had been veiled when I first saw it.

"Just as we were among the first, we are the last three mortals to behold the Grail outside of the sacred isle of Avalon. Though the people of this realm served it well and faithfully for many years, they have proven themselves unworthy to have such a treasure in its midst. Thus, as its guardian, I remove it from the land of men and return it to its hallowed resting place until such time as it is again called forth by the will of the gods."

Having thus spoken, she broke two cruets over it, one of clear liquid—water from the holy springs of Avalon—and one of crimson. "This is the blood of every Grail Maiden who has ever served this holy relic. Blessed and purified, may it be purged of any defilement brought about by the hearts and minds of men, and sanctified for whatever role the gods decree for it next." She drank the contents of the cup and placed its golden veil over it.

After one more bow to the former altar, she joined us. "Let us go from here. There is only one thing remaining to do."

⚬⚬

We stood on the shore, facing the Grail Castle. To anyone watching from above, we were simply three onlookers curious about the strange fortified island, but this moment was so much more.

"Many people attempted to steal the Grail in the dark days after Camlann," Mona said. "I watched from the shadows as man and woman alike—rich, poor, Christian, Druid, Saxon, and Briton—attempted to take the cup. But it refused to budge from its place of veneration. Just as it knew our hearts when we drank from it and assumed the most appropriate shape for us to understand, so too did it know the hearts of those who came to it. That is why only I was able to remove it. I suspect the two of you would have been able as well, in my absence. So that no trace of the Grail remains except in the memories of this generation, there is one last thing we must do."

Mona reverently placed the Grail in Aggrivane's hands. "I ask you, as one who studied with Merlin and has conducted his life with honor, to please guard this while we work."

Aggrivane looked at her with astonishment. Except for during two ceremonies with Arthur, the only people to have the privilege of holding the Grail were Galahad, Peredur, Mona, and Bishop Marius. He fell to one knee and bowed his head. "I would be honored, my lady."

Mona took my hand. "I have the power to do this myself, but I would much like you to join me. In this action, may you find peace and closure for all the many things you have suffered and those you have lost."

We each took a deep breath and closed our eyes. I sent my

consciousness downward, searching until I felt the faint thrum of the Tor, a heartbeat I could always hear if I listened, no matter how far my body was from its source.

Mona chanted in the ancient language that predated Avalon, her voice high and clear. When she squeezed my hand, I added my voice to hers, the words bubbling from my lips of their own accord, with no conscious thought on my part. My vision filled with images of angry seas, of waves growing higher and higher until they engulfed a city I did not recognize. This was the predecessor to Mona, to Avalon, the isle that had been lost beneath the waves many ages before. Then my eyes snapped open, and I beheld the sea churning, the tide lapping at the tops of the outer walls of the Grail Castle.

As we continued to chant, the wind howled, whipping up the caps of the waves until they spilled over the walls and into the castle. Rain poured down in sheets, raising the water levels even higher, until the whole castle groaned and collapsed in on itself, swallowed up by the waves in a matter of heartbeats.

Mona squeezed my hand again, and I fell silent. The chant ended on a sharp note, whose finality was unmistakable. As the echo of her voice faded away, the winds calmed, the sky cleared, and the seas settled. Within moments, our clothes were dry, as was the ground around us, as though nothing had ever happened.

I gazed out over the sea at where the Grail Castle had stood on its island. There was no sign it had ever existed. Somehow, I knew that upon the next change of tide, the causeway would be gone as well, to live on only in the astonished memories of those who would recall the strange storm and tell tales to their grandchildren of the fortress that had once guarded the holiest of treasures.

I turned away, another chapter of my life having come to a close. As we walked away from the coastline and the city, my heart lifted and I smiled. The gnawing grief that had held me in its sway was gone, as was the anger I felt toward Evina and Elga, all of the penned-up pain of my life since Mordred had caught Lancelot and I saying our farewells. It was as though years' worth of healing had taken place in the space of an hour. Somehow, in a way I would never be able to explain, the Grail had worked its magic to heal me one last time.

Chapter Twenty-One

When the mists parted, Ailis, Viviane's daughter and the current Lady of Avalon, was waiting for us, along with Helene, who had stayed in Avalon after Camlann and was now a second-degree acolyte clothed in green. For a moment, she reminded me so much of Morgan when I first came to Avalon that it seemed time had rewound itself.

But then Ailis took my hands and I was brought back to the present. I ran to her, embracing her as though she were my own mother. Aggrivane genuflected, touching his thumb to his forehead, lips, and heart.

"Welcome, beloved daughters," she said to Mona and me. "And to our brother in peace."

Mona bowed to her and removed the Grail from the sack she carried. "Holy Mother, it is done. I return to Avalon the gift the Goddess so graciously gave to us so many years before."

The Lady nodded. "You have served your calling well, my daughter. Return it to the hidden temple from which it came, that it may slumber there until it is again called forth in another age." She brushed Mona's cheek softly, lovingly. "Then take your place among your sisters and live out your days in peace, secure in the knowledge you have done all she asked and more."

With a small curtsy, Mona turned and headed toward the Tor, Helene trailing at her heels, ready to serve.

"Morgan must be so proud," I said wistfully.

Ailis smiled. "Helene will be Lady of the Lake after me. I have seen it."

The Lady took our hands in hers. "I know what you have suffered. There is no recompense I can give, but I can promise you the protection of Avalon for as long as you shall desire it."

"Thank you, Lady."

"You must be tired from your journey. Come, let us take some refreshment. There is much you should know."

She led us to a small patio outside her quarters, overlooking the orchard. As we drank water from the springs and nibbled on fresh bread, I watched the priestesses at their work. Some tended the gardens, others taught at the center of clusters of students, while many of the older women turned spinning wheels or tended looms on patios similar to ours. There was one bright patch of hair I kept expecting to see among them but could not find anywhere.

"You seek your sister, Morgan, do you not?" asked the Lady, who had been watching me.

"I do. The last I knew, she lay dying within a fort far from here. I hoped someone had saved her, brought her here to be healed. Was my hope in vain?"

"No. She is here. But you look in the wrong place. Morgan was true to her word and stayed with Arthur until the very end. He is buried here, you know."

I choked back a sob. I had not expected to find him buried here, especially since he was a Christian. "I did not know."

"You may visit him, if you like."

I glanced at Aggrivane, unsure how he would feel. He nodded. "Please."

I took a step to follow her but paused when Aggrivane whispered in my ear, "I would like to pay my respects, unless you would like a private moment."

In answer, I took his arm and led us both in the Lady's wake.

She spoke to us over her shoulder as we walked. "Arthur was unconscious when Morgan arrived here with him. Despite our best ministrations, he never again woke."

We walked on and on, through the plains and over rugged land that led into the mountains. I had never been this close to the edge of the mists before. The Tor was still visible behind us, but it looked much smaller than it did up close. Still imposing in its shocking grandeur against the surrounding lake and plains, it seemed more like a small hill than a mighty monument. When I stepped over the crest of a ridge of rocks, a shiver coursed down my spine.

The Lady noticed. "We have passed beyond the veil of Avalon. This land belongs to the Christian priests, for Morgan desired to honor Arthur's wishes to be buried on Christian soil."

From out of the mists, a small wattle-and-dub building emerged, its roof crudely made of sticks that were hardly adequate to keep out the rain. In the center, where the branches ended at the chimney hole, a carved wooden cross was fastened with twine to the sticks around it. On both sides were flowering hawthorn trees taller than the building.

So it was real. Legends I had heard all my life said that this was the building Joseph of Arimathea had constructed after he brought the Grail to Avalon's shores from Jesus's desert homeland in the east. Christians believed the hawthorn trees grew from where Joseph sank his staff into the ground and that their miraculous bloom in the middle of winter occurred to honor the birth of Christ.

The hide flap covering the doorway fluttered, and from inside emerged a stooped man dressed in a coarse, gray wool tunic, his bald pate and long beard marking him as a follower of Joseph. His smile warmed my heart. "Blessings, my brother and sisters."

The Lady returned his greeting with a small bow. "As to you, Father Edgar." She gestured toward us. "These are friends of our departed High King. They wish to pay their respects."

Father Edgar stepped forward and took Aggrivane's hands, saying something to him I could not hear. Then he was in front of me, taking my hands like a long-lost friend. I curtsied to show my respect for his faith and his position.

He beamed, revealing naked gums. "I may be old and my eyes rheumy, but I know the face of my queen. It is I who should bow to you. Welcome to the chapel of St. Joseph, my lady. If I may be of assistance, simply call. In the meantime, I will let you conduct your business in peace." He gingerly settled himself into a rickety chair next to the door and turned his eyes to the mountains, muttering Latin prayers to himself.

The Lady pointed at a clearing between two yew trees. Protruding from its base was a black stone cross. Beyond it was a mound of earth, most certainly Arthur's grave.

"When Arthur breathed his last, for a long time, Morgan refused to believe he was dead, insisting he slept still. It was only when he was buried that she accepted the truth. She grieved hard for him, but her grief was not protracted, for she soon felt a longing to return to the world." She watched me carefully, as though anticipating my every reaction. "We never thought we would see her again. Then several weeks ago, she returned to us, suffering from grave complications in the wake of a nasty wound to the abdomen she appeared to have bound up herself. She said she wished to make amends with Avalon so that she could die in the peace of both our faith and that of the Christians."

As we approached the clearing, I found that the cross had markings inscribed upon it. I narrowed my eyes, but it took me a few moments to recognize them as Latin letters inscribed in the tall block Roman style. As I struggled to make them out, Aggrivane chuckled.

"She got the last word after all," he said, admiration clear in his voice.

I furrowed my brow at him, but he pointed back at the cross. Only when I finally translated the words did Aggrivane's reaction make sense.

Here lies the great King Arthur, with his first wife.

"His first wife? Am I reading that correctly?" I turned to the Lady. "There must be some mistake. *I* was his first wife."

She shook her head. "No, not according to the laws of Avalon. Arthur laid with Morgan in the Sacred Marriage. That made her his wife in spirit long before he wed you in law."

I opened my mouth, but no words would come forth, only copious tears. After so long, our battle was over. Morgan had died in the winning and now, thanks to this inscription, everyone would know he had loved her long before I became his queen. She would lie beside Arthur forever, gaining in death what she had so longed for in life.

Aggrivane slipped an arm around me. "Do you know what this means?" He kissed the top of my head.

I shook my head.

He placed his hands on my hips, turning me to face him. "It means by the laws of Avalon, I was your first husband."

I looked into his eyes, my tears slowing then ceasing. He was right. We had been joined all along by a bond more immovable than the mountains.

"The Goddess puts all things to rights in the end," the Lady said, stepping back so we could absorb the meaning of this in private.

"Do you think we might one day be buried together?" he asked, his deep brown eyes aflame with hope.

I gazed at him, his smile melting my heart and easing my lingering doubt and pain by degrees, just as the dawn chases away the fog. So many events separated us from our first embrace on this isle. In the years between, I had won and lost his love, become queen, taken a lover and been betrayed by him, as well as my husband and the boy I considered a son, won and lost my ancestral tribe, faced down and forgiven the greatest of my enemies, only to find Aggrivane once again. Through it all, one constant remained—the soft voice of the Goddess whispering her will in my heart. Now she was telling me the time for grief and strife was over, that I could finally embrace this man without fear and without guilt and love the one I had known all along belonged to me.

In answer, I slipped my hand into his. "I do."

I rested my head on his shoulder, overwhelmed by a sense of rightness and completion. It would take time to know him anew, to let my broken heart heal and let my love for Lancelot fade enough so that I could give Aggrivane a permanent place in my heart once again. But even now, the chambers of my heart shifted to make room for him as the small, secret place I had kept for only him unlocked like a long-neglected tomb. Someday, when the sunlight and breezes of Avalon had finally chased away the cobwebs of grief, it would swell to embrace him wholly.

For once, time was not a barrier. After all, we had the rest of our lives.

Before You Go . . .

Thank you for reading this book. If you enjoyed it, please leave a review on Amazon and/or Goodreads. Word of mouth is crucial for authors to succeed, so even if your review is only a line or two, it would be a huge help.

To be the first to find out about future books and insider information, please sign up for my newsletter. You will only be contacted when there is news, and your address will never be shared.

Also by Nicole Evelina:

- *Daughter of Destiny* (Guinevere's Tale Book 1) (Arthurian historical fantasy)
- *Camelot's Queen* (Guinevere's Tale Book 2) (Arthurian historical fantasy)
- *Mistress of Legend* (Guinevere's Tale Book 3) (Arthurian historical fantasy)
- *Been Searching for You* (contemporary romance/women's fiction)
- *Madame Presidentess* (historical fiction)
- *The Once and Future Queen: Guinevere in Arthurian Legend* (non-fiction)

Please visit me at **nicoleevelina.com** to learn more.

❧◦❧

I love interacting with my readers! Feel free to contact me on Twitter, Facebook, Goodreads, Pinterest, or by email. You can also send snail mail to: PO Box 2021, Maryland Heights, MO 63043.

BOOK 1: DAUGHTER OF DESTINY

Guinevere came into my head in the fall of 1999, when I was a junior in college. I had read Marion Zimmer Bradley's *The Mists of Avalon* the winter before and, though I loved the book, I really disliked her portrayal of Guinevere. So I sought out other books about her. This led me to Parke Godwin's *Beloved Exile*, which made me wonder what happened to Guinevere before and after her life with Arthur.

I can still remember the moment Guinevere first took up residence in my head. I was sitting in a quiet stone walkway on an otherwise unremarkable morning of the fall semester when she told me she had a story to tell, one different from anything anyone else has said. It was in that moment we struck up a bargain and I decided to write my own version. Or at least that's what I tell myself. This never really was my story; it's always been Guinevere's. She's been calling the shots from the very first word.

Arthurian legend is a tough subject to write about because we don't know what is true and what is not. The Dark Ages are so named for a reason. We really don't have a lot of historical data to look at when trying to reconstruct them. What we do have, works from Ven. Bede and a Welsh monk called Nennius, are at best, a wild pottage of myth, history and legend. Separating fact from fiction is difficult, but that's also what makes it enjoyable for the historical fiction author.

Scholars and historians have been debating for years whether or not Arthur ever existed. If he did, he most certainly had at least one wife (Celtic law allowed for polygamy), and hence, some form of Guinevere would have existed as well. (Most other characters have been added over time as the stories evolved.) But in the end, does it really matter? Not to me. The legend that has arisen from the idea of Arthur has inspired countless generations, and I daresay will continue to do so. While I choose to believe that a real flesh and blood person inspired these stories, I do not ask you to believe the same, only to go with me on this fantastic voyage to the past, and I hope in so doing, learn a little about yourself. If you do, I have done my job well.

I can only separate fact versus fiction for you in the confines of this book. It began with a strong female character and so that is where I will begin my apologetics. As you read this, please remember I am not a historian (nor do I play one on TV). I am a storyteller who uses history to shape the views and customs of the world in which my stories are set.

The Picts and the Tribes of the North

The Picts are a large group of tribes who lived in the highlands of Scotland. Corinna and Guinevere descend from the British tribes directly to the south of them, those who lived between Antonine Wall and Hadrian's Wall – the Votadini, Selgovae, Novantae, and Damnonii (there were other, smaller tribes in the area, but I'm simplifying by confining the discussion to these main four).

In the post-Roman period the kingdom began to be called the Gododdin and its inhabitants the Men of the North. Little is known of the culture of these tribes, so I have taken liberties in conflating what we know about the Picts with the ways of their southern neighbors.

Corinna, Guinevere and Isolde are inspired by a matriarchal ideal that may or may not be fact. I'll let the historians hash that one out. What is true is that the Picts passed tribal leadership on through a system of matrilineal succession, meaning that the noble bloodline was counted through the female line. So if a man and woman marry but have no heirs, when the man dies, the woman's nephew (his sister's son) would inherit. We see this in *Daughter of Destiny* in Lot's eldest son Gawain being Arthur's heir, after Lot. This is because Arthur and Ana are brother and sister. This is not the same as matrilineal primogeniture, in which titles are passed from mother to daughter to the exclusion of sons, which I have chosen to have Corinna and Isolde's mother practice. There is some possibility that the Picts and the Irish (and perhaps the Celts at an earlier time in history) practiced this, but to-date evidence has not born this out.

It is true, however, that the Picts allowed their women to fight in battle. How and to what extent is lost in the pages of history. But I have allowed this fact to color the personalities of my Votadini women and give them a strength, independence and vitality that I personally believe their historical counterparts would have possessed.

Although the story of Leodgrance and Corinna is a product of my imagination, the kingdom of Gwynedd really was considered a safe haven for the Votadini tribe during this time period.

Scholars debate who was responsible for such an unusual move, so I have chosen to have that role fall to Vortigern for purposes of my story.

Corinna's burial customs are based in Pictish lore and the wording of her headstone is consistent with Roman tradition.

BRITAIN

The war-torn world in which Guinevere was raised is also based in fact. During the late fifth century, Britain was struggling to find its feet after the withdrawal of the Roman Empire. That old tribal infighting would resurface is not much of a stretch of the imagination. The influx of Saxon invaders and the raids of the western coast by the Irish are also painfully real, as was the event under Governor Paulinus that came to be known as the Rape of Mona. There is even some evidence that Vortigern could have been a historical figure.

AVALON

Avalon has long been associated with Arthurian legend. Geoffrey of Monmouth was one of the first to refer to Avallo in his *Historia Regum Britanniae* (c. 1136) and he called Avalon the Isle of Apples in the *Vita Merlini* (c. 1150). Not long after, in 1191, a group of monks on Glastonbury Tor "discovered" a grave and headstone that supposedly marked the final resting place of the great King Arthur and his wife, Guinevere. While that story has largely been discredited, it cemented the association of Glastonbury with the legendary isle of Avalon to which Arthur was taken after the battle of Camlann.

The Tor exists much as I have described it and the mist really does rise at dawn and dusk, but the details of Avalon's appearance are fiction, born out of inspiration begun by Marion Zimmer Bradley and continued through my own meditation and study. Another strong source of inspiration was *The Isle of Avalon* by Nicholas R. Mann, as well as conversations in Glastonbury with Arthurian scholar Geoffrey Ashe and Jamie George, the man who helped Ms. Bradley research for her famous novel.

The Kingmaker comet is a tradition in Arthurian legend, but I can find no factual equivalent.

The treasures of Avalon are based in the legendary 13 treasures of Britain, but again there is no proof of their existence.

I have fabricated the game/divination tool of Holy Stones. It is loosely based on a combination of chess, Chinese checkers and bird's eye view role playing games. But Druids were often consulted in matters of battle and diplomacy, so the spirit behind it is true.

The herbs which the priestesses use and the goddesses on which they call are based in historical research.

Many of the rituals and beliefs in this book were taken from modern neo-pagan and Druidic practices, which seek to recreate the beliefs of the Celts, which are largely unknown. Hence,

Aggrivane's knowledge of the stars, Guinevere and Morgan's practices of divination, the story of the Oak King and Holly King, the Beltane enactment of the Great Marriage, and Avalon's consecration and full moon rituals have some basis in fact. I have, however, chosen to put my own spin on these rituals to suit my story. Ironically, the salute which the priestesses give the Lady of the Lake is loosely based on the Catholic tradition of touching one's thumb to the forehead, lips and heart before the pronouncement of the Gospel during Mass. The Candlemas ritual that comes later in the book is of my own making, based on a mixture of neo-pagan Imbolc and Catholic Candlemas customs.

One of the biggest questions about Avalon remains how it became associated with the Christians. Tradition holds that Joseph of Arimathea, sometimes known as a tin trader, either visited the isle with his nephew, Jesus, in Jesus' youth, and/or returned there after Jesus' death, bearing vessels containing His blood and water from His side. Some say one of these vessels was the Holy Grail, while others argue it really originated with cauldron of the pagan goddess Cerridwen. Pellinor's family prophecy involving the Grail is entirely a product of my imagination. Regardless of Joseph's involvement or lack thereof, Christians did settle on the Tor somewhere between 600 – 800 AD (although I have moved their presence back to approximately 450 AD to suit my story) and remained there until King Henry VIII dissolved its monastery in 1539.

King Arthur

Arthur's lineage is based on strongly debated tradition. Read any of the dozens of books attempting to uncover his real identity and you will see how many theories there are, as well as his hundreds of supposed familial connections.

The story of Arthur's coronation, is of course, fictional, but I have based the inauguration stone on the Stone of Scone, which the Scottish used for generations in crowning their kings. The title given to Arthur, "Dux Britannium" was a real Roman title meaning "Duke or military leader of Britain" that likely would have been known to the elders during the time of my story. The title of "Arddurex" comes from Frank D. Reno's book *Historic Figures of the Arthurian Era: Authenticating the Enemies and Allies of Britain's Post-Roman King*. The other factual element of Arthur's coronation is the geis, or limitation, laid on him by the Lady of the Lake. A geis or geisa (plural) was common in Celtic custom and even more so in legend, and as is the case in this story, often led to the ruler's undoing or even death.

The hunt for the stag, portrayed at the end of the story, is also based in Arthurian tradition.

BOOK 2: CAMELOT'S QUEEN

Whereas the first book in this series was Guinevere's early life, this story is the one everyone thinks of when they call to mind Arthurian legend. And because of that, it was written with no small amount of trepidation. I knew no matter how I chose to spin the story, I would alienate or offend someone who is a purist of a tradition I didn't follow. That's one of the perils of retelling a legend like that of Guinevere and Arthur; everyone has their own image of what the story should be, of what are the essential truths and elements that cannot change.

Not only that, this story delves into a few controversial and dark issues, including rape, physical and mental abuse, and PTSD. Guinevere's kidnapping and rape by Malegant (or sometimes other characters) is part of the canon of Arthurian legend. Sometimes she goes with her captor willingly, but more often than not, she is the victim of his lust and desire for power. Just how badly she was abused (if at all) varies by the telling, but to leave this event out simply because it is distasteful would be disingenuous to both the tradition and to readers.

I have done my best to treat these issues with respect and not use them simply as plot points but to show how they affected the characters' lives and brought about change, as they do for victims in real life. Therefore, my version of Guinevere suffers both mentally and physically for a lengthy period of time after Malegant's abuse, nearly losing her mind when it is coupled with Arthur's betrayal. It is only after time and Avalon's version of therapy that she can learn to move past her experiences.

Similarly, the Battle of Mount Badon affects all of Arthur's troops as well as the victims and their families, most notably Nimue, for whom loss of her mother was the trigger of a slow descent into madness. While her brother found strength and redemption in his faith, Nimue was unable to cope. I hope that if anyone reading this story has been affected by similar circumstances, you see the care with which I have tried to handle these delicate subjects, and if, God forbid, my writing triggered any negative memories, I am truly sorry.

Celtic Marriage

As this part of the book starts out with Guinevere and Arthur's wedding, my notes begin with the history behind marriage in their time. Celtic marriage was very different from what we think of today. It was rarely done out of love, usually out of political gain for the families/tribes involved. It also was not a religious event but a contractual agreement. The laws governing marriage were set up to ensure children were protected (the stigma of illegitimacy did not exist even if a child was born out of wedlock), make clear the rights of the husband and wife, and protect the property rights of both parties.

Under Brehon Law, there were ten forms of marriage, each diminishing in importance, legal rights, and desirability. Guinevere and Arthur could have had either a first and highest degree of marriage, which takes place between partners of equal rank and property, or a second-degree union in which the woman has less property than the man and is supported by him—it all depends on how you look at it.

When Malegant kidnaps Guinevere, he is attempting to create a sixth-degree union in which a defeated enemy's wife is abducted and the marriage is valid only as long as the man can keep the woman with him. There is also a ninth-degree union which was brought about by rape. This is why, in his mind, Guinevere is his legitimate wife.

The Celts believed in polygamy, so second wives and concubines were not unknown, although how often this was practiced after the Roman withdrawal is unknown. Morgan and Arthur would have had a second-degree union because by the time he married her, she had married into a title and lands with Uriens but was not equal to Arthur. Luckily for Morgan, she was married to Arthur for a while before Guinevere returned because laws existed that stated a first wife could legally murder the second wife within the first three days of marriage. Still, Guinevere was not only Morgan's competition for Arthur's attention, she was a threat to Morgan's livelihood. In the event of Arthur's death, a chief wife had rights to her husband's estate, while other wives were governed by informal contracts that often didn't require the first wife to provide for them at all or for the husband to leave them anything. So Guinevere would have been within her rights to leave Morgan with nothing after the Battle of Camlann, but that's another story for the notes to the third book in this series.

The transactions around marriage depicted in this book are all based on Brehon Law. Dowries were very important as brides were purchased from their fathers by their husbands for what became known as a bride-price. Some of this was kept in reserve for the woman should her marriage end at the fault of her husband, so she would not be left destitute. There was also a virgin-price that guaranteed the wife's purity, which Guinevere's father falsely arranged with Malegant.

Arthur's Lineage

The family lineage Arthur explains to Guinevere when she first comes to Camelot is one of many used throughout Arthurian legend.

The ring he gave her is real. It's called the Escrick Ring. It was found in March 2013 (while I was writing this book) near York and immediately linked to "fifth-century royalty." So naturally, I tied it into my novel with fictitious symbolism relating to Arthur's ancestors.

The Combrogi and Arthur's Military

"Combrogi" is a real term found in Welsh literature that I chose to appropriate in place of the more modern Knights of the Round Table.

Chain mail really was a Celtic invention, but whether or not the Combrogi's saddles would have had stirrups is a matter of controversy. Most historians say they would not have, but at least one Arthurian scholar has put forth a hypothesis that the invention may have been carried to Britain by the Sarmatians, who were sent to Britain by the emperor Marcus Aurelius in 175 AD.

As a fiction author, I have chosen to take this unlikely possibility and spin it into a partial explanation for the Combrogi's unprecedented success in battle.

Lancelot's views on training horses may seem very modern, but they actually have ancient origins. The Greek writer Xenophon (430-354 BC) advocated the kind treatment of horses in his book *On Horsemanship*. "The golden rule in dealing with a horse is never approach him angrily. . .When a horse is shy of some object and refuses to approach it, you must teach him that there is nothing to be alarmed at. . . or, failing that, touch the formidable object to yourself and then gently lead the horse up to it. The opposite plan of forcing the creature by blows only intensifies its fear, the horse mentally associating the pain he suffers at such a moment with the object of suspicion" (28).

Like Lancelot, Xenophon also emphasizes the importance of the relationship between horse and master. "It is best that the stable be placed in a quarter of the establishment where the master will see the horse as often as possible" (20). And again, "If you would have a horse learn to perform his duty, your best plan will be, whenever he does as you wish, to show him some kindness in return, and when he is disobedient, to chastise him" (39). He emphatically states, "Far the best method of instruction is to let the horse feel that whatever he does in obedience to the rider's wishes will be followed by some rest and relaxation" (50).

The Famous Battles of King Arthur

The battles I've chosen to show are only a few attributed to King Arthur by the Welsh historian Nennius, who records twelve great victories during Arthur's reign as Dux Bellorum. There is much debate among scholars over their true dates, locations, and even who fought whom. As a fiction writer, I have picked what best fit my story and will leave it to the historians to hash out the rest.

The name Caw is closely associated with Arthurian legend. There are likely a number of men by this name. A Pictish chief named Caw really did live somewhere near Strathclyde around the years 493-570 and may even have been father of Arthurian "historian" Gildas. I have chosen to make him a rebel and conflate the details with what Nennius tells us of the battles of Arthur, "The seventh battle was in the Caledonian Forest, that is, the Battle of Celidon Coit." I have chosen to interpret that to mean the Caledonian Forest was in modern Scotland. The details of the battle are all from my own imagination, but legend has it that Arthur was victorious.

One of the two battles most people are likely to be familiar with is the Battle of Mount Badon (the other being Camlann, which takes place in next book). Nennius writes, "The twelfth battle was on Badon Hill and in it nine hundred and sixty men fell in one day, from a single charge of Arthur's, and no-one lay them low save he alone." While the name comes from the book *De Excidio Britanniae* (The Ruin of Britain) written by the monk Gildas in the mid-500s, the battle itself is likely to have been real. Someone led a decisive battle against the Saxons sometime between 490 and 530 AD that resulted in a period of peace.

That someone has come to be known in myth as Arthur and the battle called Badon. The location is a matter of much speculation, but I've chosen to go with the popular theory of it being at a hill fort near Bath, which the Romans called Aque Sullis. The use of battering rams by the Saxons is also historical. In his book *Britannia antiquea, Or Ancient Britain brought within the limits of authentic history*, Beale Poste, a nineteenth century historian writes, "We find by the History of Gildas that the Saxons had plenty of battering rams, in the use of which, they were very liberal (234)."

Celtic Views on Death and Burial Practices

The Celts believed in reincarnation. In mythology, the Cauldron of Rebirth was able to revive the dead. Pre-Christian Celts also believed in an after-death Otherworld (Annwn in Welsh mythology), a resting place between incarnations that was a heaven-like paradise.

Graves were oriented west-east. West was the direction of the Otherworld, and Christians believed that this positioning allowed the dead to face Christ when he raised them on Resurrection Day. Single-person burials were the norm, with the dead person's head facing west. Sometimes a mother and child were buried together. Bodies may have been laid in the bare earth, in a stone coffin, or in a hollowed-out log, but coffins as we think of them were rare.

OGHAM

Chances are you've heard that the Celts passed all of their knowledge on orally, which is one of the reasons why we know so little for certain about their beliefs. This is true, but the Celts did have a system of written language called Ogham. The earliest inscriptions we have in this language date to somewhere in the fourth century, mostly in Ireland, Wales, and Southern Britain. But some historians and archeologists, such as Lloyd and Jenny Laing, believe it dates back much further than that—even as far back as the Sycthians, who may have been the Gaelic Celts' ancestors dating to about 1300 BC. Ogham is mentioned often in ancient Irish myth, where it is said to have been used for poetry, Druidic spells, and even political challenges.

The main source of written knowledge about Ogham is a fourteenth century manuscript called The Book of Ballymote, now housed in the Library of the Royal Irish Academy. When written, Ogham appears to the modern eye like a series of vertical, horizontal, and diagonal lines, the number and shape of which indicate the letters. The alphabet had twenty characters arranged in series of four. Later, five additional characters were added.

The use of Ogham as sign language, which Imogen employs, is very controversial and certainly not accepted by all historians. John Matthews explains in his *Encyclopedia of Celtic* Wisdom that the fingers of the hand and certain locations on the palm represent letters or phrases. A person signing this way would use the placement of fingers across the shinbone, nose, thigh, foot, or on the palm or fingers of the opposite hand to indicate a letter, word, or phrase.

THE GRAIL

No explanation of an Arthurian legend story would be complete without talking about the Holy Grail. So many books have been written about it that I'm not going to go into theories, only explain how I came to the idea you see in this book.

I chose to have a party of knights find the Grail because tradition varies as to which one did the finding. The most popular are Galahad, Perceval (Peredur), and Bors. In my version, Bors is not included because he's not a nice person. Traditionally, though he is involved in the quest, Lancelot doesn't ever see the Grail because he isn't pure. I have chosen to force him to make a choice between Guinevere (as representative of the Goddess) or the Grail. Of course, he chooses Guinevere.

Because there are so many possibilities of what the Grail could be (chalice, cup, cauldron, etc.) and they mean so much to people who believe in them, I didn't want to alienate anyone by picking one over the other. My Grail changes because I really do believe it is whatever you wish it to be. The seals Guinevere sees on the sides were inspired by those on a small chalice I purchased years ago from a New Age store. I'm not even sure what faith it is an implement for. (If you're ever at one of my book signings, I'll have it with me, so maybe you can tell me.)

The Grail Maiden is a title usually given to Elaine of Corbenic because she bore the man who finds the Grail. However, in many of the legends, a woman or angel is guarding it when it is discovered. I have chosen to extend this idea into a kind of special suborder of the Avalonian priestesshood. The stone circle they pass as Guinevere is tracking their progress (called this book the Sanctuary of the Stars) is Avebury.

The Grail Castle can be found in the Vulgate Cycle of Arthurian legend as well as Thomas Malory's Le Morte d'Arthur. It is usually associated with Corbenic, Elaine's home, but I have chosen to make it a place that housed the Grail after the knights find it. I placed it on a fictitious island off the coast of Camelot to keep it well within reach of Arthur and Father Marius.

BOOK 3: MISTRESS OF LEGEND

The epigraph at the beginning of this book sets the tone for the whole story, which is one of warriors, war and change in Britain. It is an excerpt from "Y Gododdin," the earliest surviving Welsh poem, which is also called the "Book of Aneirin." There are two different versions of the surviving manuscript (one is shorter than the other, and generally believed to be more reliable). Cardiff MS 2.81, dates to the 13th century, but the poem itself is believed to be much older and may have first been written down in the ninth century from an oral source dating to the seventh century. Written in Old Welsh and Middle Welsh, it tells the story of the historical Battle of Catraeth between the Saxons and a motley crew of post-Roman Celts, Picts and Votadini sometime near the year 600 AD.

It is used by some to justify the historical existence of King Arthur because of the line "although he was not Arthur," as in "he was good, but not as great as Arthur." However, most scholars point out that this line could be referencing any outstanding warrior who bore that name, and also if there was someone like King Arthur whom people lauded, chances are good many babies would have been named after him, just as we do with celebrities and royalty today.

Traditionally, Guinevere is not involved in the Battle of Catraeth, for she and everyone who knew Camelot are long dead by the time of the battle or, if the story takes place in the Middle Ages, many generations yet to come. But I chose to set this battle about fifty years earlier than most scholars date it because of the Votadini heritage I have given Guinevere throughout this series. The Battle of Catraeth was the penultimate defeat of the Votadini, though here I have framed it as only the first in a line of disasters that would then end around the time of the historical Battle of Catraeth, ushering in the age of the Anglo Saxons and the formation of the country of England.

Part One: The Broken Crown

In most Arthurian stories, after Guinevere is rescued from the stake she flees with Lancelot to his castle, Joyous Gard, which has been variously placed throughout England, though one of the most accepted locations is Din Guayrdi, modern Bamburgh. From there he defends against attacks by King Arthur. Eventually, they part and Guinevere becomes a nun and Lancelot a monk, both living out their days in penance for their sin.

This ending does not suit the strong, active, willful woman that my Guinevere is, so I chose to make her an active participant in the remainder of her life and in trying to save Camelot. Guinevere's wounds are consistent with second and third degree burns. Why did she get them if she was a priestess? She couldn't control the fire and concentrate on successfully jumping onto Lancelot's horse at the same time. The ointment the priestesses make to help heal her is based on an Amish remedy still in use today. Similarly, the method of invisible ink Morgan uses on her herb and poison vials is historical, invented by Pliny the Elder. (Thanks to the American Bookbinder's Museum in San Francisco for that tidbit.)

Traditionally, when Arthur leaves Camelot in Mordred's care, Guinevere is harassed by Mordred, who attempts to marry her (sometimes willingly, sometimes not) for her power. I have kept the element of the rulers desiring her sovereignty, but I chose not to exploit the relationship between Guinevere and Mordred, as these characters never had any chemistry to me. They are in my mind, much more like mother and son, than lovers. Besides, I planned to have Mordred and Elga get together and had no desire to create yet another love triangle in this already complex story.

The convent that Elga sends Guinevere to is my own invention, although York is historically known for being a Saxon haven and then later, a capital, and was important enough to have had its own bishopric. I chose to include it as a nod to Guinevere's traditional ending as a nun, but also to provide an update on Mayda's fate from *Camelot's Queen* and to give Guinevere a safe haven during the battle of Camlann.

Religious orders, especially those comprised of women, were rare at the time, but we know from the famous example of St. Brigid and her dual monastery in fifth century Ireland that they did exist in Great Britain during the Dark Ages. The rituals the Sisters enact while Guinevere is at the convent are based on actual Anglo Saxon Christian rituals from around the year 900, as described in *The Dramatic Liturgy of Anglo-Saxon England* by M. Bradford Bedingfield. Some of them may seem familiar to Catholic readers, as the Tenebrae ritual is still used today with some revisions after Vatican II. If you are interested in the sign language used by the nuns, I recommend *Monasteriales Indicia: The Anglo-Saxon Sign Language* by Debby Banham. A few Catholic religious orders still use similar communication today during the period of their day known as the Grand Silence.

The historical veracity and date of the Battle of Camlann is the subject of much debate. It is estimated as taking place anywhere from 515 – 542 AD. Camlann appears first in written record in the tenth-century Annales Cambriae, which says it took place twenty-one years after the Battle of Badon, the exact date of which is unknown. Based on that, Camlann can be placed at 515, 520 or 539, depending on the source, although the traditional date has become either 537 or 547. Confusing things even more, the Irish Annals of Tigernach place it in 541, Geoffrey Monmouth uses 542 and the Spanish Anales Toledanos dates it much later in 580.

Scholars have been trying to definitively locate the location of the battle for years. That is one of the reasons why I portray it as a series of battles on the run, rather than being in one fixed location. Sites as varied as Somerset, Cornwall, Wales, and even as far north as Hadrian's Wall have been suggested. I chose to locate the final battle in which Mordred and Arthur are mortally wounded on Hadrian's Wall because that is in keeping with my northern Arthur. Like so much else about King Arthur and the legends that surround him, the true location is something we will likely never know for sure.

Part Two: People of the North

The People of the North is a name for the tribes that lived between Hadrian's Wall and Antonine Wall in what is today southern Scotland. There were once many tribes in the area, but by the time in which this book is set, the Damnonii, Selgovae, Novantae and Votadini were the main four. Among those, the Damnonii and Votadini were the more powerful. The titles of Votad and Votadess are my own invention, based in the root meaning of the word Votadini, which is wo-tado or wotad, which translates as foundation or support.

Mynyddog Mwynfawr and Morcant are based on historical people, while Evina, Rohan and most of the rest of the Votadini are fictional. According to Welsh tradition, Mynyddog was the ruler of the Gododdin, which was either part of the Votadini lands or another name for them. His capital is generally accepted to be Din Eidyn, which is today called Edinburgh. It is unclear if his name is a personal one or a title. He is thought to have been a brother or son to Clydno Eitin, a historical ruler of Strathclyde, who is mentioned briefly in this book. Clydno's historical son, Cynan, is also a character. Morcant is the historical Morcant Bulc, the last British king of Bernicia before it became an Anglican holding. Included in his territory was Ynts Metcault, also known as the Isle of Winds, which is today called Lindisfarne (more on that in a bit).

Traditionally in Arthurian legend, after the Battle of Camlann and the deaths of Arthur and Mordred, the country is plunged into civil war. The two main traditional contenders for the throne are King Mark of Cornwall (who in my story is dead by this point) and Constantine (who was traditionally Arthur's heir, beginning with Gildas' sixth century writing). Some authors even say Mordred had children who would have been in line for the throne, but that is not relevant to this story. For a good explanation of both Constantine's role in Arthurian legend and Mordred's possible sons, see *King Arthur's Children* by Tyler R. Tichelaar. I chose to make the two main British contenders Constantine because of tradition and the House of Rheged (Owain and Accolon) because of their historical power.

Guinevere's possession of ancestral lands in Stirling and her mother being a Votadini are based on Norma Lorre Goodrich's theory that Guinevere was a Pict born in Stirling. Goodrich is also the source for that area being Guinevere's inheritance. The marking ceremony is my own invention, as are the marks and which animals belong to each tribe. The symbolism of the feathers is also fiction, but was inspired by the traditions of many ancient cultures.

The plague that has affected the village outside of Stirling that Guinevere visits (and that we find out toward the end of the book has killed many of the inhabitants of the Grail Castle) is based on the plague of 537, also called the Plague of Justinian, which is generally thought of as the first ever recorded outbreak of plague. It is believed to have disproportionately affected the post-Roman Celts because they frequently traded with Mediterranean merchants (which is also where Sobian obtained the henna to dye her hair). It was more of a bubonic plague than the smallpox/typhus-like disease I have described. I changed it because I didn't want people getting it confused with the better-known outbreak of bubonic plague during the Black Death in the fourteenth century.

Part Three: The False Queen

The revolution in Guinevere's name was based partially off the real-life insurgency that Lady Jane Grey's family led in her name in the sixteenth century. I know that many others have happened throughout history, but that one is my historical touchstone, especially for a revolution that happened without the person's permission, as the one in this book does at first.

I have purposefully conflated the Saxons and the Angles in this and the final section of the book for ease of reading. I thought it would be awkward to try to explain the different Germanic tribes to the reader in the course of a fictional story, so I chose to attribute everything to the Saxons. In reality, what occurred during the Battle of Catraeth took place between the Celts of the Gododdin and the Angles from Denmark, who were a separate invading tribe from the Germanic Saxons.

King Ida and his sons, Theodric and Osmere, were historical personages, though Ida's reign actually began in 547. Ida did really take over the capital of Bernicia and claimed Catraeth as his own. As cited in the Anglo-Saxon Chronicle, his son Theodric led a three-day the battle against King Uriens for the Isle of Winds, what we now call the Isle of Lindisfarne. Its strategic importance is just as I have stated in this book. See Brain Taylor Hope's wonderful book *Yeavering: An Anglo-British Centre of Early Northumbria* for more information. The date of the siege is uncertain, but is usually placed somewhere between 547 and 590, depending on the source. During the battle, Morcant is said to have paid a foreign assassin to murder Uriens. Because I had already had Malegant murder Uriens in Camelot's Queen, I substituted his eldest son, Owain, instead, and identified the assassin as the fictional character Rohan.

Evina's ritual with the horses is fictional and the part before the executions begin was inspired by a post on the rituals of the Celtic horse goddess Epona. I may have stretched the bounds of Celtic law in that scene, as execution was a last resort for the Celts, who liked to settle things with fines and the creation of outlaws instead. However, I find it difficult to believe that a warrior people who were rumored to practice human sacrifice and had an obsession with the heads of their enemies didn't employ capital punishment for extreme cases.

The Lughnasa testing and training of the warriors is based in the mythical Tests of the Fianna, which Irish warriors had to pass in order to become part of Fionn mac Cumhaill's band of warriors, as well as the practices of the Scandinavian Berserkers. Examples of skills tested include the voice test (although this is not clearly defined), weaponry skill, stealth, hunting, dancing, scouting, swimming, board games, racing, harping, smithing, wrestling, and endurance of extreme temperatures, among others. For an excellent resource on what the training of ancient warriors may have been like, I recommend *Weapons and Warfare in Anglo-Saxon England* by Sonia C. Hawkes. In the same way, Calliac's Death Goddess ritual is not historical, but it is based in images of the Gaelic hag-goddess Cailleach and various incarnations of the Death Mother around the world.

The winter training that Lancelot and Guinevere put their recruits through is based on both historical and modern military training exercises. My equestrian readers will attest that ice balls are a real problem that plague horses in the winter. My main source of information for this was Equus Magazine.

Part Four: Y Gododdin

As mentioned in the opening of these notes, the Battle of Catraeth has a long and storied history, thanks to the mysterious poem "Y Gododdin," which is said to memorialize historical warriors of an actual battle between the ascending Angles and the massively out-numbered Britons. The poem gives 300 as the number of Britons (a number I have slightly increased for the purposes of my story) and scholars estimate the Anglican force at anywhere between 50,000 and 100,000. It is said that of the 300, only three survived to tell the tale. Given the Celtic fascination with the sacred number three, these numbers are more likely symbolic rather than an actual count.

The feasting hosted by Mynyddog is recorded in the poem and is typical of pre-battle rituals of the time, and similar to the feast in the epic story of Beowulf. In her article "Warfare and Horses in the Gododdin and the Problem of Catraeth" Jenny Rowland argues that the feasting may also have served as a recruiting drive for the upcoming battle. The blood bond is my own invention, but Rowland notes that "heroic vows [were] made during the feasting." The use of woad and henbane, as well as its effects, are historically accurate, as is the Celtic obsession with the heads of their enemies and the power they hold.

The nationalities of the warriors on the British side are generally accepted to be mostly Votadini from Gododdin, and those from Alt Clut's warriors, but they are also said to have come from Rheged and as far away as Gwynedd and the Pictish lands.

The location of the Battle of Catraeth is uncertain, but many believe it to be the city of Catterick in North Yorkshire. However, this is far from universally accepted, with Scottish locations such as the border of the Gododdin, Roxburghshire, and Din Ediyn (Edinburgh) proposed, as well as towns in Wales, Cumbria and Yorkshire in England. I have no opinion on the actual location and so have chosen to use Catterick. The date of the battle is generally thought to have taken place between 570-590, but as with most things during the Dark Ages, this, too, is debated, which is why I took the liberty of placing it when it fit for my story.

Assuming Catterick is the correct location, one might ask why a group of primarily Votadini warriors would travel so far south for a battle. That is a question that has plagued scholars for ages. Of course, it could have been to lay siege to a hillfort or take back disputed or key strategic land, but that is a long journey for such an effort. Jenny Rowland theorizes that the battle could have begun as a rescue mission to save the author of the poem from prison, which is one of the legendary explanations for the poem's existence. Similarly, John and Caitlin Matthews note in their book The Complete King Arthur, that it may have started as the rescue of a Votadini hostage. Both of these theories are where the idea of Lancelot being captured came from. It could also have been a raid, the like of which was very common in Celtic culture. This type of military expedition wouldn't have been important enough for the ruler to attend personally, and so it would explain why Mynyddog didn't lead his troops into battle. Other theories say it could have been a pre-emptive strike against the increasingly powerful Angles and that Catterick is just where the two armies happened to meet, rather than the original end goal.

The last point that bears exploring is the burial of King Arthur in Avalon, which is commonly believed to be one in the same with Glastonbury, England. The grave of King Arthur and Guinevere uncovered at Glastonbury in 1191 has long been thought to be a hoax created by the monks to raise money to help repair their abbey which had been badly damaged by a fire in 1184. When they "found" King Arthur's grave, it was marked by an iron cross that bore the words, "Here lies the famous King Arthur on the isle of Avalon." (Some versions also add "with his second wife, Guinevere" to the text.)

While it is nearly impossible that this find is real, it is so ingrained in Arthurian legend that I felt I could not let it pass unmentioned. So I chose to play off the idea of Guinevere being Arthur's second wife. In the story I have created, the only logical reason that such a thing could be said was if Morgan was Arthur's first wife by way of the Sacred Marriage. Therefore, in this version of the story, regardless of whether or not the grave found in Glastonbury is authentic, the marker is not the original; the first one mentions Arthur's true wife, Morgan.

⁘

If you would like to know more about the sources I consulted in writing these books, please visit my website, nicoleevelina.com, and click on the "Research" tab under the section for the book you're interested in. You may also wish to search my blog, located on the same site, for additional information on many of these topics.

About the Author

NICOLE EVELINA is an award-winning historical fiction, non-fiction and women's fiction writer whose books have won nearly 30 awards. The first two books in her Guinevere trilogy, *Daughter of Destiny* and *Camelot's Queen* were named Books of the Year by Chanticleer Reviews and Author's Circle, respectively. Her most recent book, *The Once and Future Queen*, which was named Non-Fiction Book of the Year by Author's Circle, examines popular works of Arthurian fiction by more than 20 authors over the last 1,000 years to show how the character of Guinevere changes to reflect attitudes toward women.

Her mission as a writer is to rescue little-known women from being lost in the pages of history. While others may choose to write about the famous, she tells the stories of those who are in danger of being forgotten so that their memories may live on for at least another generation. She also writes from the female point of view since the male perspective has historically been given more attention.

When she's not writing, she can be found reading, playing with her spoiled twin Burmese cats, cooking, researching, dreaming of living in Chicago or the English countryside…and of course, plotting her next book.